A Price Beyond Rubies

a novel of the Civil War

To the Loves,
Louise ... Barry

D0064018

A Price Beyond Rubies

a novel of the Civil War

Louise McCants Barry

Sunflower University Press®

P. O. Box 1009 • 1531 Yuma • Manhattan, Kansas 66505-1009 USA

© 1996 by Louise McCants Barry

Printed in the United States of America on acid-free paper.

ISBN 0-89745-201-1

Cover: Lithograph of *The Battle of Pea Ridge*, created by Kurz & Allison, 1899, courtesy The Chicago Historical Society.

Edited by Julie Bush

Layout by Lori L. Daniel

For Bill

Who can find a virtuous woman? For her price is far above rubies. . . . Strength and honor are her clothing; and she shall rejoice in time to come.

Proverbs 31

Contents

Part 2 — War, 1860-1865

Part 3 — Reconstruction, 1865-1874

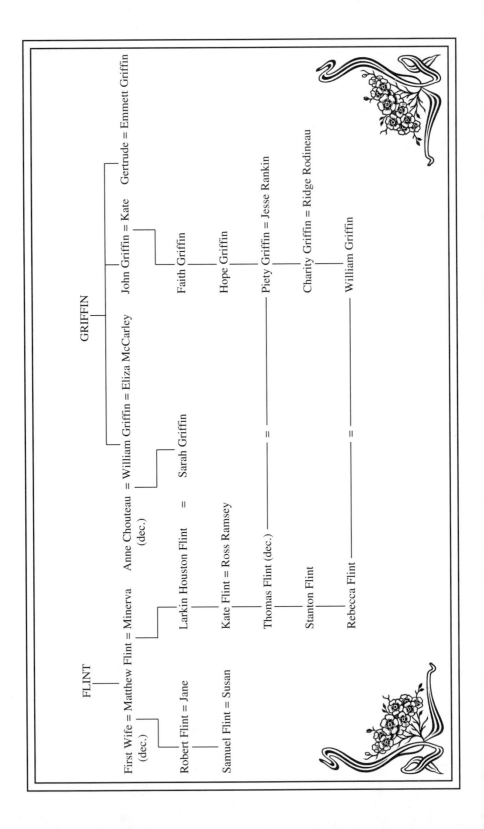

FLINT

GRIFFIN

First Wife = Matthew Flint = Minerva   Anne Chouteau = William Griffin = Eliza McCarley   John Griffin = Kate   Gertrude = Emmett Griffin
(dec.)   (dec.)

Robert Flint = Jane   Larkin Houston Flint   =   Sarah Griffin   Faith Griffin

Samuel Flint = Susan   Kate Flint = Ross Ramsey   Hope Griffin

                                          Thomas Flint (dec.) ——————— = ——————— Piety Griffin = Jesse Rankin

                                          Stanton Flint   Charity Griffin = Ridge Rodineau

                                          Rebecca Flint ——————————— = ——————— William Griffin

Preface

*IN 1980 I WAS GIVEN a long-hidden copy of my paternal grandfather's autobiography. His story has fascinated me ever since, and this historical novel is the result. Pleasant Houston Spears, on whom I have based the character of **Larkin Houston Flint**, was born in 1836, fought as a captain on the Union side in the Civil War, then went on to become a legislator and prosperous landowner in Reconstruction Arkansas. He was a wonderful fiddle player, and always did things in a big way; his house was a two-storied, twelve-room affair, built of native materials. He died in 1912 and is now commemorated by two tombstones in the same cemetery (but that's another story entirely). My* grandmother, Sarah Kitchens Spears, on whom I have based the character of *Sarah Griffin Flint,* was almost ninety when she died. I remember her fondly. She had a light step, a quick smile, and was a marvelous playmate. As a child, I considered her to be my best friend.

A Price Beyond Rubies has been developed against a background of actual events. I have tried to depict accurately the social and military history of the Civil War in Arkansas and Missouri, states of deeply divided loyalties where all too often brother fought bitterly against brother.

Although Larkin's prologues are correlated with my grandfather's autobiography, I have used my imagination freely in the development of this novel, while staying true to the spirit of the time. I have relied heavily on the large amount of Civil War oral history still extant in Arkansas during the years of my childhood, as well as on the many excellent histories that record this period.

Because I have freely blended fact and fiction, I believe my readers are entitled to know which is which:

 The real-life *Sarah* was not related to the legendary Chouteau family, nor was her name Griffin. I have invented a fictional branch of the Chouteau family in order to describe major events of the Civil War in and around the Kansas City area. Sarah's ancestor *Louis Chouteau* is fictional, as are his descendants, e.g., *Uncle Auguste.* The prototype for Louis Chouteau is to be found in recorded history in the life of Auguste Pierre Chouteau, that trader par excellence whose house of Chouteau dominated the western plains. *Aunt Bereniece,* beloved and respected grande dame of the City of Kansas, is historical, as is the much-disputed will that divided Chouteau property between legitimate and illegitimate offspring.

 The town, which was officially named Kansas City in 1889, has been called by many other names: Kawsmouth, Westport's Landing, Chouteau Landing, the Town of Kansas, and the *City of Kansas.* In the interests of clarity, for the most part I have used *Kansas City.*

The family connection of *Larkin Houston Flint* to Sam Houston is fictional. Again, a prototype existed. I am indebted to Marquis James, who in his Pulitzer Prize-winning biography of Sam Houston, *The Raven*, recounts the story of Houston's marriage to the Cherokee princess Tahlehina. I have improvised from this vignette and have shifted the dates by several years to create the fictional characters of *Morning Star* and her daughter, *Minerva*.

 For the most part, family names in Arkansas are fictional, although I have used those appropriate for the Scotch-Irish settlers of the state. *William Griffin* is a fictional character whose prototype was Richard Griffin, an early settler of Arkansas and one of my maternal ancestors. Most of the Griffin men of that period were either planters or doctors; so far as I am aware, none ran a tavern. *Griffin's Tavern* is a fictional name. The actual tavern used by both sides as headquarters during the Battle of Pea Ridge was called the Elkhorn Tavern.

 In both armies, officers of the rank of colonel and general are historical, except for *Colonel T. C. Huntsman*, who is fictional. I have tried to describe the major battles of the area — *Pea Ridge*, *Prairie Grove*, *Westport*, and *Price*'s long march into Missouri — with historical fidelity.

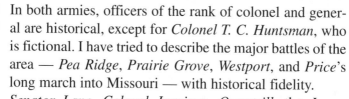 *Senator Lane, Colonel Jennison, Quantrill*, the *James brothers*, and *Bloody Bill Anderson* are historical, as are the descriptions of the collapse of the jail in Kansas City; Quantrill's retaliation in Lawrence, Kansas; the infamous *Order No. 11*; the plots of the *Order of the American Knights of the Golden Circle*; and the visit of *John Hay* to Kansas City.

The recounting of blood feuds among the Cherokees in the Indian Nation is historical, but *Ridge Rodineau* is a fictional character.

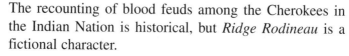 It is a matter of recorded history that a group of northwest Arkansas men loyal to the Union were ambushed and marched in chains to Little Rock, there to be given the choice between hanging or joining the Confederacy. The escape of these men is taken from my grandfather's writings. I have been unable to discover the name of the Confederate officer who commanded that operation, hence the invention of *Colonel T. C. Huntsman*, my fictional vil-

lain. The preacher, *Theophilous Massey*, is also fictional.
 Both the visit of the *Ku Klux Klan* to my grandfather and
the political maneuvers that ended the carpetbag domina-
tion of the Arkansas legislature are described in my
grandfather's autobiography.

The remarkable political strategies in Reconstruction
Arkansas that resulted in the 30-day shooting war of 1874
are historical. *Anna Strasser* is fictional. My grandfather
was never governor of Arkansas, and the characters of
Payson Clemson and *Joseph Bender* are fictional. Their
prototypes exist in the recorded histories of the state.

I have remained true to the spirit of my grandfather's narrative — and
thus a novel that by today's standards is *politically incorrect*. Because
Grandfather was considered by the Ku Klux Klan to be a dangerous radical who aided and abetted the education of Negroes, I have no doubt he
would have appreciated the irony of my position.

LMB
1996

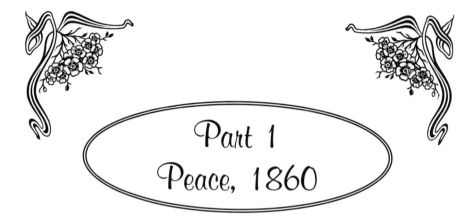

Part 1
Peace, 1860

Prologue
Larkin, 1874

I LOOK BACK and wonder what we could have done differently. My name is Larkin Houston Flint, 38 years old, a veteran of the Civil War, First Arkansas Cavalry Volunteers, Union army. As the Good Book says, there is a time for every-thing under the sun, and it is due time I take up my pen to relate the times we endured. While young and unacquainted with the horrors of war, I left behind my wife and all that I held dear to join the army. I greatly regretted the need to fight my own neighbors, but if a man is not true to himself and will not declare his own conscience, he is not worthy of the respect of a second-class coon hound and disgraces the shape of his being.

My roots are deep and my people proud. I could see no other option than to serve when I must. Even now, as I look back at the times with crystal-clear hindsight, I can think of no other recourse. If a man accepts the blessings and benefits of citizenship, he incurs the burden of fighting for the same. If he derives benefits through the decisions of his elected leaders in times of peace and prosperity, he assumes the responsibility to live with their harsh and sometimes faulty decisions as well — at least until the next election.

Hard years lay ahead. I like a good fight as much as the next man, but I have never met a Flint who took well to taking orders from another. Still, I felt it to be my duty to declare for the Union, the long-faced Bible-thumping abolitionist preachers notwithstanding.

My wife took it hard. Sarah and I had been married scarcely two years, and she was over-young besides. It seemed too hard to bear that I must ride away from her and our firstborn to fight a war that was needless at best and callously cruel at worst. Yet a man does what he must. Knowing full well that the principal instigators of this detestable conflict promulgated, planned, and fostered it to their own gain and dubious glory, I still felt compelled to go.

Both sides of instigators held the word of the Lord in their mouths and Satan in their hearts. The fruit of their labors was gall and wormwood for many a poor devil who wanted nothing more than to be left alone to live in liberty.

More than a score of years have passed since I went to war. Our government has stood for nearly a century now, and the world has changed beyond mortal imagining. Until recently I served as governor of Arkansas, a state which in wartime my father once governed. My grandfather, governor of two states and senator of one, came within foreseeable reach of becoming president of the United States in that decisive year of 1860. Had his wisdom prevailed during the sad times of my telling, the sorrows of our country would have been substantially mitigated. Yet wisdom counts for naught when passions are inflamed and tempers unloosed.

Our war tore up a wonderful country. Life was remarkably good in the middle of this century. Every white man saw opportunity all around him. Many made the most of it. The land was rich, there for the working and the taking.

As a young man I never thought to be rich. On the other hand, it was not my intent to live poor. Brilliant achievements had little place in my dreams. I would have been content to have Sarah, enjoy my family, raise my children, own my own land, and be my own man.

In spite of my heritage, I never aspired to riches or politics, nor set out to become a leader of men. Not being cut from the cloth of a follower, I long thought of myself as an independent. But the war taught me a new truth. The definition of a leader is a remarkably simple one: a leader is a man who has followers. Absent followers, no man is a leader. Throughout the years, men have sought my company and asked my counsel. I have come to accept this responsibility and to bear its burdens.

Now I am my party's candidate of choice for national office. Whether I accept that honor and bear that burden is the heavy decision that lies before me. Sarah's part is pivotal. If I am to go, Sarah must be persuaded. Long-standing differences, both of philosophy and of practice, must be resolved.

Though orators declaim in public that piece of nonsense that says, "I am the master of my fate; I am the captain of my soul," my own observation of life has been radically different. Our lives are shaped by seemingly insignificant events, decisions that seem at the time to be dependent on chance as much as choice. At the time, my meeting with Sarah seemed pure chance.

Father had stated that he was thinking of buying another fiddle and mentioned that Ansel Alewine had one for sale over at Griffin Flat. Father thought I might be willing to ride over to the upcoming square dance at Griffin's Tavern to try out the fiddle and give him my opinion. I was willing enough to accommodate him, though 20 miles was an overly long ride for a neighborhood square dance. Still, since he seemed to attach a fair amount of importance to the thing, I was not averse to pleasing him and squiring a sweet new bunch of girls at the same time. It proved to be one of the few times when Father truly outmaneuvered me. By the time I had figured out that he and old William Griffin had already talked it over and struck a deal, I had swallowed the bait, hook, line, and sinker.

When I first saw Sarah, I knew I had to have her. She had the sweetest-made little body I had ever laid eyes on — the kind of shape that makes a man ache to lay hands on her as well. Yet I was not counting on marrying so soon. At 24 I had invitations from several and service from some, and I saw no need to settle down. Sarah changed all that.

She was sashaying down the line, dancing the Virginia reel, laughing up at some long-legged besotted boy who couldn't take his eyes off her. I knew full well how he felt, but he was in my way. I shouldered him to one side, claimed her for the next dance, and took that smile for myself. She was light as a feather and sweet as honey. To her credit, I must admit that Sarah never seemed to have the least idea what kind of effect she had on men. She was innocent to the bone. Even on our wedding day, when that lecherous old federal commissioner from the Indian Nation was hard put to keep his greedy hands off her, she never had any notion of what his problem was. She had been spoiled by all her kin, and downright babied by that old black mammy of hers, but her stepmother and her pa had raised her strict and raised her right. I took one look at her pa's judgmental Presbyterian face and knew I would have to marry her to get her. As things turned out, there were remarkable bonuses attached to our union. What no man could have foreseen was the pain of our parting.

I will go to my grave holding in my heart the smile on my Sarah's face the first time I held her in my arms. Her touch lives in my dreams; but in my nightmares I live again the pain and cruelty of war. For too many years I have spent my days in the labor of Reconstruction, one mortal man attempting to heal the wounds and bear the scars that but for violent passions we would never have inflicted on each other. One lifetime may not be enough for the country, or for Sarah and myself.

Not all the passions of those times were evil. America before the war was a shining land. Our forefathers had accomplished in 100 years what might easily have taken 1,000 in the hands of lesser men. There were intelligent and energetic men in a country that was an unending expanse of land. Until the Civil War, the noble experiment of the United States of America shone like a beacon to the rest of the world. But the passions of evil annihilated the best and the brightest among us. Our generals were merciless butchers. The poor devils not killed in battle were wasted by disease, hacked on by army doctors, and killed slowly by the thousands in the hellholes that served both sides as prison camps.

I have tried over the years to conceal as best I can the bitterness that I bear. But if I were put under oath and asked my true opinion, I would be forced to observe that it is the slackers of elastic conscience who hired others to do their dying for them who are now in places of power. It is that detestable breed that I have fought throughout these years.

Were I to go to Washington, my influence would be substantial. Our country is now plagued with cheap currency, plus an influx of foreigners who will work for nearly nothing. Add to that the known fact that these foreigners are disciplined to obey without asking undue questions, and there is again a real capacity for violence in the land. These foreigners take jobs while our own people go begging. Moreover, too many now perceive free blacks to be a burden in the land.

If the most noble country in the history of mankind collapses under the weight of its burdens, it will be due to the disinterest and faltering courage of its more responsible citizens. I have no wish to have my name among these ignoble numbers.

This is no longer the country I fought for. The nation I served was a land of wide horizons, populated by a liberty-loving people. I sometimes wonder, if men now had to choose between liberty and prosperity, which way the die would be cast. Our country needs more than prosperity. If I persuade Sarah where her duty lies, so that I am able to answer my party's call to serve in Washington, I mean to spend the rest of my days working past Reconstruction toward reunion.

Persuading Sarah when she was 16 was a simple matter of a smile and a touch. The Sarah of today is a different woman. I must admit my own contribution to that difference. Sarah has carried her own share of burdens over the years. A woman expects to bear children, and Sarah has borne four living, one dead. But Sarah's burdens have been those of responsibility. My duties have frequently mandated my absences, and I having been gone overly much, the duties of overseeing our property and our household have quite naturally been passed on to Sarah. It may be that I was gone too much and cut her too much slack. Sarah, poor misguided girl, over time came to honestly believe that she could run our plantation as well as I. The old saying may well be true: the best manure for any land is the frequent footsteps of its owner. There were years when my land felt my tread too seldom, but Sarah was always there. In time she came to believe that she had authority as well as responsibility. Over the years, the sweet girl I married became a woman I could not have predicted.

Chapter 1

LARKIN HOUSTON FLINT married me on my 16th birthday. All told, 87 persons watched us wed, counting the territorial commissioner of the New Cherokee Nation, plus the two full-blood Indians brought along to wait on him, and not counting Pa's three slaves who were there to wait on the rest of us. I thought we married for love, but I was wrong. Larkin and I married for lust — lust abounding, full-measured, pressed down, and overflowing. Doubtless, love was a natural and generous assumption on everybody's part, though I was too young to know the difference. Even less did I have cause to know there **is** a difference. Larkin surely had

known many and knew better, but he would have dismissed the distinction as hardly worth the serious consideration of a grown man 24 years old.

Larkin had a lot on his mind that day. I was not his secondary interest, and before that day was done, I was to know proof by way of joy and stirrings of rapture, but Larkin's day had begun on a more serious note. He was not a man to sidestep any opportunity, and the commissioner of the Cherokee Nation, the official envoy of the United States to the Indians, was definitely there to offer an opportunity.

To most it appeared merely a nice political touch that the commissioner had ridden nearly 100 miles to pay his respects to the bride of Sam Houston's grandson. Both families were highly mindful of this honor, and my own pa had overextended himself and all his hands to see that I was wed in a manner considerate of the circumstances. From the extent of the preparations — the whitewashing, hog-killing, scrubbing, and cooking that preceded my wedding — you would have thought us to be making ready for the old general himself. Indeed, if General Houston had been up to the rigors of a 500-mile journey, who is to say he would not have come to bless and inspire his handsome descendant? This view was Pa's way of seeing things. Pa was a man in favor of conviviality and ever inclined toward life's comforts, and my wedding gave him a wonderful opportunity for both.

The best of friends and the most opportunistic of strangers were to sample alike my mouth-watering marriage supper, taste the fiery liquor, and dance to the lively music of the best fiddlers in Arkansas. Pa, ever inclined to urge all to eat and drink and wax exuberant, was never disinclined to make a future profit by doing a present good deed. My wedding made history in northwest Arkansas, along with ensuring Pa's reputation as the owner of the most favorable stagecoach stop between Little Rock and St. Louis. Perception is everything. From that sparkling January day in 1860 until the day he died, Pa was counted to be a man of substance and unstinting hospitality. Meaning mostly to do me honor, but not unwilling to do himself proud in the bargain, he made for himself a not inconsiderable sum in the turbulent years to come from the goodwill generated that day.

Pa's forethought meant little to me. Larkin was on my mind and in my heart. I counted the hours until I could actually and legally feel his touch. I fevered to be in his arms. In this last goal I was effectively thwarted by

Pa, whose fierce Scots-Presbyterian intent was to deliver me as a virgin bride to the man who had bargained for me. Between Larkin's powerful pull and Pa's vigilant will, my heart pounded and my body ached for weeks before my wedding.

My stepmother, Eliza, compounded my problems. She wore me out. Our house was a stout log building one and one-half stories high, four rooms down, three above, and a wide hall in the middle. A long covered front porch formed the entrance. Eliza undertook to clean it all as a prelude to my wedding. We aired out the great rooms, polished the brass, scrubbed the wide split-log flooring, waxed the tables, and aired the feather beds. We washed sheets, pounded out the dust and aired the heavy homespun counterpanes that covered the beds, whitewashed the upstairs bedrooms, and scrubbed the necessaries. Each morning, she set out these tasks until she exhausted me. Each afternoon found me across the wide hall in the big kitchen and keeping room, where I sewed and she cooked. I sewed by hand the hems of my new nightgowns, I hemmed the homespun sheets for my dower chest, and I altered with care the wedding dress that had been my mother's, first worn in South Carolina and carried with love over the Tennessee mountains.

No wonder I was too tired to do more than moon and yawn in the evenings, too worn down and too sleepy to risk Pa's reprimands by more than a few swiftly stolen kisses by the firelight. What held Larkin back on these twice-weekly visits I was unable to fathom, but I knew my own limitations. A small-boned girl of a scant 100 pounds can extend her efforts only so far without exhaustion. Eliza's dedication to her wifely duties mandated that she assist Pa in his goal of ensuring my virginity. Between them, they delivered an excited, exhausted, and eager bride.

I vowed to myself, having nobody else to talk with about it, that I would do nothing but love Larkin after we were wed. Though I was too modest to mention it, even to Larkin, I meant to spend both my days and my nights in his arms. Why else did people wed?

I was spared the enormous effort of cooking for the 90-some-odd souls expected. Assisted by three hardworking slaves, Eliza shone like a full moon in her own kitchen. Pa had married the Widow McCarley at least as much for her cooking as for her conjugal charms. She was a marvel. Her pies were known to all who supped with us, there being much discussion, even argument, as to whether her cherry cobbler of the buttery crust and sweetly tart juices was truly superior to her rich and creamy six-egg chess custard. Arguments ran strong in both directions and were seldom settled even after generous samplings of each.

Eliza's Brunswick stew was famed in three counties. She had brought her Virginia grandmother's prized and secret recipe for the stew to both her marriages. I was initiated into its mysteries as a part of my own wedding preparation. The first ingredient was the easiest by far to acquire. "Shoot three squirrels," the document began, then went on to list tomatoes and okra, butter beans and snap beans, turnip and onion, potatoes and corn, and spices and roots unknown to few besides the Indians. Served alongside plates of hot corn bread and rolls of freshly baked light bread, Eliza's stew was a steaming wonder. Only when she undertook to teach me the secrets of its making did I know beyond a reasonable doubt that my stepmother of seven years had surely become my friend.

The advance work of the wedding began in early December 1859, the day after Larkin spoke to Pa for my hand. Preparations started off briskly enough, but the pace stepped up remarkably after we returned from our eventful Christmas Day visit to the homestead of the Flints. Pa knew then he had his work cut out for him. That visit was a foretaste of futures unknowable, an inspection guaranteed to daunt any but the most lovesick of maidens. My innocence was my shield with Larkin's father, for Matthew Flint assessed me and found me fair. Indeed, unbeknownst to me, he had assessed me much earlier and had liked what he had seen.

I did not so readily pass muster with Larkin's proud-faced mother. I was to encounter her likeness much later in the face of my own daughter, but at the time of my wedding she was a singular force and an enigma to me. Minerva Houston Flint carried the long limbs of her father with the nobility of bearing of her royal Cherokee mother. Her face had the proud bones of that Indian princess who had coupled so passionately with Sam Houston almost a half century earlier. Her beautiful and inscrutable countenance showed emotion less frequently than that of any other woman I have known. Her age was indeterminate. A strong-visaged, rich-complexioned goddess, she gave quarter reluctantly, if at all.

The invitation (or was it a command?) to take Christmas dinner at the mountain stronghold of the Flints had been delivered by Larkin the same day as his asking for me. Seated at Pa's ample table, Larkin had polished off his second plate of Eliza's chicken and dumplings, looked down at me with his already endearing lopsided grin, then looked beyond me to Pa.

"My father asks that you and yours take Christmas dinner at his table. Sarah needs to know what she's getting into."

As if I cared about anything beyond Larkin at that point. His mother and father interested me not in the least. I knew little of them. Their valley, six miles away as the crow flies, was separated from my own by a mountain — that reach of the large and lovely Boston Mountains that served as backdrop to our parents' respective and extensive holdings.

I was to see Larkin only once more in the next ten days prior to Christmas. His second visit so flustered me that I could scarce eat or sleep. I had only to close my eyes to recapture the sight of him — just over six feet, his handsome head topping the broad shoulders and slim hips of a natural athlete, the beautifully modeled lips firmly held in control. His black hair and deep-set blue eyes were a wonderful contrast to the high fresh color of his bronzed complexion. He had only to look down on me to set my heart pounding. A smile was high praise. His touch was almost too pleasurable to bear. Those lips brushed mine as he went out the door into the darkness. It was all I could do to keep from running after him.

In short, my mind that Christmas morning was so full of Larkin that my unnatural quietness was mistakenly attributed by Eliza to be maidenly apprehension, which was just as well. Had I had any foretaste of the emotions that lay ahead of me that sparkling winter day, my spirits would have vacillated like a compass needle held by an unsteady hand.

Pa had rousted us out of bed before daylight. Eliza's Christmas gift to me was a beautiful new pair of black kid high-topped shoes, their toes accented and protected by a narrow rim of polished brass. I wore them proudly. We dressed and breakfasted by candlelight, Eliza eating two biscuits to my one, Pa, as always, claiming his eggs to be the best cooked he'd ever had. Black Zeke had harnessed the mare to the buggy and saddled Pa's big roan, for the mountain road was too steep to burden the mare with the weight of all of us. I secretly suspicioned that Pa's real reason for riding the roan was to show off his handsome new gelding, but the heft of Eliza was reason enough for his decision. Eliza was what Pa called a somewhat sizable woman, with a backside that bespoke of good use and good victuals. My easygoing Pa boosted her into the buggy with an affectionate hoist to that same backside, teasing her even as he lifted her into the driver's seat. "I swear, Eliza, when you walk you got the only pair of hips in these hills that talk to each other. One says to the other, 'You let me by this time, I'll let you by next time!' This buggy ride'll give them both a rest."

"William Griffin, that hot toddy you had before breakfast went straight to your head and loosened your tongue. Ride on, let us be, and don't fill Sarah's head with thoughts best not discussed in front of the child." But Pa was already in the saddle, the roan's hooves ringing on the frost-rimed rocks of the road. His choosing to take the steep six-mile wagon trace over the mountain rather than go around it by way of the big pike would cut some 15 miles from our journey. Pa liked adventure; he had not bargained for a long day on the road, much less for an overnight stay.

At the ford of the Buffalo River we left the big road and took the wagon trace up the wooded ravine. It was not much of a road, for not many had traveled it. Two rocky ruts with tall dead weeds grown up between led through country too rough to drive a good buggy through, to say nothing of a fine mare. We stopped every half mile to let the heavy blowing mare rest from pulling her burden. The higher we climbed, the more we marveled at the view. The sides of the road grew thick and brushy laurel with huckleberry bushes beside and bare-branched maple and oak above. Dusky green cedar and acres of pine competed for space. Through the openings above their branches I glimpsed the high-ranged mountains, dark green and gleaming in the sunlight. The woods showed wonders that day. Sunlight shafted through the early morning mist to glitter thousands of diamonds on needles of pine. The gray-blue berries of the cedars gleamed like the pearls of the Fairy Queen. Far above us on the stark limbs of a tall hickory, I spied the white berries of mistletoe. I begged Pa to gather a bunch for my Christmas gift to Larkin. I could have climbed the tree far more readily than Pa, but I knew better than to scratch up and tear my new wool challis dress, a dress never designed for shimmying up the trunk of a hickory. So my good-natured pa climbed a dozen feet, knocked off the mistletoe with his buggy whip, and presented it to me with the wish that with Larkin's help it might be put to good use by day's end. Ah, all the world was bright and sweet that Christmas morning!

The mare climbed three hours before we crested the mountaintop. I gazed down onto as pretty a site as could have been imagined. At the upper end of the long valley below us lay the Flint holdings. A large, square-trimmed log house of two stories was surrounded by maple and oak, the yard sloping down to a clear, pebble-bottomed little river that rippled in the sunshine. Already the scene was lively. The stock barn on the far bank, enclosed by a tall split-rail corral, held horses, mules, milk cows, chickens, ducks, and an ever-shifting population of coon dogs and barn cats. As I was later to learn, the establishment was not off limits to deer, raccoon, wild turkeys, and any other creature needing a meal or a refuge.

Pa halted for the last rest stop, well pleased, having brought us in good time and fair shape within sight of his goal. Gazing down at the richness of the three-mile long valley, he proceeded to educate me and instruct me in civility. "Sarah, you will be remembering that Larkin's mother is the half-breed daughter of General Houston. She is by way of being considered a princess among the Cherokee, and proud beyond knowing. My judgment is, she's hard to know and hard to please. Be mindful of the honor she intends you."

With this admonition he hoisted Eliza's willing rump back onto the buggy seat. I sprang lightly onto the space that was left, and Pa led our triumphant entry into the imposing wilderness kingdom of Matthew Pleasant Flint and his formidable consort.

Visitors to this solitary stronghold were rare enough to create a commotion. The old Negro posted as a lookout ran to open the big gate that barred our ready entry. Grinning like a possum, he mumbled, "Welcome, masta! Welcome, missuses, welcome, welcome!" The big yard was busy. Squaws, Negroes, and white hired hands were roasting what I took to be venison. There was much running, giggling, fetching, and carrying. Children played, dogs barked, commotion abounded. Larkin and his father advanced to meet us.

"Welcome to our home and our family. And a happy Christmas to all."

Matthew Flint bespoke pride and dignity in every inch of his imposing six-foot frame. To me, he appeared an old man, his full head of silvery hair worn long, framing the deep blue eyes and Roman nose that he had passed on to Larkin. Intelligence, courtesy, strength, and honesty formed his character, which had earned the trust of the Cherokee and white settler alike. If ever I gazed into the face of a born leader, it was that day on that first swift look at the face of my future father-in-law. I saw the promise of Larkin's future foretold on the countenance of his father. Separated by age but joined in temperament, they were contemporaries in both intellect and ambition. Yet on Larkin's face there were emotional subtleties that I was unable to read. His heritage from those long-dead Cherokee chiefs was already writ on his face. I was to spend a lifetime endeavoring to decipher them. All these swift impressions left me in uncharacteristic silence as I was handed ceremoniously out of the buggy. On the other side, Larkin welcomed my stepmother and Pa with a grave courtesy that underscored the importance of the occasion. We drew near the house, I on Mr. Flint's arm, and thus we approached the chatelaine of the household. She stood regally at the top of the wide steps of her own porch, dark green shrubs of bright red-berried holly defining the foundations beneath, rich throws of buffalo hides slung casually across the porch railings. Her enigmatic look encompassed me.

Through the eyes of Minerva Flint I saw how I must appear to her, a small-boned and graceful girl filled to excess with romantic notions, a girl whose dark curly hair was no longer bound neatly into its chignon but was escaping in small curls around my forehead. I silently thanked Eliza for insisting that I wear my new blue dress. With full sleeves that gathered into a deep yoke and a fitted bodice that ended in a gathered skirt, the challis matched my eyes and complemented the exquisite lace collar that had been part of my own mother's trousseau. I advanced with considerable confidence. My waist was small, my skin was fair, and my ways were lively. I was a better reader and a more graceful dancer than any girl I knew. But these attributes, however desirable, appeared not to be the ones for which the inscrutable Minerva Flint was searching.

"Enter; our house is yours."

Since she spoke the words with sincerity, I addressed her directly. "I mean to please Larkin, and to try to please you, ma'am."

Again, the penetrating eyes surveyed me. "I know you do."

Pa had his own pride. "Mrs. Flint, we are honored to be here today. In the back of Eliza's buggy there are baskets to add a few trifles to today's table. If you would be so kind as to direct me, I'll carry them into your kitchens." Trifles, indeed. Those carefully packed baskets held a whole baked ham, mince pies so rich with spirits and spices as to constitute a real danger of inducing intoxication, a magnificent pound cake with its accompanying rum sauce, plus Eliza's famous blackberry cordial. The Griffins had by no means come empty-handed.

Though I had dreamed for days of being with Larkin, I had not realized there would be such scant opportunity to see him alone. As our party gained entrance to the main house, various brothers and sisters and their numerous offspring came forward to vie for my attention. Two half brothers, Robert and Samuel, were presented with their busy wives and gamboling children, as were the married sister, Kate, with her sizable family, and the younger unmarried ones, Thomas, Stanton, and Rebecca. To most, Larkin presented me simply, saying, "This is Sarah," but to a late-arriving pair he introduced me with more definition. The noon sun was overhead when the last guests appeared. Two splendidly mounted horses came through the gate, their riders imposingly garbed in elegant pantaloons and broadcloth coats. The plumed hats of cavalrymen topped the flowing black hair and red-skinned faces of Cherokee Indians. These were Matthew Flint's brothers-in-law, invited to the Christmas holidays for reasons both political and personal. To his uncles, Larkin presented me with care. "This is Sarah," he said, "daughter of William Griffin, and, on her mother's side, granddaughter of Louis Chouteau."

It appeared to be a lineage sufficient to invite their respect. They bowed. I had never before seen an Indian bow, nor had I seen any man, whether red or white, in such elegant clothing. I was fired with curiosity, determined to question Larkin at some later point.

I very seldom thought of myself as the granddaughter of Louis Chouteau, the adventurer who had left his wife and a civilized life in the City of Kansas to make yet another fortune between the banks of the Missouri and the Arkansas Rivers. Known to all who benefited from Indian trade, whether based on furs or liquor and pioneering necessities, Louis Chouteau had been a force and an ascending power until he died. Through my mother's inheritance it was expected that someday, if the wrangling politicians in the federal bureaucracies of Washington ever settled the question, I would be eligible for a one-eighth portion of the thousands of acres of disputed lands to which Monsieur had established his claim. This prospect was not immediately likely, the matter having been debated by squabbling attorneys and their anxious clients for the past decade.

I understood, however, the significance of Larkin's introduction. The braves of the Cherokee Nation regarded the French to be their natural allies, the English to be their frequent enemies, and their current white father in Washington, James Buchanan, to be a vacillating and unpredictable source of concern. While it was of relatively minor importance to me, I was more than pleased to have been defined as having parentage that passed muster with these exotic gentlemen.

Larkin took the reins of their horses as the Houston brothers advanced toward Matthew Flint. I seized the chance to learn more. "Tell me about them, Larkin. How are they descended from General Houston?"

"The Raven is the Indian name of Houston. He is the adopted son of

Oo-loo-te-ka, a great Cherokee leader, a chief in the Tennessee mountains during Houston's young days. From the time he was a boy Houston sought out the Indians, most especially in time of trouble. I guess he cut a wide swath among them when he was a young officer. General Jackson sent him out on an Indian assignment as Jackson's personal selection. Anyhow, he saw his boyhood sweetheart again, Oo-loo-te-ka's daughter, Morning Deer, on that trip. They were young, she was lovely, and Houston married her in a Cherokee ceremony."

"How long ago was this?" As the general was famous, I had heard much of his ways and could immediately see the advantage of having the chief's daughter as a wife.

"This would have been somewhere around 1815 or so. My mother was born in 1816, and my twin uncles the next year."

My mind came back to known history. "Then how could he later on take a wife in Tennessee?"

"Morning Deer died birthing the twins. They and my mother were reared in Oo-loo-te-ka's wigwam and educated at Dwight Mission, down near the river. Houston wanted them to move in both worlds, as he has always done."

By this time, I had formed some opinion of Minerva. "And which is your mother's choosing?"

"Mother lives in the world of her choosing. And lives royally."

I knew that he spoke truth. Ever so fleetingly I realized that Larkin meant to do the same. Although I had no aspiration toward regality myself, I thereupon decided that I would cultivate an understanding of those who did. To be a princess in the midst of an Arkansas clearing suddenly seemed to be a desirable objective. Minerva had married a man well-off by territorial standards, had brought him advantageous political connections, and had been blessed with abundance. The Raven's dreams of empire were still beset by the unpredictable winds that blew from Washington, but his daughter and her husband had managed to create their own wilderness oasis.

Minerva had met her match in Matthew Flint. Older and more experienced than she, he was descended from generations of Scotsmen whose driving need for independence had carried them deeper and deeper into the interior of the continent. Born in Tennessee of a father who had himself been born in Virginia, Matthew had established himself as a man of importance long before he met Minerva. His first wife, mother of Robert and

Samuel, had not survived the rigors of their long and difficult journey over the Great Smoky Mountains and lay buried in a lonely mountain grave. Matthew had arrived in Arkansas a widower with two sons to raise, considerable capital to expend, and a need for a partner equal to the expectations of a man of ambition. The young and well-educated Cherokee daughter of the Raven had proved to be equal to these ambitions.

One of the rewards of his marriage to Minerva had been Matthew Pleasant Flint's 1832 appointment as farmer and trader for the Cherokee Indian agency. Highly resourceful, he knew how to capitalize to advantage the elements of Indian trade.

Having selected a beautiful site of land in Arkansas, he had purchased a 10,000-acre tract of virgin forest and fertile prairie at the Congress price of $1.25 an acre. This rich valley bottomland with its fresh, sweet springs contained a shallow river navigable by flatboat, as well as mountain slopes heavy with valuable timber. The Ozark Mountains at his back constituted a natural and formidable barrier from the north. The river that drained these lands flowed into the Arkansas and hence to the Mississippi and New Orleans, affording a ready road to market for the corn, hogs, and mules that were his cash crops.

In partnership with his brothers-in-law, the half-breed sons of General Houston, a monumental farming/trading enterprise had taken shape. Traders with unusual and exclusive privilege, John and Thomas Houston preferred to locate their main establishment on the civilized side of the Cherokee Nation border, at Fort Smith, on the western border of Arkansas. Their interests, however, were far-ranging and knew few boundaries. Like their father, they saw no reason why politics and profits should be mutually exclusive.

All this Larkin outlined for me as we walked toward the corral. While he led both horses, I walked at his side with my hand on his arm, careful to stay at the horses' heads.

"I'll wait outside the corral," I offered, reluctant to subject my new shoes to the muck within.

"Come with me inside the gate, Sarah." His tone did not imply a choice.

Hitching up my skirt, I walked ahead through the gate to watch while Larkin removed the saddles and bridles. With a final slap at their flanks, he sent the horses away at a freewheeling gallop. "This way, Sarah."

As he led me into the far shadows of the lean-to shed, I looked at Larkin in delight, belatedly grasping his reasons for wanting me there. Deliberately and surely he took me in his arms. His kiss began gently enough, though soon it set my heart to pounding. Never had I been so close to another. An only child and lonely girl, even one with an affectionate parent, has little call to be pressed against the body of another, and my own small body responded like a traveler coming home to a warm hearth. I melted and I glowed. He put both hands at my waist, lifting me smoothly onto a low box so that we were almost on a level. Thus, I was able to feel his muscles come to attention, emphasizing the most intimate parts of his body. One hand was at my back, another swiftly cupped my bottom, pressing my surprised but willing body to meet his as I responded to his now urgent kisses. When he finally released me I was too dizzy to stand, and I put both arms around his neck in greedy expectation.

"They'll be waiting for us. We must go in for dinner now." The disciplined look was returning to his face. "We may not have another chance today. There'll be a lot of talk at the table and later, as well. And I wondered what you'd be like."

"Am I as you thought?" I asked shyly.

"Better," he grinned. In one swift move he lifted me in his arms, carrying me across the corral and through the gate where he stood me on my feet. I floated rather than walked the considerable distance toward his father's house, there again to be scrutinized thoroughly by his family.

In relatively short order we were summoned by Matthew Flint to his Christmas feast, a feast that began with a solemn grace and lasted for the greater part of the afternoon. Roast venison, stewed beef, baked ham, baked wild turkey, relishes, yams, pickles, breads, puddings, cakes, pies, and various creamy concoctions all claimed our attention in the great room. Across the wide back hall in the big kitchen, the hired men, women, children, and squaws ate seated on the broad window ledges, on the floor, or on the few chairs that could be spared from the great room. Dogs strolled expectantly down the hall and through the rooms, dashing after the bones that the children tossed to them. Through the hall connecting the two big rooms I could see the lively children. Being only a few years beyond childhood myself, I wondered if they were having more fun than the adults. Quickly suppressing this doubt of my own adulthood, I focused my attention on the table conversation.

The taller of Madame Flint's brothers held the floor. "The scales have already been tipped in Kansas, that dark and bloody ground foretold by our ancestors. War will come, sooner than we like and sooner than most think."

"Kansas men are no different than we are. They care little about slavery one way or the other. Land titles are what they're after, and that's the point they'll fight on." Samuel Flint spoke with conviction.

The talk grew heated.

"You may be right, Sam, but the Kansas-Nebraska Act moved the slaving fight from Washington to Kansas, and emigrants there have been fighting the battles for both sides ever since. Some are fighting out of meanness and greed, but more are fighting the battles of others. I talked to a man here in Carroll County who was in St. Joseph last year. He told me he saw firsthand a shipment of 200 'Beecher Bibles' shipped to Kansas City bound for Lawrence." My pa took issue. His point was well taken. It was widely rumored that one Northern church alone, that of the Reverend Henry Ward Beecher, had shipped hundreds of rifles to Kansas, earning these lethal weapons the popular title of "Beecher Bibles."

"Southerners are sending guns, as well. Wouldn't you, if your holdings and even your income depended on hanging on to your property and your lands? And a big part of a planter's property is in slaves." Robert got in the discussion.

"Congress may be filled with smart men, but they're too long on compromise and too short on common sense. And Buchanan is no better. That Land Act of 1854 was a compromising piece of foolishness. You all know it as well as I do. Most of that land in both Kansas and Nebraska was still entitled to the Indians then, and little had been surveyed. Six months later you couldn't buy an acre anywhere. It changed hands before it even got surveyed."

"Horace Greeley is the real general of the war in Kansas. 'Bleeding Kansas' will be counted on the Union side because of his victories."

"Wars with words are one thing. Getting shot at is something else. And I'm not keen on getting killed over somebody else's slaves or over Greeley's high-flown preachings."

"Even getting shot at in an honest battle is an improvement over the hacking and murdering that has gone on in Kansas. John Brown's sneaking raids and the Pottawatomie killings were a disgrace to the Union cause. And we're apt to get the same in Arkansas before we're through — we could get it from either side."

"I said it before and I'll say it again." Sam was adamant. "Which side they fight on in Kansas has little to do with slavery and a lot to do with getting rich on land speculation. But the Kansas issue is settled. Best we pay attention to our own. Lunatics like John Brown may think God speaks to them firsthand and gives orders to kill and pillage, but we know better. We're coming down to some hard choices in Arkansas. There won't be an easy way out. We're going to have to choose sides in a war that no man at this table wants to see."

Matthew Flint responded with characteristic analysis. "Arkansas hesitates to secede. She is exposed on her entire western flank by Indian country and on the north from Missouri. Our fortunes, indeed, our livelihoods, depend on the continuance of our trade in those directions."

He was, of course, entirely correct. The fortunes of all present had been made through trade with the West and the North, through trails leading to St. Joseph and to Santa Fe or slanting obliquely toward the Cimarron. Prospering farmers, stagecoach owners, and Indian traders and Indian agents based their very existence on this westward expansion.

Pa responded, "If Arkansas secedes she will be invaded from all quarters except the south and possibly the southwest. Some of Texas may be for secession, but I cannot believe that Senator Houston will ever swear an oath against the country for whom he has been so valiant a soldier."

"Those of Little Rock look southward to the Confederacy, Mr. Griffin, and they stand to gain much if the price of cotton continues to advance." Larkin had long ceased to pay attention to me and was urgently proposing the chief cause of concern.

"Plus, the loss of slaves will cost us dear," Pa stated. "I, for one, can bear that burden. Better to lose a few slaves than to lose a country and a livelihood."

"But, William, you have but few, while to the planters their slaves are a necessity. I fear the outcome of this." Matthew Flint looked grave.

"Who is to say that all of Arkansas must choose the same wigwam? The river affords a natural boundary to the south, and Crowley's Ridge to the east. Why cannot the lot of this north half of the state be cast with the other Northern states?" The second uncle's imaginative proposal gained the attention of all.

"Why merely with the North? Why not an alliance with the Cherokee Nation?" countered his brother.

Matthew was decisive. "The Cherokee Nation alone lacks the power to command an alliance. The Cherokee Nation plus northern Arkansas constitutes a persuasive attraction for an alliance with the states of the North." The matter was discussed for the better part of the next two days, and in the end Matthew's logic prevailed. The most likely ambassadors being already present at this extended family council, the plan was defined and within due course was presented to Sam Houston's friend, the President's most convenient ambassador, the territorial commissioner of the Cherokee Nation.

Thus, brightened possibilities opened to men of substance and ambition, the men who that day dined at my father-in-law's table. And thus was my precious time alone with Larkin reduced to a few short minutes, for he was to become an essential element in their proposed plan.

Larkin was the natural choice to be their representative at the party caucuses. Of all the handsome and able Flint sons, he was the best educated. He had studied Latin and mathematics and had literally read everything he could get his hands on, even walking over the mountains the winter he was 17 to read one term at the New Arkansas College in Fayetteville. Matthew Flint's house offered a rare opportunity for learning, for his bookshelves contained riches seldom found west of the Mississippi. An eight-volume set of ancient history was displayed, along with *Elements of Euclid* and a geography book, Shakespeare, Locke, *Gulliver's Travels*, Plato's *Republic*, Hume, and, of course, the Bible. Altogether, he owned three shelves of books from which to choose. I had never seen so many books in one residence and was drawn to them as a moth to the lights.

It was midafternoon when we left the Christmas dinner table and crossed the wide hall to the opposite great room that contained the books. Dominated by the stone fireplace that filled its west wall, this room was the heart of the household. High on its walls hung four fiddles, three guitars, and one exquisitely crafted dulcimer. Between the two wide windows that admitted the light from the south were the bookshelves, and below the bookshelves was Matthew Flint's well-worn desk, positioned so as to take advantage of the best light. With its pens and inkwells and well-used account books I felt immediately at home, for I had been schooled by Pa to accurately keep his own accounts.

Two high-backed chairs with cushions and footstools flanked the fireplace. I was immediately reminded of pictures once seen in a history book, sketches of the carved wooden thrones designed for the comfort of long-dead Scottish lairds. A spinning wheel and a long trestle table with benches furnished the room, along with buffalo-hide throw rugs, many-colored pillows, and a high-posted bedstead complete with a feather bed covered by an indigo and white woven counterpane.

But it was for music we had adjourned to this room. Minerva led the way, seating Pa and Eliza in the two imposing chairs that were the seats of honor. "No more talk of war," she declared. "We'll end the day with music and cheer."

There seemed to be no clear rank as to the choice of the instruments. Larkin took one fiddle, his father another. To my astonishment Minerva was handed the dulcimer, which she carefully placed upon the trestle table. Soon each instrument had been appropriated. There followed a clanging and scraping as chairs were positioned, strings tightened, and bows waxed, but these ordinary noises were intermingled with the pluck, pluck, pluck of strings being tuned by practiced hands. At a nod from Matthew the music sprang into life, the sweet sound of the fiddles floating and pulsing the melodies. From the first lively rhythm of "Buffalo Gals" to the last haunting strains of "What Child is This?," I was spellbound, caught up in emotions too complex for my immediate understanding. Nor was I alone. The siren songs worked their magic on us all. An hour later Pa reluctantly broke the spell. "Could we have one verse of 'Auld Lang Syne' as our fitting farewell to this day?"

Larkin's violin took up the melody, but it was Minerva's lustrous contralto voice that sang the poignant words: "And here's a hand, my trusty friend, and gie's a hand of thine; we'll take a cup o' kindness yet, for auld lang syne."

Some thoughtful hand had fixed the mistletoe to the door lintel. I exited the room as in a dream, blessed by my future father-in-law's soft kiss on my cheek, stirred by Larkin's lips brushing fleetingly against mine, and guided unerringly to the waiting buggy by Pa's firm hand beneath my elbow.

Chapter 2

MY SOUL WAS SINGING. I sat down on the buggy seat eager to dream of Larkin during the long ride home, but I had another think coming. Eliza had held herself back as long as she could. Our buggy had scarcely cleared the gate before she began her parsing of the day.

"Well, Sarah, you've got your work cut out for you. If ever I've seen a woman with no give to her, it is Minerva Flint. Stiff-necked and high-headed. And I expect Larkin has more than enough of the same in him, too. I most assuredly hope you stay on that woman's good side. Still, to her credit, she runs a fine household, and I figure her to put

Matthew Flint and their children ahead of every earthly consideration, including herself. So I guess if you please Larkin, you're likely to please her."

"I please Larkin." My tone was sure. "And Larkin's land is three miles from the big house. I don't expect to be seeing her all that much. Even when I do, there'll be lots of others around. And they all like me."

Eliza was matter-of-fact. "They like your looks, they like your land — or they will once you finally inherit it — and they like what Larkin wants. They don't know you yet. The Flint women work hard. And do as they're told, all except Minerva. When Larkin says, 'Jump,' he'll be expecting you to say, 'How high?' That won't come easy for you, Sarah."

"Loving Larkin comes easy for me." I was not to be daunted, neither by her sobering words nor by my own internal uneasiness that her analysis was not that far off the mark. "But maybe you'd better teach me a little more about cooking before I have to start doing it."

"My Lord, Sarah." Eliza was instantly contrite. "I've been so busy getting the house ready I've fallen down on the job of getting *you* ready. You've never cooked a meal by yourself in your life. There's always been me giving orders to you or you giving orders to Neely."

Neely was wife to Zeke and mother to Tobe. Together these three slaves furnished the labor that accounted for the major part of Pa's business success. Zeke was the blacksmith, not only for the stage stop, but for all that lived around us within a 20-mile radius. In addition, he was general laborer for everything else Pa wanted. Along with Tobe, Zeke farmed the land, herded the sheep, milked the cows, and fed the stock. They lent their considerable strength to every profitable enterprise Pa developed.

Neely worked the garden, spun the yarn, made the fires, wove the cloth, made the soap, did the wash, cooked the meals, waited table for the stage stop travelers, and cleaned the house, all to Eliza's demanding standards. I had helped in most of Neely's enterprises, but my status had been strictly that of an apprentice, and an unenthusiastic one at that, hard work being fairly low on my interest list. With reluctance I foresaw a considerable change. Larkin owned no slaves. My life was about to take a decidedly different turn. There would be immediate uses for skills that heretofore had been substantially below my nearly-16-year-old dignity.

Eliza offered comfort and commendation straight from her Presbyterian heritage. "Remember the words of Proverbs: 'Who can find a virtuous woman? For her price is far above rubies. . . . She seeketh wool, and flax, and worketh willingly with her hands. . . . She girdeth her loins with strength, and strengtheneth her arms. . . . She looketh well to the ways of her household, and eateth not the bread of idleness." She paused, thought a while, and took heart. "We'll start your cooking lessons tomorrow, Sarah. You're smart and you're quick. Now that you're willing, you'll do fine. I'll not have Madame Flint looking down that proud nose of hers at our girl. And Larkin won't have food on his mind in the beginning, anyway!"

I giggled. Eliza gave me a sharp look and caught my blush. She began a knowing chuckle, and Pa found us laughing together, joined in that confidence that comes to women who are sure of their powers.

As always, Pa was thinking ahead. "It's going to get dark on us long before we can get home, and the weather is changing. I'm not going to put the horses over that mountain road after dark. We'll take the long way, go by the big road, and stay the night with John and Kate. It may snow tonight."

Eliza and I were in instant agreement with his good judgment, Eliza because she was tired and liked her comfort, I because my Uncle John's family were my favorite kin. A visit with them always warmed my heart.

We pulled up to their house just as the sun went down. Pa's brother, my Uncle John, came out to shake Pa's hand and make us welcome and wanted.

"Kate and the girls have been talking about you all day, wondering how things went over at the Flints. Larkin's a lucky man, Sarah. I hope he knows how lucky he is. You're beginning to remind me so much of your mother that it takes my breath away. Anne had that same sweet look in her eyes."

Aunt Kate came to the door. "Come in out of the cold. You're just in time for supper. We've been hoping all day that you all would come back this way, and the girls even saved you a Christmas orange, Sarah."

"I saved you something, too, Sarah — a Christmas hug!" My cousin Willie threw his arms around me, whirled me off my feet, and set me down in the middle of his sisters, Faith, Hope, Charity, and Piety. All started talking at once.

As usual, I started teasing Willie. "Willie, why is it that you're a foot taller than I am when you're only a year older? I can't believe they feed you any better at that boarding school than Aunt Kate does at home, but you're a lot changed. Even your feet look bigger."

Uncle John took up the teasing. "Willie's changed from a runt to a scarecrow. We can't keep him in pants and we can't keep him in shoes. I'm not sure we can afford to keep feeding him, either." He ruffled Willie's curly hair, grinning at his only son, his pride and joy.

I grinned with him. Willie was my favorite, too. The brother I'd never had, the playmate I'd always had, Willie and I had fought and argued, made up and played together since I could remember.

"Sarah, if I could figure out a way that first cousins could marry, I'd never let Larkin have you." Willie's smile was wide but his tone meant business. "But since I can't ask for you myself I'm thinking on the next best thing. Larkin's little sister Becky is a real sweetheart. How'd you like me for a brother-in-law?"

I was quick to see the advantages. "Go for her, Willie. I'm going to need another Griffin in the middle of all those Flints. But she's not very big and she's not very old. What is she, 14?"

"She is, and if I can catch her early I can train her right. You've been spoiled, Sarah. Larkin's going to have to break you in a little. Now Becky could be in training for the next two whole years while I'm off studying medicine."

Aunt Kate laughed. "Well, she's a real improvement over some of your other girls, Willie. I think you might do worse. But has Becky been told yet? Or do you plan to spring it on her as a New Year's Eve gift?"

"I'm working up to it. I haven't been studying marrying too long. If Sarah hadn't brought up the subject, it might not even have crossed my mind. But I sure could use somebody to wait on me. I can't afford a slave, and I hear that wives come mighty cheap!"

Aunt Kate had listened to enough foolishness. "Don't tease Sarah on the eve of her wedding. She deserves better out of you, Willie. And we all pray for your happiness, honey." She kissed me, held me tenderly in her arms, then led me toward the glowing hearth. "And Eliza, you must be worn out. I know how you are, and I know you've done nothing but work for weeks now. You come sit by the fire, too, and we'll let the girls wait on us. I want to hear more about the Flints. I hear that Matthew gave Larkin a quarter-section of land. A good start."

Aunt Kate and Uncle John had easy access to all the talk in the county worth hearing. Uncle John's grist mill was the only one in the county. Since Griffin's Mill was an essential element in the corn and wheat farmers' lives, it was the news center. Although Pa got a Little Rock newspaper every week, the *Gazette*, at the stage stop, and Uncle John got the *Independent Reform*, from Benton County, most people were ten times more interested in news of their neighbors than in news of the nation. So word of mouth flourished, and the Griffins had a more accurate version than word of mouth usually furnished. Pa referred to talk around the grist mill as the "Griffin Gazette."

Eliza answered, "Yes, Larkin has the land, with the cabin on it, the first cabin that was built in Carroll County, I hear. It's a good-sized one. You know, the Flints never do anything by halves. But I've been wanting to talk to you, Kate, about something else." She lowered her voice beyond my hearing, but I cared not, for it freed me up to talk to the twins, Charity and Piety. Faith was already married, and Hope would probably be an old maid, but Charity and Piety and I were nearly the same age, the liveliest trio of girls to be found anywhere.

"You've got to promise to come visit me often. You'll be my closest neighbors, besides the Flints. Ten miles won't be that far, and Uncle John will let you come if you come together." The wooded road was not safe for a woman alone, the danger being not so much the infrequent traveler as the frequent prowling of panthers and bears.

"Well, he'll let us if Willie comes with us, but it'll take a lot of persuading to get him to let us set out that far in the buggy without a man. But when Larkin comes to the mill, maybe we can ride back with him." Piety was practical.

Charity was a romantic. "Willie may be willing to ride over on a regular basis if he meant what he said about Becky Flint. Does Becky have another beau yet?"

And so we laughed and planned in innocence and affection.

We ate supper early and went to bed early, for all were tired. After considerable juggling of bed space and sleeping arrangements, I found myself on the trundle bed next to the larger bedstead that held Pa and Eliza. Near exhaustion, I had almost drifted into dreams when I caught Eliza's urgent whispers. "Will, did John say anything to you about that Casey girl from back in the mountains?"

"Well, he did mention her, Eliza. Go to sleep, woman. I'm tired out."

"But Will, they say she's with child and has named Larkin the father."

"Eliza, I am ashamed of you." Pa's fierce whisper was firm. "You ought not to listen to gossip about loose girls, much less stories made up by two-bit whores. I thought better of you."

"But, Will, I heard the squaws laughing about it today in the Flint kitchen. They thought it to be a joke."

"And now I'm twice ashamed of you for paying attention to the talk of squaws."

There was to be no putting off Eliza's worry. "Will, I talked to Kate, and John heard the same thing at the grist mill last week."

After a long sigh, Pa gritted his teeth, a sure signal of his anger. "Eliza, that Casey girl has spread her legs for every man and boy in the county that had two bits. She has been her ma's main cash crop since she was 13. A trashier family never holed up in these hills. I'd as soon believe the word of the serpent of Eden."

"Then you don't believe the child to be Larkin's?"

"Eliza, if you set that rear of yours down on a porcupine, would you know which quill stuck you? That slut has no idea whose child it is. I don't expect to ever have this subject come up again. Put it out of your mind. The subject is closed." Silence reigned.

The household slept, but I did not. Finally, lulled by the sweet memory of Larkin's kisses, I drifted off to dreams in which Larkin's violin played elusive melodies and I studied his rhythms so as to match my steps to his tune.

Things looked better in the morning. There had been a light snow during the night, but morning dawned fair. After a satisfying breakfast of Aunt Kate's buttermilk pancakes and sugar maple syrup, I felt sufficiently recovered to ask Aunt Kate some hard questions. It was not easy to find a place of privacy around so many kinfolks, so finally I simply had to state my case. "Aunt Kate, could I please talk to you for a few minutes before we leave?"

She gave me her instant attention, "You girls go help out in the kitchen. I want to talk to Sarah."

"Aunt Kate, did you ever worry before you married? Yesterday I was so happy. Today I wonder if I dreamed it, and it might not last."

She gave me a quick compassionate look. "Sarah, you've heard things, and I'm sorry for that, for I know what they were. No, I try not to worry. You're getting a fine man, and Larkin *is* a man, not a boy. He's honest, he keeps his word, he's smart and hard-working. I know what you love right now is his touch. There's many a sorry man with good looks and a sweet touch, but fortunately, Larkin is not one of these. Flint men are wild before they marry, but they settle down when they marry right, and Larkin is marrying right. He knows it, too, which goes to prove he's as smart as he looks. He knows you will be his partner."

"Is that all men want in a wife, Aunt Kate, a bed partner?"

Aunt Kate was shocked. "Not just a bed partner, Sarah. A real partner. Somebody he can count on to be on his side, through thick and thin and joy and sorrow. I don't think my John could have made it through life half as well without me, and I know I could not have been as happy without John. Partners help each other. Partners face the world together, raise their children together, work out their problems together, and stick up for each other in time of trouble. Your Pa has promised you to the man who is the catch of the county. Larkin picked well, too. You're a prize, Sarah.

"Love comes, Sarah, but not until you sacrifice some for it. You show love through sacrifice, but you get love that way, too. You don't know the meaning of the word yet, nor Larkin, either. But you will. Love will come to you both." She kissed me. "Your pa and Eliza are waiting. You need to get home and get ready for your wedding."

Pa was in a thoughtful mood as we rode along and kept his gelding's pace constant with ours so he could talk to Eliza.

"John's going to free his slaves. He thinks he'd better do it while the law still allows it. There's talk that when the legislature meets, there'll be a bill introduced to forbid it. John has had slavery on his conscience a long time. I told him he can free them up, but he won't get them off his back that easy. Free Negroes are nearly as much trouble as slaves, plus you can't get as much work out of them. He paid $700 apiece in gold for Ike and Joe, when they were boys, plus another $1,000 for their mother, and then she up and died on him after only five years. So he's been out $2,400, plus feeding them all this time. I'm not sure it makes any sense to his pocketbook. Now he's going to free them up and turn around and pay them $200 a year in wages besides. John's got a soft heart. This time he may be showing a soft head besides. He won't get rid of those boys. They don't know anything except how to run a grist mill and farm a little, and they're not bright enough to learn much more. He'll be stuck for their feeding just like he is now. The only difference is, he'll be giving them $200 a year, which they'll spend like water as soon as they get it. And they'll lay down on the job. They never have worked as hard as Zeke and Tobe, and John has let them get by with it."

Eliza was puzzled. "Then why is John so set on freeing them? Free

Negroes never have been in great favor around here. White men don't trust them, and slaves can't afford to be around them."

She was right. The free Negro was considered to be a poor example to the slaves, and especially liable to influence by abolitionists if they could read, which Ike and Joe could not. Free Negroes came in for suspicion from all quarters. Since they were frequently used by abolitionists to stir up trouble among slaves, the law provided severe penalties for free Negroes found in the company of slaves. Even entertaining a slave in his own cabin made a free Negro liable to a fine of up to $100 or 30 lashes. No free Negro in Arkansas was apt to have $100, nor wanted 30 lashes. Such a law cut him off from contact with his own kind.

Pa continued to worry. "John says his conscience is bothering him. He says he feels it's not right to have the power of life and death over others' lives. He tells me he and Kate have been praying for an answer."

"There is no good answer." Eliza was first and foremost a practical woman. "If they free those two, John and Kate would be better off without them. They could work white hired hands for the same money. Freeing Ike and Joe and trying to keep them around is the worst thing they can do, for Ike and Joe will be suspicioned by all the whites, they won't be able to visit with any of the slaves, and they're not able to look after themselves. John will still have their care, he won't have their value, and he will be in for a mess of trouble."

"He knows all that, and it's still heavy on his mind. If he forgets the money he paid for them, sets them free, and heads them off north to Missouri, he thinks he will simply be shifting his burden to somebody else. Joe barely has enough sense to keep to the big road without somebody else's directions. Ike is some brighter, but not much. And John is responsible because he has bought and raised them."

Eliza replied from the heart. "John and Kate and their children are all the family those boys know. They don't have anybody else. Why on earth does all this have to come up now?"

"Because Ike and Joe want their own women. They want John to buy them some wives and let them have the same home comforts that white men have. They have the gals picked out, too. John is a good man, and he's between a rock and a hard place."

"That's not going to change your thinking any about our own slaves, is it, Will?" Eliza decided to put her worrying closer to home.

"I don't know, Eliza. I'm going to ride on home ahead of you girls and get the place ready for tonight's stage. Maybe work will clear my head. I'll see you when you get home." Pa rode off, his back straight and his brow worried.

This was the Christmas of 1859, and if any of us could have guessed how the fears of all would have focused our lives in the next few years, we would possibly have quailed and grown fainthearted. Abolitionists came much closer to home than any would have liked. Good men like my pa deplored them, for they wanted authority to change our lives but cared little for the responsibility of working out the problems after the change. Yet, I and all my kin felt the plight of the slaves to be unjust. Whites and blacks both worked hard, but whites had the precious gift of freedom. Whether the freedom of blacks was sufficiently valuable for whites to die for was another matter.

But politics and abstract justice took a back seat to practicality when we got near home. As our buggy forded the creek that formed the eastern boundary of our little community, I was struck by the astounding thought that the next two weeks were likely to be my last two spent in the only home I had ever known. Suddenly, even the buildings looked dear.

Eliza clicked the mare into a quick trot, and we pulled up in front of our home at noon. The stage was due at five o'clock, and we all had work to do. Eliza went straight to the kitchen to light a fire under the stew pot and set Neely to a lively pace. I was put to work peeling potatoes and slicing ham, and we let slavery take care of itself while we took care of business.

Yet even as I worked alongside Neely in the big kitchen, I thought of how much I owed her. Unlike Ike and Joe, Neely and her men were smart and quick. Besides, Neely's loving heart had been the mainstay of my life after my mother died. I thought back to the day of my mother's funeral, when Pa was bowed down by a lonesome grief that left me somewhere out in the cold, cut off forever from my mother's love and cut off from Pa by his remote and solitary grieving. For a few weeks after my mother's death I had stayed with Aunt Kate, but one spring morning Pa had appeared with Neely in his buggy, ready to take me home again. From that day, when I was six, Neely had been my surrogate mother, seeing to my needs, soothing my pains, and giving me the true affection of her warm and generous heart. I loved Neely, and she loved me. If she had been mine to free, would I not have owed her that freedom? And did Pa not owe it to her now? The law in Arkansas was hard on free Negro and slave alike, and men of conscience were struggling with problems not of their own choosing. Neely and Zeke and Tobe were capable people. As free Negroes they could make a living anywhere. Maybe Pa ought to let them go while he could.

I pushed these thoughts to the back of my mind. "Neely, you've got to show me how to do the hard parts of cooking. I've got to learn to do more than I've been doing."

"Lord, I never thought to hear you say it! Our chile done turned over a whole new leaf! Just shows what having a man will do for a gal!" Neely laughed until the tears ran down her face. "Lord hep us! Your world gonna be turned upside down!

"But we ain't gonna start tonight. Miss Liza not gonna like it if you burn de corn bread or mess up de biscuits when we's feedin' folks from de stage. Clear out now and let me get moving. I needs to be cookin' up a storm. We gonna have our hands full in a few minutes."

Neely was right. We heard the silvery blast of the coach horn, the driver's signal that he had crested Lemley Mountain and had begun his mile-long descent into our valley. We formed an efficient welcoming party, Tobe and Zeke ready to unhitch and feed the horses, Eliza and Pa and I on the long porch to welcome the passengers. Neely alone stayed inside, coaxing her brick fireplace oven to the temperature for baking the biscuits.

The stage rolled in on schedule, quickening the pulse of our entire mountain settlement. We always received news of the nation when the stage came in. Both Springfield and Little Rock had telegraph communication, Springfield with St. Louis, Little Rock with Memphis. Only the stage from the southwest, through Fort Smith, was without this link with civilization. But since what the southwest lacked in refinement it made up in rambunctiousness, news was equally interesting and frequently more rowdy from that direction.

This coach from Springfield was full. The passengers appeared to be well acquainted, which was not surprising. They had been cooped up together, three passengers to a seat, for a full 12-hour day. The front passenger seat faced to the rear so the occupants could talk, and woe betide the passenger who hoped for solitude. Among nine interior travelers, garrulous traveling companions were the mathematical expectation.

This winter day, all were tired, dusty, and cold. The upper half of the coach consisted of open framework with thin leather curtains that could be buttoned down to the solid panels below. In winter, even when the curtains were buttoned, snow, rain, and cold entered freely. The passengers had endured the bracing experience of the stinging light snow throughout the day and emerged with an exhausted look.

Once inside the tavern, the talk was lively. Pa and the stage driver, Bill Hawes, exchanged business news. The driver was the bearer of glad tidings. "The Overland Stage Route is all set to open again next month. That last 100 miles of mountain trail over the Sierras has been opened. They finally found a pass they could grade a coach trail through. Get yourself ready, Mr. Griffin; your business is about to pick up considerably."

"How many miles is this route, all total?" Pa asked.

"The longest stage and mail route in the world! It will be 2,795 miles, they say, nearly 3,000 I figure, counting in the detours and backtracks and river fordings that those surveyors in St. Louis never estimate or pay us extra for. There'll be service twice a week, like last year. You're going to have a full house around here, counting in passengers you're already handling over the Butterfield Trail."

Pa's mental calculator had already been activated. "What's the fare now?"

"Fare $200. Time 25 days; 140 stations along the way. Which reminds me, I've been carrying your new contract for same." Bill handed an important-looking document to Pa, who carefully placed it inside his writing stand before turning his attention to the wants of the other men warming themselves before the fire.

"Gentlemen, may I offer you a drink on the house? This is a great time for the Griffins, great beginnings. My daughter is to be married soon, the Overland Mail Route from St. Louis to San Francisco is to begin again this next month, and I offer a toast to the future." From among the travelers a tall man in well-worn clothing responded. "Ah, the future! I wish I could see a country peopled in peace and expanding in prosperity. But I'm afraid the prospect is dim. We not only have our own North and South ready to fight over slavery, the news is that we have the French ready to use any excuse to grab Mexico, and we have that tight-fisted queen on the throne of England interested only in the profit to be made from our conflict. I drink to the future, but I'm leery of our enemies and I pray for the country."

Pa was an optimist. "There is a way out of this, and the way leads straight to Sam Houston. If Sam Houston were to become President, we could rest assured he would find a way out of this mess we're in. A

Southerner who loves the Union would be bound to find a path on which to lead us forward."

Their talk flowed with the whiskey, blended with Eliza's good food, and continued unabated until bedtime. Travelers occupied my bedroom, so I again slept in a trundle bed next to the larger one of Pa and Eliza. Pa this night was in an exuberant mood.

"Girls, sleep well and sleep happy. Wise men are going to move heaven and earth to get Sam Houston where he belongs, which is leading this country. What fools men are to fight over slaves when prosperity for all is so nearly within our reach!"

Chapter 3

THE SOLEMN CLANGING *of the church bells was the overture to my wedding. The cold winter air carried their summons for miles. Kith and kin responded in such numbers as to fill the church. In my ears the bells rang only one word: "Lar-kin; Lar-kin; Lar-kin." When I saw him standing at the altar, waiting for me to walk* down the aisle on Pa's right arm, I thought him to be as beautiful as a god. His new broadcloth pantaloons and dark frock coat clothed him in unaccustomed elegance. I lifted my eyes to meet his and found favor in his sight. Larkin's deep blue eyes were the eyes of a man who knew exactly what he wanted.

My wedding dress had been twice worn, first by my grandmother, then by my mother, and the silk was aged to a creamy ivory. The lace of the yoke formed a ruffle around my shoulders, repeated in a deep flounce around the hem. The dress was my heritage, but my life was my own, and on the day I turned 16 I handed it into Larkin's keeping in the simple ceremony designed to ensure our union.

Pa placed my hand in Larkin's. We turned to face the preacher.

"Dearly Beloved . . ." the preacher began. "Wilt thou, Larkin, take this woman to be thy lawfully wedded wife . . ."

His response was firm. "I do."

"Wilt thou, Sarah, take this man . . . for better or for worse, for richer or for poorer, in joy and in sorrow, in sickness and in health . . . wilt thou promise to love, honor, and obey? . . . Forsaking all others . . . as long as ye both shall live?"

I was seized by an emotion so strong as to transport my mind out of my body, lifted by a powerful feeling of the significance and transient quality of the moment. For seconds, when time was suspended, I felt myself to be elevated above the scene, gazing objectively down on the ancient ceremony, watching myself and Larkin. I could see myself, young and trembling, eyes sparkling with emotions powerful but as yet imperfectly understood, joined by the hand with a man of compelling magnetism, a man of unusual qualities. This fleeting perception was quickly replaced by my realization that my response was expected. My mind returned to my body in time to hear my own voice whisper, "I do." Larkin slipped his ring upon my finger.

The preacher continued, "I now pronounce you man and wife. What God has joined together, let no man put asunder. Let us pray." No sound of trumpets could have been sweeter than the voices of the congregation as the notes of the doxology lifted and swelled to conclude the ceremony.

Ushering out their honored guest, the commissioner of the Indian Nation, Pa and Eliza led the way back to our home to begin the festivities that had been so long in the making. By the time Larkin and I arrived, the mood had already shifted from solemnity to celebration.

The house looked wonderful. Pa and Eliza had been up long before daylight preparing the food and arranging the lustrous pine and cedar boughs that now decorated each wide windowsill and fireplace mantel. Glowing red-berried holly and waxy white-berried mistletoe intertwined with the gray-blue branches of cedar. Festive candles glowed against the twilight, and richly hued red velvet ribbons had been formed into swags and bows to accent each arrangement. I was proud of us all: proud of Eliza for her hard work in bringing our home to such a festive polish, proud of Pa for his unstinting generosity, even proud of myself, for had not my own mirror told me that in my wedding dress I was a happy beauty? Surrounded by the variously festive sounds of the guests at my wedding feast, I prayed devoutly for the knowledge and grace necessary to fulfill the new role that I had so quickly accepted a scant hour earlier.

As if in answer, Larkin came to my side, putting his proprietary arm around my small waist. His touch sent such a surge of joy pulsing through my body as to leave no room left for speculation about any future other than that which was most immediate — the first of a lifetime of nights in his arms. I moved happily and lightly around the room, confidently welcoming the many who had ridden for miles to be a part of this day.

Suddenly I was filled with appreciation of my good fortune. Having lived all my life among people for whom life was stern and simple but good, I took for granted the privileges extended by my father's position. The beautiful mountains that hemmed us in contributed much to the isolation and sense of community of the settlement in which I had grown up. Though far from ordered and more pompous social customs, there was an established social structure, and the people I knew lived well. I did not miss what I did not know.

I was acquainted with the self-reliance forged by necessity and well-acquainted with our neighbors, at least half of whom were related to me by blood, through Pa or by extension through Eliza. There was my Aunt Gert, whose home was two miles away, widow of Pa's oldest brother. Cousin Alta and Cousin Ed lived a mile in the other direction. We knew their strengths, tolerated their weaknesses, and understood their situations in ways incomprehensible to those not bound by ties of blood and circumstance.

I caught a glimpse of Minerva holding court. Among the assembled country women she glowed, an exotic full-breasted red robin surrounded by wrens and sparrows. Her dress was a lustrous gray taffeta that heightened her rich complexion and emphasized the still-youthful contours of her regal figure. Her air was that of majestic dignity, as though she was lending an august presence to an altogether auspicious occasion. In contrast to Eliza, whose efficient bustling always included those in her proximity in her cheerful conversation, Minerva sat in self-contained silence.

Those around her paid deference by attempting to ensure her comfort and entertainment.

Her own daughters, Katie and Becky, were not in evidence, however, for each had more pressing concerns. Katie, the mother of three small children, was busy with them in the back room, but Becky was talking to my cousin Willie, looking up into his good-natured and intelligent brown eyes as though he was the only person in the room.

As we moved around the room I felt surrounded by the love of family and affection of friendship. These people had literally known me all my days. Aunt Gert had taught me to sew and to knit; Cousin Ed had taught me to read, for he was schoolmaster as well as farmer. The Lemleys, the Joneses, the Stricklands, the Stobaughs — all were part and parcel of the fabric of community that until now had formed the pattern of my life. How strange that ceremonies should so simultaneously enrich and impoverish our lives. Soon I was to move away into a settlement unknown to me, to be a Flint, and to live alone with Larkin in a cabin three miles removed from his nearest neighbors. Accustomed neither to personal solitude nor to the total care of a household, I was now about to join the ranks of adults who assumed these responsibilities. I wondered if I was ready.

Surprisingly, it was Minerva who seemed to understand my misgivings. I felt her regal presence beside me, her arm linked with mine. "Shall we drink a toast together, Sarah?" I motioned to Tobe, who poured two glasses of wine.

"To your future, and to my new daughter." She smiled, the first smile she ever gave me. I bowed in quick harmony of spirit and looked into dark Cherokee eyes filled with understanding. "Sarah, you are moving now around the wheel of life, the magic circle. Sixteen is not too young to be starting when you open your heart." It was as though she had read my thoughts. Again, I was proud, and this time pride was mixed with gratitude as I walked at Minerva's side around the room. "You'll miss the bustle and the people of Griffin Flat, Sarah, but 'tis only our fears that make us alone. Open your heart, for life is before you."

I knew she spoke ancient wisdom, and once again I faced my future with confidence. Sixteen seemed suddenly to be a magic age, an age when all of adulthood beckoned and doors beyond doors waited to be opened. I touched the broad gold band that Larkin had so firmly placed on my finger. If marriage opened all doors, this earth was a source of constant marvels. How fortunate I was to be beginning my journey at 16!

When Eliza signaled to Pa that the tables were ready, he invited all to join him at the wedding feast. Extra tables had been placed in each of the two great rooms, and sideboards were heaped with the bounty of our fertile land — ham and venison, chicken and beef, pound cake and cobblers, pickles and tarts, jams, jellies, potatoes, sauces and succotash, all prepared under Eliza's skillful supervision and displayed with the artful hospitality of an experienced innkeeper.

Eighty-seven people ate at my pa's tables that day and remembered that sumptuous wedding feast as a standard of comparison for years to come. Neely and her men were kept busy passing platters, pouring coffee, filling wine glasses. Pa was in his glory, with a feast to be savored, an occasion to be celebrated, guests to be honored, and a daughter to be envied. Vast quantities of food washed down with copious draughts of wine worked their mellow magic on all assembled. In the wide hall between the two great rooms the fiddlers began to assemble, Larkin's brothers taking the lead as they began the haunting melody of "Barbara Allen." Soon, as other musicians joined the Flints, the lively lyrics of "Old Joe Clark" and "Turkey in the Straw" replaced the more romantic ballads. But by this time, sufficiently fortified with food and drink, our leading guest, the politician from the Cherokee Nation, was ready to wax eloquent about the subject that had brought him such a distance.

"Gentlemen, how can war be prevented? The Cherokees need war even less than the whites. Our only hope for development of the Indian Nation into a state of prosperity is to ensure sufficient time and resources to change from an outlaw's land into one of self-supporting farms and self-reliant people. I cannot overstate our need for a period of peace and prosperity. If you could see, as I do, the dockets of the United States Court at Fort Smith, you would understand the devilish state of affairs that now exists. I fear that the eastern edge of Indian Territory will join with your state in the making of a hell on the border. Since the beginning of the Kansas expansion, we have been subjected to a reign of terror. Desperadoes, horse thieves, murderers, and shysters have crowded out the common thieves and drunks from our court calendars and our jails. We cannot continue to invite the opportunity for criminal speculation. In order to ensure your own borders, you must find a way to help civilize that of ours."

"I agree; sir, we are drawing too close to insurrection and pillaging." Matthew Flint responded first, as was his due as the ranking landowner present. "My earnest counsel is that each man here present cast his influence in the direction of the one man who has sufficient resources to lead us toward peace — Sam Houston."

"We are agreed on the man, Matthew," my Uncle John said dryly. "It is the means we're looking for."

Larkin joined in the discussion. "Party organization is the key. The Democratic caucus system in this state is rotten, and everybody knows it. If we are to bring about a new party, it will have to be done by open and honest debate.

"There can't be any good expected from a party that is mainly a party *against*. We need a party that is *for*: for the Union, for expansion, and for the peace of mind to get about the job of making a living without fighting among ourselves."

"For too long a time we have been governed by men of marketable principles and elastic conscience. If you men started a strong push for a new party, with Houston as the avowed national candidate, there would be many who would listen, and it is the only way to keep Texas in the Union. If the assistance of the Indian Nation would be of help in your new organization, I would be honored to participate as a go-between. Perhaps the ears of the newspapers of Washington, D.C., and the state of New York are more easily tuned to the Indian Nation and to Texas than to Arkansas." The commissioner was, of course, correct.

Pa perceived the issue to be settled and had a thirst coming on. "Tobe, bring the commissioner another whiskey. Boys, can you help me clear the tables out of the room? We're going to need a lot of space when we start dancing the Virginia reel!"

In the hall the fiddles sang a plaintive backdrop to his oration as the politician summed up the arguments for Sam Houston.

"When Texas was annexed, the whole country saw the rest of the West — the Rockies, Oregon, California — as a part of her dowry. The expansion of the entire country is tied to Texas. I'm thankful for Sam Houston, and proud of his guts, for he was the only Southern senator in that whole self-serving Senate to vote against the Kansas-Nebraska Bill. If others had had one-tenth of his gumption, this country wouldn't be on the brink of war now. That bill opened the whole West, from Iowa to the mountains, to slavery."

Matthew Flint added, "Speaking from personal knowledge, Houston's main concern was not only slavery, but what would happen to the Indians in all of that wide territory. And he was foresighted to worry. All his concerns are beginning to come to pass."

The commissioner continued, "The new American party looks to Houston as the only hope of the country for union. He's got to be the only standard-bearer with tested leadership credentials. Look at the man. A senator through the '50s, then back to Texas now to run for governor. He'll win that race, too. The way he fought the slave trade in Texas this year is an example of his courage. Ever since those two cargoes of slaves landed from Africa on Texas soil, he's been a wrathful Moses and the conscience of the land. He's stated over and over again, Texas's connection is national. Not North or South. The only hope of this country is for the rest of the states to be led by this same leader."

Matthew Flint was in complete agreement. "Sir, I join you in that view, and for the most personal of reasons: I have five sons whom I do not wish to sacrifice either to the greed of the one side or the misguided views of the other. I propose two toasts: first to peace; next to Larkin and Sarah."

Matthew Flint's toast gave Pa the chance to change the subject, a chance he had been impatiently awaiting. Ready to move from politics to partying, Pa called for the dancing to begin.

The lively lilt of the Virginia reel summoned us to our places, Larkin and I at the head of the line, the commissioner partnering Minerva at the foot. Pa gave his arm to Eliza, Matthew Flint bowed to his Becky, and the dancing began. Each touch of Larkin's hand, each brilliant look from his deep-set blue eyes promised happiness. Oh, how we danced! My feet flew, and my face was never brighter than during that sweetest of dances the night we were wed. Pa's eyes filled with tears as he took his turn sashaying me up and down through the formal patterns of the reel. With a flourish he handed me back into Larkin's arms.

It was at the end of the first set that Larkin's careful planning became apparent. To the commissioner he made his manners and extended our farewells. In a low voice, for the commissioner's ears alone, he said, "Sir, I am sure Sarah and I have your permission to leave you shortly. Please know how honored we are by your presence. And please know, also, that you can count on me to serve the cause of our new party. When your future plans are laid, I will undertake whatever you and my father see fit for me to do."

The worldly old politician smiled. "Larkin, it is truly a tribute to your upbringing that you can be mindful of your country at this moment." He turned to me and spoke with evident sincerity. "Ma'am, I do most urgently and truly envy Larkin Flint this night. And I wish you both joy."

Larkin continued to carry out his plans. "Sarah, tell your Pa and Eliza good-bye without getting yourself noticed too much. We're slipping out the back way when they start up the next dance."

"Won't that be rude?"

"I don't care whether it's rude or not. I've waited as long as I mean to wait, and I mean to have you all to myself."

"But I need to change into other clothes. I can't travel in my wedding dress."

"You don't have to change. Believe me. It's all planned. Slip out toward the kitchen and go out the back door."

Outside the door stood Neely, her face aglow with love, unaccustomed tears running down her dark cheeks. "My girl's leavin' me. I betta be putting her in good hands, Mista Larkin. You betta treat her good."

"I will, Neely." Larkin was in a hurry. "Where's the buggy?"

Neely wrapped my cloak around me. "It out back. Zeke he waitin' to drive you. He'll bring you de wagon in de mornin'."

Larkin lifted me into his arms as easily as he would have lifted a sack of flour and strode down the kitchen path to the drive where Zeke sat waiting. Settling beside Zeke, he lifted me onto the seat so that I was in his lap. Zeke eased the horses gently and quietly down the dark lane, passed the slave cabin, and crossed through the back pasture.

"Where on earth are we going?" I was totally bewildered.

"Well, if you think we're going to spend our first time together in your pa's house with all our kinfolks and half the county watching and listening, you're not the smart little girl I've taken you to be. That crowd is probably planning a big shivaree sometime tonight, but they'll be shivareeing an empty bed. We're going to your Aunt Gertrude's farm. It's just far enough away to throw them off track. I doubt if we're missed for another hour. They're dancing in both big rooms and drinking and telling yarns in the hall. Each bunch will think we're with the others. When they finally miss us, they'll have no idea where we went."

"Won't Aunt Gertrude be coming back home tonight?"

"She will not. But she left her people to wait on us." Aunt Gert, a widow, had a hired hand and his wife to help her work her farm.

"Does Pa know where we're going?"

"He does not. But he knows you're in my keeping now."

Without regard for Zeke on the other side of the seat, Larkin kissed me deeply and long, his lips sweetly caressing my own. I relaxed completely to this sweet promise. Larkin's urgency was becoming apparent.

"As soon as you get back on the road, drive faster, Zeke," he instructed.

We arrived in good time. Zeke handed me down, produced a packed valise from the back of the buggy, and watched us safely inside before heading the horses back home.

The house welcomed us. Though no one was around, the room had recently been readied with a good fire, the freshly made feather bed plumped with snowy pillows and covered with a thick wool blanket.

Larkin removed my cloak and kissed me again before he spoke. "Now, love, it's time for us. Has anybody told you what it will be like?"

"Nobody. But I haven't asked, either."

"Then we'll start from the beginning. Tonight I'm going to love you, and the loving will likely hurt you. But only this once. It won't hurt again after tonight. You'll understand when we're doing it."

With quick, competent movements, Larkin started taking off his clothes. Under my stunned and fascinated gaze he changed from a civilized man to a naked god. He turned to me and with decisive fingers began the task of unbuttoning my wedding dress, starting at the top of the long row of tiny silk-covered buttons that extended down my back from my neck to my waist. "Step out of your gown, Sarah." He continued my swift undressing. "Next, your shimmy; now your drawers."

I was left standing in my long silk stockings, too shy and too startled to meet his eyes. Lovingly and slowly he began to kiss me, my eyes, my lips, my neck, moving on to my breasts. A thrilling shudder ran through my entire body, and waves of sweetness began their singing, starting deep inside me.

He lifted me inside the cold bed, his warm and naked body next to my own as he caressed me with his exploring hands, even as he again sought my lips, his tongue and his fingers each adding to my excitement. Under his delicately eager fingers the flesh between my thighs became liquid, and I felt the fingers replaced by his swollen and stiffened member — seeking entrance.

"Sarah, I meant to take you slowly, but I can't wait."

There came a painful thrust, another, and suddenly we were joined into a union so insistent, our bodies so exquisitely fitted as to leave no room for thought. I was awash in physical sensation — the remembrance of the quick searing pain, the rapid thrusting of his enormous member, the surging movements filling and claiming my body, and the beginnings of sweet feathers of feeling from within my depths. I was unprepared when Larkin gave a long moan and a mighty shudder. He clutched me to his body as though he meant never to let me go and spilled his seed deep within me.

Astonished, I lay as in a trance. Gently, delicately, reluctantly, Larkin separated his body from mine. "Go to sleep, Sarah. It will not hurt the next time. I wish I could have held back, and I will next time. Have I told you yet how beautiful you are? You're beyond words. Sleep well. Tomorrow will be easier for you, and better."

Within minutes he was asleep, but I lay in Aunt Gert's vast feather bed wondering what to do next. I could feel his liquid beginning to seep from my body onto the clean white sheets, and in bewilderment I climbed out of bed seeking a remedy.

Across the corner of the room a screen concealed a chamber pot. In the light of the dying fire I tentatively walked my naked self toward the shelter and the relief it afforded. But something unexpected had been provided for my use. On a low table stood a wash basin and pitcher, with soap and fresh towels close at hand. As I washed, I marveled that in such a short time I could have been plunged from such passion to such common concerns of urine, blood, and semen. Undoubtedly, all women went through this. In deep bewilderment, I wondered why not one of them — not Eliza, not Aunt Kate, nor even Neely — had given me any advance instructions.

I opened the valise to find my new cambric nightgown on top, packed by Neely's thoughtful hand. Slowly, I perceived that their thoughtfulness might well have extended further than I had realized. Larkin had given me an introduction beyond description. The mysteries of life were made manifest in the flesh of loving men and women, and no amount of preliminary conversation could have adequately prepared me.

Reality had been beyond my imagination. Had any attempted my advance education in matters between a man and a woman, I would have disbelieved even the most trusted teller. That the stirring joy I had been feeling for weeks had been purposed toward such piercing pain was incomprehensible. I was stunned by the realization that all the ceremonies, all the preparations, all our visitors, and all their celebrations had been focused toward this unmentionable act — an act that was publicly celebrated yet one considered to be beyond private discussion. Nevertheless, remembering those insistently sweet ripples of sensation that Larkin's caresses unfailingly evoked from my responding body, I concluded that life held mysteries within mysteries. Larkin had promised that tomorrow would be better and easier. Clearly my childhood had ended, and I had opened both my heart and body to Larkin. I climbed back into bed, snuggled next to him, and slept soundly.

True to Larkin's instructions, Zeke arrived with the wagon by the time the sun was up. We heard the rumbling of the wagon along with the sounds of doors slamming in the kitchen across the hall. The household had been up long before us. To wake in Larkin's arms was a prelude to a new world. We reached out to each other at the same moment. Larkin's grin was wide and boyish.

"Can you believe it, Sarah? From now on, I can have you anytime I want you. But maybe I'd first better talk to Zeke. Your pa will need him back at your place to wait on all the visitors. And since your pa has been considerate enough to give me his girl, I guess I'll return his kindness by sending his slave back in short order. No sense in letting them think we can't get out of bed this morning. But would you take that white thing off and let me see that perfect little body one more time in the daylight?"

I giggled, did as he asked, and gave him a little more besides. We dressed for breakfast with so much teasing and laughing that I marveled that the passionate couple of the night before had reverted to the pranks and giggles of childhood.

With an abrupt assumption of maturity we walked across the hall where breakfast was waiting.

"How does your husband want his eggs?" the hired woman asked me. I had no idea, which set us to laughing again.

"Over easy, lots of ham, and a batch of biscuits. I'm so hungry I could eat a horse," Larkin replied. "And, speaking of horses, it's time you set eyes on one more present — my wedding gift to you." He led me out the door.

There, tied to a lead behind the wagon, was the most beautiful little black mare I had ever seen. Sleek-coated and high-spirited, she had the configuration of a horse bred both for speed and endurance. I did not know then that I was looking at a quarter horse, that remarkable breed developed by the Indians, but I did know she was meant to be mine. "Dolly's already broken to ride, and she's yours. I want you riding at my side, and this mare can keep up with most. You're a lot alike; two high-spirited fillies!"

Oblivious to Zeke or to the watching hired hands, I flung my arms around Larkin's neck and kissed him soundly on the mouth. I approached the mare with more courtesy, rubbing her nose, talking to her extended ears, letting her get the feel and smell of me before I intruded too far into her space.

"We'll get well acquainted soon, I promise," I said as I left her. Again, I marveled at Larkin and at how much I still had to learn about the complex man I had married.

"I'll take care of loading up, Zeke. You'd better start back to Mr. Griffin's. If you walk fast you can get there before most of the people are out of bed. They'll likely be slow to get up this morning."

Zeke started off at a brisk pace down the road that led to my father's home, while I marveled at the efficient planning that Neely, Zeke, and Larkin had brought about. There stood Larkin's wagon, his two large mules hitched to pull it, his own saddle horse, and my newly presented quarter horse hitched behind it on short leads. The wagon was loaded with our wedding gifts, which meant that Neely and Zeke had worked long hours last night after the final indulged guest had gone to bed.

At the same time that I was filled with appreciation for their hard work, I glimpsed with consternation my own immaturity. I had done no advance planning. All my life I had relied on the efficient plans of others to ensure my keep and comfort. No wonder Neely had laughed, and no wonder that last night she had cried. I had a lot to learn. I walked back in Aunt Gert's house to eat a big breakfast before beginning our journey.

Chapter 4

IN THE CLEAR LIGHT of that cold January morning in 1860, we rode up the hill and into the meadow that framed my new home. My first sight of Larkin's place told me where I belonged. Never before or since have I looked with instant recognition on a place that reason told me I was seeing for the first time.

The long, low cabin was sited facing south with its back to a massive bluff, the harsh gray outcroppings of the mountain's broad front and rock-ribbed surface softened by moss and patterned by pine. This sheltering backdrop gave definition and character to the house. Long square-hewn logs notched with precision framed the length of my new home.

The east and west ends were braced by huge, rough stone fireplaces, their chimneys rising far above the shingled roof, blending the colors of their stones into the mountain that had been their source. Two glass-paned windows let in the south light, and the lilac-framed front door opened directly upon the large flat rock that served as entry. The cabin's stone foundation was barely visible from the front, but it sloped steeply toward the rear to a four-foot back foundation wall. The house was situated on a hill that declined abruptly to the little creek rippling at the base of the bluff.

I rejoiced in the beauty and symmetry of the scene, somehow aware of the precision of plan that had blended the building so beautifully into its setting. Bare-branched oak and hickory trees stood tall, their strength emphasized and graced by the slighter redbud and dogwood that grew beneath them in the small yard. A low rail fence enclosed it all. I could see the gray-vined tracery of wild rose and honeysuckle vines intertwining the front rails.

"Who built it?" I asked, and was unprepared for his answer.

"Father built it, but Minerva planned it. She says this house is in tune with the spirits. For those who listen."

"I'll listen, I promise. I'll love listening. In between working and loving you, I'll listen."

"Minerva believes you listen *through* living and loving, but I never have been sure when you're supposed to do it. I've always been too busy working or too tired to do much listening, and I haven't had anybody handy to do my loving with." He smiled the lopsided smile that signaled his pleasure. "Until now."

"Maybe we'll have time to listen in the evenings, after the work is done." I was an optimist.

But it was Larkin, the realist, who set the pace. "We can't listen right now. I need to get a fire going, unhitch the stock, and unload the wagon. I'll show you the path down to the spring. We have the coldest, purest water you ever tasted. The spring that bubbles out of that cave at the base of the bluff keeps milk and butter cold even in summer. Minerva thinks the spirits that watch over the house speak through the winds and the water. I can tell you, if that water is their witness, Minerva's spirits have got the coldest breath in the world!"

"I can't wait to see it all, inside, outside, in the woods, and in the cave!" I was enchanted, still intoxicated by Larkin's nearness, still remembering the pulsing fusing of our bodies, immersed in the memory of the night and the happiness of the present moment.

Larkin lifted me from the wagon, swooping me in his arms, whirling my skirts and petticoats in a wide circle, carrying me through the yard and over his threshold to set me down inside our home. I lifted my lips to his and waited expectantly for his sweet touch. But Larkin was a practical man.

"This place needs a fire going in it before I unload the wagon. The water bucket's by the back door, Sarah. If you follow the path down the hill, you can't miss the spring. Be careful of the steps down the path. There may be ice on them." He gave my bottom a dismissing pat and started toward the fireplace, where a day's supply of wood was already ricked along the wall, handy to his use.

A small ripple of surprise at Larkin's abruptness marred my delight. Still, I thought, if that's the way he is, I surely can get used to it. We'll work fast and leave more time for loving and listening later. Tightening my shawl around my slender shoulders, I picked up the oaken bucket, heavy even when empty, and started down the steep path toward the foot-log.

Underneath this narrow bridging, the creek ran musically inside its dark banks. Directly across the foot-log was the entrance to a small cave floored with large, carefully laid flat rocks. Through an opening high on the granite wall, the water flowed steadily down to the shallow pool designed for its collection, a pool rimmed by the rocks that allowed for my sure footing. I put an exploratory hand into the icy water and gasped. Larkin was right. These spirits came from a cold center deep in the bowels of the earth.

But my natural exuberance could not be damped by cold spirits. Sensing an unexpected tentativeness in the atmosphere of the cave, I addressed Minerva's spirits directly. "Please bless us, spirits. And help me make him happy."

I filled the bucket to the brim, staggering under the considerable weight of my burden, and addressed the invisible spirits once more as I made my exit. "I'll be back. Maybe after you get to know me better you'll talk to me." As I crossed the foot-log in the bright sunlight I laughed aloud, partly at my foolishness and partly in happiness, and climbed the steps to Larkin.

A crackling fire was licking at the fireplace logs, the rich pine kindling wood flickering and popping as the warmth chased the cold from the corners. Matching my actions to Larkin's, I filled the kettle on the crane and located the coffee beans and the coffee grinder. The aroma of coffee steaming toward our nostrils convinced us both that I had the makings of a competent cook and housekeeper. As Larkin unloaded the wagon, I moved around the room placing my belongings. In a lighthearted mood I rejoiced in this new world where I had Larkin all to myself.

We ate cold ham and cold biscuits and drank hot coffee when the sun was highest, but I heaped the heavy Dutch oven with coals so as to roast fresh pork and sweet potatoes for our supper. By midafternoon, the last housekeeping present had been put away, and I, too, felt that I had a place in the cabin.

A new feather bed, gift of Cousin Alta, was on the big bedstead, softening the corn shuck mattress and the taut rope springs. Aunt Kate's wedding ring quilt was its lovely cover, each patch in the design a reminder of a leftover scrap from a dress that I could identify and remember seeing on Aunt Kate or one of her daughters. The heavy new skillets from Aunt Gert were placed near the hearth; the casks of flour, sugar, dried peaches, soap, and sauerkraut were carefully placed in the small lean-to that served as storeroom.

Bright pillows from one neighbor, a new sewing box from another, and a huge skein of wool from another added color and texture to the sparsely furnished room. I set a bouquet of dried flowers on the narrow stairs that led up to the loft. In the place of honor we installed the finely carved chest that had been the gift of the commissioner. I filled it with the two new dresses and three new nightgowns that formed my trousseau, topping it with the beautiful pewter candlesticks that had once belonged to Eliza's mother. Finally, on a shelf above the chest, I placed my two treasures: the painted miniature of my own mother's lovely face and the book of Shakespeare's plays that Larkin's uncles had given into our keeping.

I looked at Larkin, our work accomplished, and waited for his signal that I had earned the right to his more tender attentions.

He came to stand behind me, put both arms around me with his hands covering my breasts, and kissed the back of my neck. Slowly he began to unbutton each of the buttons that extended the length of my plain, everyday butternut wool dress. "I'm not sure yet, Sarah, that you can undress yourself. So far, I've had to do it for you."

Within seconds we were in bed, Larkin's body covering mine, his kisses deep and demanding. This time when he entered me there was only a momentary twinge, a feel as of scraped flesh being rubbed. He paused, giving me time to come to accommodation of this vibrant intrusion, which now seemed to fill the entire space within me. Then, surely, rhythmically, and steadily he began to move me until I was aware of nothing on this earth except Larkin's body. Within minutes there was a copious gushing explosion. His whole body jackknifed; he fell on me as if he were faint; and I felt in bewilderment that although I had again been his instrument of pleasure, equal pleasure had again been denied me.

But I had misjudged him. He lifted me gently and placed a pillow under my bottom. Kneeling beside me he started the long, slow series of kisses, beginning with my eyes, then my lips, my neck, my breasts, then on to my navel and down to that little button of flesh that served as sentry to all pleasure. To my astonishment, I realized that each kiss of that magic button evoked breathtaking feelings that spread in ripples in ever-widening circles. Then, beyond denying them, beyond analyzing, beyond anything except experiencing them, came sensations of such exquisitely piercing sweetness as to transport me into a world in which there was nothing else except these feelings — these and a wild, greedy, convulsing reach for more. I heard my own voice uttering little cries. I had not known the sound of ecstasy before.

Slowly, I returned to myself and looked at Larkin with startled eyes. He teased me. "What a lot of noise for such a little girl!"

"Don't tease me now. I can't think." I laid my head on his naked chest and lay languidly in his arms, lacking the strength or spirit to do more than marvel at the miraculous bonding joy described in the marriage ceremony as "ye shall be as one flesh."

Life was too full to be believed, and I was centered with Larkin at its exultant core. On that cold January day in Larkin's bed, warmed by the glowing fire from the hearth and the sweetly ebbing feelings of our own bodies, I asked for no more of life's blessing than those that had already been my good fortune to receive.

Larkin looked over at me, my black curls tumbling over the pillow, my eyes telling wonderful truths I had not the words to express, and allowed himself a satisfied and sensuous smile. "You know why we got married in the wintertime, Sarah?"

"Because Pa wouldn't let you have me until I was 16?"

"That was part of it, but I could have dickered with him some about that point. No, we got married in the wintertime so we could have long loving times together in bed and not have to be out working in the fields from sunup to sundown. I'd be the meanest-tempered man in the world if the only time I could lay hands on you was at night after I'd spent a long day out there walking behind a mule and a plow. This way we've got a couple of months until spring."

His hand began lazily to trace the outline of my naked breasts, then to move gently over the curves of my hips and thighs. "I'm just memorizing your shape. It'll give me something to occupy my mind while I'm out there tonight milking the cow and feeding the stock." He grinned. "Well, Sarah, I don't know what to do with you. I had thought we'd have time to go riding today."

I answered him honestly. "I hate to get out of bed, but I can love you again after supper, and if I'm going to get to ride today, it'll have to be soon, before dark."

"Well, let's hit the floor, then." We jumped out of our soft circle of warmth beneath the wool blanket and stood on the cold planks of the puncheon floor to pull on our clothes. I envied Larkin his thick deerskin britches and scratchy wool shirt. Men had the best of it when it came to clothes. It would be so much easier to ride a horse if women could wear pants, ride astride, and use their legs to grip the horse. Looping one full-skirted knee over the horn of a sidesaddle kept a woman on the horse, but it effectively reduced the amount of control she could exercise. Yet I was a good rider, even handicapped by full skirts and sidesaddles, and I was eager to try out my beautiful new mare.

Larkin was not a man to dally in an undertaking. We headed briskly for the barn, where he saddled his own horse and Dolly with quick, sure movements. "We'll have time for a short run. Maybe tomorrow we can ride farther. Right now I want to find out if you girls are suited to each other."

Soon we were mounted and trotting down the road. When we reached the level stretch at the foot of our hill, we looked at each other in quick agreement and let the horses have their heads in long, easy, smooth loping strides. High-spirited and happy-hearted, we rode with the bright sun on our heads, the cold wind whipping our cheeks, and the whole good world under our feet.

I would not have changed places right then with the queen of England herself, and Larkin had the pleased and prideful look of a man who held life's treasures in the palm of his hand.

We were within a half mile of the gate of the Flint homestead when Larkin motioned me to rein in Dolly. "Let's turn around and go back. There's no need to let anybody else in our lives right now. This day is ours. There'll be plenty of other days to visit with my family. Let's go home to supper."

I was joyful. "I'll race you!"

"Sorry, I can't take you up on that. You're sure to lose on that side-saddle. Now, if you knew how to ride straddle you might have a chance of winning, though I doubt if I'd take kindly to having my bride outride me the first day of our wedlock."

"I can ride like a man. Willie taught me. We used to sneak out in Uncle John's pasture and ride bareback. I love to ride that way. Sidesaddle is a stupid seat on a horse. There's no way of guiding or gripping with your knees."

Larkin laughed. "I've been thinking of borrowing a pair of Stanton's outgrown britches to put on you. I don't know of any reason why you can't ride any way you want, so long as you stay on Flint land.

"What we do on our own property is nobody else's business. We'll be visiting Father and Minerva pretty often, and nobody will see you except family. I think I can find an extra saddle for you, too. If you ever get chased by anything or anybody on this road, I want you to be able to move fast. I'll get you fixed up with a saddle and a pair of britches the next time I get back over to the home place. Then we'll see what you can do on this mare when you have a fair chance."

We trotted our horses toward home — already I called it home — and I prepared supper for Larkin for the first time. Baked pork and sweet potatoes from the Dutch oven, sauerkraut and hoe cake, big glasses of buttermilk, and Eliza's leftover pound cake made a feast. I washed up the handsome white dishes that had been my mother's, scoured out the Dutch oven, and laid out the cast-iron skillet for cooking the morning's breakfast, while a satisfied Larkin smoked his long-stemmed clay pipe. Life was good beyond the telling. We sat before the fireplace as the fire hissed with a strong popping sound. "The fire is calling for snow," said Larkin.

"Is that why the fire makes that popping noise?"

"That noise means that the earth is getting quiet. The clouds are thick, damping down the noises on the ground and the light of the stars. We'll have snow when we wake up tomorrow."

He proved himself an accurate prophet. The snow fell softly and silently and by morning lay thick and white over the corn-stubbed fields and close-wooded forests. The smaller scrubs of cedars and pine were changed into white-shrouded mysteries, and the bare branches of long-limbed hardwoods were softened with a deep edging of white. We slept late, wakened finally by the determined lowing of the milk cow. Larkin eased himself from the warmth of our bed to the chill of the cabin and built up the carefully banked coals of the fire so that I could rise in comfort.

Soon the bright flames sent shadows dancing along the cabin walls, and a circle of warmth spread around the room. Only then as he went out the door did he arouse me. "I'll be ready for ham and hot biscuits when I get the milking done, Sarah. Do you think you can manage to get that pretty little bottom out of bed now? I'll take you rabbit hunting if you don't burn the biscuits!"

All we did those next few days was enjoy ourselves. We walked along the banks of the ice-bound stream for the sheer joy of looking at its beauty. We strode across the white and frozen fields in search of rabbits and squirrels. Larkin's two hounds bounded along, now and then tentatively sniffing at me to determine whether I was an acceptable addition to the household. He taught me to shoot a rifle and to skin a rabbit, and I read to him from Shakespeare's love sonnets by the light of the fire and in the warmth of his arms. Removed from the rumblings of the outside world, we indulged ourselves in each other. Within the space of a week, I changed from a tender and tremulous virgin into a sensuously rejoicing woman.

But even as the weeks lengthened and we laughed and loved and learned, I knew our snow-covered solitude would be brief. Spring would come soon. Larkin would hitch the mules to the plow to turn the rich earth, and I would have to undertake the tasks of a frontier wife — planting the garden, washing clothes, preserving fruit, rendering lard, leaching lye; the list was endless — but I was not eager for my free days to be over and my days of burden-bearing to begin.

Larkin was right about the advantages of getting married in January. The weather stayed cold and the wind stayed raw, but we piled logs on the fire and ate and drank and made love, hardly able to get enough of each other.

There came a morning in late February when the promise of spring was in the air. A red-tailed hawk wheeled rapidly above the meadows, seeking his meal from the morning. The first fuzzy buds showed on the pussy willows, and green shoots of poke sallet pushed through the rich, loamy ground near the spring cave. We had no more than finished our breakfast that fine day when Matthew Flint rode up the driveway. Dismounting, he kissed my cheek and handed a mail packet to Larkin as he walked through the door. "Our planning is beginning to pay off, son. The county convention of the new Union party will be convened over at Huntsville in April. I've been asked to go and read a resolution affirming Sam Houston as a candidate. The people of Texas are planning a big celebration of the 24th anniversary of San Jacinto this spring, and I've been sent an advance copy of the resolution they mean to propose. That'll be April 21st. Sam Houston surprised Santa Anna and had him on the run in 20 minutes that day. I hope to God he can outmaneuver our own country's self-serving, cutthroat politicians as well as he outmaneuvered Santa Anna's cutthroat, lily-livered troops. He's got more at stake now than he did then. The Union's a damn sight more important than Texas, though I never yet met another Texan besides Houston who thought so.

"Now it's up to us to organize Arkansas and hold up our end of the deal. I want you to go with me to Huntsville, son. You'll be a real help. A grandson of Sam Houston is a man people will want to know. I'd take it as a real favor to have you with me."

"I'll go, Father, but it will take some planning. It's a day's ride over and a day's ride back. Allowing a day for the convention, I've got to plan on being gone three days. I can't leave Sarah by herself here. She can't even milk the cow, let alone shoot a gun straight. And I need to work on my planting, though I'm hard put to do it; and somebody's got to milk the cow and feed the stock."

Matthew's brow furrowed a moment, and then he resolved Larkin's dilemma. "Either Tom or Stanton can come over and take care of things. I think I'll send Tom. That way he can take care of the planting, too, while he's here." Tom was 20, a younger version of Larkin, and I felt uneasy at the prospect of entertaining for three days a brother-in-law whom I scarcely knew.

"Larkin, could I take that time to visit Pa and Eliza? It's been weeks now, and I miss them some. Except for visiting now and then with Aunt Kate, I've never been away from home before."

Matthew Flint allowed a look of approval to show on his experienced old face. "Would that suit you, Larkin?"

"Suits me fine. It won't hurt Tom to batch it while he's here. I'd been doing it for a year before I brought Sarah home; it'll make him appreciate a wife when he gets one."

"Well, it looks like you marrying Sarah has set more than one young buck to sparking. Tom's been riding down to your Aunt Kate's himself, Sarah. He's got his eye on one of the twins. Don't know how he tells them apart, but he's bound to have ways of doing it. And your Cousin Will showed up at our place last Sunday just in time for dinner. Seemed to have a good appetite, too. But Becky got to blushing and smiling so much she barely ate a bite. We told her if she started losing her appetite over her first beau, we'd have to put a stop to her courting. She's too little to have her growth stunted at 14."

I was delighted. "I can't wait to go home and hear the news! We've got to stop by Aunt Kate's so I can see the girls. Is it Piety or Charity Tom's courting? And I can tell you that Willie always eats like a horse. I can't think that sparking would even put a dent in his appetite. But Willie's a terrible tease. It's hard to get him to be serious."

"He's serious about Becky. But the child is too young and I've told him so. He's going to have to live with my judgment on that."

"What does Becky say?"

Matthew Flint's tone broached no argument. "What she says doesn't enter into it. No daughter of mine is going to get tied down at 14. If Will Griffin is serious, he can come back in two years and ask for her then. She's a long way from being ready to be a wife."

Larkin laughed. "That's what Sarah's pa thought, too, but I guess we've proved him wrong. I believe Sarah's turning out to be right wifely, after all."

I blushed as red as a rose. Wisely, Matthew changed the course of the conversation. "Larkin, how about you and Sarah coming down home to spend the night with us before we leave out? If we get an early start we can get to Griffin's Mill nearly in time for breakfast. That way, we'll be at Sarah's pa's by high noon. We can rest the horses and head on in to Huntsville. We'll be both places long enough to catch up on whatever news there is and can take fresh news to the convention with us."

I was elated. "I can't wait, I just can't wait; I'm so glad you're going to let me go!" I danced across the room and curtseyed to my father-in-law, then to Larkin. They laughed the pleased and indulgent laughter of men who have managed to delight a pretty woman without in any way inconveniencing themselves.

As Larkin and Matthew talked politics, I started preparations for dinner, determined that Mr. Flint would carry a good report on my cooking back to the many who were bound to be curious about my qualifications.

Chapter 5

OUR HONEYMOON ENDED when the spring plowing started. We had a lot of work to get done before Larkin's trip to Huntsville. Larkin had to get the corn planted — as much as he could, anyway — before he left, and all at once I had enough work to keep two women busy. For one thing, I had to wash up all our dirty clothes and bed linens. Figuring it had been too cold outside to try to deal with the wash pot and the scrub board, I had let a good-sized stack of dirty clothes pile up on me. After Mr. Flint's visit I went to work in that department. I've been more worn out lots of days since, but that first time I built a fire under that cast-

iron wash pot, carried water from the creek to fill it, set up the two heavy wooden tubs and the bench close to the wash pot, and started in to scrub clothes on that stout wooden scrub board, I thought I might die from pure tiredness before the day was over.

Wringing out the heavy sheets was the hard part. I'd never seen it done without two people. Back home, Neely would grab one end of a hot, wet, soapy sheet and yell for whoever was handy — me, Zeke, Tobe — to take the other. One of us would twist in one direction, one in the other. It was nothing for two people, but next to impossible for me to do it alone the first time I tried it. And I knew better than to bother Larkin. He was in the fields plowing, pushing the mule hard to get as much done as possible. I gritted my teeth and kept going. The last load I put in the wash pot was the soaked cloths from my monthly mense. They had to be boiled clean, so as to be ready for the next time, and I hated scrubbing the stubborn dull stains. It was a miserable morning.

I gave Larkin a cold dinner in the middle of the day, and he didn't take well to it. "Sarah," he said, and I didn't especially like his tone nor the look on his face, "a man expects more than cold meat and bread when he's been out plowing since sunup. You can do better than this."

That made me mad. My back was killing me, my head ached, my knuckles were rubbed raw from the lye soap and the scrub board, and I still had another couple of hours to go before I was through with the wash. After that I would have to start up supper, another tiresome job. But I bit my tongue to keep the hot words from bubbling from my lips. Then I took a good look at Larkin and saw how truly tired he was, the sweat rolling down his face, and I knew that he had had a worse morning than I had.

He was getting the field ready to plant the corn, plowing up new ground, because corn likes a rich, deep dirt. Plowing would have been a lot easier if he had worked with a yoke of oxen, but Larkin didn't have the patience for slow oxen, so he used the higher strung, faster mules instead. All morning long he had been following a mule, breaking up ground, and plowing deep. He wanted to put in early corn so as to get it harvested by August to make room for sowing rye, and he wanted to get 40 acres planted before he went off to Huntsville. I was already learning that Larkin was a high-tempered, hard-driving man. And when he was tired and hungry, it was a bad combination. By that time I had found out that Larkin could harden his heart about as fast as he could harden his member. And he was formidable in both departments.

I swallowed my anger, took a look at myself through his eyes, and gave him a straight answer. "I will do better next time. I'll see to it that you have a good supper tonight. I'm tired, but not as tired as you. I'll try harder."

His mood shifted like mercury, and that quick lopsided grin changed his face from storm to sunshine. "We'll both try harder. I'll see you at sundown."

My heart lifted, coming up from somewhere near the pit of my stomach to its usual position, and I set myself to the job of finishing the wash and starting our supper. Eliza's Presbyterian teachings were paying off, I thought to myself. A soft answer does turn away wrath. And yet, on a deeper level came the certain knowledge that I would face that cold, hard look again when I displeased my husband. I resolved then and there to make his happiness my everyday study.

Calling on what little strength I had left, I fried up sausage for supper, baked a hot pan of corn bread, and cooked up a custard in the Dutch oven. When Larkin finally sat down to the table, I handed him Pa's standard remedy for all life's temporary ailments, a good dollop of Eliza's blackberry wine. I was rewarded by the sweetest look that ever graced the face of a tired and handsome man, and, exhausted as I was, I glowed for the rest of the evening. The secret is to study him all the time, I thought. I'm going to have to learn to understand him. It won't be easy.

I made up my mind to learn everything I could from Neely and Eliza. Life seemed to be one lesson right after another, but I reminded myself that the last few weeks had been one joy after another. I was too worn out to waste time on any more philosophy. I went to sleep that night the minute my head hit the pillow and woke up the next morning beside a rested and reasonable husband.

Larkin got his corn planted in record time that spring. I put in my first garden and did a remarkable job of it, if I do say so myself. By the end of March we had things in good shape, ready to leave on our trip in clear conscience. Brother Tom showed up on schedule, and I was able to find out which twin he was courting.

"It's Piety," he said.

"I'm surprised. Charity is always so much fun, and Piety is always so practical. I thought you'd pick Charity."

"Fun is fine for a square dance or a picnic, but I ain't looking for a dancing partner. Piety suits me just right!" Tom's tone was that of a man who has made up his mind.

Larkin was ready to leave, saddlebags packed and horses ready. "Let's go, Sarah, and leave Tom to think about his courting."

We set off in high spirits, loping the horses along the three-mile stretch of woods that led to Larkin's home place. Sunshine lit up the creamy blossoms on the dogwood and the purple-tinged buds of the redbud. Birds sang and crows cawed and swooped far above us, perennial signs that the earth was again preparing her mantle of green. Matthew Flint greeted us with his usual warm courtesy as Larkin kissed his mother's cheek and I dropped her a formal curtsey. To my amazement, Minerva held out her hand. "You don't need to curtsey any more. You're in the family now, and it's our job to make you feel welcome. Sam and Robert rode over with their families to take supper with us. Come in and get better acquainted with us, Sarah."

I did as I was told. Working side by side with the squaws in the big kitchen were the two other Flint wives, Susan and Jane, with their children playing around their skirts.

Susan, wife of Sam, gave me a sisterly hug. "You look wonderful, Sarah. You were beautiful on your wedding day, but there's something about you now that's glowing. I believe Larkin must have done a few things right."

Again, I blushed, unable to think of an answer. What was between Larkin and me was not up for discussion. Not wishing to be rude, I changed the subject. "Isn't Kate here?"

"She's in the family way again, poor thing, and not feeling good. Three babies in three years is too much, and that husband of hers ought to be castrated." Susan rolled her eyes. "I don't know why she wanted him in the first place. He'd already had three babies in a row by his first wife — wore her plumb out. He was over here courting Kate before that poor dead woman was cold in the ground. Too strong an appetite, that's what I think. Kate's going to have to learn to say no."

Jane laughed. Looking pointedly at the children playing at Susan's feet, she asked, "Like you do?"

Susan was a good-natured woman. "Let's finish dishing up the supper and call the men to the table. Flint men have got big appetites in more than one department, and right now they've got food on their minds."

All ten Flints adjourned to the supper table, the squaws assuming the task of waiting on us in one room while feeding the children in the kitchen. Talk was lively, and I realized from the flavor in the air that the men had done a little judicious sampling of Matthew's excellent corn whiskey. Amid their talk of weather and crops and hogs and corn I found a chance to ask Becky, "Have you decided you like Willie? I hear he's trying to court you."

A look of pure joy lit up her face. "I thought he'd never get around to noticing me, and now that he has, I can't think of anything else. Father is not willing to promise me; he thinks I'm too young. But I know what I want."

"I guess Willie does, too. He told me last Christmas he had you picked out."

Becky's beautiful dark eyes misted with tears. "You're a blessing for a sister, Sarah. The others laugh at me and think I'm a baby."

"Well, you may seem a baby to them, but you're not one to Willie. But if I was you I'd spend some time learning how to run a household — don't come to it as unready as I was. I wish that I had learned at home from Eliza and Neely instead of trying to figure out most things by myself."

When the meal ended, the Flints, as seemed to be their custom, adjourned to the other room for music. Larkin's violin still hung on the wall, and as he took it from its peg he touched the wood with loving fingers. Matthew Flint, as always, called the tune. "Only a little music tonight. We have to get off by daylight tomorrow."

"What'll it be, Larkin? You choose."

"Let's try the 'Cherokee Circle.' "

The lively, lilting sounds of the fiddles filled the air, rhythms too complex and chords too haunting for my immediate understanding. As the last minor chord echoed in the room I asked, "Who wrote it?" and was not surprised at the answer, "Minerva."

I marveled again at the intricate strands that bound this complex family. The Larkin who evoked such haunting music from his violin was the same man who for the past week had been hauling manure and fighting his mule and who was on his way toward a political maneuvering tomorrow. And the woman who had written the elaborate melody I had just heard was the same woman whose father was a famous senator and who still believed that spirits inhabited the cave that was our springhouse.

The next morning we were up and mounted and ready to ride by the time the sun rose. With Matthew Flint to my right and Larkin to my left, we set off at an easy canter, the horses' pace smooth and flowing. In the first light of morning, the birds sang their greeting to the sun, and clouds of mist hung above meadows rimmed by virgin forest. Delicate blossoms of wild plum mingled with the beauty of redbud and dogwood as we rode through the glory of an Ozark spring morning.

We got to Aunt Kate and Uncle John's house just as the family was sitting down to breakfast. Aunt Kate kissed me, everybody hugged me, and in a matter of minutes we were all seated at the big table eating fried eggs and hot biscuits.

"You've never put away such a breakfast before in your life, Sarah," Aunt Kate noted approvingly. "You keep that up and you may finally put a little meat on your bones."

"Sarah works too hard to gain weight," Larkin replied. "I didn't know what a hard-working wife I was getting."

Aunt Kate's wise eyes searched mine, and I smiled at her. "It's a miracle, Aunt Kate. I'm finally getting good at something besides reading and dancing!"

Something like relief showed on her face, along with questions unasked and unanswered. The men kept up such a steady stream of political talk that I barely had a chance to ask the really important questions. "Piety, are you really going to marry Tom? Is Willie truly serious about Becky? Does Charity have a beau yet?"

"Yes to all three questions, and I'll tell you all about them when you come back through here next Sunday. I see Mr. Flint heading for his horse, so you'd better get out there, too. I already know enough about Flint men to know they don't expect to be kept waiting." Piety hugged me even as she pushed me out the door.

The ten miles to Pa's house was an easy downhill ride. It was a glory of a morning. The wind was keen and fragrant with the first sweet scent of peach and plum. The blooming trees, tender and lovely against the nearly bare-limbed staunchness of hickory and oak, scattered their delicate petals on the wind. We rode with the sun on our faces and the wind at our backs. Newborn lambs wobbled in the misty meadows and larks sang their morning praises, while in the tall overarching trees that lined the road the bluejays and sparrows kept up their morning chatter. I waved when we passed an occasional plowman following his yoke of oxen and rejoiced in the fresh new day. To canter with Larkin down the big pike on a beautiful Ozark morning was to know one of life's real joys, and my heart sang its own private and personal praise song.

Pa and Eliza literally welcomed us with open arms. Pa hugged me so hard I thought he would break a rib, and Neely came rushing out of the kitchen shouting for joy. "Praise de good Lord, my baby's come home! Lemme see my baby's face in de daylight! You is a sight for sore eyes!" And then, after a critical inspection of my happy face and my callused hands, she turned to Larkin. "She doin' good. Look like I can put my hex signs down for now, anyway. She doin' good."

Pa was mindful of his manners. "Matthew, step inside and have a seat by the fire. Would you like a dram before dinner? You've had a hard ride this morning and have a harder one coming up. Eliza, would you fetch us something? What'll you have, men?"

Eliza's knowing eyes had already looked me over from head to toe. "Sarah, you've turned into a beauty. Who would have thought it? Our little, big-eyed skinny girl! Married life becomes you. Larkin, we're so thankful you let Sarah come home to visit us. We've been so lonesome for her. I don't know who's missed her the most — her pa, or Neely, or me."

Pa could hardly wait to get us seated, for he had momentous news to impart. "Gentlemen, this is a red-letter day! As a matter of fact, it is a day that, to tell the truth, I wondered if we'd ever see! Sarah, there's finally been a ruling on your inheritance. The logjam has been broken at last. Now it's only a matter of time before it's finished!"

"How so, William?" asked Matthew Flint.

"The ruling came in the mail pouch this morning. Fresh out of Washington, D.C., is an official letter from the Bureau of Indian Affairs. They've finally reached a conclusion as to how many of Louis Chouteau's offspring are entitled to inherit his lands."

We sat transfixed. For a dozen years the matter had been appealed and re-appealed through the courts and the multiple layers of official bureaucracy, the case hinging on whether Chouteau's acknowledged half-breed bastard children had the right to inherit equally with his five legitimate children, one of whom had been my mother. Bitterly contested by attorneys representing his legitimate children, Chouteau's will had specified that his three bastard sons should share equally in the lands to which he held title at the time of his death. In contrast to his famous half brother, Auguste Chouteau, who had squandered an enormous fortune during the latter years of his life, Louis Chouteau had been prudent in matters of money.

My grandfather had been an ambitious man from an extraordinarily ambitious lineage. He had set up his principal establishment in the heart of the Osage country. He and his brothers had built the house of Chouteau into the dominant position in the Southwest. At the time when the Santa Fe Trail became the richest merchant route in the nation, these enterprising traders became the most influential men, white or red, between the Missouri River and the Mexican border.

Their chief source of wealth was the bounty afforded by the West — the skins brought in by the trappers and hunters on the one hand, and on the other, the opportunities for selling desirable goods to the Indians and necessities to the white settlers who continued to push Westward in larger and larger waves. Louis Chouteau had early on won the loyalty and respect of all segments of this myriad society through honesty and fair dealing. The result had been the amassing of a considerable fortune, translated mostly into vast holdings of lands stretching down from Missouri and Arkansas and extending into the Indian Nation.

At the time of his death, my grandfather had held title to 40,000 acres, and it was for this prize that his children, both legitimate and bastard, had fought so bitterly. Although the legitimate children had argued with considerable conviction that the three half-breed sons had no basis for inheritance, the matter had been so clouded by the courts that eventually the ultimate decision had been remanded to the Bureau of Indian Affairs for its ruling on the matter.

Now, after three years of consultation, study, maneuvering, and corresponding, the massive machinery of the government had issued an edict. All eight children, legitimate and illegitimate, were to share and share alike in the holdings of Louis Chouteau. This ruling meant that I, the only child of my dead mother, had become heiress to 5,000 acres.

I sat in astonishment, unable to comprehend the implications of this new turn of events. Slowly, as I looked at the satisfaction on the faces of the adults who were the major forces in my life, I asked the obvious question. "How did it happen to come about now, after all these years of wrangling?"

The looks that passed among the three men were prideful beyond telling. Larkin answered me. "This is General Houston's wedding gift. When I asked your father for you, he asked my father to write to Houston, both to ask Houston's blessing and to ask his help. It was Houston's influence with the Indian Agency that forced them into a decision."

"But they ruled against the legitimate heirs." I was puzzled. My inheritance by their ruling had been reduced from 8,000 acres to 5,000.

"The important thing, Sarah, is that they ruled. Now the matter is settled, and the title to 5,000 acres will pass to you within weeks, rather than being dwindled and chewed on by the court costs brought on by petty-minded bureaucrats! Better to get it settled soon. If this country had gone to war before it was settled, God alone knows whether you would have ever seen an acre of land. A bird in the hand is worth a lot more than two in the bush!" Pa was firm and final.

"Where is the land? Which part of the holdings has been specified?" Matthew Flint's question was appropriate, for the lands were widely scattered.

"It's not been specified yet. The court has ordered that a 'Partition and Deed' be signed by the heirs dividing the estate property into eight equal parts. It has also ruled that the partition of the land be made among the plaintiffs and defendants and has appointed and commissioned three men without prejudice to make the partition. The partition is to be made no later than July 1, 1860, and to be binding on all concerned." Pa was elated. "Eliza, bring us a bottle of your best wine. We'll drink a toast to General Houston, and drink in pride and gratitude. He has delivered a princely wedding present, and we owe him our everlasting thanks! Matthew, when you and Larkin get to the convention tomorrow, I hope you move heaven and earth in support of Sam Houston!"

As far back as I could remember, I had known that my mother would inherit land. Now, as her heir, I tried to take on the implications of this sudden change in my fortune — tried and failed, for to suddenly come to terms with vast new wealth and responsibilities was mind-boggling. Pa handed me the attorney's impressive document, and I read it with total concentration before passing it on to Larkin.

Pa was now looking thoughtfully at me. "Sarah, this will take some doing. You and Larkin will have to go to Kansas City this summer to settle this thing. Married women can inherit property in Arkansas, but you'll still be a minor. I expect the court will transfer title to Larkin in trust as an advancement to you, his wife, since he will be considered to be your guardian. In any case, you both have a lot to look forward to, and I most heartily congratulate you both. You're going to stun your aunts and uncles when you see them in Kansas City. You look so much like your mother they'll think they're seeing a ghost."

Larkin was ready to ride. "Father, we'd best be back in the saddle if we're to make it in to Huntsville tonight."

With a triumphant smile and a quick kiss, he swung up into the saddle. We watched the straight backs and high heads of father and son as they rode briskly down the pike toward the anticipated political maneuverings.

Eliza smiled as she looked at the assured posture of the Flint men. "I'd expect Larkin to be a real force in that Kansas City gathering of your relatives."

As always, Pa took a tolerant view. "Well, if Larkin is a force, and I expect he will be, he comes by it honestly. So does Minerva, for that matter. After all, she's descended from a chief on her mother's side, and her father, old Sam Houston, didn't get to be a governor in two states by letting other people push him around. I never have seen any humble governor yet, nor senators, neither. It's not in the nature of the breed. A man's not a leader when he always has to go around begging other people to tell him what they think ought to be done. Being a leader and a force is not a mark against a man, Eliza."

"Well, then, Larkin's lucky on both sides of his family." Eliza's tone was crisp. "It appears to me he was born to tell other people what to do!"

I gave her a quick look, taken totally by surprise that her analysis was so much on the mark. Memories of my back-breaking work, my roughened and calloused hands, my eagerness to please Larkin, my constant efforts to excel in his eyes, were translated into my reply. "Well, when and if I do get my hands on any money, the first thing I'm going to do is get a hired girl. I'm working like a nigra, not that Larkin isn't, but I never expected married life to have so much hard work built into it."

Eliza did not hold with self-pity. She looked me in the eye. "My girl, you're working no more and no less than every other married woman here in these mountains. If you had to do all that work with a youngun or two hanging onto your skirts, then I might start feeling sorry for you. As it is, I'd say it's time to count your blessings. Looks like you ought to be able to afford a hired girl before you have your first baby. That is, if you're not in the family way already."

I gasped. Such frank talk coming from Eliza was astounding. "No, I'm not." I could feel my face turning red.

Surprisingly, she reached out and hugged me to her bosom. "Honey, you've got the look of a girl who's had her share of loving, and I'm proud of Larkin for making you happy. But I'm not sorry for you. Hard work never killed anybody yet. If it did, Neely and I would both be dead. And if we don't go out in the kitchen right now and give Neely a chance to talk to you, her feelings will be bad hurt. We've all missed you something awful, but I swear I think Neely has missed you the most."

We walked through to the big kitchen, but Neely was not there. Through the kitchen window we watched her as she rushed down to the pike to shoo with her apron a turkey hen and her brood across the road and out of harm's way. From there she went down the path to the springhouse, through the fragrant mint and the violets, to bring back butter for the fresh rhubarb pie she was in the process of baking. When she came back, sweating and smiling, she folded me in her embrace, then she held me at arm's length for a long inspection. Seemingly satisfied with what she saw in my face, she again inspected my hands. "You doin' all right. Happy face, rough hands, slim waist — dat ain't bad. Now you can set and talk to me and do easy work while I gets supper ready for de stage to come in."

So I told her about the garden and about my first time doing the wash, and my burned biscuits and my good custards and what fun it was to ride my beautiful mare. As we talked we peeled potatoes and pounded hominy grits and made pie crust, with Neely rushing outside at regular intervals to baste the great side of beef on the barbecue pit. Up at dawn, she had been cleaning and baking and frying and churning, the sweat rolling down that strong face to trickle onto her ample bosom. Eliza generously left us to our confidences. Finally, I said, "Neely, there are so many things I still need to learn. Will you teach me how to make soap and how to put up sauerkraut? And I'll need to know how to keep the birds away from the fruit when it's spread out to dry, and how to make jelly. I wish I had paid more attention last summer."

Neely took her time with her answer. "Honey, you don't haf to do it all right de first time. Mista Larkin, he can't 'spect too much too soon. Seems to me he tell you what he want and he tell you what he need. You doin' fine, honey. Go in and spend some time with Miss Liza and your Pa. We not careful, dey be gettin' jealous."

As I went out the door, Neely grinned from ear to ear, and to my amazement summed up. "Hey, once you gets dat land, honey, things gonna be evened up some. You ain't gonna get no upper hand, but you ain't gonna have no hand tied behind your back, neither! From now on, you ain't gonna haf to jump near as high ever time he say frog!"

I had to do my visiting with Pa and Eliza as they worked, for the stage was due in another hour. "Eliza," I asked, "who is Charity's new beau?

Aunt Kate didn't have time to tell me much. But Charity looks mighty happy."

"He's their new hired hand. Rode in from the Indian Nation one day looking for work. Said he'd grown up around a grist mill. John put him to helping Ike and Joe. John says he can outwork and outthink both slaves put together."

I laughed. "That might not be too hard to do." Although of good disposition, neither Ike nor Joe was noted for industry. "But why did Charity take a shine to a hired hand? She can just about take her pick of any boy in the county."

Pa entered into the conversation. "This man's not your usual drifter hired hand. I'd say he's got Indian blood in him, and he's far too well educated to be an ordinary laborer. There's more to his situation than meets the eye."

"He's got a story behind him, that's for sure." Eliza was reserving judgment. "He's fine looking, he's well spoken, and he's hardworking, but I'd want to know a lot more about him before I'd let him start courting my girl."

Pa, always a temperate man, took his time before answering and chose his words judiciously. "There's a lot going on in the Cherokee Nation right now. Always has been bad blood between the two factions who came out West over the Trail of Tears. The bunch that negotiated that treaty with Andrew Jackson has always been hated by the other, the one that John Ross leads. There was a big blood-brother killing back in 1839, shortly after the Eastern Cherokees got to the Indian Nation. I hear stories that both sides are gearing up again. Indians have deep hates and long memories. All the talk about secession now and all the gearing up to war is liable to be causing old wounds to fester amongst the Cherokees."

I took a deeply personal view. "Larkin's people won't be caught up in these old feuds, will they? I haven't heard any mention of it around them."

"I shouldn't think so. Larkin's living like a white man, which he mostly is, and his Houston uncles in Fort Smith are neutral. Larkin's grandfather, old John Jolly, had the foresight to move out here 20 years ahead of the Trail of Tears crowd. Oo-loo-te-ka, his Indian name was. I always thought he probably was a mix of both white and Indian. He led 6,000 or 7,000 out to Arkansas and the Indian Territory long before my time here. It must have been 1817 or 1818 when the first Cherokees took up land here."

"Why did they come so early?" I was puzzled but not surprised. My limited experience with Minerva and the Flint men had already taught me they were not cut out to be followers.

"My understanding was that Houston influenced that early move. Remember, he is Oo-loo-te-ka's adopted son, as well as having been Andrew Jackson's friend. Houston had fought alongside the Cherokees in the war of 1812, under Andrew Jackson. He seems to love them both. My best guess is that Houston and Jackson and Oo-loo-te-ka made a deal. They were all smart men and could see what was coming. They wanted to get the Cherokees out of the reach of the white men. Things looked a lot different back then. Fifty years ago, nobody thought this country would ever be settled by the whites. When John and Kate and I crossed the Tennessee mountains 24 years ago, we found virgin forests and peaceable Indians. Mostly rich Indians, too.

"They say old John Jolly lived like a king. He owned slaves, he planted cotton, and got rich shipping cotton downriver to New Orleans. Then he would ship trading goods upriver back to the Cherokee Nation, making money both ways. He was a shrewd old man. Never would speak English, so he constantly put people in the position of trying to guess what he was up to."

"I'd say Minerva comes by her ways naturally." Eliza's tone was dry. "But I'd like to get back to the here and now. What does all of this have to do with young Ridge Smith, Brother John's new hired man? If Smith is his real name, which I'm beginning to suspicion it's not."

This time Pa was firm. "So far as we are concerned, Eliza, his name is Smith and that's all there is to it. We don't want to bring harm to a fine young man by casting doubt on him, much less do we want to be causing blood to shed. If he's from the Stand Watie side of the Cherokee feud, he has good reason to flee the threat of murder and to hate John Ross. A generation back, Ross's followers marked four men for death over that Trail of Tears Treaty. Killed three of them. Stand Watie was the only one who survived.

"I used to know the Ridge family when they lived in Fayetteville. John Ridge was one of those three men who had been murdered over in the Indian Nation. After that, his widow moved to Arkansas for the safety of her children. Folks said she had lived like a wealthy woman in the Indian Territory, but she didn't live that way in Fayetteville. She had six or seven children. I don't know what happened to them, but the Ridge family is close kin to Stand Watie. When you get two smart Indian chiefs like Watie and Ross ready to fight to the death, there's always danger, especially if you're blood kin to either side.

"We'll stay well out of this, Eliza. We won't speculate about young Smith's beginnings, and we won't gossip. John and Kate are fine people. We are going to mind our own business."

When Pa used that tone, the subject was closed. Eliza and I, recognizing reality, turned to a lighter subject.

"To think that Larkin and I will be going to Kansas City! What do you suppose it's like? Pa, you went there. What was it like when you were there?"

"Sarah, it's big and it's noisy and it's full of all kinds of people. It's also home to a lot of your kinfolk, decent folks, and proud as Lucifer. They take great pride in the Chouteau family in Kansas City. It'll be an experience you'll never forget, especially with Larkin at your side."

Eliza laughed. "I wish I could be a mouse hiding in a closet in Kansas City just so I could hear what those Chouteaus have to say to their half-Indian brothers."

"I don't think they're going to be high-nosed or high-handed around Larkin. Not more than once, anyway."

Eliza's shrewdness in matters of human nature was always evident. "They have no quarrel with Larkin. They've always expected to share the inheritance with you, Sarah. Just look on it as a rare chance to get to know your kinfolk."

"Good advice, Eliza." Pa beamed at his sensible wife and leaned down to pat my cheek. "Daughter, it is so good to have you back home. We've missed you sorely. I wish Larkin and Matthew would take a week for their journey so we could keep you longer."

I rose to help Eliza and Neely in the kitchen, awaiting an opportunity to talk to Pa, for I had developed a wonderful plan, one that would require his consent and cooperation.

When I was alone with him, I seized my chance. "Pa, if I'm really going to own property, could I buy Neely from you? What I'd like to do is buy her freedom."

"Sarah, I wish I could say yes." There was a look on Pa's face such as I had seldom seen, a look that spoke both of compassion and bitterness. "The law won't allow Neely's freedom. We're four months too late. January 1st of this year was the last day free Negroes could live in

Arkansas. Any found in the state after that date will be sold into slavery for one year and then resold into permanent slavery. The law has been changed, and it has been made harsh. To free Neely now, even for a day, would likely put her in the hands of slave traders and hard masters before all was over."

"We've all got to ride out the storm that's coming." Eliza moved swiftly to Pa's side and took his hand in a rare gesture of tenderness. "Don't blame yourself, William. Neely doesn't blame you. Sarah doesn't either, I'm sure. You take too much on yourself. A man does what he can, and you do far more for your slaves than most. Don't look back and blame yourself anymore. We've got enough to do to look ahead and get braced for what's coming."

"Eliza, you're right, as always. And what's coming is your good fortune, Sarah."

Eliza was ready for a change of subject. "I have a gift, too. This day is yours to do with as you please. A married woman has little chance for a day of her own, and this one is yours. Be lazy, go visiting, do nothing, do everything, but please yourself all day!"

"My goodness, Eliza," I gasped, "what a present! I don't think in my whole life I ever did exactly as I pleased all day long. I may not know what it feels like."

"Time you found out." Again, Eliza's tone was crisp. I hugged her gratefully and smiled into her understanding eyes before heading out the door to saddle my mare and feel the winds of freedom.

Down by the springhouse I picked a bouquet of violets to place on my mother's grave, wrapping their stems in wet moss. By the time I picked the flowers, Tobe had already saddled Dolly for me. I cantered down the road holding the violets in one hand and the reins in the other, the light April breeze and the warm sun lifting my heart.

A half-mile ride brought me to the churchyard, where my mother lay amongst friends and relatives, their graves clustered as closely as their lives had once been. I traced with my forefinger the dates that defined her too-brief time: Anne Chouteau Griffin, 1825-1850, plus the one word that my father had chosen to place below the dates: "Beloved." Standing there in that quiet space, I kissed the violets before placing them on the green mantle of grass that separated me from my mother forever.

But the day was too beautiful and I was too full of life to stand and remember. Leading Dolly to the church steps, where she was easier to mount, I sprang back in the saddle to canter up the beautiful stretch of road that led toward Aunt Gert's house.

To my right rippled the bright waters of a mountain stream, rushing and gurgling over its shallow rock-plated bottoms, then deepening and widening into larger pools before rushing once again down the mountain slopes. Tall, big-leafed sycamore trees dipped their branches toward the water, curtseying their graceful limbs toward the cottonwoods and sweet gums that competed for space near the creek bank. I counted five or six shades of newly minted green leaves — the light green of sweet gum, the darker green of oak, the lush wide leaf of the shaggy-barked sycamore, the bluish deep green of the pine and cedar, all contrasting with the grape and honeysuckle vines above and the darkly glossy huckleberry bushes below. Squirrels and rabbits darted among the boulders of the mountain to my left. The bright bush of a red fox flashed briefly in front of me before dashing into the safety of the trees.

It was a day for rejoicing. I thought of Larkin, talking politics and listening to speeches, shut inside the stuffy walls of a political convention. Surely, I thought, he can't be enjoying himself all that much. He'll be so glad to get back.

As things turned out, I was only partially right. Larkin was glad to get back home, and he proved to be wonderfully glad to bed me again. However, his first real taste of politics had already made him a convert for life. I should have seen it coming, given all that Houston blood flowing through his veins. Larkin was born to be a leader, born to influence others. He took to politicking like a duck takes to water.

As Larkin described it to me later, his day was spent shaking hands, getting acquainted with half a hundred new men, and listening both to impassioned speeches and to shrewdly argued and logical persuasions. His long day had concluded with the inevitable hearty eating, companionable drinking, and self-serving maneuverings of both the able and the mediocre. Having accomplished his mission, that of naming Sam Houston as the convention's choice, Larkin felt his day to have been an unqualified success.

Chapter 6

 *ON SUNDAY, Griffins go to church. I had not realized how much I had missed these Sunday services until I walked down the aisle with Pa and Eliza to sit in our accustomed place. The dear and familiar rituals began. The preacher read out the hymns line by line, the words of each hymn blending solemn pronouncements with promises of joy. My kin and their neighbors sang in harmony, united by the melodies of the music and the certainties of their beliefs. Religion was the bedrock of their lives, their bulwark against the hardships of this world, their hope of joy in the next.*

I immersed myself in the sounds of the service. The long and fervent prayers of personal petition, the drawn-out and frequently repetitive sermon of the traveling preacher — all these warmed my heart. I was at home with my own kind. Even the hard, wooden split-log bench on which we sat for two hours seemed tolerably comfortable. When the sermon was finally over and the last "Amen" was said, Eliza reached across Pa and took my hand.

"You've missed it more than you thought, haven't you?"

My reply was straight from my heart. "I've missed you all more than I thought. But Larkin makes up for it."

It was Pa's hospitable habit to invite the traveling preacher for dinner, along with Aunt Gert, Cousin Alta, Cousin Ed, and anybody else he decided on the spur of the moment to include. He had no trouble collecting his usual crowd, for a mouth-watering Sunday dinner at Eliza's table was one of life's certain pleasures.

Larkin and his father rode up to the gate just as Eliza and I were setting the table. Forgetting the dignity that a married woman is expected to exhibit, I rushed up to Larkin and threw my arms around him.

With a smile and a triumphant glint in his eye, Larkin took charge. Whispering quickly in my ear, "Later, Sarah, later," he put an arm around my waist and led me firmly back across the veranda and into the assembly of relatives, where he and his father immediately became the center of attention.

"Well, Matthew," Pa asked, "is there hope for the country? How does it look for Houston?"

"I'm hopeful, William. The *Arkansas Gazette* sent one of their reporters all the way from Little Rock to cover the convention. For once, northern Arkansas may have had an influence far beyond its own borders. The *Gazette* is going to support Houston. Their editor is even planning to go to the national convention. He thinks there is a real chance for Houston."

"Will there be a state convention in Arkansas?" Cousin Ed, the schoolmaster, asked the question and waited intently for the answer.

"There is to be another in Little Rock at the end of this month. I'm to be a delegate. The timing is urgent, for the national convention date has already been set for May 9th."

"Where is it to be? Will you be attending, do you think?" Cousin Ed, ever mindful of political matters, was a considerable student of history.

"The party leaders have rented a vacant Presbyterian church in Baltimore, Maryland. The Democrats will be meeting a few days earlier in Charleston, so we'll know who their candidate is before we pick ours." Matthew spoke like a man who was sure of his ground.

Unexpectedly, Preacher Massey went on the attack. "Northerners must be a godless lot to let a Presbyterian church go unused. For shame, I say!" Tall, gaunt, and rugged, our circuit-riding preacher was a man with a substantial appetite and an unswerving antagonism to sin. "Though I was born in the mountains and expect to die in the mountains, I have always tried to pray for the godless in the North who have the misfortune to live in the cities. But when the people stop using a Presbyterian church, they go too far." Eyes flashing, he paused to consider a punishment appropriately vindictive.

"Sir, I doubt things are that bad." Larkin addressed the preacher straightforwardly. "My understanding is that the Presbyterians in Baltimore built a fine new church. Their old one will not be vacant for long before another congregation finds need for it."

"You sound like you were part of the planning committee," Pa spoke approvingly, proud of his new son-in-law.

"In a way I was, and I sure wish I could go with Father to the state convention. But I just don't see how I can spare the time. Father is sure to get nominated to go on to Baltimore, and it's about a two-week trip each way. Whether he goes by steamboat to St. Louis and then takes the train, or whether he boards the train at Memphis, it's going to take up more than a month. I can't spare a month at crop time."

"There's work of importance to be done here at home, son." Matthew spoke as if he were laying out Larkin's future. "We've got the editor of the *Arkansas Gazette* on our side, but what we need is the goodwill of the men who'll be doing the voting. The old Democratic party in this state is corrupt. They're going to be out there buying votes and laying the groundwork for lining their pockets later. I'd like you to come as far as Little Rock with me, so you can meet the other men who'll be working to get Sam Houston elected. I don't ask that you go on to Baltimore. But I am asking for one more week here in Arkansas." Matthew, who had for years been his county's representative to the state legislature, had clearly laid his plans.

Larkin glanced at me and a look of pure mischief came into his eyes. "Sarah, it appears to me you're going to have to learn to milk that cow. If I'm going to be out and going again, I've got to teach you a lot more than what you know now. And your aim has got to get better on that rifle. If you have to fight off panthers or prowlers, I want you to be a sure shot."

"I don't have to learn to plow, do I?" I was only partly joking.

"No, but I could probably find a hoe handle that would fit your hand pretty well."

Now it was Aunt Gert's turn to become indignant. "For shame, Larkin, for shame! Going off and leaving that pretty little thing for a week is bad enough. Laying out all that work for her to do while you're gone and treating her like a field hand is too much! Sarah, you come right back here and stay with me while he's gone!" Her eyes flashed as she shook her finger indignantly at Larkin. "There's no call for matrimony to turn Sarah into a slave!"

Wiping the grin off his face, Larkin did his best to appease Aunt Gert's wrath. "I was teasing Sarah, ma'am. Truly I was. Minerva can send some of her household to stay with Sarah while I'm away. Or it may be that Charity and Piety can come for a visit. I won't leave her by herself. You're right. Sarah's too dear to be treated so. You can rest easy, ma'am. I don't aim to put politics ahead of my responsibilities."

Even so, Aunt Gert was only half persuaded. After dinner, as Larkin and Matthew Flint and I prepared to mount our horses, she gave me one more piece of advice. "You keep your eye on that young man, Sarah. He's a man who's always going to get his own way. And too good-looking by half. He bears watching."

I kissed her wrinkled cheek. "I mean to keep an eye on him."

All three of us were smiling as we rode down the pike. "Sarah," Matthew said dryly, "what your Aunt Gert lacks in a sense of humor she makes up in her sense of justice. You Griffins strike me as a mighty protective clan. Larkin, I'd advise you to tread lightly around Sarah's kinfolks until they come to know what a joker you are. I wouldn't much want you to stir that preacher up, either. He may or may not be close to God, but he appears to be too close to old John Brown for my comfort. God knows, the country doesn't need another of that fanatical breed."

"The country's got a lot of breeds of men that I could do without." Larkin was serious. "I've about decided that 10 percent of the men in this country are busy stirring up trouble for the other 90 percent to fight about. All I want is that Sarah and I can be left alone, live our lives, and prosper like you and Minerva have done. That's not too much to ask of life, but I'm beginning to think our hopes are hanging by a thin thread. If Houston's not named as a candidate, God knows what's ahead. If your Aunt Gert can't stand the thought of you being by yourself for a week, Sarah, I wonder how she'd take to the idea of my having to go off to war and leave you behind?"

I looked at him in horror. "Let's change the subject. This day is too pretty to spoil. I can't bear to think of it."

As we forded the Buffalo River, Larkin looked toward the fork of the road. "Father, what do you say we take the short way and go home over the mountain? I've been away about long enough."

Riding spirited horses over the mountain brought us into the Flint Valley in record time. We left Matthew at his gate in order to head straight home, for Larkin seemed driven by an urgency I could not fathom. When we finally rode up to our own gate he reined in his horse, looked mischievously at me, and grinned his heart-stopping grin.

"If we hadn't gotten here soon, I would have had to take you right by the side of the road, Sarah. Actually, that might not be a bad idea sometime. You might enjoy the feel of green grass tickling your bare bottom!"

I laughed aloud, finally understanding his haste. We walked hand in hand inside our own doorway, where a warm late-afternoon sun was slanting in through the western windows. My arms went around his neck. His kiss was so loving, so tender, and so filled with yearning that I opened to it like a flower. We built together a rising intensity of passion that spilled its surging pleasure in waves of unbearable joy. I cried out with wonder, with sensations so intense they could not be sustained and be bearable. We grasped each other's bodies as the final spending and ebbing waves left us equally limp, and smiled into each other's eyes, beyond words, beyond thought, beyond anything except bonding and feeling.

We lay spent, holding each other in sweet ownership, until the mooing of the cow reminded Larkin of milking time and reminded us both that the horses still stood saddled and hitched to the gate. We laughed as we dressed. Larkin pronounced the obvious analysis. "Sarah, if politics does that much for our love life, it might be worth it for me to run for office!"

Still laughing, we resumed the work and rhythms of our lives. I have never in my life been happier than I was that tender April evening in 1860 when I was barely past 16.

But life had to go on, and there was work to be done. Larkin worked like a dog in the few days remaining before he left home again. Matthew rode over a couple of times to work out arrangements for Larkin's absence. When finally it was all settled, Larkin hired Ike, one of Uncle John's slaves, to cultivate the corn and look after the stock. This promised to be a good solution, for Ike was to ride up with Piety and Charity, who would stay with me. I would not have thought anything would have made it up to me for Larkin's second absence, but Piety and Charity's visit came close. We had a purely wonderful time. Four days we worked and sang, talked and dreamed. Actually, we talked and dreamed more than we worked and sang, but we did manage to make up a batch of soap and get a year's supply of candles dipped.

Aunt Kate had taught her girls a lot more than Eliza had taught me in the hard work department. Probably because Neely was always handy, strong and smart, Eliza and Neely had over the years found it easier to do things themselves than to teach me. Aunt Kate and Uncle John only owned the two male slaves. The daughters of their household were trained in competence and in generosity of spirit by their parents' example. On this visit, Piety and Charity tried to pass their competence on to me. I learned a lot, including how much hard work it took to make soap.

Larkin had brought me a present from Minerva before he left, and I couldn't wait to see the girls' faces when I put it on. She had sent me a pair of Stant's outgrown pants and a shirt, so I could ride astride and work around the place in comfort. Larkin had laughed when he brought them but turned thoughtful when I modeled my new britches.

"I don't know whether to laugh or cry," he said. "That sweet little bottom of yours is so shapely in those britches that I can't have you wearing them in front of any men except family."

"Well, how am I going to wear them in front of Ike, when Piety and Charity and I are working around the farm?"

"Slaves don't count. Ike knows he's a dead man if he so much as looks at you crosswise. Just be sure you only wear them to work in and to ride on our own land."

The day we made the soap I was up early, putting on my new britches before the girls were even awake. After they got over their shock, they giggled themselves into hiccups, but I kept the pants on anyway. Working around a fire all day while wearing wide, heavy skirts can get hot and hazardous. But I was ready for work in lots of other ways, too.

I had already leached the lye the day before. Larkin had built me an ash hopper, a little trough made out of hickory wood, lining the bottom of the trough with corn shucks so the water would drip out slowly into the wooden bucket beneath. I filled the hopper with fireplace ashes, poured water over it, and by evening had plenty of lye for our project. Actually, I was pretty proud of myself for having so much forethought.

We started making soap right after breakfast. Eliza had told me to save all my grease, and heaven knows we had plenty, what with all the frying I had been doing for four months. We put the lye in the water in the wash pot, built a good fire, and started adding the grease and stirring the pot. We had a stout wooden stirring paddle with a long five-foot handle, but you'd be surprised how heavy a handle can get when you have to constantly stir.

We took turns for hours, the sweat pouring off our faces. The sun got hot, and we got hot, but finally we were done. The boiling thickened the soap until it was like jelly, then we poured it into an old churn, put in some ginger leaves to make it smell good, and felt truly pleased with ourselves.

The sun was so hot that temptation got the best of us — we decided to try out our new soap in the creek. Charity had the idea first. "Let's go bathe in the creek. The sun's been shining on the water all day. It'll be warm enough if we wash fast."

Piety was horrified. "What if someone sees us?"

My arms were aching, my back was tired, and I knew the water would feel good. "Nobody can possibly see us except Ike, and I'll go give him orders to stay in the far field until I call him." I walked down the length of the field, gave Ike his orders, grabbed some towels and a cup of the new soap, and headed down the creek bank with the distinctly delicious sense that we were about to turn into sinful pagans.

"Promise and cross your heart never to tell another soul." Piety was coming around.

We promised, then shed our clothes on the creek bank. At first we shut our eyes and refused to even peep at each other. Then Charity slipped on a moss-covered rock, falling with such a splash that we laughed until we hurt. We played, splashing water all over each other, and cavorted like the innocent children we were. Even so, conscience prevailed. We cut our time short, climbed back into our clothes, and walked up the hill happy and refreshed. Larkin was due home by dark. Piety had every confidence that Tom would ride along with him, so it was time to start cooking a man-sized supper. Piety and Charity went on to the cabin to start up the fire, while I walked down to the lower field to see how Ike was coming along with his plowing.

I nearly missed seeing him. If I had been a minute later, he would have already been back between the plow handles where he belonged. As it was, I crested the hill overlooking the cornfield and stopped in the shade of a hickory to get a rock out of my shoe. Still bent over, I looked down the field to see the droop-eared mule hitched to the plow, tethered by its reins at the end of a corn row. The mule stood like a statue, now and then twitching its ears against the persistent flies. Crows swooped, jays called, a squirrel darted ambitiously around the unmoving feet of the stolid mule, but Ike was nowhere in sight.

Then I saw him climb up the creek bank and head back toward the plow, his britches soaked to the waist, his movements slow and stealthy, his walk as deliberate as though he was stalking unsuspecting prey. In that split second, my mood changed from contentment to cold fear. Concealed by the shadows of the big hickory tree, I froze in horror. Belatedly I understood the scene before me: the abandoned mule meant Ike's deliberate disobedience, his defiance of all the rules that shaped our lives and held us safe.

I knew he had been spying on us. I could imagine him wading carefully up the creek, concealing himself when he came within hearing range of our splashing and cavorting, positioning himself for a full view of our delicate and naked flesh. While we had been innocently giggling, turning our backs on each other so as not to gaze too fully on our private parts, Ike had been lasciviously feasting on the sight of our tender bodies. Charity and Piety and I were now fixed as pictures in his private gallery, images he could call up at will to be partners in the lewd reaches of his imaginations. It was a realization so repugnant as to bring a spasm of nausea to my throat.

Still frozen with shock, I watched as Ike resumed his plowing, stumbling along behind the mule with the uncaring gait of a man whose mind is totally unconnected to his task. I waited until he had reached the end of the furrow and had turned his back to plow in the opposite direction before I left. Quietly I slipped back down the hill toward the cabin, my steps slowed by the horror of the choices that lay ahead of me.

Each option was unthinkable. To tell Larkin and Tom of Ike's spying was to sentence Ike to death. To let his action go unchecked was to open the door to the possibility, from that look on his face, that any one of the three of us might be violated, and to the certainty that we would live in constant fear of it. To tell Uncle John, Ike's owner, without telling Larkin would be both disloyalty and stupidity. Larkin would never forgive me for discussing an intimate action with another man, even a kinsman. I walked in anguish toward the house. Piety and Charity were working around the hearth, Piety rolling out piecrust, Charity washing rhubarb. Charity took one look at my face and put her arms around me.

"What's wrong, Sarah? You look like you've seen a ghost! What happened?"

I told them. Maybe I should have kept it to myself and carried the burden alone, but I could not. Besides, Ike was a member of their household, a constant presence in their lives, far more a threat to them than to me.

Piety's response was predictable. "We should never have gone in the creek. It's our fault. We knew better."

"What's done is done. This was no accident. Ike knew what he was doing. We've misjudged him, all of us, thinking he was only slow. Being dull doesn't keep him from being dangerous. Now we'll have to watch him all the time."

Charity's imagination had begun to fill in my sparse description. "I think I'm going to be sick." She sat down slowly, her face as white as the now-forgotten piecrust.

Piety spoke from the deep core that formed the relationship between the races. "We've got to tell Pa. It will have to be his choice. Pa won't kill Ike, like Larkin and Tom would, but he won't keep him, either. He can't keep him, knowing that Ike has seen us naked on purpose, and not knowing what he may want to do next."

"Wouldn't it be better to tell Ma and let her tell Pa?" Charity had put my own thoughts into words. Maybe Aunt Kate could handle the matter easier than we.

"We're grown women, about to be married. We've got to tell Pa ourselves, and he will keep it quiet. But it lays a terrible burden on Pa. If he sells Ike, Pa will feel he has passed the problem to somebody else. If he sets him free, Ike will have to leave the state. He's liable to rape the first woman he can get his hands on if he thinks he can get by with it."

Piety looked at us both. "I know what Pa will do first, and it's what we ought to do. He'll pray over it. We better pray over it, too, and pray harder than we've ever prayed before." We held hands, closed our eyes, and offered up our own petitions. Finally, Piety broke the silence. "Help us, Lord God. Amen."

My eyes were wet. I saw tears running down Piety's cheeks. But Charity's eyes were dry and clear. "The truth is, we haven't been safe any of the time. We thought we were safe. Probably Ike has been wondering for years what we look like without our clothes on. Remember, he and Joe have been pestering Pa to buy them wives. There is no easy answer to this, but I don't intend to lay blame on myself."

"Will you tell Uncle John the minute you get home?" I was fearful, reluctant to keep such a secret from Larkin, even more reluctant to face the consequences of his knowing.

Piety answered, "Yes, and he will tell no one. I hope he won't even tell Ma. Just as I hope you won't tell Larkin, Sarah. No good can come from burdening Larkin. And a good deal of harm could happen — to all of us. I think from now on we'd better pray to bear our burdens. I guess silence is one of those burdens. Telling somebody else is like passing the burden from our backs to theirs, but in this case it mostly seems to be Pa's burden. I feel sorry for him, and even more sorry for Ike." She spoke as if the thing was settled, but I was already caught up in a new worry.

"What if Larkin doesn't get back tonight? It's nearly dark. I thought he'd be back by now. What if the stage couldn't get through on time? Sometimes bridges get washed out. The creeks may be flooded if the rivers are backed up. This is a bad time of year when it rains a lot, and we don't know what kind of weather they're having down around Little Rock, or what the roads are like." My words opened a new chamber of horrors.

"We've got to make plans. We don't have much time. The cow needs milking; Ike will be up here looking for his supper soon. If Larkin is not back by dark, Ike will figure he'll not be back tonight, and if Larkin's not back, we're in danger. Ike had a sly, slick look on his face. He's big and strong, but he's not smart. Our only chance is to outthink him."

"Sarah, you can't go down to the barn alone to do the milking. Send Ike to do it when he comes up for his supper." Piety began, as always, to deal with practical tasks. "Charity, finish the pie and slice up some ham while I make corn bread. We're going to feed Ike so much he'll get sleepy early. Sarah, are your guns loaded? We may need them before the night is over."

I looked at her with pure astonishment. In the space of an hour we had changed from careless girls to grim women preparing to protect our lives. Only minutes earlier it had been unthinkable to us that Larkin should shoot Ike in cold blood. Now, with the stark prospect of rape before us, we were considering killing Ike ourselves.

"This feels like a nightmare. Sarah, are you absolutely sure that Ike spied on us? There couldn't have been some other reason for him to be in the creek?"

"I'm sure. It wasn't only that his pants were wet and the mule was hitched up; it was his face. I felt like throwing up when I saw his face."

"Then we'd better get the guns ready."

How quickly the familiar can become forbidding. When Ike shuffled up to the back door for his supper, I handed him the milk bucket. "You'll have to do the milking tonight, Ike. Mr. Larkin's not home yet, and I'm too tired. I'll give you your supper after you milk the cow."

"Yessum." He walked toward the barn with a slow, shuffling gait, the milk bucket held slackly in one enormous hand. I was struck by his size — the broad back, sturdy legs, his entire body muscled by years at the grist mill, lifting heavy bags of grain. I realized he could sling any one of us around as easily as he could toss a sack of corn. I shut the door to the cabin and we began to plan against the unthinkable.

Dark was coming on, and still there was no sign of Larkin. When Ike handed me the foaming bucket of milk, I gave him a full plate of beans, fat meat, and corn bread in exchange. This time he did not look me in the eye but took his plate over to the shed and began to wolf down the beans like a starving animal. I called over to him, "We'll have the pie done in a little while. You can come back for cobbler when you finish the beans."

Straining the warm milk as fast as I could, I carried the pail down the steep steps and across the swinging bridge to the springhouse. Piety and Charity would keep Ike occupied until I got back, feeding him rhubarb cobbler. Even so, I needed to hurry. Once inside the cave, my mood shifted like lightning. "Spirits, help me," I prayed in earnest, petitioning these unknown ancient powers as if they were handmaidens to Almighty God Himself. My mind cleared as though in instant answer to my fervent need. I became as analytical as if I were working on an algebra problem, and as cool. One word was writ large in my mind: PLAN.

On swift feet I carried the answer of the spirits back to the cabin, racing up the stone steps to begin our grim preparations.

Ike was slouching back to the shed where he slept, the empty smeared pie plate on the back porch bench testifying to his greedy appetite.

Piety and Charity stood at the front windows, staring with fading hopes at the empty road. Charity looked at us with a solemn eye. "We've got to eat some, whether or not we have any appetite. Larkin isn't coming tonight, or he'd be here by now. So we'd better get ready for the worst."

Piety answered, "We'd better act as natural as we can. If Ike sees we're suspicious, it likely will cause him to be cautious. We'll have more of a chance if he acts like his usual dumb self than if he comes up with some big plan. And there's always the chance we're wrong. Maybe he means to leave us alone."

"And maybe he means to rape us." I spoke calmly. "What he'll do is try to get us one at a time. We can't even go to the privy by ourselves now, or go out without a gun. We might as well bring this thing to a head and force it out into the open. We can't worry like this too long."

"Whatever he means to do, he'll do tonight. He'll think tonight is his big chance, since Larkin didn't get home. God alone knows how long this thing has been building up in him."

We worried separately and planned together as the dark shadows of night concealed the familiar landscape. We searched the road in hopes of seeing Larkin and Tom. Finally, we faced the truth. We were on our own.

Larkin's guns were primed and ready. I took the heavy shotgun down from the rack above the fireplace, laid the pistol on the table by the bed, moved one chair so it would face the door on the north wall, and positioned another so it would face the south door.

"He'll not try to get in through the windows. He's so big he's liable to get stuck. He'll try to break down the door."

"I don't think he can. These doors are stout. The bolts are strong. This cabin was built to last. The only way he can get in is to bust the door off its hinges, and I don't think he's that strong."

"Surely he wouldn't be such a fool. Even if he could get in, he would be a perfect target. Even a pistol would bring him down at close range. The shotgun would tear him apart. Surely he knows that."

"He doesn't know we're even suspecting him, let alone waiting on him with a shotgun. He'll figure on scaring us and surprising us, just as we're counting on surprising him."

Again, Piety spoke up with the voice of reason. "We may be wrong. Sarah, you may be wrong. Maybe you mistook what you saw, and even if you didn't, Ike may let go of any ideas he had. He's nearly too lazy to get worked up about anything."

"No man is ever too lazy to get worked up about having a woman." I spoke out of deep conviction. "If I'm wrong, then let's be thankful. If I'm right, we've got to be ready. I doubt if any of us can get to sleep, but one of us ought to try. I'll take the shotgun and sit facing the front door. Charity, you take the pistol and sit against the other wall, facing the back door. Piety, you put the poker on the floor by the bed, and see if you can get some sleep. One of us, at least, may as well lie down and see if we can rest."

We took our stations, and the hours passed. A pale, thin sliver of a moon came up, bringing little light and no comfort. I think I almost dozed off, the shotgun cold against my feet. It was the sly sound of cautious bare feet that I heard first, then breathing, heavy, panting. Through the open window I caught his rancid smell — a smell of grease and sweat and the long embedded grime of his body. He was on the other side of the wall behind me. It was Charity who was opposite him, Charity who would have to shoot him.

Fear flashed through my body. For one helpless instant I was frozen, incapable of action or thought. Then in a swift surge of sanity, my brain took over. I looked across the room where Charity sat in the shadows. As if in answer to my questioning fears, she aimed her pistol toward the window on my right.

I froze.

He was coming in through the window. Stealthily, silently, his massive shoulders filled the space. The pale moonlight silhouetted his bulk and provided a target. The click of Charity's pistol was his first clue regarding his reception; the roar of her gun was the last sound he heard. He fell like an ox, gravity propelling the massive trunk of his body onto the cabin floor, his feet still outside, his bent knees angled over the window ledge in a grotesque posture of subservience.

With shaking hands I lit the bedside candle. Somewhere, a woman screamed, an anguished cry of pure terror. With complete detachment I recognized the voice as my own. On the other side of the room Piety lit a second candle, carrying it in stony silence to stare at Ike.

He was buck naked, his black flesh gleaming in the candlelight, a length of rope clutched tightly in one massive fist, a butcher knife in the other. Blood was pouring from the massive hole in his back. Gurgling, groaning sounds came from lips curled back from blackish-purple gums. His face, contorted in agony, reminded me of a wolf, a wolf caught in a fatal trap. With one last fearful gurgling rattle, his head flopped forward, signaling his death.

We stood as if turned to stone, unable to think or to act, reluctant to touch him or to accept the reality of his death. Finally, I broke the silence.

"His blood is on all our hands, Charity. Just because you were the one who had to pull the trigger doesn't mean that it's your conscience any more than mine. I planned how we'd shoot him, and Piety loaded the guns. We're all in this, and we all lived through it. Instead of being sorry we had to shoot him, let's look at the other side. Let's be thankful to God we didn't get raped and killed."

Piety's tone was brisk. "And let's get to work. Let's drag his body out in the yard. He's already bled all over the floor, and there's blood on the wall. It's time to deal with what we've done."

Finally, Charity spoke, her voice as clear as the waters in our cave and as quiet as if she were in church. "I don't feel like I did it. When I saw him start through the window, I felt somebody else take over my hands. It was like strong hands guiding my hands. Somebody else's hands aimed the pistol, and somebody else told me when to shoot. They even pulled the trigger. I had help."

This time it was I who called for prayer. "Let's get down on our knees and be thankful." And on my knees I made silent entreaty to the spirits and to the Lord to make me worthy of their help.

I wanted to drag him face down, so the girls would be spared the sight of his enormous black member. I bent over to grab one muscular shoulder but drew back in surprise.

"I can't get a grip on him. He greased his back and shoulders."

"That's so he could slide through the window and not get stuck. All these years we've been wrong about Ike. He wasn't as stupid as he looked. He was lazy and probably acted dumb to get out of work."

"His was not the plan of a slow man. That rope, for instance. He could have used it to tie two of us up while he raped the other."

"Or he could have used it to strangle us, one at a time, while we slept."

He was so heavy that we finally had to put the rope under his arms and around his shoulders. I pulled on the rope while Charity took one of his arms, Piety the other.

It took all three of us to drag Ike's heavy body across the room, out the door, and onto the front yard. We pulled him as far as the fence, where the sweetness of the wild rose was poignant contrast with the stench of his body. I went down to the barn and got a sheet of canvas, an old wagon tarp, to spread over him, weighing its edges down with rocks so the dogs would not be able to get to him.

By daylight we had finished scrubbing the floor and the wall of the cabin. I made a good, strong pot of coffee. We sat down at the kitchen table to face another day.

"We might as well get on with our lives. We're no worse off than the pioneer women who settled this land. They fought and killed Indians; we fought and killed a man who was trying to kill and rape us." I spoke the truth as I saw it.

Piety took charge. "I'll milk the cow. Charity and Sarah, you cook breakfast. I expect Larkin will be home today."

"Tom likely will come with him. They can dig a grave."

"We have work to do. The cow is lowing; the stock are waiting to be fed. Charity, would you go out to the woodpile and split some kindling for the fire?"

She put us to work, that wonderful remedy for woe and sorrow. She made us sit down at the breakfast table to go through the motions of eating. Charity had cooked oatmeal. I thought maybe I could swallow some, but I was unable to get anything past the big lump in my throat. In silence we went through the motions of our morning.

When the barking of the two hounds signaled their arrival, we rushed to the gate to welcome our men. Three riders appeared: Larkin, Tom, and a tall and handsome stranger I knew instinctively to be Charity's beau. We rushed into their arms. Only when we began to tell our tale of horror did the tears start to flow.

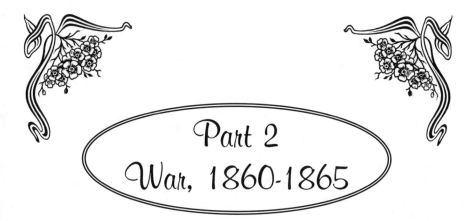

Part 2
War, 1860-1865

Prologue
Larkin

OUR WHOLE WORLD shifted that summer. Father and I set off for Little Rock in a state of confidence that I have seldom experienced since. I was young then; I refused to believe that rational men would deliberately vote to tear the country apart when we had the option of choosing a hero like Sam Houston to hold us all together. I know now that arrogant egos are seldom limited by rationality. At that state convention in the spring of 1860 I met my nemesis, one T. C. Huntsman, a man who was the personification of arrogance. I disliked him on sight and grew to despise him the more I got to know him.

The convention business was perfunctory. Father was one of the four delegates named to represent Arkansas at the national convention in Baltimore. Because selections for the state legislative posts were pretty much cut and dried, the remainder of the agenda consisted of nominating candidates for the various congressional districts. Father had already been re-elected to the state legislature for the past seven terms and had no personal interest in national office. For these and other reasons, his support and counsel in that direction were sought by several. Even so, he was somewhat taken aback to be solicited by a total stranger. A little strutting banty rooster of a man, Huntsman collared us in the hotel corridor and confidently named himself as the party's best choice for Congress. He then requested Father to place his name in nomination for the post.

Father responded courteously that a hallway introduction seemed insufficient background from which to launch a nomination and suggested that the motion be made by someone with whom Huntsman had a deeper acquaintance.

The man's response surprised us both. "I'm well known to all here in Little Rock, sir. It is you from the backwoods who lack knowledge of me. I plan to run for Congress this year. I'd prefer to run with your support. I'm offering you the chance to link your name with mine."

Father took in the measure of the fellow — the bold eyes, greedy lips, pompous stance — and his eyes glinted. When he finally spoke, his tone was dry.

"Overreaching ambition can be a dangerous condition. I fear I must decline the opportunity to advance your own, sir." We turned and walked away. As we did so, the editor of the *Arkansas Gazette* fell into step beside us.

"Do you know that fellow's background, Matthew?"

"Never saw or heard of him before."

"I'm afraid we'll be hearing a lot of him in the future. The man's on fire with ambition. Comes from somewhere over close to Memphis. He's new to Little Rock, but he's determined to get himself elected to Congress and doesn't seem to care which party or platform gets him there. He's a firebrand and a secessionist and he's all out for war. He's too loose-lipped for my taste. Told me to my face that war furnishes a quick avenue to fame and fortune."

"Appears to me he's a man whose ambitions greatly exceed his qualifications," was Father's succinct reply.

We dismissed Huntsman from our minds, for we had more pressing concerns. Father caught the stage for St. Louis, there to take the train for the ten-day trip to Baltimore and the national convention. I took the westbound stage and headed home to Sarah. I spent most of the stage ride calculating finances, tallying up the worth of my own farm, figuring my expectation from this year's crops, and speculating on where the soon-to-be-acquired Chouteau land would be located and how it could be used to best advantage.

The next morning I rode on to Griffin's Mill to pay John Griffin for my week's use of his slave and to talk over a proposition with my longtime friend, Ridge Rodineau. Ridge at that time was caught between a rock and a hard place. Orphaned son of a chief of the Cherokees, nephew of another, and sworn blood enemy of a third, Ridge had recently left the Indian Territory on my advice for a more hospitable environment. With the help of John Griffin he was now carving out a new life under a new name — Smith.

Our lives had been joined since we were boys of 18, when we had gone on a Colorado cattle drive together. Cattle drives separate the men from the boys. Ridge was the best friend I ever had or will ever have on this earth.

I had been able to persuade him that Arkansas could use his talents far more effectively than could his bloodthirsty relatives in the Cherokee Nation. I needed a business partner; Ridge needed a new life. Now seemed the right time to take him home and introduce him to my wife. We spent the better part of the day discussing business possibilities, after which we rode on over to my home place, visited with Minerva, and picked up Tom. The next morning we headed home to Sarah and the twins.

As things turned out, when we got to my farm the first order of business was to bury that murderous bastard the girls had shot. We dumped him in a hole in the ground like the mad dog that he was and took up the task of getting the girls settled down. Ridge and Tom managed the soothing of the twins without too much difficulty, but I had my hands full with Sarah. Looking back, I see now that things were never the same again. Sarah lost her innocence that day. In some strange and complicated way, the killing caused her to question every aspect of our lives. She was never again the compliant girl of that past winter.

But time swiftly moved on, and events came up too fast for comprehension or introspection. We had the bad news from the Baltimore convention by telegraph long before Father got home, of course. When the message came to Griffin Flat, William Griffin saddled up his horse and rode over the mountain to tell me in person. "Lark," he said, "they nominated the wrong man. The country will be ruined, and in the end it will be every man for himself.

"There's no way out of this now. Houston was our only hope. I despair of democracy. When a thousand mediocre men prefer to be represented by one of their own rather than electing a true leader we've lost entirely. The National Union party nominated Senator Bell of Tennessee. He's a lackluster man and a party hack, but he's a party hack who remembers his friends."

William Griffin and Eliza accompanied Father when he returned from Baltimore. My brothers Robert and Sam came with their wives. My sister Kate was there with her husband, Ross, as were Willie Griffin and Ridge Rodineau. When we were all assembled, Father began to speak, his eyes shadowed by the sorrow he felt in his soul.

"Some people scorn the idea that there will be bloodshed as the result of secession, but let me tell you, bloodshed is coming. After a sacrifice of millions in treasure and thousands of lives, the South may win, but I doubt it. The Union will win, but at a cost that we today can barely imagine. Can the Flint family stay neutral? For a while. There will even be an opportunity for us to plan and to profit. It's time for us to start planning. We've got hell ahead of us. We've got the choice of going through hell and making money or going through hell and coming out paupers. At the end, our profits will be bitter fruit if so much as one of our lives is lost.

"But it may be that some of you, even now, have no wish to stay neutral. Know that every man at this table today will always be welcome here, regardless of your choice. I ask your vow of loyalty to each other, now and for the future, before I ask your choice. I ask your handshake and your solemn word to be bound as a family. Blood ties come first in the Flint family."

He then polled the delegation, exactly as he would have done in the legislature, starting with my oldest brother, Robert. "I'm neutral," said Robert.

"We understand that," replied Father. "I'm asking that you search your soul and reckon your future leanings when the day comes that neutrality is not possible and you have to fight."

"Union," replied Robert.

"Sam?"

"I'm neutral, but when push comes to shove I'll have to go with Arkansas. In the here and now, I'm going over to Fayetteville and read law in the hopes of staying neutral as long as I can. When this is over, this family will need a good lawyer."

Father then addressed Kate's husband, Ross Ramsey. "How do you stand, Ross?"

"I have no intention of fighting. Not on either side. They'll have to shoot me to get me. But before they shoot me they'll have to catch me, and these hills have many a hiding hole."

Father's eyes glinted, but he continued with his roll call. "Lark?"

"Neutral as long as possible; Union when neutrality is not possible."

"Tom?"

"Northern."

"Stanton?"

"Northern."

"Willie Griffin?"

"I've got to go with Arkansas. A man can't in conscience benefit from years of medical training at state expense and then refuse loyalty to the state that trained him. My loyalty is not to the South, and God knows it's not to slavery. My loyalty is to Arkansas."

"Ridge?"

"Union. That's why I left the Indian Nation. Stand Watie, my dead father's brother, is a fire-eating rebel. My father's blood enemy, Chief John Ross, is right now a Union man, though he's apt to turn the way the wind is blowing. This leaves me no place to stand in the Indian Nation. I'm not neutral. I'm for the Union. And may God have mercy on us all!"

That day we swore an oath with our hand on Father's Bible, an oath that bound us all in family loyalty throughout the years to come. William Griffin swore the oath as well. "Matthew," he said, "let me join you. I side with the North and with the Union. On the other hand, I'm too old to bear arms, and I have no son to fight for my family. Permit me the honor of sharing yours."

"None of us can afford the luxury of neutrality for long," replied Father. "We have a year at the most. Regardless of which side wins the presidency — and you can be sure it won't be Senator Bell — there will be war by next summer. Profits will be made in the beginning. Great profits can be ours if we choose the right enterprises. If the war drags on, and I expect it will, there are ways we can both help the Union and help our family. I had a ten-day stage ride to think this over, and here's my proposal.

"Both armies will need mules, meat, and corn. They'll need uniforms and arms, too, but we're in no position to take advantage of that need. The first three needs we can supply. While others are talking and wondering and campaigning for office, we're going to be buying up every mule and mare and jackass we can get our hands on. We've got 10,000 acres on which to feed them, breed them, and hide them. No sense in advertising our efforts.

"Lark, you and Ridge ought to be able to organize this. Your experience on that Colorado cattle drive in '54 ought to come in handy now. It has been my observation that every experience in life can be put to good purpose sometime. What you learned when you were boys can make a real difference now. I expect Fort Leavenworth will become a major command post when the Union gets organized for war."

Ridge laughed. "I wouldn't want us to put into practice everything we learned. We had a few wild times along the way. But you're right. Herding mules over the few hundred miles to Fort Leavenworth ought to be easy as compared to herding cattle to Colorado."

So we planned and studied and organized ourselves against the future every man had reason to dread. Robert, Tom, and Stant were put in charge of the farming operation. Father was chief overseer of all operations.

Father proved to be right. We made good money and we made fast money. Ridge was the smartest horse trader I ever worked with. He had the patience of a saint where there was the chance of making a dollar. Many a day I watched him dicker with the farmers who had driven their mules to the market in their county seat. His usual strategy was to get friendly in the morning, lose interest during the middle of the day, and offer one-half the mules' value about the time the sun went down, just when their owners had faced the prospect of a long, tired, empty-pocketed drive home. We made quadruple profits all year. Ridge paid half of the mules' worth, we fed them at no expense a few months on the open range, and I sold them at Fort Leavenworth and Fort Scott and Fort Smith for twice, sometimes three times, their value.

Events definitely came on too fast for easy assimilation that summer. Sarah and I took the stage to Kansas City in July for the settling of her inheritance. Sarah cut a wide swath in Kansas City. Beauty can turn heads anywhere, but a beautiful young rich woman commands real attention. For about 24 hours in Kansas City I felt more like Sarah's husband than I felt like myself. The Chouteaus treated her like a visiting princess, and she took to it like she had been born to a royal bloodline. As for myself, I got the courteous treatment usually accorded to the prince consort. It was a wonder they didn't expect me to walk two steps behind.

Fortunately, our visit was brief. This state of affairs was easily remedied and soon mitigated by a change of venue.

Sarah's portion of the land was situated in three parcels — 2,500 acres of river bottomland lying just south of the Arkansas River in Arkansas, three sections of mountain land in the Arkansas Ozarks, and one section of comparatively useless prairie in the middle part of the Indian Territory. I was pleased with the distribution. The mountain land was considered to be rich in minerals and contained a middle-sized and reasonably profitable zinc mine. The bottomland was prime and farmed for cotton.

Altogether, I was well satisfied, and all the more pleased at the news Sarah had been saving to tell me: she was expecting our first child. Why she put off telling me until we were homeward bound, bouncing around in that rough stage coach, God only knows. I suppose she could not avoid my knowing after she began vomiting. My poor little girl had a rough trip home. When we finally arrived at her father's tavern, I had to carry her off the coach. She was as pale and limp as a baby bluebird.

However, Eliza and Neely brought her around in short order, and by morning we all rejoiced together at our good fortune. I expect I was the chief rejoicer. Matthew Houston Flint was born February 16, 1861. I have loved him without reservation from that moment.

After Lincoln was elected President, Arkansas split into two camps. Most people did not own slaves and had little interest in slavery, yet slaveholding rabble-rousers managed to inflame their passions on the pretext of high principle. Chief among these rabble-rousers was T. C. Huntsman, who had managed to get himself elected to the Congress of the United States and thereafter fanatically devoted himself to tearing apart the nation he had been elected to serve. Aided and abetted by every fire-breathing secessionist preacher he could find, Huntsman, from January to March 1861, organized a series of public meetings in every county seat in northwest Arkansas.

When such a meeting was scheduled in Yellville, Father and Ridge and I rode over to engage Huntsman in public debate. He was preceded on the platform by none other than that hard-hearted old hypocrite of a traveling stump preacher from Griffin Flat, Theophilous Massey. For the first hour, Massey threatened with hellfire and brimstone all who did not fall into line for the Southern cause, but after he had warmed up to his subject, he got personal. He singled out Father in particular as one given over to godless ways, a heathen wife, and Union leanings.

Father's response was prompt. Though 20 years older than Massey, he stepped up on the platform, called Preacher Massey a lying bastard, knocked him flat, and gave him the clear option of leaving town or facing worse. In matters of his own self-interest, Massey's judgment was acute. He slid off the platform, turned his back to the crowd, and took off at a fast lope.

Father rolled down his sleeves, bowed to Huntsman, who was taking it all in from his seat on that same platform, and addressed the stunned and silent crowd.

"I thank Almighty God that this nation is founded on the bedrock principle of separation of church and state. How I worship my god, or how you worship yours, is not the issue here today. The future of your country is at stake. I beg you to beware of self-serving fanatics, preachers or otherwise."

He then turned to Huntsman, bowed again, and addressed his adversary coolly. "Sir, I believe you are the next scheduled speaker."

Father stepped down from the platform. We walked out of that assembly to the sound of cheers and applause. The Yellville newspaper reported that Huntsman was prevented from speaking by the boos of his audience and left promising retaliation.

The president of the Arkansas legislature, David Walker, convened that body in April of 1861 to vote on Arkansas's secession from the Union. Five negative votes were cast, one being Father's. Walker begged the five to reconsider and to make it unanimous. Much pressure was brought to bear. In the end, Father stood alone and cast his one vote for the Union.

But the end of the convention was not the end of confusion and argument. Though their elected representatives had voted to remove Arkansas from the Union, individual men and women were not persuaded of the merits of the Confederacy. Most of our neighbors were worried and torn and would greatly have preferred the option of neutrality. I stayed neutral as long as I could until the Confederate Congress passed the Conscript Act, forcing every man between the ages of 18 and 35 years to join some company and go into camps, subject to orders of General Hindman, commander of the Trans-Mississippi District. My neutrality was over.

I joined the Union army in October 1861 and was commissioned as a captain in the cavalry. Though I was in a few skirmishes the first few months, I did not see real action until March 1862, when I slipped home on leave to visit my family.

We had assembled at Father's place on a Sunday morning, a beautiful day remarkable for the clarity of the bright blue sky above and the unseasonably warm air around us. Our wives and our children were with us. Father was attempting to organize a "peace society" composed of non-slave-holding citizens of good moral character who wished to remain neutral. Word leaked out in the wrong places and produced disastrous results.

Minerva had directed the women to spread great trestle tables under the trees. On those tables was placed the delicious food of our Sunday dinner. We were feasting in easy fellowship when we were taken completely by surprise. A troop of armed Rebel soldiers came dashing out from the concealing woods and surrounded us. Egged on by that black-hearted coward of a stump preacher, Theophilous Massey, the soldiers fired their guns in the air, yelled, and rounded up men, women, and children with no regard for comfort, courtesy, or decency. Then into the yard rode their leader, that Satan in human shape, T. C. Huntsman, erstwhile U. S. Congressman, now Rebel colonel.

"Chain them up, men!" he yelled. "And march the dirty Yankee dogs to Little Rock!" Twenty-seven men were chained together that day, every man and boy over 15.

Father stepped forward to face his captors. "Huntsman, we are peaceably assembled on private property. You and your men are breaking the law."

Huntsman's response was a ringing slap across the face. "Tie that old man up. He goes nowhere. Chain him and lock him in his own barn. Guard him."

The Rebels took an ordinary log chain, fastened it around our necks, and linked us together two by two, with the long chain running down the center of the column. Thus they forced all 27 men to begin our toilsome march. As matters developed, the brutality of our captors was matched only by their commander's stupidity, for he soon discovered this disposition not at all favorable to marching. We were rechained by the wrists so that our movement might not be so impeded. Herded like desperate criminals, we were marched away from our weeping women and children and headed toward the kangaroo court of the Rebel governor. After a ten-day march to Little Rock we were offered a clear-cut choice — join the Confederate army or be hanged for treason. I was not in uniform and was not known to the Rebels as a Union officer. Not one of the others was guilty of any crime save that of attempting to live in peace in times of evil passions.

We learned some hard lessons of life on that forced march, chief among them being the value of duplicity in the opposition of evil. In the course of a few god-awful days, we abandoned the rules of civilization in favor of the law of survival. In short, we duped the governor, stated our loyalty, and were packed off to join the Confederacy. While we were still chained as one body, we swore an oath to each other to escape at the first opportunity, join the Union army, and exact our revenge on the man we now reviled — one T. C. Huntsman.

The self-same day that we chained men falsely swore our Confederate loyalty, we heard stories that struck new fears in our hearts. While we had been on our forced march to the South, a great battle had been bitterly fought, with Griffin Tavern at its center. The Battle of Pea Ridge, folks called it. Neighbor had fought neighbor; kin had fought kin. By mid-March, the retreating Rebels dragged in to our camp, telling tales of the stink of the dead and the shrieks of the dying, left behind by the hundreds. Even as I feared for William and Eliza Griffin, I convinced myself that Sarah and our son had been untouched by the battle, separated and protected by the six-mile width of mountains too steep to drag a cannon over.

But the silence from home became too deep and too ominous. Weeks dragged by as my many letters went unanswered, and I reluctantly faced the horrors of my imagination. I literally had no idea of the whereabouts or the safety of those I loved the most. In the grip of these terrible fears, my brothers and Ridge and I began to form a plan to escape from the Confederate army.

I finally saw a way out for us. To a man, the conscripts were miserable and inclined toward mutiny. What we did, all 27 of us, was to sympathize with the conscripts and urge them on to mutiny. When they talked about home, we made them more homesick; when they worried about being killed or maimed, we made it sound probable; when they wondered how they could slip away, we talked about how easy it would be.

I traded my supper many a night for the chance to play a violin that one of the fellows had brought along. Each night I played the saddest and sweetest tunes I could think of. Men who were already moody became desperate and morose. Many wept around their campfires. Finally, some fellow got his nerve up and broke the tension. The mutiny started right after dark.

The men took the regimental flag and marched up and down through the troops, calling out, "All who are ready to go home, fall in." For a time it appeared that the whole layout was as good as gone. When the color bearer took his exit with the flag heading west, about 200 men left with him, including all my brothers. As soon as they were one mile out of camp, the 25 out of our bunch gave the others the slip as planned, heading northeast toward home.

I had to stay behind. My brother-in-law, Ross Ramsey, was sick with the bloody flux that night, out of his head with a raging fever. There being no way to transport him without jeopardizing the fate of the other boys, Ridge and I shouldered our responsibilities as their elected leaders. Ridge led the other boys out; I stayed with Ross. By the time Ross got well, we were deep in Arkansas Rebel country, and he went wild again upon finding out that he had missed his chance. I promised him to lay plans and to go over the hill with him as soon as we got near friendly territory again, but we had to be eternally vigilant. The Rebels were now on the alert. Colonel Huntsman became a wild man when his officers finally had the guts to tell him about the desertions. In retaliation, he sent 1,000 men in pursuit and captured many as prisoners, 125 in all. These were brought down to our camps to be guarded and to serve as reminders and examples to the remaining. The poor souls were treated like brutes. They were kept in camps in an open field where there was nothing but the bare ground, and their rations consisted of whole quarters of raw beef thrown down on the dirt, without any kind of fuel to cook it with, or salt to season it, and no bread or even a substitute. Soon the news reached camps that the Yankees were near on forced march. The prisoners were double-quicked out in great haste while the balance of the regiment lost no time in getting ready to follow, so away we went in the drenching rain. We did not stop for shelter, as the propelling power of Union soldiers that actuated our hasty flight was too close for comfort.

This was about the 20th day of October 1862, at which time Ross Ramsey could no longer stand it and tried to slip out on his own. He was caught by the home guards — those worthless wretches.

On the night of the 21st we camped on Mulberry Creek, then on the 22nd we got to Horse Head Creek, eight miles west of Clarksville. There on dress parade we heard the orders read: Ross Ramsey would be shot on the 24th. I swallowed my pride, went to the colonel, and begged for Ross's life. The colonel lied and promised to consider my request.

On the evening of the 24th, as I stood shivering in the cold, I watched the Rebels shoot my sister Kate's husband. The brigade was drawn up in an old field just below Spadra's Landing. Ross was brought out in a two-mule wagon, followed by Captain Adkinson and a detail of 12 men. All my life I will remember the dazzling brightness of their guns. The wagon was stopped and Captain Adkinson took a plank out of the wagon, setting one end on the ground and leaning the other end against the top edge of the wagon bed. The poor doomed man, yet shackled, crawled down and stepped a few paces out from the wagon while it was driven away. The guard was then drawn up and formed. Ross turned toward the guard, apparently undaunted, and with as much fortitude as if he knew not what his fatal results were, faced the detail, standing in a position of a soldier without arms. He looked at the 12 men without a quiver or change of fiber, as though all things were smooth and lovely. Captain Adkinson deliberately stepped up to Ross and crossed his hands on his breast. Ross shook his head and put his hands down. Then the captain took out of his own pocket a white handkerchief and aimed on putting it over the eyes of the doomed man, but again Ross shook his head. Ross looked at me, standing a few feet away, and in clear and manly tones said, "Tell Kate my last thought was of her."

Then the captain stepped to the side of the guard and commanded: "Ready; aim; fire!" And so they did. Down went poor, unfortunate Ross, a victim to Rebel oppression, unrelenting outrages, and his own hatred of violence.

By November, I had made it over the hill. There was no need to stay. Ross was now beyond my help. My intentions were to check on my family and rejoin my old Union regiment, in that order. I traveled by paths and through the woods and made it home safe, taking eight days to go 100 miles. What I found seared my soul. Griffin's Tavern was burned to its foundations. My wife and son were gone, as were Father and Minerva. I nearly went crazy trying to find my family, but by the time I got home, the news was so old and my people so badly scattered that I finally gave up in despair. It seemed useless to stay.

I acquired a good horse and rode in haste to try to rejoin my old regiment. On December 5th I contacted the Union army, where I was able to furnish pertinent information to my commanding officer. Two days later we fought the Rebels at Prairie Grove. I never would have believed that I could find satisfaction in killing my fellow man, but every fiber of my being demanded revenge. Looking back now, after more than a score of years, I must confess that was one battle where I lusted for the kill. I projected the face of Huntsman on every Reb and killed more of his surrogates that day than I am now willing to remember. From then until the time I had news of my family, I forced myself to focus on war. I had no other choice.

Chapter 7

IF I LIVE TO BE 100, I will never get it through my head why it is women can't have the same rights as men. Nineteen people sat at Matthew Flint's long dinner table that Sunday after he got back from the Baltimore convention, but only ten had opinions that he counted. As he went around that table and asked each man which side he would stand on, I had to grit my teeth to hold myself back.

From her place at the far end of the table, Minerva caught my eye. "Sarah, will you help me dish up the desserts?"

Surprised, I followed her out to the big summer kitchen, the sweet June breeze cooling my cheeks as we walked through the dogtrot that separated the square log summer kitchen from the main house.

"Which side do you stand on, Sarah?" Her question astonished me. Never before had she expressed the slightest interest in my political opinion.

"I don't know. In the long run I'll have to stand with Larkin. But that's not the point. The point is, how I stand counts for nothing. And how you stand counts for exactly the same amount. It's not right. We didn't even get asked. The men don't even think to go through the motions of asking. Why is it, with brains as good as theirs and feelings as deep as theirs, we don't have any voice? We might as well be Negroes."

"Sarah, I forget sometimes how young you are." Minerva's tone was analytical, without inflection or affection. "The plain truth is, women's views don't count because we don't have to fight for them. Women don't go to war. Men do. You will not be called on to lay down your life, but every man at that table will have to choose the side he's willing to die for."

"Will the black men fight?"

"I doubt it. I don't believe there is any way of making them fight. Slaves don't have any property to protect, not much to gain if they win, nothing to lose if they don't."

Minerva's keen gaze assessed me. "It's not like you to get your back up, Sarah. You're not yourself. What you girls went through when you had to shoot Ike has changed you more than I thought."

Even as I fought them back, tears stung my eyes. "I'm so afraid. I can't stand to be by myself. I follow Larkin around all day. I'm scared to let him out of my sight. I can't sleep at night unless he has his arms around me. Even then, I don't sleep much. I haven't had enough sleep to put in a thimble since that night two weeks ago when we shot Ike. It's not just rape I'm afraid of now. I'm afraid of everything — panthers and bears and strangers. I'm afraid to walk through the woods by myself. I'm afraid to stay in the house by myself. I jump when a squirrel runs across a window ledge."

In a rare act of tenderness, Minerva put her arms around me and patted my shaking shoulders. "Little Sarah, you're taking this hard, and you've held up so well in front of the family that none of us realized how bad you've been hurting."

"Except Larkin."

"Larkin isn't going to talk to us about your private concerns. We didn't raise him that way. But I should have guessed, and I should have asked sooner. I can help you, Sarah. I can give you something to help you sleep."

Minerva turned to the squaw who was at the back table washing up dishes and spoke to the woman in Cherokee. The old woman put down her dishrag, wiped her soapy hands on her apron, picked up a wicker basket, and headed out the door for the woods.

"I've told her which herbs to pick. She'll simmer them while we visit after dinner. When you go home tonight you can drink the brew before you go to bed. You will sleep tonight, and after a few good nights of rest you will be more yourself again. I can help you sleep, Sarah, but I can't give you your courage back. You've got to do that for yourself. Courage is not the absence of fear. Only the stupid of this world are without fear. Courage takes grit. Courage means facing up to your fears and going ahead anyhow to do what needs to be done. Every man at that table is going to be praying for courage, and you'd better be doing the same. You're going to be on your own too much in the years ahead, Sarah. Larkin can't be with you all the time, and he can't hold you every night. He's going to be gone a lot, whether he's making a living or fighting a war. He needs a wife who will pull her share of the load."

Her rebuke stung. Pride came to my rescue and stiffened my backbone. "I'm going to do better, Minerva. I'm going to try for courage more than I've ever tried for anything except pleasing Larkin. And I'm beholden to you. Going without sleep has made me crazy. I don't want to be crazy. I want to be happy."

"There are many roads to happiness, but fear will never take you there. Cowards hold back and go nowhere. Pray to your spirits, Sarah. They can help you."

"They've already helped me. I wouldn't be alive now, or Piety and Charity either, if they hadn't helped me."

Her discerning eyes softened as she smiled on me for the first time. "Life is opening another door for you. You've had a bad scare, but that's no excuse for being a coward the rest of your life. You have it in you to become a fine woman. Don't hold back. You can't be a happy woman if you keep acting like a scared child." She continued, "Matthew believes we all have trial by fire ahead of us. All the more reason for us to choose to be happy every chance we get. Now, let's take the desserts in, before Matthew loses patience."

We carried in the big bowls — sweetened strawberries, fluffy mounds of whipped cream, delicately seasoned custard sauce, hot buttered biscuits for shortcake, plus a big blackberry cobbler pie for those few not satisfied with strawberries.

After dinner the men sat around under the shade of the big walnut trees as they smoked their pipes and discussed their plans. We women washed the dishes and put the food away for the cold supper Minerva would serve before sundown. When the last dish was clean, Minerva carried her dulcimer outside, Larkin and Tom and Matthew tuned up their violins, and the lively melodies of their fiddling coaxed our hearts toward happiness. But when it was time to head home, my pa changed the tune. "Could we close with a hymn to mark this day?"

Minerva struck a chord in a different key, and her rich contralto soared in a hymn of hope. "Abide with me: fast falls the eventide; the darkness deepens; Lord, with me abide."

Willie stepped over to Becky's side as his clear baritone joined Minerva in duet. Other voices took up the melody. By the end of the last verse, we were all joined in that powerful hymn of entreaty, each of us asking God to bless us and spare us in the days ahead. When the last note was borne away by the breeze, Matthew pronounced an "Amen" of benediction. In spite of my fears, fatigue, and worries about the future, I rode the three miles home with an easy heart. After supper, I drank Minerva's potion and slept like a baby for the first time in two weeks.

Larkin had the milking done and the coffee made before I woke up the next morning. By the time I had put my clothes on, he had sliced long strips of bacon and was stirring up batter for flapjacks. Shamed, I put my arms around his neck, kissed his beautiful mouth, and made him a promise I have kept to this day. "From now on, Larkin, I'll carry my end of the load. Being afraid won't keep me from doing my work. When you go out in the field today, I'm going to hoe the garden. These last two weeks I've let the grass grow so high it's choking out my cucumbers and tomatoes. If I don't clean out the weeds now, we won't have anything to eat next winter. I think I may already have lost my strawberries."

His look of pure relief told me how deep his worry had been. Patting my bottom with a practiced hand, he grinned down at me. "Let's see how fast you can slap flapjacks in the skillet. We both need to get moving. While I was away politicking, the grass nearly took over my corn crop. All that time wasted, my crops growing up in weeds, my wife nearly killed, and all to no purpose. We're going to have war anyway. When I see how little difference one man can make, I wonder why a sensible man even wastes his time trying. After all the politicking and speech-making this summer, a lot of smart men are going to cast some mighty foolish votes. There won't be a decent candidate in the bunch. Whoever gets named president will likely do a piss-poor job. What it takes to get elected in this country and what it takes to run it well are two different things.

"But I've got to get the field work done. Sarah, I'd appreciate a good stack of flapjacks along about now."

I filled his plate, poured his coffee, and got on with my own day's work.

I missed my mense that week, but I didn't think too much about it. Considering all I had been through the past month and how high-strung my nerves had been, I thought it best to wait and see before saying anything to Larkin. Soon I had a more compelling reason to be shut-mouthed about it. The letter everybody had been waiting for finally came from Kansas City. The Jackson County commissioners having reached their decision on the appropriate partitioning of my grandfather's estate, the heirs were duly summoned to convene for the reading of the partitioning and the legal transfer of titles. A trip to Kansas City was the opportunity of a lifetime, and I had no intention of missing my chance to play a starring role in the family melodrama. Travel by stagecoach was considered hazardous for a pregnant woman, mainly because of the jolting, bone-bruising ride over the rocks and ruts. Summer travel involved additional penalties of heat, dust, bugs, and thirst, along with being cooped up in tight quarters with sweat-soaked strangers. Had I so much as hinted that I might be expecting, Pa and Larkin would have forbidden me to go. The prospect of staying home while Larkin looked after my interests might have seemed entirely suitable to the menfolk, but it was unthinkable to me. I meant to go and to have a good time while I was there.

My traveling clothes were ready and waiting. Eliza had bought a beautiful length of fine wool serge, cloth so light and lustrous that the rich gray color gleamed in the sunlight. Aunt Kate and Eliza had selected and studied for hours an elegantly simple pattern and had cut into the expensive wool only after numerous measurements and consultations. Finally, it was decided that I would have two dresses cut from the same pattern, the first made of linen, which would be easier to cut. After the lessons learned from the making of the linen dress, then the wool dress would be tailored. As a result of their patience and cautiousness, I was the proud owner of two beautiful new dresses. I planned to wear the linen dress on the journey and the wool dress for the important business in the lawyer's office.

I was tingling with excitement the morning we boarded the northbound stage at Griffin Flat. Larkin handed me inside the coach with a flourish and appeared actually to enjoy the looks of envy he got from the five men who were to be our traveling companions. I was relieved that there was not a full nine-passenger load, which would have made for close and sweaty quarters. As the only woman, I was allocated the choicest seat next to the window and facing forward. While Larkin talked crops and politics and peace and war with the men, I speculated silently as to what we could expect in the big city world of my Chouteau relatives.

Three days of fast 80-mile-a-day travel brought us to Westport, the stop closest to the City of Kansas. As we clattered along on the crowded pike that led into town, Larkin tried to prepare me.

"You're liable to see nearly everything here in Westport, Sarah. When Ridge and I came through on our cattle drive six years ago, I'd never seen such a rough and crowded place in my life. Don't be afraid, but stay close to me. They've got a lot of respectable women here, but there's plenty of the brassy kind, too."

I was fascinated. "How will I tell them apart?"

He laughed. "You won't have any trouble telling them apart, Sarah. Those that have wares for sale will be advertising them." I soon saw what he meant.

We pulled into Westport late in the day, when the hot July sun cast long shadows on the noisy and crowded streets. Tall prairie schooner wagons loaded with trade goods and pulled by stolid teams of oxen competed for road space with drovers cracking their whips over herds of hogs and cattle, moving the animals along the pike to the slaughter pens. A slave auctioneer was finishing up his day's work at the slave block on one of the main corners of town across from the three-story brick tavern and hotel that was our destination.

As I stepped down from the stage I saw a nearly naked young Negress being led away by her new owner. Three coal-black Negro men, chained by the wrists, followed behind her. In front of us, a sunbonneted woman in a calico dress drove a wagon while her husband and sons walked beside it. Another tired-looking woman yanked her little boys away from the hooves of our horses. The square was teeming with people: well-dressed men in frock coats; half-naked Indians with roached hair and painted faces; farmers with their broad-brimmed hats, suspendered trousers, and weary wives; traders, gamblers, and cattle drovers; and soldiers from nearby Fort Leavenworth. All walked in the hot sun along the plank sidewalks and the crowded streets. Leaning out of the open windows above a wooden saloon, laughing women with bare shoulders and red lips called to the men who caught their eye.

The fierce orange sun nearly blinded me as I stepped out of the coach. Steadied by Larkin's hand, I stood in front of the big red brick hotel and stared at the well-dressed gentleman who was smiling at me, his arms stretched wide in an expansive gesture of welcome.

"So this is our *petite* Sarah. I would have known you anywhere. Monsieur Flint, welcome! Madame, welcome!" With exquisite courtesy, he bowed to Larkin before focusing his attention on me. "You are as lovely as a wild rose, my child, and the image of my dear dead sister!" With a light kiss on each of my cheeks and a firm arm around my shoulders, he deftly separated me from the other passengers and led me toward the shade of the hotel lobby, leaving Larkin to retrieve our valises and follow us inside.

"I am your Uncle Auguste Chouteau, your mother's eldest brother, here to welcome you to the entire family. Indeed, now that you are here among us, our family is complete. We have longed to know you, little Sarah."

Belatedly, he turned his attention to Larkin. "Sir, permit me to introduce myself, and to apologize for my tardiness in not doing so sooner. I must confess to having eyes only for my niece, who is cast in the beautiful image of her late mother. I am Auguste Chouteau, at your service. Permit me to offer you the hospitality of my household, and to assure you of the welcome of my brothers and their families." Having appraised and approved of my husband, he extended a hand of genuine hospitality. "Welcome to Westport, Monsieur Flint. May you and Sarah enjoy it and visit it often!"

Larkin's confident handshake was hearty. "Your world is a lively one, sir, and appears to be mighty prosperous. Sarah and I are not accustomed to so much hustle and bustle. Are things always this lively?"

"Ah yes, monsieur. In fact, Westport may have already passed its peak. The Oregon Trail emigrants have mostly gone on. However, the Santa Fe trade remains prosperous, and settlers bound for California and Colorado continue to keep us busy. But already my brothers and my great-aunt have decided to relocate their affairs in the City of Kansas, three miles distant. We have regular steamboat traffic there now, a great boon to business."

He smiled, "Now that many of my family have relocated their residences away from the river bottoms and up on the bluff, they find themselves to be very comfortable. The Chouteau neighborhood is called Quality Hill, and our Aunt Bereniece, widow of our Uncle François, presides as grand dame of the city. The entire family is invited to dine with her tomorrow evening, after we meet with the lawyers and the commissioners. She wishes to have a dinner of celebration, and she wishes to see you, Sarah. Now that our own mother and father are gone, my brothers and I regard our Aunt Bereniece as the head of the family." His eyes twinkled. "Dealing with tomorrow's lawyers will be good training for dealing with your Aunt Bereniece, Sarah."

My uncle extended his next invitation to Larkin. "May I persuade you to dine at my table tonight, sir? I am a widower and without children. I would be honored by your company. My home is a mere six blocks away."

"I think not, Mr. Chouteau, although Sarah and I appreciate your kindness. Sarah has had far too little sleep on our journey. The accommodations were hot and crowded and not up to the standards she was expecting. The stage stops were pretty sorry establishments. We've not seen anything in a class with Griffin's Tavern. I expect Sarah is more tired than she has been willing to admit. Though we appreciate your offer, I think we'll be well advised to have a quiet supper and a good night's rest."

Larkin spoke the simple truth. I had been miserable on both nights of our journey, and especially miserable the night before. In a shack of a stage stop I had been expected to share a bed with two other women in a small, hot bedroom, where the sheets had not been washed since accommodating their last occupants. The smells of travel had been strong on both my bed partners — the sour smell of unwashed, sweaty women.

From the lumpy strawfilled tick that served as our mattress had come the unmistakable odor of dried urine, a memento left by some long-gone bedwetter. My stomach had heaved, and after a spasm of nausea I had deposited my own contribution to the smells of the room in the slop jar in the corner. After hours of wakefulness, I had taken a blanket from the foot of the bed, placed it on the floor, and slept the rest of the night away from my snoring bed partners. I had taken great pains to wash away my fatigue and had not complained to Larkin. I looked at him now in astonishment. He reads me too well, I thought.

Evidently, my worldly uncle was equally experienced in understanding women, for he examined me again, this time more objectively. A tender smile softened his worldly old face, as he readily acquiesced with Larkin's decision.

"A wise decision, I expect. We will look forward to seeing you tomorrow. I'll have my carriage here at nine o'clock. It's a three-mile trip from here to the courthouse, and we are due there at ten. Since I am the only Chouteau of the name who still maintains a Westport residence, it will be my privilege to convey you to the City of Kansas tomorrow." My uncle tipped his tall beaver hat. "I bid you good night and good rest."

We watched his self-assured exit as he bowed to acquaintances and tipped his hat to their ladies.

"Am I anything like the Chouteaus, Larkin?"

"Well, you've got the same black curly hair, and you and your uncle are both short. But I hope to God you never get that fat, Sarah. Keeping you shapely may have to be my goal in life. But I have to admit, he walks like he owns the earth, and you do, too. So maybe you're more kin than I thought."

In search of a good night's rest, we found our room at the back of the top floor of the hotel. It looked down on the wagon yard, which was adjacent to the huge log warehouse with the name "Chouteau" painted over the main entrance. Built in the old French fashion of upright logs pounded into the ground side by side, the warehouse extended the length of the block and looked as sturdy as a fort. Tall schooner wagons were lined up in front of the wide warehouse doors. As Larkin and I leaned out the window and watched, we recognized much of the cargo. Hams, sides of bacon, barrels of flour, beans, cornmeal, and coffee, along with bolts of cloth, guns, hardware, harnesses, ropes, and wooden boxes of merchandise were handed along in a practiced rhythm by sweating Negroes.

"A man named Majors does most of the transport business out of Westport now." Larkin spoke like one who had studied the situation. "He runs this big trail operation, plus a meat-packing business besides. Makes 50 percent profit on each trip. He has special wagons made; won't use anything except oxen to pull his wagons. His wagons are so big and loaded so heavy it takes a team of 12 to pull one wagon, and he runs 25 teams to a wagon train, plus a full set of spare oxen."

"You sound like you know him."

"Father and Ridge and I have been studying the situation. I need to talk with Mr. Majors while we're in town. If we're going to run a business out of Arkansas in corn and meat and mules, we need the right connections at this end of the trail."

"I thought you just said he only uses oxen."

"That's what he uses now, because Indians aren't interested in oxen and won't attack the wagon trains to get them, like they do for horses and mules. But when the army starts organizing for war, they'll need mules. We figure a man smart enough to run a Santa Fe Trail operation will be smart enough to organize the effort to equip and feed the army.

"Let's wash up and go down to supper, Sarah. No sense staying up here in our rooms when we can watch how things are done in the big city."

I brushed the dust out of my hair, shook the dirt out of my fine linen dress, washed my face, and took Larkin's arm to descend the broad stairs in style. It seemed to me that all eyes were on us as we walked past the bar and the gambling tables toward the big dining room at the rear. I had never seen such a variety of men in my life. Dirt-stained, leather-chapped cowboys sat with white-collared, frock-coated gentlemen. Indians dressed up like white men watched farmers and traders and soldiers and trail hands. Flashily dressed men with soft white hands dealt their cards with practiced flips of their wrists. The few women in the room glanced at me with hard eyes and scant interest, but the looks of admiration from the men were sufficient to stiffen my spine and cause me to move swiftly through the noise and smoke to the comparative quiet of the big dining room. A tall, plainly dressed woman walked toward us, her hand extended in friendship. "Welcome to Harris House. My name is Henrietta Harris. I run the kitchen and dining room and Colonel Harris runs the rest of the place. Most people call me Aunt Hennie. Pick a seat anywhere. As you can see, we've got six long tables here, and most nights they're full, so sit with anybody you like. We'll try to fill you up."

Larkin turned the full force of his best smile on Mrs. Harris. "I'm Larkin Flint, Miss Hennie, and this is my wife, Sarah. She used to be a Griffin. Her father is William Griffin. Maybe you've heard of Griffin's Tavern, on the Butterfield Stage run?"

"What I hear is that Miz Griffin makes the only pies west of the Mississippi that bear comparison with mine. And they tell me that her Brunswick stew is better than mine. Welcome, indeed! You make a mighty handsome couple, but I wish you had brought your ma and pa with you. We'll try to serve you a supper as good as you're used to at home."

She indicated our places and motioned to the waiting slaves, who began to pass heaping platters of food in front of the ten people around our table. Steaming sweet corn served on the cob, green peas in cream sauce, cabbage cut into cole slaw, tiny new potatoes dripping butter, radishes, tomatoes, lima beans, fried okra, and green onions accompanied buffalo steaks, crisp from the grill, and tender pink slices of ham baked with brown sugar and molasses. All this was complemented by freshly baked rolls and bowls of sweet butter. It was a feast to remember. I ate in good appetite, listening with fascinated interest to the variety of conversation flowing around me.

At the far end of the table, a portly, red-faced man with a bristling gray mustache was speaking with an accent I had never heard before. "How long will it take me to get to the Rockies, boy? They tell me you know the territory."

The slender youth seated at my right answered him readily. "It takes us three days, but we're talking 24 changes of horses and eight riders."

I turned my interest to the boy beside me. "Do you ride for the Pony Express?"

"Yes, ma'am. My name is Willie Cody, and I ride for Mr. Majors. I've been working for him since I was 11, ma'am. You might say he's been like a father to me. Every now and then he likes to have us boys come into town for a few days so Aunt Hennie can fatten us up a little."

Larkin looked at young Cody with undisguised interest. "I'm told that Majors never asks for U.S. Cavalry escort for his wagon trains nor for his mail runs. Why is that?"

"Our wagon trains don't have mules, nor horses, nor whiskey, so we ain't too interesting to the Indians. But we do carry guns on the trail, we do keep the wagons chained together at night, and we do keep strict watches. There's no feeling in this world like a lonesome night watch on a cold New Mexico mesa with a sky full of stars blazing right above you. A man feels like he can reach up and grab his own star."

An army officer addressed Larkin. "Majors has done something remarkable. He has translated his religion into reality and made it pay off financially. His drovers have to swear not to drink nor curse nor beat their animals. When they're on the trail, his wagon trains never stop closer than a half-day's ride to a saloon. The men get paid on Sundays, but they get paid for attending outdoor prayer meetings. His profits now run in the millions. Last year he hauled nearly 10,000 tons of freight and had 5,000 men on his payroll. The man's got an empire that goes all the way to California. He has made piety profitable."

Young Willie looked over at the officer in calm assessment and took him on squarely. "And I'm proud to be on his payroll. You can call it piety; I call it decency. I hope for your sake you have a boss who's as fine a man as mine is."

The man smiled. "I join you in that hope, my boy, and turn my eyes in interest to our forthcoming election, when you citizens will decide on my commander-in-chief."

Willie Cody stated his views in a matter-of-fact voice. "Well, I can't vote, 'cause I'm not old enough, and Miz Sarah can't vote, either, so it's up to the rest of you. Seems to me the whole country could benefit from a Sunday prayer meeting. God knows, them Washington politicians could take some major benefits from spending a few nights on top of a mesa shivering under the stars. Maybe then they'd have sense enough to appreciate what a wonderful world we've got going for us, and not spend so durn much time figuring out ways they can mess it up."

Chapter 8

LARKIN WOKE UP EARLY, *ready to get going, but I saw no need to leave the bed. It was barely sunup. I could hear the clang and clatter from the already-busy wagon yard beneath our open window. I wanted to bask in the knowledge that somebody else would cook our breakfast and do the work of the day. This trip might be my chance in a lifetime to have somebody else wait on me hand and foot, and I meant to make the most of it. My Uncle Auguste was not due for another three hours. I saw no need to get moving, but Larkin had other plans.*

"I'm going to head over to the wagon yard, Sarah, on the

chance of finding Alexander Majors about. I'd advise you to get your clothes on if you expect to have any breakfast. When I get back we'll go down to the dining room together. I don't want you going down there by yourself. Nobody's going to mistake you for a fancy woman, but I don't want any of those characters to mistake you for an unprotected woman, either. Westport's got a reputation for roughness, and this day's too important to mess up.

"Get up and get yourself ready. Don't you care that our whole future is going to be laid out by a bunch of big-city lawyers today?"

"Not as much as you care, I guess." I smiled at him with appreciation. "Actually, I care a lot more about you than I care about land or trading mules or all these other things. But if I'm going to have to get out of bed to make you happy, you can count on me to do it. I think I'd like a bath this morning. Why don't you have them bring me up a tub of hot water, so I can be clean when I meet all my relatives?"

I meant it. My elegant new dress deserved a clean body inside it. Larkin had managed to look well-groomed with a basin and a jug of hot water, but I needed more. I felt like this might be my last chance for pampering.

"Sarah, that bath is going to cost me an extra dollar, but I'll have the tub sent up anyway. Just be ready when I get back, and keep your fingers crossed that we end up with our right share of the good land today." Larkin was so preoccupied with his calculations that he strode out the door without so much as a wave of his hand.

After I had washed away the stains and smells of travel, I felt ready to face whatever the day had to offer. When Larkin returned in good time and high spirits, I met him confidently. Although he did not mention my appearance, I saw more than one look of appreciation in the eyes of the other men in the dining room. I felt like the gods were smiling on us that hot July morning, and in my heart I was smiling right back at them.

Arriving promptly at nine, my voluble Uncle Auguste handed me into his carriage, seated himself beside me, and directed Larkin to a seat beside the coachman. While being driven like a princess through the busy streets, I began for the first time to understand my own family's roots.

"Four generations of Chouteaus have traded in this part of the world," my uncle began, "beginning with old Auguste Chouteau, who landed on the banks of the Mississippi in 1764 as a boy of 14. Your Great-Aunt Bereniece came to the City of Kansas in 1821 as the bride of François Chouteau.

Your grandfather joined them in establishing Chez les Causes. By 1824 this settlement, the City of Kansas, was such a success that when General Lafayette honored St. Louis with his presence, he sent personal greetings and congratulations to the western outpost of the brothers Chouteau."

"Did Great-Aunt Bereniece know my mother?"

"She watched your mother grow up. I'm the eldest of the five children; your mother was the youngest. As the baby and the only girl, your mother was the center of the family, as I expect you will be today. What a pity that your part of the property will be so far removed from us here in the Chez les Causes."

I looked at him with astonishment. "How, Uncle Auguste, can you be so sure as to the location of my part of the land? The commissioners will not inform us of their decisions for another hour yet."

His worldly look recognized my innocence. "These commissioners are politicians, my dear, and they ply their trade in Kansas City, not in the Indian Nation, and not in Arkansas. Let us just say they were amenable to certain suggestions and guidance in their distributions. There are many of the Chouteau family here; all of us have long memories not only for favors rendered but also for mistakes suffered."

I giggled. "So Larkin's been on pins and needles for nothing. It's all settled, and you made sure of my part of it."

"Let us say that we looked after your interests, my brothers and I, as well as our own. We are a close family, geographically as well as spiritually, except for you. And now we have a chance to know you."

Ahead of us was the levee, holding back a wide river on which rode two steamboats. Around the huge piles of freight that lay on the docks swarmed the Negroes, greasers, Indians, roustabouts, merchants, and drummers whose interests converged on the river. A brass band tooted in welcome as one of the steamers pulled in. The pulse of the scene quickened as hustlers approached each arriving passenger, vigorously touting Kansas City's two hotels.

Uncle Auguste smiled at my enjoyment. "I knew you would find this exciting, child. You may not know it yet, but commerce is in your blood."

"What are those signs those men are carrying, Uncle?"

"They're hotel advertising. One is the Free State Hotel; the other is the Pro-Slavery Hotel. More accurately, we locals call them the Border Ruffian Houses. Those who know the ropes avoid both and take a carriage for Westport and the Harris House. We will go on to the courthouse now, where the commissioners will be expecting us, but I could not resist showing you the pulse of our city."

I had only a moment alone with Larkin before we entered the courtroom. "Larkin, we're going to be pleased with our portion. My uncle says so."

Larkin grinned. "And will your half-breed uncles be pleased, as well?"

"You know, he didn't mention them."

"Take my arm, Sarah. Let me escort you in. I'm tired of walking two steps behind. We'll walk in like husband and wife and find out our future."

There followed a flurry of introductions as we met my other three uncles Chouteau — equally talkative and well dressed, but shorter and younger versions of their oldest brother, Auguste. The air was thick with the smoke of cigars, and through the haze I glimpsed the official-looking commissioners. Apart from the bustle stood the three half-breed uncles, their slender bodies lounging casually against a table, their dark eyes carefully empty of emotion.

The commissioners received our undivided attention as their chairman began his careful reading of the property allocations. What it all boiled down to was that the Kansas City property was divided among my four legitimate uncles, each of whom received a 640-arpent strip of land fronting on the river and extending back through the city, plus an additional 4,360 acres of variously located farmland to comprise the stated sum of 5,000 acres for each heir. My holdings were to consist of two portions in Arkansas, one along the river, the other in the Ozarks, plus one section in the territory of the Indian Nation. The half-breed uncles received 5,000 acres each in the Indian Territory.

To my amazement, all present seemed pleased. The bastard uncles had inherited what was clearly the least valuable land, yet they made neither murmur nor protest. They slouched up to the table, made their signatures of acknowledgment, and walked out the door, leaving their representative to work out the details of title transfer. No word had been spoken between legitimate and illegitimate brothers at any time during the sessions. Neither had I greeted my half-breed relatives. I was the only woman in the room. It seemed obvious to me that the men expected little from me except my signature and my silence, both of which I provided.

There followed a flurry of signatures and transfers of paper. In his role of my husband and legal guardian, Larkin carefully followed each transaction. I was proud of him. His questions were thoughtful, his analysis quick. It pleased me to see expressions of respect and approval on the faces of my experienced uncles. When the last paper was finally signed, Larkin and I returned to our hotel. This time we had the carriage to ourselves.

"Why weren't my half-breed uncles angry, Larkin? Clearly, they got the short end of the stick. That dry red-clay land out in the Indian Territory can't be worth much. And they didn't say a word."

"Sarah, they got exactly 5,000 acres apiece, more than they ever expected to get. Their hopes were so dim before General Houston forced this decision that they could have lived their lives out and still be wrangling over that will. They were glad to get anything, and your hard-bargaining Kansas City uncles knew it. No wonder the Chouteaus got rich. That decision today was a masterpiece."

"I don't see why. My uncles in Kansas City got exactly the same amount of land as we did. And our land along the Arkansas River bottom is bound to be far better than any here in Missouri or over in Kansas."

"You're right about the value of the land. We got the best farmland in the lot. But that's the point, Sarah. I'm a farmer. I can take good land and make it prosper. They are merchants and will have to depend on others to farm their land. What they are interested in is commerce. That property they acquired today is measured in old French arpents, a long, thin strip of land, about an acre. The French laid out their cities in arpents, running back from the river. I'm willing to bet you a ten-dollar gold piece that the brothers Chouteau today got title to a big hunk of the best downtown real estate in the City of Kansas. It may not be that valuable today, but it will be pure gold in a few years, the way this town is growing."

"Then why don't you begrudge it, Larkin?"

"Because I'm not a merchant. I have no interest in living my life shut up in some room buying and selling and conniving and scheming. I wouldn't want to live in this town, not even if we had ten arpent strips right down the middle of it!"

I laughed. "Which is just exactly what Uncle Auguste inherited today."

"He can have it. Nope, we're better off in Arkansas where we can do as we please. I don't want to live my life as a merchant, eternally trying to please other men. Your uncles are mightily shrewd people, though, and we're beholden to them for looking after our interests."

"My guess is, they feel beholden to you for looking after theirs. If you hadn't married me, General Houston would not have pulled the right strings. So it's a fair trade."

"And you're the prize at the center, Sarah. When we get back to that fine hotel, I may be able to think of a few ways to show you how grateful I am."

We both laughed. We climbed up those hotel stairs so fast we were breathless.

Hours later, when we were ceremoniously introduced to my Great-Aunt Bereniece Chouteau, I was sure she knew exactly how we had spent the afternoon. After her polite assessment of Larkin, she took my hand in both of hers. "Daughters are a rarity amongst the Chouteaus, my child, so they are especially cherished. I myself have given birth to nine sons, but only one daughter." Her knowing eyes appraised Larkin as though to read his past and future in one swift look. "We treat our daughters gently, sir, in the hope that fate and their husbands will be inclined to do likewise."

"As you know, ma'am, I cannot answer for fate." Larkin's entire attention was focused on my aunt.

"Which is all the more reason why tenderness in a husband is a quality devoutly to be hoped for. Sarah, permit me to introduce you to my daughter, Marie. She will see that you get to know her many brothers and their wives. Larkin, I wish to know you better. Tell me your plans. How will you choose to deal with Sarah's inheritance?"

Marie laughed as she took my arm. "If your husband is not intimidated by Mama, then he'll be the only man in this room who is not. She rules with an iron hand, one little five-foot queen amongst all these men. She could give lessons to Queen Victoria, and no doubt she will if their paths ever cross. But what we would have you know, Sarah, is that the body of our little queen mother contains the world's most tender heart, along with a steel backbone."

"My Uncle Auguste has told me some of her history," I responded. "She came here as a teenage bride, surrounded by servants; she had four sons in the first five years and lost two to cholera in the same summer."

"What he may not have told you is that she nursed French and Indian alike that summer, and personally baptized 75 Indian children so that they might die in God's embrace. Chez Kansas had no permanent priest at that time. Our father said, 'We have no priest, but God gave us a saint.' Mama endured suffering and has triumphed over disasters. We have ceased to question her wisdom."

Marie smiled. "Nor does Mama hesitate to share her wisdom with those in her family. Do not be surprised if you and Larkin have the benefit of her excellent advice before the evening is over. She likely will not feel that short acquaintance should limit her insight."

"Looks to me as though she's learning a lot about Larkin already. They're deep in conversation." I was intrigued. The sight of Larkin being intimidated by anyone, let alone an old woman of 15 minutes' acquaintance, was a novel one.

Soon I was too busy enjoying myself to spend time speculating about Larkin. As Marie guided me among my talkative aunts and uncles and cousins, I was the center of their undisguised attention, the object of their affectionate curiosity. My own curiosity was at least equal to theirs. Clearly, they viewed the evening as their opportunity to welcome me into their vigorous and voluble midst. That I was a naive girl from the backwoods seemed only to add to the warmth of their interest. As we moved among the crowded high-ceilinged rooms with their polished floors and graceful furniture, I found myself wishing I could meet each person quietly and separately, so as to study and better understand my new family. Their clothes, their conversations, their ways, this big luxurious mansion — all were foreign to me. Yet they were so well integrated with each other that when one asked a question, two or three answered it, each supplying an appropriate portion of the conversation. As they laughed and sipped their wine and argued and agreed with each other, the noise level in the room rose and blended. Their sounds reminded me of a congregation singing familiar hymns in harmony.

Larkin was smiling down at Great-Aunt Bereniece while listening intently to Uncles Auguste and Pierre. Uncle Auguste was holding forth. "Alexander Majors's Pony Express is a brilliant achievement. The man's a genius at organization. He put the whole deal together in less than two months, hired 400 station helpers and 80 riders, bought the fastest horses in the country, and built nearly 200 new relay stations."

"We met one of his riders last night," Larkin replied. "A skinny kid by the name of Cody."

"I don't doubt that he's skinny. It's the only kind Majors will hire. He's got an advertising poster that says it all: 'Wanted: young, skinny, wiry fellows not over 18.' Every ounce counts when you're trying to outrun Indians. Majors has found tough young boys, mostly orphans. He tells them up front they may risk death on a daily basis."

"What kind of horses did he buy?" Larkin waited intently for the answer.

"Mostly mustangs."

"Then he's a good judge of horseflesh. I hope he's as good a judge of mules. The Flint family expects to be dealing in mules these next few years, and I took the opportunity to call on Mr. Majors before breakfast this morning."

Pierre Chouteau's eyes flickered. "Mr. Flint, I take it you have decided to consider yourself a member of the family. We are honored to have so quickly gained your trust. I wish you well. If we can help you, permit us to do so."

"I can use some analysis, and I'd be grateful for it. So far as I can tell, this Pony Express is a flashy operation, but can it make money?"

"I doubt it. It's good for our businesses, good for California, good for the country. In fact, I think it's good for everybody except Majors. The government ought to subsidize him, but most likely it won't. He's apt to lose his shirt — all out of honor and patriotism. I hope for his sake his other holdings make money for him. He's going to need some profitable sidelines."

"Well, it's our hope to set up one. We think mules and meat and corn are going to be money-makers."

Uncle Auguste beckoned to Marie and me. "Sarah, this is a day of rejoicing for me. To have gained you as a niece is an answer to my years of prayer. To find you married to so astute a man is an unexpected blessing." Putting an arm around each of us, he led Larkin and me into dinner, and seated me on his right. By the end of that evening I had been on the receiving end of more compliments, more attention, and more downright flattery than had ever come my way in my entire life all put together. I was petted and praised and consulted and encouraged to express my opinions.

The evening ended with a series of toasts — to the day, to the future, to Larkin's grandfather, Sam Houston, and to me. My head was spinning as I bobbed down for my farewell curtsey to my Aunt Bereniece. Her question caught me off-guard.

"Sarah, do you know what Larkin wants out of life?"

My blank look must have supplied the answer.

"It is obvious that you are trying hard to please him, my dear. Pleasuring him is fine, and easy when you're young, but what does he want from you in the long run? What does he hope for out of life?"

"Aunt Bereniece, if only I knew, I wouldn't have to spend so much time studying him. I could be helping him get it."

"Exactly, child." She sighed. "If only you lived closer. He's a husband worthy of your efforts, and no doubt will father fine children. Yet I would wish him to be more forthcoming in confiding his hopes and his plans to you. You will be in my prayers. I expect you to write and tell me the name you choose for your firstborn."

As my Uncle Auguste escorted me to his carriage, he seemed overcome with emotion. "Sarah, please know that my home is yours. Should you ever need shelter, should you ever need comfort, should you ever need protection, please regard me as a surrogate father."

So marked was the change in his mood from the gaiety of the past few hours that I protested his concern.

"But, Uncle, have you not today already made sure of my inheritance and my comforts?"

"No man can read the future, my dear, most especially in these unsettled times. Promise me. Promise to write often and to keep us in your heart. We will in the future regard your husband as a member of the family. We think you chose well. I speak for us all when I urge you to regard yourself as a loved member of the family, but I speak for myself when I say that you are to regard my home as your own."

He handed me into the carriage, turned to extend his hand to Larkin, and instructed his coachman to take us directly to the Harris House. The southbound stage was scheduled to leave at daybreak. Larkin put my thoughts into words. "When we get on that stage tomorrow, Sarah, we'll be going back into a whole different world."

Chapter 9

When a woman is expecting her first child, she feels like she is the center of the world. Never before or since in my entire life have I had such feelings of my own importance. I focused inward on my own belly. Every flutter, every pain, every joy took on deep meaning. Changes swirled all around me that late summer and fall of 1860, but it was nigh on to impossible for me to take the same interest in the events of the outside world that I took in the changes in my own body.

I took a detached interest in the passions and politics of the forthcoming elections, but only in those events that

seemed likely to affect me directly. In September, Larkin bought a buggy
so it would be easier for me to get about. I went with him to an all-day
rally over at the county seat. People had come in for 30 miles around.
There were dressed-up women in crinoline and hoop skirts, farmers' wives
in calico and sunbonnets, frock-coated men in top hats, and men with gal-
luses holding up pants that needed patching; all gathered in front of the
courthouse, ready to be persuaded. Each party was well represented by
men running for local office, hanging on the coattails of one national candidate or the other.

There were four major political parties, each one supporting a different
candidate for president. I knew little and cared less about any one of
these men. The Democrats had split by this time. The Northern Democrats had nominated Douglas; the Southern Democrats, Breckinridge; the
new National Union party, Bell; and the Republicans, Lincoln. Few of
us in Arkansas knew anything about any of them. Of course, none of
those men came to Arkansas. Three of them claimed to be for the Union.
Only Breckinridge was open to the possibility of secession, but what
these candidates promised in the campaign made little difference. When
all their fiery stump-speaking, rabble-rousing representatives got through
with their oratory, what it all boiled down to was this: the country was
about to choose between the Union without slaves or slavery without the
Union.

Lesser men jumped on the bandwagon of each candidate. At the rally
we attended, a fellow by the name of Huntsman ranted and raved, then
pumped up and scared the crowd until he had most of them believing that
three of the four candidates were either deficient or deformed. He swore
that Lincoln had the heart of Satan — that some had even seen horns
beginning to sprout on his forehead; that Douglas lacked guts; and Bell
lacked sense.

I began to think we all lacked sense. Standing around in the hot sun listening to the empty promises of self-serving loudmouths seemed an insult
to our intelligence. Strangely, Larkin actually appeared to enjoy it.
Although most in the crowd were strangers to me, Larkin knew many.
Dozens came up to shake his hand. I began to feel tired and light-headed
and wondered how I could persuade Larkin to leave when he was obviously enjoying himself so much.

"You're having such a good time," said I, "I'm surprised you're not up
there making a speech yourself. You're smarter and better-looking than

any of them. Especially that blathering Huntsman. He's got a face like a fish. He's all lips."

"Well, if those lips keep moving, he's going to get himself elected to Congress. He's not up there pumping the crowd up for slavery and Breckinridge — he's pumping them up so he can get himself elected to Washington."

"Then why don't you debate him?"

"I can't afford politics. Not yet, anyway. A man needs money to be in politics, whether it's honest money he's made himself, or dishonest money he's managing to skim off somebody else. This is no time for me to be out running for office. I need to be making a living."

"Well, I don't see that it would cost anything to debate a few of these big-mouthed politicians. Seems to me if you talked sense to this crowd, they might appreciate the change."

Larkin gave me his full attention. "Sarah, I swear you never stop surprising me. I think maybe you've got a point there. The next time that conceited windbag schedules one of his debates close to us, I may just take him on. You're right. It won't cost a dime, and it might just make a difference."

"Then you'd better pay close attention to his rantings. Maybe you'd better move up front. For my part, I mean to sit in the shade with Pa and Eliza and drink lemonade. This baby doesn't want me to stand around any longer in the hot sun."

Clearly, Eliza had been waiting to talk to me.

"Sit down, girl; it's bad for you to be standing around like that in the heat. I've saved you a seat in the shade, and your Pa will go get you a glass of cool lemonade. We've been worried. You look a little peaked. How are you feeling?"

"I'm fine, Eliza. I've felt life already. The baby lets me know he's there pretty often now."

"Are you still waiting on Larkin hand and foot? Maybe you ought to rest more."

I smiled. "No more than you wait on Pa."

Her tone became anxious. "Sarah, your pa and I have talked a lot about this, and we think you need to get a hired couple in. With Larkin's plans for traveling all over the upper part of this state and parts of Missouri and Kansas besides, you've got to look ahead. We can't help but worry. Has he talked any to you about any changes? When is he planning to go look at your new land, especially that big tract down south of here by the river?"

"He's going to go inspect the bottomland as soon as his corn crop is gathered. He thinks I ought not to go, even riding in the new buggy — he thinks the trip would be too hard on me. After the way I carried on during that stagecoach ride back from Kansas City, it looks like my traveling days are over until after the baby comes."

"Traveling with a new baby won't be easy, either. I hope Larkin's not aiming to move until you've had a chance to get strong again. In fact, your pa and I would feel a lot better if we knew more about what his plans are. We worry."

"I don't think he's got it settled in his own mind, yet. I know Larkin thinks this is not a wise time to move so far down south, especially not into a part of the state where most folks are all for slavery and secession. It's hard to know the smart thing to do. It's hard to manage a big plantation when you live half a state away from it. On the other hand, it would be even harder to live where our neighbors suspicioned us because we hold for the Union. If those who live on those big cotton plantations are anything like that loud fellow who's been up there on the platform for the past hour, they think everybody that's for the Union has the heart of the devil. How is it that these people have got themselves so worked up?"

"Sarah, if I could answer that question, I'd be smart enough to be president myself. Let's talk some about what you're going to do when it's time for the baby to be born. I wish I could loan you Neely for the winter, but I just purely can't do it. Mr. Griffin and I need her so much at the tavern, I don't think we could operate it without her.

"Your Aunt Gert would love to come stay with you, but I've discouraged her. She's old and apt to get sick and be more trouble than help. One thing's for sure. You can't stay in that lonesome cabin by yourself while Lark travels all over half the country. Your pa would love for you to come home and stay with us, but I told him flat out that it wouldn't work. If you moved back home, your pa would treat you like a baby, and you're beyond that now. You and Lark have got to come up with a plan, and you'd better do it soon."

I smiled, "Eliza, I've been too happy to worry. Maybe I'd better start."

Fear of the future was everywhere. Charity and Piety began to make plans for a double wedding in December after all the crops were laid by. Larkin and Ridge ranged far and wide that fall and winter, buying up mules and hogs and corn for later resale at Fort Smith and Fort Hays and Fort Gibson. Larkin's brother Sam went over to the academy at Fayetteville to study law and took his family with him. Becky begged her father to let her marry Willie Griffin that fall. Matthew Flint consented to Tom's marrying Piety, but he absolutely refused his permission to Becky, because she was still too young.

The Flint household became the hub of a far-flung enterprise. Larkin and Ridge crisscrossed a wide area and, as Eliza anticipated, were gone a lot.

By this time, Ridge had started using his true name, Ridge Rodineau. He didn't think it right for Charity to get married under a false name. I very much liked Ridge. He was big and honest and smart. If Larkin had to be gone at all, I was glad he had Ridge as his partner.

Larkin and I had our first real showdown over those trips. It was the first time I ever stood my ground with him. He had it all worked out in his mind that I would move over to the Flint compound and stay with Matthew and Minerva while he was out and about. He planned to move Tom onto our farm to look after things.

I put my foot down. I flat out refused to budge. It took very little imagination for me to picture what life would be like for me as the young pregnant daughter-in-law in Minerva's household, and I didn't like what I saw. I would be classed along with Becky, as a girl with few responsibilities and little authority. I had no intention of leaving our cabin, and I told Larkin so. That hard look I had learned to dread glinted in his eyes.

"Sarah, try to look at this sensibly. The way I've got this thing figured out, it won't cost us a dime. You'll have Minerva and Father and Becky and Stanton for company, so I won't worry about you when I'm gone. Tom can manage this farm nearly as well as I can. It may be that after he marries Piety, I'll sell him this place, anyway. We could live the winter with Father and Minerva and move south to our new Chouteau land down on the Arkansas River after the baby is born. Can't you see the advantages?"

"I can see the advantages to you. You can wheel and deal and come home when it's handy for you without having to give the least bit of thought as to how I'm doing while you're gone. And I suppose you think I ought to be happy to be in your father's house and they will be happy to have me. But it won't be that way. I've spent this whole year learning to be a woman, and I'm not willing to be a girl again, or to live under some other woman's roof, even Minerva's. It's not that I don't like Minerva. I like all your family. But I like being in charge of my own household." I paused, praying for love to soften the hard lines of his jaw, hoping to see some sign of tenderness in his eyes.

"Sarah, you can't stay here alone. If you got sick you might lose the baby, all by yourself here without any human closer than three miles away."

"Then hire somebody. Everybody else in our families have people hired to do the hard work. If you're going to be trading mules all fall and winter, you're going to be making money. Surely some of it will belong to you, else why do it at all? I'm not planning on moving in with Minerva and your father. I love this place and I love you and I'm staying right here."

"You're putting me in a real difficult spot, Sarah. I've already talked it over with Tom and with Father. They're counting on it."

I was furious. "Without talking to me? I'm your wife, Larkin. How dare you make major decisions without even bothering to find out how I feel? How dare you!" I was shaking with anger.

Larkin's eyes flashed fire. He grabbed his hat off the peg, slammed the door behind him, and headed down the path to the barn. Soon he was galloping his horse down the road without a backward glance.

I sat down on the porch, watched him ride down the long driveway, and tried to think things through. Finding the right hired man and woman would not be easy. This was not the time to buy a slave couple. Larkin was against slavery, anyhow.

So that narrowed our choices down to a white couple. Finding one that would work and be trustworthy would be hard, even assuming that Larkin meant to come around to my way of thinking. Still, I meant to hold out, no matter how Larkin felt about it. Sitting there in the cool shade of the long porch, watching the bees buzz around the tall pink hollyhocks that lined the rail-fenced yard, I prayed for wisdom, but I also prayed for strength. I thought about the married women in the family. When Eliza had her mind made up, Pa listened, mainly because Eliza was as much his partner as she was his wife. He had to have her to run the tavern right, and he knew it. Then I thought of Minerva and wondered how two strong-minded souls like Matthew and Minerva had managed to accommodate their lives to each other so as to work so well together. There must be lessons there. Still, I reflected, Minerva had come to Matthew as his equal, bringing great political advantage with her.

Confidence flowed inside me as I began to consider the advantages that had come to Larkin through me. I settled back to think. Our child fluttered inside my belly. All things considered, I hoped it was a son. There was no question but that men had the upper hand in this world.

I sat there and tried to reason it out. Clearly, poverty was not partnered with power. Equally clearly, Eliza's power was not based on money but on her competence and Pa's love and respect. Minerva's power was solidly grounded in her own sense of worth and Matthew Flint's recognition of it. So money alone was not sufficient. Marriage to me had brought Larkin the prospect of wealth. Now it was up to me to earn his respect. As I saw it, the time had come to stand up for myself.

I went down to the peacefully rippling creek, bathed in its clear water, dressed in clean clothes, poured myself a cool glass of buttermilk, and sat back down on the porch to wait. Larkin would have to come back by sundown to look after the stock.

By sundown I had begun to have my doubts. The cow was already lowing down by the barn. I could picture her udder heavy with milk. Out of simple kindness to the cow, I was about to pick up the pail and start for the barn when I saw two riders coming up the hill. Becky and Stanton, grinning from ear to ear, jumped down from their horses and yelled, "Surprise!"

"You get two instead of one tonight, Sarah! Larkin had to go over to Newton County, so he sent us to keep you company. Stant's going to look after the stock, and I'm going to cook our supper. All you have to do is to look pretty and get waited on. After supper you can watch me beat Stant in a game of checkers."

My laugh matched theirs. "I'm surprised, all right. And after supper I'll beat you both in a game of poker. We'll see if I've learned how to bluff. Is Larkin coming back tomorrow?"

"He said he'd try to," Stant said, "but we promised to stay until he gets back. He's fixing to hire somebody to help you out here on the farm, and he heard about a widow woman over close to Jasper. He took a team and a wagon with him, so I figure he thinks there's a good chance of moving her back here in short order."

Pure relief washed over me — relief so strong it made my voice crack and my knees weak. I began to order Becky and Stant around like slaves, claiming I would need practice. We laughed and joked until bedtime, three children, playing at being grown-up. I was the oldest one, and I was only 16.

In the middle of the afternoon of the next day, Larkin rode in. Behind him was a loaded wagon driven by a half-grown boy. A big-framed, sunbonneted woman got down off the wagon seat. Larkin introduced them.

"This is Monnie Homer, Sarah, and this is her boy, Ned. He's 12, and his ma tells me he's a hard worker. Monnie's kin to some of Ridge's relatives. They've been making their home in Jasper since Ned's pa died last year."

"If you can call living from hand to mouth making a home, I guess that's whut Ned and me have been doing. Living mostly on the sufferance of kinfolk is another way of looking at it. We're glad to be here. I mean to be of hep to you, Miz Sarah. Ned and me like to earn our keep."

I liked her on sight. Nearly as tall as Larkin, she had the lean look and strong hands of a woman acquainted with hard times and hard work. Her straight-lipped broad face was saved from homeliness by a pair of deep-set, intelligent eyes. I held out a hand of welcome.

"I'm glad to have you. We'll do fine together."

Larkin started giving orders. "Becky, show Monnie the stairs to the loft. We'll make pallets for them to sleep on up there until we can get another room added on the house. Stant, help Ned unload their things. Ned, water and feed the mules before Stant drives them back to Father's place. Monnie, Sarah will show you where the smokehouse is so you can slice up some ham for supper. Stant, when you get back home I want you to spread the word that we'll be having a cabin-raising four weeks from next Saturday. That'll give us time to get things ready. Ned and I'll be hauling logs for the next few weeks, so we'll all be busy."

Becky, laughing at Larkin, reached up to pat her big brother's sunburned cheek. "Sarah," she said, "I wonder how you stand such a bossy man. Of all us Flints, is there a one of us that's not good at giving orders?"

I smiled into Larkin's eyes and spoke the truth. "He suits me just fine."

Chapter 10

*LIFE GOT SUBSTANTIALLY EASIER af-
ter Monnie and Ned came to work for us.
Even when Larkin went off on four- or five-
day mule drives, I was not as put out as I
expected to be. The bigger my belly got and
the closer I came to full term, the smaller
the world became. By Christmastime, my
world had shrunk to the baby and me and to those who
loved us the most. I was aware of the outside world, naturally, but mainly I focused inward. Monnie took over all the
hard work of the household and seemed glad to do it. Ned
did the milking, fed the stock, slopped the hogs, and carried
water. Before long it seemed natural to have them around.*

By November, Larkin had drawn up plans to add a wing onto the cabin. We put on a big log-raising so as to get most of it built in two days' time. Larkin took the bold approach and nearly tripled the size of our home. He designed the new wing with two stories joined like an L to the house, each floor nearly as big as the main house. Most of the west wall of the first floor was dug right out of the side of the hill and made out of rock like the house's foundation. The north and east ends were log to match the original cabin. We wound up having a place to be proud of.

On the day of the log-raising, Minerva was overseeing the operation every step of the way. Some women might have minded her presence, but I didn't. Remembering that it had been her careful plans and true eyes that had produced the symmetrical beauty that I so loved in our main cabin, I was glad of her help, and told her so.

"Minerva, I'm beholden to you. Larkin and I will have more room than we'll know what to do with, and you've planned it so well that the new wing will set into the side of the hill like it grew there. Larkin's worked mighty hard cutting these logs and shaping them up, but he gives you the credit for planning the place. He says every window will look out on the creek below and the mountain above. I feel blessed."

Minerva's face softened in a rare smile and she spoke with an openness I was not often privileged to share. "We're all blessed, Sarah, and that baby is a major part of the blessing. It's hard to believe you're the same little lovesick curly-headed girl that took Christmas dinner with us last year. If this good weather holds, we can get this place finished in time to take Christmas dinner here with you and Larkin this year. But right now, I need to be out keeping an eye on the house-raising."

Wagons had been rolling into our yard since right after sunup. Aunt Kate had brought a quilting frame, set it up at the far end of my kitchen, and women were sitting on all sides of it quilting and talking. At the other end, over by the big hearth, Eliza was directing the dinner preparations while half a dozen women worked and talked at once. I caught Becky's eye. "What do you hear from Willie?"

"Willie thinks that since Mr. Lincoln has been elected, the country will be at war by next spring. He's studying as hard as he can to be ready, for he's sure that he's going to be needed. The South doesn't even have an army, much less army doctors. Willie feels it will be his duty to volunteer when war comes."

"Becky," I said, half angry and half fearful, "I don't want to hear about war. I don't even want to think about war. I'm about to have a baby, and that's all I can think about now."

"Everybody understands that, Sarah. Minerva says all women are that way with their first baby. But war is coming soon whether you think about it or not. That's all the men talk about now. Why do you think Larkin really wanted to move you over into our big house? It was because he feels like he will have to go off and leave you and the baby behind, and you will be isolated up here with that big bluff behind you and no neighbor closer than us, three miles away."

"Well, I won't be alone now, anyway, because Monnie and Ned will be here. Monnie's as big and strong as lots of men, and Ned is big for his age. But I don't think things will be that desperate. Even if they should become so, I don't want to think about it now."

"Well, you can't get away from it. War is all the men will talk about."

She was right. At the end of the day when the tired men sipped their whiskey and gathered in for their supper, they talked and worried. With the election over and done, the talk was *when*, not *if*, war would come.

"By the time Mr. Lincoln is inaugurated, most Southern states will already have seceded," stated Matthew Flint. "The newspapers are full of nothing else. Any day now, South Carolina will lead the march. Their legislature is already in session."

"Arkansas and Missouri won't rush in to join them. There are too many of us neutral, too many of us favoring the Union." Larkin was convincing, his eyes somber, his manner thoughtful.

"Already, I am receiving solicitations from both sides. The planters will have their way in that convention, and Arkansas will go with the South. It's only a matter of time. And Arkansas plus Missouri are critical states." Matthew's tone was matter-of-fact.

Pa took issue with Matthew's statement. "I can't see two backwoods states being so critical. Why do you say so, Matthew?"

"Because northwest Arkansas and southwest Missouri will be the breadbasket of the armies west of the Mississippi. Planters go around preaching that cotton is king — and that may well be true in peacetime — but a hungry man can't eat cotton. It's corn and hogs both armies will be needing and fighting for. Both sides will fight like hell for control of the food supply."

Ridge Rodineau spoke up. "I see your point, Mr. Flint, but I would argue another position." He spoke with respect, for no man liked to flatly contradict Matthew Flint. "I see California as the key."

"How so, Ridge?"

"California's got the gold. The South will have to buy its weapons abroad, and it will need gold to do it. England will sit back and play both sides against the middle and sell to whichever bunch can pay in gold. When I was in the City of Kansas the last time, I heard a lot of talk about shoring up the army outpost in California and a lot of worry about how hard it will be to haul gold across the mountains in wartime. God knows, it's hard enough in peacetime. What do you hear, Lark?"

"I've heard two totally different points of view. When I went down to central Arkansas last month to inspect the Chouteau land, I talked to a bunch of the neighboring planters. To a man, they're convinced they'll be better off without the Washington government than with it. They're thinking that seceding will get rid of a lot of taxes they don't get any benefit from. To my mind, they're taking a damn shortsighted view, but they don't seem to care about much of anything except making money from cotton. As to what I hear in Kansas City about gold and California, the news there is more encouraging. I hear that Mr. Alexander Majors is already working on that problem. The more I do business with that man, the more impressed I get."

Larkin expanded his statement. "He managed to get the news of Mr. Lincoln's election to California in record time, eight days by Pony Express. That whole Pony Express operation fits into this puzzle somehow. One thing's for sure, Majors didn't set it up to make money. They say he's losing his shirt but determined to keep the operation going anyhow. The last time I stayed at the Harris House I saw that little skinny Cody kid again. He just about worships Mr. Majors. I figure Majors to have connections in high places. He seems to be close to a Congressman Blair from St. Louis, and men say Blair is a staunch friend of Mr. Lincoln."

Ridge agreed. "You're on target, Lark, but I'd not rule out that Captain Lyon from Fort Riley. He's mixed up in the planning, too, and my guess is he's tough as a boot and on fire for abolition."

Larkin's brother Tom spoke up. "I know one thing — slavery is not problem enough to warrant a war. If our new President aims to be a real leader, he'd better come up with some plan to do something with the Negroes. He can't just set them free. Where would they go? Supposing Mr. Griffin here sets his three slaves free. If they go up north to Illinois, they'll just be flogged and sent back. They can't go up to Missouri or over to Mississippi, because both states have got laws keeping free Negroes out. This country's got a problem without a solution. Here we are, letting the Irish and the Germans and anybody else from over there in Europe come in and go right to work, and we can't seem to find a place for the Negroes who were born here."

Pa agreed. "And it's a damn shame. I'd rather have Zeke and Tobe working for me than any damn foreigner. They're smart and they're honest and I trust them, which is a damn sight more than I can say about these sneaky outsiders that are moving in on us. I wouldn't go live in Kansas if they gave me the whole state. They've got a wild-eyed bunch over there. On both sides."

"Well, I hear from Mr. Majors, who got it from Mr. Blair, that our new president will call for colonization of free Negroes in the first speech he makes." Larkin spoke with assurance.

"He can call for it all he wants to, but calling for it and getting it are two different things. Take my three people, for instance. I can't believe for a minute that Neely and Zeke, much less Tobe, would want to be shipped over to Africa. Why would they want to go across the ocean to live amongst strangers? This is the only home they know. I wish Mr. Lincoln well, but I hope his solutions on other problems are smarter than what I've heard so far."

I had heard about all I could stand. "Larkin," I said, "could you persuade the men to come to the table and eat? The corn bread is getting cold and the biscuits nearly so. We've got spareribs and barbecue and squirrel stew."

Larkin smiled at me. "You make your point, Sarah. We ought to eat before the food gets cold. Mr. Griffin, would you ask the blessing?"

So we ate and we visited and laughed and worked, but in the back of our minds we were always worrying about war. Piety and Charity wed Tom and Ridge on Christmas Eve. Tom moved Piety into the house his brother Sam's family had left vacant when Sam went over to Fayetteville to read law. Larkin asked Ridge to move over to Lunceville to oversee the zinc mining operation I had inherited, so Ridge and Charity loaded up a big wagon and left the day after Christmas. Larkin stayed close to home the rest of the winter. I was so near my time that he was afraid to be out of earshot.

Just when I was beginning to think that I was permanently pregnant, my water broke and the pains began. Larkin saddled up in record time and tore off down the road at a fast gallop to get Minerva. Monnie put a kettle of water on to boil, sent Ned out to the barn to shuck corn, and settled down to wait with me. Soon the pains got sharp. I began to dread them and to fight them.

"Yore making things harder than they need to be, Miz Sarah," Monnie said. "You've got to get control uv yurself. Breathe deep, through yore stomich. Let yore breath hep you. That baby's got to fight to come out. Hep him. Don't fight him."

She put her hand on my belly so as to feel my contractions and began to hum a tuneless little song, "Rest, wait, breathe — rest, wait, breathe — rest, wait, breathe." Soon I had my breathing under control, the rhythm paced and eased by her strong hands holding mine. As minutes passed and lengthened into hours, the pains sharpened, but her steady tune never ceased as she lent me her strength and her calm assurance. By the time Larkin returned with Minerva, the contractions had grown fierce.

The next several hours were a mixture of pain and sweat, blurred by the draughts of the potions Minerva kept forcing past my lips, but regulated by Monnie's steady monitoring of the rhythms of my breathing. Finally, as the pains began to cut through my very bowels, Minerva shifted her strategy. "It's time to push, Sarah. This child is ready to come out. Help him, Sarah; push hard."

"I can't," I moaned. "It'll kill me. The pain is cutting me up inside."

"You can. And it won't kill you." Minerva's tone brooked no argument. "Push and help that baby out of there."

Again it was Monnie who coached me. "Grip my hands, Miz Sarah. Squeeze and push. When I say push, give it all you've got. He's nearly out. A few more pushes'll do it." She began to count, "One . . . wait . . . *push;* two . . . wait . . . push . . . three . . . wait . . . Now!!!"

My child tumbled into Minerva's waiting hands with such force that she gasped. She laid him on my belly, still attached by the pulsing cord. I took his sweet little hand in one of my own and let love wash over me.

If I had to sort out and name the few perfect moments that have punctuated my life, surely that first time I held my child's hand would rank at the top. This time the tears in my eyes were tears of joy. I slipped into exhausted sleep. Monnie told me later that even as I slept I smiled.

Chapter 11

BY THE TIME Mr. Lincoln was inaugurated in March, seven states had already seceded from the Union and established the new government they called the Confederacy. Events started happening so fast that Larkin set up a system so he could stay informed. It became Ned's job to ride each evening over to the Flint homestead to bring back newspapers, letters, and rumors that might have been delivered there.

On April 15, Mr. Lincoln called on the states to raise 75,000 troops to suppress the rebellion. Arkansas refused to provide its quota. Within a week, Matthew was summoned to Little Rock as a delegate to a secession convention. This convention voted Arkansas into the Confederacy, with Matthew Flint's vote being the only one cast in opposition. Ned brought the news to Larkin the evening of May 8, 1861.

Baby Matt was nursing at my breast and Larkin was smoking his after-supper pipe, smiling with pride at the baby's greedy sucking, when Ned came riding up the long lane. After Larkin read his father's dispatch, his face took on an expression of despair I had never seen there before.

"It's done. Arkansas has cast her lot with the Confederacy. Every man will have to choose now which side he aims to fight on. I might as well get my affairs in order. Arkansas is already calling for troops to fight off the invaders. Lincoln is calling for troops to suppress what he considers to be the rebellion. Everything and everybody I love is right here in Arkansas, but I'm going to have to fight on the other side."

I felt like a knife had been stuck in my heart. "Larkin, you can't go off and leave us. Surely you won't have to. Pa says that some men can buy their way out of fighting. He says rich men have always been able to buy their way out of wars."

Larkin looked at me like I was a stranger. "And some men have always been able to lie and some men have always been able to steal. Surely you would not have me be without conscience, Sarah."

I wept. "Then we are different. I would lie and I would steal to keep you here with Matt and me."

"You don't mean that. You're not thinking straight and you're not talking like the Sarah I married." He walked down the path to the barn and leaned against the rails of the pasture. There he stood, looking off into the distance until the sun had sunk behind the mountain.

I put the baby to bed, wrapped my shawl around my shoulders, and went to stand beside him in the twilight. "Tell me what you're planning, Larkin. Tell me what you want me to do. Surely you don't mean to harden your heart against me? I can't be blamed for loving you, nor for wanting you here. But I won't make things any harder for you than they already are. Let's plan together. How much longer do you think you can stay home?"

"When I do join up I'll have to go to Missouri to do it. Missouri is already torn apart, with feelings so strong on both sides that neighbors are already fighting neighbors. A company of infantry from Fort Riley, Kansas, has already been sent to St. Louis, spoiling for a fight. With both sides itching to tangle, it'll come soon in Missouri. I don't think things will move so fast here in Arkansas. With any luck, I'll be able to stay out of it until after the crops are gathered in this fall."

"It may not be so easy to get to Missouri if they actually start fighting up there, unless most of the fighting is right around St. Louis."

"The fighting won't stay localized around St. Louis. Both sides will try to capture the capital, so they can claim the whole state. That'll bring things a lot closer to us. But the Mississippi River will be the real prize for either side."

"Well, thank God, the Mississippi is a long way off. Let's push our worries to one side. We'll have plenty of time to be miserable later on. For now, could we please try to be happy?"

We did our best. The weather was wonderful that summer of 1861. The crops flourished, little Matt grew plump and sturdy, the mares gave birth to record numbers of healthy mule colts, and we did our best to preserve the good life that in earlier years we had innocently taken for granted. Yet even as we waited and worried, the forces of violence were moving relentlessly toward battle.

The fighting began in June in Missouri. Most of the people there were caught between a rock and a hard place. They believed in secession as a matter of principle; but as a matter of practice, they themselves were reluctant to leave the Union. Torn between their loyalty to the Union and their bedrock beliefs in the right of each man to defend his own property, most agonized over the hard choices that confronted them. Most Missourians did not personally want secession; still less did they want to fight their Southern neighbors who had chosen to secede. It was this basic neutrality that brought on their agony, for both the North and the South saw Missouri as a prize to be claimed. The St. Louis Arsenal was the early focus for both sides. Two great Virginia armories at Norfolk and Harper's Ferry had already fallen into the hands of the Confederacy. Armies could be raised easier and quicker than guns could be manufactured, and further seizure of forts and arsenals would be disastrous. It was essential that the one in St. Louis remain in Union hands.

In Kansas, the fiery Nathaniel Lyon had already fought his way up to general. Bold action on his part secured the armory, but it incited Missouri's Southern sympathizers to action. General Sterling Price, once the governor but now commanding the Missouri State Guards, turned the Southerners into an efficient Confederate force. Missouri had become a war zone.

Most of Missouri remained under control of the Union. Only the southwest quarter was held by the Confederacy, but it posed a formidable threat. A respected Texas Ranger, General Ben McCulloch, led 800 Rangers northward and so excited the imaginations of the Texans that his troops were increased by thousands of Confederate volunteers as he moved toward Missouri. When the popular Price and the tough McCulloch joined forces in southwest Missouri, the newspapers began confidently to predict that the Confederacy would soon reclaim Missouri.

By August, my cousin Willie Griffin had volunteered for duty as a medical officer. He was assigned to the staff of General McCulloch, now commander of the Confederate forces in Arkansas and Missouri. From Willie's letters back to Becky, it was abundantly clear that the Rebels were on the march.

We're a motley assortment. I have a spiffy smart uniform with two rows of brass buttons and braid on my collar, as do the other officers under General McCulloch. I thought I looked handsome to the point of superiority until I laid eyes on the Third Texas Calvary. Such a bunch of dudes you've never seen in your life. Everything about them shines, from their horses' flanks to their leather boots. Their flags are silk, and they hold their heads high. They've got confidence to burn and enough arrogance to spread around for the whole Confederacy. Right next to their camp is a mob of ragged Missouri men armed with squirrel rifles and pistols. They've got long hair, ragged britches, and, in some cases, bare feet. Even so, these Missourians seem to be better off than some of the enlisted men from Arkansas. These poor devils have no tents and no guns. If you can picture these men along with a few thousand painted, warbonneted Indians from the Indian Territory, you'll have some idea of the circus I'm traveling with. In theory, the Indians are led by General Albert Pike, but I've met their real commander, a fellow by the name of Stand Watie. He tells me he's uncle to Ridge Rodineau.

I may not be able to write for a while. We're on the march and covering ground. Give my love to all at home.

Your Willie

When Becky finished reading Willie's letter to us, Larkin looked at me, his jaw set and his eyes sad. "Well, here it is, Sarah. Both sides will be fighting over Missouri. Regardless of who wins, Arkansas will be the next battleground. The winner will start marching in our direction."

The news of the war was not good on the national scene. A terrible battle had been fought at Bull Run, Virginia, and the Confederacy had won a victory. The newspapers reported that the entire Federal forces were routed. The record of the Federal army at Bull Run was a listing of errors, combining an unwise strategy with poor execution. The Confederates, holding their position against great odds, rejoiced in a victory so decisive. Closer to home, a big battle just outside of Springfield, Missouri, had nominally been won by the South, but at a terrible and bloody cost to both sides. It was not a time that a man could go off confidently to fight for the Union side, but by September Larkin had made up his mind.

"If I stay home much longer, I'm liable to find myself conscripted into the Confederate army. I've got to go now, while most folks still think it to be a short war. The North is not licked, Sarah. Not by a damn sight. I've got to join up while it's still possible to get away without raising too much suspicion."

Feelings ran so high in both directions that Larkin decided it best not to let folks know when he joined up. Instead, we gave out the word that he was going to drive a herd of mules out of Kansas City and across the Rockies for Mr. Majors. Larkin figured that could account for his long absence from home without forcing the issue in people's minds that he was actually off fighting in the Union army. Things had heated up so that families on one side no longer spoke to their neighbors of the other persuasion.

We made what plans we could. Larkin arranged for his brother Stant to ride over every night to help Ned with the stock. Tom took over the job of harvesting the corn, and Larkin undertook to drive the herd of mules north to Kansas City. Not having any idea how well provisioned he would need to be when he joined the army, Larkin carried as much with him as he could.

In his saddlebags we put three shirts, three pairs of wool knit socks, three pairs of drawers, a heavy wool coat, two pairs of pants, and an extra pair of heavy mud boots. He carried his rifle behind his saddle, strapped his big Colt revolver around his waist, stuck a dirk in his belt, and coiled up a 50-foot length of rope along with the two wool blankets that would be his bedroll. Besides these necessities he took as much food as he figured his horse could bear: a ham, a skillet, a big batch of cold biscuits, and a poke of ground coffee along with a tin cup and a coffee pot. On top of it all he carried his fiddle in a leather pouch.

Matthew and Minerva and I were the only ones who knew what he meant to do. After he got to Kansas City, he turned the mules over to Mr. Majors and headed back down into southern Missouri. In late September 1861, he joined the Arkansas Volunteer Cavalry, Grand Army of the Republic, and was elected a captain.

I had a lonesome time of it that fall and winter. Baby Matt began to walk early and took his first toddling steps before Christmas. I ached because Larkin could not be there to see him do it. Matt was a handsome baby, headstrong and adventurous, with Larkin's eyes and my pa's smile. We had to watch him every minute once he began walking.

Minerva encouraged the baby's willful ways. "He'll need all that curiosity and gumption when he gets older," she said. "Besides, he comes by it honestly. Larkin always has done exactly as he pleased." She paused, and her look was shrewd. "And, Sarah, it might just be barely possible that you may tend a mite that way yourself."

I looked at her in surprise. "I've spent my whole life having somebody else telling me what I ought to do."

"Until lately. It appears to me that you're getting to be good at managing your place without Larkin. I mean that as a compliment, Sarah. You're running things well. Tom tells me that when the corn crop was gathered, you were right out there in the barn tallying up each man's fair share of the harvest. Stant says you keep Monnie and Ned busy all day. Your fences are in good repair, your hay crop is in the barn, your woodpiles are racked for the winter. You've got enough hominy and potatoes and dried peaches and dried apples to feed a family of ten, besides all the beans and turnips you've stored. I'd say Eliza trained you well. You've been too busy to feel sorry for yourself, too, which is all to your credit."

"Most of the time I'm too tired to feel too sorry for myself, which, I guess, is the main reason I'm working so hard. But today it's hard not to feel lonely for Larkin."

We were gathered for Christmas Eve at the Flint homestead, with Larkin's the only empty chair. My eyes filled with tears as I remembered the happy day only two years ago when he had introduced me to his family. Yet I had reason to count our blessings, nevertheless. Although the Union forces and their Rebel counterparts had been marching and skirmishing across southern Missouri, keeping each other in states of confusion, no major battles had been fought since Larkin joined up. So far as I knew, Larkin had been spared the horrors that lurked in my imagination.

But as 1861 drew to its close, the enormity of the war was becoming painfully apparent to all. The South's dream of a swift and relatively bloodless split from the North had turned into a nightmare. The North's expectation that the slaves of the South would turn against their masters and launch an insurrection proved to have been a wishful speculation. Both sides had grossly underestimated the brutality and bloodiness of their decision. Terrible tales of robbery and rape, burning of homes, and murder of civilians began to be told, as Jayhawkers and Bushwhackers roamed over southwest Missouri and northwest Arkansas.

Uncle Auguste, writing to me from Kansas City, had described the results of wanton destruction:

> Both sides have robbed and plundered the peaceful and unprotected families left at home, taking their food and clothing and, in some cases, burning their homes. By the hundreds, women and children, old men and boys, are finding their way to Kansas City, barefooted and starving. At the same time, Southern sympathizers here are trying to move their household goods, their slaves, and their stock out of Missouri. Most seem to be heading for Texas, where they seem to feel they will find a sympathetic environment. I send you my love, and my hope that all is well with you and yours.

In addition, Uncle Auguste had sent me a magnificent gift, an exquisite cameo brooch circled with diamonds. His card had read, "This brooch belonged to my dear wife. Please wear this in the knowledge that the entire Chouteau family rejoices with you and Larkin in the birth of your son."

As I pinned the brooch on my dress that Christmas of 1861, I thought back on the joy of my Kansas City visit and on the land I had acquired as a result of that visit. I would have traded every acre to have had Larkin safely home and in my arms, but such a trade was not one of my options.

The talk that Christmas Day was grim. Lawless foraging parties from both sides, often wearing official uniforms, took vengeance against their hated neighbors whose only crime had been loyalty to the other side. Larkin had sent his father a letter describing the results of a Jayhawker raid on the Missouri town of Osceola. By coincidence, a letter from Sam had come that same week, describing burnings and lootings in Arkansas. Matthew Flint read the contents of Larkin's letter to us:

I've been thru Osceola many times. It used to be a pretty town. It had a courthouse, fine homes, and well-stocked stores. This trip, the place looked like the outskirts of hell. The shell of the courthouse was still smoking, for it had been built of limestone and heavy timbers and had been slow to burn. Three houses were left standing in the whole town. In the yard of one, a sad-looking fellow was loading his household goods onto a wagon, so I stopped to query him as to the cause of the disaster.

"Friend," I asked, "did a cyclone strike this town?"

"Would to heaven that it had," he replied. "God would undoubtedly have been more merciful than the Jayhawkers."

It turned out that a fanatic by the name of Lane, an abolitionist, rabble-rousing senator from Kansas, had actually obtained an official letter from President Lincoln to raise an army of volunteers. What Lane had not told Lincoln was that his real purpose was pillage against Confederate civilians. The fellow I talked to said he actually heard Lane tell his men that "everything disloyal, from a crowing rooster to a brindled cow, must be cleaned out."

Well, to make a sad story short, the Jayhawkers accomplished just that. Nine Osceola men were tried and shot in a trumped-up court-martial charge. The town was completely looted. Lane took everything of any value — food, furniture, contents of the stores, slaves, horses, cows, hogs, mules, wagons, and carriages. These Jayhawkers were evenhanded — they ruined Confederate and Union sympathizers alike.

"Friend," said I to the man, "where do you aim to go?"

"I'm aiming for St. Louis," said he. "I aim to give my firsthand report to the Union commander at St. Louis. He has a right to know it when men wearing the colors of our country disgrace the name and uniform of America. They made me ashamed of the human race. I would go join the Confederacy, except that I hear that their Bushwhackers are every bit as evil."

"What did the Jayhawkers do with their spoils?" I asked.

"They loaded up the whole lot and headed back to Lawrence to enjoy what they stole. They drove off with a thousand head of stock, and a couple hundred slaves. But the crowning disgrace was that a bunch of them got so drunk they couldn't even walk. Their wagons were loaded with uniformed men — I refuse to call them soldiers — so falling-down drunk they had to be carried."

Father, I know, and you know, that there are Southern Bushwhackers who are no better. I beg you to see what you can do to take precautions as best you can against similar circumstances. We need to make sure all our women can shoot, and we need a way to alert each other. I hope to see you soon. My love to all.

Sam's letter presented the other side of that same coin. Matthew read it aloud.

I sure hope I turn out to have the mind of a lawyer, for it's clear to me I don't have a mind like a general. This town has been mighty near ruined by big-name generals this week, most of them Southern. If they keep coming in here to Fayetteville on the pretext of protecting us, the generals are liable to kill us all before they're through.

The Yankees have been on the march in Missouri. They've got a new general named Curtis. He pushed General Price all the way down here to Fayetteville. The whole town turned out to welcome "Old Pap" Price. I have to admit that Price looks exactly like a general ought to look. He's big and handsome — hair like silver — seems to like everybody except Yankees. Great at politics, I hear. Well as I said, the whole town's been outdoing itself to lay out the red carpet for Price, and, truth to tell, he appears to believe it's his right to walk on it. Things were all rosy for a while.

But when General McCulloch got to town the fighting began, and they weren't fighting Yankees. These two Confederate generals, McCulloch and Price, appear to be natural-born enemies. Price's men were complaining all over town that McCulloch's bunch won't support them. They said McCulloch won't fight a lick north of the Arkansas border. The Texans claim Price's Missouri army is a bunch of riffraff. Both sides wrangled the whole time they were in town. It made me glad I haven't had to join up as yet. It would be a hard choice.

However, we didn't appreciate how easy we had it. When the two Confederate generals were done arguing with each other, they got together and started retreating down to the Boston Mountains. The retreat sent the whole town into a state of flux. Grown men went crazy and started packing up their household goods, loading up their wives and kids in their wagons and heading south. You'd have thought the devil himself was about to be loosed amongst us, though it's fair to say the generals themselves brought on most of the commotion. When the retreat started, the generals opened up their commissary stores to all who could carry their supplies away, soldiers and civilians alike, not wishing to leave behind anything the Yankees could use. I saw one old woman running down the road with a squawking chicken in one hand and her valise in the other. She yelled with every step her feet hit the road. It was hard to tell which old hen was squawking the most!

One thing I observed that day: humans love to plunder other humans, and the lust for loot makes sane men go crazy. Wild mobs cleaned out the army stores in record time, but that wasn't enough to satisfy them. They got a good taste of pillaging and kept going. By the end of the day, mobs had broken open and cleaned out nearly every store in town. The mob was wild, and there was little or no protection from the Confederate army. In fact, part of the army was part of the mob.

As the Confederates headed south, and half the town decided to follow, civilians began to realize they needed more horses and mules to haul off their goods. These they tried to buy from those of us not leaving. The price of horseflesh quadrupled between breakfast and noontime. I sold my team of mules for $600 in gold.

As you may well surmise, Susan and I didn't rest too easy

that night, but sleep we did, and it was well that we did, for worse followed with the morning. We woke to the sound of gunfire and bombshells. "It's the Yankees," Susan screamed.

But it wasn't. Turned out that McCulloch had sent his cavalry back to burn up and blow up any buildings that the Yankees might have used for headquarters. The whole Female Academy was burnt in the name of Southern salvation, along with many of the other substantial buildings in town.

I was over there after the firing started. Folks said that McCulloch made a clear statement of purpose in front of witnesses. "Any man who won't burn down his building in the face of the enemy deserves to have it burned down around him!"

Well, as I said, it appears that one side or the other means to kill us for our own good. The next day the Federal army rode into town, and the Stars and Stripes flew on the public square. I was surprised at the numbers of those who publicly rejoiced to see it there, but their rejoicing was to be short-lived. The Feds have now withdrawn, the Rebels are back, and these who got too vocal in their Yankee enthusiasm have been packed off to Fort Smith to be tried for treason. Neighbor now regards neighbor with suspicion and fear. This is especially directed at those few of us who have managed not to declare our loyalties yet.

I'm trying to hang on until the school term is over, though I may not be able to. Father, please have Stant drive me over two teams of mules as soon as the roads are passable. I expect to sell one team, but the other I'll use to move Susan and the boys back home when the time comes.

Matthew did his best in response. He designed a horn telegraph, securing a cow's horn to every house, which was never to be blown under any circumstances except that of danger — whether from Bushwhacker or Jayhawker. When the horn was blown, the next house would blow theirs, then the next, and so on until the news reached the farthest extremes of our family's settlement. By this strategy, the horses and cattle could be run to the brush and the men could take precautions in due time.

"Father," said Tom, "I think it best that we expand this plan to include our neighbors. I think you ought to invite them in to organize your telegraph system."

Matthew agreed. The date to explain the system was set for January, but we had such a heavy snow that the whole thing was postponed until the first thaw. By that time, Larkin had come home.

Chapter 12

HE RODE UP THE HILL with a grin on his face and a light in his eyes, and the whole place came alive. By the time he was halfway up the hill, his hounds began to yap and whine their welcome. Ned came rushing out of the barn and Monnie stopped stirring the stew pot and stepped out on the porch to take a look. The baby started yelling, and I stood by the front gate smiling like a Chessy cat, my heart pounding like a trip-hammer. Larkin was barely out of the saddle before I was in his arms, swooped up and swung around in such a wide circle that my petticoats billowed like sails in the wind. When he put me down he kissed me like we

two were alone in the world. My knees buckled so that I had to hold on to him to keep my balance. Six months he'd been gone. If ever there was a man glad to be home, it was Larkin Flint on that sunny Saturday in February.

When he finally turned me loose, he shook hands with Monnie and Ned, then turned to little Matt, who was by this time silently holding onto Ned's hand, his eyes big as saucers.

Larkin hunkered down on his heels, reached out his hands to Matt, and smiled that sweet lopsided smile that always gladdened my heart. Slowly, thoughtfully, Matt toddled into the circle of his father's arms.

"Thank you, God, thank you, God," I whispered. To Larkin I said, "If I were Neely, I'd be shouting for joy."

"Go ahead," he replied, "I feel like shouting, myself. I don't think I've ever been so glad about anything in my whole life. All I want to do right now is to look around and see everybody and everything again. I've pictured every inch of this place in my mind's eye so many times. Now I want to walk over every foot of it. Get your shawl, Sarah, and put a coat on Matt, and show me how you've wintered while I've been away." So, carrying Matt in one arm, with the other around me, Larkin walked from house to barn and creek to field, inspecting his kingdom.

We had a happy supper that night. Monnie dished up squirrel stew with dumplings, followed by fried peach pies, and Larkin ate like a starving man. As he dined, he talked, and we basked in his approval. "Ned," he said, "you're doing a fine job with the stock. The mules look good, the hogs are fat, and you've got a plentiful supply of corn already shucked and ready. You're doing a man's work. Mighty good, for a boy of barely 13."

Ned's grin was somewhere between embarrassed and proud. "Well, I try. And I got two good reasons fer trying. If I was to slack off on my work, Ma would be on my back like a duck on a June bug. And my other reason is, Miz Sarah is trying to learn me to read and to cipher. We study most evenings. It wouldn't be right to hold out on her when she's trying so hard to learn me my letters."

"Well, it seems only fair for me to help Monnie's boy, when she's such a big help to me with mine," said I.

In response, Monnie reached and took Matt in her arms. "Baby, how would you like to stay with Ned and me tonight? Would you like to go sleep down in our room, and look out the winder and find yurself some deer and possums?" Matt put his hand in Monnie's and toddled off with barely a backward look, leaving Larkin and me alone together for the first time in half a year.

That night he took my body like a starving man takes food. Even in his sleep, he held me next to his heart. We slept entwined, our naked limbs seeking each other throughout the long night. At daybreak he woke, and with the old, sweet tenderness I remembered, he began slowly and surely to love me.

The sun was bright and warm for a February day. We made ready to ride over to the Flint homestead for the gathering of Matthew's neighbors.

It was a worried crowd that assembled that day at Matthew and Minerva's place. Though the war had begun to touch each family, most hoped to be spared for a few more months before making irrevocable commitments to one side or the other. Most citizens opposed the conscription law, fearing that once the Confederacy had drafted the state's able-bodied men, these same men would be sent outside the state to fight. The idea that a man would fight to defend his own land was one thing — the idea that he would be sent hundreds of miles away to defend some other state's land, leaving his womenfolk defenseless, was quite another. People waited and prayed for the war's speedy end.

Political rumors had already begun to spread. Matthew was no longer associated with the state legislature, having refused to serve under the Confederacy; however, his sources of information still appeared to be remarkably reliable.

"I hear," Matthew stated, "that when the conscript law is passed, there will be many exemptions: all state employees, all Confederate officials, all mail carriers, river pilots, and telegraph operators, all preachers and teachers and employees who work in hospitals, all pharmacists, and all planters who own more than 20 slaves. The exemption list is longer, but that's the gist of it."

"Good God, Matthew," said one neighbor, "that list is an open invitation to evasion. Half the men in the state will feel a call to preach, and the other half will come up with a sudden need to teach. The lawmakers have exempted themselves and all their kinfolk. The only ones left on the list are people like us — small farmers without slaves."

"What I think is we're up a creek without a paddle. People like us can't get exempted. Even if one of us could scrape up enough money to buy 20 slaves, there ain't 20 Negroes in all of Carroll County, and there's not a one in Newton County. This law's going to be framed to draft men like us and exempt the very ones who voted Arkansas into this mess." The speaker was Robert, Larkin's oldest half-brother. Dryly, he continued, "It appears to me that Sam is the only smart one out of the whole bunch of us. Here he is over at the academy reading law, and if there's any breed the law will find a way to exempt, it's the lawyers. Maybe we ought to all go to law school."

"It's too late now, brother," replied Tom. "Things are going to heat up around here soon. I've been trying to follow this thing through the newspaper reports, and I'm afraid the Confederate generals are pretty soon going to stop fighting each other and start fighting the Union army. When that happens, this part of the state is liable to get too hot for comfort."

"That's so, Tom," agreed Larkin. "General McCulloch and General Price have been at each other's throats ever since they've had to work together and share a command. Each one has wintered in Richmond, each telling his side of it to Jeff Davis. Now Davis has decided to get smart. He's named a man to be commander over both of them — fellow by the name of Van Dorn, nephew to old Andrew Jackson. McCulloch and Price can like it or they can lump it, but they've got to do as he says. The way I see it, even though both sides have been holed up this winter, they're liable to come out fighting any day now."

His words were prophetic. It was such a warm day that we had eaten our dinner out under the trees. We women had just gone inside to wash the dishes when there commenced such a commotion as to throw a scare into us all. We heard yelling and shooting and horses neighing all around us. I ran to the window in time to see a circle of armed men spring out of the woods and rush toward us, their guns pointed, their bayonets gleaming in the sunshine.

A tribe of screaming Comanches could not have made more noise. We were caught totally unawares. One minute the men were taking their ease with their neighbors; the next they were staring down gun barrels. We women rushed out, but by the time we got outside, the Rebel soldiers were already placing chains around the necks of our men. To see the strong and handsome Flint men being ordered around by two of the ugliest men God ever created was to doubt my own eyes. Preacher Massey, with his long stringy hair, hooded eyes, and tall bony frame stood by the side of the fish-faced politician we had listened to more than a year ago at election time. Now the man was wearing the uniform of a Confederate colonel, his eyes bulging and his full lips dripping saliva as he screamed his orders.

Rough hands pushed us women back into the house and slammed the door, cramming 30 of us and a like number of children into the same room. I grabbed little Matt, holding him up in my arms to keep him from being accidentally trampled underfoot. The sounds — the screaming and moaning of the women, the frightened cries of our children, the yells of the men outside — turned the room into a chamber of horrors.

After what seemed like an eternity, the door was opened. When we ran out for a look, we faced the guns of our captors. Looking beyond our jailers, I saw the long line of our chained men disappearing around the bend in the road. Bile rose in my throat, along with terror so acute as to leave me speechless. But worse was soon to follow.

Colonel Huntsman, at the head of his column of cavalrymen, was giving final orders to his remaining troops.

"Men, bring out the traitorous Matthew Flint and hang him in his own yard." He then addressed Theophilous Massey, who was standing nearby with a look of satisfaction, contemplating the destruction and heartache his scheming plans had wrought. "Preacher Massey, I leave the task to you. Since I must ride back to join my main army, you may oversee the successful conclusion of this day's good work." He then turned to his men: "Corporal, hang the traitor when Preacher Massey gives you the order." He turned and rode away, leaving a detachment of eight men to carry out his evil design.

Four of the men then brought Matthew forward, his hands chained behind his back, his eyes flashing fire, his silent lips set in a grim line.

Minerva stepped forward to stand at the top of the steps of her porch, her tall figure commanding the attention of every man in the yard below and every woman on the porch behind her. Her eyes were fixed with terrible intensity on the self-righteous face of Theophilous Massey, who stood at her feet.

"Touch Matthew Flint at your peril!" Her voice sounding like the trumpet of an avenging angel, she evoked the ancient curse of her ancestors upon the man who was the instigator of our pain: "Theophilous Massey, may your death make known the deeds of your life; may your heart know the pain you have caused others to suffer; may you die in agony; may you seek salvation without ceasing; may the knife that pierces your heart be aimed by your own hand!"

Then, in a voice so terrible that her words sent chills along my spine, her finger pointed like a sword at the heart of the preacher, she summoned all the furies to her aid: "Spirits of wrath, strike down this man of evil, that we may know thy power, and that the earth may be cleansed from the harm he has wrought!"

She paused, her face terrible in her anger, and waited for an answer. As though in response to her plea, there came a clap of thunder immediately above our heads. I gazed in astonishment at the sky, which had turned a dark and forbidding gray. Again, she addressed her gods, while Theophilous Massey stood transfixed and silent, his face now pale, his mouth working.

"Strike down this enemy, make known thy power! Strike fear and death into the heart of this false and evil man!"

With one wrenching movement, Massey attempted to break the power of her spell. With an abrupt jerk, he turned his body and pointed a long bony finger toward the corporal holding the noose that was ready to be placed around Matthew's neck. The preacher's mouth moved, his eyes darting back to Minerva, but only raucous, garbled sounds could be heard. Minerva's trumpeted command came once more, "Touch Matthew Flint, and you die!"

Massey's mouth contorted, his hands clawed at his throat, and to our utter amazement, his long frame jerked in convulsion, his body collapsing in the dirt at Minerva's feet.

Minerva's voice rang out once more. "Corporal, unchain Matthew Flint! Leave this property, lest the gods include you in their vengeance. Leave now before you seal your own fate!"

The man did not need a second invitation. Throwing the key to Matthew's padlock on the ground, the corporal took off at a run, his men following on his heels, leaving Theophilous Massey behind, struggling for breath amongst his enemies. Minerva rushed down from the porch, stepped around Massey like she would have stepped around a dung heap, picked up the key, and released Matthew from his chains.

Matthew's words came from deep within his soul. "Thank God! The Almighty was with you, Minerva. Now we must pray that He does not turn His face away from our sons."

"You must ride to the nearest telegraph office and implore the governor to intercede. He knows you and thinks well of you. Surely he will listen to you, Matthew."

"I doubt it. He's also a politician, and a politician without much power. He can command the troops from Arkansas, but that Colonel Huntsman was dressed up as a Confederate officer. He does not take orders from the governor."

"But neither does the governor take orders from him, Matthew. Let us go to Little Rock, where you can plead the case of our boys in person."

"Mother," screamed Becky, "if Father shows up in court when that devil of a colonel is around, the colonel will hang him! If Father stays here, then it may be months before they find out he is still alive. You go and plead the case for the boys!"

"Becky," Matthew's voice was stern, "do you really believe yourself to have a father who would hide behind the petticoats of your mother?"

He turned to Minerva. "We'll go immediately. If we push the horses to their limit, we can reach Griffin's Tavern in time to catch the morning stage to Little Rock. From the tavern, we'll send telegrams to the governor and to General Houston. He may be able to intercede for the boys. With God's help and Houston's clout, we may be able to negotiate their release."

Minerva surveyed our situation. "This will leave the girls without white men to protect them. With our hired men gone off in chains, along with the others, this place is going to be left with three squaws and one old Negra man to do the hard work."

She turned to old Moe. "Moses, I know you're too old to do much work yourself, but you've got a good head on your shoulders, and you can remind the women about what ought to be done. You're in charge. Mr. Flint and I will hold you to blame if things are not done right around here."

She continued her planning, turning to Robert's wife. "Jane," she ordered, "you take one of the squaws and go over to your place tonight. Tomorrow you can drive your milk cows, your hogs, and your horses back over here. You girls are all going to have to live here in the same compound. You'll be safer and better off. Kate, you do the same."

Kate objected. "But, Mother, two women can't drive hogs and cows and horses all at the same time."

"Then make three trips of it. Don't waste my time in foolishness, girl. You're going to have to do a man's part until the men of our family get back. Piety, I'd rest easier if you and Charity would do the same."

She turned to me. "Sarah, do you mean to stay here or go with us to your pa's place?"

"I'll go to Pa and Eliza."

Matthew then surprised me by giving Becky an option. "Becky, do you want to stay here or to go with us?"

"I'll go with you."

In summation and dismissal, Matthew turned to the other women, wives of our neighbors. "Remember our cow-horn telegraph system. Each and every one of you is welcome to come over in time of need; we've all got to help each other and pray for each other."

"Father," asked Kate, "what do you want us to do with Preacher Massey?"

We looked at Massey's motionless body, still contorted in grotesque posture, face down in the dirt.

Minerva answered, her tone like iron, "Do nothing. There may yet be breath in his worthless body. If he is already dead, he is beyond our help. Even if he yet breathes, he is not deserving of our help. If by morning he is still in the yard, drag his body out into the woods. We cannot permit his stench to foul us more than it already has."

Within the space of half an hour we had saddled our horses and packed what clothing we could lay our hands on in the saddlebags. We took to the main road, for it was too dangerous to ride over the mountain trail at night. Minerva slung a little hammock over my shoulders so that Matt could ride in it when he got sleepy, like the Indian women carry their papooses.

"I'll help carry him, Sarah, because I'm stronger than you. He's big for a one-year-old, and his weight will be heavy for you. We'll take turns."

Once we got on our horses, we held them to a fast pace. We rode hard and talked little, our unspoken fears being so terrible we were unwilling to put them into words.

The sky darkened and the wind blew cold. Matt began to cry.

"Could we stop for a little while when we get to Griffin's Mill? My Aunt Kate could cook up a bowl of hot mush for the baby. It wouldn't take all that long." I asked as much for myself as for him, remembering the comfort of Aunt Kate's arms in times of earlier grief.

"We'll count on it, Sarah. We could all benefit from a little rest." Although Matthew's tone was kind, his face was remote, his mind on the obstacles we faced.

But rest was not possible, for more horrors lay ahead. As we topped the hill overlooking Griffin's Mill, the smoke and flames of massive fires leaped upward toward the twilight sky. The mill was in flames. Uncle John's barn had already been burnt down to smoking piles of rubble. A quarter of a mile to the east, flames were shooting out the roof of the forge and blacksmith shop. To the north, the remains of the general store smoldered. All that was left of the town's cotton gin and sorghum mill were red-hot twists of molten metal.

As we rode closer, we could see that the 10 or 12 houses of the settlement were still standing. At each burning building, frenzied men and women were running to and fro, trying to save what they could from the flames. Although we recognized some familiar faces among Aunt Kate and Uncle John's neighbors, we rode on as hard as we could. Pushing our tired horses to a gallop, we pulled up in front of Uncle John's front porch. Aunt Kate was applying salve to his blistered hands.

"John, did the Jayhawkers do this? I wouldn't have thought they could get down this far!" Matthew asked.

My Uncle John spoke slowly, shock and bitterness coming up from deep within. "Matthew, I would never in a million years have thought it to be possible. No, this was not the work of Jayhawkers, nor of Bushwhackers. This town was torched by our own side. General McCulloch, the very same general my own son serves, ordered our destruction."

My crying question was addressed to my Aunt Kate. "But why? Of all the family, you all are the only ones who side for the South. Was it a mistake? Did they mistake you for somebody else?"

Uncle John's eyes streamed with bitter tears of rage and frustration. "Ben McCulloch is conducting a scorched earth campaign. He sends out his cavalry day and night with supply wagons. What they can use, they take. What they can't use or haul off, they burn. It makes no difference to them whether we're for the North or for the South. He means to leave nothing behind that will aid the Northern army."

Minerva pronounced judgment. "The man's a fool, and a fool without heart. What he's done is to make sure you and Kate starve for the rest of the winter and to make sure all the rest of us starve throughout the coming year. If people can't grind their wheat and corn, they'll go hungry all next spring and summer and fall. He's made sure to starve out the very people he's supposed to be fighting to protect."

Uncle John turned to us, his face devoid of hope. "What kind of a world are we in? When a man who's supposed to be fighting to protect us decides to ruin us for our own good, what kind of life do we have ahead of us?"

"But what terrible thing brings you out in this cold?" Aunt Kate's look took in our sad faces, our weary bodies. As we told her, she wrapped her arms around Becky and me, turning once more to Uncle John. "Dry your tears, John. What has happened to us can be borne. We've lost the mill, true, but our neighbors will help us rebuild it. They need it bad, and the grindstone is still there. We'll build again. We've started over before. But what's happening to the Flint men goes far beyond our problems. It goes beyond belief and beyond the ways of civilized people. I feel like those men are dealing with the devil in human form."

"You've put your finger on it, Kate," Matthew replied. "The jaws of hell have been opened. We can all pray for help, but my experience has been that God helps those who help themselves. As for my family, we've got to get moving. If the horses hold out, we'll make it to Griffin Flat by midnight.

"John, you must ride up to my compound tomorrow and help yourself to what flour and corn and meat you need. The girls will be mighty glad to see you. It may be some time before they see us again, so I'd appreciate your keeping an eye on them."

We rode off into the darkness, the road barely visible to our straining eyes. The baby slept as we four adults searched for sure footing on the road ahead.

Chapter 13

With a thin moon shining above us and a keen wind whipping our faces, we rode north on the wire pike, Telegraph Road, as folks had taken to calling it after the wire had been strung. We were within five miles of my pa's tavern when our horses shied and balked. The road ahead was completely blocked. Massive fallen tree trunks, underbrush, and rocks loomed high above our heads.

Matthew's reaction was that of a man pushed to his limits. "You women turn back. Go back to Griffin's Mill. John and Kate will take you in. I'll take to the woods and get around this. There's little time to be wasted here."

"The girls and the baby should turn back, Matthew," Minerva agreed. "But I'm going with you. I can make my way in the woods as well as any man. I'm going wherever you go."

"I never thought the day would come that I would send two girls and a baby out in the dark without protection, but so be it. God help you. Take my pistol, Sarah. I don't think you'll have cause to need it, but take it anyway."

I took the gun, putting its wicked weight in my saddlebags along with the baby's diapers. With a quick kiss for each of us, Matthew and Minerva dismounted, led their horses into the woods, and disappeared into the silent darkness. Becky and I turned our tired horses around and spurred them back down the same road we had come.

"Becky, there's another way to get to my pa's tavern. It'll take longer, and I don't expect we can travel it after dark, but there's a wagon road that crosses over the creek and goes over the ridge that runs alongside of Griffin Flat. I mean to try it tomorrow, after we get some sleep and get baby Matt something hot to eat."

"Well, I'll go with you," she said, "though your Aunt Kate and Uncle John barely have enough food left to feed themselves."

Suddenly, Dolly lifted her head and neighed. Becky's horse snorted in alarm. By the dim light of the waning moon we could make out the forms of horses and riders advancing toward us at a steady pace. Two abreast they rode, the clanking of their weapons, the creaking of the saddles, the steady thuds of their horses' hooves announcing their approach.

The alarm of Dolly's neighs made escape impossible. We pulled our horses over to the side of the road. My heart was pounding heavy thumps, my mouth as dry as sawdust. The baby woke up and his screams pierced the air. Rough hands grabbed the reins of our horses. Darkly silhouetted figures pointed menacing pistols at our chests.

"State your names and your business and be quick about it!" The speaker's voice was loud and harsh, but before I could reply the man who had grabbed Dolly's bridle reins yelled. "My God, Lieutenant, these ain't Yankees! We've captured ourselves two girls and a baby!"

The Confederate officer rode forward. "Speak up, ladies, and explain yourselves. What business brings you out on a night like this?"

Becky answered, her tone as clear as ice. "We came from Griffin's Mill, which was burnt to the ground today. We were trying to make our way to Griffin Flat, but we had to turn back, for the road ahead is blocked."

"Who are you?"

Again, her tone was clear and cold. "My fiancé is Captain William Griffin, now serving as medical officer to General McCulloch, of the Confederate army. This is my sister-in-law, daughter of William Griffin, owner of Griffin's Tavern up ahead. We were attempting to find food and protection there. You men have left loyal folks to starve in despair at Griffin's Mill."

The questioner turned to me. "And what are your loyalties, madam? Speak up!"

I answered him with the bitter truth. "My husband is with Colonel Huntsman. I do not know where he is." He did not need to know that Larkin was with the Confederacy by force only. "I was seeking the protection of my father's roof, but the road ahead is blocked. Please let us pass. Surely, you can see that two women and a baby pose no threat. Our horses are tired to the point of exhaustion. In the name of simple kindness, let us go back where we came from and stay with our relatives."

"Ma'am," he replied, "not only will I let you proceed, but I will give you a safe conduct pass in the event you are stopped by others. There's apt to be a lot of activity on this road tonight. I doubt that we'll be the last patrol you'll encounter."

By the light of his torch he scribbled on a scrap of paper, handing it to me with a salute of dismissal. Becky and I resumed our weary journey, grim necessity keeping our tired bodies awake. Within the hour we understood the need for our safe conduct pass. The muffled rumble of wagon wheels, the reverberations and the cadence of hundreds of marching feet, the snorts of horses, and the grunts of heavily laden men carried toward us on the cold night wind.

"That's no patrol," said Becky. "That's the Confederate army coming. Let's get our horses into the woods. There's no room for us to ride on the road, anyway, until they get past."

We dismounted and led our horses into the thick trees, me carrying my sleeping baby on my back. There we stood, shivering, waiting for the relentlessly pounding lines to march past.

"Becky, those men are headed for battle, and this march could last all night. Worse, we're apt to be caught in the middle of it. If you'll help me carry the baby, I think I can find the way to the wagon road."

We picked our way through the woods for half a mile before we found the road, the bushes and briars whipping our hair and our hands. I don't know about Becky, but tears of pain and fear rolled down my face the whole way. When we finally emerged from a thicket and saw the bare ruts of the roadbed, I felt like kissing the ground. We mounted up and pushed our tired horses north.

An hour's ride brought us to the big creek. "We'll have to ford it." I said grimly. "There's no bridge. The water's deep, but usually not too deep to cross on horseback."

"We've come this far, so we'll have to go on. But my horse is harder to manage than your Dolly. Let me give you my reins," Becky said. "You go first and lead my horse across. I'll put the baby on my back. If the water is too deep we may have to swim for it."

So in this fashion we crossed, the waters belly-high to the horses. Within minutes, both horses were safely climbing the steep bank on the far side of Little Sugar Creek. As they snorted and pawed the ground, I handed the reins back to Becky.

"Thank God, the worst is over! It's less than five miles now. We've been through so much, but soon we'll be safe with Pa. All we have to do is grit our teeth and hold on. If we give the horses their heads they'll take us on in."

"We'll see about that!" Harsh voices rang out. Menacing dark forms emerged from the trees and grabbed the bridles of our horses. My heart lurched like a wild thing, and my baby's startled scream pierced the air. I felt the muzzle of a gun barrel against my back.

"Who are you?" my voice was a thin wail.

"Twenty-fourth Missouri, Union army, ma'am. But that's not the issue here. I asked the question first. Who in the hell are you, and what in the hell are two women and a baby doing in this place? You're asking to get yourselves killed, ladies. Where did you come from?"

We told him the simple truth. There seemed no other choice.

"Ladies, you've not improved your position by coming here. In fact, you've jumped from the frying pan into the fire. But we'll take you to our major, and I guess he'll take you on to Griffin's Tavern."

The second man spoke for the first time. "We're the forward scouts for this night's little distracting action. The major has got a detachment of men a few miles up the road cutting trees and throwing up a roadblock. We're here to see that nobody interrupts him." He turned, "I'll stay here and watch the road. You take the women to Major Weston. Not that he'll be too glad to be receiving company, but we've got to do something with them. We can't keep this crying kid up here in the advance guard. If he keeps that racket up much longer, he'll wake up the whole Confederacy."

Becky spoke up, "Wouldn't you yell, if you were one year old and hungry and thirsty and scared and tired out?"

Surprisingly, our captor laughed. "Ma'am, I know exactly how he feels. The only difference is, I ain't one year old. I'd yell, too, if I thought it would help things. Come on, let's go see the major."

A short ride brought us to the foot of the ridge. The thuds of axes, the grinding of saws, the crashing of trees, and the shouts of hardworking men signaled the spot where the roadblock was being erected.

Our captor told us to dismount as he went for his major.

"Who in God's name have you brought me?" The officer looked us over.

The corporal explained our situation. "They're trying to get home, sir. One's the daughter of Squire William Griffin. They've been through a day and a night that's beyond believing. Bless their pretty hearts, they thought themselves to be riding to safety. I thought I'd leave it to you to tell them what's ahead."

The major assessed us in one penetrating glance, his intelligent eyes taking in both our determination and our exhaustion. "Very well, we'll take you with us. Griffin and his wife have been very good to us this past week while we've been quartered with them, and I guess we owe it to them to help their family come home. But, ladies, the truth is, we may not be doing you a kindness. There's a big battle brewing. You're apt to find yourselves closer to it than will be comfortable. I ought to send you back, but I'm afraid you're too exhausted to be sent down that hazardous road."

Becky spoke up. "The big pike is more hazardous than you may know. There's an army of Confederates marching north on Telegraph Road."

The major was clearly astonished. "Then this moves our timetable up by 24 hours. Finish this job in double-quick time, men. When that army hits the Telegraph Road block, they're apt to try this way next! I've got to move fast to get word to the colonel. Can you women hold out to ride another hour? If you can, I'll detail the corporal here to convey you around this ridge and turn you over to your father at Griffin's Tavern. I'll tell him you're coming, for I'll be there long before you. You may have helped the situation more than you realize. Thanks to you, we've got real news now, news that's got to be figured into the colonel's plan."

He was on his horse and gone before we had time to thank him. "Let's mount up, too," the corporal said. "I'll put the baby in front of me and carry him on in with me."

I felt as if I were close to the breaking point when the corporal kindly added, " Ma'am, if you can hold on a mite longer, I'll take you home to your pa."

He was as good as his word. At two o'clock on the morning of March 7, I reached the shelter of my father's home. They tell me I fainted when I slid off my horse and into Pa's outstretched arms. More likely it was simple exhaustion. I was vaguely aware of Eliza's soft voice humming the baby to sleep, Neely's kind hands slipping a nightgown over my head, and the blessed softness of a feather bed under my tired body. After that, I slept safely in my father's house.

The thunder of cannons woke me. I screamed, instantly alert, as I looked frantically about for the baby. Neely laid a reassuring hand on my shoulder. "Baby's right here. No need bein' scared on account of him. Baby's been fed and washed, too. Him ready for de day. Best you do de same. Dis gonna be some day. Dis gonna be a day we wisht we ain't never saw. Git up, Miss Sarah. Git yourself fed and ready. We's in de eye of de storm."

I reached for clean clothes from the chest beside my bed, opening the drawer to find the shirts of a stranger. The familiar room of my childhood had become unfamiliar.

"This here's the major's room now, him and his captain. Captain say he don't think they'll be gettin' much sleep anytime soon. Sounds like he know what he's talkin' on. Hurry up, Miss Sarah. Lemme feed you some breakfast while I got somethin' to feed you with. Pears like both sides got their eyes on your pa's tavern."

Across the room Becky was dressing, her movements quiet and quick. I followed her example, washing my dirty face and brushing my hair as fast as I could. Outside, the noise increased in intensity. The staccato sounds of rifles answered the distant cannon. In the yard, men saddled horses, clanked weapons, and yelled commands.

"Come on down to de kitchen. It de only room we got left, now dat dem Yankees using de rest of de house. Your pa and Miss Liza even sleeping in de kitchen now."

As we entered the kitchen, the major came forward.

"We are in your debt, ladies. Thanks to you, we received knowledge of the enemy's movements last night. When I sent out patrols, they checked out the Confederate position exactly as you reported it. Your night of hardship and your smart spying, to say nothing of the way you fooled the Rebs into letting you turn back toward Griffin's Mill, has made a mighty big difference in our fighting this day. I wanted to say so in person. May not get a chance later on." With a quick salute he was gone, his slender body erect as he strode out the door. We all began to talk at once. Pa got the floor, because his voice was loudest. "Where in the world are the Flint men? How in God's name does it happen that you two and the baby are out by yourselves?"

Becky told them the story, not omitting the role of their black-hearted preacher, Theophilous Massey.

Eliza's rage was fierce. "When I think of the times I have fed that yellow dog at this very table, I wish I had put strychnine in his biscuits!"

Even in times of peril, Pa could tease. "Eliza, if we could take knowledge from your hindsight, the war would already be won. But what I can't understand is how Minerva worked her spell on him. I have to believe she killed him, because you girls saw it, but in my experience I've seen no man nor woman work with the powers of God. As a Christian, I'd have to pray over this for a long time before I could come to terms with it."

Eliza was quick in her analysis. "I've seen many a one made sick by their own mind, though I've seen fewer made well by their own thinking. And Preacher Massey had a palpitating pulse and a racing heart on many an occasion. He told me so many times. Except he thought it to be a mark from God, sent to help him get people all excited and roiled up during altar calls at camp meetings."

"In any case, good riddance. He's gone and no loss to the church. I'd like to have a preacher who would spend more time preaching love and less time on hellfire and brimstone. Seems like we're about to face fire ourselves, girls. Let's make what plans we can." Pa looked at the turmoil in the yard. "Matthew and Minerva didn't make it here last night. Most likely they rode on ahead of both armies. As near as I can make it out, the Northern army has been camped around here for over a week. Our tavern is headquarters for a bunch of recruits whose terms are almost up. General Curtis thought it only fair that they get the safest posting. Except today it's not looking so safe. We're at the back of the main army. General Curtis himself is quartered over in the town at Pratt's store. One bunch of officers is in your Aunt Gert's house. All over town, the Federals have taken over the houses for their officers. You girls didn't see them because you got here in the dark, but the whole town is full of soldiers' tents. They number in the thousands.

"What I'm able to piece together goes something like this: The Confederate army is marching north, but they can't come up the wire road because Curtis blocked it. Now the Rebs are flanking around the detour, the same one you girls took. It's blocked, too. Colonel Dodge — now there's a smart one — couldn't sleep last night and personally ordered that second roadblock, the one you ran into, and had it built by midnight."

Eliza interrupted, "William, one roadblock can't hold back an army. The one side can tear it down as fast as the other can build it up."

"Not quite, Eliza. Dodge built it in a strategic place, the men say. He's moving his guns and his cavalry right this minute to back up that roadblock. You'll remember there's a deep ravine and steep mountain ridges on either side of the road just north of where it crosses Sugar Creek. That's where his defense is. The Rebs will have a hard choice — it's either go through his guns or go over the mountains. And those mountains are such rocky ground not much grows there but wild twisted scrub oak and pea vine. It's not called Pea Ridge for nothing. That's wild country."

My baby's safety was of far more importance to me than battle plans. "What you're saying is that the Yankees are to the south of us and the Rebels are trying to come in to the north of us and that we're here caught in the middle with nowhere to run."

"That's right."

Becky went to the heart of it. "We're going to have to hide, aren't we? How much more time do we have?"

"Maybe two hours, Major Weston thinks. Neely's busy stocking the cellar right now. This trapdoor that leads to the cellar is your route to such safety as we can offer, girls. Price's men will be here by noon, Weston thinks. McCulloch's forces a little after that. You women and the baby are going to have to stay down in the cellar. I know it's tight quarters. Neely's got food, water, and a chamberpot already down there. There are quilts on the floor for pallets."

"Pa," I asked, "where do you aim to stay when the fighting starts?"

"Right here, Sarah. If it gets too hot to handle, I want to be here. I don't aim to be down in the cellar. It's no place for a grown man."

"William, that's not your main reason. We've been married too long for you to fool me. Don't even try it. You're staying above ground in case the guns catch the place on fire. You're staying up here so you can open the trapdoor and get us out in time."

Pa grinned. "Eliza, if you get any better at reading my mind, I may just have to stop doing my own thinking and turn the job over to you. No use in both of us working so hard at making plans. Pity you can't read the intentions of the enemy as well as you can read mine. General Curtis could certainly use you today." He kissed her cheek. "Get to work, woman. God knows what we've got ahead of us."

Pa had one more thing on his mind. The noise around us had grown loud. The yard filled with tense-faced officers mounted on pawing horses. The road began to rumble with the sounds of marching feet and groaning gun wagons as the men of the Union marched north to meet their enemies. In the midst of all of our worries, Pa summoned Neely and Zeke and Tobe. "This has been on my mind and my conscience too long. It's time I signed the papers to set you free. They've been drawn up for over a year now, and I should have signed them long ago."

He stepped into the big keeping room, where a dozen blue-coated officers pored intently over their maps.

"Might I ask three of you gentlemen to take one minute of your time to witness my signature? I'm aware that from your standpoint my timing is poor, but my slaves are heavy on my conscience today, and I would not want to face my Maker without setting them free."

"And I would not have it on mine that I refused so worthy a request." In one swift motion the colonel arose. "Major Weston, would you join us, please? Colonel Dodge?"

Pa was true to his word. In a matter of minutes he had signed the papers, the officers had witnessed his signature, and all three of our people were legally freed from bondage.

"When this battle is over, you are free to do as you will," Pa said. "Remember us with kindness, and we will always remember you."

Tobe and Zeke stood like men of stone, but Neely's face was covered with tears.

"Lord a-mercy, Mista Will, what do us do next? Where does we go?"

"Neely, I don't know. And that worry has held me back from freeing you sooner. But I've prayed over this and wrestled the problem around until I've come up with one bedrock truth: being free means you get to make your own choices. It's not up to me to tell you what to do, nor even to solve your problems, much as I wish I could. Being free means you're on your own, same as I am. When this battle is over, you can make up your minds which direction suits you best. But right now, we'd better start thinking about saving our necks. There's room for all the women in the cellar here. Zeke, there's room for you and Tobe in the springhouse. It's not as good a protection, but if you stay low and hug its rock floor, you'll have a three-foot wall on three sides of you."

Zeke looked at Neely. "Woman, I'll be praying for you. I's making tracks for dat springhouse. Looks like I's gonna spend de day on my knees anyways." He took off, dodging around the hooves of the horses that now completely encircled the house.

"Reckon I'll stay right here, Mr. Will. If you ain't hidin', I ain't hidin'. Reckon I ought to be of some hep to you and to yourn, and maybe to dem as is in here bossin' de battle. And besides, you may need some hep we ain't countin' on. Dis bids fair to be a scary day."

Pa held out his hand and shook Tobe's hand, the first black man's hand he had ever shaken in his life. "Spoken like a man, Tobe. Now let's help these women and the baby get down in the cellar."

"Not yet, Pa," I begged, "not until things get worse. There's no need to be down there in the dark any longer than we have to be."

"Sarah, don't argue. Haven't you been paying any attention to what's around you? This place was full of officers ten minutes ago; now there's a scant handful left. The cavalry's riding out. If you don't have any sense about your own safety, get little Matt down there!"

Even as he spoke, the ground shook beneath our feet. One hundred feet away, our smokehouse exploded with a blast that burst with unbearable force upon our ears, the building demolished by a cannonball that had been aimed at the tavern. The air was immediately filled with the shrieks and yells of charging cavalry, as the troops of General Curtis drove their fire into the face of the belching guns. Frantic with fear, we scrambled into the cellar, Eliza, Neely, Becky, baby Matt, and myself — too scared to think, too numb to pray.

Chapter 14

FEAR BLOTS OUT *nearly everything else. When we first scrambled down the stairs to that cold cellar, I was too scared to think about anything except saving little Matt and me. The five of us — four women and a baby — huddled on the clammy damp slabs of the cellar floor and braced our backs against the rough rocks of its walls. After a while I got rational enough to grope around in the cold dark until I found the pile of quilts. As I clutched the baby on my lap and wrapped the quilt around both of us, my fear-numbed brain began to recognize and sort out the sounds of terror from the battle above and around us. The thunderclaps of can-*

non, the whine of bullets, the harsh explosions as shrapnel met its targets, the crash of muskets, the shouts and curses and shrieks of agony of soldiers in pain too terrible for a living man to bear, the earsplitting neighs of wounded horses — all these compounded into an explosion of horror.

Later, I was to find out that control of my pa's tavern had been the goal of each side and that having some few hours' advance knowledge of the Confederate march northward had contributed substantially to the Union change in battle plans that day.

The massive roadblocks that had so hastily been thrown up during the previous night served their purpose, delaying General McCulloch's army by three or four hours. When McCulloch's Confederates reached the open fields on the west side of town, the Federal army met them.

The tired Confederates arrived to face a rain of deadly fire from the cannons of the Northern army, yet they rallied and through fierce fighting worked their way around so as to catch the Union troops in the flank. With the disciplined Texas Cavalry on their right and General Albert Pike's Cherokee Indians whooping and screaming on their left, the Union infantry was swept away from its supporting cannons. Some artillery troops turned and ran, leaving the Indians in command of the field and of weapons new to their experience. As they captured the "wagons that shoot," the Indians grew exuberant, running and yelling, scattering in all directions, entirely devoid of discipline.

But help was on the way for the Union men. Colonel Dodge's brigade dashed through what remained of the town. By the time the Confederates had mounted a new cavalry charge, they were faced with Dodge's cannons. Shot and canister raked both cornstalks and men as the Confederates fell back into the safety of the woods. There General Pike was able to regroup his rowdy Indians.

Again the tide turned. General Pike led the redskins in an attack on the Union's left. The surprised Yankees were suddenly surrounded by hideous, howling savages, their painted faces resembling the hounds of hell. Fighting with guns, tomahawks, and bows and arrows, fighting without plan or discipline, the fiendishly painted Indians shocked and confused the Federal troops, who fled in dismay.

The Indians plunged like gleeful children into the havoc of their victory, scalping the fallen, the dead, and the dying. Engaged in their scalping, they were unprepared for the assault of a regrouped Union artillery. Exploding shells, debris, and disciplined Union fire panicked the Indians, who scattered to the shelter of the woods. Their leader, General Pike, was left without an army to command.

By this time, the exhausted Confederates and the outnumbered Federals were hopelessly intermixed, as brigade smashed into brigade, and most were so hard hit that they could do no more than save themselves. More Union troops arrived, wheeling their cannon into place. In midafternoon, these troops met General McCulloch's Texans head on. McCulloch was killed. Within the hour, his second-in-command, General McIntosh, was killed. This left General Pike, lawyer, politician, and erstwhile leader of the Cherokees, in command. Mastering what men as could be persuaded to follow him, he led some of the troops in retreat, searching for the remaining Confederate generals. Other Confederates simply turned back and headed south for home, tired, hungry, and grieving for their fallen comrades.

Thus, one wing of the Confederates floundered into retreat while the other, Price's Missourians, made powerful advances from the north. These troops headed directly for the high ground of the tavern where we were hiding.

Those of us in the cellar lost all track of time as we crouched and waited in our dark hole. Our fears kept us quiet. It seemed totally unsuitable to attempt to talk when the very air above us was thick with the horrible sounds of fighting and dying men.

Suddenly, the trapdoor opened. Two strangers were pushed down the steep cellar steps. As quickly as it had opened, the door was slammed shut again.

Eliza was the first to speak. "Who are you? What is going on? Why are you here? Where is my husband?"

"One question at a time, madam," replied the speaker, his cultured tones as calm as though he had strolled in from a tea party. "My name is Knox, reporter for the *New York Herald*. My colleague writes for the *Missouri Democrat*. We have joined you without ceremony on terms not of our own choosing. All is confusion; all appears to be lost. The Confederates are charging over the brow of the mountain — Pea Ridge, I believe you locals call it — and they have the scent of victory in their nostrils. Already, Union troops are retreating down the slope, hastening down the Telegraph Road, leaving all behind — their equipage, their supplies, their tents, their food, and their fallen comrades. As for your husband, madam, I cannot say for sure. For hours we have been assisting the army surgeons with their terrible tasks. Your home has become a Union hospital, madam, though it may soon become a hospital for the enemy. Colonel Grenville Dodge's men are all that stand between us and oblivion.

"Words cannot do justice to the bravery on both sides that I have seen this day. Officers are fighting right along with their men, exposing themselves as freely as they require it of their troops. God may not give either side the victory this day, but He has given abundant courage."

Neely, her nerves at the breaking point, interrupted his monologue.

"Then you betta hopes He give you some courage, too, Mista man. Because I's got to use de chamberpot, and I ain't gonna use it wid you in dis hole wid me. You git yourself back up dem steps."

"Woman," he replied, "try not to be stupid. Do you think I am down here by my own choice? I was shoved down here by Major Weston. He'll shoot me if I go back up. Empty your bladder and be quick about it. Obviously I cannot see you in this dark."

All at once I was furious. "And, equally obviously, you have little concern for our feelings. Neely has as much right to her feelings as you have for yours. If you are too cowardly to climb out of the cellar, I'll go up the stairs ahead of you. I am quite sure the major will not shoot me."

"No, but the enemy may do so. What you women don't seem to understand is that any human above ground is in mortal danger now. This tavern is about to change sides. The Confederates are within minutes of capturing the premises. There's likely to be hand-to-hand combat in the tavern, in spite of the dead and the dying now occupying much of it."

"It gonna be worse den you thinks in here when I lets loose." Neely's voice rose in a sob. "Heaven hep us all. I can't hold it back no more. I's got to git to dat chamberpot!" Her bowels rumbled as the sickening stench of her unrestrained diarrhea filled our nostrils. The air in the cellar, already chokingly close, was so filled with the smell of her excrement as to make breathing unbearable. Waves of nausea rose in my throat. Finally, I could fight it off no longer; the need for fresh air became too strong. I handed the baby over to Eliza, pushed open the cellar door, and faced new horrors. The bloodied bodies of wounded men lay all around me, their cots packed together so closely as to barely leave space to walk among them. Through the open doorway of the big keeping room I could see the operating tables, the army surgeons attempting to save the lives of the wounded through the grisly options available to them — amputation; cauterization; probing for the metal of shot and shrapnel; and sewing up the gaping holes inflicted in battle, often without any anesthetic other than whiskey.

The operating room was a bloody island in a raging ocean of violence. I could see the broad back of my own pa as he assisted the Union doctors. Even as I watched, the team began another operation.

"More ether, Mr. Griffin."

"How much, Captain?"

"Just a few more drops ought to do it. Be sparing. It's precious stuff."

"Now the saw. This leg has to come off." Pa handed the surgeon a short silver saw, its handle gleaming in the light. The doctor, his back bent over the inert form of his patient, began his unnatural work. Suddenly the wounded man shrieked, the high, shrill sound of unmitigated agony.

"Hold him, boys," the doctor yelled. "A few drops more, Mr. Griffin. This man's big. Takes a lot to put him under. Hand me the knife. We're nearly through here. Now the file. As soon as I clean and smooth off this end of bone, we'll cauterize."

The sickening stench of burning flesh signaled the end of the process. The patient's shrieks subsided as the ether took hold.

"Carry him into the kitchen, men, and bring on the next patient." The surgeon's tone was emotionless.

My pa spoke up. "Captain, I'd suggest you check on what's going on in the yard around us. Looks to me like your army is about to leave you behind and your patients as well."

But Pa had misjudged the mettle of the Federal commanding colonel. We heard the fierce fire of an advancing Union skirmish line as blue-coated men swept past the tavern, heading north into the very teeth of the Confederate troops on the hill above.

A messenger rushed in the tavern door. "Orders from Colonel Dodge, Captain. We're going to retreat and you've got to evacuate. Colonel thinks this skirmish can hold off the Rebels long enough for you to load up the wounded on the wagons and head south. Better look lively. The colonel says there ain't much time! The wagons are coming up the hill behind me."

The surgeon turned to Pa. "My thanks, Mr. Griffin. You've done a re-markable piece of work here today. You've got a real talent. I've never seen anybody learn how to give ether to a patient as well as you have in such a short time. And my thanks to your darky. He's a good man." The surgeon turned to the busy orderlies, already carrying out the litters of the wounded. "Show a little pity, men. What little anesthetics they had won't hold long. Don't be so rough. Give each man who can swallow it as much whiskey as he can get down his gullet. They'll need to be numb for the journey. God knows how far we've got to haul them."

"Not all that far, Captain. Colonel Dodge means to hide out for the night in the woods south of here. We're not quitting — not by a long shot — we're just regrouping to fight again tomorrow!"

My pa turned in my direction, seeing me for the first time. "Get back down in that cellar, Sarah, and for God's sake, keep that baby down there! Have you gone crazy? This is no time to be sticking your head above ground!"

I stood my ground. "Pa, I just heard the corporal say there would be a little time to load up the wounded. I've got to clean up the cellar while that's going on. Neely's made an awful mess down there. I need soap and hot water, and I've got to get the others out long enough for Neely to clean herself up."

Tobe came around the corner, his clothes covered with blood. "Miss Sarah, do my ma need me?"

"No, but she needs hot water and soap, and lots of it."

"Dat we got. We been using it all day cleaning up all dem messes of blood and guts."

The doctor spoke again. "You've been fine help, Tobe. Wish I could borrow you from Mr. Griffin, here, and take you along."

Pride rang in Tobe's voice. "No need to borrow me. I's a free man now. You gives me time to hep out my ma, and I'm on my way wid you. 'Bout time I stood up to be counted on."

"Tobe, I won't ask you to join us in retreat. You're too good a man to be treated so. But if we come back through in victory, I'd be proud to have you as an orderly. It won't be too much longer before Congress authorizes Negroes as soldiers. They're already debating it. You're a good man, Tobe!"

Amidst all the noise and frenetic action, the surgeon calmly took his leave. "Good day, Mr. Griffin. Tobe." He bowed in my direction, "Good day, madam." We saw his straight back as he marched to the last wagon, took his seat beside the frightened driver, and disappeared in a cloud of dust down the hard-fought road.

"Hurry with that hot water, Tobe," I yelled. "We've got to clean up the cellar before the Rebels take over the tavern." One by one they came up the cellar ladder — Becky, Eliza, and the two newspaper correspondents. The talkative one had barely reached the tavern door before retching all over the porch.

"Bring some of that water over here, man," he yelled at Tobe.

"You can clean up your own mess, sir," said Eliza crisply. "I'll not have you giving Tobe orders. You wait on yourself. Run out to Neely's cabin, Tobe, and bring your ma a change of clean clothes. Do it while it's quiet in the yard. Time's precious, here. Sarah, let that baby down and let him run around on the floor while he's got a chance to do it. He's been cooped up too long!"

My pa came over to put his arms around me. "Sarah, even with your dirty clothes and your horrified face, you looked like an angel to me when you climbed up out of that cellar. Thank God we're safe so far. I need a big kiss from my girls before you all go back down."

Eliza grinned, "Well, William, I'm not what you'd call in the habit of kissing filthy-faced men, but I guess just this once I'll make an exception." She yelled down. "Neely, are you decent? If you are, bring up the slop jar, light up a candle to try to clean up the air, and we'll all get ready to come back down there."

The silvery sound of a bugle split the air. "It's retreat! The colonel is giving up!" Pa exclaimed.

"More likely, he's not so much giving up as retreating to fight again tomorrow." The war correspondent spoke with conviction. "But, ladies first. If you don't head for the cellar soon, I'm apt to dive in ahead of you!"

"Coming, Pa?" I asked him.

"No, daughter, I'm facing them above ground. They won't fight much longer today. It gets dark early this time of year. They'll be lighting their campfires soon, trying to eat and rest a little before tomorrow's battle. I'll call you when things calm down. Most likely, the Rebels will be here soon."

Within the hour we heard a new set of noises: the heavy tramp of feet as men marched across the floor above our heads; the harsh sounds of barked orders; the clank of weapons; the commotion of men and weapons and supplies on the move. Eventually, the door above our heads was opened.

"Come on up, girls," Pa called. "We're judged to be safe for the night, and we have a new set of visitors." One by one Pa handed us up the ladder — Eliza, Becky, little Matt, and me. Neely climbed the stairs next, her skirts flouncing in the face of the New York correspondent who was following close on her heels. Pa did the honors with formality. "Ladies, may I present General Price and General Van Dorn? They will be headquartering here."

No two men could have been more unlike than the two generals standing before us. The tall, massively proportioned General Price was a handsome man with silver hair, frank blue eyes, and an open countenance. He was clean-shaven in an age when beards and mustaches were the norm.

He bent his tall body in a graceful bow that included us all. "Ladies, my pleasure." Although I had no way of recognizing it as such, the accent was that of a cultivated Virginian. With a slight gesture, he turned to the second man, Major General Earl Van Dorn, commander of the Confederate Army of the West.

This man, too, was handsome, strikingly so, his eyes burning with an intensity absent from the open countenance of the older general. Small in stature, erect, with dark, wavy hair, his eyes showed acute alertness, plus a jaunty recognition of his own superiority. The energy pent up in his tautly erect body seemed constantly to be seeking an outlet. A quick smile showed beneath his trim mustache. "I am honored, ladies."

Van Dorn then turned to Pa. "Sir, will you and your ladies dine with General Price and me this evening? We must plan on an early meal, for we have much work to do before we sleep."

Pa's dignity matched that of the general. "We accept your invitation, sir, but first I feel compelled to acquaint you with our views. Sarah's husband is, even as we speak, a victim of the misguided actions of one of the officers under your command, a colonel by the name of Huntsman. Larkin Flint and his brothers and neighbors are being marched to Little Rock in chains, having committed no crime and having given no offense. Sarah and Becky, tell the generals what happened to the men of Carroll County."

We told our story. Price's eyes showed flashing indignation, his naturally chivalrous instincts sympathetic to our predicament. But Van Dorn's response was chilling.

"In times of war, ladies, neutrality is not possible. It is, in fact, the most dangerous of all positions, affording the protection of neither side and leaving you open to invasions from both."

He turned to me. "I cannot help your husband, madam, nor would I, if I could. Though it pains me to say so, your tears cannot soften my heart. I hold no admiration for Colonel Huntsman, nor am I betraying confidences when I say so, for my opinion of him is well known. Still, I will not interfere with his methods."

His dark eyes looked intently into mine. "I do ask for a truce at your father's table this day. We are your guests. You, in turn, are either our prisoners or under our protection, depending on your view of the matter. It is my philosophy in war to be grateful for each day that God continues to give me life."

Van Dorn then turned to Pa. "Mr. Griffin, I believe I now understand where your allegiance lies. I offer my hand in truce for this night."

It was an uneasy assembly that gathered around Pa's table that evening. The two generals usurped Pa's place at the head and Eliza's at the foot. General Van Dorn had placed Becky on his left and me on his right, from which close proximity he courteously attempted to draw us into what I recognized as social small talk. He had a reluctant dinner partner in me. To my mind, no sane person should have been expected to carry on a civilized conversation, distracted as we were by the sounds that surrounded us.

Gray-uniformed men had already scrubbed away the blood of their enemies. Now they worked purposefully to set up the room as a hospital to receive the Confederate blood that would flow in tomorrow's battle. From the woods and fields encircling us we heard the cries of the day's fallen. They lay on the cold ground begging for water, for relief from misery, even begging for the comfort of a caring hand. Though the window, shut tight against the chill air, muffled their agonized pleading, the very faintness of their cries added to their urgency.

The rich food of the general's table was dust and ashes in my mouth. Worry about Larkin caused any words I might have had to stick in my throat. Pa, recognizing my predicament, took over the conversational duties for the family.

"My nephew, Will Griffin, the betrothed of Miss Rebecca, here, is a surgeon serving under General McCulloch. I would expect there may be a fair chance of seeing him soon, as it appears that Griffin Tavern will again be used as headquarters and hospital. Who is to be Will's commander, now that General McCulloch has fallen?"

General Price was the first to respond. "I must defer that question to General Van Dorn. My knowledge of General McCulloch's plans has frequently been incomplete. Regrettably, his planned line of officer succession was outside my scope of information." Price's tone was cool, his manner detached. I was reminded of Sam Flint's letter and its references to the animosity between Price and McCulloch. I looked at General Price's face and saw arrogance writ large upon his handsome countenance.

Van Dorn was quick to respond. "McCulloch was a man's man, able and brave, as tough in body as in mind. His men will miss him sorely. I respected the man, and I respect his memory.

"As to his successor, the news is bleak, indeed. McIntosh assumed command, only to be killed himself within the hour. Albert Pike was next in line."

Van Dorn's tone grew icy. "Regrettably, General Pike could not be found at this time of great need. He is, however, due here even as we speak. When he does report in, I fear I must ask you ladies to excuse me. My business with him is urgent." His face grew grim at the prospect.

We excused ourselves as quickly as manners would permit and returned to the kitchen, now the only space available for the use of the Griffin household. I was exhausted and ready for bed, but Becky had grown so excited at the possibility of seeing Willie that she persuaded my indulgent pa to postpone our bedtime.

Soon we heard the commotion of voices in the next room. Becky, immediately alert, opened the connecting door a crack in the hope of gaining information about Willie. In the educated accents of New England, a deep voice announced, "Brigadier General Albert Pike reporting, sir." We peeped through the crack in the door, hoping to see Willie, as well. But the newcomer was alone.

The man we saw was not a stranger. Silently, I motioned for Pa to join us as we stared through the door. There in front of us was the unmistakable bulk of my wedding guest of two years past — the former commissioner of the Cherokee Nation, now a Confederate general. With our eyes glued to the crack, we gazed at General Albert Pike in fascination. He was a huge bear of a man, having long curly hair that flowed around his shoulders and a full gray beard that was in marked contrast to the dark mustache that framed his red lips. General Price, himself a tall man, was dwarfed by comparison. General Van Dorn appeared to weigh no more than half as much as his newly arrived subordinate. But the smaller Van Dorn unleashed enough fury to quail an entire regiment.

"Brigadier general, indeed! For shame, man, for shame! You are a disgrace to the Confederacy, a shame to the entire South, not worthy to call yourself a man, much less call yourself an officer. As of this moment, consider yourself to be stripped of your rank, entitled to no more honor and recognition than that of the savages you pretend to command. May you rot in the tortures of hell! I mean to see you court-martialed. If it is within my power to do so, I mean to see you shot! To permit those savages you claim to command to scalp the fallen — and that includes scalping the helpless wounded, sir — has disgraced not only your name but my entire command. You may look like a man, but you have the soul of a yellow cur! To lead your men from General McCulloch's hard-fought victory to an unnecessary and cowardly retreat — I shall never forgive you, sir. You have shamed us all. I mean to charge you with treason."

He turned to General Price. "Sir, he is in your custody. Get him out of my sight!" Van Dorn grabbed his cape. "I'll be out with my troops." The door slammed behind him.

The appalled General Pike turned toward General Price. "For God's sake, man, give me some help. You know I'm not a coward. You know my men did their very best this day. My God, my poor starving men marched through the night without sleep, they fought without food — unless you can count parched corn and raw turnips as food — and still they whipped the Yanks for most of the day. The tide turned on us after McCulloch fell. Hell, man, I don't deserve a court-martial because McCulloch got shot! It was the Yankees who shot him, not me! What ails Van Dorn?"

Price's response was frank. "He knows all that. It's the scalping that set him off. He thinks those scalping savages disgraced us all and him in particular. He's damn touchy about his reputation, and there were New York newspapermen here today. He means this war to be his personal stepping-stone to glory. He's burning with ambition, and he means to earn a world-class reputation. Now he fears that your scalping Indians have earned him world-class scorn and dishonor. Additionally, Van Dorn's a sick man. He's been running a high fever throughout this entire campaign. Some of what he just said was the fever speaking. Bad combination — high fever and high temper."

"I swear to you, General, only one Yankee's scalp was taken," Pike lied. "I've already sent a note of apology for that to General Curtis."

"Another mistake, sir. General Van Dorn is not one who takes it lightly when one of his subordinates apologizes to an enemy general. Your day has been filled with misfortune. Your apology should have been cleared with your commander first. However, none of these mistakes is, in my judgment, grounds for a court-martial."

"Then you'll help me?"

"I'll make it possible for you to help yourself. I'll remand you to Fort Smith, where you'll be in friendly territory. You won't be charged until General Van Dorn has time and opportunity to do so. That might never happen. He usually cools off about as fast as he heats up. You're a good lawyer. Good luck!"

Price stepped to the outside door and instructed his aide. "Colonel, provide General Pike with a fresh mount. Detail four men to accompany him to Fort Smith. They are to vacate the premises before daybreak."

General Pike extended his hand. "Sir, you are a true gentleman. I trust posterity will be kind to you and to yours, in the same measure as you have shown your kindness to me this day. My thanks, sir." He saluted.

The huge man turned, his movements surprisingly graceful, and walked out the door.

Chapter 15

We were up, dressed, fed, and waiting for the dawn while it was still dark outside. I stepped into the backyard to fill my lungs with crisp morning air. I wanted to look one more time at the world around me before going back down into the clammy confinement of our cellar. As I stood there shivering, I saw the unmistakable bulk of General Albert Pike emerge from the barn, followed by his four guards. I wondered at the size of the horse required to carry so massive a burden and then looked in awe at the enormous stallion that was now being led out of the barn. Horse and rider, their combined weight easily a balance for the

four average-sized men and their mounts, preceded the guards south down Telegraph Road. The general sat erect in his saddle, every considerable inch still the commander of his regiment.

I had turned to go inside when my attention was diverted by a line of hospital wagons making its way into our backyard. A young officer leaped down from his seat beside the driver and began to issue crisp directions to his orderlies. I would have recognized his voice anywhere. "Willie!" I screamed in a tone that brought our entire family rushing out of the kitchen. It was Becky, running with the grace of a young deer, who reached him first.

"Becky, Becky, is it really you?" Willie asked his question so joyously that he might have been seeing an angel. Becky melted into his arms, the expression on her face bringing tears to my eyes. I turned to Pa and Eliza, "Let's go back in the kitchen. They'll have little enough time together to-day as it is. Let's give them what few moments we can."

Soon they walked through the kitchen door, Becky's eyes shining like dark stars, her lovely fine-boned features glowing as though a candle had been lighted within. Willie shook Pa's hand and hugged us all.

"I've learned lately to take the bitter with the sweet, but today's the first time I've ever started off getting the sweet before the bitter! I'd think I was dreaming, except that it's all too complicated to be a dream." He paused, one arm around Becky, even as he talked.

"Uncle Will," asked Willie, "are you still a justice of the peace?"

"Yes," replied Pa, "though it's a duty not occupying me overmuch. Why, Willie, are you asking such a question?"

"Because I want you to marry Becky and me. Right now. Before the shooting starts again and before we have to live through another day of hell. I've been carrying our marriage license in my breast pocket for months now, carrying it against the time I would finally get back to Becky. Now, by God's own miracle, she's here in my arms, and I aim to marry her."

Stunned, my pa protested. "But Willie, we may none of us live through the day. This is not the time for marrying."

It was Becky, her eyes shining with unshed tears, who answered him. "When I enter eternity, Mr. Griffin, I mean to go into it married to Willie. Nothing else in this life is as important to me as he is. We have little enough time, sir. Barely enough for you to say the words. Please, sir, would you marry us now?"

Pa stepped to the door of the adjoining room. "Gentlemen, may I request the presence of two of you as witnesses to an important event? My nephew, your surgeon, has asked that I unite him in marriage to his childhood sweetheart. We need witnesses. I promise the ceremony will be brief." The sound of cannon rang in the distance. "Exceptionally brief," Pa amended.

General Van Dorn pushed away from his breakfast table. "It's six-thirty in the morning, Captain," he admonished Willie. "Have you no sense of propriety?"

"Sir," replied Willie, "I apologize for the untimeliness of our request, but I'm asking out of a strong sense of urgency. Will you honor us by your presence?"

"Your emotions are commendable, sir, if somewhat inconvenient. I would perhaps refuse you, Captain, but I cannot refuse the look in your young lady's eyes. I accept." Van Dorn continued. "It will be my pleasure to give the bride away."

I looked at Becky in a new light. She was a beauty, her slender body moving with unconscious grace, her glossy dark hair braided in one long straight plait that hung down her back, her beautiful dark eyes a striking contrast to her creamy complexion, her lovely features as perfectly molded as those of the face on my cameo. Though Becky was married in the plain dress of homespun that had been her garment for the past three days, and Willie was clothed in a worn uniform splotched by the dried blood of the previous day, the love on their faces transcended both their clothing and their surroundings.

As Pa solemnly intoned the mystical words, "I now pronounce you man and wife," and Willie bent to kiss his bride, the cannons began their loud, fierce thunder. Generals Van Dorn and Price, hastily scribbling their signatures, swiftly returned to their duties in their headquarters room, but not before each had claimed the privilege of kissing the bride.

"I figure we've got an hour, Uncle, before they begin bringing in the wounded," said Willie. "After we drink a toast to my bride, do you suppose Becky and I could have the rest of that hour to ourselves?"

So we drank a toast of Eliza's best blackberry cordial. "To your future, new happiness, and long life," toasted Pa, "along with our prayers to the Almighty that He may grant you these and bring us all safely past today's horrors."

A continual cannonading commenced, as the guns of Curtis's Federal army attempted to wrest from the Confederates their gains of the day before. Price's Missourians responded with a concerted infantry and cavalry attack. In the fields outside, men in gray met men in blue in bloody hand-to-hand combat. Inside the tavern, for the second day, we found ourselves surrounded by a roaring, smoking, shrieking inferno.

"Head for the cellar, girls!" Pa yelled, grabbing baby Matt and thrusting him into my arms. Once more we scrambled down the steep cellar steps. "Becky, be quick!"

"No, Mr. Griffin," Becky replied. "I mean to stay right here by the fire and talk to Willie until they start bringing in the wounded." And she did. In spite of Pa's pleading and Willie's advice, Becky sat on Willie's lap in front of the kitchen fire as they whispered their future hopes. But within the hour, Griffin's Tavern was once again a combat hospital. When Becky opened the cellar door and came down the stairs, I could hear close at hand the cries and piteous pleading of men in agony. Torn between fear and hope, we sat in the dark to wait out the day.

By midmorning, the sustained gunfire had diminished to sporadic shots, and the roar of battle had lessened so that individual sounds could be interpreted. From the yard outside came the rumble of wagons and the yelling of commands. From the rooms above us came the tread of heavy feet. In the distance we heard a mighty explosion. We were later to learn that a Confederate ammunition caisson had exploded, further reducing Van Dorn's already insufficient supply of guns and ammunition.

Within minutes, the cellar door opened. Pa called down, "Girls, I believe it is safe to come out. I don't know which will be hardest on you, the stench and confinement of the cellar, or the sights you're going to see all around you up here."

We climbed the stairs and once again faced unexpected horrors. With the exception of Willie and two other Confederate doctors, there was not a single Confederate officer in sight. Generals Van Dorn and Price were gone. All evidence of their belongings had disappeared. Their desks, maps, and chest had been replaced by the cots of the wounded. Blood ran down from the operating tables and seeped through the floorboards. Willie's shirt was covered with blood, as was that of my pa, who once again had placed himself in the service of the wounded. Tobe, down on his hands and knees in the kitchen, was attempting to scrub up the blood that covered the floor. Army orderlies moved purposefully among the cots, preparing for the evacuation and transport of their wounded patients.

"Is the fighting over? Where have they all gone?" Eliza's question spoke for us all.

Pa's face was sad. "It appears to be over for now. So far as we can tell, the Federals won this day, though both sides have fought so fierce that it may be they both lost. Anyhow, the Confederates are retreating down the Huntsville road, and a madder bunch of men you never saw in your life. One minute they were winning; the next, their officers sounded retreat. They're madder than hell, and mad at their own officers to boot. The Federals are expected any minute."

"Then why are you still here, Willie?" I asked. "Didn't you get ordered out, along with the others?"

Willie's reply was terse. "Look around you, Sarah. I can't walk out the door in the middle of surgery. We're not through here. These men need help."

I threw open the door and looked past our yard to the battlefield beyond. Earlier in the day, strong, young soldiers at the peak of their manhood had struggled fiercely. Now the fallen, the broken, and the bleeding called piteously for water. Where tall hickory and staunch oak had stood among green-needled cedar and pine, the trees were now debarked and splintered, shorn of their leaves and branches, their bare trunks still standing, pointing at the gray and chilly sky. Combat equipment, broken and abandoned, littered the fields and pasture. Dead horses swollen into grotesque shapes shared the ground with the fallen men. A pall of smoke hung over the grisly scene. Burial details and stretcher bearers from both armies worked their way among the fallen, segregating the corpses into two piles — the blue and the gray.

The wounded were not segregated. Under orders from General Curtis, each wounded man, from either army, was to be taken to the nearest field hospital.

Eliza came to stand behind me. "There's work for all of us here today. I mean to do what I can to help, even if it's no more than giving a drink of water to those pitiful, suffering soldiers out there."

An older surgeon, his face sagging with fatigue, responded. "They would be grateful, ma'am. And so would I. There's more work to be done than there are hands to do it this day. I expect we'll have more doctors later on, when the Federals re-occupy this place, but as you can see, the needs of those men are immediate."

So we went to work, all three of us — Eliza and Becky and me. I handed baby Matt into the care of Neely, hoping and praying that he was too little to understand or remember any of the horror around him. Then I tied my shawl around my shoulders, took a cup and a bucket of water, and went out among the fallen men to offer them what aid and comfort as could be obtained from cool water and a caring hand. I did what I could throughout that cold and cheerless day, the gray clouds overhead threatening each hour to drench the poor souls on the battlefield. Some of the dead lay without coat or shoes, their garments having been stripped from them by their own fleeing comrades. The living shivered and suffered in the wind, awaiting their turn for attention by the surgeons. Finally, by the end of the day, the last living man had been transported to the two makeshift hospitals set up in Pa's tavern and barn.

As I returned to the warmth of the tavern, I found myself strangely calmed. Though I was tired to the bone, I no longer felt full of my own troubles. Instead, I silently thanked God for sparing me and mine and asked His compassion for the suffering men who had survived the battle at such tremendous cost.

Neely's big kitchen table served as supper table to us all that evening. The Federal officers having returned, we again dined with officers of high rank — General Curtis, Colonel Dodge, Colonel Bussey, Colonel Sigel, and Colonel Osterhaus. In a gesture of true chivalry, General Curtis had extended his invitation to include Willie and the other two Confederate surgeons who had worked ceaselessly and without regard to color of uniform.

"Gentlemen," said Curtis, "permit me to offer you my thanks for your work on behalf of our wounded, and to reciprocate by offering you the liberty of neutrality while we are under the same roof. I have exchanged communiques with General Van Dorn. We have agreed on surgeon and patient exchanges tomorrow morning. Wagons will have safe conduct passes through Union lines. General Van Dorn will do the same for ours. And, now, may I offer a toast? I understand there was a marriage ceremony in this same room this morning. Ladies and gentlemen, shall we drink to the bride and groom?"

In thanksgiving for being spared for yet another day, and in hopes for happiness for Willie and Becky, we drank deep. The talk at Pa's table flowed as freely as in former and happier times.

Willie addressed the stern-faced General Curtis. "May I offer my congratulations to you as well, sir? You have been victorious against a worthy adversary. You undoubtedly must feel the pride of victory this night."

Curtis's tone was sad. "I feel no pride, Captain Griffin, unless it is the pride of duty. Care and grief weigh heavily on my soul; it is duty that carries me through, not pride. Even as we speak, the vulture and the wolf now roam amongst the fallen. Dead friends and foes sleep in adjacent graves. But I am grateful to you doctors, and to you, Mr. Griffin, and to you ladies, for your compassion to the wounded."

The older doctor responded, "I fully understand and share your philosophy, sir." He continued, "What I will never understand is man's seemingly compelling need to wage war on his brother."

My practical pa had listened to enough philosophy. "What I can't understand, General Curtis, is why the Confederate forces abandoned the field this morning. To me, the battle appeared to be evenly matched. Some might say even going in their favor."

"It's an amazing story, sir, and one that will probably always remain a mystery. General Van Dorn ran out of ammunition. His supply wagons did not arrive to support him this morning. For all his bravery, for all his abilities to lead and to inspire, he appears not to have planned for support and supplies. No army, no matter how brave, can remain in the field without ammunition."

"But the supply wagons were right behind our hospital wagons! I know for a fact they were less than a mile behind us when we started out this morning!" Willie's tone was incredulous.

The general was adamant. "Nevertheless, it was lack of Confederate ammunition that brought on their retreat, for we were evenly matched today in bravery and fighting ability. It was war to the knife and knife to the hilt. A bitter day, even though it is ended well."

Colonel Sigel spoke. "My scouts tell me their supply wagons are now at Camp Stephens, 12 miles distant, which means the wagons must have turned around and changed direction, instead of following your hospital wagons, Captain Griffin. Very strange, indeed. Did you encounter any messenger when you drove in this morning, anyone who might possibly have redirected the wagon train? I'm curious. It seems so unlikely."

"Only General Pike and his retinue headed south. Pike looked mad enough to bite nails in two. Didn't speak and barely returned my salute."

The teutonic Colonel Sigel was puzzled. "What would possess Van Dorn to send one of his generals south at this time?"

Pa answered him. "Pure, unmitigated anger. Yesterday, in yon very room, Van Dorn chewed Pike out, called him a disgrace, and ordered him to Fort Smith."

"For what, Mr. Griffin? For what?"

"For allowing the Indians under his command to scalp the fallen on the field of battle. Pike claimed otherwise, but Van Dorn feels Pike's Indians disgraced the Confederacy."

"And so they did, Uncle Will. I saw their work with my own eyes. Yesterday, as today, I tended the wounded on both sides. Living men were scalped, to say nothing of those already beyond feeling."

"That's as it may be, Captain Griffin, but the inability to command half-wild Cherokee Indians does not necessarily mean the man's a disgrace. There are few among us who would volunteer for such a command."

It was Pa who summed up the situation for the colonel.

"Van Dorn cut Pike's pride to the quick. Albert Pike's a politician first, a smart lawyer second, and a proud man, always. His loyalty is to Arkansas and to those Indians he represents. In his eyes, Van Dorn is no more than the smart-aleck little snot of a nephew of Andrew Jackson — not dry behind the ears, yet. I doubt there was ever any love lost between those two. As it is, there'll be bad blood there from now on."

Surprisingly, the somber face of General Curtis lightened in a hearty laugh. "Friends, let us thank God for proud men who inadvertently serve our own cause, and thank God that General Pike's Indians chose to give their allegiance to the cause of the South!"

"And now," Curtis continued, "Captain Griffin, it will be my great pleasure to excuse you and your beautiful bride. I feel sure you have more than war and politics to occupy you this night."

I have never in my life seen a woman look happier than Becky Flint Griffin as Willie led her across the hall and up the wide stairs to their bridal chamber.

Chapter 16

BY MIDMORNING, the last Confederate hospital wagon had rolled out of Pa's yard. Willie had said his good-byes as lightly and as easily as though he was counting on being back with us by supper time. Only his eyes betrayed him, and I tried hard not to look at the pain that showed there. Pa asked the question that was on all our minds. "Where do you think you'll be heading, Willie? And which general are you following, now that McCulloch is dead?"

"It's all speculation, Uncle, and we'll find out for sure when we catch up with General Van Dorn's headquarters. We're under orders to head east from here. Doesn't make a lot of sense to me, but we'll head east, anyway. Good-bye, all. Gotta go."

He swung my squealing baby around in a big wide circle, kissed Eliza, squeezed me in his usual bear hug, shook Pa's hand, tipped up Becky's brave face to brush quick kisses over her eyes and trembling mouth, and swung up into the seat beside the driver. We saw him smile and wave as the last wagon went around the bend in the road.

As we walked back into the house, Pa asked a Union officer another question that lay heavy on all our minds.

"Not wishing to sound inhospitable, Colonel Dodge, but do you folks have any idea how much longer you'll be needing to use Griffin's Tavern?"

"Good question, Mr. Griffin. Why don't you put it directly to General Curtis? I'll ask him if he can spare you a moment." A smile crossed his handsome face. "And I'd be obliged, sir, if you would inform me of the general's answer."

General Curtis, standing a few feet away, responded readily. "We'll evacuate tomorrow morning, Mr. Griffin. I recognize that you will be ready to see us go, but I fear our departure will not simplify things for you as much as you hope. We are withdrawing to the north in order to care for our men and replenish our supplies. If my scouts have supplied me with accurate information, a major portion of the enemy's forces are headed east, no doubt in the expectation of shoring up the Confederate forces on the other side of the Mississippi. Others are headed southwest, probably hoping to hold the Arkansas River at the Oklahoma border.

"Speaking as your guest, albeit an uninvited one, I wish to thank you for your many kindnesses. But speaking as a military man, I would be less than forthcoming were I not to warn you of the likely consequences of our withdrawal from your premises."

"What consequences, sir?" Pa was clearly amazed. "What consequences could be worse than being in the midst of such a battle as we have just endured?"

"The consequences of living in a no-man's-land, sir. With both armies occupied elsewhere, and the town of Griffin Flat devastated, you will be removed from all protection. You'll have neither the protection of military troops nor the protection of the proximity of friends and neighbors. In short, I foresee internecine warfare in the borderland. Rascals and robbers, villains and scoundrels, the dregs of humanity will fill the void. They will soon begin to prey on those who are remote and defenseless. I wish you well, sir, and I regret that my message is so pessimistic. Now, if you will excuse me, there is much to be done."

Pa remained undaunted. "Well, girls, that's as it may be. But we can't sit around cowering in the corners. He's right. There's much to be done. For one thing, we need to find out how our neighbors fared. I'll walk over to the town. I doubt we have a horse left to ride, so it's shank's mare. Tobe, you go over to my sister-in-law's house and find out how Miss Gertrude is faring."

"I'll go with you, Pa, if I can get somebody here to keep an eye on baby Matt."

"I'll look after him, Sarah." Becky's face was wet with the tears she had held back at Willie's leaving. "I need to be busy and I don't feel like working. Come on, baby, let's go out to the barn and find out what's left out there."

Pa and I walked down the path in silence and turned west on the big pike toward what was left of the settlement. Two buildings were still standing — Pratt's store and the house belonging to my cousins Ed and Alta Watson. The schoolhouse, the church, the homes, the barns, the sheds, the smokehouses — even the privies — had been blown up, knocked down, or burnt.

"I wonder who's left alive?" I said.

"Damn few, I'd think," was Pa's terse reply. "And those that are still alive are probably fixing to leave. What have they got left to hold them here now?"

We walked up the steep road that led to Cousin Alta's house, where smoke was coming out of the chimney and people were milling around in the yard. Cousin Ed saw us coming and ran down to meet us.

"How are things at your house, Will?"

"We're all alive, and the house and barn are still standing. Who's left?"

"Most of us are alive. Alta and I stayed in our cellar through the whole thing. Most folks in the town holed up in the basement at Pratt's store. It's got thick rock walls, and it's deep. Clate Hays tells me that by actual count, 44 white folks and three slaves were down there for two days. Pretty close quarters, but they're all alive."

Cousin Alta was in her kitchen dishing up bowls of hot mush. Her hug was loving, but her face was grim. "It's a long road to Texas."

"Texas?" Pa was astonished. "Why on earth would you head out such a distance?"

Cousin Ed answered him. "Texas is friendly territory. Folks can put down roots, make a crop, and start over."

I was struck with an idea. "Cousin Ed, why don't you and Cousin Alta settle on some of that Chouteau land that I inherited? It's not all that far from here — about 100 miles south. It's close to Lewisburg Landing, up the river west of Little Rock. Larkin says it's wonderful land. Now that Larkin's away, my Uncle Auguste is trying to manage it from 500 miles distant, and I know he'd appreciate having somebody he could trust actually living on the land. It would be a kindness to Uncle Auguste and to Larkin, too, to have you and Cousin Alta there." The more I thought about it, the better I liked the idea.

"Sarah, you always were the smartest pupil I ever taught!" Cousin Ed's face showed both relief and pride. "Taking charity has never been my style, but I don't believe this would be charity. I think I can be of help to you and Larkin."

Cousin Ed held out his hand. "We'll shake on it, Sarah. It's a deal. I'll write your uncle as soon as we settle in there, and I'd appreciate your doing the same."

Pa smiled at Cousin Ed. "Well, even an ill wind blows some good, it seems. Ed, I appreciate this. And I know Larkin will. We'll hold you in our prayers."

"Then you won't consider going with us?"

"Ed, I can't. There's not only Eliza and me to consider, there's Sister Gert to look after. She's too old to make any kind of trip. I can't leave my dead brother's wife alone to shift for herself on that big farm. Besides which, I don't truly have any notion of living anywhere except right here. I wish you well. We'll miss you all, but I purely don't want to live anywhere else, war or no war. I'll send Eliza over to say good-bye."

Pa shook hands all around, I hugged friends and relatives for the last time, and we went back home to break the news to Eliza. Eliza set out on foot to bid her farewells, but when she came back she was riding Dolly! I could not believe my eyes.

"What kind of miracle is this, Eliza? Where on earth did you find my horse?"

"I didn't find her. Cousin Ed found her wandering around in the brush down by the creek. He knew her by the blaze on her forelock — you know,

Ed's always been good with horseflesh — so he caught and bridled her and sent her back to you."

"Amazing, completely amazing," said I.

"Amazing stories are all around us. While I was over at Alta's house, Washington Ford's old Negro came staggering in too scared to talk. He had hid out in Ford's storm cellar three days, and in all the commotion, folks had forgot about him. When they finally went and found him, the poor old soul had been struck dumb with fear. Can't say a word. Just mumbles and cries."

"We may all be mumbling and crying before this is over, Eliza." Pa's tone was sober. "I see Tobe coming, so we'll have news of Gert."

Tobe was grinning from ear to ear. "Miss Gert's well, and she bossy, and she got a cellar and smokehouse full of grub. Ain't nobody robbed her or roughed her up none. An' her jest a little bit of a thing!" His tone was admiring. "She done outsmarted 'em all!"

"How did she manage?" Eliza asked.

"After de fightin' commenced an' de Yankees done gone off an' left her, Miss Gert put up a sign on her door. Kep' 'em all away ever since."

"My Lord, Tobe, one sign on a door won't keep folks away, let alone soldiers." Eliza was not convinced.

"It do iffen de sign say cholera in big black letters." Tobe grinned again. "It fooled me, too. But I figgered I had to go in, anyhow. There she be, middle of de bed, nightgown on over her other clothes. Turned out she had a loaded pistol in hand under her quilt. She send word to you all to come over in de mornin' after de Yankees leave here. She got a ham to give you, and some taters. She some little lady, she is!"

"Well, cholera sign or not, she can't stay on that big place by herself, with her hired help long gone and no neighbor closer than two miles away." Pa, torn between admiration and exasperation, spoke to Tobe. "Tobe, you may as well count on spending your nights over there."

Tobe, his face solemn, faced Pa squarely. "Mista Will, I cain't. I ain't gonna be here but dis one more night. Come sunup, when de Yankees pull out, I'll be goin' along. I ast de colonel, and he say he'll take me along til we meet up wid a Negro regiment. There's already one over in Kansas, and one comin' up from Louisiana. I'm aimin' to jine up wid de first one we come across. I shore hate to leave you, but dis is a thing I's gotta do."

"You're a free man, Tobe, even if I can't seem to shake the habit of bossing you. You do what you need to do."

Zeke came forward. "I'll stay wid Miss Gert tonight. Neely and me not going nowhere. Not now, anyways. I'll go. I knows you ain't gonna be able to git her to come over here. I'll stay nights at her place. 'Sides which, iffen she still got a henhouse and a smokehouse, it's mor'n ussens got. Might be, she'll see it as a fair swap."

"Well, Zeke, that'll work as a stopgap measure, but it won't work for long. Miss Gert can't stay by herself, and the sooner she realizes it, the better. I'll go over tomorrow and try to reason with her." Pa had clearly had all the surprises he could stand in one day. "I don't know whether to laugh or cry when I think of Gert in that bed with her loaded pistol under the cover."

We learned to live from day to day that spring, and from hand to mouth. Aunt Gert's smokehouse kept us in meat, her flour barrel kept us in bread, and our own hard work and ingenuity kept us in everything else.

Between them, Yankee and Rebel armies had eaten us out of house and home. Worse yet, they had burnt, killed, or run off every hen, cow, mule, and hog Pa owned. The barn was nearly stripped clean. The stock was gone, and the harnesses, the plows, even the most ordinary tools — hoes, buckets, baskets — were scarce as hen's teeth. If we had not had Aunt Gert's farm to fall back on, we would have been forced to pack up and leave like everybody else. As it was, we went to work and found our salvation in working until we were too tired for worrying.

Pa hitched Dolly to the plow and broke ground for our garden. It hurt us all to see my beautiful, high-spirited mare harnessed in such a way, but it had to be done. Eliza and I put in a garden; Neely leached up a batch of lye, made a kettle of soap, and cleaned up the entire tavern from top to bottom; Pa and Zeke plowed up 40 acres; and Becky put on a sunbonnet and went right out to the field with them to help plant corn. Through it all we waited and prayed for news of those we loved, but news was hard to come by.

The Griffin Tavern of that spring of 1862 was as unlike the Griffin Tavern of the past as a dried-up tadpole puddle is from a rain-freshened bayou. Where once we had had twice-weekly stage stops and mail deliveries, the busy fellowship of 200 neighbors within a two-mile radius, plus a steady flow of travelers up and down Telegraph Road, now we had solitude so deep that each time Pa's hounds barked, we jumped up to find the reason.

Mostly, the road was used at night by the military, when it was used at all. Such daytime traffic as was on it was usually some hard-pressed farmer, anxious to ride fast to wherever he was going and to get back home before dark.

Finally, my gregarious pa could stand our isolation no longer. "Girls," he said, "I'm going to ride over to see Kate and John, then on over to the Flint compound. I've had all the worrying and wondering I can stand. I'll be gone overnight, so sleep with your guns by your beds, and keep the hounds close to home so they can let you know of any prowlers."

He rode off early the next morning, obviously happy to be in the saddle instead of trudging down the corn rows between the handles of his plow. We could hardly wait for his return. When the hounds began to bark the next afternoon, we all ran out on the porch to meet him, each of us hoping and praying for good news, each inwardly braced against the bad.

"They're all fine," he called out, even before he got off his horse. "Get that scared look out of your eyes, girls, and give me a chance to tell it all."

Becky spoke what was in her heart. "Is there any mail? Has anybody managed to get any word to us?"

Pa looked at her with pity. "Not from any of the men, Becky. But there is a letter from Minerva. She and Matthew made it through the lines to Little Rock and met with the governor."

He handed the letter over to Becky. Eliza handed Pa a sip of whiskey, recognizing from his wary look the nature of the news the letter contained.

> Your father and I are in good health and moderate spirits. Events here have not developed to our liking; however, there are still possibilities of improvement. The governor steadfastly refused to intervene in releasing our men from the Confederate army, since he claims they took the oath of Confederate allegiance of their own volition and fair compensation for release from their chains. We have learned that all are with General Huntsman's army, and that they are being permitted to serve without prejudice. Your father says this means they will be given the same treatment as the other enlisted men, whatever that is.
>
> Your father's situation is less than favorable. The governor declared him to be a traitor to the Confederate cause and has remanded Matthew to Fort Smith for military trial. Matthew, of course, is arguing that such action deprives him of his constitu-

tional rights, inasmuch as he has never been in the military. We have sent numerous messages to friends and family, including my father. We travel to Fort Smith next week, there to await events with as much fortitude as we can muster. Be brave, girls, and support each other.

Becky burst into tears. "I can't bear to think of Father locked up in some miserable jail cell, alone and defenseless."

Eliza's response to Becky was as brisk as it would have been to me. "Don't cry before you're hurt, Becky. I doubt that your father will be alone. After all, Minerva has two brothers living in Fort Smith. I know that he is too brave a man to allow himself to be miserable. More likely, he'll be treated with more courtesy in Fort Smith than in Little Rock. Fort Smith's a military town, most likely with a lot of Union sympathizers."

Pa agreed. "Becky, Eliza's right. The governor is helping Matthew as much as he can without bringing a hornet's nest of Confederates swarming around his own head. He'll come out of this, you mark my words."

"Tell us about the others, Pa." I was eager for news. "How are the girls doing, over at the Flint compound? Did you ride over to see about Monnie and Ned? Tell us about Aunt Kate and Uncle John and the girls."

"Kate and John are fine, as you might guess. The girls are working like men, right along with John. John went over and borrowed food from the Flint women, just like we borrowed from Gert. The women are making a crop. John is working day and night to build the mill again. His neighbors are helping. They think they'll have it up and running by harvest time. And Piety and Charity are both back at home with John and Kate."

Eliza grinned. "Too many women under the same roof, eh?"

"Well, the twins both claim that their mother and father need them to help put in a crop. That's what they told the other Flint women, and that's what they told me. My guess is, they feel more at home with their ma and pa. There's a mighty bossy bunch of women all gathered in under one roof over at the Flint homestead — begging your pardon, Becky. Sam's wife and her two boys are back with them now. Sam decided it was time to sign on with the Confederacy. He's already been sent east, but they think he wasn't sent in time to get mixed up in the fighting at Shiloh. So far, Sam's letters to Susan are the only ones that have made it back home.

"Things are too quiet, too quiet everywhere I've been. There's trouble brewing. I'm afraid those generals have marched off and left us to the tender mercies of rogues and rascals. John's worried, and so am I. This road's too quiet in the daytime and too busy at night for my comfort. I want you girls to start carrying a gun with you when you're away from the house. It's time we faced facts. We're on our own, and we've got to be wary."

Chapter 17

SUMMER WAS SO BEAUTIFUL that year that it took my breath away. Tender green grass blanketed the battleground — our yard, the woodlot, and the meadows where so much blood had been spilled. Pa and Zeke went out with a crosscut saw and took down the trunks of dead trees.

"*I can't stand to see those scarred tree trunks pointing at the sky,*" *Eliza had said.* "*They remind me of cemetery monuments. It's like living in the middle of a graveyard.*"

"*We'll be needing wood for next winter, anyway,*" *Pa had replied.* "*Might as well get these sad reminders out of sight.*

But we *are* living in the middle of a graveyard, Eliza. Each night I pray for the poor boys who were killed here, and I pray they fell to good purpose. But nature goes on, and so must we."

Nature outdid herself that spring and summer. The wisteria vine on the porch was a blanket of purple, wild roses climbed all over the fence rows, and the healing green of new leafed trees and grass was all around us.

One June morning we heard the steady hoofbeats of a mounted patrol, and Pa stepped out on the porch to meet them.

"Sergeant Harold Jones, Confederate army," said their leader. "I have here a general order from headquarters, Trans-Mississippi District, to be posted for the information of all citizens. This policy is in effect until further notice." Within minutes he had nailed the paper on the wall beside the tavern door, remounted his horse, and led his patrol on down the Wire Road.

"What on earth was that all about?" gasped Eliza.

"Read it," replied Pa.

General Orders, Hdqrs., Trans-Miss. Dst.
No. 17   Little Rock, Ark.   June 17, 1862

I. For the more effectual annoyance of the enemy upon our rivers and in our mountains and woods, all citizens of this district who are not subject to conscription are called upon to organize themselves into independent companies of mounted men or infantry, as they prefer, arming and equipping themselves, and to serve in that part of the district to which they belong.

II. When as many as ten men come together for this purpose, they may organize by electing a captain, one sergeant, one corporal, and will at once commence operations against the enemy without waiting for special instruction. Their duty will be to cut off Federal pickets, scouts, foraging parties, and trains, and to kill pilots and others on gunboats and transports, attacking them day and night, and using the greatest vigor in their movements.

III. Captains will be held responsible for their men, and will report to these headquarters from time to time.

By command of Major-General Hindman.

"Well, I've read it now," replied Eliza, "And I still don't know what this General Hindman means to accomplish by this."

"What this does, Eliza, is to give every cowardly rascal left in the country a license to kill and steal. It means the scum of the land can legally organize into bands, call themselves vigilantes, rob who and where they please, and kill anybody who stands up to them, then claim that they legally killed Union sympathizers."

I remembered Larkin's letter of the summer before. "But, Pa, haven't the Jayhawkers of the North already been doing this up in Missouri?"

"You can't divide scum by a state line, Sarah, nor by whether they wear a blue uniform or a gray. They're all evil. The difference is, now, in the South, this order makes it legal to be evil."

Eliza, ever practical, made an instant decision. "Well, this settles it. Gert has got to move over and live with us. She can't keep on living by herself, putting Zeke to the trouble of going over every night to sleep on her premises. Whether she likes it or not, she's moving."

Pa agreed. "But you tell her. I'd as soon try to move a swarm of bees!"

So Aunt Gert moved in and brought along her cow and her chickens. It took a considerable load off my mind, for she took over the care of little Matt while I worked out in the fields. They made a wonderful pair. By fall Matt had learned all his letters and could count all his toes and could talk up a storm. Aunt Gert took the entire credit. "If I'd-a known how good I was with younguns, I'd-a prayed to the Lord to send me a dozen. I figure to have Matt reading by next summer!"

Next summer was too far off for me to even think about. By morning light I prayed for news of Larkin. At the end of every long day, I pushed my fears to the back of my mind, rocked my little boy to sleep, and prayed for us all.

Becky's letters from Willie were full of hope. "Our situation has changed wonderfully from what it was in the spring," he wrote.

> Our men are being supplied with small arms and artillery on a continuous basis. The country here in Mississippi is fertile and beautiful, though a little too flat for my taste. The people treat us like saviors and heroes. They think our generals to be wise and audacious — you must remember, they don't have a chance to know them up close and personal. This fellow Van Dorn is a ladies' man of the first water and has found consider-

able opportunity to polish his skills! I now begin to hope that I might even get to see you before too long. We're all getting our hopes up for a speedy victory. Rumor has it that we're headed for a place called Corinth.

    Your loving husband,

    Major Will Griffin.

The same mail had also brought a letter to me from Cousin Ed, now settled in as overseer of the Chouteau land down south on the Arkansas River.

It's a different world down here. The river runs wide and deep. They say it floods nearly every spring; however, a good strong levee protects your land. Evidently in the past, the Chouteaus have had excellent renters. The rents consist of a portion of the cotton produced. This system offers excellent returns in times of prosperity, but it is my duty to report to you that the expectation of profits is bleak this year. There is no feasible means of getting your cotton to market.

There is considerable irony in all of this. Cotton is now selling on the New York exchange at 60 cents a pound. Before this war broke out, it sold for around 7 cents a pound. Shipping it out and selling to the Union is illegal here in the Confederacy, yet there is absolutely no market here.

The landowners here have convinced themselves that this war is being fought over slavery, but I believe it is being fought over cotton and tariffs and class hatred of governmental control.

At any rate, control of the Mississippi River is now the key to shipping cotton. Each side has the other checkmated. No wonder that both sides want Vicksburg so badly. It is the key to commerce.

If I could figure out a way to ship your cotton bales to market, you would be a rich woman. Unfortunately, such is not the case. I continue to wrestle with the problem.

I do sincerely hope all is well with you and yours.

Pa laughed. "If that's not just like a Scotsman! Not a word about Alta and not a word about how they're doing. He's taking his new duties too seriously. Making money out of cotton right now is like getting blood out of a turnip. If anybody can do it, I'll bet on old Scotch Ed Watson! But don't hold your breath, Sarah."

"That's the last thing I'd be holding my breath about, Pa," I replied. "We need a lot of things more than we need gold. I can't see that gold would do us much good right now. What could we buy? We're in need of meat and flour and eggs and milk and no place to buy them. There's nobody living within five miles of us now, and even if there was, I wouldn't have the gall to try to buy their food right out of their mouths. I know we're not going to starve, for we've got a good garden and a good corn crop and a good hive of bees. But, I can tell you, gold is not nearly as close to the top of my list as a good slice of fried ham and a plate of Eliza's hot biscuits!"

I had just finished milking early one September morning and was walking toward the house, the heavy bucket of milk still frothy and steaming in the cool air, when a man walked out of the woods. Fear choked me and nailed me to the spot. As he came closer he began to run toward me, then to wave, his ragged, gray-uniformed arms flapping in the air. Pa's hounds started growling and barking.

"Call off your dogs, Sarah, it's me! It's Ridge! Don't you know me, Sarah? Call off your damn dogs before they take a leg off of me!"

You never saw a gladder man in your life, nor a hungrier one. Ridge Rodineau picked up that heavy milk bucket in his big hands like he was lifting a tin cup and drank deep, gulping the foaming milk like a starving man.

"I mustn't hog all the milk. Tom and Stant and Robert are out in the woods, and they're just as hungry as I am." He waved toward the woods. "Come on out, boys! It's Sarah!"

"Where's Larkin?" I asked, my heart pounding like it had a life of its own.

"He had to stay behind to look after Ross Ramsey. Ross has the bloody flux. But they'll be along as soon as Ross is able to travel. You can begin to look for Larkin in a couple of weeks, we figure. But, right now, can you feed four starving men? We managed to sneak away with some dried corn in our pockets, and we've been living on corn and wild grapes for eight days now. Wait till you see Stant. He's grown up out of his britches, even living on army grub. You'll barely know him."

The three happy, ragged scarecrows who came running out of the woods bore little resemblance to the handsome men who had marched off in chains seven months before.

"We can't hug you, Sarah, we're crawling with wood ticks! Sleeping in the woods don't improve a man's smell, much, either!" Tom was so happy he was grinning from ear to ear. "But do you think your pa could spare us some hot water and soap along with some grub? I'd kind of like to be cleaned up before I get close to Piety!"

Well, to make a long story short, we had a wonderfully happy morning. Eliza cooked and Neely scrubbed clothes and the rest of us talked our heads off.

"What are your plans, boys?" Pa asked.

"After we see our families, we'll join up with the Union army. We figure on getting horses at Father's place so we can join the cavalry. No Flint likes to walk when he can ride, and Ridge feels the same. We figure on a few good meals and a change of clothes, then heading north. Don't fret, Sarah, Larkin will be along shortly. If four men can maneuver through the woods, it'll be twice as easy for two."

Aunt Gert came up with an idea. "You boys don't want to wait here for your wet britches to dry. I've still got a chest of my dead husband's clothes. Ten years they've been in that chest, but they're still good. He was a tall man. They'll fit you as well as the clothes you boys wore in here. Zeke can fetch them and you can be on your way. I know you want to get home." She grinned. "You boys are beginning to fidget. No point in letting you leave here in wet britches!"

So we sent them off with full stomachs, wearing my Uncle Emmett's homespun britches.

"What'll I do wid dese old ragged uniforms, Miss Liza?" Neely asked.

"Put them in the store room after they dry out. We'll use them for mop rags. Looks like we can't afford to waste anything anymore, even those miserable gray rags."

We were all cheered by their visit. I started to count the days when I could reasonably expect to hope for Larkin's return. But something was brewing. Ominous sounds began to be heard during the dark nights. Bands of riders traveled up and down the Telegraph Road. Pa tried to remain cheerful. "No news is good news, girls. Let's not cry before we're hurt."

There came a day when our fears materialized. Zeke was away; Pa had sent him over to Aunt Gert's farm to pull up turnips. Six men rode up to

Pa's gate and helloed the house. "Stay inside, girls. I don't want them seeing any of you if I can help it," admonished Pa.

"Are you William Griffin?" asked their leader.

"I am."

"My name is Captain William Quantrill, official appointee of General Hindman, Trans-Mississippi District. I am commandeering your foodstuff in the name of the Confederate army! Boys, search the barn; Cole, you and Frank search the house! Dick, you go slap a bridle on that pretty mare I see out there in the barn lot! Hurry up, men, let's get moving. You wouldn't happen to have a jug or so of good corn whiskey, would you, Griffin?"

"I would, and it's yours for the taking. But for God's sake, man, don't take all our corn. It's taken us all summer to put by enough to eat to keep us alive next winter. Show a little pity, Quantrill. Take the horse, take the whiskey, but leave us enough to eat to hold off starvation."

They paid no more attention to Pa's pleas than they paid to the wind blowing through the trees. All six men dismounted. Three went lurching off in the direction of the barn. Their leader, followed by the two he called Frank and Cole, pushed Pa to one side, flung open the front door, and staggered through the house. They found us cowering in the corner of the kitchen by the fireplace.

"So that's what you're hiding in here, old man!" Quantrill's red-rimmed eyes glared like a hawk, while his thin lips twisted in the grin of a wolf. His smell was disgusting — the fumes of whiskey mixed with the smells of filth and sweat. Chewing tobacco had stained his big teeth and matted his drooping mustache. His eyes darted around the room as he slouched over to the fireplace to spit an ugly dark brown stream onto the coals.

"Two pretty girls and two worn-out old women — three, counting the darky!" His voice surprised me. Even slurred by whiskey, he spoke in the accents of an educated man, and a Northern one, at that. "Ladies, I'm forgetting my manners." He leered at us. "These two gentlemen are Cole Younger and Frank James." He turned to the men. "Looks like there's nearly one apiece for us, boys, if you're not too choosey. The little curly-headed one's mine. You boys can fight over the rest of them! You better search the place first, though. No telling what they've got stashed away in this big house. But tie up the old man before you start in. I may need to question him some."

The one named Quantrill kept his guns on us, while the other two tied Pa up to a straight-backed chair.

"Now, old man, I don't have much time, so don't waste it. You're bound to have some gold hidden around here somewhere. A man that owns a big place like this is bound to have prospered over the years. It's an easy choice, man. Your gold for your girls. You tell me where your gold's hid, I'll keep the boys from playing with your girls. I might as well tell you now, the boys are apt to get a mite rough with them. Women have been mighty scarce where we've been; you're not likely to enjoy having to watch it."

Pa's face was gray as ashes.

"After I tell you where the gold is, what guarantee have I got that you'll ride off and leave my girls alone?"

Quantrill took his time about answering. He walked back over to the fireplace and spit another slimy brown stream onto the coals. Then he grinned.

"Beats me, old man. Looks like you're going to have to take my word for it. Surely the word of an officer and a gentleman ought to satisfy you." He paused. "Don't waste more of my time, old man. Where's your gold?"

"It's down in the cellar in one of the stone crocks. West wall, top shelf. The crock of honey next to the back has gold pieces down at the bottom of the crock. Take them and go. I'll not argue with you over gold, Quantrill, but in the name of God, leave my girls alone!" Pa was begging, his eyes filled with tears.

The man called Frank came staggering down the stairs, a jug of whiskey in one hand, bundles of blankets under his arms. "Bill, this place has just about been picked clean. There's nothing much worth cartin' off up here 'less you take the feather beds. They're more trouble than they're worth. Here's a few blankets." He slung them down the stairs.

"Unless the boys in the barn have found more than I think they did, this place ain't got much, for all its size!" He looked around. "Well, it does have pretty women. That ain't all bad."

Quantrill seemed to be in a hurry. "Get down those cellar steps, Frank, and bring up that honey jar. Old man Griffin, if you're lying, I'll put a bullet through that heart of yours."

While we waited, my little son took action. Wiggling out of my restraining hands, Matt walked over to Pa, climbed on his lap, and put his arms around his neck. He then looked Quantrill squarely in the eye. "You ugly," said Matt clearly. "You ugly."

The man called Cole laughed until he hiccuped. "Well, Bill, I've been thinking that myself, but I hadn't got around to mentioning it. Now that I think on it, you shore ain't gonna be winning no beauty prize!" He laughed again, took a deep swig of whiskey, and passed the jug over to Quantrill. "Here, Bill, comfort yourself. Maybe whiskey will help cure your ugliness!"

Quantrill grabbed the honey crock, pouring its contents out on top of Eliza's clean kitchen table. Sure enough, five gold pieces were stuck to the sweet amber honeycombs. "Wash them off, woman," he ordered Neely.

"Don't you think we might ought to ride on, Bill?" asked the one called Cole. "It's apt to get dark on us long before we make camp. And I've got a strong hankering to ride out of here, women or no women."

"Well, I still ain't satisfied. The gold don't come out right. Five pieces for six men don't compute. Tell you what. We'll draw lots. Odd man out don't get no gold piece, but he gets to pick himself a woman to have fun with. Come on boys, we'll draw straws."

He grabbed the broom from the corner, broke off six straws, and palmed them in his filthy hands. Grinning, the men drew straws, their greedy faces leering at us where we huddled by the fireplace. All five drew short straws.

"Well, you lucky men get the gold."

"How'd that happen, Bill? I want to see your straw." Cole was not convinced.

With a triumphant snort of laughter, Quantrill produced the last straw — a short one. "I made sure I'd get a girl. You fellows seemed happy enough with your gold up until a minute ago. No woman is worth a gold piece this big, anyhow. Happens I'm feeling like a little sport tonight." He reached over and grabbed my wrist.

"You boys go on out and mount up, all except Cole. Cole, you take the women out in the other room. Keep your gun on them. We'll let the old man stay and watch. The kid, too, since he's got a ringside seat."

One of the others grinned, "Well, Bill, since you're going to have an audience, how about letting me watch? I figure I might learn a thing or two if I could see you in action!"

Pa interrupted, his voice a cry of despair. "Wait, man, there's more gold on this place. I'll give you all of it, I'll tell you where it all is, only turn loose of my daughter. Let her go free, and you can have a small fortune!"

Quantrill paused. "You lie. How can you guarantee me, old man?"

"You let the women go free, and the baby boy. Keep me here as a hostage. If you don't find gold where I tell you it is, you can kill me."

Quantrill laughed. "Good try, Griffin. Your life for theirs. But suppose I let them go, and there's no gold. I've lost out on some sweet loving, and all I'll get is the pleasure of killing you. As it is, I can kill you anytime I want to. And I'm by no means convinced you've got any more gold."

Finally, I found my voice. "Let's try it the other way. Let Pa go free, and my baby, and the other women. Let them walk out the door and go free. You can take me then. You've got a sure thing."

"By God, girl, you've got a head on your shoulders!" Quantrill's eyes glowed like black coals. "Untie the old man, boys, and march this bunch of women out the door with him. Make tracks, all of you! This offer's got possibilities!"

Pa's cry was anguished. "Sarah, don't do this! He's going to kill us anyway. Don't die in dishonor! You other women leave, and take the baby! Do as I say! *Leave*!!"

They were marched out the door, crying and pleading — Aunt Gert carrying Matt, the guns of the Bushwhackers prodding them forward.

The man called Cole came back inside the kitchen. "Bill, whatever you're going to do, do it and let's ride. Time's wasting here, and we're liable to find a Yankee patrol riding up on our backside if we fool around here much longer."

Quantrill eyed me critically. "I believe you'll have to keep till I come back, girlie. Right now, maybe it's smart to ride on. But you owe me one. At that, you might be worth a gold piece. But I hate it when I get cheated of too much fun. It makes me mad."

Coldly, deliberately, with all the hate in this world focused in his eyes, Quantrill walked to the door, turned, took his pistol, and shot my father through the heart. Still tied to the chair, Pa's body fell at my feet as Quantrill's gang galloped off down the Wire Road.

Chapter 18

A FREEZING DRIZZLE FELL on us while we buried Pa. We lowered him into the ground in a coffin Zeke made from the boards of our old blown-up smokehouse. We blanketed his grave with the dark red and gold leaves of maple and sumac. I read the service from Pa's Bible, and we all prayed. But the cold, hard pain in my heart did not ease. We walked back from the churchyard in a silence broken by Eliza's sobs, only to find a Union patrol searching Griffin Tavern.

Outrage gave me a voice. "What on earth are you doing?" I screamed.

"Which one of you is the owner of this house?" The questioner wore the insignia of a sergeant in the Union army.

Eliza's shoulders shook in another spasm of weeping. She gestured in my direction.

"It belonged to my pa. He was killed yesterday by Bushwhackers. We just finished laying him in the ground. So I guess we own it." I went over to Eliza and put my arm around her waist as I again asked the question. "What are you doing here now? Why weren't you all here yesterday when you could have done us some good? My pa is dead and now your men are searching our house! Explain yourselves!" By this time I was shaking with fury.

"We're following orders, ma'am. It is my duty to read to you General McNeil's orders concerning Bushwhackers and the telegraph":

BUSHWHACKERS BEWARE!
Headquarters Dept. of the Frontier

The organized forces of the enemy having been driven out of the country in our rear, and there being none on our lines of Telegraphic and Mail Communications, except that common foe of mankind — the guerrilla and Bushwhacker — and the cutting of telegraph wires being now the act of these men alone — men who have no claim to be treated as soldiers, and are entitled to none of the rights accorded by the laws of war to honorable belligerents — it is hereby ordered that, hereafter, in every instance, the cutting of the telegraph wire shall be considered the deed of Bushwhackers, and for every such act some Bushwhacking prisoner shall have withdrawn from him that mercy which induced the holding of him as a prisoner, and he shall be hung at the post where the wire is cut, and as many Bushwhackers shall be so hung as there are places where the wire is cut.

The nearest house to the place where the wire is cut, if the property of a disloyal man, and within ten miles, shall be burned.

By Command of
Brig. Gen. John McNeil

Pausing, the sergeant cleared his throat, then, gathering his resolve, he continued. "Ma'am, it is my duty to burn this house. The telegraph wire was cut yesterday, one mile up the road from here. This is the nearest house. We've already hung a Bushwhacker on the telegraph pole where the wire was cut, and it's time now to carry out the rest of the general's orders."

Becky found her voice at last. "But Mr. Griffin was a Union man! Everybody knows he was a Union man! That order doesn't say to burn the nearest house! It says to burn the property of the nearest disloyal man! Everybody who knew Mr. Griffin can testify that he was loyal!"

The sergeant's voice was firm. "We don't see it that way. And neither will our colonel, ma'am. We've found four Confederate uniforms hid in an old trunk in your storeroom. I count four white women here, and I count four Confederate uniforms over there. I don't know where you've got your men hid, but I do know a Reb uniform when I see one. I'll give you ladies ten minutes to get your things out of the house. And at that, I'm giving you extra time, because you've got a little boy there. Whatever you can carry out in ten minutes, you can keep. What's left will be burnt."

He took out his pocket watch. I handed little Matt over to Aunt Gert's trembling arms, and we all raced in the house to grab what could be saved.

As the sergeant lit his first torch, I made one more appeal. "You're making a terrible mistake! My pa was Union to the core. He was killed yesterday by Rebel Bushwhackers! Don't you understand what we're telling you?"

"I understand orders, ma'am. And I carry them out. Even when it's not easy. If you was to walk down that road a mile and take a look at that poor Reb prisoner now dangling by his neck on yon telegraph pole, you'd understand carrying out orders ain't always easy. Nor pretty, neither. That Reb boy wasn't any happier over being hung than you are about having your house burnt. Better stand back, ma'am. I'm through talking!"

Within minutes, flames were shooting through the roof of the solid home that had been our rock of Gibraltar. The soldiers rode back up the road to report to their colonel, leaving us to sit on the ground and watch the final flames grow dim. It was Zeke who focused our grieving thoughts back to more immediate concerns.

"Where we gonna haul dis stuff we save, Miss Liza? And what we gonna haul it wid? We ain't got no horse left. Best we git movin'."

Aunt Gert answered him. "The answer is plain. We'll move it to my house. What's mine is yours, Eliza. What's not so plain is how we're going to get it there."

We all turned to Eliza, but she sat still as a statue, the tears still running down her face. I answered Zeke.

"We'll go out to the barn, Zeke, and get Pa's cart. And his buggy, too. At least they're still there. We'll load them up and pull them ourselves."

Neely looked at me with appreciation. "Dat my girl. It ain't gonna be easy, but it ain't gonna be as bad as doing widout."

We loaded the cart and the buggy and harnessed ourselves between the shafts. Zeke and Neely took the cart. Becky and I hauled the buggy while Eliza pushed. Aunt Gert walked slowly, holding Matt by one hand, leading the cow with the other. One backbreaking step at a time, we hauled our possessions over the two miles of wagon road to Aunt Gert's house.

That night before I went to sleep, I thought it through. My pa had been the one person on this earth that I could unfailingly count on to be on my side, through thick and thin, through right or wrong, whether I pleased him or whether I pained him. I had been as sure of his love and protection as I had been sure of the sun's rising. Now I was on my own with a child of my own. Even as I lay in the shelter of Gert's house, Larkin might be lying on the cold ground, a fugitive from the Confederate army. Or he might be in some raging battle. Or he might be dead. Even given the best of circumstances, if he was still alive and lucky enough to get back to see us, any visit would be but a brief stop on his way to rejoin his Union regiment. I lay awake, the raw welts rubbed by the buggy harness throbbing through my chest and shoulders.

"Any way you slice it," I thought, "I'm on my own, and it's up to me to look after myself and little Matt as best I can. Women in these mountains now are at the mercy of God and man. It's clear I can't fathom the mind of God, but it's time for me to stop expecting any mercies from men. What's left prowling around these mountains are less men than beasts." I thought of Quantrill and his vile face, and I was filled with such fear and hatred that I lay shaking, too tired to sleep, too angry to pray.

From her bed across the room, Aunt Gert spoke to me. "I'm going to get up and fix you a hot draught to put you to sleep, Sarah. You've nearly reached your limit. Poor child."

She stirred up the fire and soon returned with a steaming hot cup of a bitter brew. "Drink it, honey. You need to sleep. There'll be plenty of time to plan and worry when it's daylight. You're too dazed, too tired, and too heartsick to do any clear thinking now. Save that for when your mind is clear."

I drank her brew and sank gratefully into blessed release. We were all improved by a good night's sleep. Breakfast was hearty, and we had plenty. We ate mush with milk and thick, sweet sorghum molasses. The world looked somewhat more bearable in the bright sunshine than it had during the dark of night. I faced them all and told them what was on my mind.

"I'm going to take Matt and go to Kansas City to stay with my Uncle Auguste until this war is over. I'll not leave for a few days, until you all get settled in, but I need to get going soon. It's nearly November now. I need to leave before winter." I waited for their arguments.

Eliza spoke first. "Sarah, I feel like you're my own child, and I don't think you ought to go. In the first place, I doubt that you can get there. There'll be soldiers on the roads and Jayhawkers, and Bushwhackers. What's likely is they'll kill you or else they'll rape you so you wished you were dead, and baby Matt will have nobody. I'm not so much thinking of myself — God knows I'm not, though I don't know what I'll do without you — I'm thinking of you and the baby. I know you wouldn't go if your pa was alive."

"I'm in more danger here, Eliza. That Quantrill will be back. Even though he'll find Griffin Tavern burned, he's smart enough to figure out that we're likely to be close by. He'll be back for sure, and who knows how many others just as bad. I don't think these outlaws will rape you and Aunt Gert, and they won't hang Zeke or rape Neely, for they don't put them in the same category as white men and women. But Becky and I are in peril." I turned to Becky. "Will you go with me?"

She came over and put both arms around me. "Sarah, I love you like a sister, but I can't go with you. Willie could never visit me or even get letters to me if I moved up into Union territory. The Union army controls all the northern part of Missouri. I can't separate myself from the chance of seeing Willie. But if I were in your place, I'd try to go. I don't blame you for trying, Sarah, but I'm afraid you'll never get there."

Eliza spoke again. "You're welcome to live with us, Becky. It would be our joy to have you here."

"I'll be better off over with Willie's parents," Becky responded. "I know Mr. Griffin already has too many women on his hands, but I think Willie will feel better if that's where I am. Though I don't know how I'm going to get there."

"You'll walk, girl, how else!" Aunt Gert's patience, never great, had worn thin. "Being on your own is not necessarily fatal! I've lived alone and lived to talk about it. Let's stop this worrying and whining right now and start planning on how best to get on with what we've got to do. If a bunch of men sat around whimpering and whining, we wouldn't think much of them. Appears to me we're each called on to play a man's part." A rare smile lit up her face. "Sarah, I can get along without you, but I sure don't see how I'm going to be able to part with baby Matt!"

"Here's what I'm planning," I said. "You won't have to part with Matt for a few days yet. You all need a mule, and I expect Monnie and Ned have managed to hang on to our livestock. I'm going to walk over the mountain — it's only six miles; I can make it in one day if I leave the baby here with you. I'll stay there a day, get things in order as best I can, saddle a mule, and come back the third day. I thought I'd start tomorrow."

"I'll go, too," Becky said. "That's a wild road, and I'm a good shot. I couldn't face Larkin if I let you go off by yourself and get yourself killed by a panther. I'm going, too, and that's all there is to it."

We started out at daybreak the next morning, anxious to get moving while the good weather held. I strapped Matthew Flint's pistol around my waist. Becky slung Pa's rifle over her slender shoulders. We moved along the road at a brisk pace. Gradually, our hearts grew happier.

The glorious fall colors of the Ozarks blazed around us, the reds and golds and deep russet leaves blending their radiance under the bright blue of the late October sky. Squirrels skittered around our feet, improvidently scattering their acorns in all directions. Overhead, we saw the graceful vee of wild ducks heading south toward their winter feeding ponds. With the shed needles of pine spreading a golden carpet for our feet and the brisk breeze singing steadily through the trees, the world seemed once again to have hope and joy enough to balance the pain. We walked undisturbed until we topped the mountain that overlooked the Flint compound.

A woman was walking up the steep road, moving with the loose stride of one born in the hills. We sat down on one of the massive boulders by the side of the wagon trail and waited.

She was not much older than we were, a tall, rawboned girl. Colorless eyelashes framed her washed-out blue eyes. She stopped to visit with us in the time-honored way of hill people. "You girls lookin' fer work?"

Her question surprised us both.

"Work?" said Becky.

The girl grinned, her mouth widening in a sly acceptance of our response. "Maybe you'ens don't call it work, but that's whut it is. You'ens try takin' on five or six Reb soldiers in one night, and you'ens will find out whut I mean. Spreadin' yore laigs that many times can plumb tucker a gal out."

Her critical look assessed us both. "You'ens shore yore up to this? You ain't virgins, air you? Where do you gals come from?"

I answered her. "We're from Griffin Flat. Who are you?"

"Name's Ocie Casey. Born two miles down that road in Booger Holler. Lived in these hills all my life, but I'm aiming to move. Whut I'm doing right now is I'm on my way to see my ma afore I go."

"Why are you moving?" I was still trying to get my bearings.

"These dang Rebs ain't got no real money. All they got is Confederate scrip. It's worthless. Cain't even trade it fer nuthin'. One uv t'other gals tells me the Feds air over to Fayetteville, and them boys pay in shore 'nuff money. I'm aimin' to head that way soon as I see my ma one more time. So you'ens can move into my tent. It ain't much, but you ain't gonna be too lonesome. I got a good trade. Pity they ain't got real money."

"Where is your camp?" Becky had finally found a chance to get a word in edgewise.

The girl grinned again, a sly leer that transformed her face from plain to lewd. "Jist about one foot away from the Flint family property line. That hard-headed hellion that's bossing all them Flint women won't let us camp girls set foot on Flint land. Here them Reb soldiers is camped all over the place and them fancy Reb officers are housed right there in the big house, and that mean-hearted woman took after me with a poker and swore she'd knock my head off iffen airy one of us girls spread our laigs on Flint land. Bossy hypocrite! Thinks she's so high and mighty. Hates the men, too. They say she hates every man in the Reb army since they shot her old man."

"They shot her man? Are you talking about Kate Flint? Has her husband been shot? Ross Ramsey?" Becky's eyes were wide with shock.

"You'ens know them? Who be you?"

"Our name's Flint, too. We're kin."

Ocie Casey's pale eyes reassessed us both. "I ort to have knowed it. You Flints all look alike. Course, it's the Flint boys I've mostly knowed." She grinned again. I was beginning to dread that sly grin. "And knowed 'em well. Guess I mainly knowed Lark the most. When you see Lark, tell him Ocie Casey ain't forgot him!"

With a flip of her dirty skirt, the girl stepped off the road and ducked like a rabbit into the briar patch, moving along the faint path that wove around the tangled grapevines of the underbrush.

I stood there stock-still, watching Ocie Casey's back as she dodged down the mountain path through the briar patch. Her words had hurt like barbed wire whipped across bare skin, and my brain was trying to deny what my heart knew to be real. "She must be lying," I argued aloud, "for surely the officers would not allow a bunch of harlots to follow the soldiers around from camp to camp. All the officers who fought at Griffin's Tavern were gentlemen. Every one of them — whether they were Northern or Southern. They wouldn't allow a bunch of filthy, nasty women to camp right alongside of soldiers." My skin crawled as I remembered the sly leer on the girl's face when she had mentioned Larkin.

Becky's voice was calm. "I don't think she's lying, but I don't think she's important. What worries me is Kate and her problems. If that nasty girl is telling the truth, and Ross has really been shot, how on earth did Kate learn of it, and where is Lark? Kate will be wild. Six children to look after, and Father and Minerva away in Fort Smith, and Sam's wife and Robert's wife on her hands, to say nothing of all their children, and to have the Confederate army camped in the house besides! She'll be wild. Let's walk fast, Sarah. I hate to find out what's ahead of us, but I can't stand not knowing. Surely, Sarah, after all the grief and troubles we've been through, you're not going to waste any more thoughts on a piece of trash like that Ocie Casey, nor on her kind. Let's walk faster. It's all downhill from now on. I wonder what really happened to Ross. If he's truly dead, Kate will be unforgiving. She's always been crazy about Ross."

We walked on in a silence broken only by the sad, muted cries of the birds and the persistent thin singing of the wind. A gray-blue mist hung over the mountains that loomed in forbidding layers in the distance, though the sun shone on the green-pined slopes immediately around us.

Memories and worries are not too different from mountains, I thought. They're vivid up close, dark barriers on the horizon. I looked up at the bright sky, shook off my doubts, and reached out to grab Becky's hand.

"Becky, it may still turn out better than we think. Someday we're going to look back on this and wonder if it really happened. When this war is over, we're all going to be happy again. I'm going to have to make up my mind to deal with trouble as it comes. It's time I stopped borrowing trouble. You're right, that filthy girl and her kind are the least of our problems."

We topped the ridge that overlooked the Flint compound. The tents of the Confederacy dotted the dried-brown acres of meadow and pasture like ripe white bolls of cotton on the stalks of a brown cotton patch. The sentry posted at the gate came forward to meet us, his curiosity showing openly on his face.

"State your names and your business."

"Rebecca Flint Griffin. This is Sarah Flint. This land belongs to my father, and we're here to join our sisters and their families. Are they still in the house? Where are the Flint women?" Becky's tone was civil, but her dark eyes flashed in a look so like Larkin's that I gasped.

We walked on through the gaggle of soldiers camped on the Flint pastureland, their shelters skimpy rectangles of cheap canvas slung over primitive poles. Already the men were preparing their suppers. The cast-iron skillets that rested on the coals of their campfires sizzled with fresh cut pork. Heavy iron stew pots swung over glowing coals. The hearty smell of corn bread wafted from Dutch ovens. My hungry stomach growled; my mouth watered. It had been over six months since we had taken good food for granted.

Becky's eyes flashed fire. "And while these scruffy men are eating up Flint hogs and stewing Flint beans and baking Flint corn bread, we have faced starvation over at Griffin's Tavern! How dare these motley men eat up all the food that Kate and Susan and Jane have spent the summer growing!"

She marched past the sentry soldier at the door of her father's home as though he had been a house slave, past the astonished Confederate officers lounging in her father's study, and on through the passageway to the big Flint kitchen. I followed on her heels.

There in the kitchen were the Flint women, their tired bodies bent over the hearth. With difficulty, Susan was straining to lift the heavy stew kettle from its hook above the huge fireplace. Jane, at her left, was carefully placing glowing coals on top of the Dutch oven, which was used to bake the biscuits. Kate was turning a dripping beef roast as it sputtered its fat on the coals of the right side of the hearth. All three looked exhausted.

"Where are the squaws?" Becky demanded. "Why aren't they in here doing the heavy lifting? Has that lazy bunch of officers stuck you girls with the job of waiting on them hand and foot?" At the sound of her voice, all three whirled around, and we were all caught up in the rushing words of reunion.

"That arrogant General Hindman has put both us and the squaws to waiting on him hand and foot. When they're not slaving for him, the squaws are waiting on that horrible Colonel Huntsman." Kate spoke as clearly as though the objects of her denunciation were not within hearing range. "All three squaws are kept busy washing and ironing and cleaning and slaving from dawn to dusk."

"Kate, what happened to Ross?" I asked the question urgently. "And what do you hear from Larkin?"

Kate's eyes turned dark and hard. "Those murdering devils had Ross shot. They claimed he was trying to escape. We don't know where Larkin is; he's not here in this camp, and we think he'd be with this army if he were still with the Confederates."

"How did you find out about Ross?"

Her tone was loud, and her ringing voice carried easily to the next room. "That black-hearted Colonel Huntsman had the eternal gall to write me a letter bragging about what he had done, claiming that Ross was shot as an example to what he called 'other potential deserters'! To think that he and his kind have the colossal nerve to camp out in Father's house and eat Father's food, while Father himself is in that vile Confederate prison in Fort Smith! It turns my stomach every time I let myself think of it!"

Susan spoke in a whisper. "They won't be underfoot many more weeks. They're planning another big battle before Christmas, hoping to run the Yankees completely out of Arkansas. They talk and brag all the time about how they're going to do it."

"Do you hear from Sam?" I asked the question anxiously.

"He's with General Van Dorn. Some place called Vicksburg. He writes he'll probably be there a while. Seems as though they're holed up for the winter. We don't know where the others are. None of us has had a letter from Robert nor Ridge nor Tom nor Stant since they came through here last month."

"I'm not going to stay here tonight," I decided out loud. "I'm going to walk on over to our place, Larkin's and mine. If you give me a piece of corn bread or a biscuit, I'll eat it as I walk. I'm anxious about Monnie and Ned."

"You don't have to walk, Sarah." Kate's tone was matter-of-fact. "We still have mules. The Confederates probably have plans to steal them when they leave, but for now they're ours. It's the one thing we've got they can't eat. But you'd better get going before dark. There's more danger in these woods than panthers anymore. In fact, I'd choose an honest panther over a lying Confederate any day!"

Susan flinched. I marveled at her patience with Kate. Then I felt a fresh rush of sympathy for us all. Willie and Sam with the South, the other Flint men with the North, and all of us trying to stay in the same family. I saddled a mule, kissed all the women good-bye, and rode with trepidation toward my own home.

Chapter 19

NED'S SHARP EYES spied me long before I saw him. He came running down the
road to open the gate, his freckled face
grinning from ear to ear. I held him off at
arm's length before I hugged him. "You're
growing out of your clothes! You're nearly
as big as a man, Ned! How's your mother? Are things going all right for you?"

"She's fine, and she's right behind me."

I turned to see a smile of pure joy lighting up Monnie's
leathery face. "Thank God, Miz Sarah, yore safe and sound.
How's baby Matt? Is he talking yet? Does he remember us?
Do you know where Mr. Lark is? Me and Ned visited with

the other Flint men when they was through here. Whut a pity that Mr. Lark stayed behind to hep out Ross Ramsey, whut with Ross gettin' hisself shot anyhow, pore man! How's yore folks?"

I started to cry as I told them, gulping and hiccupping like a child. Monnie put strong arms around my shaking shoulders.

"Child, there'll come a day when it won't hurt near so much. Do you recollect how it hurt when you birthed baby Matt? How the pain was so sharp you thought you was apt to die of it? But that pain don't hurt you none now, and the hurt from losin' yore pa will fade, too. One of these days you'll recollect all them good times, and the bad times will jist nearly fade out. Come on in and set by the fire whilst I feed you. It gits dark on us quick this time of year, and Ned and me will be takin' you for a walk after supper."

"What do you mean, taking me for a walk?"

"Ned and me done took to sleeping in a cave. We found ourselves the best big old hidey hole in these whole mountains. Safe as a church. Ain't nobody gonna look fer us there."

Ned chortled with laughter. "You know, Miz Sarah, how Mr. Larkin always said yore spring had such a cold breath? Well, the reason we feel cold air comin' out of that water is that there's a big cave back there behind it. I was out squirrel huntin' one day and fell in a big hole, and durn if it didn't turn out to be a tunnel into the biggest cave you ever seen in yore life.

"They's a little river, and a flat floor, and it's dry with high walls — heck, they's a place as big as a barn in there. We got bedrolls in the big cave, and enough grub hid to live on fer a while if we had to."

"Are things that bad, Monnie?"

"They've bin mighty hard fer the gals left behind, them as is enduring this war. Most menfolks either tuck off to fight, or tuck off to the hills. Them Bushwhackers have tuck to killing every man they find, old ones and younguns, too, and robbing the pore womenfolks out of house and home."

There was iron in her voice. "Them Bushwhackers are mean to women. Mighty mean. But Ned and me have managed to fool 'em so far. Every night, soon as we milk the cow and eat, we hide the stock in the woods, hobble 'em, take whut we need fer the night, and go sleep in the cave. Any Bushwhackers that sneaks around the house in the night ain't gonna find much here but cold corn bread and cold ashes! Things that I know you set a lot of store by have all been hid out in the big cave, things that wasn't too big to git through the tunnel on the front end."

When I walked through the front door of our house, I felt as comforted as if Larkin had put his arms around me. His presence was everywhere. Monnie had emptied the room except for the largest pieces — the bed, the big chest, the tables. But something new had been added: a huge panther skin was displayed along one wall, its length stretched out to formidable proportions.

"Tell me about the panther."

"When you and Mr. Lark didn't make it home from Mr. Flint's place last February, me and Ned started in to git worried. Soon as we finished the milking the next mornin', we climbed on the mule and rode out to look fer you all. 'Bout a mile down the road from here we came up on this here big panther growlin' and snarlin' and rippin' the innards out uv a man. Cuffin' him and pawin' him around like the beast would uv played with a rabbit. I shot the panther. After we got a good look at how the pore feller was sufferin', it turned out I had to shoot him too. I put the pore feller out of his misery. The panther had tore his guts out, but he was still moaning. It was that ol' Preacher Massey. Looked like from his tracks he had crawled his way along the road 'til the panther jumped him. We buried him there in the woods. Me and Ned tanned the panther hide. I ain't never seen one as big in these parts. It's purt near eight feet from nose to tip of tail. We kind uv thought Mr. Larkin might like seein' it."

That night in the cave I wrapped myself in a warm blanket and lay safely down to sleep on a comforting corn-shuck mattress. There on the cave's limestone floor, I prayed earnestly for us all. For the first time in many months, I felt peace flow through me like calming waters.

We had a hard day's work ahead of us the next morning. Ned went out to the barn and cleaned up the buggy, greasing the wheels, oiling the leather, and polishing the brass to a shine. I meant to undertake my journey in as much style as I could manage.

I took up a shovel and went out to the smokehouse. Two hams and a shoulder were already hanging there from a recent butchering, dripping their grease directly onto the loamy ground beneath. Two feet down I heard the sound I was listening for, the thud of my shovel hitting solid rock. I called to Monnie to come help me, and together we dug out the flat slab that Larkin had placed so carefully to mark the container beneath. Next we dug the dirt away from the vessel under the rock.

"Help me lift this out, Monnie," I said. "It's too heavy for me to do it by myself." Together we hefted the heavy stoneware crock out of the ground.

Monnie's jaw dropped open. "This here's one uv yore milk crocks from yore springhouse. This here's a half-gallon crock! Good God, woman, has that thing got gold in it?"

I took a knife and scraped away the wax that sealed the close-fitting lid of the crock, then carefully lifted the lid to reveal the gold coins, our treasure that Larkin had so carefully hidden.

"Miz Sarah, why air you showing this to me? This here is big treasure. You could uv dug this up by yurself. Why air you lettin' me know this?"

"Because we're going to carry it to the cave and we're both going to know where it's hid. That cave's safer than this smokehouse. I saw what the cannonballs did when they hit my pa's smokehouse. When they tore it up they tore up the ground, too. Hurry. Let's get moving."

I took a leather pouch out of my pocket and filled it with the heavy coins. We carried the remainder to the cave and hid the crock carefully behind one of the many glittering stalactites flanking the high limestone walls. As we walked back to the cabin, I handed five gold coins to Monnie.

"These are yours — $100 gold pieces. They are for you and Ned. There's not a bank in Arkansas now, and there's not apt to be one you can trust for many a year yet. Hide these gold pieces as best you can, and use them as you see fit. I'm depending on you and Ned to keep this place up in good shape for Mr. Larkin and me. It may be a long time before either one of us gets back. If Mr. Larkin has a chance to get back here before I do, take him out to the cave and show him where we hid that crock.

"Don't tell Ned. Bushwhackers are liable to torture men and boys, but I don't believe they torture women. They rape women, but I've not heard any talk of torture. I'm trying to take what precautions I can for you and Ned.

"It may be years before this war is over. And the way Ned keeps growing bigger, he'll be forced into joining up with the army before too long. You'd be welcome to move over with the Flint women if Ned joins up."

Monnie's tone was final, "I ain't moving nowhere." Abruptly, Monnie changed the subject.

"We got some thinking to do today afore you hit that long road tomorrow. Miz Sarah, you air too purty to start out by yurself, and that's the long and the short of it."

"Well, I'm planning on a few changes. I thought I'd sew these gold pieces into a pillow and pad up my stomach so as to look like I'm about six months along. I don't think anybody, even a Bushwhacker, is going to go poking a pregnant woman in the stomach!"

Monnie's face was thoughtful. "That ain't enough. We got to make you look ugly, and that ain't gonna be easy. Whilst you sew up that there pillow, I'll pack up grub fer yore trip. And I'll think on how to ugly you up."

In the middle of the day we sat down to a mouth-watering feast. Monnie had fried ham and baked hot biscuits. I ate like a pig, savoring every bite.

"Monnie," I said, "this is the first bite of biscuits I've tasted in months. We didn't even try to grow wheat this year, and we ate up all of Aunt Gert's flour last summer."

She smiled. "Bet you ain't had ham in a while, neither. I'm packing up a sack of flour and a ham, and a side of meat fer you to be takin' to yore stepmother."

That afternoon I made ready for my journey, sewing Uncle Auguste's beautiful cameo into the pillow along with the coins, packing up clothes for my little boy and me, trying to meet our needs with compact bundles that could serve us on the long and complicated journey from the danger-filled mountains of Arkansas to the comparative safety of Westport.

Monnie interrupted me. "Miz Sarah, I done got it figgered out! I'm gonna ugly you up so that yore own kin won't hardly know you! And there ain't gonna be no horny outlaw botherin' you, on account of I'm gonna make folks hate to look at you! Sit down, and jist put yurself in my hands!"

She convinced me. I sat down at the kitchen table while she applied her cosmetics. She covered half my face with the dark red semi-permanent stain of pokeberry juice, running it in a jagged line from my forehead down across my nose, my mouth, and my neck. Next, she took Larkin's goosequill pen and carefully outlined with ink-dark lines the edges of the blotched red of the dye, creating lines and delicate etchings in ragged patterns on the soft canvas of my skin. Next, she produced a beeswax candle, its color exactly matching the wine-colored stain of the pokeberry juice. From the soft dripping of the melted wax she created ridges and puckers on my skin, outlining in bas-relief the demarcation of my discolored pigment.

When Monnie's work was finally finished and she triumphantly handed me the mirror, I gasped in horror.

"I've never seen anybody so disfigured! I'm going to scare my own baby! People will flinch every time they look at my face! I look like I've been burned and scalded!"

"You got that right," Monnie chortled. "If a man's gonna hate to have to look at you, I'm doubting he's gonna be all that interested in rapin' you. An' you lookin' pregnant besides.

"It won't stay this way fer too long," Monnie continued. "It'll wear off in a few weeks. And you'll have to put new wax on mighty near every day. Best you stay away from the fireplace, too. That wax job'll melt iffen you get too close to the heat. But I think you'll fool many a man. Ugly women ain't too apt to grab their fancy! And iffen I do say so myself, Miz Sarah, you're about to find out how it feels to be bone ugly!"

"Even that devil Quantrill wouldn't look at me now," I exclaimed.

"You don't have to worry none about Quantrill fer a while, nohow, Miz Sarah." It was Ned who spoke. "Folks over at the Flint place say he done took off and went to Virginia."

"How would they know?"

"Him and his men report to Colonel Shelby, and Colonel Shelby's head-quartered in Mr. Sam Flint's house. I go over and do what I can fer the Flint women, and they hear all the news. Some of them officers brag and gab whilst they eat. They say Colonel Shelby's a smart, close-mouthed one, but that mean Colonel Huntsman brags up a storm."

"Why on earth would that Quantrill have any business going to the Confederate capital?"

"They say he's jealous. Shelby got a promotion to colonel. Now Quantrill wants a promotion too. Shelby wouldn't recommend him, so Quantrill cleaned hisself up and took off to plead his own case. So he ain't gonna be nowhere near you. You may see Colonel Huntsman, though."

Monnie agreed. "Pore Miz Kate is near to bustin', she hates Huntsman so, and here she has to cook for that ol' booger man every day. I surprised she hasn't poisoned him by now."

Ned continued, "Quantrill left his men behind, but they're mostly gone in the daytime, or too drunk to be payin' much attention. I sneaked over to their camp early this morning and brought back a good horse fer you to use. Figgered you was entitled to one, beings as how they stole yore Dolly. Picked out a good one, too. They've stole so many they're careless. Hobbled 'em and left 'em in plain sight. When you leave here you can drive out in style."

He grinned again. "Miz Sarah, you may leave here an ugly woman, but you'll shore be a stylish ugly woman!"

We laughed until we hurt, all three of us, the laughter healing like good medicine. That night in the cave I again slept in peace and hope, and when I bid them good-bye the next morning I left full of confidence that Larkin and I would return to find our home in their good hands.

If I had needed anymore proof of the effectiveness of Monnie's handiwork, Becky's appalled look the next morning was evidence enough. I marched into the Flint house preceded by the uneasy young sentry who had challenged me at the door. Once inside, I insisted on being ushered into the presence of the commanding officer. As it happened, the senior officers were assembled for breakfast in the big Flint keeping room — General Hindman, General Marmaduke, Colonel Huntsman, and Colonel Shelby.

The sentry announced my arrival just as Becky came hurrying in from the kitchen with a big platter of biscuits.

"Beg pardon, sir; begging your pardon, General Hindman, but this lady insists she has to speak with you."

The general turned impatiently in my direction, bold eyes flashing with annoyance.

Becky took one look at my disfigured skin and bulging stomach and dropped the biscuit platter, scattering biscuits and broken crockery over half the room. The general's mood quickly shifted from annoyance to anger.

"Corporal, have you no judgment? What do you mean, letting this civilian interrupt my breakfast? Madam, state your business and be quick about it!" His penetrating gaze surveyed my ravaged face and made no attempt to conceal his repugnance. "What is the nature of your business, madam? Be brief!"

"I request a safe conduct pass through Confederate lines to Little Rock. I can no longer count on the benevolence of male protection in this part of the state, and I desperately need to relocate to Little Rock to join other family members." I lowered my eyes modestly toward my bulging belly. "I need to start as soon as possible. My buggy is packed and waiting outside. My only request is that of a pass of safe conduct."

"Madam, if you are a true daughter of the South, why should a pass through Confederate lines be necessary? I assure you, my army intends no harm to the women of the South." His tone was cold, his eyes impatient.

I answered him in honest anger. "General, six days ago your men murdered my father in cold blood in his own home, stole my horse, took our food, and threatened me and my female relatives with death and dishonor."

"You lie, madam." His tone dismissed my testimony.

"General, do you have a Captain Quantrill who rides under your command? And does he have men named Frank and Arlie and Cole and Newtie who ride with him? General Hindman, I have a father in his grave and a home burnt down to its foundation because of the actions of men under your command. As God is my witness, a safe conduct pass is little enough to ask in return!" My voice shook in anger. I fixed my eyes on his, and he was the first to blink.

"Hand me pen and paper, Shelby." The general scribbled the pass as Becky returned with fresh biscuits. Through the doorway I could see the amazed faces of my other sisters-in-law. As I took the pass and turned to leave the room, another officer arose from the table.

"Colonel Jo Shelby, ma'am. I believe I can offer you something beyond the safe conduct pass." His looked with compassion on my ugly scars. "I can offer you the safety of a military escort for at least a portion of the way." He turned to General Hindman and addressed him formally. "With your permission, sir. Quantrill, as you know, is under my command. In my judgment, an escort is the least we can do in the way of reparations."

General Marmaduke spoke for the first time. "That will not be necessary, Shelby. In two days' time a portion of my forces will be headed in that general direction. Madam, I can offer you the safe conduct assurance of a considerable force of men, plus my word that your complete privacy will be assured during the journey. Corporal, call my aide and see that the appropriate arrangements are made."

Tears came to my eyes. "Sir, I do truly thank you. And you, Colonel Shelby." I bowed and followed the corporal out of the room.

Through it all, Colonel Huntsman continued his greedy attack on his plate of breakfast ham and eggs, as little interested in my needs as he would have been in the misery of a mouse in a trap. I lowered my eyes to conceal the hate I felt in his loathsome presence.

With the competent assistance of General Marmaduke's young aide, my travel plans were soon decided. I explained my need to pick up baby Matt, so it was arranged that I would leave immediately, preceding the Confederate forces down the pike, pick up my child, and rendezvous with

General Marmaduke's cavalry at Griffin's Mill, two days hence. Thereafter, my buggy would be a part of their caravan, proceeding with the
troops on their week-long journey to Little Rock.

Once these logistics were agreed upon, it was not my intent to linger.
Within minutes, Becky had said her good-byes to Kate and her sisters-in-law and climbed onto the buggy seat beside me. Kate tethered one
of her young mules behind the buggy.

Becky was full of news. "Sarah, Kate says the Confederates are planning a big winter offensive. She spends all her waking hours working and
listening. She says that Union forces now hold Memphis, Tennessee, and
Helena, on the Arkansas side of the Mississippi River. Kate says half the
men camped around our home don't have guns; the rest have only got
shotguns."

"Kate would make a good spy." I thought of the hate and the zeal in her
eyes, and I had no trouble imagining Kate as an official scout.

"She'd be working as a scout right now if she didn't have those six little
children to raise. She wants us to get word to the Federal generals about
what Hindman is planning."

"And what would that be?"

"He's trying to retake the valley of the Arkansas. They need our part of
the state to feed the rest of the state, and the army as well. The other offi-
cers call Hindman's plan his 'darling project.' He wants to rule over all of
Arkansas. They say he's not all that different from that big fat General
Price, who wants to rule over all of Missouri. They're both politicians.
Kate says Colonel Shelby and General Marmaduke want to win for the
Confederacy, but that horrible Colonel Huntsman is in it for himself — all
he wants is gain and glory!"

"So what is Kate pushing us to do?" I had a feeling that more was coming.

"Sarah, you're going to be in Little Rock, and sooner or later on your
way to Kansas City, you're going to get to Helena. The Union occupies
Helena. Kate hopes you can send a telegram to General Blunt or to General Herron so they'll know what Hindman is planning. Hindman needs
northwest Arkansas. They say there's wheat, corn, potatoes, apples, hogs,
and five flour mills — enough to feed Hindman's Confederate forces all
winter. A big fight's coming before the real bad weather sets in. Kate says
it'll be over around Fayetteville, somewhere."

"I'll do my best to get word to somebody important on the Union side."

I gritted my teeth, exactly like Pa. "And I hope with all my heart that some good Union man will manage to kill Quantrill!"

Chapter 20

It was a ten-day march for General Marmaduke's forces from northwest Arkansas down to the river, and an easy ten-day buggy ride for baby Matt and me. A bright sun tempered the keen air, warming the grand old mountains and lightening my spirits. Each night my tent was pitched at a discreet distance from those of General Marmaduke and his staff. Each morning and evening an orderly brought food to Matt and me from the officers' mess. With meticulous courtesy, the general had invited me to dine at his table, but I had thought it wise to decline.

Matt thrived on the journey, and so did I. There were no cows to milk, hogs to slop, stock to feed, wash to do, or fields to work. Other hands cooked the food, fed and watered my horse, pitched my tent, made my fire, and fetched my water. Matt and I rode in our buggy by day and slept in our tent at night, effectively isolated from the men while still enjoying the privilege of their protection. Of the many who served our needs, not one man could bring himself to look directly on my disfigured face and swollen belly. I became accustomed to averted eyes and uncomfortable silences when necessity forced our routine interactions. For me, the journey became a time for rest and renewal. For baby Matt, it was a time of pure delight. The reticence the men felt in my presence was not extended to my little son. Evening after evening, he was the center of attention as the men sat around their campfires, smoking, remembering, singing, and storytelling. The same men who were made shy and uncomfortable around me were warmed and delighted by Matt, and they vied for the chance to hold him on their knees or carry him on their shoulders.

The campfire is to men on the march what the evening hearthside is to a family at home, a place for rest and sociability. Though the night air was cold and keen, I disciplined myself to stay a long way from the comforting warmth of those glowing fires. The wax of my facial disguise could never have survived such proximity. So while I stayed in my tent and shivered in my close-wrapped shawl, Matt was carried around from campfire to campfire, a lively little reminder to those rugged men of the children they had left behind.

We reached Lewisburg Landing on the Arkansas River on November 15, 1862. There General Marmaduke and I took formal leave of each other.

"Sir, please accept my heartfelt appreciation for your courtesy, and please express my appreciation to your men for their kindness to my child." I meant every word sincerely. I had managed to travel the most dangerous portion of my long journey, the rugged no-man's-land of the Boston Mountains, with the Confederate army itself as my security. Even more surprisingly, I no longer considered those courteous and decent men to be the enemy.

The general bowed. "Madam, I did my duty. I would advise you to retain the safe conduct pass you received from General Hindman. As you and your little son continue your journey, it may yet prove to be of some use to you. I wish you Godspeed." He paused. "I admire courage and enterprise, madam, whether in men or women. Good-bye, Mrs. Flint. I wish you well."

I stood there on the banks of the wide river and considered the next leg of my journey.

Directly south and across the broad Arkansas River lay the flat, rich riverbottom land I had inherited. The city of Little Rock was 50 miles away to the east. At my back, to the north, stretched the high bulk of the Ozark Mountains, and to the south in the hazy distance one lone mountain rose abruptly above the plain, its forbidding bluffs looming in perpendicular majesty. The road ended at the river bank. As I watched, a ferryboat pulled up to the landing. As I drove my buggy down to meet the boat, a strong sense of my ancestry swept over me.

I addressed the ferry owner with considerable confidence.

"I'm looking for the Chouteau plantation. Can your boat take me there?"

His shrewd eyes appraised me. "Ma'am, when you cross the river, yore there. As far as you can see, up and down the river, the land on yonder far bank belonged to Chouteau. That there by the mountain, too. It's all titled to Chouteau."

"But I don't see any buildings across the river. Does anyone live near the landing?" I was puzzled. Cousin Ed had assured me that he was living on the plantation.

"There's buildings there, way over at the base of yon mountain. Them Frenchmen was stingy. Didn't want to waste good cotton land on dwelling space. Their overseer's house is on that first hilly rise at the base of yon mountain." He pointed. "Are you wantin' to be ferried across? If so, let's go."

I looked at him doubtfully. "Are there no bridges?"

"There sure are, ma'am. They's a bridge down at Little Rock and they's a bridge on west, upriver a hundred miles at Van Buren." He held out his hand. "That'll be ten dollars, ma'am. In gold. I won't charge you any extra for hauling yore horse and buggy."

Once aboard, I looked more critically at the ferry. "This is a mighty big flatboat to be hauling just one buggy. Looks like it was built for a larger load."

"Yore right, ma'am. This here's a stern-wheeler, built to carry cotton. It's a 50-bale carrier. A fine boat. I've hauled many a bale on it, down this river and on down the Mississippi."

"Then why aren't you still using it to haul cotton?"

The old face grew grim. "Ain't no cotton to be hauled, ma'am. Well, that ain't quite the way of it. There's cotton, all right, most of it hid out so General Hindman can't find it and burn it, but the folks that own the cotton don't have no place to sell it. Can't get it to market. It's against the law to sell cotton to the Union — a man can get throwed in jail for doin' business with Yankees — and there's nobody left with any money to buy cotton here in this part of the South. Flatboats can't get past the Yankees if they go south to New Orleans, and the same if they try going north to Memphis. We can float down the Arkansas River to the Mississippi, but it don't do no good. General Hindman's got a fort built there. Them Rebel soldiers got orders to burn every bale they can get their hands on." He paused, then continued. "My name is Hern. You might say I'm a neighbor. If you need a boat again, I might could hep you out." He tipped his sweat-stained hat. "Good day to you, ma'am. Right down that road a mile. First house you come to, after you pass the slave cabins."

Barking dogs announced our arrival. My Cousin Ed handed me out of the buggy with astonishment written plainly on his fine-boned Scottish face. Cousin Alta, following close on his heels, asked the questions that delicacy forbade a gentleman to ask. "Sarah, why are you traveling at such a time? And what on earth happened to your face? I'm surprised your pa and Eliza would even think about letting you ride so far in your condition!"

Cousin Ed's worried eyes surveyed me. "Child, come in and tell us about it. Come in and sit by the fire. Come in and let us share your troubles. Nothing but terrible times would bring you so far."

Cousin Alta's tears flowed and Cousin Ed's eyes flashed fire as I told them of Pa's dying and of the burning of Griffin Tavern.

"There's gumption in you, girl, and a good head on those slim shoulders. I wouldn't have believed one girl and a baby could have made it safely through those devil-infested mountains." Cousin Ed's hands shook in agitation. "And I find it hard to believe that you can make it safely from here on to Kansas City. But it may be that what's ahead is likely to be easier than what's behind you. How can we help you? How do you mean to go on from here? And why did you decide to take this long, roundabout way to get to Kansas City? You've chosen to go south, east, north, and west, instead of going northwest."

"I figure it's the only way the baby and I have any chance at all," I replied. "The mountains in northwest Arkansas and southwest Missouri are crawling with outlaws — scum in human form. When we're moving with the army, we'll have the protection of law and order. Whether Union army or Confederate, it makes not too much difference. There's more danger in those woods from Bushwhackers and Jayhawkers than there ever was from bears and panthers."

"What are your plans, Sarah?" Cousin Ed's tone was calm, but his wrinkled old face was alive with interest.

"I've got General Hindman's safe conduct pass. That should take me on east of here, through Little Rock and as far as Helena, on the Mississippi. Once I get there I won't need his pass, for Helena is held by the Union. Then I can board a steamboat and go north to St. Louis, then west by stagecoach or steamboat to Kansas City. After Helena, I'll be in Union territory the entire way."

Cousin Alta smiled. "Sarah, it happens I can find a few pokeberries around here. Looks to me like that face of yours is going to need a fresh batch of red dye before you start out again. How your pa would laugh if he could have seen you outfoxing that mean old General Hindman! If you fooled him, you can probably fool the others. Hindman's the most feared man in Arkansas right now. Everybody's afraid of him, and lots of people hate him, including some of his own men."

"Alta's right," responded Cousin Ed. "People here in Arkansas have suffered about as much under Hindman as they would ever have had to suffer at the hands of any conquering enemy. Since he took over as commander of the Trans-Mississippi District, we've had a terrible time of terror here. Hindman's burned all the cotton he can find. He has thrown decent men in jail for trying to argue with him to save their own barns from being burnt. As a schoolteacher, what I hold against him the most is what he's done to free speech. If a man speaks out against Confederate policies, he's apt to find himself looking out through jail bars. He's trying to shut down the *Arkansas Gazette*, the one newspaper that dares to report his doings. So far, though, the *Gazette's* still being published. "

"I'm hungry for news," I responded. "We haven't gotten a newspaper in Griffin Flat for months now, nor much mail, either. The first thing I mean to do when I get to Helena is to ask the Union commander there to let me telegraph Uncle Auguste. I figure he can find out where Larkin is. If Larkin managed to get back to his old regiment, he wouldn't have any way of getting word to me so long as I stayed in Griffin Flat. I've got to make it to Union territory to have any contact with Larkin."

Cousin Ed's look was appraising. "Sarah, you're a smart woman, and a strong one. I wonder if the Lord will forgive me for the proposition I'm about to put to you.

"I can see a way of getting your cotton to market. You've got 40 bales. Last year's crop is out in the barn. This year's crop is still in the pasture hidden under haystacks. There's not room for this year's crop in the barn. With the protection of your safe conduct pass, we could load all 40 bales on old Pete Hern's stern-wheeler and float it down the Arkansas River to the Mississippi, then turn north and go as far as Helena. That smart Union general at Helena can arrange for cotton to be shipped up the Mississippi to Memphis to market."

"Cousin Ed, you just told me that General Hindman had this part of the state under martial law. Won't Pete Hern be afraid to let us use his boat?"

"Hern's for the Union. Got a boy fighting up in the north with Phelph's cavalry."

"Do you actually put that much faith in my safe conduct pass, that one little piece of paper?" I respected Cousin Ed's opinion, and I listened carefully to his answer.

"I do, because Hindman has outsmarted himself. Folks are afraid to argue with him or with the orders he issues. Hindman's planning a big battle in northwest Arkansas. He won't be around these parts for weeks, and he can't be reached by telegraph where he is. Nobody can check with him about that safe conduct pass, and I'm gambling his soldiers won't argue when they see his signature. Besides, we'll cover the cotton over with tarps. I think it can be done.

"Sarah, we're talking $10,000 in gold, payable when this war is over. If cotton is selling for 60 cents a pound in New York, they'll be paying at least 50 cents in Memphis. At 500 pounds each, that's $250 a bale. With $10,000, you and Larkin can make this place the finest plantation in the western part of the state. When this war is over, you could really give Larkin something substantial to come back to. Think it over tonight, and give me your answer tomorrow."

By morning, my mind was made up. Over the breakfast table we started planning the trip.

"We can't even begin to plan, Cousin Ed, unless that fellow agrees to carry us on his stern-wheeler. It's going to be a big risk for him. He may not feel up to it."

"Sarah, he and I have been talking this idea over ever since last summer when Grant and Sherman got control of Memphis. We just couldn't see any way to get past the fort that General Hindman has built down at the mouth of the Arkansas River. But your safe conduct pass can open that door for us."

I was beginning to grow enthusiastic. "Can't you just picture Larkin's face when I get a chance to tell him we'll have a fortune waiting for us after the war?"

Cousin Alta brought me back to earth. "I can picture your face if we don't stain it up with another dose of the pokeberry juice. I may not be able to do as good a job as Monnie did, but I'm sure going to try. And, don't forget, you've got to take food. It'll be a long trip. How many days will it take, husband?"

"Floating downriver we can make good time. Hern estimates 40 miles a day, which means four or five days from here to Helena. Plus, we've got to figure in that we'll be stopped by Confederate patrols. It'll be a week's trip all the way to Helena, and another couple of days on up to Memphis. Once Sarah sells the cotton in Memphis, and gets on a regular steamboat, it'll be ten days to St. Louis, and ten more from there to Kansas City. More than a month on a boat, I'd say, if all goes well."

"Well, once Sarah gets on the steamboat at Memphis, there'll be plenty of food. She'll be in Yankee country then." Cousin Alta's tone was matter-of-fact. "You-all will need a ten-days' supply going up, and another ten-days' to get back. You'd better take a side of meat and a sack of corn-meal. I'll send dried peaches and fresh apples. I'm glad Matt is as old as he is. Milk and butter are going to be scarce, for you may not want to risk putting in at the river banks to get fresh produce."

"I'll leave that up to Hern. He knows the territory and we don't. One other thing. We can't afford to have Sarah do the cooking and melt that wax. Looks like you're about to have a plumb restful trip."

I laughed. "Well, I hope you're better at cooking than I think you are, Cousin Ed. Else we're going to be starved out before we ever get to Helena."

"I'm counting on Pete Hern doing the cooking," Cousin Ed responded. "He's been running boats up and down those rivers for 30 years. Before I go talk to him this morning, let's talk money, Sarah."

"What do you think is the fair thing to do, Cousin Ed?"

"Well, all cotton brought in to Memphis is purchased on contracts for payment at the close of the war. That's the law. You can see why the Union has to enforce it. If they paid Southern planters in gold now, that money would almost certainly find its way to the Confederate treasury. So payment is deferred. General Grant encourages this buying of cotton. His policy is to drain the South of its supply. What few foreign loans the Confederacy can get are based on cotton for collateral. Grant's trying to cut these loans to a minimum. I can assure you that you'll be warmly received by Grant's subordinate officers after we get to Memphis.

"I believe the fair thing to do is share both the risk and the profit. I think it would be worth 20 percent to you to get your cotton to market. Twenty percent of $10,000 is $2,000, and I'm proposing that Hern and I share that equally. We'll none of us get anything until the war is over. But I think the North is bound to win, and I'm willing to wait. So is Pete Hern."

We shook on it and started getting ready. We wanted to get going while the good weather held. "How are you going to find darkies to get those heavy bales loaded up?"

"I'm going to pay their owners. Most cotton planters are having trouble taking care of their slaves this winter; it's been so long since they've had any real money. Confederate scrip is nearly worthless. They can grow their own food, but they need a little money for clothes and tools and equipment. These plantations are looking mighty shabby around here." He looked over at me. "A $20 gold piece placed in the hands of the right owner would buy us all the slave labor we need to load every bale of that cotton."

Chapter 21

OUR BOAT PULLED AWAY FROM *Lewis-burg Landing at dawn on the morning of November 20. Matt was wild with excitement, jumping and running and squealing until I finally had to fix up a little harness and a tether for him so I could make sure he didn't fall overboard. Once Captain Hern had the steam up and got the boat moving, it was a feeling like no other. The boat moaned and palpitated like a live thing, bearing downstream at full speed, smoke curling up from the tall chimney stack, the paddle wheel throbbing and churning the waters. The waves rolled high, and our spirits rose to meet them. For the first time in my life I witnessed*

enthusiasm and eagerness beneath the dour Scottish exterior of my prim Cousin Ed. For me it was a remarkably easy day. I watched the waves spray the drooping, leafless branches of the great willows on either shore. I gazed at their companions, the bare-branched sycamore and sweet gum trees. Occasionally, we glimpsed magnificent plantation homes situated facing the river. Captain Hern anchored that night at a lonely bend in the river.

"This spot doesn't have a human settlement within five miles, to my knowledge. We're not likely to attract any attention here. Just the same, I think it wise to take precautions. Tonight we'll stay on the boat and eat a cold supper. Mr. Watson, I think we ought to take turns keeping watch."

So a pattern was established. I took first watch, Cousin Ed the next, and Captain Hern the last. The night was uneventful, and I was awakened before dawn by the throbbing of the steam engine as Captain Hern fired it up for our journey on down to Little Rock. We had discussed the matter thoroughly and agreed that our best course was that of a matter-of-fact approach to whatever authorities we encountered. By midmorning, Captain Hern prepared to dock at Little Rock to present his boat-ownership papers to the Confederate military authorities. After a fresh application of wax and pokeberry juice, I dressed in my black dress and bonnet, held my child firmly in my lap, and watched Captain Hern lower the gangplank to the wharf. Cousin Ed marched down it, his purposeful stride that of a man bent on important business. Within half an hour he had returned and given Captain Hern the signal to cast off. It was noon and we were far downstream, eating the cold ham and corn bread that Cousin Alta had packed, when I finally asked the questions that were heavy on my mind.

"You were back so soon. It must have been easy. What did they say at the dock?"

Captain Hern permitted a grin to crease his leathery face.

"Yeah, Mr. Watson. Tell us. I can't stand not knowing another minute, but I'll be durned if I was going to be the first one to ask the question."

Cousin Ed spoke carefully, choosing his words with Scotch economy. "Wouldn't have been seemly to brag. Fellow on duty seemed to have me mixed up with somebody else. Wearing my good Sunday suit must have fooled him. Fellow seemed to get the impression I was representing somebody important. Said he wouldn't want to be the one to put an obstacle in my path. Seemed considerably impressed by General Hindman's orders."

Captain Hern spoke up. "What in tarnation does that piece of paper say, Mr. Watson?"

"Says, 'Permit bearer to pass, and extend every courtesy. By order of Major General Hindman, Commander, Trans-Mississippi District.' One more thing. The fellow did ask me who I represented."

I was getting impatient. "And what did you tell him?"

Cousin Ed permitted a twinkle to appear in his canny Scottish eyes. "Under close questioning, I allowed as how I represent the house of Chouteau. Fellow waved me right on out the door. Even gave me this morning's paper to entertain me on the trip. If he'd had a red carpet handy, I think he would have rolled it out, too!"

I began to laugh. "That man thought you were in cahoots with General Hindman — or, rather, he thinks the Chouteau firm is in cahoots with General Hindman. He thought you were representing a cotton speculator! Cousin Ed, how did such a strict Presbyterian work himself up to tell such an out-and-out fib?"

"It's no fib, Sarah. You're a Chouteau by birth, and I represent you. If petty bureaucrats find it to their advantage to close their eyes to the possibility of profiteering, it won't be the first or the last time it happens. There have always been men who make money out of other folks' misery. Now, let's read the paper. The fellow said it's full of news about General Albert Pike and the latest mess he's stirring up. And let us most earnestly pray that we'll find the same sort of fellow on duty at Arkansas Post when we get down to that new fort at the mouth of the Mississippi."

I occupied myself by reading the front-page story of the *Arkansas Gazette,* which reported the latest development in the ongoing saga of the troubles of General Albert Pike.

"Cousin Ed," I asked in amazement, "it says here that General Pike has brought charges against General Hindman, plus General Hindman's commander, General Holmes. How can that be? Didn't General Pike get his command taken away after the Battle of Pea Ridge?"

"Not that I ever heard of, Sarah. Don't know where you got that notion. He fumed around a while over at Fort Smith. General Van Dorn took the bulk of his command east of the Mississippi and appeared to have forgotten all about Pike. If there's anything a politician can't stand, it's being out of the limelight, and Pike's been trying to get back in it all year."

"The Federal expedition against Vicksburg has failed. General Burnside has been made commander of the Army of the Potomac. That army is south of Washington and north of Richmond at a little town called Fred-ricksburg." I sighed as I read. "Even allowing for this to be a Southern paper, and bound to be one-sided, the news for the North is not good. They're checkmated on the Mississippi, and this sounds like they're not doing any better in the East."

"Don't discount that General Grant too soon, Miss Sarah. They's a lot of in-fighting going on amongst the generals. On both sides. Whether it's Hindman and Holmes fighting Pike in the Confederacy, or Grant and Sherman and Burnside bickering in the Union, them big shots have a hard time remembering who it is they're supposed to be fighting." Captain Hern thought a while. "But I'd say this war is going to be won or lost on the Mississippi. And I'm betting my money on the one that's the meanest and toughest. That's General Grant. Them Rebs are holed up on top of the bluffs at Vicksburg, but they're cut off from their supplies, and Grant's mean enough to starve 'em out. It'll be a long, hungry siege for them pore suckers."

I was instantly alerted. "But that's where my Cousin Willie is — he's with Van Dorn at Vicksburg."

Hern gave me a compassionate look. "Like I say, this war will be won by the general who's the meanest and toughest. And we better get our-selves toughened up. Tomorrow we'll put in anchor at Arkansas Post. We'd better hope our luck holds out. Tomorrow's the turning point of this trip. If we get past that fort at Arkansas Post by sundown, we can ease on out to the Mississippi and head north toward Memphis under cover of darkness."

The weather held, and our luck held with it. Captain Hern threw out the gangplank at Arkansas Post in late afternoon. I was so nervous my stom-ach was tied up in knots, but Cousin Ed stepped down that gangplank like a man who expected to get exactly what he asked for. Handing his stack of papers to the sentry on duty, his tone brisk and confident, he stated his business.

"I need a word with your commanding officer, sentry. A private word, if you please. Kindly convey me and my papers into his office."

Within the space of half an hour he emerged from the office, signaled to Captain Hern to cast off, and marched briskly back up the gangplank. It was almost dark by the time the boat had covered the few remaining miles down the Arkansas River to the Mississippi. Matt and I watched Captain Hern's skillful handling of his steam barge. With great care he navigated a slow turn against the current to head north against the strong force of the mighty Mississippi. Finally, late in the evening, when Captain Hern had decided we were far enough upriver to anchor the boat, I asked Cousin Ed about his dealings at Arkansas Post.

"How did you do it, Cousin Ed? What were those papers you showed the sentry? I didn't know you had any papers."

Cousin Ed lit his pipe. In the brief glow of the flared match, I could see his old face soften in an almost boyish grin.

"Happens I did have papers. Got a big stack of them. Captain Hern and I've been giving this job a lot of thought these past few months, so I had plenty of time to plan ahead. I wrote your Uncle Auguste last summer and asked him to send me a stack of stationery — Chouteau letterhead and blank bills of lading. Figured I'd look more official when I did any kind of business, since I was a newcomer in that part of the state."

"So you used that Chouteau letterhead to put together a fake set of papers?"

"Not altogether fake, Sarah. I've got an accurate and completed listing of every bale we've got on board. Each bale of cotton is listed precisely at its official ginned weight."

"What do you mean, ginned weight?"

"What it weighed when the bale left the cotton gin. Average bale weighs in around 500 pounds, but they vary some." I could hear the pleased note in his voice. "You know what schoolteachers are like, Sarah, when it comes to details. Anyhow, I made up a set for whoever wanted it, along with a set for us, and a set for the port authorities."

"My goodness, no wonder that stack of papers was so thick! You must have been filling them out for hours! What made you think of doing it?"

"Figured whatever fellow was stuck with being in charge of an isolated and undermanned fort would want to make sure he had covered his backside — begging your pardon for the language, Cousin Sarah. If it's reassurance for his decisions a man's needing, there's nothing like an official stack of papers. The thicker the better."

Captain Hern was still puzzled. "So you got that pore sucker to bite. You gave him a thick stack of papers. How did you hook him? How in the world did you talk him into letting us go down the river?"

"Made up another set of papers. He thinks we're bound for New Orleans to ship all this cotton to England and help out the Confederacy. Got a bill of lading made out to Port of New Orleans."

"Now, Cousin Ed, something's fishy there. That man knows the Union's holding the river south of here, all around Vicksburg. He wouldn't authorize one barge to try to run a Union blockade."

This time Cousin Ed could not restrain himself. For the first time in my life, I heard my dour old Scotch cousin laugh out loud. "Fellow thinks we're in the buccaneering business. I told him we had a wagon train of four big wagons waiting for us north of Vicksburg, 12 oxen to the wagon, each one ready to haul ten bales apiece. Got the idea from hearing Larkin talk about Mr. Alexander Majors's big wagon trains. Told him Chouteau Enterprises out of Kansas City was masterminding the whole thing. Told him the wagons were going to loop around Vicksburg and be met by another boat 50 miles south. Told him it was all hush-hush and top secret."

"You spilled out all that and then told him it was top secret?" Captain Hern's tone spoke volumes.

"No, Captain. Give a man more credit than that. I let him force it out of me. I asked him to telegraph Chouteau Enterprises for confirmation; I swore him to secrecy; I insisted on knowing the name of the officer he reports to. Fellow questioned me ten minutes or so before I let him in on how we're going to do it. Only one problem left, as I see it."

"What's that?"

"Fellow was so impressed he's bound to blab about it sooner or later. When he does, some of the other planters may actually take up the idea and try to do it. We better hope Grant manages to take Vicksburg before too long."

I laughed out loud. "Cousin Ed, you do beat all. You've got the makings of an actor. I've never seen you take a swallow of whiskey in my life, but what do you say to one now? I want to drink a toast to all three of us."

"Don't mind if I do. But just a wee dram to celebrate."

"How far is it on to Helena?" I was eager to begin the next part of the journey.

"Another couple of days ought to do it. Looks like the weather is turning in our favor."

"How can you say that when it's turning cold and the wind is threatening to blow up a rain?"

"Nothing dampens most folks' ambitions like a cold, soaking rain, Miss Sarah. None of them folks that live on the banks is going to be rushing out to hassle us if they have to slough through cold rain and mud to do it. We'll batten down our hatches, fire up the engines, eat our cold meat and corn bread, and git ourselves upriver to Helena."

Light, fluffy flakes of snow were falling when we walked down the gangplank at the Helena wharf. Little Matt ran around like a puppy off his leash, trying to catch the flakes with his quick little fingers.

"He doesn't remember seeing snow before," I said to the blue-coated soldier who handed me off the stern-wheeler.

"He's a mighty fine little fellow, ma'am," replied the soldier. "Looks like he's ready to run for a while. Kids don't take too well to being cooped up, even when they're on a good-sized boat like this one."

Cousin Ed had come to the point immediately. "I need to see your commanding officer, sir. And Mrs. Flint, here, requests an interview with General Curtis. She is an acquaintance of the general and needs to see him on a personal matter of some urgency. Captain Hern will stay with the boat. We welcome your inspection of its cargo."

I had made as good an appearance as possible for my audience with General Curtis. I had melted the disfiguring wax and scrubbed on my face until the wine-dark stain of the pokeberry juice had lightened to a deep pink. Cloaked and bonneted against the falling snow, I approached the Union army headquarters outfitted in my black silk mourning dress, its wide skirts belled out by hoop skirt and crinoline, its severely high neckline softened by my mother's lace collar. I had decided to maintain the disguise of my bulging belly until I had safely arrived in Kansas City. It provided the safest hiding place for the gold coins that I could think of.

General Curtis's headquarters was an impressively handsome, tall-ceilinged, white-pillared brick home. Genuine concern showed on the general's homely face as he came forward to greet me. He wasted no time in small talk. "Mrs. Flint, what troubles bring you here, and how can I be of assistance to you? Please sit down and tell me your story."

"General Curtis, I ask your help in finding out whether my husband has been able to escape from his Confederate captors and rejoin his regiment in the Union army." I briefly outlined the happenings of the past several months.

"Madam," he replied, "it shall be done, but the task may take some time. Where can you be reached, once my staff has completed their inquiry as to Captain Flint's whereabouts?"

"Sir, I plan to journey by steamboat to Kansas City, there to make my home with my mother's brother, Auguste Chouteau, until this war is ended." I handed him a piece of paper. "This is the address of Chouteau Enterprises. Uncle Auguste can always be reached through them."

The general looked at me thoughtfully and spoke his mind. "I consider it unwise — perhaps impossible — for a woman in your advanced stage of pregnancy to attempt such a long journey."

I gasped. No Southern man would have acknowledged that he recognized the pregnancy of a woman outside his family, much less would he have mentioned the condition in her presence. But General Curtis sat sternly, waiting for my response, his high-domed forehead wrinkled with concern, his bushy eyebrows and graying sideburns giving him the appearance of a tired old owl. I had no choice except to tell him the truth.

"Sir. I am not expecting a child. This bulk at my midsection is a pillow, and it contains enough gold to pay for passage to Kansas City and living expenses for me and my young son. I thought it best, given my youth, that I take what steps I could to ensure our safety and privacy."

His look of concern was replaced by one of admiration. "By God, madam, if the men on my staff had one half of your tactical ability and ingenuity, we could figure out how to beat the enemy quickly and end this bloody war! Give your uncle my best personal regards. Pity you're not a man. You could help him run the house of Chouteau!"

"Sir," I replied, "running the house of Chouteau is not on my mind. It is my husband who is my concern, and with all my heart I thank you for your willingness to find out information about him. The news that he is alive and well would be the greatest Christmas gift that could be granted me."

"Madam, I pray that I can be the means of granting you that gift. In the meantime, I can offer one of lesser value. We have a convoy of empty supply boats scheduled to depart for Memphis this afternoon. These boats can offer safe conduct to you and safe passage to your barge all the way to the Port of Memphis. I can assure your safety as you travel upriver, and I trust I will be able to supply you with the information you requested." He rose and ushered me to the door.

I looked at my surroundings. "Such a handsome house you're headquartered in. A real contrast to Griffin's Tavern."

This time General Curtis's look of satisfaction was unmistakable. "This is the home of my chief opponent, General Hindman. I derive a not inconsiderable amount of satisfaction out of using his luxurious home as my headquarters." He bowed. "Madam, believe me when I tell you it was a true pleasure to see you again."

The journey to Memphis was uneventful, and our business there was readily and profitably accomplished. Matt and I said reluctant good-byes to Cousin Ed and Captain Hern as we boarded the handsome steamboat bound north and northwest for St. Louis and Kansas City.

With quick handshakes both men took their leave, and my little son and I took our places among the many who believed themselves to have urgent business in the distant cities to which we were bound.

I kept to myself as much as I could for the entire 20-day journey, avoiding both the curious eyes of the men and the more direct questions put to me by the women. This last was not easy, since we women slept and washed and dressed in the close proximity of crowded cabins. Still, I managed to maintain my distance, both in the cabin and at mealtime.

Among the many who crowded the wharf at St. Louis were newsboys hawking their wares with signs that read, "Big Battle Fought in Northwest Arkansas. Casualty Lists Available Here." Carrying Matt in my arms, I rushed down the gangplank to buy copies of newspapers, then hurried back on board the steamboat. With my heart in my throat, I read the casualty lists. The name Flint was not there.

Bold headlines told the story. "Bloody Battle Fought at Prairie Grove." General Blunt and General Hindman had fought each other with well-matched fury. Hindman and his army had retreated to the south under cover of darkness early on the morning of December 8. Casualties had been heavy on both sides. Adding those killed, wounded, and missing, the Confederates had lost over 1,100 men, and the Union had lost over 1,300. Union troops under General Blunt were now camped near the battlefield, prior to launching a campaign to invade the Arkansas River Valley and secure Arkansas for the Union. Meanwhile, General Hindman was leading his ragged, half-starved, and demoralized army toward Little Rock. The Federal artillery had been fired with devastating accuracy at Prairie Grove and with terrible effect against the Confederacy.

I read each newspaper article with meticulous attention, searching for names or details that would serve as clues to Larkin's whereabouts. His regiment, the First Arkansas Cavalry, had been among the first of the Union troops to encounter the Southern forces, having been ambushed by Quantrill's raiders early in the battle. Quantrill's men, dressed in false colors, were wearing the Union uniforms of captured Northern soldiers. My pulse pounded with anger as I read of Quantrill's sneaky strategies. I was fiercely glad to read that the Union army had emerged victorious. If, indeed, Larkin had managed to rejoin his regiment, he must have been in the thick of the fighting, and I prayed for his safety and for news concerning him.

On the afternoon of December 22, 1862, ten days out of St. Louis, we arrived at the wharf of Westport's Landing. Viewed from the banks, our arrival must have been a magnificent sight. The boat advanced with flags flying, smoke curling up above the treetops from the two huge chimney stacks. We swung around the bend, the great engines pulsing, the waters churning, the deep-mouthed melody of the whistle singing like a mighty and joyful wind, the loudly pealing bells signaling our successful arrival. From the wharf a brass band took up the rhythm, the loud, clear music of the trumpets accentuated by the throbbing tuba and the pounding drum. The great gangplank began its curving swing and gradual descent to shore. Boxes and barrels, hogsheads and cotton bales were rolled and bumped along its surface. Matt and I joined the moving parade of passengers that began exiting the ship.

I strained my eyes for a glimpse of my Uncle Auguste's tall silk hat and portly figure, but he was not to be seen among the crowd. As I stepped onto the wharf, a tall Union officer turned toward me. Straight as a Cherokee arrow, his dark beard and dark hair prematurely streaked with gray, his blue eyes made more striking by contrast with his deeply tanned complexion, Larkin Houston Flint held out his arms to me.

Chapter 22

OH, THE JOY WE GAVE each other, that Christmastime of l862! Joy in the morning, joy in the evening, and the dear good Lord above knows how much joy we took during the long, cold nights! Through the rich blur of it all — the talking and laughing and remembering and crying, through eating and drinking and visiting and loving, through parties and dinners and singing and dancing — ran such a sweet, deep core of joy that I could only marvel at the miracle of it.

Uncle Auguste gathered the entire Chouteau family into his Westport mansion on Christmas Eve. Candles gleamed in each tall window, evergreen ropes of pine and cedar swung from the wrought-iron railings of the handsome entry, wreaths hung on the stone columns on the street. Carriages filled with talking and laughing Chouteau relatives drove up the wide avenue. Again and again the wide front door was flung open to admit silk-hatted gentlemen and their crinoline-skirted, fur-bedecked ladies. Inside, Christmas greens were swagged in ribboned garlands, candles danced among the cedar and mistletoe entwined around polished chandeliers, and the great hearthed fireplaces warmed us all with the cheerful blazes of stout pine logs.

In the high-ceilinged dining room with its paneled walls and oval mirrors, a long mahogany sideboard held the steaming wassail bowl of Christmas cheer. Bustling starched-aproned Irish maids served crystal glasses of sherry from trays of gleaming silver. Larkin and I stood in the wide hall with Uncle Auguste. There we greeted each guest, from the eldest, my Great-Aunt Bereniece, on down to the youngest baby, the newest child of my Cousin Marie. I had to pinch myself to make sure I was not dreaming. Could the girl I saw reflected in the hall mirror possibly be me? She wore a rich, hoop-skirted gown of black velvet, the neckline cut wide to expose her white neck and shoulders. An exquisite cameo on a band of black velvet accented her delicate throat. Her face was flushed and radiant with happiness.

"Larkin," I whispered, "it's been scarcely two months since I buried my pa, and I thought that day I would die from the sorrow of it. How can it be that I am so happy so soon after his death?"

He gave me his full attention. "And it has been less than three weeks since I was in the thick of battle, so bloodthirsty that day that I was half-crazy, trying to kill every Rebel within reach, not knowing where you were or whether you and the baby were alive or dead."

Oblivious to the relatives who surrounded us, Larkin took me in his arms and kissed me soundly. "From now on, Sarah, I aim to kiss you every time I feel like it. Life is too short and the times are too risky to hold back when we have a chance to be happy."

"Our little Sarah may be the biggest risk-taker of us all," said Uncle Auguste. "Sarah, it turns out that you were only a few leaps ahead of the hounds when you sold that cotton in Memphis. General Sherman's army embarked out of Memphis four days ago — for all practical purposes, Sherman has commandeered the entire Mississippi River for his army's use. The day before he left he issued an order making it a crime to buy or deal in cotton. Sarah, if you had been three weeks later getting to Memphis, you would not have been permitted to board that steamboat headed for St. Louis. The Good Lord was looking after you." He paused and smiled. "And looking after your pocketbook as well. Behind that pretty face, you've got quite a head for business, my girl."

"Well, it is hard to find a Chouteau who is not interested in business," agreed my youngest uncle, François. "Which is fortunate, considering the situation we're in. What with supplying the needs of those settlers who persist in moving west, and supplying the increasingly heavy demands of the army quartermasters, we're uncomfortably close to being shorthanded."

"A minor worry, François." Uncle Auguste's tone was reproving. "Surely not one that will induce sympathy from either Larkin or Sarah, nor most of the good folk living outside Kansas City in rural Missouri. While we are protected by Federal troops, those in the countryside have been terrorized."

François was not easily swayed. "I personally believe reports of Federal depredations to have been highly exaggerated. Perhaps the Southern guerrillas have acted outrageously, but not their Northern counterparts. I suspect that most refugees have abandoned their homes from groundless panic and blind terror rather than actual danger."

"Federal depredations are real, and Union troops fully capable of brutality." Uncle Auguste spoke sternly. "The Seventh Kansas Cavalry is a case in point. If Colonel Jennison, their commander, is killed, he will surely roast in hell. While he claimed he and his men were foraging, in actuality they were stealing and burning with a vengeance worthy of the devil himself. This war has brought out both the best and the worst of men."

"For a man who can barely read and write, that Colonel Jennison has got a remarkable imagination." The speaker was my Uncle Louis. "Take what he did over in Independence, for example. Herded every white man in town into the public square, then rounded up all the darkies, dressed them up in Federal uniforms, and had them march in military formation around the captured whites. Next, he read them all a proclamation that his Seventh Kansas Regiment was about to throw a 'shield of protection and defense' around all loyal men."

"The man's a disgrace," Uncle Auguste said grimly. "I make it my business to know something of the background of the men the house of Chouteau does business with. Jennison has gone from rags to riches in the short space of less than two years.

"That day he and his men left Independence," he continued, "they marched their swaggering way back through Kansas City with a train over a mile long — darkies, horses, mules, oxen, and a dozen or so wagons filled with loot. Men say he takes the silver and gold and jewelry for himself and parcels out the spoils that are too large to be hidden."

"Disgraceful as the looting is, it's petty thievery when compared with that ridiculous deed of forfeiture that Jennison has come up with. How a mere colonel, and an ignorant one at that, can bluster and blunder his way into such power is beyond my comprehension. It is that deed of forfeiture that's making him a rich man."

"That's a term with which I am unfamiliar." Larkin's statement was directed at Uncle Louis.

"Thank God the idea has spread no farther than the Kansas City area. It's a document put out by Colonel Jennison as an instrument of the Federal army. It's designed to force each man suspected of being a Rebel to turn over his property to the U.S. Government, the conveyance of such to be null and void if the signee can subsequently give proof of his active loyalty to the government."

"Who decides as to the loyalty?" Larkin's tone was dry.

"Jennison does. Might makes right. He calls it his 'loyalize or obliterate' policy. Legally speaking, of course, the deeds are worthless and made under duress. My brother François is correct after all. Too many good men are off fighting. Too many who are venal and corrupt remain here to plague us."

"What do you think of Senator Lane, Uncle, and what part does he play in Jennison's success?" Larkin's question surprised me.

"That's a hard question to answer, Larkin. Jim Lane's a paradox. I can usually peg most men, but Lane's a breed apart. He's a born leader, a natural fighter. They hate him in Missouri as much as they love him in Kansas. He's a remarkable orator — very moving. They say he's a wild animal in combat, an old-time evangelist on the platform. I know for a fact that when he was elected as senator from Kansas, he didn't have enough money to buy shoes for his children. We outfitted him on the credit when he made his move to Washington. He's produced a remarkable record there for a man so recently out of the prairie. I'm told he has Lincoln's ear on occasion." Uncle Auguste sighed. "It is not always easy to tell the sheep from the goats. The fact that Lane is far superior to Jennison by no means qualifies him to be giving advice to the President of the United States."

"Honest Union officers are outraged at the lies of Jennison and Lane, and rightly so," Uncle Louis observed. "It will be instructive to find out what sort of records he produces in real combat. Fighting a fierce and well-armed enemy is considerably different from robbing old men and women and children. But what of more recent news?"

Cousin Marie's husband, a tall man in the worn blue uniform of the North, answered the question. "Sherman's troops have landed 12 miles up the river from Vicksburg and have destroyed the railroad there. Sherman has performed a miracle. He's floated thousands upon thousands of men down the Mississippi, to say nothing of the Negroes that climbed on board the boats as they moved down the river. There's talk of Sherman's men being able to take Christmas dinner in Vicksburg tomorrow."

"That'll never happen." Larkin's tone was sure. "General Grant's main railroad supply depot fell to the Confederacy a few days ago. Holly Springs, I believe its name is. My brother Sam fights with Van Dorn on the other side, so I try to follow the action around Vicksburg as much as I can."

"Well, that leaves Sherman in one hell of a position. He's got that big army down there in the swamps around Vicksburg, and Grant's withdrawing instead of advancing to join him. I'd never in a thousand years guessed that little Van Dorn to be a match for Sherman and Grant." Cousin Marie's husband looked somber.

It was Larkin who answered. "In the long run, he won't be. I'm told that Van Dorn's not too smart. He was at the bottom of his class at West Point. But he's brave, and his men like him. They say he's a great soldier. My commanding officer says if Van Dorn had as much sense as he has guts, he'd be unbeatable.

"My guess is, Grant and Sherman will prevail in the long run, but not anytime soon. Van Dorn's got bluff-top fortifications, and our Union troops are going to be wading through swamp and mire, poor devils, with Rebel guns trained on them every miserable step of the way. That country around Vicksburg is a quagmire, and our boys are about to be shot at like swamp rats."

Uncle Auguste was a man who looked for reasons. "Why do you suppose it was that Grant and Sherman were so poorly coordinated? Looking at it from the standpoint of a civilian, I can't understand Sherman taking off so fast on water without making sure of Grant's land support."

"There are those who claim that Sherman wants glory more than anything else. Maybe he wanted to be the only one to capture Vicksburg. Glory can be a strong motivator for some men," Uncle Louis observed.

"Glory is going to be mighty cold comfort to those poor devils sloughing through those swamps tonight. I'd like to propose a toast to them and to us." Larkin raised his glass. "To a speedy victory, and to all who bring it about! And to family and friends, and the joys of reunion! And finally, to Uncle Auguste, for opening his home to my wife and son!"

Aunt Bereniece appeared at my side. "A remarkable man, your Larkin. A complex man." She paused, then smiled. "It is our custom on Christmas Eve to go as a family to midnight mass. I had intended to fold you and Larkin into the bosom of the family by inviting you to experience as visitors the peace and joy of the mass. Upon reflection, I expect you might prefer to stay here and experience a more private communication. It is your choice."

"Aunt Bereniece, I've never been inside a Roman Catholic church, and neither has Larkin. I would like to go, and I expect Larkin and I are both in need of God's grace. We have not been in church for so long. But we won't know how to act, when to stand, when to kneel, what to do."

"Visitors are neither expected nor encouraged to go through the rituals, Sarah. Simply open your hearts, and receive God's blessings."

"Aunt Bereniece, would you include Minerva and Matthew in your prayers tonight? Uncle Auguste believes your prayers have a special power. If they do, then the Lord will listen, and He will help Matthew Flint."

"The Lord will listen, of that I have no doubt. But I do not presume to predict His actions, Sarah. Nor should you. The Lord has brought you through tribulations to Kansas City. He has brought Larkin here safely to you. Let us be thankful for His goodness without presuming to dictate His decisions." Again, she smiled. "It will be my pleasure tonight to take you and Larkin and little Matt to your first mass. And I will most certainly pray for Matthew Flint, and for all those in need — your poor stepmother, Eliza, alone on Christmas Day; the mothers and wives wondering about their men off at war; and the widows and orphans who wonder no more. Larkin offered his toast to the men on the battlefronts. I will offer my prayers, to mingle with the many others who are this night praying for peace."

So it was that Larkin and I found ourselves on Christmas Eve sitting in the hard pew of an unfamiliar church, little Matt asleep on Larkin's lap. As I looked at the thick stone walls and high-beamed vaulted ceiling, at the richly robed priest and the overpowering crucifix, and listened to the glorious soaring music of the choir, I felt the power of the place enveloping my senses and uplifting my soul. Afterward, as we walked through the cold, starry night to Aunt Bereniece's carriage, I looked up at Larkin, and for the first time in many months I saw the gift of peace reflected in his face.

Later that night, in the shadows of our canopied bed, we loved each other so deeply, so gloriously, that our pleasure was beyond my remembering. I delivered myself up to his strength with pure gladness and lay there peacefully afterward, flooded with a joy that gradually ebbed into a deep and renewing sleep.

The days and nights of Larkin's military leave sped by too quickly, the precious hours allotted to us spilling out of the hourglass of time. All too often the demands of others lessened our time together, demands that Larkin seemed neither to resent nor attempted to diminish.

Although my wise Uncle Auguste made no attempt to impose his own routine upon our lives, I found myself adapting easily to the ways of his household. For his part, Larkin took it for granted that his days would be spent attending to business and that our meals and our evenings would be spent with the various members of the large and lively Chouteau clan and their guests.

It was remarkable the number of people Larkin came to know during those brief two weeks with us, and equally remarkable how many of them came to dine at my uncle's hospitable table. Whether he went to the Union army headquarters or to the offices of Chouteau Enterprises or to the establishment of Mr. Alexander Majors, Larkin's visits frequently resulted in additional dinner guests. I often learned more news at the table than I did from the newspaper.

On the day after New Year's Day, Larkin's commanding officer dined with us. Larkin introduced us proudly. "Sarah, this is Colonel Phillips, commander of the First Regiment, Arkansas Cavalry Volunteers. Sir, this is my wife."

The tall, tired-looking man bowed gracefully over my outstretched hand. "Madam, I am honored." He then turned his attention to my uncle. "Sir, I appreciate your kindness in including me at your table this evening.

I hold Larkin Flint in high esteem. It is a pleasure to meet his family. I have some knowledge of your enterprises, and I welcome the opportunity to hear your views at this critical stage of the war."

"Critical, indeed," replied my uncle. "New Year's Day 1863 will go down in history as a watershed time."

"Why, Uncle?" I asked, seeing no reason why I should be excluded from the conversation.

"Because yesterday President Lincoln signed his Emancipation Proclamation, and that signing is going to have far-reaching results."

Colonel Phillips agreed. "I shouldn't be surprised if time does not show it to be a turning point in the history of the country. And perhaps the war as well."

"That one document is going to help a lot of people make up their minds." Larkin spoke thoughtfully. "I expect Lincoln's main reason for doing it now is to keep France and England out of this war. They'll no longer be willing to recognize the Confederacy. To do so would be to endorse slavery. It looks to me like Lincoln has drawn a clear line they'll be unwilling to step over."

"He's drawn a line, all right. Whether or not it's so clear is a matter of debate," Uncle Auguste added. "I read the entire document carefully when the Northern newspapers published it last September. You no doubt were denied all access to Northern newspapers while you were being held by the Confederates, Larkin, but we in the Union had a chance to become very familiar with this proclamation. What Lincoln has done is to free only the slaves of the Confederacy, not those in border states, and not those in territories retaken by the Union. Any slaveholder in a Union state still has legal title to his property. It's a political document, and a remarkable document."

"Let me see if I understand the reasoning." Larkin had a smile on his face. "Lincoln's position is *not* that a man can't justly own a slave; his position is that a man can't own a slave unless he lives in the Union."

"Well, at least the Northerners won't be able to sell any more of their darkies down South. My pa used to say that's the way the Yankees took care of their darky problem." I thought on Neely and Tobe and Zeke and wondered what lay ahead for them.

"I'm somewhat surprised that Lincoln decided to pursue this course of emancipation." Uncle Auguste looked thoughtful.

"Legally, he's on solid ground." Colonel Phillips spoke with assurance. "Lincoln's position is that he can free these slaves under his war powers and that these war powers extend only to Rebel-held territory. So he's permitting the Union slaveholders to keep their property. He's pleased the extreme abolitionists like Frederick Douglass and William Lloyd Garrison; he's served notice on the South that when the Union wins this war, their slaveholding days are over; and he's made helping the Confederacy an unpopular cause in France and England. Not a bad piece of work for one document!"

"Well, if I understand you, sir, I'd say the document's got certain problems. Men like me in the South are going to be a lot less interested in volunteering to fight to free the slaves than they would be in volunteering to fight to preserve the Union. The Union's worth dying for. I'm not sure the slaves are."

"Larkin, you've gone to the heart of it." Uncle Auguste's tone was sober. "That's exactly the drawback. But Lincoln's an astute man. He believes the benefits far outweigh the risk. Already the common laborers in the North, most especially recent immigrants — the Irish, the Germans — hate and resent the free Negroes. They see these black men as competition. The free Negro does not have a fair chance in the North. Even with victory, his position will not improve. In fact, it may worsen."

"I'd be most interested in your opinion of Lincoln's views on the place of Negroes, Mr. Chouteau. Do you believe that Lincoln feels the black race to be inferior to the white?" Colonel Phillips waited for my uncle's answer.

"There can be no doubt that Lincoln detests slavery. I am convinced that he believes, as all of us here at this table believe, that slavery is wrong and unjust. Whether he thinks blacks to be inferior to whites is an entirely different question. This is the belief of most men in this country, and I expect that Lincoln shares it."

I thought on Neely, a woman every bit as smart as any of the white women she had been working for all her life, and my heart ached for her. Then when I looked around the table and came to terms with the fact that every man there considered himself to be superior to me, my heart ached some for myself.

Having listened intently to the views of the men, I ventured again into their conversation. "Why is it that the president chose this particular time to issue his proclamation? Why didn't he do it early on in the war?"

Larkin answered me. "He had to wait until he could speak from a position of strength. When McClellan beat Lee at Antietam last September, the tide finally turned in the North's favor. Thank God! When Lee whipped the socks off the North at Bull Run early on in the war, he set off a Southern winning streak that didn't end until the Battle of Shiloh last April. Yet even after that bloodbath of Shiloh, Lee kept on winning. Last August he fought at Bull Run again and chased the Union again nearly back to Washington. After a year and a half of war, the Union is finally on the road to winning now, and it was Antietam that was the turning point. Thousands of poor devils gave up their lives at Antietam, on our side alone. I'd prefer to think they died, not for slaves, but for the Union."

"I agree," replied Colonel Phillips. "When I look back at the Battle of Shiloh and realize that our country lost more good men there in two days of fighting than we've lost in all the wars that America has fought before, my blood runs cold.

"Having said this, I would be less than fair were I not to point out that the free men of America make up a fighting force unexcelled in bravery, in tenacity, and in intelligence. For all its faults, democracy has produced real men, and I am proud to command them!" The colonel's voice rang out. "As a case in point, I look back to our recent battle at Prairie Grove, in Arkansas. On the morning of the seventh day of December, we were facing Shelby's troops. I'll warrant that no better men and no better officer than Shelby can be found in the entire Rebel army, and my own men knew that and knew what they were up against. Still, when I gave the signal, my men splashed through a creek, jogged across a cornfield, and went up that slope at a dead run. They surged over the crest of that hill like a stream that had broken its banks, and Shelby's advance line crumbled. But we were up against brave men and seasoned troops. Shelby rallied his men and countercharged, and my men fell back.

"Then straight through my Union center rode Larkin Flint, waving his hat and yelling to his men to follow him back up that slope. And they followed him — straight into that hail of steel they followed him, into the bloodied clashing of hand-to-hand combat they followed him. Some to their death, and all to their glory, they followed him. I reformed my other units, and together we fought the Rebs back, foot by foot, until twilight silenced the battlefield. That night the cold battle-moon cast its white glow on the twisted shapes of hundreds of fallen men, but, let me tell you, sir, they were as brave and worthy a group of men as God ever put on this earth!" The colonel turned to me. "Madam, I brevetted your husband to the rank of major on the spot, and no man ever deserved it more! You have every cause to be extremely proud of Larkin Flint."

"Sir," I replied, "I have always been proud of Larkin Flint, and I expect I always will be." And I smiled through my tears at the man who would soon kiss me good-bye and ride back again to war.

Chapter 23

AUNT BERENIECE BEGAN my education the day Larkin left. Less than an hour after Larkin's ramrod-straight back had disappeared from my sight, the plump figure of my determined little great-aunt came marching through the door of Uncle Auguste's dining room.

"Sarah, I will not permit you to sit around and drink coffee and feel sorry for yourself."

Startled, I set my cup back down on the table, wiped my tear-reddened eyes, and sat up straight.

"It is high time you learned the arts of supervision. Your Uncle Auguste is delighted to have you grace his home, and

there is no doubt he will take joy from your presence, whether or not you decide to be useful to him. But you could fill a real need and at the same time prepare yourself to manage your own future responsibilities by taking on the management of your uncle's household."

"That can't be too hard to do, Aunt Bereniece. I've grown up watching Pa and Eliza manage the tavern. I've been running our farm with one hired woman and her boy since Larkin went off to war. Surely, running a big house like this can't be all that much harder to do."

Her worldly old eyes looked straight into mine. "Child, you have already been through grief and terror, and it is greatly to your credit that you have not only survived, but triumphed. But when this war is over you will again live in a world that is run by men and for men. I propose to train you to manage an extensive household, to be an exceptional hostess, and to carry out Larkin's business plans on the occasions when he cannot be present. In short, I wish to train you for the life that lies ahead of you."

So my training began. I learned to shop and to supervise, to plan and to delegate. I learned to be a good hostess for my uncle's many guests and to deal with the unimportant and obscure rules that society has developed for social occasions.

Uncle Auguste's guest list was as varied as his interests and ranged from young Bill Cody on the one hand to the archbishop of the diocese on the other, with a wide assortment of politicians and pundits in between. Uncle Auguste's great skill lay in ensuring the ease and comfort of each person who dined at his table. I learned that even the most eminent and distinguished personages are only human. Under the vigilant tutelage of Aunt Bereniece and the warm encouragement of my uncle, I learned not only to preside as his hostess at formal dinners but also to manage his household for his comfort and convenience.

Although the rules of polite society appeared considerably more curious and complicated than the logical rules of algebra and grammar, my aunt was pleased with my progress. But even as I concentrated on learning the ways of the privileged, outside our comfortable world the war continued. Men fought and died; women wept; and children went hungry.

By late February I was able to write Larkin that I was again with child. Our letters crossed in the mail, and his contained Minerva's news concerning Matthew Flint.

The request for your father's trial was finally granted and

took place before the general advocate of General Hindman's army on January 20, 1863. You will rejoice to hear that your father was completely exonerated of all charges. Your heart would have been warmed by the outpouring of public sentiment expressing support of your father's position and commendation of his character. His friends rode day and night, once the news of his trial date had been set, to reach the courtroom to testify and to express their support. Many old-time friends were in the audience, legislators with whom he served many a term, heeding the call of friendship — some intense Southern sympathizers among them. Here below are the charges made against Matthew:

> Charges: Treasonable and seditious conduct.
> Specification 1st: That he, Matthew P. Flint, did have in his possession a Union flag and did on occasion display it on the flagpole at his residence.
> Specification 2nd: That the said Matthew P. Flint did cause his neighbors to assemble and did offer comfort and support to them.
> Specification 3rd: That the said Matthew P. Flint did refuse to receive Confederate Colonel T. C. Huntsman into his home and did make seditious remarks with reference to same.

> All of this occurred on or about the latter part of February 1862.

> Witnesses to the prosecution:
> Theophilous Massey
> Artemus Crawford
> Haswell Mosby

To our immense amazement, General Albert Pike came forward and urgently requested that he be allowed to give testimony on Matthew's behalf. In a speech so eloquent as to bring tears to the eyes of the ladies present, Albert Pike spoke of Matthew's honesty and kindness, his unfailing love of country, of the happiness and contentment so evident in his home, and of his caring concern for the welfare of his neighbors. Finally, in summation, Pike addressed the last charge, that of Matthew being unwilling to receive Colonel Huntsman in his home. Turning to the many assembled in the courtroom, he asked,

"My friends, were you to have had the gift of prophecy, so that last year you could have known what you now know, how would you yourselves have viewed that colonel of the Confederacy, that disgrace to the the Trans-Mississippi District, that wolf in sheep's clothing, Thomas Huntsman? Had you known that he would cause your crops to be stolen, your homes to be burned, your lands to be forfeited, your daughters to starve, and your sons to shed needless blood, not to advance the cause of Arkansas, but to advance his own ruthless lust for power — I ask you, examine your hearts — would you have received him as an honored guest into your own homes? My fellow citizens, Matthew Flint is guilty of nothing other than wisdom, wisdom that enabled him to accurately read the character of a man who is — even as we speak — leading the Confederate army into the jaws of despair and despondency. My friends, if it were your choice to choose your neighbors, and if the choice lay between the silver-headed man standing before you, a man with honesty and intelligence written large upon his face — I ask you, would you choose tall, dignified Matthew Flint, or would your preference extend itself to that little, strutting banty rooster of a man who disgraces the uniform of the Confederacy, Colonel Thomas Huntsman? My friends, think what your own choice would be!"

General Pike sat down to ringing applause. Matthew was forthwith acquitted of all charges. As for General Pike, whatever others may say as to his conduct, both during and before the war, he will always be welcome in our home, for it is to him that we owe Matthew's freedom. Public sentiment is now on our side, and we rejoice in the prospect of returning home as soon as possible. If all goes well, we should be home by early March.

But even as I was rejoicing at Matthew's release, there came news of a truly disturbing nature. All along I had harbored the fear that Larkin would be sent east to fight with Sherman or Grant. And in fact, General Grant did call on General Curtis for all available men to help with the siege of Vicksburg. I prayed most earnestly that Larkin would be spared the horrors of that battle.

To fill the vacuum created by the withdrawal of his troops from the Indian Territory and northwest Arkansas, General Curtis called in a brigade of "Pin" Indians — Cherokees sympathetic with the North who showed their loyalty by wearing two pins in the lapels of their coats — and Kansas Negroes, and ordered these red and black men to take the posts vacated by Union soldiers. This unprecedented move pitted full-blooded Indians and Negroes of the North against the Confederates —Stand Watie's mixed-bloods and Quantrill's guerrillas. To my horror, Colonel Phillips was assigned to command the Union's new border patrol. Quite naturally, he took Larkin along on this newest assignment — where the enemy would likely be led by the bloodthirsty William Quantrill.

To my surprise, Larkin's letters to me were optimistic.

> These red and black men are equal to the job. Colonel Phillips's column of 2,500 men has reestablished Union authority in the Indian Territory, protected the loyal Cherokees like Ridge, repudiated the treaty made by John Ross with the Confederacy, and outlawed Stand Watie! Not bad, for a few weeks' hard riding! Ridge is with me again. He's a captain now, and no better man ever rode a horse! Kiss little Matt for me and take good care of yourself. I will write as frequently as events permit.

Amongst Uncle Auguste's wide circle of associates, the policies of the Union military government were the subject of much discussion. Vigorous measures had been taken by the Union to try to control the civilian population and to cope with the increasing costs of combating the Confederate guerrilla war. Misguided measures, my uncle thought them to be, and he grumbled and worried about their consequences.

"These outrageous assessment boards will turn every honest businessman in town against the Union and do nothing to deter the secret Confederate sympathizers from their spying and skullduggery!" His outburst came as he read his morning newspaper.

"What now, Uncle?" I asked.

"General McNeal has levied heavy fines on the 'disloyal' citizens of each county in western Missouri. Our own Jackson County has been let off easy, with a fine of $15,000, but he's fined Platte County, practically next door, a huge sum of $85,000."

"Why, Uncle? Jackson County has Kansas City in it, and Platte County is mostly farms. Shouldn't it be the reverse?"

"It's retaliation, Sarah. The general believes Platte County to be full of Confederate sympathizers. I expect it is. But these fines won't make them less sympathetic. Quite the contrary. But, at that, we've much to be thankful for. Last summer General Schofield assessed St. Louis $500,000 to clothe and arm the militia. The effect on business there was disastrous, to say nothing of the effect on morale. I have played a considerable role in organizing a committee of citizens to petition President Lincoln that these assessments cease."

"But, Uncle, surely the people are willing to help clothe and feed the very militia that defends them!" I thought of Larkin, and his brothers and Willie, and wondered at the injustice of a population unwilling to support the troops who were fighting to protect them.

I continued. "I've had letters from my family today. They are all undergoing such hardships that I feel guilty up here in the North doing nothing to help out. Kate is running the entire Flint operation, Monnie is making a crop to keep bread on the table, Piety and Charity and even Becky are helping Uncle John run his grist mill. My 70-year-old Aunt Gert is working alongside Eliza and Neely and Zeke — they butchered a hog last month to eat on during the rest of the winter. I feel useless being pampered when Larkin is off fighting and all my women kinfolks are working."

"New times require new responses, my dear." With a sympathetic kiss, Uncle Auguste picked up his tall silk hat, wrapped his cloak against the chill wind, and stepped briskly toward his waiting carriage, leaving me to contemplate the contrast between my new luxurious life-style and the one I had left behind me in Arkansas. Such a strong feeling of homesickness swept over me that tears came to my eyes. I missed them all. I laid my head down on the crisply starched damask tablecloth and cried.

When Aunt Bereniece arrived, her response to my tear-stained face was brisk. "We will call today on one of my best friends, Amelia Montgomery. She is mother-in-law to your Cousin Marie. So we'll drive from Westport back into Kansas City to make our calls today. The fresh air will no doubt do you good. You really must not permit yourself to become discouraged, Sarah.

"Speaking quite frankly as your surrogate mother, I believe pessimism to be a trait that is extremely unbecoming in a woman. Men of responsibility in this world are entirely capable of generating their own doubts as they ponder the wisest courses of action available to them in an uncertain world. To have their women worried and afraid and doubtful of their wisdom is demoralizing at best. Let your presence be a source of cheer for your Uncle Auguste, and, by all means, see to it that your letters to Larkin are full of hope." Then she changed the subject.

"I thought you might enjoy a drive through the downtown section. As you can see, our city is thriving. Five thousand people now live in Kansas City."

We drove past tall two- and three-storied red brick buildings crowding each other for space along the avenues leading north to the river, past the stores, past the Jackson County Courthouse, past the newly built hotel and the imposing army headquarters.

"I do believe that wartime inspires the cultivation of the musical arts," remarked my aunt. "There is, of course, the seamier side of the arts. And here in Kansas City we have more than our share. The large numbers of enlisted men necessitated by the army's headquarters here have given rise to some distressingly common performances — minstrel shows, circuses, even dance-hall girls — but one hopes these are kept to a minimum.

"Over to the left, Sarah, you will see the Kansas City headquarters of the Western District of the Army. General Schofield, commander of the district, is a personal friend of your Uncle Auguste. You may perhaps have met him."

The large brick building that served as district headquarters was set back from the street. A tall iron fence enclosed its courtyard, and heavy iron gates protected its entrance. Its narrow windows looked out on scenes of purposeful activity. Civilian gentlemen exuding airs of prosperity and importance walked to and fro, their narrow broadcloth trousers, silk hats, well-polished boots, and fur-edged cloaks giving testimony to their monetary achievements. Blue-coated officers, buttons polished, boots shined, hard-edged caps set firmly on erect heads, strode briskly past the various civilians. Some wore the voluminous capes designed for the winter — the enveloping short-shoulder capes giving double protection when buttoned against the cold wind.

In contrast to those wearing more conventional clothing were the colorful characters who truly defined the border town of Kansas City — drovers in broad hats, flannel shirts, rough wool jackets, and homespun trousers tucked in cowhide boots, their knives and pistols worn in their belts. Rough and ready these men might be, but they were the backbone of commerce in the West, where trade in cattle and horses and mules formed an essential component of the economy.

Mingled amongst the officers and various civilians were the high-crowned hats set precariously above the dark faces of Indians, their long braids dangling below their befeathered and bedecked headgear. I nudged Aunt Bereniece. "Do you suppose it's against the law to issue a well-fitting uniform to those Indians? Look at them! They're all wearing coats that are either too big or too little! Either their sleeves hang down over their hands, or they don't reach much beyond the elbows. And they're split down the back so they can move their arms! What a motley mess they are! I wonder why they are here. The Indians don't seem to be doing much of anything except sitting around. And look at those women over by the side entrance. What on earth could they be doing here?"

"We will assume those women are servants, Sarah. It is the kindest assumption one can make. Surely, my dear, you must realize by now that there will always be fallen women who serve the carnal appetites of men. I shall speak to my nephews about the unseemliness of allowing these women to congregate in public. I am sure the civic leaders of Kansas City will not wish to permit these poor, unfortunate women to ply their trade in broad daylight on streets where they are apt to accost respectable gentlemen. I shall mention this forthwith." Her lips tightened. "The devil is always among us. I believe we have had enough sightseeing for today. Turn west on Second Street, coachman. We will call on Mrs. Montgomery and my daughter, Marie."

We headed west toward the top of the steep hill that overlooked the river. Deep gashes had been dug to build the road, but even so the horses were heaving as they climbed the bluffs. Built of sturdy brick, the solid two-storied homes of the town's ruling class crowned the city. "These homes look like they were built by people who have come to stay," I commented.

"Quality Hill, this section is called. Ironically, it over looks the West Bottoms, where your ancestors first established the town. The Bottoms has become a slum since the terrible floods a few years back. I frequently remind your Uncle Auguste that God has marked out by topography the lines of growth of Kansas City and that he would do well to move up here with the rest of the family. But he clearly prefers Westport. Here we are, my dear."

Aunt Bereniece's wide hoop skirts sailed across the sidewalk that led to the white-pillared porch of the Montgomerys' handsome brick residence. The white-aproned maid who opened the heavy walnut door led us down the hall and into the Montgomery sitting room, where Amelia Montgomery and Cousin Marie rose to greet us. After the usual pleasantries were exchanged, my aunt lost no time in speaking her mind to her old friend.

"Amelia, if you can bring yourself to discuss so distasteful a matter, would you please ask your husband to use his influence to banish those wicked camp followers from the streets of downtown? To see those shameless fallen women walk openly along our sidewalks is an affront to decency! Surely the city can take action."

"Actions may very well be taken, Mother," replied Marie, "but possibly not for the reasons you have in mind. There is growing concern that these women are also spies — learning secrets from Union men and relaying information to the Confederates, most especially the Bushwhackers. Rumor has it that outlaws like Quantrill and Anderson send their favorite prostitutes back and forth from headquarters to Bushwhacker hideouts. There is already considerable discussion as to humane ways of stopping this spying. You will remember, Mother Montgomery, that last summer when Quantrill captured Independence, there was much talk that women there conspired to betray their own town to him! A disgraceful, shameless, and motley bunch of women, I imagine, if they can stoop to consort with the kind of men who associate with Quantrill!" Marie paused. "The world's oldest profession, given a new twist. But, of course, spying is most successfully accomplished by educated people. I doubt that the contributions of prostitutes amount to much. After all, they have access only to the most common enlisted men, who know very little about plans and maneuvers.

"I should think the observations of your father-in-law, for example, would be of considerable interest to General Schofield at this point, Sarah. Is he recovered from having spent this past year confined in a Confederate barracks?"

"Minerva writes that he is quite well, although he tires easily. I have the impression that it is my sister-in-law Kate who really runs the place now. Minerva has resumed the managing of the household, and Kate has become Matthew Flint's right hand. Kate's a smart woman. She's bitter, and she has a right to be, but she's doing a man's work, buying and raising mules, and this past month she herded them over that long road north to Fort Scott and sold them to the army."

"That's incredible, Sarah. I've never heard of anything so daring. Who helps her?"

"She's rounded up a few half-grown boys too young to be drafted into the army, boys whose families side with the North. And my hired woman's boy helped her. Ned's 14 now, and big for his age. But her main help was Ned's mother, Monnie. Monnie's as tall as a man, and tough. Actually, I ought to have said that Kate and Monnie both managed that mule drive. I'll bet it was something to see. One hundred and fifty miles, through the ice and cold of January, over the ruts and trails of the steep Ozark Mountains, hiding behind the rocks and trees of the hill country over the border in the Indian Territory, until finally they got up into the comparative safety of Kansas.

"In fact, if it were not for Kate's mule drive, I would not have had any news from home. As you know, it is against the law to correspond with anyone living in the Confederacy. If I still lived in Arkansas, I could never have any letters from Larkin. There's no mail delivery now between the North and the South. But Kate let everyone in my family know about her trip and carried letters to Fort Scott, where the commanding officer could mail them on to me. Kate's a good woman, in spite of her toughness. She even took the time to write me a note about Larkin's brothers. They're all fighting in the East now — Sam is at Vicksburg, on the Southern side; Robert and Stant are at Vicksburg, too, but fighting under Sherman for the Union. Tom's been sent a long way off — he's with General Buford, somewhere in Pennsylvania, Kate thought."

"Your sister-in-law has more grit than most men. I could never have managed a mule drive. Nor could any woman that I know. You must be very proud of her." Marie's tone was sober.

"I'm proud of her and sorry for her. She's going to grieve over losing her husband the rest of her life, and I think she may be bitter for as long. There's not much forgiveness in Kate. Not that she's not a good woman. But she's a match for any of the Flint men in toughness."

The elder Mrs. Montgomery smiled. "That may be quite a statement.

I'm told that your Larkin is a remarkable man. He's making quite a name for himself."

"Sarah, when it comes to toughness, you have your own special gift," Marie agreed. "The difference between you and Kate is one of tactics — you worked with men and through men, and Kate worked in opposition to them — but you both accomplished your intentions. You may sweeten your strength with a little sugar, Sarah, but it's still strength!"

I smiled and reached across her wide-spread hoop skirt to take her hand. "Marie, I'm so glad I have you in my family here in Kansas City."

Chapter 24

IN EARLY SUMMER OF 1863 Larkin wrote to me from Fort Gibson, deep in the Indian Territory, where the Federal army with its blacks and its Indians was firmly in command.

I have the feel of victory in my bones. It's a feeling I haven't had before, and I can't explain it now. All I know is, I can sense the curtain rising on all four military theaters at once — and I count ours here west of the Mississippi as one of those. Arkansas is about to get squeezed by the Union pincers — from Helena on the Mississippi and our army here on the western edge —

and this time we'll prevail. I am as sure of this as I am sure that by the time our next son is born I will be with you to welcome him!

I read his letter with a mixture of hope and doubt, my body heavy with pregnancy, my mind already looking ahead to late September, when I expected to be confined. The curtains of the drama of war were indeed rising — Robert E. Lee was reported as being on the march into Pennsylvania, while in Vicksburg the starving troops of the South were surrounded in bitter siege.

It was the first of July, a hot, humid summer in Kansas City. My legs had swollen, and I felt enveloped by an unexpected weariness. My weight gain had puzzled us all. Fatigued and tired, I wondered if I would be able to carry this baby to full term. Larkin's hopeful letter was a welcome sign. I tried hard to share his optimism.

Cousin Marie was a great help to me that summer. Her calm cheerfulness, her thoughtfulness, and her abiding intelligence were a godsend. Marie had invited little Matt and me to spend the day with her on the Fourth of July, and I had gratefully accepted.

"Marie, please don't think me disloyal when I say this, but I'm not sure I'm feeling up to another all-day-long Chouteau family holiday gathering. There's so much talk and so much noise, so many children running around, so much food and so many people asking me how I'm feeling and telling me how I should be feeling that I get exhausted just thinking about it. It will be a blessed relief to spend a quiet day with you."

Marie smiled. "I thought so. But it's only because you're so far advanced in your pregnancy that you have this great heaviness and weariness. The real Sarah — the one I know best — loves people and crowds, even thrives on them. You'll be yourself again as soon as this baby is born."

We sat there under the shade of the great elm trees in the Montgomery backyard, sheltered from the hot, fierce sun, idly watching the bees buzzing among the tall hollyhocks that flowered in front of the wrought-iron fence enclosing the property. Toward the back, the lot ended abruptly at the edge of a bluff overlooking the Missouri River. From our chairs on the parched grass of the lawn we could see across the river to the flatlands of Kansas that stretched toward the horizon. It was only a matter of time before our talk turned toward the war. "Who would have thought it would not be over by now?" Marie's voice was filled with anxiety. "Two years, and still no end in sight."

I thought of Willie and of Sam, doggedly fighting on the Confederate side at Vicksburg, gradually being starved by Grant into submission, and of Marie's husband, Victor, who with Robert and Stant Flint were with equal stubbornness outside of Vicksburg pressing for a Union victory.

It was as if Marie read my mind. "At least, Victor has food and water in plenty — I'm so thankful for that. He writes that they are on General Grant's northern flank. They have the shelter of the woods from the burning summer sun, they're well supplied with food — General Sherman insists on that — they have found wonderful deep springs of good water, and the men improve daily in health.

"But the reports from the Southern side are appalling. Starvation is stalking the streets in Vicksburg. All the beef is reported to be gone, and all the pork. What meat the Southerners have comes from cooking rats and mules. The people have dug caves in the hills to hide in. Most of the people are living now on stewed peas and beans."

"I want the Union to win, Marie; how could I not? Yet my heart aches for Willie, starving there, and for Sam. Why is it that no other Southern general has come to help them at Vicksburg? And what happened to General Van Dorn?"

"As to why there has been no help, I would guess it is mainly due to mismanaged Southern generalship west of the Mississippi. Victor thinks Marmaduke and Shelby to be superb leaders. But Hindman has been discredited, and his successor is no better. And, as to Van Dorn, his end is worthy of a novel." She smiled.

"What happened to him?"

"He was shot by the jealous husband of some poor foolish woman who let Van Dorn seduce her. They say that the man slipped into the Confederate lines, called on Van Dorn formally, shot him, and escaped without a trace. Victor thinks the whole thing is pitifully funny, but he always has had a grudging admiration for Van Dorn. In the meantime, I wish we had some fresh, cool air and some fresh news."

As if in answer to her hopes, Marie's mother-in-law rushed out on the lawn carrying a newspaper in her hands.

"Girls, come read the papers! God has answered our prayers with *two* great victories! Vicksburg has surrendered, and the fighting there is over! And the North has won a terrible battle in a little town in Pennsylvania called Gettysburg! How remarkable an omen it is that both should happen on the eve of the Fourth of July! Get down on your knees, girls, and send your prayers to God in thanksgiving! It appears that the tide has finally turned! God has granted overwhelming victories to the Union!"

I thought of Larkin's premonitions of victory. Out of my memories flashed a picture of the fields around Griffin's Tavern after the battle there: the agonized broken cries of the living, the blood, the stench, the grotesquely sprawling postures of the dead left unburied in the haste of the retreat. I wept for the price paid for victory and prayed that we could all live once again the good life we had left behind in pursuit of war. As I looked across the yard at little Matt, happily digging in a sandpile and chattering with the young Irish maid who had been instructed to keep an eye on him, I thought on Matthew Flint. Three of Matthew's sons had been in the fighting at Vicksburg, and one at Gettysburg.

When the carriage came for Matt and me that afternoon, Uncle Auguste came along as well.

"I thought it best to escort you personally, Sarah. The entire town is rejoicing in the good news of a double victory, and some of the rejoicing is likely to take a rowdy turn before the night is over. I thought perhaps we could forego the family picnic tonight and settle instead for a quiet supper at home."

"I'm so glad you feel that way, Uncle. Somehow, I would rather pray than celebrate this evening. I'm praying for Willie and Sam. I'm so afraid they will wind up in one of those terrible prison camps. Doesn't surrender mean prison camps for those who lose?"

"It may not this time, Sarah. The North may not have enough prisons to hold them all. Reliable estimates of the size of the Confederate army at Vicksburg place their strength at over 30,000 men. Grant is by no means a sentimental man; however, he is a practical man. He can't shoot them now that they have surrendered, and it would be both uneconomical and inconvenient to take on the burden of feeding them. I shall await the news of his decision with great interest. In the meantime, however, I must ask you to keep a firm grip on little Matt. This street is becoming crowded; I fear our carriage may get jostled."

We drove south along Grand Avenue, past new wooden warehouses and a few old brick commercial buildings. A crowd of jeering men had gathered around one building, a crowd that overflowed the sidewalk and obstructed the traffic of the street. Women looked down and waved from the windows of the building, some laughing, some screaming retorts to the taunts and banter of the men below on the street.

"Uncle, what on earth is going on? Who are those women? And why are there bars on the windows? That building looks like a jail."

"It is a jail, unfortunately. The Union army has decided that Bushwhacking must be stamped out, and these women are in jail for the crime of spying, of sheltering Southern guerrillas, and of giving them information."

I was appalled. "The Federal government has put women in jail? Why, Uncle, it is unthinkable!"

"Many things are unthinkable in wartime, my dear. They are not randomly selected women. Some few are respectable — although they are the mothers and sisters of outlaws — but most are hardened women of the streets, women who ply their trade around army camps."

"It is hard to imagine respectable women being put in jail. They must be totally mortified, especially to be cooped up with harlots."

"My dear, your language is bold. But, yes, most of those women are harlots. It is my understanding that the decent women are few. The mother and sisters of Jesse and Frank James, and the sisters of Bill Anderson, the two Munday girls, and a female relative of Cole Younger are among them. Notorious men, all of them thought to be members of Quantrill's despicable band, yet their female relatives are said to be respectable. General Ewing treats these women with consideration. They are housed on the third floor, apart from the harlots. You will notice that the windows of the third floor are quiet. Only the harlots on the second floor are waving and screaming at the men in the streets."

Remembering Quantrill's lascivious lips and ruthless eyes, I shuddered. "I can't imagine why any woman, even a harlot, would serve as a spy for Quantrill."

"The reason is all too simple, Sarah: money. These women sell themselves to Union soldiers, learn what rumors they can about troop movements, supplies, and plans, then ride south into the leafy hills where Quantrill has so many places of concealment. They sell themselves plus their new knowledge to the guerrillas. They are a blight on the earth. If the ground could open up and swallow them all, it would be a blessing for the Union." His face stern, my uncle looked steadfastly ahead.

Then, to my astonishment, as the coachman slowly maneuvered our carriage through the crowd on the street, I heard a shrill voice calling my name.

"Miz Flint, Miz Flint! Look up this a-way, Miz Flint!" The woman's voice was stridently insistent. Shocked, I looked up toward the bars of a second-story window, straight into the pale eyes of Ocie Casey. "Please tell me, Miz Flint," she yelled, "is Lark still alive?"

If she had hit me on the head, she could not have stunned me more. Deeply shamed, I willed myself to silence, but I lacked the power to control my whole body. I sat there in the buggy seat in the hot July twilight, shaking like a leaf.

Meanwhile, the horses trotted down the new macadam road that connected Kansas City to Westport. Only after we were safely inside the privacy of Uncle's high-ceilinged parlor did he ask the obvious questions.

"Can you bring yourself to tell me what that was all about, my child?"

"There's so little to tell, and yet I'm afraid even that little bit is too much, Uncle." As succinctly as I could, I described the chance encounter Becky and I had with Ocie Casey the previous year. Then I went back into times past and dredged up the repressed memory of Eliza's worried recitation of the Flint squaws' gossip and my pa's emphatic repudiation of her story.

"Oh Uncle," I concluded, "I know it's better to rise above my suspicions, and I know it does no good to worry about such evil women, but my heart is aching, to say nothing of my head. I feel like I need to go to bed. I wish I could stay in bed and sleep and not have to think or to worry."

"That is readily accomplished, Sarah. Tomorrow you will be able to put that vulgar girl's question into perspective. Whether she is merely acting out of malice, or whether she harbors a genuine, if unreciprocated, interest in Larkin, that girl has no place in your life. Nor should you waste another minute on thoughts regarding her. Let sleep heal you, my child."

"Aunt Bereniece says that which pains instructs, but I'm not sure where the instruction is, right now."

"I would suppose she means that pain informs us as to those things that are truly important. And Larkin is truly important to you." My uncle smiled gently. "But you already know that, Sarah. Sleep well."

The next morning brought such news as to put all else into perspective. The casualty lists were being published. The names of the dead had begun to come in over the telegraph wires. On July 1, the first day of the fighting, Thomas Andrew Flint had died at Gettysburg. We were later to learn that

Tom had died quickly and gallantly on a Pennsylvania hillside, having delivered an urgent message from General Buford to General Reynolds in the face of a massive Rebel advance. Tall, blue-eyed, high-tempered, warmhearted Tom, dead at 23, would never again walk the Arkansas hills he loved nor hold Piety in his arms. The Flint family would forever be incomplete. I wept to think of Larkin hearing the news in his camp on the western prairie and remembered with gratitude that Ridge Rodineau would be there to help him bear it.

Within a few days, the newspapers carried accounts of the Vicksburg surrender. General Grant had allowed the defeated Confederates the honor of marching to the front with flags flying while they stacked their arms. The men then marched back again as prisoners until paroled. Only after the parole was signed by each soldier was each man's status changed from prisoner to parolee. The Rebels were then free to march out of Vicksburg to begin their long journeys home. Officers were allowed their regimental clothing, their side arms, and one horse. Rations were to be drawn from the Confederate commander's stores; the sick and wounded were to be released as soon as they could travel.

Grant had not only won a stupendous victory but had extended terms of honor to the vanquished, an army of 27,000 men. Furthermore, he had avoided the necessity of depleting Union supplies by feeding the enemy he had conquered.

In my imagination I could picture Sam Flint starting out on the long journey back to the hills of home, and I could picture Willie Griffin waiting with his wounded patients until they, too, were able to travel. And I could imagine Piety's anguish as she came to terms with the knowledge that Tom would never come home again, not even his body, for he would rest forever on a hill in Pennsylvania. Finally, I was able to root out of my heart the poisonous suspicions that Ocie Casey had planted there about Larkin. "Let him come home alive, Lord," I prayed, "and I promise to let go of my jealous thoughts and old suspicions."

Larkin's next letter was dispatched from Fort Smith on the western border of Arkansas.

We've seen a considerable amount of action and have taught old Hindman's replacement the same lesson that arrogant Hindman learned last December. I am convinced that General Blunt is a match for any general the Rebs can come up with west of the Mississippi. On July l6th we marched all night and struck the Rebs at dawn, took 57 prisoners, all of the Rebs' supplies, and had the satisfaction of seeing whole companies of Hindman's slack-jawed conscripts desert like rats. They ran down that dirt road so fast they kicked up a column of red dust all the way to the river.

Tom did not give his life for naught. We're winning this war now, and it was Gettysburg that turned the tide. I have requested a furlough in September. It is my expectation to be at your side when our next child is born.

The hot and humid days of summer lulled me into an apathy that Aunt Bereniece, with her unrelenting energy, countered as best she could. "You must walk each day, Sarah. You need to walk in the fresh air. You must form the habit of rising early, so as to walk while the morning air is still cool."

On the morning of August llth, I rose early. Even accustomed as I was to the oppressive heat in Kansas City, this day promised to be a scorcher. Already, with the sun only an hour up in the sky, I could feel the heat beginning to build. Conscientiously taking Aunt Bereniece's advice, I walked slowly along the narrow graveled alley that separated the lots of Uncle's prosperous neighborhood. I waved to his neighbor across the alley, the Reverend Flowers, as he came out of his house with his milk pail, walked to the small shed at the back of his lot, and sat down beside his patiently waiting cow.

"Uncle is right," I thought; "Presbyterians don't pay their preachers a living wage." The reverend and his wife had the use of the big rectory but such a meager salary they could not even hire a yard man for their two-acre lot.

All at once, the silence of the morning was broken by the sound of horse's hoofs. A single rider in Union blue galloped down the street, leaped from his horse, slung the reins swiftly over Uncle's iron hitching post, and began pounding on Uncle's front door. I walked toward him as fast as I could, dread of his news already clouding my senses.

By the time I had reached the front door, Uncle was hastily walking down the stairs, traces of the lather of his morning shave still visible on his face. He looked in anxious inquiry toward his urgent messenger.

"Mr. Auguste Chouteau?"

"The same. What is it, man? What brings you here?"

"Sergeant Ramsey, sir. I bring an urgent message from Major Plumb. Your building on Grand Avenue has collapsed. The one between 14th and 15th Streets. It's gone, sir. Fell down right after the sun came up this morning. The timbers buckled, the brick walls bulged out, the foundations gave way, and the whole damn thing collapsed right down to the ground. Major Plumb requests you come right away."

"My God, man, that's the building the army rented from me to use as a jail! There were women in there!"

"Yes, sir. The major asks that you come right away. General Ewing should be there by the time we arrive. And the army doctors."

"Tell me now, man. What happened to the women?" My uncle turned to the gaping maid standing in the back of the hall. "Bridget, call for my carriage. Get it immediately." He turned back to the sergeant. "How many women are hurt? Did they have any chance of getting out?"

"Four dead, sir, that we know of. Major Plumb's men are still digging, sir. A dozen or more badly hurt, crushed, mostly trapped. They couldn't get out of the windows, you know. Had to run down the stairs. The women on the top floor had it the hardest. They couldn't make it down the stairs in time. The walls teetered and bulged, just like an earthquake. The major thinks those crowds of men were there to conceal the digging that was going on. We found tunnels under the building that undermined it. There's just a heap of red dust and rubble down there now, with screaming women still under the piles of bricks and timbers."

The sound of Uncle's buggy wheels turned our attention toward the street. On the sidewalk behind me the Reverend Flowers was standing, his kind old face contorted with horror, his milk bucket still in his hand.

"May I ride with you, Mr. Chouteau? Those women who are still alive may need what comfort my prayers can give them."

"By all means, Reverend." My uncle indicated the seat next to his own. Hatless and coatless, their faces set and grim, the two men headed north toward the wreckage.

The noon sun was hot and high above us when the Reverend Flowers came back.

"Mrs. Flint, I hate having to ask this of you, and your uncle hates it even more, but we both think it best that you come down to the hospital that has been set up next to the wreckage. There's a woman there who is dying, a woman named Ocie Casey. She feels that she needs to talk to you. She's begging. She wants to die in peace. I know this is hard, but your uncle asked that I fetch you. Will you come? The woman likely will not last the day."

I looked down at my swollen belly, hugely extended by nearly eight months of pregnancy. It had been months since I'd been out in public in mixed gatherings. My mouth went dry with dread. There had to be something concerning that woman that Uncle felt he couldn't handle. I could not begin to imagine what that could be. I straightened my shoulders. "Yes, I'll come."

We rode in silence through the crowds lining the streets, past the armed soldiers guarding the rubble, and past the screams and moans of the women still entombed under the heavy timbers. We stopped at the door of the hastily improvised hospital in the nearby building. There my uncle met us. Taking my hand in his own, he led me down the row of cots to that of Ocie Casey. Her face, always pale, was completely drained of color. "Her back is broken," my uncle told me, "but she refuses morphine to blot the pain until she has talked to you."

Even then I could not like her. I sat down heavily in the chair provided and looked down at her face, twisted now with pain and fear. "I've come. What do you want?"

The pale eyelashes fluttered. Her eyes looked directly into mine with such urgency that I flinched. "Look after my little boy. Promise me. He ain't gonna have nobody now. Promise to look after him."

"Why are you asking me?" But even before I asked the question I knew the answer.

"He's a Flint, that's why. You'll know it the minute you lay eyes on him. He's with my ma, but she's bad sick now. She ain't got no money excepting whut I send 'em. And she's got two others uv her own. They'll starve." The pale eyes looked urgently into mine. "Promise."

"The child is Larkin's?" Hard as it was to ask the question, I had to hear the answer.

The grimace of a grin passed like a shadow over her face. "I ain't fer shore whose he is. Might be Larkin's or might be Tom's. One 'er t'other. Them's the only two had any cash money that summer and fall of '59." Again, that shadow of a grin as she remembered. "My boy's a Flint, fer shore. It's writ all over him."

Suddenly the girl's body was racked with a spasm of pain. She coughed, and bright red blood spewed out of her mouth. Unexpectedly, I thought of

Piety as she had calmly and briskly dealt with the reality of Ike's death, quietly directing Charity and me as we dragged Ike's body out of the cabin. I could see Piety's competent hands as she scrubbed Ike's blood off the floors.

And I knew that with Tom dead, I had to spare Piety any further grief. She had enough to bear as it was. This much I could do: I could accept the child as Larkin's. Tom was dead. No possible good could come from adding any more to Piety's load of sorrow.

The girl's tone was urgent. "Promise. I ain't got much time left." Finally, compassion came to me.

"I promise. He'll be looked after. Where is he? Where does your ma live?"

"She's still on the home place. She's sick and Pa's dying. Pa's been shiftless all his life. He's crippled. He ain't no help to her; he's worse than useless."

"What's your boy's name?"

Again, the grimace of a grin. "Named him Jefferson Davis Casey." Another spell of coughing shook her, and more blood came out of the twisted mouth. Her eyes opened again anxiously. "I didn't dream it? You did promise?"

"I promised. Here's my hand on it." Slowly, with every cell in my body recoiling from having to touch her, I reached out my hand. I picked up her limp and freckled hand from the blanket that covered her broken body, and shook it. Her eyes closed.

"I'll take the morphine now." Her voice was calm.

It took both Uncle Auguste and Reverend Flowers to support me as I willed myself to walk from the hospital back to the buggy. "That which pains instructs." The refrain ran through my mind all day and most of the night until I finally found the blessed relief of sleep.

The next morning I wrote to Matthew and Minerva, hopeful of early mail delivery now that the Federal army again occupied the northwest part of Arkansas.

A young woman named Ocie Casey died yesterday in the collapse of a jail here in Kansas City. She called for me before she died and told me that she has a child in Arkansas. The boy lives with his grandparents only a few miles away from you. I promised her I would look after this boy. I will count it a favor if you would see to his well-being until such time as Larkin and I can return to Arkansas and assume the responsibility for the boy's care. I am thankful that I can count on your understanding and on your discretion in this matter.

I thought long and hard as to what to write to Larkin, and in the end I wrote nothing at all. There would be time enough to tell it when we were face to face.

Chapter 25

QUANTRILL EVENED THE SCORE within ten days' time. One of the dead girls was the sister of his lead scout; another was the sister of Bloody Bill Anderson. Ocie Casey was one of Quantrill's favorite whores. Their deaths provided the motivation he needed to whip his men into a murderous rage.

From all over Missouri, Quantrill organized his raid of revenge. Men of various persuasions were, for once, joined in common cause — outlaws, organized guerrillas, pro-slavery farmers, even two companies of Confederate cavalry. On August l9 they jogged into camp at Pardee's farm in

Jackson County, only 20 miles from Union headquarters in Kansas City. Bill Anderson was there, along with Frank James, Bill Gregg, and Cole Younger, each vowing to outdo the other in the bloodletting carnage of retaliation. On the morning of August 20, 1863, 450 men rode out. Their destination was Lawrence, Kansas. They carried a death list of their proposed victims. Heading the list was Quantrill's Jayhawker counterpart, Senator James Lane of Lawrence.

Shortly after the sun came up on the morning of August 21st, the blood-thirsty yells of the outlaws broke the early morning silence of Lawrence. Most people were still asleep when the killing and burning began. Houses were torched, men were shot, families robbed and left homeless. When the outlaws rode out of Lawrence at midmorning, they left behind 183 men and boys dead and 250 orphans. The town was littered with the bodies of those gunned down in cold blood. The smoking ruins of nearly a million dollars worth of destroyed property smoldered in the hot sun.

While the women and children fought the flames and agonized over their dead, the wily senator who had been the chief target of Quantrill's wrath rode into Kansas City. Once in the headquarters of the Union army, Senator Lane's demands for Union vengeance prevailed over the usual good judgment of General Thomas Ewing, the Federal commander of the Kansas City Military District.

What the senator demanded was nothing less than the depopulation of the rural sections of the Missouri counties adjacent to the City of Kansas, the farms and small towns thought to be giving aid and information to Quantrill and his Bushwhackers.

Four days later the senator's reaction became the law. On August 25, 1863, General Order No. 11 was posted:

Headquarters, District of the Border
Kansas City, Missouri, August 25, 1863

General Order No. 11
    I. All persons living in Jackson, Cass and Bates Counties, Missouri . . . except those living within one mile of the limits of Independence, Hickman's Mills, Pleasant Hill, and Harrisonville, and except those in that part of the Kaw Township, Jackson County, north of Brush Creek and west of the Big Blue, are hereby ordered to remove from their present

places of residence within 15 days of the date hereof. Those who, within that time, establish their loyalty to the satisfaction of the commanding officer of the military station nearest their present places of residence will receive from him certificates stating the fact of their loyalty, and the names of the witnesses by whom it can be shown. All who receive such certificates will be permitted to remove to any military station in this district, or to any part of the State of Kansas, except the counties of the eastern border of the State. All others shall remove out of this district. Officers commanding companies and detachments serving in the counties named will see that this paragraph is promptly obeyed.

II. All grain and hay in the field or under shelter in the district from which the inhabitants are required to remove within reach of military stations after the 9th day of September next will be taken to such stations and turned over to the proper officers there, and report of the amount so turned over made to district headquarters specifying the names of all loyal owners and the amount of such produce taken from them. All grain and hay found in such district after the 9th day of September next not convenient to such stations will be destroyed.

III. The provisions of General Order No. 10 from these headquarters will be at once vigorously executed by officers commanding in the parts of the district and at the stations not subject to the operation of Paragraph I of this order, and especially in the towns of Independence, Westport, and Kansas City.

IV. Paragraph III, General Order No. 10, is revoked as to all who have borne arms against the Government in this district since the 21st day of August 1863.

By order of Brigadier-General Ewing:
    H. HANNAHS,
    Acting Assistant Adjutant-General

Almost immediately, Order No. 11 was seen for what it was — a tragic mistake, the vengeful brainchild of the cruelly clever senator from Kansas, the climax of a dozen years of bloody infighting between Kansans and Missourians.

My Uncle Auguste, appalled at General Ewing's decision, organized a committee of prominent citizens to bring pressure on Ewing to rescind Order No. 11. More than a dozen men gathered in Uncle's parlor on the evening of August 25, men who had staked their faith in the future of Kansas City. Some I had met; others I knew only by reputation. R. T. Van Horn, editor of the newspaper, was there; Alexander Majors; Thomas Swope; T. A. Smart; Dr. Lester; the Reverend Flowers; Colonel Coates, home on leave from the Union army, and Mr. Lykins, his next-door neighbor; Hamilton Montgomery, Uncle Auguste's attorney; Mr. Harris; and George Caleb Bingham, artist and politician.

Their mood was grim. My uncle opened the discussion. "You men have made Kansas City what it is today. For the past ten years, while Kansas Jayhawkers and Missouri Pukes have kept the countryside of both states inflamed, you men have built Kansas City — you have opened banks, founded newspapers, conducted mercantile businesses, organized a railroad company, brought in the telegraph, and built hotels and streets. Your energy, your faith, your sound judgment have been demonstrated time and time again. Now, I ask you to join me in persuading the Union commander, General Ewing, to rescind his disastrous order. It will lay waste the countryside, it will ruin the lives of thousands upon thousands of farmers and small-town citizens, and it will be ruinous to the economic future of Kansas City. I ask that we agree to use our combined influence on General Ewing."

"I couldn't agree more, Auguste." The speaker was Van Horn. "This Order No. 11 will result in disaster. Men will not peaceably move away from their farms merely because some overbearing blue-coated idiot of a Union officer orders them to do so. Much less will they peaceably agree to see their homes burned and their wives and children homeless. This order will make Southern sympathizers out of neutral men and make vengeful partisan fighters out of those who are already in sympathy with the South."

"The guerrillas will not be affected by this order. It's an ill-conceived and diabolical plan. Ewing's Folly, it ought to be called."

"Lane's Bloodletting might be a better name. Lane has wanted to humble Missouri for years. He's always at the bottom of any scheme of violence, and he's at the bottom of this. That damnable document has his stamp on every line."

Of them all, only the Reverend Flowers came to Lane's defense.

"Gentlemen, I was in Lawrence the day of Quantrill's massacre. Quantrill was not avenging the deaths of those poor women here in Kansas City. He was slaughtering for the thrill of it. Killing Kansans is his idea of a blood sport. He relished it, and so did his men. They say that Bloody Bill Anderson vowed to tie a knot in his silk sash for every man killed that day. I personally saw him tie five knots. Folks said when he rode out of town, that sash had 20 knots in it. For him to wear the uniform of the Confederacy is a disgrace to civilization."

It was the newspaperman who questioned the reverend. "How was it you lived to tell the tale, Reverend? Didn't Quantrill gun down every man in sight?"

"I was staying at the City Hotel. The Stone family owns it. They're friends of my wife's. For some strange reason, Quantrill spared that hotel. Some say that one of Quantrill's spies was there amongst us. He burnt the Eldridge House, and he marched all the men out of the Johnson House, torched the hotel, and shot them in the street. The Bushwhackers were diabolically methodical. They spread out in groups of six or eight, street by street, house by house. They knew the town, too. They killed a doctor, a state senator, a newspaper editor, and the mayor all on the same block. Gunned them down in cold blood, then had the gall to tip their blood-stained hats to the weeping widows and rode on to further slaughter."

"Then why didn't they gun down Lane, if they were so well informed? He was in town, home from the Senate for the rest of the summer."

"They did burn Lane's house, but he wasn't in it. I was told Lane got out in his underwear and hid in a ditch in his pasture while his wife lied to Quantrill and swore that Lane had gone to Leavenworth the night before."

Van Horn spoke again. "Why Lane continues to have the ear of President Lincoln is totally beyond my understanding. But he does have it, and that makes him doubly dangerous. I predict that our combined influence will not prevail to make General Ewing change that order."

"Ewing's a stubborn man, that's true. But he's politically ambitious."

"He's ruined himself, then."

The Reverend Flowers concluded his narrative. "Men, Lawrence that day was a burning hell. While businesses burned, looted goods were scattered all along the streets. I saw two young boys, sons of the newspaper editor, dragged away from their father's bleeding body only to be mercilessly pistol-whipped by one outlaw, then shot to death by another. It was all over by nine o'clock in the morning. Those fiends rode out with their packhorses loaded with stolen goods. That raid can never be justified on the basis of revenge. It was blood sport and robbery."

Colonel Coates summed it up. "And the man who was the focus of it all, Senator Lane, intends to make rural Missourians a pawn and to continue the game. Order No. 11 will make legal what Quantrill has been doing as an outlaw. This order will make Missouri a no-man's-land. And, I agree with Auguste, it will be devastating for Kansas City. Whether we oppose this order on humane grounds or whether we oppose it on economic grounds, we must all oppose this Order No. 11."

Their opposition proved to be fruitless, but their predictions were chillingly accurate. Within ten days' time, thousands of bitter, dispossessed country folks found their way to Kansas City.

As Uncle had foreseen, the impact of Order No. 11 on the businesses of Kansas City was disastrous. The city grew in population, but the growth was mostly due to hungry country people with few resources other than the land they had left behind. Uncle, himself, became bitter.

"This town could have survived an attack of Asiatic cholera easier than it can survive this damnable Order No. 11! My business is being blockaded by both sides now. That stupid order has cut off all food supplies within a 40-mile radius. We will not be able to fill our military contracts. All construction will soon stop, if it hasn't already. Kersey Coates told me he's going to stop all work on that magnificent hotel he is building, even though the foundation is already in. He plans to let it stand. And General Ewing had the infernal gall to try to rent that foundation from Coates to stable the horses of the Army headquarters."

"Surely, Uncle," I argued, "you exaggerate."

"Sarah, with all my heart I wish that I were exaggerating. Alas, I am stating the truth. Already, only ten days after the order became law, gold and silver coins have disappeared from circulation. I am conducting business with scrip. Our warehouses are emptying fast, and when they are empty, it will be virtually impossible to replenish our supplies. You need not worry about my being shorthanded at work, Sarah. If things continue as they are, the house of Chouteau will close its doors within the year!"

I was appalled. "Uncle, please tell me it is not that bad!"

"Sarah, you should know me well enough to realize that I neither exaggerate nor equivocate. Already, my brothers and I are making plans to dismantle our businesses. My younger brothers will search for other ventures outside of Kansas City."

"Uncle, if I were not here as a burden on you, would you begin another enterprise elsewhere?"

"No, Sarah. The City of Kansas is my home, and in the City of Kansas I have built a fortune of some consequence. Here I will live and die, and it is my great pleasure to have your company." He smiled at me. "And the company of your children."

And, indeed, I felt as though the birth of this next child was imminent. The weight of this pregnancy was now such a burden that I could barely climb the tall stairs to my bedroom. I longed for my labor pains to begin, and I longed for Larkin. Each day I hoped for news of him, but there was no word from the Indian Territory.

When the news finally came, I was completely unprepared for it. Uncle had just finished his breakfast, little Matt was playing in the side yard, and I was lingering over my last cup of coffee when we heard the loud rap of the heavy brass door-knocker.

Even as Uncle escorted the solemn-faced Union chaplain into our dining room, my mind refused to accept the horror his visit implied. "Mrs. Flint, it is my duty to bring you General Ewing's compliments, ma'am, along with sad news concerning Major Flint." He handed me the letter.

Dear Madam,

I regret to inform you that your husband, Major Larkin Houston Flint, has been missing in action since the morning of August 15, 1863, and is presumed to be dead.

Major Flint was attached to a small party of 16 officers who were detailed to acquire certain information regarding the "wild" Indians of the plains. Whilst on the mission his detachment was ambushed by a war party of Osage Indians of overwhelmingly superior numbers. As the situation proved to be hopeless, the Union commander was forced to raise the white flag of surrender. Said flag notwithstanding, the savages scalped and/or killed the entire party with the exception of two officers. Major Flint being one of the two officers not present and accounted for at the scene of the massacre, it is my official conclusion that he is missing in action. Rest assured that I shall keep you informed when and if further information is forthcoming.

And please accept my personal condolences on the loss of a

splendid soldier, a remarkable man, and my personal friend. With deepest sympathy, dear madam, I remain,

John Phillips, Colonel
United States Army
Headquarters, Army of the Frontier

"But this doesn't say he's dead!" I cried the words both in hope and in anguish.

Uncle looked at me with pity. "Sarah, under the circumstances described in this letter, death may possibly have been a friend."

"No! I won't believe it! And I won't look on death as a friend! Pray for him, sir, that we'll see him again!"

The chaplain's eyes were compassionate. "I will pray for you all."

My mind retains very little memory of the next few days. Unwilling to accept the reality of the horrors implied in the colonel's letter, I sat in numbed silence, unable to think, unable to plan, unable to sleep.

As she usually did, Aunt Bereniece assessed the situation and took charge.

"Sarah, you must come to terms with this, and you must eat and sleep, else you will do harm to the child you are carrying. If Larkin is dead, your loss is indeed great. But it is no greater than that of thousands of grieving women throughout the land. If he yet lives, you have no cause to grieve, and every cause to trust that God will return him to you."

Her words stung. "It's not knowing that numbs me so. I keep picturing him being captured and tortured. These are pictures in my mind I can't talk about, or even stand to think about, but they're always there in the back of my mind."

"Put them out of your mind, child. Surely you realize that you can't keep this up. Look to the future."

I looked her squarely in the eyes. "That's what hurts the most. All I see in the future is emptiness. I can't stand to think of a future without Larkin in it."

"Your future is far from empty, Sarah. You have one son, and soon will have another. Your future contains responsibility. And, while you may be unable to accept it now, your future will contain joy if you accept your responsibilities and continue with your life. For example, your own child deserves better from you. Look out the window at little Matt, sitting on the porch alone, with no child to play with, no adult to talk to. Surely, you are not going to give more time to your grief than you give to your own son!"

She reached over and put both arms around me. "Child, pick up your burdens and walk." She kissed my cheek with a tenderness that brought back childhood memories of my long-dead mother.

"I have instructed the coachman that I am to be sent for immediately when your labor begins," she said, taking her leave. "Dr. Lester is competent, of course, but he cannot substitute for family. I will be here when you need me."

I walked across the back porch to the steps where my little son waited for my attention. "Let's walk across to Preacher Flowers's barn and look for kittens, Matt. His cat is about to wean them, and I expect there are some kittens there that would like to be played with."

So life began again as I learned to live one day at a time. News from the war was scarce, whether from the East or from the operations along the Mississippi. Only the Indian Territory reported actions of any consequence. General Blunt had marched through the Indian Nation, hunting down the Indians who were Confederate allies. By the first of September, Blunt had marched in triumph into Fort Smith, on the western edge of Arkansas. I tried to picture Larkin alive and well, riding into Fort Smith with his old brigade. When my imagination refused to comply, I focused instead on the maps, which showed all of the Indian Territory and Kansas and western Arkansas north of the river under the Stars and Stripes.

By early September, Federal troops had occupied Little Rock. As always, my reaction was personal. Now I could expect to get letters from home and hear news from those I loved. At the same time, I now had no further excuse to postpone the duty of writing to Matthew and Minerva to tell them about Larkin. But nature intervened and delayed my writing.

My water broke in the middle of the night. By the time Dr. Lester arrived, my pains were coming hard and fast. Aunt Bereniece hurried in the door in time to hold my hand as I began to bear down in response to the long contractions that pushed the baby through the birth canal. This time I needed no encouragement to push hard. As I gave myself over to the demanding process of birth, I almost welcomed the physical pain. It provided a welcome focus, dispelling the grief that enveloped me.

Old Dr. Lester was matter-of-fact. "One more push ought to do it. Come on, girl, push this baby out!"

Moments later, "It's a boy; a healthy, squalling boy!" His tone was as joyous as though he was delivering his first baby. "Here, Madame Bereniece, I'll hand him to you to be washed. Now, Sarah, let's see what I can do to clean you up."

I gasped. "Doctor, I'm getting more contractions. Strong ones!"

I gave myself over to the demands of my body and began again to push. The startled doctor shouted in delight. "By God, girl, you've got another baby coming through!" Within minutes he had delivered another healthy boy. Later, with the downy head of a black-haired baby boy cuddled in each arm, I smiled myself to sleep.

All along I had planned to name my next son for my pa; so I named the twins William Griffin Flint and Auguste Chouteau Flint, and called them Will and Gus. For a while our entire household revolved around them. Matt lost interest in playing with kittens, being far more fascinated by the wiggles and wails of his demanding baby brothers.

During the days I was kept so busy that I was forced to push grief and worry to the back of my mind, and at night I was so tired I fell asleep every chance I got. Uncle continued to visit General Ewing's headquarters on the chance of learning further news of Larkin, but by this time most of the Federal forces were marching east from the Indian Territory, headed for Little Rock. The trail was cold.

I did the best I could. Aunt Bereniece was a big help. Cousin Marie was a frequent visitor and seemed to love helping me with the babies. One hot September afternoon we were seated in the side yard, under the shade of the big elm trees, a baby on each of our laps, Matt playing at our feet.

"You continue to believe Larkin is alive, don't you, Sarah?" Marie asked the question gently.

"I do. I think I would know it if he were dead. I think I would feel it. So far I haven't had any premonitions or dreams that tell me he's gone. I have to believe he's still alive."

"I understand that, Sarah. I truly believe that if my Victor were to be killed, I would have some signal, some sign, some knowledge that he had actually departed this earth. I know this sounds presumptuous, but I think somehow Victor would let me know."

Even as we spoke, we saw the Union chaplain stop in front of the house and loop his horse's reins over the iron hitching post. Seeing us in the side yard, he advanced toward us. My heart lurched in my breast, but his face was lighted with a smile as he handed a telegram into my trembling hands.

"He's alive, Mrs. Flint. He walked into Fort Riley, Kansas, three days ago. The fort commander there sent a messenger east to Fort Leavenworth, where the army has a telegraph station. Major Flint is safe, ma'am. It says so right here."

They told me later that I slid out of my chair in a faint and that the chaplain's quick action saved my baby when he caught both of us in his arms. I do remember laughing and crying and talking and reading the telegram over and over: "Major Flint alive and well at Fort Riley. Details follow."

Our sounds of rejoicing roused the neighborhood. Preacher Flowers and his wife rushed over. Uncle was sent for. Aunt Bereniece came within the hour, her extensive grapevine of information having already informed the entire Chouteau clan of our happy news. Of us all, only Marie maintained her calm tranquility, seeing to the babies, watching over Matt, supervising the serving of coffee and cakes to the neighbors and relatives who filled the house, and, finally, reminding me of my responsibilities.

"You must calm yourself, dear, else your milk will dry up. The twins are ready for another feeding, and I wonder if you are as ready as they are. You're remarkable, Sarah. I have not seen you shed one tear during these long, terrible weeks when you have been waiting and wondering. And now, when you are rejoicing, you are crying as freely as you are smiling." She kissed my cheek. "Good night, Sarah. God must be watching over you and yours."

In late September the letters came pouring in, a virtual flood of words. Larkin's came first, and I read it like a thirsty man drinks water.

September 15, 1863

Dear Wife,

By this time you will have received the news both of my misfortune and of my safe deliverance. I greatly regret that you were subjected to the sadness of the first report, and rejoice with you that I am alive and safely arrived at Fort Riley, where the fort commander assures me that my request for a furlough will be granted as soon as my health deems it to be practical.

Now to recount the times we have endured for the past four weeks: Whilst our forces under General Blunt and Colonel Phillips continued to be successful in assuring Federal authority in the Indian Territory, rumors began to reach us that the Confederates were inciting the wild Plains Indians of Kansas against us. Colonel Phillips, feeling it a necessity to find out what truth there was to these rumors, asked for a party of volunteers to reconnoiter the situation. Sixteen of us rode out that day, including Ridge Rodineau and myself. But within the week, 14 of us were dead. We had ridden stealthily for over a hundred miles. Now and then we passed a few disinterested snake-eyed, half-wild savages, but mostly all we saw was short-grass and buffalo chips.

On the day we met with disaster, we had nooned in the shade of some oaks. A couple of motley-looking braves approached on horseback, begged for food and liquor, and offered to lead us to their village to powwow with their big chief. Our officer in charge, being none too sure of his bearings, agreed. I remember that Ridge made protest, but was overruled. We mounted up and rode west, directly into the trap the wild Indians had waiting for us. Scarcely five miles away we encountered hundreds of the painted fiends, swooping down over the hills toward us.

We wheeled around, headed east, and rode for our lives. Within a mile we encountered a dry creek bed, a six-foot gully gaping in our path. My horse stumbled and threw me off, which seeming misfortune turned out to be our saving grace. There was little time to change plans. The horse's leg was broken, so I prepared to hole up and kill as many Osages as I could before I met my Maker. But Ridge thought different. He stopped and yelled at me to climb on his horse. I argued with him.

"That horse can't carry the weight of two men."

"Don't be a damned fool, Lark. And don't waste any more time arguing, or we'll both be dead." I climbed on behind him.

It was a big, strong stallion and bore its double burden better than I expected, but even so, we fell behind the others. We saw them reach the Verdigris River and head north along its banks. By this time they were a quarter of a mile ahead of us and the Indians less than a mile behind us. When we got to the river we dismounted, and instead of following our comrades north, we whipped our horse and headed him north, slid down the river bank, and headed south down the river on shank's mare. We dodged and hid under the bluffs and underbrush and put as much distance as we could between us and them. We kept going for three or four miles, then hid under a brushy bluff and waited until sundown. There the two of us held a council of war and planned our strategy. We had our pistols but did not dare to shoot them. We had four days' worth of rations apiece. We were in double jeopardy — in Bushwhacker outlaw country and in savage Indian country, and both bunches were inclined to kill us first and inspect our credentials later. We decided our only chance of survival lay in heading north to Fort Riley, 100 miles distant. Accordingly, we started our wet trudge up the Verdigris River at twilight, it being too risky to walk overland or wade the river in the daylight.

There was a full moon that night, and we waded along at a fairly good clip until we came to a sandbar where the river had widened a half mile or so. There in the unearthly glow of that pale moonlight we found the bodies of our slain companions, along with the white flag of surrender they had raised. I will spare you further description of what we found, Sarah. Yet I will admit that, even as we recoiled from the horror of what we saw, we helped ourselves to the rations in their knapsacks. It was well that we did so, otherwise we would surely have died from starvation. We dared not so much as shoot a squirrel, much less light a fire, on our trek north. I owe my life to Ridge Rodineau, but we both owe our survival to the beef jerky and corn pone we took from our fallen comrades' mess kits.

Ten nights we waded up that river until it ran out of water. We undertook and survived a hazardous 20 or 30 miles on foot, then ran into the Neosho River and followed it north to within a three-day walk on in to Fort Riley. They tell us we looked like ragged skeletons when we got to the stockade, but we made it in good spirits and good time. I'll tell you this much, Sarah, I don't ever aim to eat another bite of beef jerky as long as I live. I'm not going to be too keen on wading up any more creek or riverbeds, either!

Tell little Matt I hope to see him soon! And kiss him for me. By now it may be that our next child has been born. I long to see it, and I long to see you.

I started counting the days — even the hours — until I would see him again. The twins flourished, so much alike that we had to keep a ribbon tied to Gus's wrist to tell them apart. My own spirits were so high and my body recovering so rapidly that I felt like singing and dancing. For this precious interval, God had smiled on me, and I spent my time happily making plans for Larkin's furlough.

In the meantime, the letters continued to arrive. I heard from both Minerva and Eliza on the same day. Eliza was full of family news:

Dear Sarah,

I rejoice in the chance to let you know we are all still in the land of the living, and in tolerable health, and I trust that you are enjoying your new life and all is well with you and yours. I have a lot to tell you, so will make it as brief as I can.

Your Aunt Gert is feeling puny. She hasn't been strong for a long time, but she is strong in mind if not in body, and lines up work for all of us to do while she is lying there in bed. Neely and Zeke are doing as much work as any four darkies you ever saw — they work from sunup to sundown. I try to keep up with them, and between us all we do right well. We have good crops, a good garden, two pigs in the pen, a cow, and a fair number of chickens. Your Uncle John and Aunt Kate rode over and spent a few days. They brought us enough fine-ground wheat and corn to see us through the winter.

They say the Feds are coming across Arkansas and that Old Price is on the run. This summer we've seen a lot more people going up and down the Wire Road. Mostly they've been ragged and hungry Rebel soldiers, tired of fighting and headed for home. Your Aunt Gert calls them quitters and deserters. I suppose they are. I feed them what we can spare and give them a drink of cold water. It's been mighty hot down here.

I can tell you this. I'll never let another Bushwhacker rob us blind and take our food right out of our mouths. I'm a mighty good shot now, and so are Neely and Zeke. Even Gert is ready to gun down her share, whether it be Jayhawker or Bushwhacker. She still keeps that big loaded pistol under her pillow, day and night.

Kate says the girls are fine, except Piety. She's taking Tom's death mighty hard, and it's making it all the harder for her that she has no child to remember him by. Poor girl. My heart goes out to her. Willie hasn't made it home yet, but they're all in hopes he'll show up soon.

Gert talks about baby Matt every day and wonders if he remembers her. We all send our love. Write us all your news.

Minerva's letter was as good as a newspaper, for she wrote of happenings throughout the entire state:

Dear Sarah,

Before I write of family matters I will attempt to tell you something about the war in Arkansas. Little Rock is now occupied by Federal troops, under the command of General Frederick Steele. He is reported to be a superior type of officer, and is proving to be both wise and humane in his administration of conquered territory. Already, he has approached Matthew to assist him in forming a new civilian government; however, Matthew believes such a move is premature. Many once-loyal Confederate politicians are now hastily turning their coats and declaring their belated loyalty to the Union.

Things are far from quiet in northern Arkansas. Confederate Bushwhackers are still out in full force, scavenging the land, pillaging the crops, and terrorizing the people.

And now to family news: Sam has returned and is with us once more at the family compound. He is eager to resume the practice of law and plans to remove his family to Little Rock for that purpose. We will miss them but rejoice in his safe deliverance from the war.

Some days my mind plays tricks on me. Twice now I have looked out in the early morning light and for a moment I have thought I have seen Tom riding up the hill toward home. I have felt his presence strongly on both occasions. I have formed the habit of rising with the sun and standing on the piazza each morning in the hopes of glimpsing once more that elusive phantom that is all that I have remaining of my high-spirited Tom.

I assume that by now you have learned of the death of my father, last July. It was not unexpected. As long ago as last January he anticipated his end. In my last communication from him, my father apologized that poor health prevented his traveling to Fort Smith to conduct Matthew's defense in person, explaining his selection of General Albert Pike as surrogate defense. Even in his last illness, my father maintained his loving interest in us all.

And now as to the last item of family news: Matthew and I have complied with your request regarding the Casey boy. We found old man Casey dead and the old woman dying. We have brought the boy to live in our home. He is tall for his age, has black hair and pale blue eyes. He is quick and lively, and eats like a half-starved wolf cub, but he will have little to do with any of us except the children. With Kate's six, Sam's three, and Robert's two, we now have 12. We will, of course, care for the Casey boy as our own until such time as you direct otherwise.

The entire family joins me in expressing to you our affection and admiration, and the hope that you have by now been safely delivered of another healthy child. Your are in our hearts.

Rereading all three letters, I was struck by the strength of character of each writer — Larkin, Eliza, and Minerva — and I could only hope and pray to be as worthy an adult as they had already proved themselves to be. It seemed to me that I had done little these past two weeks except play with Matt, eat, sleep, and breastfeed the babies. It was time for me to resume the management of the household.

I hired a young free Negro to live in and look after the children. Her name was Linney, niece to Dessie, the cook. Linney was a mulatto, bright-skinned and bright-eyed, and I thought we would do fine. At first, the two Irish maids balked at being on the same footing with her, but I put my own foot down and they saw the light. When they absolutely refused to share their third-story attic bedroom with her, I fixed up an alcove off my own bedroom for Linney to sleep in until the twins got old enough to sleep through the night. Uncle smiled, stayed above the squabbles of women, and opened a bottle of his best champagne the first night I came down to dinner to resume my place at his table.

"Ah, Sarah, I've missed your good company at the dinner table. Your absence has made me all the more grateful for your presence. And I expect that Larkin will soon be able to join us. Is there recent news of him?"

"He has been granted a month's furlough effective October 15, so, allowing four or five days for the journey, he expects to arrive here on or before October 20. I'm counting the hours!"

"Obviously," my uncle smiled.

"Now, Uncle, please catch me up on the news here in Kansas City. I feel as though I've done nothing but change diapers and feed babies for the past few weeks. What is going on in the real world? Has Order No. 11 truly affected business to the extent you predicted?"

"I am sorry to report that my powers of prophecy were appallingly accurate. Compared to Order No. 11, the border war of the past ten years was no more than a serious inconvenience. The financial panic we are beginning to experience will ruin some businesses. Even worse, the tightly knit frontier spirit of our town has been replaced by distrust. Up until now, neighbors could live as friends even though they held different loyalties in their hearts. Now, Federal troops have gone from house to house, forcing each householder to swear loyalty to the Union, and in some cases, to prove it. The household of Reverend Flowers, next door, is an example. Last week, when the Union delegation stopped at his door, the Reverend readily took the oath of loyalty, but his wife balked at the language and refused to swear on the Bible. The upshot of it was that idiot of a general ordered her deported to Clay County on the other side of the river. The troops actually forced that little fat 60-year-old woman to pack her bags and move out of her husband's home! I personally drove her and the reverend to the ferry boat. When the boat pulled out, that bossy woman was still giving the reverend orders as to how often he should wash and change his underwear! She didn't shed a tear, but the reverend cried all the way home!"

I should have been ashamed of myself, but I laughed until the tears ran down my cheeks.

"Surely, Uncle, they won't make that poor stubborn woman stay north of the river!"

"No, Sarah. Rest assured that steps were taken. I sent a personal telegram to General Schofield, district commander in St. Louis, as did every influential Presbyterian man in this town. She came home yesterday and started washing the reverend's underwear the same day."

"I have had little time lately to read newspapers. Tell me about your business, and tell me about the war."

"Trade is stagnating. Two of my brothers are already considering starting businesses in other locations. It is rumored that the abolition of a sep-

arate Kansas City military district will take place shortly, which means
that General Ewing will be transferred elsewhere. If the army does not
transfer him out, George Caleb Bingham will drive him out. Bingham is
spending his entire energies — and they are considerable — writing,
speech making, and politicking — attacking Ewing and Order No. 11."

"What of the war news, Uncle?"

"It is grim. A terrible battle has just been fought in Georgia at a place
called Chickamauga. The Union army was defeated, and the combined
losses on both sides were so terrible as to be beyond comprehension,
losses comparable to those at Shiloh last year. Reports put the number of
casualties at over 35,000. This can hardly be described as war. So many
men dead amounts to butchery. Surely, before God, this country should
have found a better way to settle this argument than killing the best and the
bravest of its men."

"Uncle, is it Grant who is so harsh? I've heard him called the Butcher."

"Sarah, the facts are that both sides have their share of butchers. In the
Battle of Chickamauga, the Union had 16,000 casualties; the Rebels
18,000. Partisans can give any interpretation they wish, but the blood
flowed freely from men on both sides."

"I worried so when Larkin was sent to the Indian Territory. Now I feel
grateful. He may be in less danger there than he would be east of the
Mississippi."

"There will be a lot of action in the western Plains, but I expect that in
the overall scheme of things, Larkin may be better off dealing with wild
Indians and Confederate raiders than being with Grant. Both sides are desperate now. Lee cannot hold out indefinitely. He does not lack courage, but
he does lack men and supplies. The next year will be decisive." He paused.
"And, of course, it's an election year. That means we have not heard the
last of the diabolical senator from Kansas."

Chapter 26

 *I HAVE NEVER IN MY LIFE seen a gladder look on any man's face than that on Larkin's when he finally held us all in the circle of his arms. Matt had run to meet him while Larkin was still dismounting from his horse, and I followed close behind, a baby carried proudly in each arm. Somehow he held us all in his embrace, and for the first and only time in all the years I have known him, I saw tears of joy running down the bronze cheeks of Larkin Houston Flint.*

Words cannot tell the joy that pulsed through us, although many a word was spoken in our trying to tell it all to each other. It had been more than ten months since we had

parted; we tried to make up for lost time during the precious month we now had together.

"What was the worst, Larkin, of those three weeks when you and Ridge dodged the savages? Was it walking up those dark rivers at night, or starving during the daytime, or being eternally afraid for your life? Tell me about it, so I have some idea of what you went through."

"Sarah, it wasn't the hunger, although I hope I never go through another time in my life where my belly feels like it's about to gnaw right through my backbone. And it wasn't my feet, though some nights every torn blister felt like some fiend was sticking a knife blade through the soles of my feet. It wasn't even the fear of death. God knows I'm not ready to die, but it's not so much the hereafter that I'm afraid of. It was the fear of not living — of never seeing little Matt again, or watching him grow big; never knowing or seeing this next child," he paused, and touched each downy head, "as it turned out, these next children; and never truly settling down with you to live our lives together. What hurt the most was the thought of missing out on the rest of life. So I kept walking, one step at a time, and so did Ridge. I expect his reasons were the same as mine."

He paused, and his face grew grim. "Then, too, fear is a powerful persuader. You must remember that the savages had already scalped the heads of 14 good men. I just wasn't ready to have my own head of hair added to their bloody collection."

His face changed. "Sarah, tell that light-skinned little darky to come take the children and look after them for a while. I want you to myself."

He took me with a stunning swiftness and urgency. "Sarah, I can't hold back any longer. It's been too long."

I cried out, but his pressure was so intense and his urgency so insistent that, even as I willed myself to silence, and my body began its gradually remembered responses, his passion exploded as violently as it had begun. Only afterwards, as he held me in his possessive embrace, did he show tenderness.

"Oh, Sarah, I couldn't help myself. I expect that for you it felt like our wedding night all over again, didn't it? I won't take you by storm again; I promise. Just lie here naked, love, and let me hold you for a while. God, how I've wanted to feel your sweet little body next to me. We've got a month of loving ahead of us, Sarah. Next time it'll be like it used to be with us."

It was when I was lying there in his arms that I told him about Ocie

Casey and her little boy. "Larkin, what's done is done. The child has got to be raised by somebody. Minerva will look after him until we get back to Arkansas. After that, as I see it, he'll have to be our responsibility. Every day I pray for the grace to make me equal to it."

When he finally spoke, his words surprised me. "It'll be as hard for me as for you, I expect. I never thought to raise a woods colt, much less to cause you to have to raise one of mine. If I thought he was Tom's, I think it might be easier. It would be good to have Tom's line go on. But we'll never be sure, will we? One thing I am sure of, Sarah. You're better than I deserve. This may be the only time I ever say it, so listen and believe that I mean it. I'd be a ruined man if I had to go through this world without you." Tenderly, sweetly, and slowly he kissed my lips. "I love you, Sarah, with all my heart, I love you."

Later, as we sat in front of the fire in my bedroom, Larkin holding one twin, me with the other at my breast, I questioned him further. "Larkin, why do you think it is that nature made men so different from women? Why is it that men have such strong needs for women's bodies, and girls don't even know they have a need for men? And why is it that the whole world sees this as being the natural way of things? My pa would have died of shame if I had lain with a man before we were married, yet, as I think back on it, he took it for granted that you had lain with women — as, I expect, most men do."

"I think God made men and women for two different purposes, Sarah. The world gets populated only when men spread their seed around, and men are made so they'll spread enough to keep the next generation coming." He grinned, the first time in many a month that I had seen that dear lopsided grin. "As the Good Book says, when the sower sows his seed, some falls on fertile soil, and some on rocky and barren ground. Until he's married, a man hopes he's sowing on barren ground, but he usually gets too randy to worry overmuch right then about the state of his crops!"

"Then why is it that women are expected to be so pure?"

"To be blunt about it, Sarah, a man wants to pass his property down to his own children. And, unless his wife is absolutely pure, he can't be totally sure they *are* his own children. I think it's that simple." He looked at me, eyes flashing. "Add to that, I would kill any man who trifled with you."

"That's another thing that puzzles me. Why is it, Larkin, that men are so quick to fight, and women are not? I don't see any cause to believe that women are all that much more moral than men, regardless of what every-body says about how pure and sweet womenfolks are."

"As I see it, nature put women on this earth to bear children and look after them until such time as they can look after themselves. Nine months plus a lot of years goes into the process. Look at you right this minute, with a babe at your breast. If women had to go out to fight or do their own hunting, their children would starve. So I think nature put most of the fighting blood in men for a reason. Men even fight sometimes for the fun of it, but women don't."

I thought back on the past few years. "But when a woman does fight, she fights to protect what's hers, and she fights to kill. Right now, for in-stance, my Aunt Gert keeps a loaded gun under her pillow. And I still have your father's pistol, the one he gave me that terrible night that Becky and little Matt and I set out for Pa's tavern." I shook my head. "Fighting is far from being my idea of fun. But Arkansas is full of women now who could shoot to kill if they had to. When their men come home from war, they're not going to find many sweet little helpless women left. Women may still take pride in being pure, but they've had cause lately to grow a whole lot of steel in their backbones."

Larkin reached over and exchanged babies, taking one full and sleepy baby from my breast while handing me his hungry twin. Again, he smiled at me. "Sarah, do you know, I think you just described yourself. From now on I aim to treat you with the respect you deserve!"

That night as I dressed to preside over Uncle's dinner table, my mirror confirmed what I already knew. The love of a man does wonders for a woman's looks. I buttoned again each of the tiny cloth-covered buttons that fastened the lovely gray wool dress Aunt Kate and Eliza had made for me more than three years before. Although my breasts were fuller, the waistband hooked as neatly around my middle as it had done when I was just 16.

Uncle beamed proudly at us when we walked down the stairs. "What a handsome couple you make! The entire family of Chouteau is eager to congratulate you on your safe deliverance, Larkin, but it was my judgment that you would wish to postpone extensive family gatherings. We are en-titled to at least one evening without guests, so I can rejoice with Sarah on your safe return. She has missed you more than words can tell, but I, too, have missed you. I am eager to hear your opinions. These are momentous times."

Larkin inclined his head gravely toward Uncle's exuberant face. "First, sir, permit me to express my appreciation once more. I continue to be deeply in your debt, and not only for your kindness in sheltering my family. Sarah has just told me of the collapse of your building and the dying request of the woman Ocie Casey. I deeply appreciate your discretion and your tenderness to Sarah."

Uncle held up a silencing hand to cut short any further words on the subject. "What's done is done, Larkin. I see no need to speak more on the matter. Every man can look at his past and find room for improvement. Let us speak of other topics."

"But what actually caused that big brick building to collapse, Uncle?" I asked.

"When we dug out all of the rubble and got down to the basement, we found tunnels leading out on two sides, both the north and the south. We now think — Major Plumb and I — that the Rebels had dug tunnels under the buildings so the girls could escape. Whoever was doing the digging — and it was likely the work of many — lacked any knowledge of engineering principles, for they dug out the very bricks that formed the foundations of the building."

"But why two? Wouldn't one tunnel have done it?"

"Our analysis is that after going through all the secretive backbreaking work of chiseling through the north foundation, the Rebels found that they had entered a stronghold, the basement storage room. The only access to that room from within was through a heavily padlocked door. It was used as a vault by the two merchants who rented the space on the first floor. One can imagine their disappointment when the diggers realized that all their picking and shoveling had been for naught and they had to begin again!"

Larkin, ever practical, asked in surprise. "How could that much digging escape the notice of the guards? There was bound to be noise in the doing of it."

"The women must have been in on the plot. Night after night they yelled and flirted and flaunted themselves at their windows so as to keep a loud crowd of men surrounding the building. The yells of the mob concealed the noise of the diggers. Major Plumb tells me the women had pestered him for the privilege of visiting the stores during the afternoon, and he had obliged, taking the precaution of placing a guard at each of the street level exits. Their plan was simple enough. The women planned to descend to the basement and slip out through the tunnels while their guards thought they were shopping for trinkets and ribbons. I have no doubt that Quantrill masterminded the entire scheme. The lives of the women meant little to him. It is bloodletting he lives for."

"Well, he's done that in plenty." Larkin's tone was hard.

Uncle went on to other events. "You are aware, I am sure, that Lincoln has now named Grant to be commander of all of the Union forces in the West. Grant has already replaced Rosecrans with Thomas."

"My brothers Robert and Stant fought under Thomas last month at the Battle of Chickamauga. They wrote to our father that General Thomas stood like a rock. I expect they'll both be glad of this change in command. One thing is sure — Grant's not in it for the glory. Grant's in this thing to win. He won't focus on capturing cities. It'll be winning battles he'll set his mind to."

"What do you hear from Arkansas, Larkin, now that the Union holds Little Rock?"

"Father reports that Lincoln seems to be closely monitoring events there. It's hard to imagine how Lincoln finds the time or the strength to do all he has to do. Seems that he is working out a plan of reconstruction. Several Union meetings have already been held in the northwestern part of the state. The crowds attending these meetings were large and enthusiastic. Several prominent men have already sworn an oath of allegiance.

"Still, there are bound to be many who will go to their graves hating the Union and admiring all who fought against it. And it may be that those who stayed at home and didn't fight will be more bitter than the soldiers. Most of us who have faced fire have come to respect the men we're fighting against. I wonder what the country will be like when this war finally ends. The seeds of bitterness are buried deep."

I thought of Larkin's sister Kate. "Maybe deeper in the women than in the men."

Uncle changed the subject. "Larkin, what is the state of things in the Indian Territory now? What of those Indians who cast their lot with the Confederacy? And what has happened to the many who were hounded off their lands because of their loyalties to the North?"

"Thousands upon thousands are still in Kansas. Others are still farther north. Senator Lane is making his usual righteous noises about wanting to help his dispossessed red-skinned brothers return to their lands in the Indian Territory, but that's because Lane's anxious to get them out of Kansas. There'll soon be a big push to get the northern Indians moved back to their treaty lands, I expect. The Indians will need to get started by February or March so they can get back to their lands in time to plant their spring crops."

Uncle was a man who looked at legalities. "What about the land once owned by those Indians who joined the Confederacy? I am assuming the government's position to be that those who fought for the South broke their treaties with the United States and forfeited their lands."

"Exactly. Which means there will be a lot of land up for grabs in Indian Territory. That's another reason Senator Lane — slippery rascal that he is — is trying to push as many Indians south as he can. He's trying to move them off of that rich Kansas prairie land and down to that red dirt in the Indian Nation. Now that old John Ross is in Philadelphia and Washington, Lane stands a good chance of doing exactly that." Larkin summed it up. "While the northern Indians die from smallpox on their Kansas reservations and the Confederate Cherokees starve on the trails as they try to escape south to Texas, that so-called friend to the Indians, Senator Lane, profits from their misery.

"Yet for every rotten politician in this country, there are hundreds of honest men," Larkin continued. "Surely, when this war is over, honest men will manage to reestablish themselves in government. Otherwise, it will all be for naught. I have told Ridge more than once that when the war ends, he's going to be obligated to be a leader among the Cherokees."

Uncle looked squarely at Larkin. "And do you not see a similar set of obligations for yourself? Arkansas will be as torn and impoverished as any state in this Union and deeply in need of honest and intelligent leadership. Do you not see a duty to serve your country in peace as well as in war?"

"Not until I get my own affairs in order and my own family settled in. Once this war ends, there's enough work ahead of me in Arkansas to keep me at home for many a year. That land Sarah inherited is mighty good land, no question about that, but it's got to be worked by somebody before it can produce. White men may be willing to sharecrop another man's land for a while, but they'll move on as soon as they get a chance. The Lord only knows whether darkies will be willing workers once they are free to come and go as they please. It's going to be a different world down there in Arkansas."

I didn't take issue with Larkin very often, but I felt obliged to do so now. "Neely and Zeke have been free for nearly two years now, but they've stayed right there with Eliza and Aunt Gert and worked like dogs. Not that Eliza hasn't worked just as hard."

"They haven't had much choice so far. Where could they go where things would be better? But when this war ends, they're apt to see things in a different light. And they'll not be alone. The South is not going to know how to treat darkies as free men, and the North's not going to want to deal with them at all. Even those pious-mouthed abolitionists up in New England will keep on talking righteous about darkies up there, but they'll want us to keep them all down here."

"All the more reason for you to consider the duties of leadership yourself, Larkin. When you come to the choice between living under a system run by politicians for their own glory and profit or of assuming the responsibilities and the yoke of government yourself, I most sincerely hope you will think long and hard on the choice. I fear that my cynicism is all too apparent when I say this, but the end of this war will tempt many a man to reap the spoils of victory. For every honest statesman like Abraham Lincoln, there will be a dozen profiteers like Jim Lane."

Larkin answered him thoughtfully. "Arkansas has lost a lot of good men, and will lose a lot more before this war is over. Now that Grant's the commander, he's apt to force this war to a bloody finish. I have no doubt the war will end in Union victory, but it won't come cheap. When it's over, there may not be enough good men left in Arkansas to form a government."

"Ah, but there will be, Larkin. President Lincoln is about to propose a plan that is simplicity itself, but a plan that recognizes the scarcity of good men. My sources in Washington tell me it is already being discussed. They are sworn to secrecy as to details, but they all agree on the mercy and intelligence of the proposal." He paused. "When you say your prayers tonight, Sarah, include a prayer of thanksgiving for a leader like Lincoln. I do not know of another man in public life today who has the breadth of wisdom that he commands. That the country produced such a man is a triumph for democracy; that the country recognized and elected such a good man is a real miracle."

Chapter 27

THE SECOND DAY Larkin was home, I gave him the present I had been saving as a surprise. I figured that seeing his twin baby boys was surprise enough for the first day, but the next morning I surprised him all over again. During the past year I had hung on to as many of my gold pieces as I could, spending them frugally and carefully when I had to part with them. But Larkin's letter about his escape changed my attitude about money. After I got that letter, over and over again I pictured him on Ridge's horse, riding for his life, the Indians gaining on them with every pounding hoofbeat, Larkin's own horse and all his possessions already abandoned on the barren

prairie. So with Uncle's help I went out and searched the City of Kansas until I found the one gift that I knew would gladden Larkin's heart. I paid an old German cabinetmaker $100 in gold for a fiddle so beautifully crafted that the old man had tears in his eyes when he handed it over into my keeping.

When I held the fiddle out to Larkin, surprise and joy vied for dominance on his handsome face. He stroked the glowing wood and carefully balanced the bow. Then with his eyes half-closed, he bent his black head over the instrument, his entire mind and body concentrating on the singing sounds that he coaxed into life with his skillful fingers. As the music surged and soared, the violin sang a melody I had never heard before — a wonderful mingling of sorrow and joy. It was almost as if the music was telling the secrets of life, giving voice to the silent sufferings, the quick joys, the glad times, the sad partings, and the hopes of tomorrows. Quick tears stung my eyes as I listened. When he finally laid down the bow, I went over and put my arms around him.

"I've never heard you play that way before."

"The song's been running through my mind for weeks now. I wasn't sure I would be able to make the sounds come out the same way they've been singing in my mind, but it came close."

"It's more beautiful than anything I have ever heard."

He put his arm around my shoulders and ran his fingers through my hair, his look of rapt concentration now replaced by a boyish grin. "Thank God you're prejudiced, Sarah. I couldn't stand it if you weren't!"

Then his tone grew sober again. "This song's for Tom. I think of it as 'Tom's Tune,' but I guess I'm going to have to find a better name for it. But let's change the tune, now." He picked up the bow again and began such a lilting rendition of "Old Dan Tucker" that Matt began to giggle and dance around us, old Dessie came grinning out of the kitchen to stand in the hall and clap her hands and sway, and Linney sashayed down the long hall with a twin on each arm to stand and pat her foot in the wide parlor archway. We all got carried away, made girlish by the lively fun of the music. I caught little Matt by both his hands.

"Come on, Matt, you can pardner your mother!" Giggling and glad, we skipped our way down the hall and back. Dessie and Linney clapped, and all of us sang to Larkin's fiddle.

"Old Dan Tucker went to town . . ."

"Swingin' dem purty gals round and round!"

When he had finished, Larkin put the fiddle in its case as tenderly as I would have put a baby to bed.

"I've said it before, and if I keep on being lucky, I'll have many a chance to say it again, but you do amaze me, Sarah. Yes, ma'am, you surely do." He was grinning from ear to ear.

Later, he put on his blue officer's coat with its double row of brass buttons marching down the front, picked up his braid-trimmed cap, strapped on his pistol, and picked up his riding crop to go down to join Uncle Auguste in the world of men and commerce. But as he walked down the path toward his waiting horse, he was still whistling "Old Dan Tucker."

The days flew past, one sparkling, bright day after another. I never remembered seeing the skies look any bluer and I never felt the days go by faster then they did that blessed month we had together in the fall of 1863. Frost painted the trees and lifted our already happy hearts. Every day was a jubilee for me. Fall's colors ran riot in every direction, and I was ever mindful that the crimson and gold and wine-red and umber leaves were nature's passionate prelude to winter. We gloried in the beauty of the days — the warm sun, the crisp winds, the vivid scattering leaves, the tang in the air chilled by the cold, starry nights, nights where we lay deep in the warm pleasures of my big four-poster bed.

Every relative we had competed for the pleasure of hosting a gathering in Larkin's honor. We all tried to keep things as calm as we could in the face of the worrying news that continued unabated from the world of war. Of course, Larkin was the center of attention at every family assembly. Over and over again, folks gathered around, sometimes asking for music, sometimes asking his opinions, but always seeking his company.

One evening as Larkin moved across the room to join the group of men who were waiting to claim his attention, Cousin Marie turned to me. "He's a very special kind of man. Does he know how superior he is?"

"Do you mean, does he have the big head?"

"That's not exactly my meaning, but that's a fairly good down-home way of putting it, I suppose."

"He has the gift of truly focusing his attention on the person he's talking to. Look at him now, over there listening to Uncle Louis in that circle of men." Marie smiled her gentle smile. "Our Uncle Louis is not precisely my idea of a fascinating conversationalist, but Larkin is listening as though he is deeply interested in whatever it is Uncle Louis is giving his usual strong opinion about."

The editor of the newspaper was interrogating my uncle as to his future plans. "I am told, Louis, that two of your brothers are leaving to begin new businesses in California, but that you and Auguste will remain here in the Midwest. In which direction will your new venture lead you?"

"Geographically, Van Horn, we will all go in the same direction — West, where the future of the country lies. One brother will go to California, one brother to Colorado. I shall not reveal the nature of their plans. That is for them to do, if they choose to.

"My own plans I shall freely tell you. I shall establish a branch of Chouteau at Fort Larned in Kansas, for the purpose of buying and selling buffalo hides."

"What!" Van Horn was incredulous. "With a history as outstanding as that of your family, and with interests so varied, you mean to tell me, man, that you are going to concentrate on dealing in buffalo hides?"

"Indeed I am. And I will tell you frankly that there will be an enormous market in buffalo hides once this war is over. I speak of this now only because I know your discretion in matters of business. I shall, in the beginning, establish an ordinary trading post, ostensibly to accommodate the needs of Fort Larned. But the ultimate goals will be the buying and selling of buffalo hides."

"The shrewdness of the brothers Chouteau is legendary. I will not argue with you, but I must confess that I see little opportunity for profit there. The plains are full of buffalo and the plains are full of Indians. So far, they've both been more of a hindrance than a help."

It was Larkin who answered him. "Sir, there are many who look on the Indians as a threat. Speaking as one who has both fought them and fought alongside them, I hold an opinion somewhat more complex, but that is neither here nor there. I myself am one-quarter Cherokee, and proud to have that blood in my veins. Yet less than three months past I was in terror of my life from wild Plains Indians who scalped and beheaded 14 of my friends and comrades. My boyhood friend, the man to whom I owe my life, is himself half Indian. I know no finer man.

"Yet having said all this, I will tell you that I believe that when this present war is over, another will begin. Indeed, it is already beginning. We will war against the wild Plains Indians. And the buffalo plays an important role. I believe Louis Chouteau is exhibiting exceptional commercial foresight."

Van Horn's perceptive eyes looked directly into those of Larkin. "Is there a solution to the Indian problem?"

"The solution is assimilation of Indians into the general society of our country. Packing them off to loaf and languish on reservations is not the answer. No man can keep his pride when he lives off the dole of another. And for their part, the Indians have got to master the ways of the white men, for white men are now in the majority. It's not a question of wanting to do it; it must be done.

"The Cherokees have already adapted to the white man's ways. Some have thrived. Look at John Ross, and Stand Watie, and the Rodineau family. Some have failed, as is true of any group of men. The solution is to have a policy of government that rewards the Indian who will cast his lot as a free and independent man, the same as the white settlers. The solution is to make sure that each Indian has the same chance as each white man, and then to let them all sink or swim."

"That'll never happen. The Indians won't see it and the white men won't want it. And it's the white men who vote. Your solution takes too much time, Major Flint — a generation or so, plus patience and hard work on the part of the Indians, along with more tolerance and less greed on the part of the white settlers. Voters will lack the patience for your solution."

"Of course, to be fair, these Indians are going to have to be allowed a vote, too," said Larkin. "If they're going to be expected to be independent, it's only fair to let them vote. That means they've got to be educated."

Van Horn looked grim. "That will never come to pass, Flint. And I still haven't heard how those buffalo hides figure into this equation."

"When this war between the states is ended, the next war is going to be between the white men and the Indians. And the United States Army is going to be on the side of the settlers. Right now the Plains are filled with Indians and with buffalo, and the Indians depend on the buffalo for the majority of their needs. The policy of our future will be to make the Indian absolutely dependent on the U.S. government for their every need. Either the buffalo or the Indian must go. We're not going to be able to handle the Indians so long as they've got plenty of buffalo. In the long run, the government's policy will be that it's a more humane thing to kill off the buffalo than to kill off the Indian.

"Mark my words," Larkin continued, "there'll be a lot of dead buffalo lying around on that prairie before the government's able to get those Indians corralled on reservations."

Mr. Van Horn looked over at my Uncle Louis. "There's something I'm missing here, Chouteau. You're not planning to set up a new business just to help along the subjugation of Indians. What is the piece of the puzzle that I'm missing?"

My uncle, looking as solemn as if he were in church, leaned back and prophesied. "I have it on good authority that tanned buffalo hides make excellent belting for machinery, the best so far discovered. When this war ends, the entire country will expand. Factories will flourish and industries yet unconceived will create a great demand for heavy machinery. Wheels cannot turn without belting. Everything we have said to you tonight, Van Horn, has been said to you in the strictest confidence."

Van Horn smiled. "Louis, you promise me you'll stay out of the newspaper business, and I'll promise you to stay out of the hide business. And may we both prosper!"

"Certainly you both stand a better chance of it under that arrangement." Uncle Auguste smiled on both gentlemen.

"But Larkin, your analysis is indeed bleak. Not only bleak, but inhumane. And I wonder, speaking as one whose family's beginnings in commerce were based primarily on trade with the Indians, if these new settlers have any right to consider themselves to be a superior race. It is a moral question of some magnitude." Uncle turned to the frail old priest standing on his right, his spiritual leader and close friend. "I would be most appreciative of your views on the subject, Father."

"As you know, Auguste, when I came first to Westport Landing I ministered to Indian and white men, alike. To be as precise as possible, I found the behavior of one race to be as pagan as that of the other. The early settlers were unwashed and unshaven, given to the most horrible imprecations and blasphemies, ignorant, loud, armed to the teeth, all too ready to drink and ready to fight. Furthermore, being men without families, they were all too ready to wench. Mostly Scotch-Irish, of whom I will admit I have an insufficient understanding. Though they lay claim to being Methodists and Presbyterians, in my own observation they came closer to being heathen." The priest paused. "But that was long ago. No doubt the new settlers will be an entirely different breed of men."

Uncle looked decidedly uncomfortable. "Father, I had perhaps neglected to mention it earlier, but my nephew, here, Major Flint, is himself of Scotch-Irish extraction. Larkin, you should be aware that Father Benet has given of his talents and labored for the Lord in our rough frontier for nearly 40 years. The kinds of people who were early attracted to the City of Kansas have not necessarily been of the highest caliber." He paused, clearly wondering how to proceed.

Larkin laughed heartily, to the obvious relief of my uncles. "Father, I would not for the world attempt to take issue with you. It's true that I am Scotch-Irish, and am proud of being so, for more than most I am aware of the obstacles and the heartaches implied in that heritage.

"History teaches hard lessons. Four hundred years ago, when France was already civilized enough to produce a Sun King, the Scotch lived in a mountainland harsh with poverty, ignorance, and near-anarchy, ruled by feudal lairds who fought each other at the drop of a hat.

"I have no doubt my people then were as dirty as the Indians now are, and as superstitious. But they were also a gritty, high-tempered, fun-loving people. My impression is they were mostly willing to live and let live and greatly enjoy the doing of it.

"Some of us are ignorant, some are learned; some are hardworking; some are louts; some are saints, and some are sinners. But all are proud, and quick to fight. Not a bad breed of men to settle a new land, but a breed that is likely to be hard on the Indians, when it comes to competing for land they both want."

Van Horn looked at Larkin with respect. "No harder than the Germans and the Swiss, is my guess. The whole of Europe is going to be looking our way, and hungry men from one country will be just as desperate as another. I would agree with your analysis, Major, but I would add one more element. The Scotch-Irish, in my experience, are both a religious and a warlike people and singularly resistant to taking orders from any man."

"No wonder the Rebels fight so well." Uncle Louis summed it up. "Most of the South was settled by the Scotch-Irish. Grant has his work cut out for him. The breed of man you just described, gentlemen, will fight until he drops."

"I know that, sir, better than most." His shoulders squared and his jaw set, Larkin bowed to the group, took my arm, and we walked together out into the cold night air.

Chapter 28

LIFE WENT ON AFTER Larkin left. Both armies settled down into winter quarters so their men could recover their strength and make ready for the spring campaigns. A lot of letters went back and forth that winter. Matthew Flint was deeply involved in President Lincoln's plans for amnesty and reconstruction, so I had reliable news of the many changes taking place at home. Minerva's Christmas letter was full of hope about the changes for the better.

Dear Sarah,
I write you now from Little Rock, where

Matthew and I have taken up residence.

President Lincoln's steps have been both wise and just. Matthew feels Lincoln's plan has an added advantage in that it is easy for all to understand. On December 8, 1863, Lincoln offered full pardon and restoration of property rights (except for their slaves) to such "Rebels as would swear an oath of future loyalty to the Constitution of the United States." The President's plan for design of the new government is simplicity itself. When the number of newly loyal voters is equal to ten percent of the number who voted in the presidential election of 1860, these loyal people are entitled to establish a new state government.

Progress has been rapid. I have written all the children of the very considerable honor that President Lincoln has bestowed on their father. President Lincoln has named Matthew Flint the provisional governor of Arkansas, in recognition of Matthew's vote being the only loyal one cast on that spring day in 1861 when the state legislature voted Arkansas out of the Union.

A new state convention will meet on January 4, 1864. Matthew says the main work of this body will be to take the old state constitution and amend it so as to abolish slavery, repudiate the Confederate debt, and provide the people of Arkansas an opportunity to take the oath of loyalty to the Union.

Becky tells me she is writing you the family news, but I must tell you myself of my remarkable experience the morning we left our home to journey to Little Rock. The day was November 25, Tom's birthday. As was my habit, I had risen with the sun and was standing on the porch looking down the long drive to the gate. Little Jeff slipped out of his bed and stood at my side. We stood in silence, my every thought being centered on memories of my dear Tom.

Then I saw him. He came riding up the hill again, but this time he seemed to be searching — whether for something or for someone I knew not which. Suddenly his eyes spied little Jeff, half hidden behind my skirts. A smile appeared on his face, and he waved in recognition. To my everlasting amazement, Jeff raised his little arm and waved at Tom in return. Tom's glance then shifted to me, and in far less time than it takes to write it, he looked straight into my eyes, raised his hand to his forehead in a formal salute of farewell, wheeled his horse around, and disappeared into the morning mist.

I insisted to Matthew that Jeff accompany us to Little Rock. He is here with us now and is gradually becoming accustomed to the town and to us. I must admit there are times when I feel that I am trying to domesticate a young fox, but Jeff is a joy, nevertheless. Matthew sends his love to you and to all your family. We hope at some future time to have the honor and pleasure of meeting the relatives who continue to be so gracious to you.

Three times I read Minerva's letter, each time marveling anew at its message. Into my mind flashed one of Pa's favorite philosophies: "God works in mysterious ways, His wonders to perform!" Is a vision made visible to the eye any less or any more real than a vision that flashes through the mind? I pondered it often but spoke it to none.

Becky's letter was filled to the brim with love of Willie and love of life.

Dear Sister Sarah,

Willie got home for Christmas, riding up to Griffin's Mill on the back of a ramshackle, swaybacked mule that had a belly slung so low that Willie's feet nearly dragged the ground. I will never in my life see a more beautiful sight than my freckle-faced, curly-headed Will Griffin jumping down off of that tuckered-out mule.

You would have thought it was the Second Coming the way we all carried on. Your Aunt Kate shouted as though the Lord had just sent a tongue of fire to hover over her head — well, that last statement may be an exaggeration, but not by much. Your Uncle John hugged Willie so hard I was afraid he would break a rib. Hope and Piety and Charity took turns hugging and laughing and crying, and through it all Willie grinned that old easygoing grin we had missed so much.

We had such a hard time finding any time to ourselves that after he had been home a week, Willie and I moved out. You'll never guess where we are now! Willie thought up the idea, and it has turned out remarkably well. We are honeymooning in your old cabin — yours and Larkin's. Actually, it's too big to be called a cabin, but anyhow, that's where we are. Ned joined the army last month, leaving Monnie by herself, and Willie persuaded her to go over to Jasper to visit her sister and family for a month. Monnie was glad of the chance for a visit with her sister; she's been lonesome for Ned, so the visit will be good for her. In any case, she had not spent a night away from the place since that day they first came over three years ago.

Kate gave Ned the best horse she owned so he could ride off in style. He's headed for Fort Smith to try to enlist in Larkin's regiment.

So, your warm house is once again sheltering a honeymoon-couple. At the end of the month we will go to Fayetteville, where Willie plans to establish his medical practice. He says that when he hangs out his shingle it will be time for me to start calling him Will instead of Willie. In the meantime, though, each day we spend together seems too good to be true.

I read and reread Minerva's and Becky's letters before sending them on to Larkin. This was a time when Larkin's premonitions of Union victory were beginning to be substantiated by events of the war. When Grant had won that mighty battle in Tennessee in late November, he had split the country vertically, separating the eastern part of the South from the West along the Mississippi River. Now, in January, General Sherman began his long march, first heading south, then heading from west to east across the Confederacy, trying to split the country horizontally. In late January, President Lincoln had again reorganized his army west of the Mississippi, transferring the bitterly resented General Ewing and replacing him with a man of proven qualifications, General William Rosencrans. Influential men in Kansas City lost no time in welcoming this clear-eyed, hard-headed general to their city.

Uncle Auguste was invited to a dinner given in the general's honor by the newspaper editor. Mrs. Van Horn was kind enough to include me in her invitation. I dressed with care, for the assembled guests would be as well dressed as any I had ever seen. I wore the elegantly simple black velvet dress that had been Aunt Bereniece's Christmas gift upon my arrival in Kansas City. It was a matter of considerable satisfaction to me that the dress still fit. Lifting the rich cloth of my crinolined skirt, I descended the stairway to the wide hall where Uncle waited with my cloak.

"Sarah, there is no doubt in my mind that I am escorting the most beautiful woman in the City of Kansas this evening. I suspect our new general will be considerably impressed."

"Uncle, you and I both know how prejudiced you are." I laughed up at my fondly beaming uncle. "I expect the general has a lot more on his mind than dinner parties. But I'm honored to be invited, just the same. Do you realize that this is the first time I have gone anywhere without my babies since the twins were born? I may not know how to act without a baby on my lap!"

Uncle wrapped my cloak around me. "How fortunate you are, dear girl. A handsome and capable husband, three fine children, and only last month we celebrated your 20th birthday! And how fortunate I am to have the blessing of your presence in my household." With a flourish, Uncle offered his arm and escorted me out to his carriage.

The party was well advanced when we arrived. I was delighted to see Cousin Marie across the room, her lovely face intent as she conversed with two men of considerable presence — the two Toms, Uncle called them, Thomas Swope and Thomas Smart. The guest of honor stood in front of the fireplace. Even had he not already appropriated the central position in the room, his commanding presence alone would have established his importance. A tall, dignified, broad-shouldered man, General Rosencrans's face was that of one accustomed to power and made stern by responsibility. My impression was of dark, thick hair and a full beard and mustache that enhanced rather than concealed a firm mouth and strong jaw.

Our host introduced us. "General Rosencrans, may I present Mrs. Flint? Mrs. Flint's husband, Major Larkin Flint, serves in the Indian Territory under Colonel Phillips. I believe you have already met her uncle, Auguste Chouteau."

As I curtsied in response to Van Horn's introduction, I looked up into a face dominated by intelligent eyes and accentuated by a strong, aquiline nose. A warm smile altered the general's sternness. "Madam, I have already been informed of your husband's miraculous trek up the Verdigris River. He is widely regarded as a brave and resourceful man. Having now met you, I realize again how extremely fortunate a man he is." He turned to Uncle Auguste. "Sir, I am delighted to again have the honor of meeting with you. I hope in the near future to have the opportunity to consult with you regarding some problems in the area."

"General, you have only to designate a meeting time. My time is yours to command." My uncle was sincere in his statement. This new general was no novice, like his predecessor, General Ewing, nor did he appear to be unduly influenced by the maneuverings of the fanatical and self-serving Senator Lane.

Talk flowed among those who sat at Van Horn's richly appointed table that evening. The conversation was dominated by the general but was freely entered into by all the men present.

The general went to the heart of the matter. "Gentlemen, I have been told that the country to the north of here is mostly filled with disloyal citizens, not only Confederate sympathizers, but also men who once served in Price's army and have now returned to their homes. Deserters from the South they may well be, but their sympathies are still with the South, and my sources feel there are enough of them to pose a threat. I'd be most interested in your views on this matter. Should you prefer to speak with me privately, I will honor your decisions."

Van Horn responded. "We're all honorable citizens, sir, each and every one of us. And I, for one, have no compunction about stating my views.

"We call these men the 'pawpaw militia,' men manipulated by the Bushwhackers. I suspect that, if the truth were known, they probably have already formed an underground organization of some kind."

"Pawpaw?" The general looked puzzled.

Thomas Swope answered him. "The pawpaw is a fruit native to the Ozarks. It grows on low trees in the mountains. They say the guerrillas eat pawpaws and possums when the going gets rough. In other words, the Bushwhackers use pawpaws, and they use these clandestine citizens for their own ends."

"It is a great element of disturbance in Missouri. The state is, and has been from the beginning, populated by two major classes of citizens — radicals, that is to say abolitionists, and conservatives, people who hold a preference for the Confederacy and for slavery. These pawpaws are in league with General Price. Always have been. Price's main goal in life is to be governor of Missouri again, and he keeps raiding into Missouri every chance he gets."

My uncle looked across the table to Hamilton Montgomery, Marie's father-in-law. "Ham, have you heard anything about a secret society up in the northern part of the state?"

"I have, Auguste, and what I have heard has caused me considerable worry. I hear there's a widespread network of secret lodges, and their avowed purpose is to organize. When the time is right, they plan to assassinate. And I hear people like us are the targets."

Uncle replied solemnly. "That's the gist of what I've heard, except for one substantial addition. I've heard that these folks have friends in high places in Washington, traitors so well placed as to be above suspicion. I would caution you, General Rosencrans, to employ men in whom you have complete and utter confidence when you undertake to investigate this."

The general looked as hard as iron. "Sir, even if these Rebels are leagued with the powers of darkness, and even if this delicate business of getting to the bottom of their plot requires a trip to hell, I am determined to ferret it out! The lives of too many good and honorable men are at stake."

Later, as we rode home through the snowy night, I asked Uncle Auguste the question I had held back earlier. "Uncle, how did you come to know so much about these people north of the river?"

"Sarah, remember last August when the wife of Reverend Flowers got deported because of the damnable Order No. 11? She boarded with some people up at Weston who mistakenly took her to be of Rebel sympathies. They didn't realize that she had been brought up a Quaker and had refused on principle to swear on her Bible about military matters. In any case, the women where Mrs. Flowers stayed babbled freely. The Reverend Flowers told me that there is an organization of secret lodges masterminded by some former congressman that Lincoln expelled for treason at the beginning of the war. This treason is not confined to the backwoods of Missouri. Would that it were!"

"Why, then, Uncle, is it only now that the situation is being dealt with?"

"It is because General Ewing did not believe the political preferences of these 'backwoods people,' to use his term, to be important. I personally went to him with this information when Mrs. Flowers returned. Ewing dismissed it as the trivia of gossiping women." Uncle paused. "Ewing is entirely too much under the influence of Senator Lane. But this new general is his own man, Sarah, if I'm any judge. This is an election year. We'll see a lot of action before too long. Let us hope that God grants the country both peace and justice during this coming year."

"Uncle," I asked, "can you honestly tell me that the end of this war is in sight? All I read and all I hear comes down to bitter fighting, terrible losses, with one side claiming they've won one time, the other the next time, but mostly, aren't they killing each other in about the same numbers?"

Uncle's shrewd old face was sad. "Yes, child, each army is killing the other in numbers that, overall, are approximate. The best and the finest men in the country are sacrificing themselves in a war that should never have been fought. But, as I stated, this is an election year."

"How can the person who is elected determine the victories of the war, Uncle? Both sides are already fighting as hard as they can."

"Ah, it is the reverse, Sarah. The progress of the war will decide the election. Not in the Confederacy — Jeff Davis was elected to a six-year term. He does not have to waste one iota of his energies on an election this year. But Lincoln's candidacy will rise or fall with the tide of Union victories. The Democrats of the North are already crying out for the need to sue for peace. They believe the war to have been a failure. When the nation votes next fall, men will in effect be voting on whether to sue for peace and drop out of the war, or to fight on to victory at all costs."

"Are you telling me, Uncle, that Lincoln will have to spend his time campaigning this year?"

"On the contrary. I am told that Lincoln, shrewd and honorable man that he is, plans to continue to spend all his time and energies on the war and let his record speak for itself. His many critics will jump into the fray and campaign against him, but Lincoln's face is set forward. He will ignore the arrows aimed at his back."

"Well, my stepmother, Eliza, would say that it's always darkest before the dawn."

"We will most devoutly hope that to be true in the present case. In any case, good night. I was enormously proud of you this evening, my dear."

He handed my cloak to Linney, and I walked swiftly up the stairs, where my hungry twins awaited me. As I suckled their demanding little mouths at my breasts, I thought of the many mothers who had sent their sons off to war and needless sacrifice. How many, I wondered, thought this war to be worth the awful price that had already been paid? And if I myself could vote, I wondered how strong the temptation would be to opt for peace without victory.

Chapter 29

THE LETTER FROM Eliza came in early March. I tore it open with eager fingers, for it had been almost a month since I had had news from home.

Dear Sarah,
I have sorrowful news to communicate.
Your Aunt Gert is dead, a victim to the war and to the forces of evil. I will try to tell you about it as straightforwardly as I can.
As you know, the Federals have proved victorious in northwestern Arkansas and have chased

General Price and his Rebels down south of the Arkansas River. The upshot of this is that this part of the state has been left open to the raids of lawless and evil bandits who would rather raid and steal what others have worked for than go out and earn their living by the sweat of their own brows.

We have heard of a lot of killings lately — a dreadful slaughter of what few old men and boys that are left in these parts, plus stealing and burning and destruction like you would not believe.

And now I will tell you about the grievous times we have endured here. It was one week ago today, on February 10, that it happened. Neely had already fed your Aunt Gert her breakfast, your aunt having felt too poorly to get out of bed. Neely and Zeke and I were just getting ready to sit down for our own breakfast. I long ago gave up the custom of making Neely and Zeke eat at a separate table. We work together and we eat together, except, of course, when we have company. Anyhow, in rushed these two big Bushwhacking men, smelling to high heaven of whiskey and filth, their guns drawn. They demanded breakfast.

"The table's set," said I. "We'll feed you what we were going to eat ourselves."

They sat right down, grabbed every bite we had with their big, dirty hands, and gobbled it up like pigs, while Gert glared at them from her bed from the back of the room. Then one of them pointed his gun at Neely and me while the other rascal got up and grabbed Zeke and dragged him over in front of the fireplace.

"Now," said he, "you women are going to give us what gold you've got hid around here."

The one who had grabbed Zeke tied up his hands and feet and stuck the poker in the fire to heat it up.

"Now don't tell me you all ain't got no gold, because every time you tell me that I aim to warm up this nigger's feet with this here hot poker!"

We begged him to spare Zeke such fearful pain, but to no avail. That fiend took off Zeke's shoes and made ready.

"It's buried in a fruit jar in the henhouse," said I. "I'll get the gold, but don't torture that poor helpless darky!"

We were all crying and screaming, and I think the rascals believed me, but that devil of a man stuck that red-hot poker up against Zeke's bare foot anyway. Poor Zeke let out a scream the likes of which I hope to never have to hear again. I ran to the henhouse and grabbed the fruit jar and ran back with it and threw it at the outlaw's feet.

"Here," I said, "it was my poor dead husband's, but it's yours now. Just leave us alone."

But the one holding the poker just grinned. "Well, now, woman, we've got the gold, we got our breakfast, and I reckon it's time we got a little fun. Me, I get my fun by hearing niggers holler. Old Newt, over there, he likes to have his fun with women. We'll take our fun one of us at a time. He'll hold the gun whilst I have my fun; I'll later on do the same fer him." He picked up the poker and headed for Zeke.

All at once your feisty little Aunt Gert, who had been too weak to get out of bed, summoned all her strength and brought that big pistol of hers out from under the covers and shot that torturing outlaw right through the heart. Even as that one fell, the other outlaw whirled around and turned his gun on Gert and shot her dead.

I grabbed the poker and hit that second outlaw on the head with all my strength. He dropped like an ox, but I was not sure he was dead.

"Neely," I said, "I need to hit him again, but I don't know whether I can bring myself to do it or not."

"I can," said Neely. She went out in the yard and got the ax and hit that murdering devil on the head. After that, there was no doubt that the man was dead.

So your brave little Aunt Gert is gone, staunch to the end. I miss her more than words can tell.

Gert had changed her will this past month whilst your Uncle John and Will were here to witness it. She left 160 acres of her land to Neely and Zeke and the rest of it to me. We will all three stay on right here in Gert's house in the foreseeable future. Life is too hazardous to live apart. Write to us soon, for we all miss you so.

Even as I wept for Aunt Gert, grim news from other places arrived to claim my attention. Larkin was reassigned to fight an enemy fully as dangerous and far more treacherous than the Rebel army. When Grant and Sherman drew away most of the Union soldiers east of the Mississippi, the vast stretches of Western plains were left unprotected. Wild Indians, made bold by opportunity, began to prey on all whites, especially stage lines and wagon trains. Traveling west, whether to Santa Fe or Denver or Salt Lake City, became perilous. Companies formerly assigned to fight against guerrillas in Oklahoma, Kansas, and Arkansas were reassigned to the Plains to fight off the wild tribes of Sioux and Cheyenne and Arapaho. As always, Larkin's letters were designed to keep me informed without causing me undue worry.

April 1, 1864

Dear Sarah,

Well, I have news to impart. Since I have as of last month been promoted, you may in future address me as Colonel Flint without fear of contradiction. This has come about mostly because of our reassignment to head north and west to punish the hostile Indian raiding parties operating along the Santa Fe Trail. Consequently, we will not have a permanent base. We're liable to be anywhere from Fort Larned in western Kansas to Bent's Fort in Colorado or even Fort Union down close to Santa Fe. This is not an assignment I take lightly, but I doubt the Indians to be any sneakier than outlaws like Quantrill. The good news is that Ridge is with me. He's now a major, and I am convinced he will be an invaluable aide in this hostile Indian Territory.

Ned is with me, too. He came riding into Fort Smith three months ago on one of the finest horses you ever saw. It was Kate's farewell present to him. As always, he has learned quickly and well. He's big for his age, nearly as tall as I am. I don't think the boy is 16 yet, but he has the makings of a soldier. I'll try, for Monnie's sake, to take good care of him.

I suppose the news has now reached you that in the March election in Arkansas, Father was voted as governor and will head the new loyal state government. He has written to me that his main focus will be on development of a sound fiscal policy and the organization of a militia for citizen protection. He's right. God knows Arkansas needs a decent system of law and order.

Do not worry about me, Sarah. Kiss our boys for me, and remember always that I love you all.

I did worry, of course. What woman wouldn't, knowing her husband was facing vicious savages? But I told myself the Indians were no more vicious than the Bushwhackers.

There was no lack of news regarding the war that spring. In mid-April, Grant suspended all prisoner-of-war exchanges with the Confederates, his intent being to further weaken the Confederate forces. I realized how fortunate it was that Willie and Sam had been captured earlier rather than later. Hereafter the men who were captured, whether Confederate or Union, would be doomed by Grant's decision to the living hell of overcrowded prison camps.

In the East, General Grant began an all-out assault on Virginia while General Sherman continued to destroy everything in his path as his huge army marched across the South. Larkin's brothers Robert and Stant were part of that massive march. I wondered what it was like for these two decent men to be a part of an army committed to the daily destruction of property of the women, children, and old men left behind to starve on these burnt-out Southern farms.

The Union successes east of the Mississippi in the spring of 1864 were not matched by similar successes west of the river. Down in Louisiana, a massive Union army marched north while an accompanying fleet of gunboats moved up the Red River. A second Union army, led by General Frederick Steele, marched south from Little Rock to Shreveport. Their objective was to sweep into Texas and effectively occupy all of the Confederacy west of the Mississippi. It proved to be impossible to accomplish. The Federal forces marching down from Little Rock were met by three Confederate cavalry divisions and barely escaped disaster. General Steele marched his men back north to Little Rock and concentrated on occupying northern Arkansas. General Price, operating from a base in southern Arkansas, always eager to use any excuse to invade Missouri, saw his opportunity to lead a Rebel raiding expedition north into Missouri.

With the Red River operation written off as a failure, and with the wild

Plains Indians a constant threat on the prairies, a decision to make a major raid on Missouri could hardly have come at a worse time for the Northern armies west of the Mississippi. Over in Kansas, thousands of Indians with Northern sympathies, displaced from their lands early in the war, made ready now to move south back to their Indian Territory in time to put in their spring crops. Larkin's regiment was assigned the task of assisting the superintendent of Indian Affairs in organizing the expedition. He wrote an exasperated letter:

May 1864

Dear Sarah,
    It turns out there are all kinds of duties connected with being a colonel, and I am up to my ears in one I never expected. My regiment is assigned to protect upwards of 5,000 Indians — men, women, children, plus their mules, wagons, bedding, food, chickens, ducks, and dogs. Their supply train alone is 300 wagons long. In addition, old people, nursing mothers, and babies ride in the wagons. The rest of them walk — making 2,000 riding and 3,000 walking. By my actual count we already have at least 500 puppies frisking around, and if I'm any good at judging these things, we're going to have a few dozen new babies born along the way, as well.
    It's an interesting exercise. There is always the prospect of danger, for Stand Watie and Quantrill are both out there in the bushes somewhere. They don't want the Indians, but they do want the supplies. Counting the wagons the Indians ride in plus the supply wagons, this wagon train is six miles long. Guarding this motley bunch is a tactical nightmare.
    My job is to get them from the Sauk and Fox reservation in Kansas down as far as the border of the Indian Territory. There we will rendezvous with troops from Fort Gibson and they will take over. The transfer can't come too soon to suit me! Kiss our boys for me, and remember that I love you.

    In Missouri, the rumors about plans for insurrections and secret societies of Confederate sympathizers began to be heard more and more frequently. In Kansas City, people whispered about them and even began to call them by specific names. The Sons of Liberty, some said the secret lodges were called. Others said they were the Knights of the Golden Circle and were armed and dangerous. But no one seemed to have specific knowledge. The result was a climate of distrust and suspicion as neighbors eyed each other and wondered if there were plots in the making.

Then one day Uncle Auguste's solemn mood shifted. He came home with a smiling face and jaunty step. "Sarah," said he, "prepare yourself for a social event of major significance. Kansas City is soon to be honored by a representative of President Lincoln, selected by the President himself. His secretary, Mr. John Hay, will visit our area and assess our situation. He is expected within the week. My friend Van Horn is again entertaining in General Rosecrans's honor, for Mr. Hay will be personally escorted by the general. Is your new gown finished? If not, you have only a few days remaining for your preparations."

I smiled, partly in anticipation of an event of such importance, partly in response to Uncle's interest in my limited wardrobe. Last month he had insisted that I select three dress lengths in order that I might be gowned in some approximation of the style of other women in the Chouteau family. Consequently, I was now the pleased owner of a fine shimmering silk gown in garden hues, as well as two cool and dainty summer dimity dresses.

"Tell me once more, Uncle, why Mr. Hay is coming so far from Washington, and what does he expect to accomplish in Kansas City?"

Uncle surveyed me astutely. "Sarah, I will tell you what I am able to discuss. Mr. Hay's visit has come about because General Rosecrans believes there are so many Confederate sympathizers in northern Missouri as to pose a major threat. The general began his investigation shortly after his arrival as commander of the Missouri district. And, of course, he succeeded in detecting a subversive plot.

"Arms are being shipped into the area and placed in the hands of a secret society, called the 'pawpaw militia,' in towns all across the northern part of the state. These people are eagerly awaiting the reappearance of their leader, General Price. The big question is, when will Price begin his march to Missouri? Rosecrans needs to know the plans of these secret societies, and he needs reinforcements for his own army in order to prevent the occupation of Missouri by Rebel forces."

"Uncle, I understand all of that. But my question remains, why is Mr. Hay coming here to Kansas City?"

"Because President Lincoln trusts Hay completely. The President needs an assessment of the situation by an unbiased observer.

"There is deceit lurking in high places in Washington. It is a great compliment to General Rosecrans that the President is sending his personal secretary on such a long journey. And it is an accurate measure of the importance of the issue."

The scent of flowers and fresh cut grass was sweet as we rode up the steep streets of Quality Hill. Lush white peonies framed the trim front lawns of the impressive homes that crowned the hills overlooking the city. Pink roses lined the brick walk that led to the entrance of the Van Horn mansion. Mr. Van Horn, standing at the entrance to greet his guests, reached down to pick a perfect pink bud, which he handed to me. "Please wear it, my dear. I don't know which is lovelier, you or the rose!" Van Horn grinned. "And even your Uncle Auguste is looking cheerful this evening! How good to see you smile again, old friend!"

At the far end of the long drawing room I saw the guest of honor. John Hay was a small man of athletic build, handsome, and surprisingly young. I judged him to be only a few years older than myself and wondered why the President had so few trustworthy men that he was moved to select so young an ambassador.

With his hand firmly on my elbow, Uncle steered me along the length of the room. "Mr. Hay, may I present my niece, Mrs. Flint?"

I looked into his handsome face, a face that made no attempt to disguise his attraction to me. "Mrs. Flint, had I realized that Kansas City was blessed with such beautiful women, I would have begged the President to extend my visit!"

Such frank appreciation was infectious. "And, I, sir, am unaccustomed to such compliments, but I am delighted to hear that you find Kansas City to your liking."

Even a married woman of 20 enjoys a compliment, and it was with great difficulty that I erased the smile from my blushing face before turning to make my manners to the dignified General Rosecrans.

We were a group of ten that evening — General Rosecrans, Mr. Hay, Cousin Marie and her husband, his parents, the Van Horns, Uncle, and I. John Hay's mission had been to determine the nature and the limits of the secret societies in the small towns and rural areas of Missouri. Much was discussed during the course of the evening, but none of us present inquired with any specificity as to the details of Hay's mission. We were all too aware that the lives of many would hang in the balance and that the war was moving steadily closer to Missouri.

Events of that summer and fall revealed the details of a plot that had at its core assassination of civilians and insurrection against the military. The plot was both sinister and elaborate. Over 20,000 Missouri men, sworn to loyalty to the Confederacy, were pledged to rise up and join General Price when he made his long-awaited appearance in northern Missouri. The signal for this uprising was to be given at the Democratic Convention in Chicago on the Fourth of July. Simultaneously, an insurrection was to take place in Kansas, Missouri, Illinois, and Indiana. Officials loyal to the Union were to be assassinated, and the arsenals, forts, and public property were to be seized. A general Northern invasion was then to be launched by those Confederates west of Georgia. After Hay had hastened to Washington to make his report to President Lincoln, the Democratic Convention in Chicago was postponed. But the Confederate schemers in Missouri were unwilling to see their plot delayed.

Events began to heat up fast in Missouri. On July 7, the hostile flag of the Confederacy was hoisted in Platte County, just north of the river from Kansas City. From that time on, until after Price had come and gone, murder and pillage became the byword of the Order of American Knights of the Golden Circle north of the Missouri River. Volunteers flocked to the Union banner to combat this new threat. Suspicion and danger marked the daily lives of those left at home in the rural parts of the state.

Price did not launch his raid on Missouri until September, and I expect that I was one of the first to have news of his raid. Cousin Ed, down in Arkansas, had sent me the news in his end-of-the-summer report letter.

September 1, 1864

Dear Sarah,

Your Cousin Alta joins me in hoping that all is well with you and yours. We are in excellent health and moderate spirits, encouraged by the new loyal government in Arkansas, and hopeful of a foreseeable end to this terrible war.

But in that regard I feel obligated to tell you of a recent experience of mine. As you know, there is no bridge across the Arkansas within 60 miles of here, which fact makes it a matter of some diligence to transport an army across the river.

Last week, however, it was my fate to see a sizeable army consisting of thousands of men being marched and ferried across the river. An army in full array is a noble sight, whether Union or Rebel, and I could not forbear watching its stately procession.

I glimpsed it first from the top of your mountain, from which vantage point the view is unobstructed for some 40 miles. The line of march was clear. The long column was headed north by northwest. From the massive size of the column I surmised the army to be Rebel, there being no known Union army left below the river in Arkansas. With that as a basis of reasoning, I concluded that the logical place for their crossing the river would be in the vicinity of Dardenelle, 30 miles upriver to the west, the people thereabouts being predominately loyal to the Confederacy and the river there being served by a good-sized ferryboat. Besides which, the bridge at Van Buren and the bridge at Little Rock were both in Union hands.

Consequently, I descended the mountain as fast as my horse could carry me and hastened to find Captain Hern. Having been persuaded of the importance of the matter, Hern fired up his engine and ferried us both upriver in record time. Once docked at Dardenelle, Captain Hern cooled his heels and passed the time of day with the local ferry owner whilst I made my way over to Hallum's cotton gin to do some close dickering regarding the possibilities of ginning this year's sparse cotton crop. Whilst we were thus engaged, the usual noises accompanying a mighty column of marching men began to make themselves heard. Along with the local townsfolk, I hastened over to the river bank to gape at the proceedings.

There I found Captain Hern engaged in serious negotiations with the Rebel colonel who had ridden in at the head of the advance contingent of cavalry. Hern immediately involved me in the discussion.

"Mr. Watson, this here colonel wants to use our boat to ferry this here big bunch of men across yore river. Says it's most likely going to prove out to be a two- or three-day job. I told him he'd have to deal with you. That you'd be the one to have the final say."

That Rebel colonel turned and yelled, his face red and his voice loud. Miss Sarah, I will spare you the man's profanity, which was considerable. In essence he said, "You hard-headed donkeys, try to get through your thick skulls that I am not *asking* to use your ferry, I am *telling* you that I am commandeering your ferry in the name of the Confederate army and my commanding officer, General Price!" He then looked at me. "How much time do you calculate this operation to take?"

I looked up at him, where he sat astride a massive stallion, and gave honest answer.

"Why, Colonel, wouldn't you expect that would depend on the number of men you've got to carry across? I don't know that I'm the right person to answer that question."

The colonel turned to his aides, so mad I thought he might be afflicted with apoplexy. "These ignorant louts here in the backwoods — useless as vermin and lazy as hound dogs! Look at these two — one whittling and the other scratching! May God give me the strength and patience to deal with their stupidity! Commandeer their ferry! The regular ferry is already being loaded up. Let's get this operation moving!"

"Colonel, sir," said the aide, "I lack the knowledge to operate the engine. We'll have to commandeer the boat's captain as well."

"Then do it, man! Don't waste any more of my time!"

Hern stood up slowly and looked the colonel in the eye. As cool as a cucumber, his voice flat and low, he gave answer. "You can shoot me, Colonel, but you can't commandeer me. And shooting me wouldn't hep you much, would it? That there boat ain't gonna run of its own accord."

The colonel looked at me. "I'll shoot you both unless one of you rascals operates that ferry."

I drew myself up in my best schoolmaster stance and replied. "Colonel, you may riddle me with holes if that is your pleasure, but no bullet of yours can add one iota to my fund of knowledge. I assure you, sir, that I have no knowledge as to how to operate that steam engine. However, may I suggest that the problem is one of miscommunication? Captain Hern did not refuse to operate the boat. Rather, his decision rests on your satisfactory negotiation of the terms of the contract. And for that, I need some knowledge of the size of the operation. How many men require passage?"

After a long pause the colonel gave answer, his face red, his voice hard, and his eyes mean.

"Twelve thousand men, plus their mounts, plus equipment."

Captain Hern responded with a factual analysis. "My boat can carry 25,000 pounds. Yon ferry over there, the regular boat that plies this crossing, can do about the same. That means each boat can carry about 100 men, counting their gear. Takes an hour to get across the river and back, plus you need to allow some extra for loading and unloading. Figger 20 trips in a 24-hour period. We're talking three days, just to get the men across, plus extra days for your artillery and horses and supply wagons. Plus, I can't go forever without sleep. I figure this to be at least a five-day job."

"All right, then. Get moving!"

I held up my hand. "Wait one minute, Colonel. We need to discuss terms. Captain Hern here has a hungry family. So do I. Our labor comes at a price."

"My God, man, you try my patience to the limit! Name your price! Whatever it is, I will pay it in scrip redeemable by the Confederate Treasury. Let's get moving here!"

Captain Hern sat back down. "My old woman can't eat Confederate money. And I can't buy anything with it, neither. Afraid it's no deal after all, Colonel. Mighty sorry! I thought for sure we'd be able to do business."

The colonel got down off his horse to shake his fist in Hern's face, meanwhile yelling profanity of the most vile description.

When he finally paused to get his breath I interjected a comment. "Colonel, may I suggest another form of payment? Your commanding general is well known to set a lavish table and to maintain a bountiful supply train. Captain Hern and I most respectfully request that we be paid in food — flour, salt, tobacco, lard, sugar, cured meats. It is my suggestion, sir, that your aide and I calculate the total number of crossings required and that he be authorized to compensate us on that basis from your supply train."

Well, in conclusion, Captain Hern and I spent six whole days engaged in aiding and abetting the Confederacy, in exchange for which we were well compensated by the finest of food that the Confederates had stolen from our fellow citizens to the south of us. We will undoubtedly ask the Lord to bless it to the nourishment of our bodies during this coming year.

Two final notes: (1) We had the distinct honor of ferrying General Price himself across the river. The man is massive now. I would guess him to weigh more than 300 pounds, the visible results of liberating the finest of foods from the lands of a starving people. Too fat to sit on a horse, he now rides in a carriage driven by a proud little darky. No ancient emperor of Rome could have been more comfortable with command than that massively handsome general sitting tall atop his specially reinforced buggy seat.

(2) Immediately upon my arrival back home, I saddled up my horse and rode to Union headquarters in Little Rock. There I was able to furnish General Steele with an accurate account of the strength of the Rebel army that is, even as I write, headed north to Missouri. May God bless you and keep you. Your Cousin Alta sends her love.

Chapter 30

GENERAL PRICE took his own sweet time about invading Missouri. From the rumors that began to filter in, his progress sounded more like a prolonged picnic than an enemy invasion. Gregarious and inclined to good living, Price's plans appeared to be sufficiently elastic to allow time for eloquent speech making and enthusiastic feasting as his army moved slowly northward through Arkansas and Missouri. As the Federal garrisons in Arkansas allowed his journey to continue uninterrupted, people in both states wondered and waited.

Assuming that the people of Missouri needed only the

strong presence of a Confederate army to inspire them to rise up and declare their loyalty to the Southern cause, Price advanced at a leisurely pace toward St. Louis. But he found the land to furnish very little in the way of acceptable food and forage. By then, the southern portion of Missouri was destitute and desolate. There, Price's magnificent long column of cavalry met up with ragged women and barefoot children, their few belongings piled on oxcarts headed south.

Price encountered his first real resistance at Pilot Knob, a small Union fort 80 miles southwest of St. Louis, commanded by General Ewing. Although his garrison of 1,000 men was outnumbered 12 to 1, Ewing decided to fight and delay Price as long as possible to allow for the transport of Union reinforcements to St. Louis.

Price's army marched in to Pilot Knob, pitching their tents between the 600-foot-tall volcanic core of iron on one side of the fort and Shepherd's Mountain on the other side. When Price finally fired his first big gun, the sound came almost as a relief to the tense men waiting inside the fort. Ewing's guns fired back, and four solid rows of gritty Confederates started the fight, moving forward on foot, their ragged uniforms flapping in the brisk September breeze. Ewing's men in the outer trenches waited grimly until the Confederates were in rifle range, then mowed them down like wheat before a scythe. Again and again the Rebels marched forward, some yelling abuses, some yelling revenge for Ewing's Order No. ll.

By nightfall, the bodies of 1,500 killed and wounded Rebels sprawled in the outer trenches around Pilot Knob. The slaughter was so intense that the defending Federals told each other that the Rebs had been doped by having been issued rations of whiskey mixed with gunpowder.

When darkness fell, General Ewing called his officers into conference. Their own casualties had been proportionately heavy, more than 200 men killed and wounded. But in one day's fighting, the Federals had set a record for casualties inflicted on the enemy — a ratio of seven to one. Furthermore, Price's army had been delayed for three days, sufficient time to allow Federal reinforcements to prepare for the defense of St. Louis. Believing he had done enough, under cover of darkness, Ewing spiked his guns, laid a long fuse to his powder magazine, covered his drawbridge with canvas to muffle the sounds, and marched his men out into the night. He then headed west for Rolla and the railroad terminal. When the last Union soldier disappeared into the night, the rear guard lit the fuse.

Price renewed his attack at dawn, the loud explosion within the fort having served only to convince him that he should proceed cautiously. It was two hours later before his men discovered, to their surprise and chagrin, that not one Federal man remained inside. Shelby and Marmaduke rode out to pursue the escaping Federals, but Price remained behind to enjoy the bright sunshine of a Missouri autumn.

Meanwhile, those of us living in Missouri wondered and worried. General Rosecrans pressed every available Missouri man into Union service. Provost marshals even stopped soldiers on furlough and hurried them back into active duty. Agitated by the Knights of the Golden Circle, Rebel sympathizers of all descriptions had swarmed to march with the Confederates at the news of Price's so-called invasion. Uncle Auguste began to spend more and more time at home with me and my children, allocating no more than a few hours each day to business.

"Sarah," he said, "I fear that Kansas City may yet be in the eye of the storm, and I most earnestly beg you to remain close at home with your children. Who can tell when the arm of Satan will strike out! In spite of all of General Rosecrans's efforts, Rebel spies may lurk where we least expect them."

His voice changed. "Men in Missouri nowadays are being brutally tortured and shot by the outlaws attached to General Price's army. While Price's main army avoids St. Louis and advances from Rolla to Jefferson City, and hence west, fighting little and pillaging much, his guerrilla bandits are committing the most cold-blooded murders imaginable."

"Southern officers under General Price are committing these acts?"

"Not the regular officers, Sarah. Men like Shelby and Marmaduke and Fagan would never condone such outrages. No, it is men like Bloody Bill Anderson, wearing the uniform of a Confederate captain over the heart of a vulture, who are behaving like wild beasts. While Price fought at Pilot Knob, Anderson's gang attacked a railroad train at Centralia. He took 22 unarmed Union soldiers off that train, most of them on sick leave, and shot them in cold blood. He scalped some of them, then put their bodies on the railroad track and forced the engineer to run the train over them. The man's a fiend in human form.

"Keep your boys close by your side, Sarah. I place little faith anymore in the kindness of mankind, nor in the rules of civilization. Yet there are misguided people in rural Missouri who persist in treating these outlaws as conquering heroes."

"But, Uncle, how can they be conquering heroes? Price has not won a battle! He hasn't even fought one, except for Pilot Knob."

Uncle's smile was bleak. "Wishful thinking is the foe of logic. While General Price and his long supply train picnic their way across our state, the war is being won in other arenas. General Sheridan has driven the Confederates out of the Shenandoah Valley of Virginia, devastating that entire beautiful region and depriving the Confederates of their one remaining source of food for the coming winter. Atlanta has fallen to Sherman. Where Sherman's vast army will move next is beyond my conjecture, but you may be sure devastation will follow in his wake.

"For General Price to present himself as the conqueror of the Western arena assumes much. The man's popular, but he's no strategist. My sources tell me that Price lounges on a Turkish carpet for his midday repast, sipping his brandy and waving to his men as they march by."

"Then how can he have any hope of victory, eating and drinking and waving?"

"Price has three fine commanders, Sarah. Fagan and Shelby and Marmaduke are intelligent, dedicated men. Born in Missouri, they are commanding troops who are also natives. These men will fight to the death to repossess territory they see as their own."

In early October, Price cut the telegraph lines to Kansas City and began his slow march toward Kansas, having decided not to fight for St. Louis nor for the capital of Jefferson City. As he moved west the Federal armies gave chase, 9,000 infantry marching under General A. J. Smith and three brigades of cavalry riding under General Alfred Pleasonton.

Still enjoying the autumn sunshine and the adulation of his well-wishers, Price made no effort to increase his pace as his army moved toward Kansas. In Kansas City, General Curtis, commanding the Department of Kansas, gathered several thousand militia and amassed them at the state line, one mile west of Uncle's home in Westport. General Blunt, more aggressive than his commander, General Curtis, prepared to march out to intercept the enemy. Uncle stocked his cellar with food and water and medical supplies. He went daily to mass as we waited and prayed.

Ten days the Federal troops waited in Kansas City while the jovial commander of the Confederate troops feasted his way across Missouri. Uncle Auguste, perceiving that time was dragging for the Union officers, invited General Curtis and staff to dine at his table. Dessie outdid herself that evening, serving a roast of pork delicately browned and succulently tender, garnished with the last and best vegetables from our garden. The fall apple crop had been abundant, and the meal was concluded with a deep-dish apple pie, sweetened with sugar, fragrant with cinnamon, and topped off by rich whipped cream.

The dark-eyed General Blunt looked over at me. "I am told, madam, that you had firsthand acquaintance with General Price during the Battle of Pea Ridge. What was your impression of the man?"

"Sir, I was barely 17, sorely worried for the safety of my husband and filled with sorrow for the blood that had been shed that day. Still, my impression was that of a big, handsome man with gallant manners. And he is a kind man. He was kind to General Pike."

General Curtis looked at me. Finally, a twinkle appearing briefly in his shrewd old eyes, he remarked, "God works in mysterious ways." He then looked over at Uncle Auguste.

"I have formed a considerable admiration for your niece's abilities, sir, and for her excellent judgment. I must tell you gentlemen that it is with considerable relief that I hear Miss Sarah's assessment of our Confederate opponent. A foe who is remembered for his handsome face and his kindness gives us some room for hope. And our recent information confirms Miss Sarah's analysis. Our scouts tell us that Price seems to lack all knowledge that our armies are gathering to oppose him. The man does not even deploy scouts — not in advance, and not to protect his rear. His confidence is truly phenomenal. He appears to completely trust in his popularity and in this secret organization of his — the Knights of the Golden Circle."

Uncle smiled. "When a man begins to believe his own propaganda, he is asking for trouble. Let us pray that he continues to believe in his own invincibility. If God grants the Union the victory in this coming battle, all the country west of the Mississippi will have been secured for the Union."

Blunt looked at Uncle. "For now. But the wild Indians of the Plains are still a force that must be reckoned with." He turned to me. "And I would be remiss, madam, were I not to comment on the splendid organizational work your husband is performing in that regard. As a soldier, Colonel Flint stands very high in the opinion of the army."

General Curtis responded. "Having had the pleasure of renewing my acquaintance with Miss Sarah, I count it my loss that I have not had the pleasure of meeting her husband. I believe I am the only person in the room who is unacquainted with Colonel Flint."

"I count him to be a born leader, sir," replied Blunt. "He is a man of strong will and ardent temper, but his every word and action testify to the self-discipline he has acquired. Larkin Flint is a man of great resolution."

I smiled at the gentlemen. "In other words, my husband is the exact opposite of General Price. That being the case, what you have to do in laying out your own battle plans is to figure out what Larkin would do if he were in Price's place, then figure on Price doing the opposite!"

General Curtis smiled, but his eyes were thoughtful. "Miss Sarah, I will reflect on your comment. I surely will." He rose. "We must with reluctance leave this festive gathering and return to our duties. The next few days will undoubtedly see a resolution to our situation."

Uncle shook his head as the blue-coated backs of our guests disappeared into the cool October darkness.

"Sarah, we should feel well protected. We have thousands upon thousands of Union troops bivouacked to the west and to the south of us, and two of the Union's staunchest generals headquartered within six blocks of us. Sleep well, my dear."

Each day, dawning bright and clear, saw more columns of militia march in from the west to swell General Curtis's volunteer army. Then, one sunny morning the sound of bugles and the insistent beat of drums quickened the air and excited our household.

Matt came running in from the yard. "Let's go watch! Let's go watch! There's lots of men and they're marching out! Let's go watch, Mother!"

He pulled me to the front yard. Two blocks to the north on Westport Road, long lines of men in blue were marching east. I grabbed my shawl, yelled at Linney to come with us, and ran hand in hand with Matt to watch the troops head off to fight.

It was a golden, sunny day. The purposeful tramp of the men stirred clouds of gray dust beneath their feet as they headed east along the road that stretched over the wooded hills, stone-fenced fields, and apple orchards that formed the country between Westport and the Little Blue River. The Reverend Flowers and his wife came to stand at our sides.

"What's your regiment, men?" The preacher's fine voice carried readily in the morning air, and the men answered him in unison: "Sixteenth Kansas, ready for a fight!!!" I realized then that the battle would begin somewhere outside the city. I prayed with selfish fervor that my little boys and I might be spared being engulfed in the horrors of the battle.

Suddenly I heard my name. "Miss Sarah! Miss Sarah! Is it really you,

Miss Sarah?" A fine-looking Negro sergeant marched beside his troops. I found myself looking straight into the excited eyes of Tobe. Quickly, he broke step and ran toward me.

"Ma wrote me you was here. I kep' hopin' and hopin' I might see you. Is dis here little Matt? Oh, Miss Sarah, you do look fine!"

"You do too, Tobe. You look splendid. This is Linney. She helps me with the twins." I turned to the Reverend Flowers and to Linney. "Tobe used to work for my pa. We're family to each other."

Linney took in the sight of him — his finely shaped head, broad shoulders, and intelligent features — and made up her mind on the spot. "You come back and see us, boy, when this war is over!" Her beautiful face smiled straight at Tobe. "I'll be lookin' for you."

Even as he prepared to run forward to rejoin his regiment, Tobe yelled his answer. "Barrin' a bullet, I'll be back!"

I looked at the Reverend and shook my head. "Preacher, did you ever in your life see a quicker courtship?"

He smiled. "That wasn't a courtship, Miss Sarah. It was a meeting of the minds. But, I'm wondering, just how long did it take you to be swept off your own feet by that handsome husband of yours?"

I laughed, the happy memories bubbling up. "About the same length of time. One look and one smile and I was a gone goose. I was in Larkin's arms dancing the Virginia reel. By the time the dance was over, I was in love."

"And where is Colonel Flint now, my dear?"

"He's in the Colorado Territory. I'm thankful he's there instead of here. I never thought I would say such a thing, but I don't think I could bear to see Larkin ride out to battle."

"Ah, well, Miss Sarah, many a woman has felt the same. Let us pray for all our men. I expect General Price is in for a surprise. Those men look ready, and their commander looks adamant."

In the meantime, Price's unwary army moved slowly toward Kansas. On October 18 his forces encamped at Lexington, 40 miles east of Kansas City. While the Rebels slept, General Blunt marched his wing of Curtis's Union army to meet them. Their first encounter with Price was on the morning of October 19, an encounter that was the prelude to five days of continuous action. Most of the time Price was forced to fight with his army facing in opposite directions, for Rosecrans had designed the operation so as to catch the Confederates in a vise.

Pleasonton's cavalry, almost 9,000 men, came charging over from St. Louis. At the same time, Blunt's forces were arrayed against the Rebels on the west. A day's march behind, A. J. Smith's Union infantry were closing in from the east. A commander who was less single-minded would have headed south for Arkansas at that point, but Price's overconfidence indicated otherwise. His cavalry pushed on, oblivious to obstacles. Soon, Price ordered his men to fight on foot as infantry. Amidst intense combat, they headed west for the Kansas border, where they found Curtis's men holding a line that extended 15 miles. Curtis sounded his attack at dawn on October 23, and the Battle of Westport began.

Chapter 31

SUNDAY MORNING, October 23, dawned cold and clear. As the sun rose above the low hills to the east of Westport, its rays struck points of fire from the thousands of gun barrels and bayonets of Union soldiers. The men were already finishing their breakfasts and striking their camp in the meadows to the south. I stood at my upstairs window and watched as they resolutely began to pull themselves together for the coming battle.

Where only the day before a mile-wide city of tents had been stretched from Westport down to Brush Creek, now I saw grim-faced men engaged in the practical acts of preparing themselves to fight — wrapping their blue trousers tightly around their ankles, then pulling their heavy woolen stockings up over; buckling and tightening their belts; shifting their canteens and their blanket rolls; snapping and resnapping their gun locks as they tested and retested their well-used rifles. Then, as far as I could see, troops began to fall into line, standards flapping crisply in the quick wind, officers on horseback exhorting their men, steeling their will to face their enemy and end the week-long series of skirmishes.

The long blue lines of Curtis's men began their steady tramp as they moved south in the face of Price's Confederate guns, now trained on them from the hills and bluffs beyond Brush Creek. Three of the South's best divisions awaited Curtis's attack: Shelby, Fagan, and Marmaduke. Separated by Brush Creek and a heavy growth of timber, both armies expected this day to be decisive.

Safely south of the battlegrounds, General Price consumed his breakfast of eggs and bacon and biscuits in old Boston Adam's farmhouse while pondering the advice of his generals. Faced with overwhelming numbers, Fagan and Marmaduke had counseled retreat. Shelby had urged a fight. Price had taken the advice of all three. He had ordered his precious wagon train of looted supplies to turn south so as to be safe in case of retreat, but he had ordered his men to mount up for a general offensive at dawn.

To the north in Westport, General Curtis stationed himself with his telescope on the roof of the Harris House and ordered a general advance.

How can I describe the hellish sounds of their battle? It was like a storm, with the crash of thunder and bright glare of lightning and the shrieking of howling wind and the clatter of iron hailstones from the massive Confederate guns on the bluff. Dense black smoke darkened the sky as the guns belched living fire from their mouths, fire that ripped through the bodies of the blue-coated men who marched to meet it.

The guns of the Union army roared in response. And these were but a background to all the other sounds that defined the day, including the shriek of projectiles, the long sharp hiss before their final roar of rage. With the aid of Uncle's own telescope I could see solid shot strike tall trees and splinter them like straws; strike battery horses and knock them over, spilling their vitals and blood upon the ground; strike living men, sending them through the air to shriek in agony before their death.

Within half an hour, the Union men were driven back. Curtis then called for his horse, having decided to lead the charge up the timbered hill himself.

It was at that moment that God granted an advantage to the Union forces. An old man, doggedly determined to speak personally with the general, limped up to Curtis just as the commander was preparing to mount his horse.

"They's a ravine behind that hill yonder, a holler that runs deep, and twists around way into the far side of yon hill. Iffen you take yore men up that holler, General, you all can sneak up on yore enemy's backside. I'd take you myself, but I'm purt near too old to do it. Jist lead yore men whur I point you, head out and angle southwest fer purt near three-quarters of a mile. Then off to yore left you'll see a deep ravine. That there holler winds around right up to the top of the ridge where them Confederate guns are planted. I do believe, General, that yore men can sneak up on their backsides iffen you go up that holler!"

Curtis ordered the tough little Indian fighter General Blunt to lead his seasoned regiments up the ravine. General Deitzler's thousands of Kansans were ordered to advance straight across Brush Creek when Blunt's men opened fire. The maneuver worked. The untried Kansans fought like veterans. Blunt's men came up out of the ravine to find themselves on the top of the ridge, having outflanked both Shelby and Thompson. Blunt began firing down the Confederate lines, while Deitzler's long blue line of gritty Kansans marched steadily across Brush Creek and over the crest of the hill beyond. In the meantime, General Pleasanton, immaculate West Pointer and brilliant cavalryman, had bombarded Price's rear until past midnight and was now closing in on his army.

By one o'clock the following afternoon, General Price's royal return to Missouri had turned into a rout. Fagan and Marmaduke hurried southwest in full retreat, headed for the flimsy protection of the Indian Nation. Only the men commanded by the fiercely stubborn Shelby continued to battle, fighting around the stone fences of the brown fields, gallantly spilling their own blood to cover the retreat of their chief commander, General Price.

The short October day was drawing to a close when Shelby discovered General Pleasanton on his flank. Shelby's order rang out: "Men, mount and fly!" They rode with the wind, leaving behind their wounded in the field hospital, John Wornall's fine brick mansion, and leaving behind forever 800 of Shelby's best cavalrymen, their dead bodies sprawled on the fields south of Westport.

The war for Missouri was over. Nearly 30,000 men had fought in the battle. Price had lost 2,000 men, plus ten of his big guns. Moreover, he had lost General Marmaduke, who had been captured by Pleasanton. Price's army had been routed. Price's defeated and exhausted men started southwest on a forced march, the road behind them littered with their abandoned guns and clothes. Their wagons burned, their spirits at rock-bottom, they deserted and headed for home, battalion after battalion. Price sat in his reinforced wagon seat and rode on into the bleakness of the October evening, still wondering at the turn of events. His royal progress across Missouri, his schemes for the Knights of the Golden Circle, his expectations of the people who were to have risen up and acclaimed him victor had all given way to bitter disaster.

The desolate trek across the Indian Territory changed the mood of Price's men from affection to rebellion. Accustomed to the bountiful and ever-present supply wagons that had been the trademark of Price's generalship, the men grew bitter as they starved on their diet of acorns. Some died; others deserted in droves. Only 6,000 troops staggered on foot behind their commander as he rode in his wagon back behind the Confederate lines in Arkansas in early December. For the rest of the war, Missouri was not disturbed by the Confederacy. The Battle of Westport was the last major battle fought west of the Mississippi. Meanwhile, we who lived in Westport cared for the wounded and buried the dead who had been left behind.

Along with other civilians, Uncle Auguste had gone out to the battlefield at the end of the day to help bury the dead and bring back the survivors. As I put my little boys to bed and waited for Uncle's return, I remembered all too clearly the ghastly scenes following the Battle of Pea Ridge. I thought of Pa's courage and Eliza's and Neely's compassion, and I prayed again that I would be granted some measure of both.

When Uncle finally came home, his usual calm assurance was gone, replaced by the grim, gray look of one who has seen horrors. Behind him walked two men carrying a bloody litter on which lay a blue-uniformed soldier.

"Put him down in the kitchen, men, until we decide on the appropriate place for his bed." Uncle seemed uncertain as to his next move.

"This man is unconscious now, Sarah. He has fainted from the pain. But when we first found him he was quite coherent, and he begged to be brought to you. He once belonged to your father, he said, and he feels sure of his welcome with you. As, indeed, he should." Uncle sat down heavily, his face tired and sad. "The decision is yours, Sarah. He has a long recuperation ahead of him. Where shall we place the bed of this black soldier?"

I looked at Tobe's unconscious face and at his long body collapsed on the bloody stretcher, and I thought of Neely's many years of tenderness to me. "Put him in the family room, right across from the parlor. The fireplace there will keep him warm. Winter is coming, and it wouldn't be right to put him out with Dessie and Udger in that cold room over the carriage house. Darky or not, he's got to be in a warm room or he will get pneumonia. Where is his wound?"

"His thigh is broken, ma'am." The young soldier holding one end of the litter looked tired enough to drop in his tracks. "The doctor's set it already. Shot right through the bone, they say, but it was a clean shot. This here's a good man, ma'am. Brave. I've soldiered with him across Tennessee. This here man's a hard fighter, even if he is black. There ain't many black men I'd be willing to take orders from, but this here man is one of 'em."

"What regiment are you with, soldier?"

"Seventh Kansas, ma'am, and we need to be getting back. There's other wounded men to be carried off, and more to be buried."

Uncle looked at me, his face lined with fatigue.

"Sarah, I now know what meaning there is behind the words 'living hell.' As we walked the battlefield in the early twilight we saw the wounded mixed with the dead, and the Rebels mixed with the Northerners, some crawling about begging to be put out of their misery, others already consigned to oblivion by a merciful God. Hundreds of men are lying in those fields to the south of us. Some were trampled under the wheels of their own horses and cannon in the fury of the Rebel retreat.

"I must go back now to assist with the burials. We are trying by lantern light to separate the blue from the gray so as to bury them in death according to their choices in life." He paused. "Though it seems to matter less and less all the time. No doubt, God will know His own."

I sat by Tobe's bed to wait for Uncle's return. Even though Tobe's leg had been set and splinted, I was afraid to leave him. It could take but an instant for a semiconscious man to move or attempt to stand and thus undo the careful work of the army doctors. It was after midnight before Uncle came home. Again, he was not alone.

This time the orderlies carried a gray-uniformed man upon their stretcher, a man whose eyes and head were wrapped with so many bandages that he looked like an Egyptian mummy. Preacher Flowers walked beside Uncle Auguste, his tall, gaunt frame bent to support my exhausted uncle.

"Put this man's stretcher beside the other one, men. Sarah, will you rouse the maids? We'll need another bed."

"Uncle, is this man someone else that we know?" I looked at the worn Confederate uniform and at the smart captain's cap that now lay on the chest of the unconscious man.

"No, we don't know him. But I can tell you he has more grit than any man I have ever met. The Reverend Flowers and I found him on the battle-field, deserted by his comrades, who no doubt believe him to have been killed instantly. He was shot in the left temple and probably rendered unconscious. But when we rolled him over, thinking him to be dead, he regained consciousness and said, 'If you fellows will help me, I'll get up and walk to the hospital tent'! Which, to our everlasting astonishment, was exactly what he did, the Reverend supporting him on one side, I on the other."

"But that's only the beginning of the story, Miss Sarah." Preacher Flowers took up the tale, his voice awed. "This man refused to be chloro-formed. He directed the surgeon in tracking the bullet. It had gone through part of his eye and lodged behind his nose. It was only after they had extracted the ball and the crushed bone behind it that he finally consented to be chloroformed. He bore the pain like a Stoic of old. The surgeon told us that without this man's courageous assistance in tracking the bullet, the operation could not have been successfully performed."

"Will he be blind?"

"Certainly so in his left eye. But there is great hope for recovery in the right eye. He must be kept quiet, with both eyes bandaged, and utterly still, until his wounds have healed."

"You can understand, Sarah, why I insisted on bringing him here. A man of such courage merits every consideration."

"Oh, Uncle, I do understand. And I am so grateful to you for giving Tobe a chance to heal properly. How could I not do the same for another? We'll take turns sitting with them. They will both need constant care for a while."

When Preacher Flowers spoke, his voice was firm. "Auguste, you must go immediately to bed. You are exhausted. I will take the first watch. At dawn I will arouse your coachman and instruct him as to what is needful.

We will divide the care of these men between our two households. But first, could we take a few moments to ask God's blessing, not only on these men, but on the many others who shed their blood this day?"

I went to bed wearied in mind and body. When the bright rays of the sun finally woke me, it was already the middle of the morning, and the household had been busy for hours. As I dressed I heard singing, a man's clear tenor, joined by Matt's childish treble. The words of an old hymn, familiar to me from many a Presbyterian camp meeting, came floating up the stairs:

"Shall we gather at the river. . . . The beautiful, beautiful river . . ."

I heard Linney's soprano take up the words:

"Shall we gather at the river. . . . That flows by the throne of God . . ."

Tobe's bass joined in at the chorus, his voice booming out the words of assurance:

"Yes, we'll gather at the river, the beautiful, beautiful river; yes, we'll gather at the river that flows by the throne of God!"

I hurried down the stairs. The room that in the dim candlelight of midnight had been a chamber of blood and despair was now transformed into a place of joy and hope. While I had slept, Uncle had directed Linney and Dessie and Udger, the coachman, in the work of bathing and feeding the two soldiers.

Tobe, sitting propped up on his cot, his splinted leg positioned carefully before him, was grinning from ear to ear. The white man's bed was empty; instead, the captain sat in Uncle's favorite chair. Matt, seated on the footstool at the captain's feet, gazed in pure delight from one uniformed man to the other, while one twin tugged at the captain's hand and the other attempted to climb on Tobe's bed. I moved swiftly to rescue the men from the pulls and tugs of my impetuous twins.

"Boys, leave these men alone! They're hurt. You can't climb on them, or on their beds!" I turned to Matt. "Your job, son, will be to keep your baby brothers away from them. You're a big boy, and you can understand me when I tell you these men can't move around. They're badly hurt, and they need to heal!"

Matt looked at me with the clear blue eyes that reminded me so much of Larkin. "They don't sound hurt. They sound happy!"

"You got dat right, son!" Tobe's deep voice was joyful. "I can't speak fer de cap'n here, but I feels like I's made my move outta hell right smash into hebben! Miss Sarah, dis ain't no dream, is it? Dem hot biscuits I jest et seemed real 'nuff, and dem eggs, too." He grinned at Linney. "I shore hope I ain't dreamin'."

I smiled at Tobe. "This is no dream, Tobe, and by the time my baby boys get through pestering you, it may not seem like heaven, either. But you do seem to have found yourself a guardian angel. It is my Uncle Auguste's good heart that you have to thank for being here. I've had reason to appreciate his kindness for a long time, and now he has extended it to you. You are in the home of a good man. He'll look after you, like Pa did."

Tobe's face changed. "Don't get me wrong, Miss Sarah, but onc't I's healed, it ain't lookin' after I's gonna need. Dis here war has learned me some things. After dis here leg gets done healing, I's 'specting to be lookin' after myself."

I felt ashamed of myself. "Oh, Tobe, of course you will. I know how much I've had to learn because of the war. For a minute I felt like it was old times and we were both back home in Griffin Flat. Of course, things will be different for you. Things are already different for Neely and Zeke. Have you heard that they have their own land now?"

"Yessum, I's heard. My pore ol' pa's feet ain't plumb healed up yet. They's gonna be a lot of men in hell wid a whole lot to answer fer when dis long war finally ends!

"But dis fine day we is all singin'! It's shore good to see you, Miss Sarah!"

I turned to the other man.

"Sir, my name is Sarah Flint. You have already met my uncle, and you made a wonderful impression on him. But I have to tell you, I could not believe my ears when I heard you all singing this morning. How can a man feel like singing when he's been shot in the eye the day before? I do find that amazing. I surely do."

I knew he was from Arkansas the minute he started to talk. "Ma'am, what I find amazing is that the Lord not only answered my prayers last night but He threw in an extra helping of kindness just to make a grand miracle of it. I was so busy praying just to live and to not be blind that I didn't even think about asking for a soft bed and a warm breakfast and good-hearted folks besides! The doctors told me last night that they think they saved my right eye. I'm hoping that if I can heal up real fast, the bones around my left eye won't shrink away.

"It's been my observation, ma'am, that despair has caused many a death. I aim to take the opposite approach and do what I can to be cheerful. Singing helps me, ma'am. I do most surely hope my singing is not offensive to you, because it is my aim to sing my way to health and healing."

I looked more closely at the man. Although the top half of his face was totally obscured by the bandages, I could see a firm chin, a square jaw, and a wide, flexible mouth.

"Sir," said I, "we'll all sing with you. I expect there'll be more joyful noises raised up in this house than have been heard for many a day, now. What is your name, Captain, and where do you come from in Arkansas?"

"Ma'am, my name's Rankin. Jesse Rankin. I come from Conway County, down on the Arkansas River. I served under General Marmaduke."

I responded to his information with pure amazement. "Captain Rankin, were you serving under General Marmaduke two years ago, about this time of the year, when he granted safe escort to me through the mountains from Carroll County down to the river?"

"I was, ma'am. Though I was a lieutenant then. Do you mean to tell me you were that poor sad girl that rode in the buggy? Then that lively little boy must be the same one that fed me my breakfast this morning, ma'am. As my own sweet mother used to say, 'Miracles never cease!'"

"Did your face heal up, ma'am? The men used to feel pure pity for you, ma'am, you being so alone and so brave. We used to sing around our campfire for you in the hopes you would be comforted. We all thought highly of General Marmaduke for giving you escort. Course, we already thought highly of him. I hate to think of him being captured yesterday. He's by far too fine a man to have to rot in prison. I expect my whole company was captured. I hold it against Grant that he's quit exchanging prisoners. It's not right. Most of my boys are about ready to take the oath and go back home anyway. They're tired of fighting a war that nobody's winning. But they're brave. They won't quit so long as Marmaduke leads them. Without him, it's a whole other story."

The resolute jaw softened in a smile as the captain changed the subject. "I'd take it as a favor if you would call me Jesse instead of Captain, ma'am. I do wish I could see you all's faces. If you all look as good as you sound, this house has got some mighty handsome folks in it. Your oldest boy, especially. Do you know that he fed me most of my breakfast? Your uncle's bringing the priest by to see Tobe and me later on today. I confess to being curious about him. I've never met a priest before. But then, to tell the truth, he may be somewhat curious about meeting a hard-shell Baptist!"

So began a most remarkable time, those days of singing and healing. There, bandaged to utter darkness, Jesse Rankin sang the greater part of each day, sometimes alone, sometimes singing duets with Tobe, sometimes with all of us chiming in. Matt was so fascinated that he sat for hours with the men, singing like a young mockingbird. Dessie and Linney never missed a chance to stop their work and join in, their rich voices rivaling Tobe's in power and depth. Each afternoon Uncle came home to the sound of music. His step grew lighter and his shoulders less stooped. Most days our house sounded like a Baptist camp meeting right before foot-washing time.

Jesse did not sing all the time, of course. Actually, he listened a lot, sang a lot, and talked very little, but in his few weeks with us, Jesse won our hearts.

We learned that he was an only child, the son of his parents' middle age, and that his people had first stepped from a flatboat onto the river bank in Arkansas at Lewisburg Landing on a hot summer day in 1817. Toward Tobe he displayed the most exquisite courtesy, insisting on taking his meals in the sick room with him, rather than sitting with us at Uncle's table, where invisible ironclad rules excluded any Negro. And Tobe responded by freely sharing the story of his life and his thoughts with this white man who in other circumstances would have been excluded from true friendship by the line of color.

My little boys were drawn to the sick room like nails to a magnet. Matt became the soldiers' errand boy, performing the many small services that neither man, Tobe in his immobility nor Jesse in his blindness, could do for himself. Even Gus and Will, mischievous toddlers of 14 months, displayed a quietness and consideration that amazed us all.

It was my guess that Linney moved herself into the room each afternoon when I removed the twins for their naps, but I took great care never to find out for sure. Clearly, she and Tobe had reached an understanding that I figured was none of my business. Uncle had formed the habit of staying at home and napping during these cold afternoons. So for a few hours each day quietness reigned. By late afternoon the sounds of singing began again. Uncle and I would come downstairs and join in. For these short weeks we were a truly harmonious household, pushing our individual worries temporarily aside.

Preacher Flowers was fascinated, but he began to worry as the time approached to take Jesse's bandages off. "Auguste," he said to Uncle one evening as they talked out of Jesse's hearing, "have you thought how Jesse's going to take it if all the singing turns out to have been in vain? Whatever shall we do if the poor boy is blind in both eyes? He hasn't even considered that possibility."

"No, Reverend, I haven't, because I've been worrying about what will happen to Jesse after he heals. Technically, he's a Federal prisoner assigned to my keeping. As we both know, General Grant has ruled that no further amnesties will be granted nor prisoners exchanged. After he has healed, I have not the heart to turn that fine boy over to army authorities to be locked up in some hellhole of a prison. I am torn, Reverend, between duty and human decency."

"Have you talked to Father Benet about it, Auguste?"

"I have."

"And?"

"Father said, 'Render unto Caesar the things which are Caesar's, and unto God the things that are God's.'"

"Do you not find that to be helpful, old friend?"

Uncle's voice was weary. "Not yet, Flowers, not yet. And the bandages are scheduled to come off within a few days."

I stepped across the hall to join them, a shawl wrapped around my shoulders against the cold November air. "Uncle, I wrote to Larkin about Jesse. I've been worried, too. His answer came in today's post." I handed Larkin's letter to the men.

Dear Sarah,

I have concluded that you undoubtedly attract battles the way a honeypot attracts bears. Who would have thought that, twice now, it would have been your grim fortune to be in the midst of terrible battles? I tremble to think of you and our boys being so near such forces of destruction. And I say that as one who has all too recently experienced the horrors of battle. Two weeks ago I received direct orders to close out the government's campaign against the wild Plains Indians so as to put an end, once and for all, to their hostile raiding parties. Acting accordingly, I planned and executed a surprise attack on the Cheyennes and Arapahoes encamped here in the Colorado Territory, killing over 500 of them in one fell swoop. Such were the benefits of the element of surprise that I lost only seven men.

All of which brings me, in a roundabout way, to the question you posed in your most recent letter regarding Jesse Rankin. As I see it, Sarah, we are in debt to the man. It was due to him and others like him that you and Matt received safe escort through the scoundrel-infested Ozarks two years ago. I have no doubt that we owe him a very great debt.

I cannot help him. I am under direct orders to do as the War Department directs. But you have sworn no such oath, Sarah. Consider this: a man in civilian clothes could board a steamboat in Kansas City, travel by water all the way to Little Rock, there renounce the Confederacy and swear an oath of allegiance to the United States of America, and hence resume a useful life. Such are the terms now extended by a generous President to all men who live in Arkansas. Rankin has as little chance of making his flight through the Ozarks on foot as you had in similar circumstance two years past. His best chance remains as described above.

Kiss our fine boys for me. I have requested a furlough for the near future. Having sustained a minor flesh wound from an arrow encountered in our recent engagement, I must wait for my leg to heal. I expect to see you soon.

Uncle smiled. "Render unto Caesar the things which are Caesar's, and unto God the things that are God's. Reverend Flowers, we're going to need a suit of civilian clothes for a tall, thin man. Do you think that between us we can come up with accoutrements appropriate for a young gentleman of means? Our young friend stands a far better chance of getting to Little Rock if he goes in style than in steerage."

"Why, Auguste, I can contribute two fine white shirts. However, truth compels me to admit that the only broadcloth suit I own is the one I preach in each Sunday. I would suggest that you stand a better chance of finding a frock coat amongst your relatives."

"Alas, all the Chouteaus are short. And there will be neither time nor opportunity to have a coat tailored. When Jesse's bandages are removed, he must leave without delay and without fanfare. Once on shipboard, he must be seen as simply another affluent young speculator politician — of whom, God knows, this war has produced a more than sufficient quantity!"

Preacher Flowers was not discouraged. "I have no doubt that Father Benet can find the necessary garments." His old face lit up with a boyish grin. "The Catholics of this town are so accustomed to have you begging in the name of charity that they won't give Benet's request a second thought."

Uncle laughed with him. "Touché, old friend! But this time, it will not be charity. I'll see Father after mass tomorrow morning. And you may be sure I shall make a donation that will sufficiently compensate for the project!"

The day was bleak and the wind was sharp the morning Dr. Lester came to remove Jesse's bandages. "It is good that the light is not bright today, young man," he remarked to Jesse. "You've been in darkness a long time. That good eye of yours will need some time to adjust to the light."

Carefully and tenderly the doctor unwrapped the last bandage from Jesse's left eye. He paused finally to peer intently, first at Jesse and then at all of us, the entire household having gathered to hear his verdict.

"Amazing, completely amazing. Captain Rankin, I am seeing a miracle. Though the sight in this eye has gone, the eyeball has not shrunk away. It is hardly even discolored! The bone structure has reestablished itself in such a way that a casual observer would scarcely know the eye to be blind!"

"Ah, doctor, though I'm grateful to you for your good help, I tend to credit a higher power." Jesse took a deep, steadying breath. "It's time now to uncover the other eye, I do believe."

The room was silent except for the snipping of Dr. Lester's scissors and the sharp, quick gusts of sleet blowing against the window panes. When the last white strip of linen was removed, the doctor spoke gently. "Open your right eye, Captain. And tell me what you see."

We all held our breath as a long moment stretched by. Again, the doctor spoke, his voice calm and low. "You may see blurs at first. Are the blurs clearing up for you? What do you see, son? Tell me what you see."

When Jesse finally spoke, his voice sounded glad beyond the telling. "I see glory, doctor! I see glory! I see the blessed faces of the finest folks in

this world looking at me from yonder hall archway. I see this big room."
He turned his head to look toward Tobe's direction. "And I see that big
man with a durn big grin that's been singing duets with me for the past
three weeks!" He held out his hand to Dr. Lester. "And I see the doctor I'm
so beholden to. Like I said, sir, I do see glory!"

Tobe's powerful bass boomed out in a hymn that nearly raised the
rafters on the roof: "Praise God, from whom all blessings flow; praise
Him, all creatures here below. . . ."

We all joined in, singing with such gusto that we sounded like the loudest camp meeting that ever came out of Arkansas. While we sang, we
stared across the room at each other. For our part, we saw a youngish man
with sandy hair that hung in curls over a wide, fine forehead. We saw light
blue eyes, a determined mouth, and a straight nose of pronounced character.

"You have the map of Scotland on your face, Jesse." Uncle's voice was
affectionate. "I would guess you to be pure Scotch-Irish. We've all wondered what you would look like without bandages — as, one would suppose, you have wondered about us."

"Well, for one thing," Jesse responded, "I've wondered whether Miss
Sarah's poor little face healed up. There's another miracle here. I don't see
a mark on it!"

I caught Uncle's cautionary look and held my peace. Some things, I was
learning, are better left unsaid and unknown.

"Sarah's presence in my house is a great blessing to me," Uncle said,
"as yours has been, Jesse. Yet there the resemblance must end. For much
as we all regret it, for your own future prospects we must soon say good-
bye to you." Uncle turned to his household. "What I have to say to Captain
Rankin is confidential. Even Tobe must be excluded from our discussions.
Captain, may I ask that you accompany me across the hall into the parlor?"

The heavy double doors of the parlor closed behind the two men. When
they emerged half an hour later, the slim invalid had been replaced by a
lanky young gentleman clothed in a starched linen shirt and frock-tailed
broadcloth coat. With an air of distinction he held his tall hat in one hand
as he prepared to say his good-byes.

The loud sound of the brass knocker on the door proclaimed that Father
Benet had arrived to drive our guest to the wharf. Uncle's face was set, and
I recognized the sign of unshed tears in his eyes. Jesse Rankin made his
rounds of farewell, hugging my boys and shaking the hand of each man

and woman, until he came to Tobe. There, instead of taking Tobe's outstretched hand, the white man threw his arms around the black in an affectionate embrace of true friendship. When he finally reached me he, extended his long, slim hand out toward mine and began to sing the old square dance song known to all who grew up in the hills of Arkansas:

> "Rise you up my dearest dear,
> And present to me your hand;
> For I mean to take a journey
> To a far and distant land!"

Clapping and singing and smiling, Tobe and I joined in the chorus that we both knew so well:

> "And it's ladies to the center,
> and it's gents around the row;
> And we'll rally round the canebreak,
> and shoot the buffalo!"

As his tall frame climbed inside Father Benet's carriage, we were all on the front steps singing our farewells:

> "Rise you up my dearest dear,
> And present to me your hand;
> For I mean to take a journey
> To a far and distant land!"

Chapter 32

THE PRESIDENTIAL RACE had been close. Lincoln had to run against two of the disgruntled generals he had had to sack earlier in the war. But the Union troops had voted overwhelmingly for him, and his margin of electoral votes was sweeping. With the smell of victory in their nostrils, Grant and Sherman began their relentless work of crushing the South. In every household across the land, women waited and prayed that the price of victory would not include the sacrifice of one of their own.

Minerva sent me one of Stant's letters, and my heart ached as I pictured the circumstances that had changed her good-natured youngest son into a relentless soldier.

Dear Ma,

We're cutting a 40-mile swath through the heart of the South. We're like a swarm of blue-coated locusts, eating everything in sight. A crow would have a hard time surviving the winter on what we've left behind in these Rebel fields. God knows what the people are going to eat, Ma, but I am resolved that the nourishment of these Rebels is not my concern. My job is to get this over with and get back home in one piece. We all have hopes of getting this war finished soon. We're headed straight east to the ocean. They're a different kind of people here. It's too bad we can't be here under friendlier circumstances.

I had prayed that Larkin would be furloughed home to spend Christmas with us, but it was not to be. The letter that arrived in mid-December dashed all hopes of an early reunion.

Dear Sweet Wife,

It had been my expectation that by this time I would be holding you in my arms, but fate has decided otherwise. The Plains Indians, far from being subdued by the winter weather and their recent losses, have been incited by their leaders into almost continual harassment of the white settlers. Thus, it is not only the wagon trains and stage coach runs and army forts that are at risk. The battle has been widened.

At any rate, as we approach this Christmas, even though we are separated by the miles and the snow and harsh circumstances, let us take comfort in the prospect of early victory and in our certain reunion. For I am convinced, Sarah, that the spring will bring rejoicing, and that I will once again hold you and our fine little boys in our own circle of love.

One cold winter day passed after another. Tobe's leg healed cleanly and well. He left to rejoin his regiment, leaving behind three little lonesome boys who pestered Linney every day to bring Tobe back to play and sing with them.

Early January brought a letter from Jesse:

Mr. Auguste Chouteau, Esquire

Dear Sir,

Please permit me once again to express to you my undying gratitude to you and your household. My mother and father join me in conveying to you our heartfelt thankfulness for your goodness. I will remain in your debt for the rest of my life, sir, and pray to God that I can so live my life as to be worthy of the opportunity and the future now granted me.

My journey home, down the rivers and hence west to Little Rock, proceeded according to our expectations. I will appreciate it if you will convey to Colonel Flint and Miss Sarah my gratitude for their sound advice in this matter. Upon arriving in Little Rock, I went immediately to pay my respects to Governor Matthew Flint and swore the oath of allegiance to the Union. Thereupon, I traveled with all possible speed west to Lewisburg Landing. Thus, I was able to take Christmas dinner at my father's table amidst general rejoicing and many prayers of thanksgiving for the Almighty's benevolence.

Immediately after the holidays I rode north to visit with Tobe's parents and to assure them of his good health. I found them to be fine folks, proud of their new status as owners of property, and full of love for Miss Sarah. Please convey to Miss Sarah the news of the cordial reception accorded me by her stepmother, Mrs. Eliza Griffin, and that of other members of her family, the John Griffin family having joined her for the holidays. I was welcomed as a member of their family, and amidst much good cheer I visited there for three days before returning to my own home to assume my duties.

Again, sir, be assured of my lifelong appreciation of your kindness.

Even while we beamed with pleasure at Jesse's news, I was again shaken with a pang of homesickness, picturing Eliza and Aunt Kate and Uncle John, Hope, Piety, and Charity, Neely and Zeke all gathered around the fireplace together. I resolutely brushed aside the self-pitying tears and focused instead on the coming year. Larkin was sure the war would soon be over. Indeed, events began to confirm his confidence.

In the West, the organized Confederate resistance was over, but the outlaw Indians moved into this vacuum so vigorously as to keep the Federal forces constantly on the alert. In the East, Sherman's army wheeled north from Savannah and began their devastation of the Carolinas, while Grant continued his ruthless press on Lee's Army of Northern Virginia.

By the time President Lincoln stood on the steps of the Capitol to give his second inaugural address, the end was in the sight of all except those blinded by bitterness.

With his characteristic intelligence and compassion, Lincoln defined the cause of the conflict: "Both parties deprecated war: but one of them would make war rather than let the nation survive; the other would accept war rather than let it perish. And the war came. . . . Fondly do we hope — fervently do we pray — that this mighty scourge of war will speedily pass away."

But the war continued until Lee's gallant army could fight no longer. On April 2, 1865, General Lee telegraphed his president the sad news. Jefferson Davis began the business of evacuating Richmond, and the Army of Northern Virginia began its last march. On April 3, the Stars and Stripes flew above the Confederate capital at Richmond. At a little town called Appomattox, Grant prepared for a massive attack. The grim and still defiant Rebels waited staunchly under their worn battle flags. On April 8, 1865, surrounded and facing starvation, a sick-at-heart General Robert E. Lee surrendered his men to General Ulysses S. Grant.

To his lifelong amazement, Stanton Flint was a witness to the historic encounter of the two generals. Stant's letter to his mother was copied by Minerva and circulated among the family.

Dear Ma,

I write you today from a little place in Virginia called Appomattox Courthouse, a little town no bigger than Griffin Flat. I'm here on account of my captain having been sent north by General Sherman with a message to General Sheridan. Ma, I was standing there at the edge of the yard today, holding the captain's horse, when up rode General Robert E. Lee with his staff. When they dismounted and marched up the walk of the good-sized brick house across the road, I got a clear look at the man I've been fighting against these past years. I expect never again in my life will I see such a fine-looking man, with silver beard and hair. His uniform was elegant, his sword sparkled with jewels, and his boots were polished. But it was his face that said it all, Ma. General Lee's face reminded me of Father's face that day Father had to watch all five of us boys be marched off with chains around our necks. I used to see Pa's face in my dreams, sick at heart and proud to the bone. Today I saw that same look on the face of the man we finally whipped.

Before too long, General Grant himself arrived. He sure hadn't gone to any trouble to get dressed up for the occasion. Didn't even have a fancy coat on. His shirt didn't look any better than the one I have on myself. In fact, the only difference between the clothes he had on and the ones I'm wearing right now was that he had a better pair of boots, and he had four stars on his blouse. He seemed not to see any of us, nor to take notice of anything except what was ahead of him.

But when I saw that plain, stern man walk up that brick walk, such a feeling of pride came over me that it was all I could do to keep from opening my mouth and shouting hosannas and crying for joy. In three years I hadn't shed a single tear, Ma, not even that terrible day when we all trudged off down that rocky road, but I ain't ashamed to say that I cried today. When General Lee finally came out and mounted his horse, General Grant and all his officers stepped out on the porch and saluted him. General Lee returned the salute and rode off, and I stood there watching with a lump in my throat as big as a goose egg, my heart pounding like a trip-hammer. It's all over, Ma. I wish to God Tom could come marching home with the rest of us. This war has killed many a fine man, but it's all over, Ma. We'll see each other soon. Give my love to Father.

As the country was soon to find out, Grant's terms of surrender were decent and considerate, concluding with the simple words, "Each officer and man will be allowed to return to his home, not to be disturbed by the United States authorities so long as they observe their paroles and the laws in force where they may reside."

Peace had finally come. Campfires smoldered into ashes, and battle flags were carefully furled. Worn and weary men of the North and the South started out on the long walk home, turning their backs on each other for the first time. Lincoln's terms of surrender had reflected the spirit of his eloquent second inaugural address: "With malice toward none, with charity for all, with firmness in the right, as God gives us to see the right, let us strive on to finish the work we are in, to bind up the nation's wounds, to care for him who shall have borne the battle and for his widow and his orphan — to do all which may achieve and cherish a just and lasting peace among ourselves and with all nations."

There was hope in the country, for most were heartily sick of war. Though a few partisan bands and their bloodthirsty leaders still lusted for blood and battle, most men laid down their arms in relief, glad for the chance to get on with their lives.

And Lincoln, their wise leader, believing that both sides shared in the blame for the war, just as both sides had borne the cost of the war, prepared to administer a peace in which both sides could begin to heal. But on April 15, an assassin's bullet ended the life of the one man capable of bringing together the two wounded halves of the country. Abraham Lincoln, that awkward, plain man whom God had taken by the hand and led to wisdom, was shot and killed. The people who had been engaged in the joyous celebrations of victory were now plunged into a massive outpouring of grief. In all of history, there had never been such national sorrow. Across the land, the people wept.

Chapter 33

WESTPORT WENT WILD *when we got the news that the war was over and the Union had won. Men shot off their guns and built roaring bonfires and shouted in triumph and danced around for joy. The news did not come over the telegraph wire until around sundown on the evening of April 12. Uncle and I were in the dining room, halfway through our dinner, listening to Linney referee the squabbles of the twins in the kitchen. It was then that we first heard the spasmodic booms of the shotguns.*

We rushed out on the porch, somehow sensing that these were noises of jubilation, and gave ourselves up to the blessed release of the worries and woes of the past four years. Our neighbors rushed out of their own houses and thronged the streets, singing and laughing, talking and crying. The most reserved of neighbors fell into each other's arms in happy greeting. Even total strangers pounded each other on the back and passed their jugs of whiskey from hand to hand.

From the center of Westport Square, where the Harris House stood, we could hear the sounds of drums and fife. We hastened to the square to join in the rejoicing. Soon the clear, high notes of a bugle sent the "Battle Hymn of the Republic" soaring up into the night. As we sang, caught up in the magic of the moment, all things seemed suddenly possible, and the doors of the future opened to promise the fulfillment of all our hopes.

Uncle's voice boomed out, "Mine eyes have seen the glory of the coming of the Lord . . ."

The crowd shouted the chorus: "Glory! glory, hallelujah! Glory! glory, hallelujah . . ."

Suddenly, I realized that Uncle had stopped singing. I looked over at him just in time to see his face twist in a grimace of pain as his body crumpled to the ground. By the time my frantic screams had galvanized the bystanders into action, he was gone. Even as I hurried by the side of the little procession that hastily carried him back to his home, I knew Uncle had no pulse. We lay him on the parlor sofa and tried in vain the few remedies I could think of. There was no use in forcing a stimulant past those rigid lips, nor pounding a heartbeat back into his limp and sprawling body. Slowly, my mind accepted what my heart already knew. Uncle Auguste was dead, gone on the very day that his prayers for peace had been answered.

Father Benet, Dr. Lester, and the undertaker all came in at about the same time, closely followed by Aunt Bereniece and Uncle Louis and Cousin Marie. Soon our somber house was nearly as crowded as the noisy streets, but there was small comfort to be had in the one and no longer any joy to be had from the other. My friend, my teacher, my substitute father, was gone. I tried to summon again the swell of joy that had rushed through me when I had first realized that the war was over and Larkin would surely be coming home, but that joy was so muted by grief that I could not recapture the feeling. Instead, I busied myself with the responsibilities that death had suddenly thrust upon me.

Uncle Louis made the case clear: "Auguste regarded you as his daughter, Sarah. He would wish us to defer to your judgment. After all, you are now the head of your household."

Uncle lay in state in the front parlor for two days and two nights, a time barely sufficient to accommodate the many who moved slowly past his casket to look in final farewell upon his earthly countenance. By the hundreds they came — the Negroes through the back door, the whites through the front.

Invariably, after their muted condolences had been spoken, Uncle's friends gathered together, talking of the end of the war and the terms of Lee's surrender and of a future with families united again. I stood there, dry-eyed, not only mourning for Uncle, but mourning all over again for Pa and Aunt Gert and Tom. In spite of all of President Lincoln's hopes and his speech about a peace with "malice toward none" and "charity for all," I feared that I would carry hatred in my heart for Quantrill and for his kind until the end of my days.

I looked again at Uncle's kind and dignified face, and I realized that not once in the two and a half years I had lived under his roof had I heard Uncle say one single malicious untrue word about his fellow man.

It was almost midnight on Friday night before I finished arranging the refreshments for the men who had come to sit with Uncle's body during this last long night of his wake. As though by some prearranged signal, his closest friends were there, along with my Uncle Louis. I was halfway up the stairs when a uniformed messenger came running into the hall. "Mr. Van Horn; Mr. Van Horn — I have an urgent message for Mr. Van Horn!"

From across the room Van Horn stood up. "Show some respect for the dead, man. What ails you, bursting in here and yelling like that?"

"The President's been shot! Mr. Lincoln's been shot! They need you down at the newspaper, sir! Word has just come in! Mr. Lincoln's dying! He's been shot in the head!"

As Van Horn ran out into the April night, fresh grief filled the hearts of those of us left behind. Uncle Louis, that dignified pillar of reserve, wept like a child, and the cheeks of all present were wet with the tears pent up through years of war and sacrifice. Dr. Lester looked at me as I stood, uncertain, wondering where to turn or what to do.

"Go to bed, Miss Sarah. Get some sleep before you have to resume your sad duties tomorrow. Grief keeps. There'll be many an hour to grieve in the future. Get some sleep tonight. Tomorrow you must bury your uncle. I'll see to it that our voices are quiet down here."

From across the room Thomas Smart rose, a decanter of whiskey in his hand. "Fill your glasses, men, for I propose a toast! To the greatest man our country has ever produced, our President, Abraham Lincoln!"

When we had gathered in the church for Uncle's funeral, the news from Washington had spread throughout the land. Abraham Lincoln had died at 7:22 a.m., the day before Easter. By the time Uncle's mourners had returned to his house after his burial, grief and speculation had fired peoples' imaginations so that they could talk of nothing except Lincoln's assassination.

Conspiracy theories were everywhere, and, indeed, there was sufficient evidence to justify them. At the same time that the President had been shot, another assassin had appeared at the door of Secretary Seward, who was ill. The assassin had stabbed both Seward and his doctor, wounding both of them.

"We're among friends here, men, so I'll say it out loud." The speaker was Hamilton Montgomery, his face grim. "The ones who will benefit from this murderous act are the radicals in Washington, Secretary Seward, and that unholy trinity of Senator Wade and Congressman Stevens and Senator Sumner." He paused, his eyes dark. "Add to that list Secretary Stanton. He's always been too close to those radicals for my comfort. It's the rest of the country that will be hurt, and the South will be hurt the most."

Preacher Flowers was not persuaded. "I refuse to think such evil of men in high office. The fact that Lincoln would have insisted on healing the nation rather than punishing the South cannot be construed as a motive for killing him. Being radical does not mean that men would plot cold-blooded assassination. You go too far, Hamilton!"

"Perhaps. But I remain unconvinced that an actor without talent, even in cahoots with a few ignorant rebels, could have brought off this vile endeavor. There is a diabolical conspiracy here. Whether the American people are ever to know the real truth behind it will be the question of the future. What we now know for sure is this: the South will be made to suffer, and all who fought for the South will be punished."

As events began to unfold, I reflected on Mr. Montgomery's analysis. Andrew Johnson proved to be no match for the radicals in Congress, and even less so for Secretary Stanton, who soon assumed the powers of a dictator.

The South was now in the grip of the revenge-seeking radicals of the

North. While the people mourned their dead President, Edwin Stanton and Andrew Johnson capitalized on the nation's tragedy by tearing up Abraham Lincoln's compassionate plan for fitting together the two halves of a broken country. Suddenly, it was as if kindness and mercy had gone out of style. New laws were passed that invited the mean and the greedy to profit from the spoils of victory.

Down in Arkansas, Matthew Flint held fast to Lincoln's vision and did his best to administer the laws of the land with decency and compassion. But he had his hands full. Andrew Johnson, a puppet of the radicals, was bent on revenge, and Edwin Stanton was without mercy. People in the South, who only a year ago had thought of Lincoln with anger, remembered his love for the country and contrasted his plans for national reunion with the policies that were now being dictated by Congress.

As Larkin and I wrote letters back and forth, making plans for our own reunion and for the resumption of our lives in Arkansas, I wondered how our new neighbors by the river would regard us once we arrived.

Larkin was resolved to build a new home overlooking the river as soon as possible. I, on the other hand, hoped to take time to enjoy again the company of our families, visiting and reaping the blessings of being together again. But Larkin was full of plans and accustomed to command. I prepared my household to be ready to journey to Arkansas whenever Larkin was able to join us in Kansas City.

In the meantime, the contents of Uncle's will added a new dimension to my plans. Once again, the Chouteau family — my three remaining uncles, Aunt Bereniece, and myself — assembled in Uncle's parlor to hear Mr. Hamilton Montgomery's solemn reading of Uncle's last will and testament. I listened in astonishment as the full measure of Uncle's affection for me was made evident.

Will of Auguste Jean Chouteau

State of Missouri
City of Kansas

I, Auguste Jean Chouteau, at this time being of sound mind and memory, and calling to mind the mortality of my body, and as God has blessed me with sundry material goods of this life, do hereby make and constitute this my last will and testament in manner and form following, hereby revoking and annulling all former wills by me made.

First, I leave to my beloved niece, Sarah Griffin Flint, the tract of land of ten acres on which is situated my present residence, along with said residence and the contents thereof, being located in the village of Westport in the State of Missouri. Also, I leave to said niece the sum of $5,000 in gold to be used by her at any time and in any manner whatsoever that may seem reasonable and proper to her, without restraint or restriction by any person or persons whatsoever.

After commending my soul to the guardian care of heaven and my body to the provision of a decent Christian burial, my funeral charges, along with any other sundry obligations that may exist having been paid in full, the remainder of my estate is to be equally divided among the children, both born and unborn, of my said niece, Sarah Griffin Flint, and is to be held in trust for said children until such time as each shall have attained his or her majority.

I hereby name my trusted friend and attorney, Hamilton Montgomery, and my beloved brother Louis Jefferson Chouteau to execute this last will and testament, in witness whereof I have hereunto set my hand and seal in the year of our Lord, one thousand, eight hundred and sixty four, the second day of February.

Signed,

Auguste Jean Chouteau

Witnesses present:
Hamilton Montgomery, Esquire
Louis Jefferson Chouteau
The Reverend Knox Flowers

I was stunned. When Hamilton Montgomery finished his meticulous recitation and turned to me in congratulations, I could do no more than swallow around the big lump in my throat.

Uncle Louis turned his earnest face to me, his voice reflecting the solemnity of his new responsibilities. "Do you not know, my dear, how much joy your children brought into Auguste's life? For a childless man to have suddenly been gifted with the presence of children related to him by blood was the blessing of his old age. In return, he wished to give your children a guaranteed inheritance."

"But why did he deed me the house?"

It was Hamilton Montgomery who responded. "Sarah, the land you inherited from your mother lies in the Confederacy, in conquered country. No man can predict with certainty the economic conditions that will exist in the South now. Arkansas has been devastated, as much by her own Confederate generals as by her conquerors, but devastated, nonetheless. And the Indian Territory is now a no-man's-land into which even hardened criminals venture with misgivings. Put simply, your uncle wanted you and yours to have access to a home where, if you choose to do so, you could live in peace and educate your children. You need not choose to live in your uncle's home. Nowhere is that stipulated. But it remains an option. And your Uncle Louis and I gave our solemn word to your Uncle Auguste that we would manage the properties to which you and your children are heirs to the very best of our abilities."

"Sir," I replied, "Larkin and I will live in Arkansas. I am absolutely sure of Larkin's wishes in that regard. Whether Arkansas again becomes, as you put it, a place where we can live in peace and educate our children will depend on whether people like us assume the duty of making it so. But who can predict where my children will live? All I know is, I am beholden to you all, and when I do leave Kansas City, it will be with sadness that I say good-bye." And even as I spoke, the hot tears began to roll down my cheeks.

Uncle Louis had already indulged in more sentiment than he was comfortable with. "Sarah, I would ask that you turn your attention to the difficult task of dispersing your uncle's household. Once you and Larkin leave, your people will be at loose ends. Your two white maids are highly unlikely to wish to go South with you. And there is the situation of the darky, Linney. Your Aunt Bereniece, I believe, will have some suggestions for you in that regard."

As soon as the men had taken their dignified leave, I turned to my Aunt Bereniece. "What did Uncle Louis mean, when he said that you had suggestions about Linney?"

"Sarah, she is expecting a child. Have you not looked closely at her lately?"

My mind did some simple arithmetic. "It's bound to be Tobe's. And that means she's four or five months along. He's liable not to get back in time to marry her before the child is born. Larkin says he expects it'll be late summer or early fall before most of the men get home."

Aunt Bereniece shook her head in amazement. "You truly are an unselfish girl, Sarah. Whether or not Linney is married when the child is born is beside the point as far as I am concerned.

"My concern, and yours, I trust, is that Linney will be in no condition to travel with you to Arkansas when you and Larkin undertake your journey. Since you will need to find someone else to care for your children, you really should be making plans."

My aunt walked firmly down the steps toward her carriage, her back straight with the conviction of one who has seen her duty and has performed it well. I headed out to the backyard to find Linney, not knowing whether to laugh or to cry.

Linney was matter of fact. "Well, of course I knowed you'd notice sometime, Miss Sarah. I've wrote Tobe. He knows, and he's glad, and we're gwine to marry when he gets by here. We's gwine to go back and live in Arkansas, too. I'd hep you out if I could, Miss Sarah, onc't we all gets there, but it ain't likely we'll live too close together, is it?"

She was right, and I knew it. I sat down to write Larkin of the far-reaching new financial developments in our lives and concluded by telling him that in the future I would be looking after the children myself. I should have known that he would look at the same problem and devise a different solution. His letter to me came back with all possible speed.

Dear Sarah,

Who would have predicted it? Certainly, I had assumed that your Uncle Auguste would most likely remember you in his will, but for him to have designated our children as sole heirs to his lucrative downtown real estate in addition to his farm holdings is generous far beyond my expectations. And your Uncle Louis, for all his dry ways, is a remarkably able man when it comes to making a dollar. Our boys' inheritance is in good hands.

As to the house, I advise you to put it on the market at once,

so as to have a good chance of having it sold by the time I arrive
in Kansas City. If you can arrange to sell the furniture as well,
so much the better. The freight of transporting those heavy old
pieces to Arkansas is an unnecessary expense, to say nothing of
the expense of storage.

I calculate that by the time we arrive in Arkansas it will be
September. Add to that the time for inspecting our place in
northwest Arkansas and visiting with our families, it will be late
fall before I can undertake the task of building our new home
on our inherited Chouteau land. It's liable to be a year from now
before we actually are able to move in, for hauling materials up
that steep mountainside will be a hard job in winter time.

As to Linney, I advise you to not abandon hope yet. It has
been my plan all along to offer Tobe the job of being my overseer. Your cousin Edward Watson is getting old. Though he's a
fine schoolteacher, I remain unconvinced that he is any good at
getting work out of darkies. I think Tobe can. Our boys will
soon need a teacher. Matt needs one now. We'll put your Cousin
Ed to teaching and Tobe to bossing and Linney to looking after
our babies and things ought to work out smooth and lovely.

Remember, it will not be too much longer before I hold you
in my arms.

I pondered over that letter a long time before I answered it, but when I
did write I had my mind firmly made up, and to his credit Larkin never
once mentioned my decision.

Dear Larkin,

I put in a late garden today, so that when you get here you
can have new lettuce, green peas, and fresh sweet corn. Everyday I picture how you will look as you come walking in the
door, and every night I remember how it feels to have you hold
me in your arms.

You are absolutely right about Cousin Ed. Teaching is what
he does best, and if we can have Tobe and Linney working for
us it will be a rare combination.

I think it better to retain Uncle's house. If you were here in
Westport you would see, as I do, that real estate is soaring in

value. Now that the war is over, houses go up in price almost daily. Uncle Louis thinks that in ten years' time, the city will be so prosperous that our boys' downtown holdings will have quadrupled in value. In the meantime, Cousin Marie has approached me wishing to rent Uncle's house. She is anxious to move under her own roof when Victor comes home, having lived in the home of her mother-in-law for the past four years.

As to the furniture, Aunt Bereniece tells me that Uncle's furniture is prized by all the family. The pieces are heirlooms, of considerable value. We are fortunate to have them in our possession. They should furnish our new home in a style rarely seen in Arkansas. I have become fond of each piece, and trust you will indulge me in my desire to have them remain in our possession. It reminds me of Uncle, to whom we owe much.

I long to see you, dear husband.

I hated to begin our new life by crossing Larkin, but he never brought up the subject of selling the house or furniture again. And I never knew whether it mattered to him or not. To me, the important thing was the war was over and we could resume our lives where we had left off.

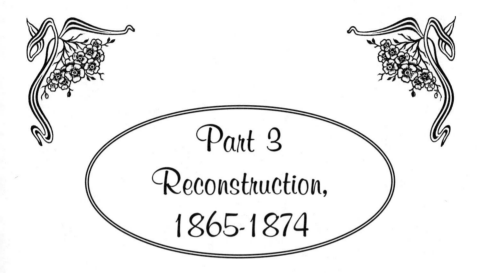

Part 3
Reconstruction,
1865-1874

Prologue
Larkin

*I WAS DISCHARGED ON August 20, 1865, after which I took the stage from Denver, arriving in Kansas City on the first day of September. This was the beginning of the happiest period of my life: the war was over, the Union army victorious, my family well and as yet alive, except for Tom. We had much cause to rejoice. It was a time for jubilation.*

Whilst in Kansas City we enjoyed a few days of celebration, then with Sarah and our wide-eyed little boys at my side, I hitched Uncle Auguste's pair of matched bays to the carriage and headed south for Arkansas. Stopping for a time at Fathers' compound, we found the entire Flint

family in congregation, at which time our celebrations began all over again.

It was mid-October before we crossed the river and set foot on the land that would henceforth be the place we called home. I worked through the winter and into the spring, directing the construction of the residence that had heretofore existed only in my mind. By the time the first tender shoots of cotton had poked through the rich loam down by the river, the house was ready for us to move into it.

The house turned out exactly as I had seen it in my imagination. I sited it on top of the bluff that formed the east end of Petit Jean Mountain and built it of native stone, tall and two-storied, with white pillars extending from the floor of the porch to the gray shingles of the roof. It became one of my chief pleasures in life to sit on that porch with Sarah at the end of each day, gazing at the magnificent view that stretched for 40 miles across the rich fields and wide river 2,000 feet below, to the green hills on the river's far bank, then beyond to the distant mountains that defined the horizon.

That first spring day we stood there, looking past the creamy blossoms of dogwood that spread like lace at the edge of the bluff, on past the gray-brown boulders, forested hills, and deep, dark blue of the most remote mountains, I lifted my eyes to the sky above and knew that I had already attained most of life's richest blessings. By summer, when pink and white blossoms began to appear on the stalks of thigh-high cotton, our beautiful little daughter was born to make life complete. I have wondered more than once if I got around to letting Sarah know how truly happy I was that year.

In any case, events on the political front began to rise up about as fast as the cotton crop, and before too long the entire state was caught up in the roughness and rankness of politics. It had all begun with Lincoln's assassination, of course.

Although Stanton did his best to sell the country the bill of goods that Southern conspirators in league with the devil and Jefferson Davis and the Knights of the Golden Circle had conspired to effect Lincoln's assassination, I never bought that idea, nor did any man that I knew. Neither did I believe then, nor do I believe now, that a third-rate glory-hungry actor and a handful of ignorant fools had the capability of outwitting all Pinkerton's detectives and the President's bodyguards. No, there was a conspiracy all right, but it was a conspiracy of those in high places, the Copperheads whose appetite for greed was exceeded only by their lust for power.

Andrew Johnson meant well, and at the last he tried hard, but the assassination elevated him far beyond his capabilities. He was no match for Congress, much less for Seward and Stanton. In the Congress, this Copperhead conspiracy was tolerated by those who ought to have been of better character. Lacking the courage to fight it, they permitted the enemies of the South to give vent to evil passions. These passions came near to ruining Arkansas.

This new radical government in Washington stuck its nose into everything, including the price of labor and even the supply of labor. At the same time that Father was governing the state with the utmost economy, preparing to present Arkansas to the Congress for readmittance to the Union in a condition of fiscal responsibility, the Freedmen's Bureau was knocking the props out from under Arkansas's private citizens and spending money like it was going out of style.

This Freedmen's Bureau, designed by a bunch of well-intended do-gooding Northerners who would have been hard put to know one end of a mule from another, much less where to put either end in conjunction with a plow, endeavored to create policies to make Negroes independent. Each Negro man was thereby entitled to 40 acres and a mule in the hopes that the many now-uncultivated acres in Arkansas would be profitably farmed. But, by the thousands, these starving and unemployed darkies had no more idea of how to handle economic freedom than my five-year-old son would have. Notable exceptions to the contrary, of whom I rank my foreman, Tobe Griffin, at the top of the list, most darkies expected the government to keep right on feeding them and clothing them exactly as their former owners had done. The only discernible difference in the darkies' minds was that they did not expect to have to work. As a result, at a time when cotton was selling for fantastic prices in the markets of Liverpool and New York, a severe labor shortage developed in Arkansas.

Cotton is a labor-intensive crop. Unlike corn or wheat, cotton takes an abundance of hands to bring a good crop to market. The weeds have to be chopped away from the tender plants on an almost continual basis from late April until the plants get big enough to crowd out the weeds — usually midsummer. I will admit there is a brief period in July and August when the crops are laid by that both master and worker can take a degree of ease, but by late August the process of picking the white fluff from the hard brown bolls begins. Then, no man can take his ease. All told, planting cotton is not a process that commends itself to the lazy. And, by the thousands, the Negroes turned lazy as they misused their new freedom, thinking themselves now exempt from the fearsome toil of their years of slavery.

Those of us with crops to bring in got desperate. I employed a sufficient number of darkies. Tobe, to his everlasting credit, was a fair, honest, and hardworking overseer, but we had one hell of a time getting an honest day's work out of men and women who felt sure that the government was going to feed them anyway.

When the last brown field was stripped down to the stalks and the last heavy bale hauled away from the gin, I solved my problem by sending Tobe to South Carolina. His instructions were to select a dozen families of industrious darkies and contract with them to relocate on my Arkansas plantation, there to farm on a sharecropping system. I agreed to furnish each family with a cabin and a 20-acre plot for their own garden and cow lot and pigpen, plus cotton acreage proportional to their ability to successfully farm it. I agreed to bear all seed and fertilizer expenses, the profits from the crops to be divided on the halves. Tobe's military train- ing had made him a splendid judge of men. He selected as superior a bunch of darkies as could be found anywhere. I paid for their removal to Arkansas and designated for their cabin sites a fine stand of walnut trees on a level piece of ground halfway up the side of the mountain. By Christmastime of 1866 we had them settled in to make ready for the spring planting.

I might mention in passing that as an additional inducement on my part, I had agreed to build a schoolhouse and to pay for the schoolteacher so as to afford their growing children the education that had hitherto been denied them. My own sons needed schooling, of course, and I figured that Schoolmaster Watson could teach a score of children about as easily as he could teach two or three, but there was more to it than that.

I have long believed that a true democracy depends on an educated cit- izenry. Whether a man is black or white, there is no way he will become responsible without some knowledge of the world around him. To give ignorant men the vote is to assure the demise of democracy. So I con- tracted with Watson to teach a six-month term, four months in the winter plus July and August when the crops were laid by.

As events developed, this last philosophy of mine soon attracted a newly formed secret society, that dastardly brainchild of Bedford Forrest, the soon-to-be-infamous Ku Klux Klan. Before too long, the Klan was on my back like a duck on a June bug, but they soon discovered they had picked on the wrong man.

There was no evidence to show that either the Ku Klux Klan or the Federals objected to the sharecropping system. The thing went far deeper than sharecropping. The Federal government was determined to raise Negroes to a state of legal parity with whites, and the people of the South were equally determined to prevent it. Schooling darkies so they could read and write and cipher was regarded by the Klan as adding insult to injury.

At the same time, the political pot was beginning to boil. Many Rebs who returned from the war could not seem to get it through their heads that the war was over and they had lost. Indeed, some of their misguided, hard-headed generals never did figure it out. Hindman and Price and Magruder, and even Shelby, rode hell-bent off to Mexico. There they offered their services to whichever side of the belligerents as would take them. I have spent more than one pleasant moment speculating on their amazement when they belatedly discovered that their vaunted generalship was not acceptable to either side!

These generals to the contrary, most men who had fought for the South came home with the mistaken notion that they could return to doing business as usual, even with the blacks and with politics so changed. To Father's intense disappointment, the Arkansas Supreme Court openly flouted the new Federal government. The ex-Confederates ran for office by the hundreds, and in the fall of 1866 they swept the legislature. In January 1867, a delegation from this new legislature proceeded to Washington to inform Andrew Johnson, and all others within earshot, of their naive views that the Arkansas Supreme Court would henceforth decide political matters in Arkansas. Of course, Johnson and the Congress set them straight in short order.

As a direct result, by March of 1867 the Reconstruction Act was in effect, an act that divided the South into five military districts and declared that no legal civilian government existed in Arkansas, nor anywhere else in the South, for that matter. This act placed Arkansas under the command of General Ord. It substituted trials before a military commission for the civil courts, and it required ratification of the 14th Amendment as a requirement for Arkansas's readmission to the Union. All these provisions were bad enough, but a further requirement was the straw that broke the camel's back and led to the activation of the Ku Klux Klan. The Reconstruction Act further mandated that "all male citizens of whatever race, color, or previous condition" (except for the many who were dis-qualified on account of having served in the Confederate army) were en-titled to vote.

Such a misguided policy would never have been forced down the throats of a conquered and decent people if Lincoln had lived. But a radi-cal and revengeful Congress, an inept president, and an arrogant bunch of Arkansas provincial politicians managed to bring about Reconstruction. The results were subversive resistance by the Ku Klux Klan, terror for the Negroes on the one hand and the incitement of the Negroes' false hopes on the other, plus the opportunities for corruption inevitably associated with one party having total control of the purse strings.

Father was heartsick. He became an old man that year. Carpetbaggers descended on us from the North and scalawags came out of the closets of the South. Over in Memphis, Albert Pike began editing a newspaper that violently opposed the law that permitted Negroes to vote. At the same time, Bedford Forrest clandestinely organized the Ku Klux Klan for vio-lence.

It was at about this time that I had my first run-in with the Klan. There had been some outrageous acts committed during this period when martial law prevailed, acts committed both by the Federal soldiers and by the Southern citizenry. Over in Pope County, the county across the river and north from us, five Republican county officials in succession were ruth-lessly killed by a vindictive citizenry. The state of health of any appointed Republican official in south and central Arkansas became precarious at best and fatal in far too many cases. However, at the same time this out-lawry was going on, my darkies and I were industriously engaged in plant-ing a record-breaking cotton crop.

Made bold by their success in Pope County, the Klan apparently de-cided to move downriver and take me on as their next target. I rode down my mountain one morning to find several posters stuck up on the oak trees and fence posts adjacent to my cotton fields. The gist of their message was plain, as no words were minced: "Flint, Beware!!! Either you drive them overeducated niggers off your place and keep your damned tongue out of politics or your wife will be a widow shortly!!!"

I took out my pencil and wrote my own message under their signs: "Trespassers will be shot! Signed, Larkin Houston Flint."

The upshot of this exchange of threats was that on three different nights, a fiery cross was burned on my land down by the river, a cross lit each night in such a position that Sarah and I could look down from our porch and see its hellish fire flaming in the valley below us.

At the end of three days, a committee of three men waited on me to ascertain what terms of truce could be agreed on. The committee, all men whose property was on the south side of the river, adjacent to my own, told their mission and expressed great concern for peace.

One man, Mr. Wilcox, spoke up and said, "Flint, you are a man of substantial reputation, and as such you are a welcome neighbor. But you and your policies are going against the prevailing sentiment of the rest of us landowners. We are here for your own good, here to warn you that those of us who are peaceable men can no longer influence the others. Many are now bent on murder and revenge. You are in danger, as are your wife and children, unless you run off your darkies. At the very least, you have got to stop teaching them to read. Good God, man, I wouldn't be surprised to hear that you're registering them to vote! We are here to call on you to be reasonable, Flint, and help us restore the peace of this part of the state."

"Ah," said I, "it is peace you desire, is it? Well, I, too, am a promoter of peace, and I know precisely how to bring it about. You fellows go home and attend to your own business, and I guarantee you that my darkies and I will attend to ours. In the meantime, I give you my word that not one darky will set foot on any property where he might not be welcome."

"Flint, you miss the point." Simpson, the second man, squirmed when he said it, but he got it out. "Our darkies are claiming that yours are better treated and better fed than ours. Whilst most of us are having the devil's own time getting our lazy niggers to shuffle out to the fields and pick up a hoe, your people are out here working from sunup to sundown. Look around you, man! Them fields of yours are going to produce at least a bale to the acre, whereas most of us will be lucky to get a half a bale. Where we've got weeds choking the life out of our plants, you've got rows clean as a whistle. Your uppity niggers are ruining the other blacks in the neighborhood. At the same time the other planters are jealous of you. Get rid of them educated niggers of yours and let us have peace."

"Well," said I, "you have just helped me change my mind. Before I will drive off my renters and ruin my cotton crop year after year just to please a set of outlaws, I will see the whole Ku Klux Klan landed safely in hell. If these white-sheeted cowards decide to put their plans into execution and come after my darkies, they are going to have to face me and my shotgun."

Wilcox, who basically was a well-intended fellow, replied. "I yet wish you well, but I have heard some very hard words from you about those fellows who are opposed to the niggers staying here. I am afraid they will have tragic results."

I purchased six .44 Colt revolvers and plenty of ammunition. I also got several shotguns and had my darkies armed and equipped as the law directs. I then told the colored men that if the Klan came back to molest them, they should kill everyone they could and that I would fight for them, but if they did not take care of themselves, not to blame me. The news soon became known about what I had done. Within a few days a preacher from north of the river called on me, and a dubious friend he was. Said he, "I have come to tell you of some bad tales they are telling on you."

"What are they?" said I.

"Well," said he, "please understand that I don't believe it at all, but they are actually telling for the truth that you have armed them niggers with guns and pistols and told them to shoot at white men."

"Pshaw," said I. "They certainly are not telling such tales as that on me."

"Yes, they are," said he. "But, I did not believe it."

"You can bet your last damned dollar that I have armed them," I replied, "and told them to shoot every damned white-sheeted scoundrel that comes here to molest them. If any of you fellows don't think so, feel free to come over some night and be convinced."

Within a few nights the Klan came. Their murdering minds effected a consequence unintended by all, for the frightening events of that night brought on Sarah's labor and the loss of a baby boy. I have neither forgotten nor forgiven this cowardly act, and I took appropriate action.

From this time on, hostilities abated, the Klan kept away, and the old feud gradually wore down. I continued to prosper and to mind my own business and to see to it that my people minded theirs. Wonder of wonders, before the election year of 1868 rolled around, my neighbors came again to my residence, this time with the intent of trying to persuade me to run as the representative on the Republican ticket to the state legislature!

As can be imagined, I had at first little inclination to get mixed up in politics, having seen my own father try and fail to achieve consensus. To my surprise, Father and Minerva and Sarah all urged me vehemently to take a part in the governmental process. I eventually consented to be a delegate to the convention charged with the responsibility of designing a new state constitution. So I stepped away from my plow, and instead of

"Gee" and "Haw" I substituted "Aye" and "Nay" and "Points of order." Before too long, I concluded that in many ways I was better off directing the mule.

We met in January 1868 in Little Rock for the Constitutional Convention, and a more motley assembly you never saw in your life. Eight Negro delegates were amongst us. To tell the truth, their conduct in general was considerably superior to that of many of the whites. Twenty-three radical carpetbaggers were very much in evidence, on the make for easy jobs and bountiful fortunes. Their leader was one Joseph Bender, a rabble-rousing, Bible-thumping preacher out of Iowa. During the war he had been chaplain to a Negro regiment in the Federal army. He had a voice like a brindle-tailed bull and was about as scrupulous as a bank robber. Then there were 30 scalawags, native Arkansans gone radical Republican, plus a handful of us who were Lincoln Republicans.

I listened through six days of back scratching and speech making, then rose and moved that the Constitution of 1864, Lincoln's Constitution, be accepted. This constitution gave the Negroes full property rights. It did not give them the franchise to vote, and neither did it deprive of voting rights those white males who had fought for the Confederacy and since taken loyalty oaths to the U.S. government. After furious debate, my motion was rejected, 62 to 10.

For the next several days the carpetbaggers and scalawags took turns making asses of themselves, until finally one of the very able Negroes again proposed the Lincoln Constitution. I led the debate, focusing on whether the newly proposed laws were aimed to help blacks or to cause them to be dominated by unscrupulous whites. Again, the motion failed, but this time the vote was 42 to 30. When finally the carpetbaggers prevailed and voted in their own harsh constitution, I and 29 others steadfastly refused to sign it.

The radicals were now firmly in power. Payson Clemson was nominated as governor. I confess to liking Clemson. I never trusted him, but it was hard not to like him. As a Union officer he had come to Arkansas by way of Kansas, having as a young man got a taste for politics under Lane and been apprenticed under Jennison to learn dirty tricks. During the war I had known him slightly, well enough to realize he was smarter than Lane and slicker than Jennison and possessed of a driving need to get to the top. This last need he had apparently fulfilled shortly after the war ended by settling down in Little Rock and marrying a girl with money.

I had not seen Clemson during the convention until the day we finished voting on the constitution, some of us having by that time adjourned to the saloon at the Metropolitan Hotel. I remember I was sitting at a table with Jesse Rankin, my neighbor and friend from across the river at Lewisburg Landing, when Joseph Bender, his big mouth roaring as usual, came strutting in by the side of Payson Clemson. Clemson promptly headed toward me, a wide grin on his face, his hand held out like he was greeting a long-lost brother.

"Bender," said he, "do you know Lark Flint? Besides being the son of our current governor, he was the best cavalry officer and the best fiddle player in the whole Union army!" Bender and I, having for the past ten days been engaged in earnest argument, were now forced to sit at the same table and assume the appearance of friendship.

Figuring two could play the game as well as one, I responded in kind. "Bender, are you sure this is the kind of company you are willing to keep? Why, if memory serves me right, Payson Clemson is the very man that set a Union army record in Kansas. Men claimed he had sampled the wares of every fat-butted whore from Independence to Abilene!"

"Now, Lark," replied Clemson, "that last has been somewhat exaggerated — as you yourself well know, having been at my side during some of said sampling. While I will admit there may now and then have been a few temptations made manifest in female flesh, if I'd actually managed to accomplish all that I got credit for, I would have died of exhaustion halfway to Abilene!" He then turned to Jesse and held out his hand. "Sir, it is a pleasure to see you again, and a fine thing for Arkansas when its Confederate sons begin to work alongside us newcomers to form a new government."

To make a long story short, such were Clemson's slick ways that Jesse and I were put in the position of acting like we were all fellow conspirators and colleagues, harboring no animosity whatsoever for the past several days of insults and invectives hurled freely at us by Clemson's henchman, old Brindletail Bender.

That night, when Jesse and I dined at Father's table, I put the case to Father. "What's Payson Clemson really like? What kind of man is he?"

"The kind of man who would rob his own dying grandmother of her last dime and cover his tracks so well you'd never find out how he did it. I've never come up against a slicker man in my life."

Jesse was a man not easily swayed by the opinions of others. "I thought today his words had the ring of truth. He seemed to be honest when he was talking about the future of Arkansas."

"Jesse, I've now had three years' experience in dealing with Clemson. You're right. The man honestly believes whatever he's telling you at the moment. He's going to tell you whatever it takes to get you on his side. He's smart as a whip, and he reads men like a book. There's only one catch: the man has no moral core whatsoever. He lies like a rug, but he never feels like he's lying, for whatever he's saying at the time is what he truly believes at that moment to be the truth. Watch yourselves, men. Clemson's charm and ambition are exceeded only by his total lack of principle. It's hard not to like him, but cover your backsides and watch your eyeteeth. He's liable to steal them right out of your head."

I had so much to tell Sarah when I got home that I kept her up half the night talking about it. The radical Republicans had picked a slate of candidates, a slate sure to get elected once the new constitution disenfranchising ex-Confederates was put into effect. Payson Clemson was nominated governor. I had been asked to stand for the legislature, and if ever a man was of mixed mind, I was, but Sarah felt otherwise.

"Larkin," she told me, "you've got to do it. You owe it to the decent men who can't vote. You can at least try to speak for justice and honest government if you are in the legislature."

"Sarah," said I, "one man can't change a majority. I'll always be a voice crying in the wilderness."

"Not so, Larkin. You told me yourself that you influenced the votes in that Constitutional Convention. They changed from 10 to 30 on your side. Your own father has stood up to terrible odds and to terrible men and still managed to make a real difference. Will you do less?"

"Minerva said the same."

"What did your father say, Larkin?"

"He said every man must decide for himself where he places his priorities."

In the end, with me hoping and Sarah praying that I was making the right decision, that spring I was elected to serve in the Republican-controlled legislature of 1868. After the election it was like Christmastime for Payson Clemson's friends. Nearly everybody got something. Clemson's supporters got cabinet posts and judgeships and appointments as tax collectors and sheriff's officers. His cronies were elected to Washington as senators and representatives. All proceeded to make ready for the lucrative tasks of lining their own pockets. Such are the opportunities in a one-party system.

On June 20, 1868, when Congress was deeply engaged in impeaching Andrew Johnson, that body took time from its foremost concern to vote Arkansas back in the Union. On July 2, Father and Payson Clemson rode to the statehouse in an open carriage drawn by six black horses. Clemson was dressed to the nines in a frock coat of finest broadcloth; Father was deliberately clothed in a suit of plainest homespun. Clemson was inaugurated as governor, after which Father walked him back to the governor's office, offered him a dram of whiskey, and turned over to Clemson the governance of the state.

The floodgates of robbery and graft were then officially opened in Arkansas. By this time, Frank and Jesse James were robbing banks all over Missouri and Kansas, but they were pikers and rank amateurs compared to Clemson's gang. Those few of us in the legislature who were not in Clemson's hip pocket could only debate the radicals, vote our consciences, and plan ahead toward a better day.

Between 1868 and 1871, Clemson and company had run up a state debt of astounding proportions — $10,000,000 on construction products alone. I was later to ascertain that of this amount spent, only a $100,000 worth of tangible evidence could be accounted for, most of this last being incomplete and therefore useless railroad beds and flood-control levees. However, all my planning and behind-the-scenes work paid off. In 1871, with the support of many radical Republicans, the enthusiastic support of the moderate Lincoln Republicans, and the clandestine support of the disenfranchised Democrats, the state of Arkansas voted Payson Clemson to Washington to serve in the Senate.

Clemson was understandably reluctant to go. After all, the man had a source of handy graft in Arkansas that had already made him a millionaire many times over. More than one man asked me my reasons for sending a known crook to Washington. My brother-in-law Will Griffin put it to me plain. "Why, Lark, are you working all over the state to send that dishonest slicker to Washington?"

"Will," I replied, "Arkansas can't afford him. We're a poor state. He'll bankrupt us all before he's through if he stays here as governor much longer. But in Washington, especially now that Grant is president, he'll have a wider range of opportunity. He may extend his talents to fleece the whole country, but he'll have a lot of competition and opposition in the

Congress. He will do Arkansas far less harm from a distance than if he stays at home and gives us his full attention."

When Clemson went to Congress, his vacated office as governor was filled by a placeholder until 1872. In that election, I was named the new governor of Arkansas, and I began my earnest endeavor to again bring integrity to Arkansas politics. I paid a high price for this decision — just how high, Sarah and I were to discover later. As it turned out, everything we held dear was weighed in the balance.

Chapter 34

 *WHEN LARKIN CAME home from the war, I could see a difference in his face. The old driving push to make every minute count had been replaced by the confidence of a man who aims to bend tomorrow to his will. Still so handsome that heads turned when he walked into a room, his features were now marked by the habit of command. Tiny lines had appeared around his eyes, and there was a vigilance to his gaze even when there was a smile on his face. The responsibilities of war had taken the last of Larkin's youth. The man he had become was a man that I loved with all my heart and soul.*

My heart leaped up when he walked in the door that September day in 1865. Such a wave of love washed over me that I began to cry for the sheer joy of his presence. But my tears were soon dried, replaced by the loving and laughter of celebration.

Within the week we had our affairs in order and were on our way home to Arkansas. We traveled light and without servants. I had arranged to ship our furniture and household goods by boat. Linney, in her eighth month of pregnancy, was in no condition to travel. Tobe had gotten back to her in late August, barely in time to make an honest woman of her before the baby made its appearance, and I arranged for them to join us later. Altogether, I was well satisfied with our travel plans, for I foresaw a ten-days' journey when Larkin and the boys and I would drive down toward the beautiful hills of home enclosed in the love of our own family circle.

Even now, I look back on those ten days and count them as one of the happiest times of my life. We rode through woods alive with beauty, the deep red and bright gold and rich bronze of the leaves defining nature's own intricate tapestry. Sunlight sparkled on the surface of each rushing stream and gleamed from the depths of the quiet pools. From the top of each mountain and the rim of each bluff we looked toward horizons of such lively beauty as to gladden our hearts and lift them toward heaven. But, as much as I enjoyed the days, I still could hardly wait for the nights.

After the last crisp bite of cornpone had been eaten and the last sip of coffee swallowed, when the campfire began to die down and our sleepy boys began to nod off, Larkin would get out his violin and play the sweet, yearning melodies of love. When we were sure the boys were sleeping soundly, Larkin would take me in his arms, his sensuous smile barely visible in the light of the waning fire. His practiced fingers warm and strong, his lips demanding, he loved me with the same passionate, soaring intensity made manifest in his yearning music. I lifted my eyes toward heaven during the days, but I felt like my body had reached there during the nights. Till I die, I will hold the remembrance of our Ozark journey in my heart.

But all things come to an end, and we could not live forever on the road. Larkin had not seen his parents in nearly four long years. The rush of reunion engulfed us all when we arrived at Matthew Flint's compound.

As he had done on my first visit to his home almost six years before, Matthew Flint came out to greet us, his silver hair blowing in the wind, his arms outstretched in welcome. His first words were to Larkin.

"Well done, son! Well done! You've made us proud!"

Larkin and his father threw their arms around each other in such gladness that tears stung my eyes.

Standing at the top of her steps, Minerva kissed Larkin on the lips, then held him by the shoulders while she stood back to look searchingly at his face.

"The years have left their mark, son." Her tone was approving. She kissed him again, this time a tender kiss on his cheek, before descending the steps to hold out her arms to me and my boys. Again, her look was searching and her tone was approving.

"And I'm proud of you, Sarah. We all are! Welcome!"

It was days later before we got caught up on news of the entire family, although most had gathered in under Matthew's commodious roof and were already engaged in the telling. We felt fortunate beyond measure to be able to come back to Matthew's house and find it substantially unchanged. Throughout the countryside we had already seen the bitter fruits of war. Where once there had been great grassy meadows dotted with fat cattle, green fields lush with the promise of abundant harvest, sturdy homes and contented families, now we saw desolation. Fields lay fallow. Briars and weeds covered the unplowed ground. The remains of burned-out homes scarred the landscape, their still-standing chimneys bearing stark testimony to the people who had been impoverished by the cruelties of war. Such cabins as remained were often empty and silent, their embittered owners having been forced to flee to other shelter.

Though we needed no reminders of the harsh price of war, such reminders were everywhere and added to my selfish gratitude that Larkin and I had been spared. Past suffering notwithstanding, we gathered with Larkin's people for a time of rejoicing and festivity.

I threw my arms around Becky, who was now proudly exhibiting the swollen belly of advanced pregnancy.

"Oh, Becky, I've got a lot of catching up to do. When is the baby due? And who else is in the family way? And where are Charity and Piety? Are they here?"

"In January. Susan's due in February. Charity and Ridge are already here, and Piety is over with Eliza. We'll send old Moe over the mountain tomorrow to tell them you're here." Becky paused, stepped back, and took a good look at me. "My goodness, girl, you do look smart! And beautiful beyond compare! Sarah, you've always been pretty, but now — my goodness — I can't get over how wonderful you look! Willie, doesn't Sarah look beautiful?"

At her side, Willie grinned and opened his arms to me. "I've decided, after years of study and close observation, that it's against the law for Flint women to be homely. Becky's right, Sarah. You're beautiful. But look around you, girls. We've got a whole house full of beauties! And I'm not going to be fool enough to tell my own pretty wife that some other woman is prettier than she is!" Willie grinned and hugged me tenderly. "But, you truly are a sight for sore eyes, Sarah! City living has put a considerable polish on you!"

I laughed. "I'm about as polished as I'm liable to get. I'm ready to start living again, and I'm sure everybody else is, too. How wonderful it is to be home!"

Stant came up behind me. "I know how you feel, Sarah. When I finally got home I kissed everybody in sight, from Father all the way down to old Moe, and all the women and children in between. What a time! Four years of war, and I'm still not old enough to vote!" Stant took Matt by one hand and me by the other. "Come on out in the other room, Sarah, and let Matt get acquainted with all his cousins. I lose count from day to day as to how many younguns there are now" — his grin teased Becky — "both seen and unseen."

Kate and Susan and Jane all came to greet me at the same time, still a handsome trio of women but by no means the happy, easygoing girls I once had known. The years had left hard marks: four years of working in the fields, facing the hot sun in the summer and the biting wind in the winter, years of constant vigilance, had taken a harsh toll on all three.

Kate still stood straight as an arrow, her proud carriage defying the ravages of work and circumstance, but Jane's shoulders were hunched, altered by burdens unrefused but nonetheless resented. Susan, the laugh lines flashing in her lovely sun-browned face, rushed to hug me.

"Well, Sarah, who would have thought that poor, pitiful girl with the candlewax scars and the pokeberry stains on her face and a pillow on her belly would come back to us a dressed-up big-city woman! We honestly did not know whether to laugh or cry that day you diddled those proud-faced generals and rode off with every last one of them feeling sorry for you!"

"All except Colonel Huntsman. That devil felt no sorrow nor any pity. I still think they gave you that safe conduct pass simply to keep you from interrupting their breakfast." Kate's tone was hard, and her eyes flashed fire.

"I wouldn't be surprised, Kate. But pity that poor man's wife, now. She has to live with him all the time. She may be the only woman in Arkansas who is sorry the war is over!" Susan laughed. "I still think, Kate, that prissy colonel was lucky that you didn't slip poison in his coffee. Own up to it. You did consider it, didn't you?"

Kate smiled, the first smile I had seen from her in many a year. "Well, the thought did cross my mind. However, I managed to come up with another idea, one that still gives me considerable pleasure whenever I think on it. The morning those overbearing men left, I laced their coffee with such strong laxative that I expect they had the trots all the way across the mountain. It did compensate me considerably to picture that arrogant little strutting general having to climb down off his high horse every few miles or so and head out for the bushes! I hear he's in Mexico now. Probably what he suffered here in our mountains was good practice for him for when he started eating Mexican cooking! I most sincerely hope so, anyway! As for Huntsman, I gave that little toad twice as heavy a dose as I gave Hindman. We heard later that Huntsman died after the battle of Prairie Grove. I'm not sure I can claim credit for killing him. We didn't hear what did."

"What's all this talk about killing? I do hope that you girls are not about to take up the practice; killing's a bad habit to get into!" Ridge came forward with Charity at his side. He grabbed me in a mighty bear hug, lifting me up and swinging me around like a child. "Sarah, I'd forgotten how little you are. You're light as a feather! Now, when I swing Charity, I have more of a sense of accomplishment!" His loving grin teased Charity, four inches taller and 30 pounds heavier than me.

"Turn her loose, Ridge Rodineau! I've been waiting for three years to see Sarah again, and I want a good look at her now!" Charity and I fell into each other's arms, smiling and crying and talking all at once.

"You sound just like Aunt Kate, but you look almost the same as you always did! Why haven't you changed as much as the rest of us have?" I meant it. Charity still looked the same.

"Well, I've changed. My shoulders are strong enough to heft 100-pound sacks of flour and my hands are so rough you could use them to grate corn, but remember, I've been living at home with Pa and Ma. The only burdens

I've been bearing were sacks of grain. They've been a lot easier to bear than the kind of burdens these girls have had to shoulder."

I looked around me and knew she spoke wisdom. Charity's face still had the fair, sweet look I remembered so well. Kate's beautifully molded mouth had settled into straight, controlled lines; Jane's had been pinched into petulance; Susan's good-natured grin remained unimpaired, but years of work and worry had erased her youth. Of us all, only Charity still retained the wild-rose freshness of her girlhood.

"Tell me about Piety. This reunion is going to be so hard for her, with all the rest of us gathering in. She'll look at all the men and remember Tom. All the Flint men look so much alike."

"She's come to terms with it. You know, she's living with Eliza now. And it's good for both of them."

From out in the yard we could hear the clanging of the dinner gong, and we assembled ourselves for our first dinner together in nearly four years. By the time we all had gathered in at Matthew's table, the floodgates of reunion had been opened. We indulged ourselves in remembrances, enhancing the best, trying hard to deal with the worst. But each one of us knew in our hearts that we had been granted the chance to weave new patterns in the fabric of our lives, and all of us were eager to begin the doing of it.

As soon as Matthew had finished invoking the blessing, he set us all to thinking about the future. "What's past is past. Whether we choose to remember the odors, or whether we choose to remember the fragrances, the war is over. I know you boys have good ideas and strong opinions. I need to hear them, and I will appreciate knowing your plans."

"Well, Father, from what I heard up in Kansas City, I'd guess that half of Arkansas is already up in Washington seeking pardons and trying to get back the titles to their confiscated property." Larkin was joking, but Sam answered him seriously.

"And the other half is down in Little Rock scheming to get control of the state government again!"

"Well," said Matthew, "there's too much truth in what you both said. Whereas President Lincoln would have remained generous in his surrender terms, Johnson is not as wise and far more harsh, and Congress is even harsher.

"I will not be surprised to see Federal troops patrolling our streets again. Be that as it may, I'd appreciate knowing your plans." Matthew turned first to Robert, recognizing his place as the oldest.

"I aim to go back to farming, and to get on with my life, and the sooner the better. And I'll have no part of politics." Robert's face grew hard. "Insofar as God gives me the strength to do it, it is my complete aim to put all remembrance of this murdering war behind me. I don't ever aim to talk about it again after today; God willing, I don't ever aim to think about it again if I can help it!"

"Lark?"

"I mean to learn to be the best cotton planter in the whole state of Arkansas. I've got a place picked out to build Sarah a house, right on top of the big bluff at the east end of Petit Jean Mountain, and I aim to sit up there and smoke my pipe and look around me in a wide 40-mile sweep and enjoy my family and mind my own business! I'm not ruling out politics, but I'm sure not ruling it in. My first aim is to get that land to producing and to look after my own family again."

"Ridge?"

"Well, to tell the truth, I'm of mixed mind. I had every intention of going back to the Indian Territory and running the ranch my father left me. The only trouble is, the Indian Territory's not civilized now. It's far worse off than before the war — far, far worse. All the scum that can't seem to settle down to work for a living seem to be making their headquarters over there. It's completely lawless except when honest men take the law into their own hands. Men joke about it now. They claim there's no Sunday west of Fort Smith, and no God west of Fort Gibson! It's no place to take Charity, and it's no place to raise children."

"Then, what are your plans, Ridge? Are you willing to cast your lot here with us?"

"Only for a while. It's not my aim to abandon my heritage. No, I've given the thing a lot of thought. Charity and I have talked it over, and here's what we're going to do. It's going to take a smart lawyer to hold his own against all the meanness and maneuvering that lies ahead in the Indian Nation. I mean to become one. I'm going to read law. Then, Charity and I will settle in Fort Smith."

"You'll not be alone in this thing, Ridge. Railroad men are desperate to get right-of-way through the Indian Territory. They're apt to be allies with you." Lark's tone was that of a man who was sure of his facts. "I talked with Colonel Dodge before I left Denver. He's got big plans for building railroads across the Plains. He had the ear of Lincoln on this; but the ear of Johnson is hardly the same thing. It's my guess the railroad interests will involve General Grant. He has more influence now than President Johnson does. In any case, railroads are bound to come, probably sooner than we think."

Sam laughed. "Another lawyer! Welcome to the tribe, Ridge! You'll find the study of law to be dry as dust, but the practice is so much fun it's almost a sin to take money for it! I'd almost rather practice law than eat when I'm hungry!"

Matthew continued his inquiry. "Stant, what are your plans?"

Stant looked down the length of the table, squarely into his mother's eyes. "Brace yourself, Ma. You're not going to like this, but you might as well hear it now." He looked back to his father. "I mean to stay in the army. I like the military life, and I do well at it. The only trouble is, I don't like being an enlisted man. All through the war I was smarter than most of the officers I had to take orders from, and I had to put up with them ordering me into damn fool situations that didn't make the least bit of tactical sense. I want you to get me an appointment to West Point, Father, so I can learn smarter ways to fight. Hell, I'm only 20. Will you do it, Father?" Stant got up from the table and put his arms around Minerva.

"I'm sorry, Ma. But can I have your blessing?"

Minerva's kiss was her answer, and Matthew proceeded to bring closure to his interrogation. He intended to make Kate his full partner in the Flint operation. "She has done a man's work these past three and a half years and looked after six children besides." Matthew looked across the table at Susan and Jane. "Not that the two of you have not been similarly burdened. But you have husbands to look after your interests now, and full lives to resume.

"Kate has not only carried on our ranching and farming interests, she has managed, even in these dangerous times, to make a profit. I mean to deed a section of land to Kate, free and clear in her own name, and to treat her in all respects as the managing partner in all my enterprises. In the near future, Little Rock will be my primary residence. Kate will have the rewards commensurate with her responsibilities here."

I looked over at Kate, who sat in quiet composure. I was struck by her resemblance to Minerva — a younger, slimmer version of the remarkable woman who had for more than 30 years graced Matthew's table. Yet there was a difference in their faces. Minerva's look was that of a beautiful woman who knows she is cherished. Kate's face, imperceptibly removed from true beauty, was that of a woman who expects to earn every step of her own way.

Matthew looked down the table to Becky and Willie. "Will, is it your intent to remain in Fayetteville?" It was. Willie had a good medical practice just delivering babies.

Larkin brought the talk back to bigger issues, wondering what the country would be like in three or four years.

Matthew had obviously thought long about the situation. "Ordinarily, son, I would say that no man can read the future. But right now there are some aspects that are fairly clear. I see three things happening: The country will have a railroad crossing its entire breadth; there will be thousands upon thousands of ex-soldiers and immigrants moving out to settle on those wide open plains; and there will have to be a fight to the finish with the Indians."

But Minerva had heard enough talk about fighting. She rose from her chair, thereby signaling the end of the meal. "Shall we play some music now?"

We moved into the other room, and at a nod from Matthew the music pulsed into life, the well-remembered melodies soaring and singing and lifting our hearts. It was hand-clapping, foot-tapping, square dancing music. The room filled with children, from Kate's 14-year-old stepson all the way down to my two-year-old twins, all singing and sashaying in time to the tunes.

When the musicians paused for a moment's rest, Larkin stepped forward. "I want to play this song for Tom." And he lifted his bow and began the poignantly beautiful melody I had first heard in Kansas City. When the last lovely note had faded, we stood in complete silence.

Finally, Minerva broke the spell. "Tom was with us as you played. I could feel his spirit in this room." Her face was calm, her beautiful dark eyes dry, though across the room I could see tears rolling down Matthew's weathered cheeks. The men hung up their fiddles and we women went back to the kitchen, our faces as solemn as though we had been in church.

Only later, when I had put the twins down for their naps, did I seek out Minerva to accomplish the duty that had been heavy on my mind. Walking down the long hall I again heard the sweet sounds of the dulcimer, sounds of the strings being plucked gently, tentatively, in the attempt to recapture the theme of the tune Larkin had played.

Thinking to find Minerva, I opened the door of the music room. Although she was seated in her accustomed place, the imposing high-backed chair by the fireplace, she was not the musician. A little boy stood plucking the strings, delicately coaxing the remembered melody from Minerva's dulcimer. Taller than my own Matt by two or three inches, the boy from the back looked so much like Matt that he could have been my own. I stood stock-still, listening until the child had played the last sure note of the main theme of "Tom's Tune." Only then did Minerva speak. "Jeff, this is your Aunt Sarah. She is wife to your Uncle Larkin." When the child turned toward me, I was struck silent. The shape of his head, the look on his mouth, the color of his skin, the black of his hair were pure Flint, all except his eyes. The boy looked at me with the pale, straight, uncompromising stare of Ocie Casey, and I was the first to look away.

"Run out and play with the others now." Minerva's tone did not brook argument.

After a long pause, Minerva addressed the issue. "Larkin saw him this morning. All three of my boys looked alike when they were little. They look alike now. Jeff looks like them, as does your Matt. Your twins take more after your side of the family. They look like your pa." She paused again.

"I know you and Larkin would treat Jeff right, Sarah. But I have to ask you another question. Can you love him?"

I searched my soul and gave honest answer. "I can care for him and treat him as one of my own and see to his needs and raise him right. But to ask me to love him is asking too much, Minerva. You're asking more than I can give."

"I thought as much, Sarah, and I mean to imply no fault on your part when I say so. I would feel the same if I were in your shoes. And it is a question I did not put to Larkin, for I did not think I wanted to hear his answer. Either way."

"Nor would I."

"Matthew and I will raise Jeff. We have come to love him, and he has come to love us. We will adopt him as one of our own. Whatever thoughts the others in the family may have had, they have had the grace to keep their conclusions to themselves. As we shall expect them to do in the future."

She rose. "The matter is settled. We will process the papers for adoption when we return to Little Rock. Insofar as the wagging tongues and prying ways of others are concerned, Jeff is the child of our old age." She smiled. "Children have a wisdom all their own. Look out the window, Sarah. Our boys are already playing together!"

I looked and saw the two black-haired little boys climbing over the tall woodpile ricked at the edge of the yard. I faced Minerva squarely. "They look like brothers."

"I do not think they are, Sarah." Her voice was without inflection.

I took a deep breath. "I mean to handle this like Robert's handling the war. I don't aim to talk about it again, and I don't aim to think about it again if I can help it. And I aim to treat Jeff right."

From the yard I heard Larkin calling me. "Sarah, let's ride over to see our home place. I'm going to saddle a couple of horses for us. Do you want to ride sidesaddle?"

I looked at Minerva, "That's another thing I don't aim to do. I don't ever expect to ride sidesaddle again."

I mounted a horse for the first time since I had left Arkansas. The air was crisp, the sun was bright, the woods were alive with color, and all at once the world looked so good to me that I started to sing at the top of my voice. Larkin laughed and joined in. We cantered along the road with spirited voices raised, "She'll be coming 'round the mountain when she comes. . . . She'll be coming 'round the mountain when she comes. . . ."

Monnie's dogs began to bark when we were a quarter of a mile away. Ned came running down the hill to open the gate, with Monnie right behind him. Even from the foot of the hill we could see that our house had been ill-used. We dismounted, so as to walk up the hill together, Monnie talking a blue streak.

"Yore gonna hate seeing the house the way it is, Mr. Lark. There wasn't no way I could keep them raidin' devils from tearing it up some. They tuck to comin' in after dark and cookin' up their grub. They knowed I was sleeping out around here somewheres, but they didn't seem to give a hoot. Fer two or three weeks Quantrill's bunch moved in and took it over lock, stock, and barrel. I was lucky the weather didn't turn too cold. We had a warm spell that year, else the pore old cow would have froze to death, hobbled down in the pine grove close to the cave.

"Them outlaws come mightily close to robbin' me uv the one hawg I had left. Whut happened was that the one old sow I had left got up too close to the house and they spied her the morning they was fixin' to leave.

That murderin' Cole Younger took one look at my hawg and took out his pistol and shot it right through the head.

"Well, I wasn't about to let them outlaws carry off that hawg. I'd-a been facin' starvation iffen I'd-a let 'em have that meat. I grabbed up the ax and stood over that hawg and dared airy one of them men to touch it. I knowed they wasn't gonna shoot me. Quantrill don't let his men shoot women. So I jist stood there and swung my ax and yelled fer them devils to keep their bloody hands off uv my hawg.

"Finally, they got tired uv fooling with me, and they was all yellin' at Cole Younger to mount up and ride, but he had to get the last word in somehow. He come swaggerin' up to where I was standing. Course he kep' out uv range uv my ax. I got purty long arms.

"Whut he done was to pull down his britches and aim his thang at me. He let loose and peed right at me. Then he grinned like an old ugly wolf and yelled out, 'Well, whut do you think uv that, old woman?'

"I wasn't gonna let him buffalo me, not after all they had put me through. 'Well,' said I, 'I'm old, and yores ain't the first tallywhacker I've ever saw in my life. But, I swear to God it's by far and away the ugliest one I ever did set eyes on!'

"I will say this fer them other men. They laughed so hard I thought fer sure they'd bust a gut. But Cole Younger got so mad his eyes purt near popped out uv his head. Them devils busted purt near every winder in the house when they left, but they didn't get my hawg. I ain't had no winder glass to put back in, but me and Ned have boarded up the upstairs winders and done whut we could to fix the floor boards. We figgered you'd tell us whut you wanted done when you got here."

Larkin smiled at her. "Monnie, you're a wonder. Not one woman in a thousand could have managed half as well as you have. It's worth more to me than you'll ever know to come back and find the house still standing.

"And you'll be interested to know that Quantrill finally got what was coming to him. He was killed last May in Kentucky, shot by Union soldiers. I have no doubt he is roasting in hell."

Larkin asked Ned a serious question. "Ned, I'm sure that the government is going to be looking for experienced men to be Indian fighters before too long. Are you liable to be interested in enlisting in the regular army after a year or so?"

"No, sir, Colonel." Ned's reply was prompt. "I reckon I'm just exactly where I want to be, back home in these here hills. Beggin' yore pardon,

Mr. Lark, but I ain't too good at taking orders, 'specially on a daily basis. Nope, I'd ruther fish and hunt and make a corn crop and mind my own business and let the army and the Indians mind theirs."

Ned looked over at Monnie, who nodded proudly. "We'uns is hoping you'uns would want us to stay on here and look after this here place fer you."

"That's exactly what I want, Monnie. But I had to ask Ned the question." Larkin looked affectionately at Ned.

Relief was writ large on their faces; Monnie answered for them both. "Our heart's set on staying put, Mr. Lark."

I reached out and squeezed Monnie's hand, for I knew only too well how she felt. Part of me would have contentedly settled back into the sweet and simple life we once had loved so well.

As we rode back toward Matthew Flint's compound, Larkin put the question to me straight. "How about you, Sarah? Would you rather stay put? Do you think you will be content to live on top of that mountain that I'm about to take you to? Will you be too lonesome?"

I took my time about answering, mindful of the possibility that the act of his asking the question implied that I had a choice.

"Larkin, I believe we're ready for the move. You're a lot different now than you were four years back. Being a colonel widened considerably the way you look at things. And I have to believe I've changed, too. Living up north in Kansas City changed me, too. We might not either one be able to take life up where we left off. I doubt that we could."

I looked at him and smiled. "Don't worry about my being lonesome. How on earth could I be when I've got you and a houseful of children?"

Chapter 35

THE SOUTH HAD surrendered and the armies had stopped fighting each other, but the hatreds remained. Nowhere were these hatreds stronger than in Arkansas. Larkin and I did not look for a kind welcome from those who would be our new neighbors. Matthew tried to prepare us the morning we left.

"You're going to see desolation. So many people went off to Texas and stayed there that you're going to see farm after farm abandoned, covered with bushes and briars. And those folks that have come back are half-starved, trying to stretch this summer's crops to last through the winter months.

"You're going to encounter a lot of bitterness, Lark. Try

not to take it personally. So many people in Arkansas have nothing left but their grudges. Their houses have been burnt, their stock stolen, and their slaves freed. They're bound and determined to blame somebody for it. It goes against human nature to expect them to remember that they voted themselves into this terrible war. No, most don't see it that way. When men look around at their own burnt-down homes and worn-out women and hungry children, they are going to resent it considerably when an outsider comes in and starts living in comfort. I hope you will not take these resentments to heart, son." Matthew smiled wryly. "I speak from considerable personal experience.

"Lincoln was right to admonish us to bind up the nation's wounds, but I'm finding it to be damn hard to govern so as to try to heal this state's wounds when a lot of the people would rather keep right on hating and bleeding."

It was our plan to stop over for a visit with Eliza before heading south over the mountains. A hard rain had pelted the land the week before we left, stripping the tall trees down to the gaunt brown forms that warned of winter. A cold wind blew at our backs, and Larkin pushed the horses hard. Every bend in the road revealed new devastation: uncultivated land gone back to grass and weeds; houses standing in disrepair, doors and shutters banging in the wind; homes burned to the ground, only tall chimneys remaining as mute testimony of past sufferings. A few gaunt and ragged people were working in their fields, grim reminders of hardships past and present.

Nowhere was the evidence more compelling than around my own pa's home. Where once in Griffin Flat there had been peace and prosperity, industry and plenty, well-built homes and sturdy public buildings, now there was nothing except crumbling chimneys and rubble-choked cellars. Three years after the Battle of Pea Ridge, not one building was left standing.

We drove on over the hill to Griffin's Tavern. There I got out of the buggy to look again at the two tall chimneys that stood as staunch memorials to my pa. Grass and vines had claimed the land, and wild grapes wound around the stones of the chimneys.

"Let's pick the grapes, Larkin, and take them to Eliza. Pa used to think she made the best grape wine in the world. It might please her to make up some wine in memory of the good times." I paused and set my jaw. "And I'm going to fix my mind on the good times. What can't be altered must be borne. I can bear things a lot better if I fix my mind on the sweet rather than dwelling on the bitter."

Larkin took a basket, filled it with grapes, and handed it up to me. "Sarah, I don't aim to do much of either. I don't see how much good is going to come from looking backwards, neither in bitterness about the bad times nor in wishful thinking of the good times. My face is set forward. Where you look around and see desolation, I look around and wonder why these folks haven't already gone to work and started cleaning up these places. I can't figure this out. Arkansas men don't lack for spirit and gumption. I fought with them, and I fought against them. Yank and Reb, they fought like tigers.

"I can't figure out why they're not already out in these fields fighting these weeds and reclaiming what's theirs. For most, their land is all they've got left. Wouldn't you think we'd have seen more work going on around these places? I'll bet things are different when we get over to Eliza's place."

He was right. Although the paint on the house was peeling, the fence rows were clean, the fields had been plowed and laid by for the winter, and big stacks of wood had been ricked against the cold. Bright bushes of holly glowed against the dark green of the cedars that still stood sentinel beside the sturdy front door of the house. Now the door was flung open, and out rushed a slender woman with snow-white hair.

Larkin, already preparing to help me out of the buggy, turned to her, his surprise showing in his voice.

"We're looking for Mrs. Griffin, Mrs. Eliza Griffin. Does she not live here now?"

Eliza's hearty laugh rang out, and Eliza's familiar voice answered. "She lives here, she's wonderfully glad to see you, and she welcomes you back home!"

I had one foot on the buggy step and one foot on the ground, and I was so shocked I dropped the basket of grapes. As Matt sprang down to rescue the grapes, I ran over, grabbed the woman by both arms, and turned her so as to get a good look at her face. Out of the sunburned face of this slender woman gazed the clear and honest eyes of my stepmother.

"Eliza, is it really and truly you? I've never seen such a change in anybody in my life. If ony Pa could see the way you look now!" I looked more closely and saw the red, rough hands, the brown skin, the sturdy bones of one who was well acquainted with hard work.

"Sarah, remember that I used to tell you that hard work never hurt anybody? It turned out that I was speaking the absolute truth. But in those days, believe me, I didn't have any idea of how truly hard work can get when you're out in the fields making a crop."

"And your hair, Eliza. When did it turn white?"

"That same winter that Quantrill shot William and the Yankees burned our house and you left, Sarah. I've heard folks say that shock can turn the hair white, and I do believe I'm living proof."

She held out her arms to Larkin. "Welcome! I want you and Sarah to feel at home here. Come as often as you like, stay as long as you like, and always be sure of your welcome!"

Larkin found his voice. "Miss Eliza, you're a beauty. How much weight have you lost?"

"Well, I don't rightly know, Larkin, for the only scales we've got are those out in the barn where we weigh the bushels of corn, and I'm a tad too tall to fit in a corn basket, but I'm guessing that I've lost 40 or 50 pounds. It's hard to tell. I've picked up a considerable amount of muscle, though." She bent down to Matt. "Feel my arm muscle, Matt. See how hard it is?"

Again, her remembered laugh rang out. "Lark, I doubt that there's a fat woman left in Arkansas by now. I will admit, some got skinny by sitting and starving and whining, but Neely and I were unwilling to starve and too tired most days to waste our breath whining. You'll find Neely has changed considerably, too. We've not either one of us tasted a custard pie in over three years, Lark! What few eggs we had we saved to put in the corn bread. And Neely swears she has dreams about pound cake with rum sauce on top of it!"

"And when I's not dreaming about sweet things to eat, I's dreaming of my sweet baby girl!" Neely's voice was so glad and her hug was so hard that we both started laughing and crying at once. "Lemme see dese here boys. Lord hep us, Miss Sarah, dem twins is de spittin' image of your pa. They got Griffin wrote all over their faces!"

"And baby Matt is not a baby anymore." Eliza looked at Matt again with respect. "Matt, would you feel like you might have a hug for your old granny?"

I laughed. "Eliza, you look less like a granny than any other woman I've ever seen in my life. You don't look much older than I do."

"She do look good. I keeps tellin' her dat." Neely was emphatic. "But,

Miss Sarah, tell me about Tobe's new wife. Me and Zeke been anxious to hear your verdict. How's a city gal gonna take to Arkansas ways?"

"Ah, Neely, she'll do fine. I'll tell you everything I know. We're going to be here long enough to get it all talked over. But, first, I want to see Piety. Surely, she's here?"

"I'm here!" Piety's clear voice rang out. "We thought we'd let Eliza welcome you first, so as to give you a true surprise." She hugged us all.

I had been anxious about seeing Piety again, for I had feared to see how the sad lines of grief and bitterness had changed her, but the sweet face she turned toward us was tranquil. I put my arms around her.

"Oh, Piety, in a way I've dreaded this whole reunion, wondering how I would feel if I were you, having to watch all the other men come home to their wives, and thinking of Tom buried so far away."

Her eyes were calm. "Please don't feel that way, Sarah. What kind of woman would I be if I wanted everybody I love to have to go through the same kind of pain I've had to go through?"

I looked over at Eliza. "Do you suppose Aunt Gert's spirit is around here somewhere enjoying our reunion?"

"I wouldn't be surprised. And your pa, as well. Sometimes I feel their spirits so strong I can almost believe they're talking to me."

"Well, then you ought never to feel lonesome and always to feel loved."

"I do, Sarah. And you should, too. But enough of this kind of talk. I want to hear all about your life in Kansas City, and I expect Larkin is ready for his dinner. We can all visit while we work. I don't aim for Larkin to go away hungry from my table."

I settled in to enjoy our visit in Eliza's house like I would have basked in the fragrance of a bouquet of sweet roses, but one thorn turned up. That thorn bothered me considerably.

Eliza was busy setting the table for dinner, counting out the plates, carrying in the silver, when Neely stopped her in her tracks.

"Miss Liza, you ain't carryin' in de right number of plates."

"Well, I've got six, Neely; I thought Sarah would probably feed the children early out in the kitchen."

"Miss Liza, I knows and you knows dat me and Zeke has got in de habit of eatin' at de same table as you, and I knows you don't want to do nothin' to hurt our feelins, but I's telling you right now, it won't do. Mista Lark ain't used to eating wid darkies, and he don't expect to be gettin' used to it, and I ain't gonna have my baby girl made miserable whilst she's visitin' us. So I'd take it kindly iffen you'd carry two of dem plates right back and put 'em on de kitchen table. I's gonna wait on my baby girl, and I's gonna wait on your table like I used to, and dat's all dere is to it."

Eliza, clearly uncomfortable, took issue. "Neely, Mr. Lark might as well get used to the idea. Didn't he just get through fighting a war to give you your freedom?"

"Fightin's one thing. Eatin's another. We has got a long row to hoe afore white men set theirselves down to break bread with us darkies." Neely walked over and put her arms around me. "My girl got her hands full as it is. We ain't gonna push things."

She marched over to the stove and started the careful work of dropping the dumplings into the stew pot. "It gonna take a lot more den a war afore white men is willin' to set down and eat wid blacks. An' I don' aim fer my Zeke to git his feelins hurt, nor fer Mista Lark to git his back up, and dat de end of dat!"

We stayed only the one night, for Larkin wanted to press on before the weather turned ugly. I felt like our visit was too short, but I knew Larkin would not rest easy until he had reached our destination and begun the job of building our new house.

As we climbed into the buggy seat, Piety handed Larkin an envelope. "Larkin, to all intents and purposes there's no mail service left up here in the mountains, so I'd take it very kindly if you would see to delivering this letter for me. It's to Jesse Rankin. We've been in some correspondence with each other since he came up here to pay his respects to Neely and Zeke. About the only way we can make sure a letter gets through is to send it with travelers. The mails are worse than useless these days, at least in this part of the state."

"I'll be glad to take it, Piety. It's my understanding he'll be practically a neighbor to Sarah and me, and I meant to ride over anyhow to make his acquaintance. This will give me a reason to go sooner."

Astonished, I looked over at Eliza. "And you let me stay the whole night under your roof and did not let on one word about Piety being courted by Jesse Rankin?" I turned to Piety.

"We used to tell each other everything! I can't believe you didn't tell me about Jesse! Has he been back up here to see you since that first visit? Do you like him? My boys loved him. They may not know what he looks like without his bandages on, but I'll bet they would recognize his voice anywhere." I was halfway aggravated with Eliza and Piety both. "Piety, I can't believe you didn't tell me you were courting!"

Piety smiled, her dimples flashing. "Sarah, I'm not sure yet whether this thing is a courtship or a friendship. Don't start making more of it than it is. Jesse's been up here twice now. That's it, so far."

Larkin grinned and picked up the reins. "Ladies, you've given Sarah so much to think about that you may have brought on a miracle this morning — I wouldn't be surprised if she stays quiet for at least an hour or so!" He tipped his hat, clicked to the horses, and we headed south toward our new circumstances. Larkin was right. I spent the whole morning thinking about how good it would be to have Piety as a close neighbor.

Four days later we had crossed the mountains and reached Lewisburg Landing. Captain Hern's ferry was anchored at the river bank. Cousin Ed emerged from the little shack by the side of the road at about the same time Captain Hern walked down the gangplank. They shook hands all round, Cousin Ed performing introductions.

Larkin held out his hand. "Gentlemen, I am in your debt. And it is my aim in future years to find opportunities to repay you. Your kindness to Sarah and my son — as well as your shrewdness — have made a world of difference in our lives."

Cousin Ed found sentiment to be an embarrassment. "No call to dwell on the past, Larkin. You would have done the same." With an abrupt change of subject he steered the conversation to the future.

"I've proceeded according to your instructions, Lark, and lined up stonecutters and carpenters and three teams and wagons. But finding enough darkies to do the heavy work of felling trees and quarrying stone is going to be hard to do!"

"I would have thought different, Mr. Watson. I would have thought there would be plenty of men looking for work."

Captain Hern answered. "Arkansas has got plenty of men, all right, and far too many of them starving, to say nothing of their starving womenfolks and younguns. I never thought I'd see the day when men would rather starve than work, but we got a hard winter coming and a mean situation brewing."

"Does the trouble stem from the Freedmen's Bureau?" Larkin's tone was thoughtful.

"Not all of it. Both blacks and whites feel bitter — the whites because they lost the war and have come home to misery, and the blacks because the government promised them far more than it could deliver."

"Well, they've got freedom," I said. "Isn't that what was promised?"

"What most darkies remember is that the government promised 40 acres and a mule to every black man. There ain't enough land and there ain't enough mules to come anywhere close to keepin' that big-mouthed promise. It was all political palaver."

Hern's face was grim. "Most niggers is worse off now than they was, but they ain't figgered it out yet. They think they can rely on the government to hand them a living. Until they get it through their woolly heads that there ain't no more handouts out there, it's going to be durn hard to get a day's work out of them."

Lark turned to Cousin Ed. "Mr. Watson, what do you think? Is there a solution?"

"Well, the way I see it, Lark, you're going to have to find white men to do the work. We've got three white men in this state for every black. Whites in Arkansas don't take well to taking orders, most especially from a Yankee colonel, but they do recognize a gold piece when they see it."

Larkin had heard enough. "All right. Let's take my wife and boys on over to visit with her Cousin Alta, and we'll begin our planning. I want to get the rafters raised by Thanksgiving and the walls up by Christmas. But right now, I need to get Sarah settled in, and I need to ride over to Jesse Rankin's plantation to pay my respects. Tomorrow we'll get started."

I looked ahead toward the mountain looming in lone majesty above the flat black earth beside the river. I stared up at the massive gray-rocked cliff that defined the east end. The site Larkin had chosen for our home commanded a breathtaking view of three counties. As I gazed up, I realized that from a military point of view, the location was virtually impregnable. The mountain ran 20 miles east and west along the river and was accessed on the east end by the narrow road that laboriously curved in sharp bends up the steep slope to end abruptly at the top of the granite bluff.

"Is there another road up that big mountain, Larkin?"

Cousin Ed answered. "There's one at the far end, nearly 20 miles west. Actually, Petit Jean is more of a mesa than a mountain. It's nearly flat on top. Good land for ranching. There's even a lake up there. Most is still virgin forest. But there is no road across the top. Once you move up there, you'll just about have your own kingdom, Sarah. You're going to be living amongst some of the most beautiful scenery on this earth, but some folks would think that view to be mighty lonesome, too."

Larkin's mind was elsewhere. "Let's plan on crossing the river tomorrow to make contact with those carpenters and stonecutters you've hired. Right now I want to visit Jesse Rankin. We've got a lot to accomplish."

Larkin came back the next morning, well pleased with his visit. I was full of questions. "Tell me about Jesse. I'm anxious to know what kind of a place he lives on. What are his people like? Has he asked Piety to marry him yet?"

"I swear, Sarah, you girls have got the curiosity of a magpie where courting is concerned. How would I know whether or not he's asked Piety? I don't read minds. Though it would be a mighty useful skill, it's one not yet granted to me." His tone was teasing, but his next words were serious.

"I take Jesse Rankin to be a good man. He's made me a mighty decent offer. Says he feels he owes his life to your Uncle Auguste and to you, and he wants to repay his debts insofar as he can. He's already gone out of his way to contact men that he knows — white men, mostly. Nearly all of them fought on the Southern side, though some few, like Captain Hern's boy, fought for the North. He says these men need work, for they need hard money to feed their families this winter and buy seed and fertilizer to put in their crops next spring."

"They may need work, but are they willing to work for a man who fought for the North?"

"He's found seven men who are. And he says that he'll make eight. I wanted to turn him down insofar as his personal help, for I know he has more than enough to keep him busy on his own plantation. Besides, I know he's not willing to accept any money for himself. What we finally agreed on was this: he's going to introduce me to these seven men — I figure most of them to be his kinsmen — plus he's going to bring over a crew of his own darkies to cut the timber and quarry the stone."

"Were these darkies his slaves?"

"They used to be, and they still expect him to look after them. He's got them on a sharecropping system. I'll pay his darkies in hard coin. He'll furnish them the land and the seed and the fertilizer next spring, and they'll split the profits from next year's crop 50-50."

"What does Jesse's plantation look like? In case Piety does decide to be courted, what kind of place would she be living in?"

"Big. Good land, big white house — well, it used to be white. It needs paint now. Rankin's land faces the river, on the north bank, about two miles west of Lewisburg Landing. His pa and ma are getting old and his ma seems sickly. Fine folks, though. They all sent you their regards, Sarah, and Jesse sent his special remembrances to our boys. Seems as though he feels he knows them well."

I felt greatly relieved. "Maybe, Larkin, we'll be well accepted by our neighbors, after all. When they work with you, they'll get to know you."

"I don't want you to get your hopes up too much. Jesse's men are all from the north side of the river. These plantation owners here on the south side were all Hindman men, I believe. Time will tell. Let's take on one task at a time."

Larkin worked wonders in the next few days. Within a week's time he had a small army of men, both black and white, working up and down the side of that mountain, felling trees, quarrying stone, improving the mountain road so teams of oxen could drag their heavy burdens to its summit. Cousin Alta marveled at it. "I've never, in all my life, seen a man as good at getting work out of other men! He's got Rebels and Yanks working together without fighting, he's got stonemasons and carpenters and day laborers and painters all so well organized that they're working like busy beavers. That house is liable to be done before the snow flies."

Day by day, the house took shape. Each evening it became Larkin's pleasure to hitch up the buggy and take me up the steep road so we could look together on the progress that had been made. I had given up riding horseback once I was sure I was again with child, and the daily buggy ride became my chief recreation.

Linney and Tobe and their baby girl and Uncle Auguste's furniture all arrived the same day. The furniture came upriver on Captain Hern's barge. Tobe proudly transported his family with two fine-looking mules hitched to a new wagon. As usual, Larkin had thought well ahead.

"Tobe, there's a fair-sized house already built for you close to the big house. You'll find it's ready for you and Linney to move into."

I had talked with Larkin about the location when he was first laying his plans. "Wouldn't it be better to have Tobe's cottage built down the mountain closer to the cabins of the field hands?"

"Nope. I want Linney to be handy for you, and I most particularly want Tobe's cottage to be within shouting distance of our house. There'll be future times when I'll have to be away from you and the children. It's my intention to rely on Tobe for your protection. Besides, I mean to set him apart from the other darkies. If I built his house near the field hands, they might not give Tobe his due as my overseer. Not that we have any field hands recruited for next year's crop yet. Now that Tobe is here, that's my next order of business. Work on the house has proceeded slower than I had thought. By the time it's ready, it'll be nearly time to start plowing."

Our house stood tall and strong, the square-cut gray stones of the walls accented by glossy white shutters. On the front, tall white marble pillars rose the full two stories to support the gray slate shingles of the roof. On the day we moved in the furniture, I turned to Larkin and took his hand. "Don't carry me over the threshold, Larkin. A woman that's six months' pregnant probably shouldn't be lifted much, anyway. I want us to walk through our front door hand in hand. We've started a whole new part of our lives, and I want to mark the moment."

Larkin took my hand in his, then raised it to his lips and kissed it tenderly. "From this day forward, Sarah, we're going to be living in our own home with our own children. I've held the hope of this day in my heart for four long years, by many a lonesome campfire."

The sweet, white clustered flowers of wild plum trees and the deep wine glow of the redbuds edged our yard and framed our house like grace notes. In the woods nearby, the tall, straight hickories and oaks showed the green buds that promised an early spring. In the yard, clumps of bright yellow jonquils lifted their faces toward the sky.

Hand in hand, Larkin and I walked through our wide front door together.

We had so many people visiting us that spring and summer after we moved into our fine big house that some weeks I felt like I was running a hotel. "It's a good thing I had Eliza's training at Griffin's Tavern," I said to Larkin on one of the rare evenings when we had our home to ourselves. "Else I don't think I could keep up with all the company we've had."

"Sarah, you're a wonder," he replied. "Here you are, only a few weeks away from having another baby, and you're as bright-eyed and bushy-tailed as though you were on your way to a party."

"Well, in a way, it's been one party after another, ever since we moved in. I'm glad, actually. But in the meantime, I've got to get more kitchen help. Linney is just about run ragged. We need to find us a cook, and whoever we get will have to live up here on the mountain."

"I know you're right, but it's not going to be easy." Larkin grinned. When he spoke his next words, I knew he was teasing, but there was an edge of truth just the same. "It would sure be a lot easier just to go out and buy a slave that was a good cook and put her out in the kitchen and tell her to get to cooking. No wonder all these people up and down the river keep looking back and whining about how good it was in the old days."

We were sitting on the wide porch that ran across the width of the back of our house. It overlooked the long lane that looped around the outbuildings — the low storage sheds, the brick smokehouse, the stables, the garden, and the sturdy four-room cottage occupied by Tobe and Linney and their baby girl, all outlined by the red glow of the setting sun.

"I wonder what Tobe would say about the old days," I said. "Working for you can't be too much different than working for Pa. Tobe's still working like a dog and still taking orders."

"Most men take orders, Sarah, one way or the other. I'd say Tobe's a lot better off now, and I'll warrant he'd say the same if you asked him. Now he's got freedom of choice. Any day he decides he does not want to work for me he can quit, go down to Little Rock, join up with the Army of the Frontier, and head out west as a Buffalo Soldier. The army would be glad to get him, and Tobe knows it."

"Why didn't he do that when the war ended? Why did he come back to Arkansas?"

"For the same reasons we did, Sarah. Arkansas is home."

The day Matthew and Minerva were expected, my boys and I stood on the massive bluff above the river and watched the big steamboat dock at our landing. Soon their buggy rolled past the rich fields and began the steep ascent over our mountain roadway. Part of that road had been hewn out of solid rock. Where it passed the waterfall that came spilling down the gray granite bluff, the grade became so steep that most of the time passengers chose to get out and walk so as to spare the horses the extra burden of hauling them. There were three switchbacks until the final bend attained the top of our mountain. There Larkin had designed the road in a great curve that circled past the front entrance to our house on around to the buildings in the back.

We had planted a hedge of spirea to border our home. Wide, curving stone-slab sidewalks led from our porch to openings in the hedge on either side of the house. I had planted flower beds to edge these walks, and already the deep blue phlox mingled with the pink of cloves, and the blue of native columbine, the white of verbenas, and the red-orange of day-lilies.

When Matthew's buggy crested the mountain, we were standing at our doorway in welcome. Gazing around in pleasure, Matthew looked first at us and then at our view. "I have no doubt this is the finest view in Arkansas. My congratulations!"

Minerva, her eyes focusing on the house, on our flowers, and on our happy faces, held out one hand to Larkin, the other to me. "I rejoice for you. You've worked hard. May you always live in such peace and prosperity!"

Within the hour, a second buggy rolled into the driveway, followed by a third.

"Did you bring friends, Father?"

Matthew gave a half-serious answer. "A governor hopes to be surrounded by friends, frequently finds himself to be surrounded by well-wishers, and all too often discovers himself to be in the company of neither. I expect these people are your neighbors, son. We will hope they mean to be friends."

Out of the first buggy stepped a stocky, red-faced man, his hand outstretched in friendly greeting. "Sir," he said to Larkin, "allow me to introduce myself. My name is Ben Wilcox, your neighbor downriver to the east, around that first big bend down yonder." His hand pointed off in the distance. "Here is my wife, Phoebe, and coming up in the buggy behind me, my wife's brother and his wife and her sister. We've been meaning to come up and welcome you to this part of the world. We hear that you folks hail from up in the northwest part of the state. We're proud to make your acquaintance, and proud to have you as neighbors." His appraising eyes took in the house and the driveway and outbuildings. "You've worked wonders. This is a mighty handsome place."

As we set ourselves to the task of making them welcome, another buggy pulled up.

"This here's my brother-in-law, Seth Simpson, his wife, Nellie, and his wife's sister, Varina. Seth lives over on the south side of the mountain. His land's next to mine."

"Welcome, sir." Larkin's strong arm assisted the women out of their carriages. "Welcome, ladies. Please come inside and allow us to make you comfortable."

While Larkin saw to the introductions and went about the business of making mannerly small talk, my mind was racing ahead to the more urgent business of how to stretch a dinner intended for four adults so as to feed nine. Quickly, I proceeded to the kitchen to consult with Linney.

"Them two little spring chickens I aimed to fry up ain't no way gonna stretch to feed nine grown-ups and four younguns, Miss Sarah. I already seen the way little Jeff is growin'. Him and Matt is already out climbin' trees. Them boys will bring back big appetites. They're liable to eat nearly as much as a man. What'll I do, Miss Sarah?"

"Slice up some ham and fry it, and we'll give these people ham and hot biscuits and new potatoes and green peas. Thank goodness for the garden! We'll have to fill out the table with green stuff, radishes and green onions and lettuce. Is that peach cobbler big enough to stretch to feed all of us?"

"It is if I slather a big glob of whippin' cream over the top. We'll make out all right, Miss Sarah. Two of them women look too skinny to have big appetites, anyhow, though the other is good-sized."

"Well, the men don't look skinny. That Mr. Wilcox looks strong, like he works hard and eats hearty. And that other man looks like he never turned down a second helping in his life."

Linney giggled. "Well, he do look portly, and that's a fact. I'll make up a pone of corn bread, too. One way or the other, we'll keep at it till we fill him up."

When we finally sat down to the dinner table, the talk was lively. Wilcox, in good humor and good appetite, was eager to hear Matthew's political predictions. "Tell us, Governor, how do things look for Arkansas? How long do you think it's going to take before planters like us get on our feet again?"

"Economically, the war has set the state back 20 years. Indeed, most folks were far better off 20 years ago than now." Matthew was matter-of-fact.

"Well, I want to applaud a recent action you people down in Little Rock have taken."

"What's that, Wilcox?"

"Reforming the penal code. A smart decision, I say, changing the law to substitute public whipping for confinement in the penitentiary. It costs a lot less to whip a man than it does to lock him up and feed him. Cuts down on petty crime, too. I think the legislature did the right thing."

It was Simpson who responded, and his look was self-satisfied. "It's against the law now for a white man to flog darkies when they don't put in a decent day's work; however, I whip when the whip is called for. Then I get on my horse and ride over to Squire Willis and pay my fine and get on about my business.

"It ought to be if a darky won't work, he won't eat. Now, with the government feeding them, sometimes a man has to do a little flogging to let 'em know who's the boss."

Not wishing to hear any more talk about flogging, I changed the subject.

"What regiment were you with in the war, Mr. Wilcox?"

"Gordon's Regiment, Confederate Cavalry, ma'am. I served under Colonel Anderson Gordon, ma'am, and proud of it. As it happened, I got hit by a Minié ball and got discharged early. I still limp and I still ache some, but I've got both my arms and both my legs, and that's a lot to be thankful for."

Larkin smiled at him, the look of one old soldier to another. "Exactly. When the war ended and I looked around Father's table when we all got home, and saw my three surviving brothers and myself and counted four men and eight arms and eight legs, I knew we had been blessed."

"Well, not everybody feels blessed, I want you to know!" Simpson's sister-in-law spoke up, her agitated little mouth and flashing eyes signaling her anger. "With my poor husband in his grave at Chickamauga and my fields covered with briars and my plantation house burned to the ground before my very eyes and most of my darkies gone, I can tell you, sir, I do not feel blessed!" Once begun, her tirade flowed unabated.

"And my poor cousin, Varina Davis, wife to our imprisoned president, cowering up in Canada, relying on the kindness of strangers to feed and clothe and educate her children while her poor husband rots in your Yankee prison, do you think she feels blessed?"

Simpson, pausing to accept another serving of whipped cream on his juicy cobbler pie, attempted to stem his sister-in-law's bitter complaints. "Now, Vinnie, it's hard to imagine Varina Howell Davis cowering anywhere, Canada or anyplace else. I sure wouldn't want her wrath headed in my direction, I know that."

His sister-in-law was not one to be quieted readily. "And, Governor

Flint, I would certainly agree that the war set Arkansas back 20 years. Twenty years ago, Papa owned a plantation so big it stretched for miles down this river valley. He had over a hundred slaves. My sister and I" — she waved her hand across the table at Mrs. Simpson — "were waited on hand and foot. My poor papa never dreamed that his girls would ever have to lift a hand to wait on themselves. And even the thought of turning loose hordes of ignorant nigras to move where they pleased around this country would have put him in his grave!"

Minerva had heard enough. Turning to the portly Mr. Simpson, she interrupted his sister-in-law's tirade. "And where did you serve during the war, sir?"

"I did my duty at home, ma'am. Arkansas law wisely exempted from service those of us with large land holdings and more than 20 slaves to oversee. I felt it my bounden duty, since my brother-in-law Wilcox and my brother-in-law Churchill were both off fighting, to stay on the land and look after all three of our plantations." He paused, his glance lingering for a moment on the embarrassed face of his sister and the petulant faces of his wife and her sister. "And, of course, to look after my womenfolks."

The impassive faces of Larkin and his father registered no emotion other than courteous attention, but the face of Ben Wilcox turned beet red as he lowered his eyes to give his full attention to the cup of coffee he was drinking.

"You Yankees have no idea the suffering you've put us through." Mrs. Simpson addressed her statement to Larkin.

"Ma'am, we've all been through suffering. Suffering was not limited to one side or the other, but I'm hopeful we can put the past behind us, harvest a good crop this year, and get on with the business of living. I imagine every man here feels the same. Arkansas can't afford to have its people divided any longer. There's already been too much blood spilt and too much property destroyed. As I see it, it's time for both sides to make an effort to get along."

Mrs. Churchill tossed her head. "Well, Mr. Flint, that's fine for you to say. It's really too bad you don't have the ear of President Johnson so he could have the benefit of your thinking. My poor cousin Varina Davis has written her heart out to him in letter after letter, begging him to pardon Cousin Jefferson, but to no avail. Johnson is as hard-hearted as the devil himself." She looked pointedly at Matthew Flint, her mouth quivering.

"There are entirely too many unworthy men in high places. Andrew Johnson is not fit to wipe Jefferson Davis's boots. When an ignorant tailor has the power to sit in judgment on cultivated gentlemen, this country has a dismal future, sir! In the meantime, please spare me any of your fine talk about getting along!"

I looked down the table toward Larkin, who sat now in cold silence, the hard glint of anger showing in his eyes.

"Mrs. Churchill," I said sweetly, "I am so glad to have the opportunity to meet a member of the Davis family, for I am sure you can set us straight as to how those ugly rumors got started about Mr. Davis when he and Mrs. Davis were captured." I paused, smiled at Larkin, and proceeded.

"Of course, I never for one moment believed that a fine gentleman like Mr. Davis would stoop to disguising himself and dressing up like a woman to avoid capture, even if the Northern papers did picture him wearing a hoop skirt and pantaloons. I would never believe such a slander. So humiliating for Mrs. Davis, I'm sure. I am so puzzled as to the widespread reports about Mr. Davis's disguise." Again, I smiled sweetly. At the far end of the table I could see Larkin's face relax in mischievous enjoyment as he prepared to witness Vinnie Churchill's discomfort.

"Well, the enemies of the South are everywhere!" Her little face swelled up like a banty hen with its feathers ruffled, her gray-blonde curls fluttering as she replied.

"Cousin Jefferson has had the misfortune to be terribly misrepresented by a malicious Northern press, and my Cousin Varina even more so. The truth is, it was raining the night Jefferson and Varina were captured, and Cousin Jeff picked up his wife's cape by mistake and put it on over his own clothes. Then, unfortunately, he could not find his hat, so Cousin Varina, always mindful of her dear husband's welfare and comfort, and unwilling for him to be exposed even for a moment to the cold rain, took her own bonnet and put it over his head, solely for his protection, of course. I assure you, sir, that while his hostile captors may have inadvertently received the impression of a woman's form, my Cousin Jefferson is not a man to choose to hide behind a woman's skirts! Now I am aware that those newspapers did report that Cousin Jeff was wearing a hoop skirt, but I assure you, sir, they lied! Jefferson Davis is a saintly man who has been much maligned."

"Madam," replied Matthew, "I agree he has been much maligned. As was our President Lincoln. It is my understanding, however, that the door to a pardon has been opened by Johnson but that Davis has refused his options."

"Ah, yes, you are correct, sir. Cousin Jefferson feels the terms to be intolerable."

"What are they?" I asked.

Matthew gave answer. "President Johnson has suggested that Jefferson Davis write him a letter asking for pardon. It is my understanding that when and if that letter arrives, a pardon will be granted."

"But surely, sir, you can see why Cousin Jefferson cannot ask for a pardon! To ask to be pardoned is to admit guilt! And no Southerner worthy of the name regards the Confederate cause as a cause for guilt! It is an intolerable idea!"

"Let me get this straight, ma'am." Larkin's face was so smooth and innocent that I had to look close to see the twinkle in his eyes. "Your cousin Varina is writing all these letters to President Johnson asking him to pardon Jefferson Davis, but Davis is unwilling to write and ask for a pardon for himself. Is that the way of it? There are some who might see it as paradoxical that Davis is willing to have his wife do for him what he is unwilling to do for himself."

Seth Simpson snorted, a sound made up in equal parts of scorn and laughter. "Flint, if you knew Varina Howell Davis, you would not find the situation in the least paradoxical! That woman has done exactly as she pleased from the day she was born! Jeff Davis can no more keep a rein on Varina than I could hold back the Arkansas River in a spring flood!"

Wilcox laughed. "I agree. I have always thought President Davis and President Lincoln to be a lot alike, not only because of their many virtues, but also because of their strikingly similar choices in wives! From what little I know about the two women, Varina Davis and Mary Todd Lincoln are as alike as two peas in a pod! Neither one of them ever saw a dollar she didn't ache to spend! And both so strong-willed they would have given Napoleon a run for his money! I hear that Mrs. Lincoln has gone plumb near crazy since the President's been shot. Not that the poor woman had far to go!"

So, gradually, Wilcox led the talk on to general topics and safer conversational ground. Before too long, our neighbors took their friendly leave.

Larkin looked over at me, a pleased grin lighting up his handsome face. "I swear, Sarah. You are something else! That spoiled woman probably hasn't figured it out yet that you came close to insulting her while she was sitting at your own table! Hoop skirts and bonnet on Jefferson Davis! I'll bet it'll be a while before Nellie and Vinnie try to mess with my girl again!"

Chapter 36

I DON'T KNOW WHY it is that the sex of a newborn child is so important. You would think that after a woman goes through the agony of bringing a child into this world, she would be so glad to get a healthy baby she wouldn't much care whether it was a boy or a girl. But that's not the way of things. When Minerva laid a perfect little baby girl on my belly, I would have shouted for joy if I hadn't been too tired to make a noise.

"I want to see her face," I told Larkin. "Who does she look like?"

"She looks like one of ours, Sarah." He was grinning

from ear to ear. "She's a homely little thing, but I guess we'll have to keep her!"

Tenderly, he lifted my shoulders, positioning my pillows so I could get a good look at the baby he now placed in my arms. She was so beautiful that I gasped in delight.

"She looks like you, Larkin. Or, maybe it's Minerva she looks like."

"What are you going to name her, Sarah?"

My answer came promptly, for I had given considerable thought to the matter.

"Her name is Victoria. I'm going to call her Tory."

"Well, that's not exactly a common name, but this baby already looks like a princess, so if that's your choice, so be it."

"That's not her entire name." I had made a swift decision. "She looks so much like you that her full name is going to be Larkin Victoria Flint." I positioned my baby girl's beautiful little mouth at my breast and gave myself over to the sweet sensations of motherhood.

I suppose there comes a time in every good marriage when you get so used to being together that you almost take happiness for granted. We worked hard and we prospered that year. Naturally, we had some problems, but I left the worrying to Larkin. Larkin had so much trouble getting what he considered to be a decent day's work out of his field hands that some days he gnashed his teeth in frustration. I was run so ragged chasing after the twins and keeping an eye on Matt and tending to the baby and helping Linney cook and clean and put up food for the coming winter that some nights I would fall into bed in exhaustion. But these were minor tribulations. Most days I was so full of hope and happiness that I sang as I worked and smiled when I rested.

While Larkin's cotton crop that year was not up to his own high expectations, he still made more bales to the acre than any man we knew up and down the river except Jesse Rankin. Altogether, Larkin shipped nearly 200 bales to market. Captain Hern and Cousin Ed hauled four full 50-bale loads down the river on Hern's boat to Little Rock. When Larkin came back from his first encounter at the cotton broker's office, he wore the pleased look of a man whose expectations have been met to the fullest. That night after supper as we sat on the porch, Larkin smoked his pipe and grinned in remembrance.

"Sarah, that Cousin Ed of yours is the shrewdest old Scotchman that ever sat down at a bargaining table. I've always thought I was a pretty good hand at horse trading, but your old skinflint cousin beats anybody I've run across so far. From now on I'm going to send him down the river without me. He doesn't need me. I can do more good here at home getting the fields picked and the cotton ginned into bales. Now that I've got the process set up, I don't need to go on every trip.

"Cousin Ed jawboned those mealy-mouthed, hard-eyed Little Rock cotton brokers into paying us 70 cents a pound for cotton when it's only selling for five cents more in New York. He's proving to be worth his weight in gold." He smiled in satisfaction. "Seeing him in operation with Captain Hern was nearly worth the trip. Along with teaching our boys to read and write, I sure hope he teaches them how to strike a hard bargain. That alone will be worth the money we pay him."

Larkin looked over at me. "Sarah, we're going to find us a cook. You look worn out, and with the price of cotton as high as it is, we can surely afford to find you some help. Next month after Piety and Eliza come down for their visit, we'll drive over to Lewisburg Landing and see if we can locate someone. If we can, Eliza can teach her to cook."

I laughed. "Well, we'll all fare better if she takes lessons from Eliza instead of me. I have to admit, cooking's not my strong point."

"But organization is. This place is running like a top. The house is always clean, the flower beds are always pretty, the garden's got enough stuff growing in it to feed three or four families, and you're wearing yourself out preserving and putting up food for the winter. I think you could come up with enough work around here to keep three or four women busy. It's not my aim to wear you out from hard work, Sarah." He paused, his voice discouraged. "If that bunch of lazy darkies would work half as hard as you do, we would have made enough cotton this year to make us rich. I've got to get better workers for next year."

"Where will you get them, Larkin? And how are you going to persuade them to work?"

"I've got an idea on where I'll find them, and I think I know how to do a better job of getting work out of them. As I've studied this thing, I've become convinced that the trouble lies more with me than with them. I haven't been treating them like I would treat a bunch of white men, nor has Tobe."

"What do you mean? Of course you haven't. How could you? They are black."

"Ah, that's the nub of it, right there. Until these Negroes have the same hopes and the same laws and the same treatment as white men, and until they know that I have those same expectations of them, they're not going to work well for me or for any other man.

"There are two things I'm seeing more clearly all the time, Sarah. I've got to select my people better. I've got to look for men who want to better themselves. Then I've got to work out a system where the hard workers get a fair share of the profits."

"But, Larkin, that's the sharecropping system. You just described it."

"Ah, but there's a hitch. Some years there won't be much profit. There'll be years when we'll have droughts, there'll be years we'll have floods, there'll be years we'll have boll weevils. They've got to expect to share the risks and take their losses, just like white men. I can't expect to take all the profits, but by the same token they can't expect me to bear all the losses. We need another side to our operation. We're too dependent on cotton. Any sharecroppers we get are apt to be too dependent on me. And on top of it all, I need to manage that zinc mine you inherited up at Lunceville."

I smiled at him, for I had been waiting for Larkin to get around to mentioning the mine. "Larkin, why don't you sell it? Uncle Louis writes me that men are going into the railroading business right and left and making fortunes in the doing of it. That zinc's got a use now far beyond what it once did. Men use it somehow to mix with iron to make steel. Cousin Marie's husband, Victor, is making money hand over fist manufacturing shovels. Those poor Chinese men digging their way across the country are using his shovels."

"Poor devils. If they're wearing out shovels as fast as they're wearing out men, no wonder Montgomery is already a rich man. They tell me that in three years' time, this whole country will be linked by rail. It won't be too long before the railroad is as far west as Kansas City. Already, the one that's been started on the West Coast has been cut through that first mountain range in California. Probably every mile of track has Chinese bones beside it. Sometimes I think that men like Jay Gould and Cornelius Vanderbilt and Leland Stanford are the real leaders of this country. I wouldn't be surprised if every official in Washington sings to their tunes.

"But, that to one side, what's to be gained by selling a zinc mine at the very time it could be getting profitable?"

"Three reasons. First, you're a good bargainer, Larkin, so you could sell it high. Second, you hate mining and you love farming and ranching. The

top of this mountain is ideal for ranching cattle. It's flat, it's good pastureland, it's well watered, and it's big, and I expect you could buy up the
rest of it for nearly nothing. I wouldn't be surprised to find out that you
could sell that zinc mine for enough money to buy up half this mountaintop. Third, if you and Tobe ran a ranching operation on the top of the
mountain and a cotton plantation down at the bottom on the river, you
wouldn't worry much about bad years and boll weevils. I think you could
attract people to work for you who were smart enough to work in both
operations, if they could have a fair share of the profits.

"I expect the profits would be considerable. You ought to be able to
compete favorably with any rancher in Texas, to say nothing of those farther out west, because you'd be assured of grass and water. Then, too,
you'd probably have a shorter drive to market than any rancher in the
country. One of these years they'll finally get that railroad finished across
Arkansas. It stands to reason the track will be laid alongside the river. It'll
be far easier to build a roadbed along the flatland than try to blast it
through the mountains. Regardless of which side of the river they build it
on, you've got a mighty short cattle drive." I smiled at him. "And you've
been mixed up in cattle drives since you were 18."

There was a long silence. When at last he spoke, there was real admiration in Larkin's voice. "By God, Sarah, if you'd been born a man you
probably would have run the whole Chouteau operation. I've been too
busy making a living to see the big picture. You're absolutely right. And
the place to go to sell that zinc mine is in Washington!"

"Washington? Why on earth would you want to go there to sell it?" I
was astonished, for I had envisioned turning over that task to my Uncle
Louis. Immediately I squelched that thought and paid attention.

"Washington is where the big money men go to pull the strings of power. Now that Johnson is President, Washington is the greed capital of the
country. It's not New York. New York's where the robber barons have their
headquarters, but the giveaway center is in Washington.

"As soon as this crop goes to market, I'm heading for Washington, and
I'll send Tobe to South Carolina to recruit us some new people." He
paused, his eyes flashing in excitement. "Sarah, I've said it before and I'll
say it again. You are a remarkable woman!"

"That's good, and I'm glad. But I'm not following your reasoning. Why
South Carolina? That's a long way off to go to get Negroes."

"The land's worn out in South Carolina. The big plantation owners have leached it out planting rice and cotton. Stant told me that when he marched across the South, he could see the signs everywhere. Smart black men will know that. If an 18-year-old boy like Stant could see it, then men who've been trying to farm it will know it, too. Arkansas land is still rich, most especially here along the river. I figure the ones who are ambitious enough to risk the move are the ones we need." He grinned the happy, confident grin of a man who sees the solution to a hard problem. "We'll let Tobe pick some ambitious workers, and I'll find some greedy zinc mine owners. When are Piety and Eliza due? That might be a good time for me to make the trip."

We had a letter from Piety the week before they arrived, the letter of a woman whose mind is made up.

> Dear Sarah and Larkin,
>
> Eliza and I will be arriving on the stage the first of October and I'm going to marry Jesse Rankin the next Saturday at his plantation. We've asked Charity and Ridge to come down from Fort Smith. With Jesse's parents and you two and Eliza, we'll have a family wedding. Jesse and I have talked it over — we talk everything over, that's one of the remarkable things about Jesse — and we don't think having a big wedding is the right thing to do. But Jesse says we may as well count on having a big wedding supper that night, for all his kinfolks will be bound and determined to come and meet his new wife, whether or not he invites them.
>
> It's been nearly six years now since I married Tom. In some ways it seems more like 60, and in other ways it seems like yesterday. But I've found a sweetness in Jesse Rankin that I don't aim to miss out on.

How good it was to have such cause for celebration! Jesse met the stage and carried Piety and Eliza up our mountain in his buggy. That same day, Larkin met the steamboat that brought us Ridge and Charity. Our house was soon filled with talk and ringing with laughter. I don't know who was the happiest. Jesse stayed right with us, not even going back to his own home until the day they were to be wed.

It took two buggies and a wagon to carry all of us to Jesse's plantation that Saturday morning, what with all the changes of clothes for the women and the children, plus Piety's two big trunks. Jesse had ridden off three hours ahead of the rest and stood waiting to greet us as we rolled up the long tree-lined driveway to his home.

The big white-columned plantation house lacked only a coat of paint to make it handsome. Jesse's explanation was aimed at Ridge and Larkin. "This year's cotton crop will go for a new roof and a new barn. I'm hoping that next year's crop will be sufficient to paint the place." To Piety he said, "Welcome home!" And his heart was in his eyes. He carried her over the threshold and on down the long hall into the parlor where his parents waited.

When it was my turn to meet Jesse's frail little mother, I stepped forward in front of her chair and curtsied with my baby held in my arms. "I wanted you to see my baby girl, Mrs. Rankin, and my little boys. My boys love Jesse so much, and I thought you might want to hear them tell you how they sang with him." I presented them proudly — tall Matt, his smile already showing the gap where he had lost his first tooth, my sturdy, boisterous, sandy-haired twins, and finally my beautiful baby.

The perceptive blue eyes belied her frail body. "How fortunate you are. It has been our joy to raise one fine son; to try to imagine that joy quadrupled is nearly too much for an old woman."

I handed the baby to her outstreched arms.

"Jesse told us that when he opened his eyes in your uncle's parlor and looked across the room and saw your face, he thought maybe his eyes were playing tricks on him. He honestly thought that being without his sight those long weeks had somehow caused him to see things differently. He said he truly hadn't remembered there was such a beautiful woman in the world." She smiled. "But now that he's met Piety, I do believe he's convinced your whole family is beautiful." She looked searchingly at the baby. "This child looks so perfect. What do you call her?"

"Well, I had every intention of calling her Victoria, but everybody in the family has taken to calling her Larky. Even Will and Gus."

Jesse's father stooped over to pick up the baby. "I'll venture to suggest she will feel herself honored. I take your husband to be a remarkable man, Miss Sarah. We're pleased to have you as neighbors. Jesse thinks highly of him, as do our other kin, the men who helped him build your house. When you're working with a man, it does not take too long to form an opinion."

It turned out to be a purely wonderful day. As Jesse put it, "We have music and joy, and tears of remembrance, toasts to the bride, and love in abundance." By the time the rest of the Rankin clan gathered in at supper time, Jesse and his parents had already made us feel like members of their family. Invariably, the talk turned from times past to speculation about the future. Some were optimistic, but Jesse's father did not share their optimism.

Jesse's cousin Clayte, a man whose empty right sleeve bore testimony to the arm he had left behind at Vicksburg, outlined his hopes.

"I tell you, men, this thing's about to take a turn for the better. This past election proves it. Thank God we've got old Albert Pike on the state supreme court now! It looks to me like our new legislature is solid for the old Arkansas. We're going to run every money-grubbing carpetbagger out of the state, now that tried and true Arkansas men are running things again."

"I'd say you're overly optimistic, Clayte." Jesse's father's tone was firm. "The South lost this war. For a bunch of high-handed local men to pass laws in complete defiance of the laws of the United States is about as wise as a rabbit poking a big bear with a sharp stick. That new legislature is about to bring disaster down on Arkansas."

"How do you see it, Larkin?" The questioner, Jesse's uncle, waited quietly for Larkin's answer.

"There are a lot of die-hard abolitionists in the North just waiting for an excuse to clamp an iron vise down on the South. Mr. Rankin's right. Defying Congress right now is about as smart as poking a thorn in a bear's paw. I guess I'm somewhat surprised at Albert Pike."

"I've known Albert Pike a long time, and I count him as a friend." The elder Mr. Rankin spoke thoughtfully. "He's one of the smartest men who ever counted himself to be an Arkansan. But, as smart as Albert is, his pride is even bigger than his brain. He can't get it through that hard head of his that, for once in his life, he's come up on the losing side."

Jesse's father looked at his brother, a smile on his face. "Remember, Ezra, how Albert looked that first year he taught school up in the hills northwest of here? Tall as a giant, handsome as Apollo, ragged as a scarecrow?" His voice grew young as he reached back in his memories.

"That would have been back around 1832 or so. Pike had already cut a wide swath — he'd been across the Santa Fe Trail with Charles Bent, toughed it out amidst some of the wildest land and wildest men to be found anywhere, and showed up hale and hearty in the spring. On top of all that, not only did he still have his scalp firmly attached to his head, he had authored a batch of poetry besides. Poetry good enough to get published."

"I always heard that he wrote poetry, but I never saw any in print." Larkin was immediately interested.

"Right across the hall in my library there's his book, published in Boston, and bound in good leather. Albert went to Harvard for a while before he headed West." Again, Mr. Rankin smiled.

Larkin answered him. "The Flint family is in his debt. It was thanks to Pike's defense that my own father was acquitted of Huntsman's charges of treason. Every Flint of the name is beholden to him for that. But, even so, I would earnestly wish he could see the reality of his present disastrous advice to the people of Arkansas."

"Well, in response, I would have to say that Albert has always been answerable to himself first, other authority notwithstanding. Democracy don't really suit Albert. He believes in the rule of aristocracy. Not aristocracy of birth, like the British system, but aristocracy of talent. To tell the truth, throughout the whole war he never got it through his head that he reported to anybody. I wish I could see him now working to heal the country instead of stirring up trouble by writing all those new poems of his."

"What poems, sir?" Larkin was openly curious.

Mr. Rankin walked across the hall to his library and returned with a copy of an old newspaper. "This is unsigned, but I've been reading Pike's poetry for years, and I think I know it when I see it:

> The wolf is in the desert,
> And the panther in the brake.
> The fox is on his rambles,
> And the owl is wide awake;
> For now 'tis noon of darkness,
> And the world is all asleep;
> And some shall wake to glory,
> And some shall wake to weep.
> Ku Klux.
>
> Thrice has the lone owl hooted,
> And thrice the panther cried;

And swifter through the darkness,
The Pale Brigade shall ride.
No trumpet sounds its coming,
And no drumbeat stirs the air;
But noiseless in their vengeance,
They wreak it everywhere.
Ku Klux.

The misty gray is hanging
On the tresses of the East,
And morn shall tell the story
Of the revel and the feast.
The ghostly troop shall vanish
Like the night in constant cloud,
But where they rode shall gather
The coffin and the shroud.
Ku Klux.

"Well, it goes on and on, but you get the gist of this. I'm told that old Bedford Forrest organized a secret society over in Tennessee and called it the Ku Klux Klan. It's already sweeping the South. I dread what's ahead. With Forrest providing the organization and Pike making their skullduggery heroic, it's a bad combination."

"What's the solution, sir?" Larkin's voice was respectful.

"I think you men of moderation are going to have to take some time off from making a living and take a hand in framing the laws of the land. Like your father has done, Larkin."

"Ah, but Father was put in place by Abraham Lincoln. Serving under Lincoln's one thing. Johnson's another."

"You're looking at it different than I would. I'd say your father's serving the people, Larkin. I hope you young men will think on that. I beg you not to leave the country in the hands of professional politicians." Mr. Rankin smiled ruefully. "Of course, when I was your age I was too busy making money to take my own advice! I'm 75 years old now, and I hold myself and others like me to blame for Arkansas's current sorry state of affairs.

"We've been a state since 1836. I'd like to see things improved, not for myself, but for the sake of my grandchildren. We've got the sorriest system of roads and schools of any state in the Union. And mostly because we've left the government too much in the hands of a little self-serving clique of men. For 30 years now they've manipulated the many in the interests of the few. Getting back in the Union won't change that. It's men like you who will make a difference."

His brother laughed. "Remember how it was, John, that first year we landed here, back in 1817?"

Jesse's father's eyes grew bright. "This place didn't even have a name then. Didn't get one until 1820, when Major Lewis settled in and named it after himself. I remember stepping off that flatboat with three or four others. We were all a lot alike then — on fire to get our own land and get ourselves going. I remember that Creed Wilcox looked over across the river at Petit Jean Mountain and said to me, 'Rankin, the land's as good on one side of yon river as it is on the other. I'll flip you to see which one of us takes which side.' And he took a gold piece out of his pocket. I called it heads. The thing came up heads, so I chose the north side and he took the south. It's Creed Wilcox's son who is your neighbor on the south side of your land, Larkin. Good people."

The old men smiled and shook off their remembrances.

"Come, Larkin, let's have some music to commemorate this happy time. Piety, what would you have Larkin play?"

Piety looked up at Jesse. "I'm going to let Jesse call the tune."

"Then I'm going to call for singing as well. Larkin, let's have 'Home Sweet Home.'"

After Larkin had played the melody all the way through, sending the sweet notes soaring into the heights, we all joined in, Piety's contralto blending so richly with Jesse's tenor as to seem like one voice, Matt's sweet treble, sure and clear, the Rankins singing in the harmony grounded in years of close communion.

When the last poignant note had floated out into the night, Clayte Rankin spoke slowly. "The night before one of our battles over in Tennessee, our regiment was camped right next to a little river. The Yankees were camped right across the river from us. After it got dark, the two bands started contesting with each other. First ours played 'Dixie,' then theirs played 'The Battle Hymn of the Republic,' then ours played 'Dixie' again, only louder. Then theirs retaliated. Just when we were all getting worked up with all that tooting and drumming, their band started playing 'Home Sweet Home,' and ours took up the tune. Soon, on both sides of the river, we were all of us singing together. Both sides of the river, North and South. I never heard it sung sweeter."

He paused and smiled at Jesse and Piety. "Until tonight. God bless your union!"

Chapter 37

THE WINTER OF 1866 passed in a hurry. While Larkin was off in Washington and Tobe in South Carolina, I pretty much had my hands full managing things at home. Eliza and I found a Negro woman over at Lewisburg who had the reputation of being a good cook and a hard worker. This turned out to be true on both counts. On top of all that, she was good with the children. Linney and I both got a little rest, which we certainly needed. As it turned out, we both found out we were expecting again. For me, it was too soon. I was surprised.

"I didn't think this would happen," I said to Eliza. "Larky is barely four months old. I'm still nursing. I didn't think women got new babies while they still had one at their breast."

The look Eliza gave me was half teasing and half serious. "Sarah, if by now you don't know how women get babies, then I expect you're probably not ever going to get it figured out. If I'm any judge of men, Larkin's a man who expects to be loved often and loved well." She waited, and looked me right in the eye. "And you glory in it, Sarah. So I expect you might as well get used to the idea that you're probably going to have a good-sized family. As early as you started, you may wind up with a dozen children before you're done.

"It's sure a good thing we found you a cook. You're going to need all the help you can get. Where she got the name Oppello is more than I can figure out. I've run into many a darky with a funny name, but Oppello just about heads the list. How did you find her?"

"She used to be owned by the people who have the plantation next to ours, people by the name of Simpson," I replied. "My guess is that Mrs. Simpson was a hard woman to work for. After Lincoln emancipated the slaves, every one of Mrs. Simpson's house slaves up and left. Some of them moved over to Lewisburg, and that's where we found Oppello."

"What do you hear from Little Rock?" Eliza asked the question with considerable interest.

"Matthew Flint is trying so hard to be even-handed that he works with both sides — carpetbaggers and ex-Confederates alike." I smiled. "Minerva says that Mrs. Albert Pike's got such a high temper that she had everybody in Little Rock laughing this summer. She got so mad at the Negro girl who was brushing her hair that she took in after the girl with a poker. Her husband's gone more than he's home. But whether he's home or whether he's gone, Mrs. Pike is just about the social center of Little Rock.

"Minerva may not be interested in socializing, but I'll bet they don't have any trouble recognizing that she is the governor's wife. And she says the young Mrs. Payson Clemson spends a lot of time trying to outshine Mrs. Pike. But there's a big difference in other ways — Mrs. Clemson is young and her husband has the ear of everybody important in Washington, while Albert Pike is still trying to get President Johnson to pardon him."

Eliza's listening had brought her around to a conclusion. She changed the subject by giving me some advice.

"Sarah, you've spent considerable time telling me about Minerva's acquaintances, but I've heard mighty little about your own. You need to get out and get acquainted in your own community. There's Lewisburg Landing, right across the river, no more than three or four miles away from your house. So far as I'm any judge, it's a good town with good people in it."

But before I could make plans to socialize, Larkin was home in high spirits.

"I tell you, Sarah, ours is a far better world than the one those manipulating rascals up there in Washington live in. By the time I got through dickering with Jay Gould's New York tycoons, I felt like I ought to count my teeth and my toes to make sure I still had a full set. As shrewd and shifty a lot as I've ever run into in my life. It's like coming up against a bunch of tricky Indians."

"Who's Jay Gould, Larkin? And what does New York have to do with selling a zinc mine in Arkansas?"

"He's a railroad man and a stockbroker out of New York. He controls miles and miles of track, all over the country. I didn't actually meet him, but I had a considerable amount of dealings with a fellow that works for him. Fellow by the name of Strasser. So far as I could figure out, Gould assigned Strasser to butter me up until I agreed to sell the mine to them on their terms. Strasser and his wife took me out to dinner, tried to loan me their carriage, did their best to show me the sights of Washington City, all the time acting like we were close as kinfolks." He grinned, remembering.

"Of course, I was hard put to be as accommodating as I would have liked to have been. Cornelius Vanderbilt's men did their share, too, making sure I enjoyed my stay. Between their two camps, I sure didn't have much time to myself. I figure I know now how Queen Victoria felt during the war, having ambassadors from the North and the South eternally camping on her doorsteps." His look of satisfaction increased.

"Having the benefit of their considerable persuasion, I finally and reluctantly allowed myself to be talked into parting with the mine. Remember how Ridge Rodineau used to string out his dickering for mules and not buy them until the sun was about to go down? Well, I did the reverse. Couldn't make up my mind between their two offers, Gould's or Vanderbilt's, even when the train was pulling into the station."

His eyes glinted in remembrance. "Ridge would have been proud of me. There I was, walking down the platform, valise in hand, with two short-legged, frock-coated, high-hatted New Yorkers running along on each side of me trying to keep up, bidding against each other as they trotted along.

"I had decided to go with Strasser's offer. Took it just when the conductor was about to hand me up into the railroad coach. Strasser jumped right on the train with me and rode with me to Baltimore. There we both got off and arranged to sign the papers. The money's in gold. I arranged to have it shipped to the Chouteau bank in St. Louis. There's not a bank in Arkansas reliable enough to put gold in. I figured our gold ought to be back in St. Louis where the name of Chouteau still counts for something."

Eliza laughed out loud. "Well, Larkin, I think it's safe to predict that the name of Flint will count for something, too, right along with the name of Chouteau. Unless, of course, you've provoked Vanderbilt into a shooting war. Men say he doesn't take kindly to being bested."

"Vanderbilt isn't going to waste his wrath on small potatoes from Arkansas, Eliza. Gould's his enemy. And the reverse. Both men are determined to own the country, or at least the railroads in it. I guess they think that if they buy up the railroads and the Congress, they won't need to buy up the rest of the country." He shook his head. "As I said, it's good to be home, where the air is sweet and the women are sweeter. Let me hold the baby a while, Sarah. I've missed you all!"

By the time Tobe got back from South Carolina, Larkin had his plans all made. He laid out the sites for the Negroes' cabins in a hollow square in the middle of a fine stand of walnut trees. The houses would be close together, each house facing outward into the grove.

"That's not a very sociable arrangement, Larkin. Darkies like to sit on their front porches and visit. They'll all have to go out in their backyards to do their visiting."

"It may not be sociable, Sarah, but it's defensible. With four houses to a side, it's built as nearly like a fort as I can make it. Things are apt to get worse in Arkansas before they get better. I want our people to be able to look after themselves. I have every intention of furnishing each man a pistol and a shotgun. Tobe will make sure they know how to use them."

"But how can you trust darkies with guns?" I was horrified. "They're liable to kill us all if they get mad at us." Memories of Ike seared my brain. Tales of Negro uprisings flared in my mind.

"Sarah," Larkin's tone was exasperated. "Sometimes I despair of this country. If a smart girl like you can't give black men the benefit of the doubt, I do wonder about the rest of the country. Tobe is as good a judge of black men as we're ever going to meet. He'll pick good men."

He changed the subject. "I've decided it's time we started going to church. And for more than one reason. We can worship while we're inside, but it's outside in the churchyard that folks catch up on the news of the community.

"I may yet get to be numbered amongst the faithful. The way things are going in Arkansas, I need to stay on top of what's happening."

I gave him a quick and scandalized look. So far as I could tell, he was joking.

But, whatever his reasons, from that time forward the Flint family was usually to be found in attendance at Sunday morning services. And, if I do say so myself, there wasn't a handsomer family to be found anywhere.

I don't know how many times that winter of 1866 I heard somebody say, "If Lincoln had lived, things would have been different!" But the approach Lincoln had sponsored, the approach he called restoration, was too kind, too moderate, and too sensible for the extremists on either side. I have always thought that die-hard ex-Confederates brought a lot of their problems on themselves. Arkansas tried to send a bunch of high-headed has-beens to Congress. There, along with the other has-been Southerners, all their accomplishments were negative. They antagonized and outraged the Northern radicals, men who had simply been seeking an excuse to impose the iron yoke of despotism on the South.

By the time Larkin got the cotton planted that spring of 1867, Arkansas had been placed under military rule. Federal troops once more occupied the state. In retaliation, the secret Ku Klux Klan started sneaking out in the night, pretending to the ignorant darkies that they were the ghosts of dead Confederates. Between them, the troops and the Klan pretty much kept the whole state on edge. Larkin and I stayed at home and minded our own business, except for church on Sunday, occasional visits with Jesse and Piety, and the necessary trips over to Lewisburg Landing to buy our supplies. But minding our own business proved to be an insufficient protection against the vindictiveness that was abroad in the land.

We had wonderful weather that spring. The days were warm and bright. We had just the right amount of rain — enough to cause the cotton to grow lush and tall, but not enough to cause the river to flood. Everything looked right, but nobody felt right. Every time I left home I was uneasy. Federal troops marched up and down the roads over at Lewisburg. White men stood around outside the stores in little knots, three or four to a bunch, talking in low voices, the brown spittle of their chewing tobacco aimed with deadly accuracy within inches of the boots of the Yankee soldiers. Most black men and women stayed close to home.

It was a Friday night in late May when the first cross was burned on our land. The dogs started barking around midnight, followed soon by a voice from the driveway. "Mr. Larkin, Mr. Larkin, git up Mr. Larkin!"

It was Wiley, one of the new darkies Larkin had brought from South Carolina. In one quick motion Larkin was out of bed, leaning his head out our upstairs window.

"What's the trouble, Wiley?"

"They's a big cross burning in the cotton patch jest north of your big gate. Look like dem devils wanted to make shore you all could look out-ten your winder an' see it. Iffen you come down here an' step over to the edge of your bluff you can see it plain."

"Did you see who it was that burnt it?"

"Nosir. Dey must have snuck in quiet and snuck out quieter. My old woman was up wid de toothache. She seen it first. I thought I'd orter let you know."

"You did right, Wiley." With the quick motions of a man on a battle-field, Larkin put on his clothes, grabbed a lantern, and disappeared out the door. It was nearly morning before he returned. He sat down at the break-fast table clear-eyed and grim-jawed. "They picked a good night for a burning cross to command attention. It was pitch dark out there. A good night for burning crosses, but not a good night for riding horses. The whole Klan won't ride until the moon is full. My guess is, our real troubles are ahead of us. Keep the boys on top of the mountain, Sarah, and keep them close to the house. And tell Oppello she is to start sleeping here in the big house. I want her close to you, and I don't want her sleeping by herself in that room over the storehouse.

"It's my guess the Klan leaves Negro women alone. I expect it's only the men they're trying to scare, since it's only the men who can vote. But we'll not take chances. When the Klan gathers, they stoke up their fires with memories and moonshine, and they've got plenty of both."

On Saturday, three men came riding up the mountain to visit Larkin. Our neighbor Wilcox, acting as spokesman for the delegation, addressed Larkin with courtesy as he formally requested a few minutes of his time.

Afterward, Larkin ushered them out of the parlor and strolled with the men around the barns and showed them his new herds of cattle. He was as cool as a cucumber and as friendly as ever.

Oppello, sitting on the back porch shelling peas, grinned a sly little grin as the men walked down the driveway. "Dat dere Mr. Simpson, him gettin' so fat him 'bout to bust his britches. Waddling along. Guess dey must've found dem somebody else to cook fer dem. He couldn't stay dat fat on Miss Nellie's cooking. Boiling water's more'n she's up to doin'.

"Mr. Simpson, he et everything in sight. Miss Nellie, her complain 'bout everything in sight! Mr. Simpson, he done give me a look jest now dat would've killed me on de spot if looks could kill! Probably galls him a whole heap to see me setting on your back stoop shelling your peas and him wid Miss Nellie so mean tempered he can't git nobody to work in her kitchen. Miss Nellie, she done believes dat she was born to be petted and de rest of de world born to do de pettin'! And she one mean woman when she have to wait on herself!" She giggled.

That Sunday in church I did not hear one word the preacher said — I was so busy looking over the congregation, studying the faces of the men, and wondering which ones had lit that fiery cross on our land. We held our heads high, sang as staunchly as though we had not a trouble in the world, and even invited Mr. Wilcox and his wife to take dinner with us.

"I wish we could, but we can't," Mr. Wilcox replied. "I've promised my brother-in-law Simpson to drive by his house today and carry him some liniment. He's down in his back. Strained a muscle somewhere. I promised to see Doc Handy after services today and ask him to make up a fresh bottle. Doc's liniment works wonders sometimes."

So I smiled, Larkin shook hands all round, and we strolled over and got in our buggy and headed for home.

On Tuesday night, the fire of another cross lit up the cotton field below our bluff. The next Friday night, the third cross burned. Larkin's mouth had become a grim line. His eyes vigilant and his back straight, he went about his tasks and saw to it that our darkies went about theirs. I was reminded of the tension in the air in the days before the Battle of Westport.

As the moon waxed full and the nights got bright, Larkin's step seemed to get a little jauntier. I was astonished. "Larkin, how can this be? You actually act like you want the Klan to come visit us."

"I want to get it over with, Sarah. We can't live this way forever. The thing needs to be settled. I'm going to ride over to Lewisburg today and assess the lay of the land. I need to talk to Captain Hern about some business. Today's as good a day as any."

He got back home right before dark, his coat torn by briars, his hatband ringed with sweat, and his horse so lathered up it was heaving. I was astonished.

"What on earth happened to you? You look like you've been riding through the briar patch backwards. I've never seen you ride a horse so hard. What have you been up to? Whose horse is that? And why are your britches wet?"

"Well, I think I've fooled them, Sarah. I hope so, anyway. While I was visiting with Captain Hern, the man from the telegraph office came over with an urgent telegram summoning me upriver to confer with the Union officer stationed over in Pope County. I climbed on my horse and started out posthaste. So far as all the loafers around the general store at Lewisburg know, I'm still heading out hell-bent for Pope County. What they don't know is that your Cousin Ed sent me the telegram. My judgment is, that Klan's a cowardly bunch, Sarah. They'd rather pay their visit here on a night when they think I'm gone. And they know I wouldn't leave home if it wasn't urgent.

"Anyhow, I left my horse in Jesse's barn, took one of his, hid out until it got nearly dark, rode a couple of miles upriver, swam Jesse's horse across the river, climbed up the mountain between the bluffs in that steep ravine where the creek has cut a path between the bluffs, and here I am! We'll see what the night holds. The moon's going to be nearly bright enough to read a newspaper by. I figure it'll bring out the Klan. Get me some dry clothes, Sarah, and a dram of strong whiskey. And some of Oppello's good stew I see over there in that pot on the stove. I think you'd better tell Linney and her baby girl to sleep here in the big house tonight. I'm going to need Tobe with me."

It was nearly midnight before they came. Larkin told me later they made very little noise. They had muffled their horses' hooves so carefully that half a hundred hooded men rode up that rocky road like ghosts. I would have expected them to stop at the cabins of our colored folks and deal with them first, but that was not their plan. Thinking Larkin to be gone and believing our colored field hands to be too afraid to defend themselves in Larkin's absence, the Klan rode up our mountain toward their main target. Belatedly, I realized that target was Tobe. In slow-dawning horror, my mind accepted the analysis that Larkin apparently had concluded long before. To make Tobe their victim would win them a triple victory — punishing Tobe for taking on the responsibilities of a white man, diminishing Larkin by depriving him of the competent services of the best foreman in the Arkansas Valley, and intimidating our other Negro field hands into fearful subservience.

I realized then that Larkin had all along been expecting the Klan to try to close in on Tobe. My memory flashed back to the visit of Wilcox and Simpson the week before, remembering how Larkin had so casually toured his visitors around our barns, showing them our new herds of cattle while simultaneously affording them an exact knowledge of the location of Tobe's cottage.

"He's fooled them," I thought, "just exactly as he meant to. But what if he has outsmarted himself instead? How can two men hold off the entire Klan?" My imagination conjured up horrible visions. Already the Klan was notorious for lynching darkies, lynchings sometimes proceeded by such tortures as to make their victims welcome the sight of the hanging rope.

Still fully dressed, I knelt at the open upstairs window with Linney beside me, two pregnant women staring into the bright moonlight as our husbands prepared to face their white-sheeted enemies. We knelt in silence. Only the Lord God above knew what was going on in Linney's mind.

Down below on the terrace to my right I could make out Larkin's shape and Tobe's as they crouched behind the stone wall that overlooked the road up the mountain. I realized then how well Larkin had chosen his spot.

At the bend of the road, the mountain fell off sharply to the right of the advancing horsemen. On their left, where Larkin and Tobe waited, the bluff rose abruptly for nearly 20 feet. I could picture Larkin fixing their leader in the sights of his gun. When they got close enough to hear, his voice rang out like an iron hammer hitting on an anvil.

"Halt! Any man who rides any closer is a dead man!" He waited. Down on the road below, horses neighed as their surprised riders reigned them to an abrupt halt.

"I have no quarrel with you men. Turn around! Go home! Leave me and mine in peace!" Again, he waited.

"Behind you in the dark I have two dozen armed darkies, all of them waiting for you to make up your minds whether or not you mean to go in peace. I advise you to take this chance to leave while the offer is open.

There won't be a warning next time. The next time any lily-livered, white-sheeted coward trespasses on my property, I mean to shoot to kill." Again, he waited. This time the silence was so thick you could almost cut it with a knife. Larkin addressed their leader directly.

"Don't take me for a fool, man. I won't call you by name, but I know who you are and where you live. I even know what your ailments are. Good God, man, I can even smell the stink of that liniment you've been using lately! Now I'm going to shoot over your head, just so you'll know this gun works. And by God, man, the next shot will be aimed at your cowardly heart unless you turn your crew around and head that miserable fat ass of yours down off my mountain!"

Larkin's shot rang out loud and hard. Filling the warm night were the sounds of panic and the noises of horses hastily turned and whipped into sudden flight down the rocky road that led to the safety of the river. As the reverberations of their frantic galloping faded, a new sound shocked my ears: the harsh roar of many shotguns fired in unison.

Larkin stood up and yelled toward the house. "You can relax, Sarah. That last volley was only the parting salute of our field hands. They had instructions to fire a farewell volley just so the Klan would know there was more where that came from. I figure the Klan ought to be clearing our gate by now if they haven't broken their horses' legs racing down the mountain."

Larkin stood directly below my window and spoke softly. "Go to bed now. The danger's over. Tobe and I are going to ride down the mountain and calm down our darkies. Try to get a little sleep."

But sleep was not possible. Deep in my belly I felt the dull ache that signaled the contractions of childbirth. Within the hour the contractions became stronger, and I began to be fearful, for I still had two more months to go to carry the baby to full term. Desperately, I tried to remember the few remedies I had ever heard of that would stop the premature contractions. I shook Linney awake.

"I've got to get help. We've got to get word to Mr. Lark. He needs to go for the doctor. You saddle up a horse and we'll get Oppello to ride down the mountain to my Cousin Ed's house. He can find Mr. Lark."

Linney looked at me with compassion. "Miss Sarah, I don't have no idea how to put a saddle on a horse. I never saddled a horse in my life. I'll get Oppello. Maybe she can saddle one, but I doubt it. You lay there flat on your back. I don't know anything about horses, but I know you ain't got no bidness moving around. You're bleedin' bad, Miss Sarah. Lay down. We'll git Mr. Lark's attention another way."

She walked over to the bedside table and picked up the big pistol that Matthew Flint had handed me that fearsome night so long ago.

"Pistol fire ought to reach his ears, Miss Sarah." She took the gun to the edge of the bluff, pointed it toward the moon, and fired it out into the still night.

"Miss Sarah, I shore hope we git somebody that knows how to do something for you. All I can think of to do is to lay you down and git clean rags to sop up the blood."

I suffered and bled through hours of dark agony. By the time my Cousin Ed arrived with Dr. Handy, I was past all hope, either for me or for the baby. I held tight to Larkin's hand, the one lifeline left to me in a sea awash with pain.

Finally, there was the blessed release of ether.

When I awoke, the late-day sun was streaming through the west windows. Larkin sat by the bed, his eyes red, the dark stubble of a day's beard on his jaws.

"Where is the baby, Larkin?"

"The baby's dead, Sarah. It was too little to live. It's a miracle that I've still got you. For a while this morning, Dr. Handy was afraid we'd lose you both." He came over and kissed my forehead, his lips as tender as the wings of a butterfly. "Go back to sleep, Sarah. I've got some pills to give you. They'll ease the pain. Go back to sleep."

It was a long, quiet summer, for it took several months for me to get back my strength. By September I was feeling pretty much like my old self again, but that summer of 1867 marked the end of my childbearing years. I never again conceived.

And we never again were bothered by the Klan. Cousin Alta told me that when Larkin buried our premature baby boy, he turned to Cousin Ed and said, "I want you to do me a favor. I want you to pass the word that I aim to personally kill in cold blood any murdering son of a bitch that puts on a white sheet and rides anywhere close to my land. And I want you to tell Seth Simpson that if he ever causes my family any trouble again, I aim to shoot him down like a dog."

Chapter 38

THERE ARE THOSE WHO might wonder how a woman can grieve so about a baby she never got to see, a baby she never knew, a baby that died while it was being born. But the truth is, I felt like I did know that baby. He had been living in my body and thumping on my belly, and I felt like I knew him well. I had planned to name him after Tom, for I was sure he was going to turn out to have Tom's high-spirited ways. That little grave with a rosebush planted at its head held a child that I had already held for seven months, and I took his death hard.

Then, too, I was some time getting my strength back. There were days I felt so tired and low-spirited I could scarcely drag myself out of bed. Larkin worried and Dr. Handy prescribed medicines, but the women in my family took action. Each competent one of them came and dosed me with kindness.

They took turns staying with us that summer, putting their own homes and responsibilities to one side in order to look after me and mine. Piety came first and stayed nearly two weeks, long enough for Jesse to ride over the mountains to bring Eliza down to us. Eliza stayed the entire month of July. She was followed in August by Charity, who came from Fort Smith with her new baby boy and stayed another month. By the time Becky and her little girl came down from Fayetteville in September I was nearly myself again, rejoicing in their company but feeling bad that my grief had caused them all so much worry and trouble.

"I don't know which one of you I've inconvenienced the most," I said to Becky. "Eliza went off and left her crops right at the time she really needed to be there. And you and Piety and Charity have left your husbands to look after themselves all this time so you can come down here and look after me and mine. I knew I had sweet kinfolks, but I guess it takes hard trouble to find out how truly sweet you all are."

Becky smiled. "Sarah, did you ever stop to think how long it has been since any one of us has had the time for a good long visit with each other? You and Charity and Piety haven't really had much time together since that terrible time when you all had to shoot Ike. You and I haven't visited for any length of time since that day Monnie uglied up your face with tallow and pokeberry juice and you and little Matt started out across the mountain with General Marmaduke's army. And you parted from Eliza's company with your Pa dead and his tavern burned. We've all been bonded by fire, wouldn't you say? But I wouldn't call us sweet. No, sweetness is not precisely the word I would choose."

I laughed out loud. "That's exactly what Eliza said. She looked me right in the eye and said, 'Sarah, I'll thank you to show better judgment. I'm not sweet. Nobody's ever accused me of being sweet. I'd like to think there's a better word that applies to me. Any simpering woman in skirts can act sweet.'"

Becky thought a minute. "We're supposed to act sweet, yet we're called on to face as many of life's troubles as men. We can't vote, and we can't buy our own land — not if we're married — and heaven forbid that we should think about taking any part in the government of the country we live in! Do you suppose that by the time our own little girls are grown women, men will start arguing with each other over whether women are smart enough to be allowed to vote?"

"Maybe, by then, if white men have got used to the idea that it's safe to let Negroes inside the voting booths. It kind of tickles me, Becky, the way white men rant and rave and preach and pontificate about whether blacks should be trusted with the ballots, when not one of them has given a minute's serious thought to letting their own womenfolks have the vote."

"Does that gall you, Sarah?"

"No. What galls me is that good men like Willie and Jesse and your brother Sam or our neighbor Ben Wilcox can't vote in Arkansas now, even though they've taken the oath of allegiance to the Union. But that cowardly excuse for a man Seth Simpson can vote, because he was too craven to go to war. Stayed at home, never fought, hides behind the white sheet of the Ku Klux Klan, but he gets to vote because he never bore arms against the United States! Wouldn't you think smart men who fought hard in the war would be smart enough to fight for a better peace? Lincoln never would have put the South under military rule."

"Are the Federal troops still marching around the towns? I've not been paying any attention to the outside world lately."

"They're still marching, and I hear ugly rumors that the Klan still rides, too, but I'm absolutely sure they won't come back up this mountain again. Furthermore, Larkin tells me that when Schoolmaster Watson opens his classroom door next month, there will be ten little pickaninnies learning their ABC's right along with your boys. You've paid a high price for it, Sarah, but I doubt the Klan will ever again pick a fight with Larkin Flint."

Sudden tears appeared in Becky's brown eyes. "You know, Sarah, it truly hurts me that Willie can't vote. When one of the best and most loving men that God ever put on this earth can't have a voice in his own government, it is a shame and a disgrace. Willie is the hardest working doctor in Fayetteville now. People come to him day and night to heal their bodies and deliver their babies and listen to their troubles. It nearly breaks my heart that these greedy carpetbaggers have come down swarming into Arkansas to run our state. How can men like Willie, men who were born here, who aim to stay here, and who will die here, stand up to them? Willie's not going to go around politicking and making speeches. He's too busy looking after the sick. Some days I get sad; other days I get mad. What a mess the South has gotten itself into!"

I was struck by a thought that sobered us both. "Knowing how you feel about Willie, Becky, how do you suppose Linney feels about Tobe not being able to vote? Linney could say a lot of things about Tobe that are just as true as you said about Willie. Tobe's honest and smart and hard-working and loving. And he can't vote either, as things stand now. But Larkin believes the new governmental policy is going to give Tobe the right to vote, probably as soon as the legislature meets."

"Well, that's not fair, either. I understand that Tobe should vote. But I will never agree that Willie should not."

"I know one thing, Becky, and it's this: men like Larkin and Jesse and Sam and Willie are going to have to take a part in government, whether they enjoy it or not. I mean to press Larkin in that direction. Maybe, when the time comes, he'll turn his mind to government."

It was the next summer, 1868, when the crops were laid by, before Larkin turned his serious attention to the political situation. By this time President Johnson had been impeached, tried before a hostile and blatantly partisan Senate, and acquitted by the slender thread of one single vote. Ulysses S. Grant had been nominated for President, a nomination sure to sweep him to overwhelming victory in the fall elections. Congress had finally admitted Arkansas to the Union, and the 15th Amendment was rushed into reality by the radical Republicans; consequently, black men — prepared or unprepared — were urged to the voting booth.

Indeed, throughout the world, it was as though momentous events were piling up, one on top of the other. Russian America, that vast and craggy North American outcropping of icy mountains, had been bought by the United States. Some called it Alaska; most called it Seward's Folly. The Atlantic cable was laid, and the Pacific Railroad, nearing completion, was pounded foot by foot through the forbidding granite of the Rockies.

Over in Kansas, the ranting, raving, radical Senator Jim Lane had been turned out of power by his own political machine. Despondent, he had shot himself in the head. Closer to home, Confederate General Thomas Hindman, discouraged by the indifferent reception accorded him by the leaders of Mexico, had returned to his own fine home in Arkansas. There he attempted a belated influence on the Klan and on his former followers, but such influence as he had was short-lived. Hindman was killed in his home by an unknown gunman, a coward who stood in the dark outside a lighted window and shot him while he sat at his own desk.

Up in Washington, Andrew Johnson, in one of his last acts of office, granted amnesty to the former Confederate soldiers, an amnesty never accepted by Jefferson Davis. And in 1869, Ulysses S. Grant was sworn in as President, and a boom for the corrupt began in America. These harsh and greedy times left their mark on us all.

Even after our neighbors had begged him to run for office, it had not been easy to convince Larkin that he ought to run for the state legislature. "Sarah," he said, "it'll be an exercise in futility. I know what I'm talking about. Payson Clemson is going to be the next governor. I know him well enough to know he's smooth as silk and crooked as a snake. He'll put his stamp on every piece of legislation out of Little Rock. And every law that's passed will be designed to put money in somebody's pocket, especially Clemson's cronies and business partners."

"Larkin, you may well be right. But if men like you don't stand for office, you most certainly will be right. If all the new laws are made entirely by men like Payson Clemson, then Willie and Sam and Jesse will never again have the rights that free men ought to have. I think you owe it to Arkansas to do whatever you can do for good. As things now stand, every black man in Arkansas is going to be hauled to the voting booth by men like that old Brindletail Bender and Payson Clemson, and they're going to be told how to vote. Even though most Negroes can't even read or write, they're going to be voting. You know perfectly well they'll vote however Clemson tells them to."

"What do you expect me to do about that, Sarah?"

"I expect you to work to pass laws for free public schools for blacks and whites alike. You know how few and far between the schools are in this state. I'm not saying that Negroes ought to be kept out of the voting booth. I'm saying that, whether black or white, a man ought to be educated so as to know what he's voting for. And I'm saying that ex-Confederates ought to be allowed to vote, too!"

As Larkin listened to me, a look of resolution came over his face, that iron-willed look I knew so well. "By God, Sarah, you've got a point there! It can't be done overnight, but it's a possible thing! The die-hard abolitionists will be forced to vote for free schooling! It's been the centerpiece of their politics all along! And, come to think of it, if Payson knows that

I'm close at hand keeping track of how much he's stealing, it may slow him down some."

He thought for a while. "I wonder how many other Lincoln Republicans are left in this state. I need to know who they are. There were about a dozen or so at the Constitutional Convention back in January. I wonder how many of them can be persuaded to stand for the legislature. I'll talk to Father and ask him to write some letters."

As always, when Larkin planned, events began to shape up in conformance with his planning. That spring Larkin was elected to the state legislature, and by the time he took his seat, Larkin counted 20 men in that body who could be considered to be moderates. They were of the Lincoln Republican philosophy. Their numbers were too small to get any of their own legislation passed, but there were too many of them to be ignored, and Payson Clemson continuously courted their votes.

As Larkin and I accommodated our lives to his new duties in Little Rock, there were various family members who gave unsolicited advice about our household arrangements. A letter from my Aunt Bereniece addressed the situation succinctly:

August 1868

Dear Sarah,

   While I wish to congratulate Larkin on his willingness to stand for public office, I would be remiss in my family responsibilities were I not to tell you of the serious misgivings I feel about the matter. For him to serve in the legislature is one thing. For you to maintain your residence at Petit Jean and not accompany him to Little Rock is quite another. I am truly concerned that it has become necessary for me to point out to you the obvious fact that it is the duty of a good wife to be at her husband's side. This is a matter of prayerful and considerable concern to me, most especially when I contemplate the temptations to which a man living apart from his family is apt to be subjected, temptations entirely avoidable were you to be always present and mindful of your conjugal duties.

   I trust you will give prayerful thought to the possible consequences of your domestic arrangements. The love of a good wife is the solace provided to man by an all-seeing Deity; but

man, being one of the more fallible of the Deity's creations, has
been known to stray into temptations when his good wife is not
to be found next to his side where she belongs.

I handed the letter to Larkin, half-smiling and half-aggravated. "Aunt
Bereniece thinks I ought to move right down to Little Rock with you and
let this big place look after itself. As usual, she's very willing to give me
advice for my own good."

"Sarah, you know we can't both go off. Tobe's a good man; he's smart
and he's hard-working, but he's accustomed to having somebody else
decide everything for him. It won't do to leave Tobe in charge. It's different with you, Sarah. Sometimes I think you were born knowing how to lay
out work for other people to do!" His tone was only partially teasing. "But
your Aunt Bereniece is a smart old girl. Maybe I ought to give up the
whole idea of politics, stay home, make money in the daytime, and love
you at night." He grinned, "Not too bad a life, at that!"

It was I who gave argument.

"Larkin, it's a sacrifice. I know it is for you. You know it is for me. But
the legislature only meets a few months — from November to Christmas,
then again in January and February. And Little Rock's only a day's boat
trip away. You can come home every couple of weeks. After the railroad
is finished, you can come home in half a day. And it's not as though you're
going to be doing this the rest of your life. One term — two years — ought
to be enough time to pass a new voting law and a new school law. Aunt
Bereniece is wise, and she means well, but what we decide is none of her
business."

"Well, it's settled, then." He looked down at me, the sweet look I loved
showing in his eyes. "You get more beautiful every year, Sarah. We'll
settle it this way: while I'm home I'll love you twice as much. That way
I'll compensate myself for the nights I sleep in a lonesome bed."

We loved each other so well and so deeply that night that I thought I
would faint from the power of it. Afterward I slept deep, and I slept happy.
But along toward morning there came a dream in which Larkin walked
along a crowded boulevard, and amongst the many who vied for his attention were beautiful women and dangerous men. Even as I watched, Aunt
Bereniece shook her sternly admonishing finger in my face. But in the
bright sunlight of a crisp fall morning, I pushed aside the remembrances
of my dream, climbed into the buggy so as to drive Larkin down to the

riverboat, and sent my handsome husband off to the legislature with a smile of pride on my face.

It was an important time to be engaged in governmental service, and it was a dangerous time. Thanks to Larkin's iron will and advance planning, the children and I lived atop an almost impregnable summit. There were many in Arkansas that year who had cause to wish themselves to be as well situated. Violence flared throughout the state as the time for the November presidential election drew near. Thousands of newly franchised Negroes were organized to march and demonstrate in favor of their idol, Grant, an idol whose feet of clay were already becoming evident to the bitter ex-Confederates throughout the state. These ex-soldiers were seeking ways to revolt against Payson Clemson and against the radical Republicans in Washington. These disillusioned men had their "squirrel guns" and ammunition. By the dozens they joined the Ku Klux Klan and set themselves to the task of outwitting the carpetbaggers and intimidating the blacks. Clemson responded by organizing a state militia to force his will on the people of Arkansas. The embers of hate were fanned to quick flames. In dozens of seemingly unrelated incidents, Arkansas was transformed into a mosaic of violence.

Early in the fall, a federal agent of the Freedmen's Bureau was shot and killed as he sat at a window of his office in Crittenden County. One dark night in Pope County, the men of one outraged family avenged their mother's suffering by hanging seven Bushwhackers from the limbs of the same oak tree. In Little Rock a great torchlight procession of boisterous Negroes was turned into a screaming rout when shotguns were fired from ambush into the singing, shouting ranks of the black men. Clemson's militia, composed almost entirely of Negroes, and officered by men who were partisan at best and merciless at worst, began their arrogant marching throughout the state. For every atrocity committed by these official outlaws, there came an equally brutal response from the Ku Klux Klan.

The tensions were tightened by that ancient Southern fear, the fear that white women would be violated by black men, who were now the official representatives of the governor of Arkansas. The winds of the Civil War had been but a preliminary to the storms of Reconstruction.

By Christmastime 1868, when Larkin came home for the holiday recess, there were so many threads of silver shinning throughout his glossy black hair that I was shocked. Yet his step was quick, his voice confident, and his eyes were clear. I thanked God that I had been granted the love of such a fine man, and I resolved to do everything I could to lighten his burdens.

Chapter 39

AFTER PAYSON CLEMSON got the reins of power in his hands, things began to happen fast. Within six months he had accumulated so much wealth that he had to bring his brother in from Pennsylvania to manage all his money. His government of oppression saddled a heavy expense upon Arkansas. Clemson's militia, 2,000 strong and mostly Negroes, moved around the state on their missions of terror and plunder.

Carpetbag lawyers began to reap a golden harvest as they litigated claims that legalized the spoil of scalawags and fellow carpetbaggers. Unrestricted by any kind of merit system, Clemson's appointments ranged from notary public all the way up to chief justice of the state supreme court. Very few of these newly designated officials were natives of Arkansas. Indeed, according to the *Gazette*, most had migrated to the state to hold office. They arrived in the fall with the ducks, intent on the same purpose — to feed richly off the land.

Things got so bad that most honest Republicans withdrew their support from Clemson and elected to suffer the consequences. Even the speaker of the house, unwilling to be party to Clemson's ruthless pillaging, went public in his opposition. For this act of honesty he was promptly deposed, though he remained in the legislature. With him, and others like him, Larkin forged his alliances.

Larkin labored through all of this, studying both the newly proposed legislation and the strengths and weaknesses of the men who proposed it. Eight months of the year, from early spring to late fall, he lived with me and our children on top of Petit Jean Mountain. During the winter, he lived in Little Rock.

We both worked hard. We prospered and looked forward to the time when Larkin could get his goals accomplished and come back home full-time. By 1870 it had become clear that one term in the legislature was insufficient for all that needed to be done. His first and foremost aim was well on its way to becoming a reality: an efficient system of free public education was established under the administration of a state superintendent of schools. Larkin took well-deserved pride in this success.

"I can see signs that Payson Clemson is getting careless. He's actually appointed an honest man to be superintendent of schools! The only honest appointment he's made so far! It must have been an oversight, but thank God for it! Now I can start working on legislation so that ex-Confederates can have the right to vote."

"That means you're going to have to serve another term, Larkin."

"It does, Sarah. Can you hold up under two more years of my being gone four months out of the year?"

"Well, I held up during the war, when you were gone a lot longer than that. I think you have to finish what you started. Besides, the railroad will be completed shortly. Can you imagine being able to ride 50 miles in less than half a day? You can leave Little Rock after breakfast and be home to take noon dinner with us. I can manage things during the week, and you can come home on Fridays and decide what needs to be done for the next week."

"That railroad's a mixed blessing, Sarah. I rejoice in what it will mean to us — I can see you and the children every week; we can ship our cattle to market without the expense of a long cattle drive; people can hope for easier lives when they have railroads crossing the state from east to west and north to south. But the cost is liable to bankrupt the state."

"How so? Other states have built railroads without going bankrupt, surely."

Larkin's mouth grew grim. "Other states have not been blessed with Payson Clemson and his crooked gang. Graft is not new to Arkansas, God knows. We've had it before and I have no doubt we'll have it again. But Payson is so smart and so likeable that by the time he gets through fleecing the public and floating railroad bonds and assessing taxes, he's apt to preside over the biggest transfer of funds in Arkansas's history. We're going to have the debt and he's going to have the cash. My big fear is that one of these days, he's going to get the idea of teaming up with Jay Gould, and between them they'll bankrupt the whole country! But so far, he's mostly been toadying up to Vanderbilt's representative."

"Do Gould and Vanderbilt both keep people in Little Rock? If they do, then both men must believe Arkansas to have some importance."

"Both men understand geography. They understand Arkansas is between Texas and the big Eastern markets, so the railroads have to run through it. And they understand money.

"But in answer to your question, Sarah, yes, Gould and Vanderbilt both keep representatives in Arkansas. Slick men, smart men. So long as they compete against each other, I don't worry too much. But if one or the other gets Payson Clemson hooked, then we're in bad trouble."

"So he's playing one off against the other, like you did when you sold our zinc mine."

"Exactly. And one of them is the same fellow — Strasser. Except now that he's older and richer, he's acquired a brand-new wife about 30 years younger than he is. A new asset, you might say." His grin was lewd. "She's the bait. Any fat, dumb, and happy Arkansas hillbilly legislator that gets invited to have supper with Strasser and wife at the Anthony House Hotel is going to be made to feel like he's the most important man in Arkansas. She's every bit as shifty as Strasser but a lot prettier, and she wears so many ornaments she glitters like a Christmas tree."

I felt a flash of resentment. "Are you telling me, Larkin Flint, that you have been entertained by a fat New Yorker and his dressed-up tart of a wife whilst I'm here on top of this mountain working hard and eating fried meat and corn bread with your lonesome children?"

He burst out laughing. "I sure am, Sarah. And it's about as pleasurable as sharing a feeding tank with a couple of hungry barracudas." He gestured at the room around us. "Don't you think I'd a thousand times rather be sitting here in our own dining room at our own mahogany table looking at my own pretty wife and fine children and eating Oppello's good cooking and looking out the window at the finest view in Arkansas? Don't take me for a fool, Sarah. I'll admit I still recognize a pretty piece when I see one, but I'm not such a fool as to be taken in by it."

His face grew thoughtful. "I do have a plan that I think will be of considerable help to Arkansas. Next Sunday when we have that big bunch of kinfolks here, I'm going to try it out on Ridge and Jesse and Will and Sam and Father and see what they think."

Later, looking back, I realized that a new branch of the Republican party in Arkansas, the Liberal Republicans, was born in our house that hot summer Sunday in 1870. The goals were straightforward: to give former Confederates the right to vote, to put Arkansas on a sound financial footing, to maintain a good system of schools in the state, and to get Payson Clemson out of Arkansas. The last had to be accomplished first.

"Short of killing him, I don't see how you're going to do it, Lark." Ridge was expressing the doubts felt by all. "Payson's got a gold mine here in Arkansas. I don't see how you're going to shake him out of the governor's chair."

"It's my thought that we've got a good chance to get him elected to the U.S. Senate. As you know, it is the state legislature that decides on the two men who go to Washington as senators, and this is the year to select one. What we need to do is work on the state representatives, one at a time. For this we've got to be well organized, and we've got to offer arguments that will make sense to the men doing the voting. Father, out of the whole legislature, how many men do you honestly think have the good of Arkansas at heart? Regardless of their politics."

Matthew's reply was slow in coming. "About a third, I'd say. You've got to remember, Lark, that Clemson handpicked these legislators. Most of them are cut from the same cloth he is."

Larkin continued his questioning. "How many men are so greedy that they would like to see Clemson gone just so there would be more graft money they could put in their own pockets?"

"Well, it's a sorry comment on that bunch he's put in office, but my guess is another third."

"Then there's our majority. What we've got to do is talk to people all over the state, find other men with our persuasions to lean on their own representatives, and make sure that they see advantages to making a United States senator out of Payson Clemson! It's an honor he'll try to refuse, but I don't see how he can weasel out of it if we get him fairly elected!"

Which is exactly what happened. The outmaneuvered governor was elevated by his old cronies to a position of national prominence. In the next election, in 1872, Larkin Flint was elected the new governor.

We did a lot of soul-searching about this last development. Larkin and I both were of mixed minds about it. On the one hand, his duty was clear. At that point he appeared to be the only man in the state who could work with a divided legislature for the benefit of Arkansas. On the other hand, our own operations were flourishing, the ranch and the cotton plantation not only prospering but also requiring constant attention. Our children were requiring constant attention as well. Matt, now 11, was so smart and so quick that Cousin Ed had already served notice that Matt would have to be sent off to boarding school soon.

The twins, too, were quick and bright, but their focus was less on studying than on doing. Already they were roping calves and mending fences and feeding stock, working with Larkin and Tobe every chance they got, with Larky trying her six-year-old best to keep up with all of them.

"We've got three boys and a tomboy," I said to Larkin.

"Well, I'll freely admit to my prejudices, but I'd say she's just about the most beautiful tomboy in creation," he answered. "It does my heart good just to look at her." He looked down at me, his teasing grin signaling what was coming next. "A miracle, I call it. How such an ugly mother could have turned out such a pretty little daughter is an out-and-out miracle!" And we put our arms around each other and laughed in satisfaction.

After much discussion and soul-searching, what we finally decided was that Larkin would continue to live in Little Rock during the week and would come back home every Friday. "That's what I'll do when the legislature is in session. The rest of the year, the job of being governor of

Arkansas is pretty small potatoes. I can stay here at home three days out of seven. And, now that we've got the railroad across the state, you and the children can come down and visit me when you're so inclined. Now and then you may decide you want to act as hostess at some big shindig."

"I do plan on enjoying the big inaugural ball they always have for the new governor. I can't think of too many other occasions that are worth the time and effort and money that's spent on them. I'd say that with Arkansas so nearly bankrupt, this is no time to be noted for lavish spending."

"The inaugural ball will likely be lavish, for Clemson's crew will want to go out with a flourish. Spending other people's money is what they do best. We might as well enjoy ourselves."

I stood with my children and Matthew and Minerva and watched Arkansas Chief Justice McClure conduct the inauguration from the marble steps of the state capitol. With his hand on the Bible and his eyes on the horizon, Larkin swore to uphold and to faithfully administer the laws of the Union and the state of his birth. I watched the hot summer sun turn his gray hair to silver and wondered if ever before such a young and hand-some man had been sworn into the governor's chair. The year was 1872. Larkin was 36; I was 28.

I looked over at Minerva, and for the first and only time in my life I saw tears in her eyes. My own eyes were dry and filled with happiness.

The governor's reception and inaugural ball were held in the Metropolitan Hotel, the state's finest and largest. We received our guests in the richly carpeted lobby, standing under glittering chandeliers, flanked by great marble columns accented by stately green palms potted in oriental urns. As the people filed by, men in their black broadcloth frock-tailed coats and bare-shouldered women in their elaborate gowns, I thought back to our wedding supper a dozen years earlier and marveled at the changes time had wrought.

Later, when the music began and we led the grand march to the melodies of a 20-piece orchestra, I thought back to when Larkin had played his fiddle for me alone and I had gloried in our solitude. But I set aside these sentimental memories and gave myself over to the enjoyment of the present.

My gown was a moiré antique silk, the color of moonlight, its skirt overlaid with venetian lace, the bodice cut low on my shoulders to show off the diamond-edged cameo that Uncle Auguste had given me so long ago. Amongst the gaudy gowns and flashing baubles that had been the costume choices of many of the wives of the newly rich carpetbaggers, the contrast was considerable.

Becky, her slender figure enhanced by the simplicity of the buttercup-yellow grosgrain silk dress she was wearing, smiled at me as a fellow conspirator. "I know what you're doing, Sarah. As you can see, I had the same thought. The simpler our dresses, the more we stand out in this crowd of show-off women."

She was right. Directly in front of us, a slender black-haired woman whirled and swooped to the rhythm of a waltz, her taffeta gown such a garish plaid of red and purple and blue and yellow as to give the effect of regimental flags flying. When the music stopped, her portly partner steered her determinedly in our direction, beads of sweat popping out all over his red face.

"Brace yourself, Becky." I was sure my voice had an edge to it, but I could not seem to help it. "You are about to meet the personal representative of no other than Mr. Jay Gould himself, plus his new wife. I met them when they came through the receiving line."

Larkin made the presentation with formality. "Rebecca, may I present Mr. and Mrs. Strasser? I first met Mr. Strasser in Washington some years ago." He continued. "Rebecca is my sister. Her husband, Dr. William Griffin, is my wife's cousin."

With a flip of her wrist and a toss of her curls, gestures that caused the diamonds that dangled from her ears and encircled her wrist to glitter in dazzling display, the young Mrs. Strasser managed to smile coyly at Larkin all the time she was speaking to Becky. "You Arkansans are such clannish people. I can see now why Larkin gets so lonesome down here in Little Rock, when he's so accustomed to such a large family. And my husband and I are always so happy to do what we can." She smiled sweetly in my direction, her small, even teeth reminding me suddenly of a pampered and confident cat.

"I do hope, Mrs. Flint, now that Larkin is governor, my husband and I will have the pleasure of entertaining you." She fluttered the dark lashes that framed her bold eyes. "We're so pleased to know there really *is* a Mrs. Flint. Actually, we've sometimes thought, my husband and I, that you were simply a figment of Larkin's imagination — a device to keep all those pretty girls at bay." She smiled sweetly up at Larkin. "I suppose you handsome men just can't help being so attractive." With the ease of long practice, she widened the focus of her attention to again include Becky and me. "I do hope you'll call me Anna. Just as I shall call you Sarah and Rebecca." She reached up to touch Larkin's cheek lightly, her huge ruby ring drawing our full attention to the gesture. "I really would hate to think that your new duties would keep you away from the company of your dear friends, Larkin."

Again, she favored me with her smile, a smile that did not seem to extend all the way to the predatory dark eyes that now assessed me thoroughly. "My husband and I have become so fond of Larkin. I am sure you can easily understand how charming we find him!" The unfamiliar nasal accents of East Side New York City echoed in my ears.

I kept my face smooth and my voice noncommittal. "How kind of you, Mrs. Strasser."

I smiled up at Larkin. "You did promise this dance to your mother, Larkin; I'm sure she has been looking forward to it." With a pleasant smile that did considerable credit to my Aunt Bereniece's training, I excused us both and turned my back on the Strassers.

The grin on Larkin's face made my own mood more joyful. "Well, as you can see, Sarah, not every guerrilla wears a Confederate uniform! That woman's as mean and treacherous as Quantrill ever thought of being, and doubly dangerous because she's got such a pretty face! Just for contrast, let me introduce you to Mrs. Albert Pike. She came late and missed the receiving line. Did it on purpose, I expect. That way she can sit in a high-backed chair and have a reception all her own!" He shook his head. "Women!"

At the far end of the long ballroom opposite the bandstand, the dowagers of the city held court. Seated in their center, her imperious dark eyes taking in every gesture and nuance of those who engaged her attention, an elderly lady in an old-fashioned black silk gown surveyed our approach.

Larkin bowed respectfully. "Mrs. Pike, may I present my wife, Sarah?"

Her lively eyes took careful measure. When she spoke, her voice was surprisingly youthful and her tone was warm.

"Sarah, I am delighted to meet you at last. I knew your grandfather. You have his eyes and his curly black hair. Welcome to Little Rock." She turned in explanation to Larkin. "The first families of Arkansas were few in number. My maiden name was Hamilton. At one time, when I was quite young, Sarah's grandfather Chouteau was a frequent caller in my father's home." Her eyes danced coquettishly. "He was a splendid dancer; not so tall as my Albert, but extraordinarily graceful." She looked at me in approval.

Her attention shifting rapidly, she concluded the amenities in order to discuss matters of a more political nature.

"My husband, General Pike, asks that I convey his regrets for his absence from so auspicious an occasion. As you may know, Larkin, Albert now maintains a residence in Washington, D.C., and is again engaged in the practice of law" — a wicked glint of mischief appeared in the dark eyes — "where, no doubt, thanks to your zeal and enterprises, he and Senator Payson Clemson will once again be forced to acknowledge each other's existence."

Larkin laughed. "Encounters that will be of considerable interest to both, I feel sure." His tone was neutral.

Her laughter matched his. "Sarah, in your husband I believe I have once more discovered a soul mate. Were I 40 years younger, I expect I might borrow a page from the menfolk, challenge you to a duel, and contest you for the pleasure of his company."

I smiled at her. "Ma'am, it would be a contest I should dread to enter upon." I meant it. She exuded the confidence of a once-beautiful woman, a woman accustomed to matching wits with the best and the brightest. She fixed her eyes on Larkin. "Do you plan on moving your family to Little Rock, Larkin?"

"We have decided against it, ma'am. Sarah will manage our holdings on Mount Petit Jean, and I will try to manage the governor's office."

"A wise decision. Albert and I long ago realized the wisdom of maintaining separate households. In fact, given my high temper" — she paused and grinned in delight. "Now don't look so surprised, Sarah. I know you've already heard about my high temper. Everybody in Little Rock talks about it. I know they do. As I was saying, Albert and I find our compatibility to be directly proportional to our absences from each other. Our affection, I assure you, has remained a constant in our lives, but our compatibility varies with distance."

This time I was the one who laughed out loud. "I wish I were going to be living near you, Mrs. Pike. I would enjoy being your friend."

"Do call me Mary Ann. And I am already your friend. Larkin, I wish to make you an offer, one to which I hope you will give serious consideration. When it is not convenient for Sarah to function as your official hostess, I should very much enjoy acting in that capacity. I believe you will agree, Larkin, that such an alliance will hold distinct advantages for you with the old-line Democrats, and possibly I could provide certain qualities of intimidation against the predatory spouses of the more aggressive carpetbaggers of your acquaintance." She glanced in distaste across the room at the Strassers.

"Anna Strasser is not to be underestimated. Behind that pretty face and vulgar facade there is an agile brain. But let us talk of more important matters. When you convene the legislature, Larkin, what is your first order of business?"

"To restore the vote to the former Confederates. Everything else has to take a backseat to that. Until we restore a healthy political climate in this state, we'll be forever saddled with graft and debt. As I see it, we're going to have to revive the Democrats to keep us Republicans healthy. That's my first priority. Sending Payson Clemson to Washington was only the first step. Now we've got to take positive actions in Arkansas."

Which is exactly what Larkin did. He appointed honest men, both Republican and Democrat, to the election board; he took the state militia out of the control of carpetbaggers and placed it in the hands of men native to Arkansas; then, true to his word, he persuaded the legislature to pass a franchise amendment, a bill that restored the vote to men who had fought for the Confederacy.

This last move proved to be the straw that broke the camel's back, the camel in this case being Payson Clemson, who in the meantime had been assessing the entire proceedings from his Senate seat in Washington. No one, least of all Larkin, expected Clemson to give up the reins of power without a fight, but none expected the direction from which the fight finally came.

Once Larkin had ensured that white men and colored men had equal access to the voting booth, he took the next step in his plan. He orchestrated a major move to create vacant seats in the legislature. I remember well the warm summer evening when Larkin sat on our terrace at Petit Jean, smoking his pipe and explaining his strategy to me.

"Remember, Sarah, when I asked Father how many men in the legislature were primarily there out of personal greed? And he estimated about a third. Well, it was a shrewd count. I asked brother Sam to spend time with me, over at the state house, sizing them up. Sam counts 30; my count is

35. Time will soon tell. What I've done is to exercise my powers as governor. You will remember Clemson gave himself nearly unlimited powers, and the legislature hasn't revoked them yet."

His grin was as wide and happy as that of a boy. "Well, I've declared all the new patronage appointments ready to be filled. That means every state cabinet post, every tax collector's job, every judgeship, even all the way down to justice of the peace — they're all waiting to be filled."

"And you're going to fill them with honest men." It was not a question on my part.

Larkin laughed out loud. "Ah, Sarah, that's where you're wrong! I'm in the process of offering up the entire slate of jobs to those 30 or so greedy men now in the state legislature. I'm bringing them in, one at a time, the toughest cases first. Do you remember that Payson Clemson redrew the county lines and created eight new counties in Arkansas? Well, these jobs are new, and all to be officered by appointment. I was elected on the same ticket as General Grant, and now I've got the full powers that Clemson expected to exercise himself. I've got nearly 40 lifetime appointments to pass out to the faithful."

I was indignant. "Do you mean to tell me, Larkin Flint, that you are actually offering lifetime appointments to crooked men?"

"I sure am, Sarah. What I'll do is have my private secretary, Mr. Bates, bring them in one at a time. Then I'll say, 'Sir, this session is virtually at an end. If there are any favors I can confer on you as a reward for your tireless toil in the interest of the public good, I will take great pleasure in doing so!' Well, Sarah, I am here to tell you, these radical carpetbaggers are biting at my prepared bait like fish in a millpond. They're acting like a bunch of bumpy suckers, swallowing the bait whole."

All at once I saw the light. "So all those legislative seats will now be vacant and open to be filled in this coming election. Now that the amnesty bill has been passed, it will be an open and honest election."

"You've got it. Putting those men into county patronage jobs is a small price to pay for an honest and healthy two-party legislature. I count it a job well done. Why don't you bring me a dram of that good corn whiskey Ned sent down in celebration of the governor's race? I do believe a few sips would be mighty tasty on a summer evening. And maybe you ought to put in some sugar and a few sprigs of mint." He stretched his long legs.

"Well, Sarah, I always knew the country was worth fighting for." He looked across the wide valley toward the misty blue-gray ridges of the distant mountains. From the side yard we could hear Larky's laughter as she ran with Linney's children among the fragrant jasmine bushes and bright hollyhocks in one last game of tag before bedtime. In the distance we could hear the hoofbeats of their horses as Will and Gus raced each other up the steep road. Melodies from Matt's guitar sounded softly in the twilight as he sat on the back porch and improvised his serenade of the moment.

When he looked back at me, Larkin had a look of real satisfaction on his face. "This country's not only worth fighting for, it's worth maneuvering for. I've got no apology for what I've done. On the contrary, I take considerable pride in what's been accomplished." He sipped his julep in quiet satisfaction and took my hand in a rare moment of tenderness.

I cherished the days we had together that summer. Many a time later did I look back and realize it was the lull before the storm. After Larkin went back to Little Rock, his life became so hectic and so filled with legislative manipulations that the children and I saw far too little of him. It was a lonesome winter for Larky and Gus and Will and me. Matt went off to boarding school that fall, the academy at Fayetteville. Until he left I did not realize how much of the work and the supervision of the plantation he had already begun. I missed him fiercely.

Larkin came home when he could, of course, but down in Little Rock the ship of state was rocking, and he had to be there to keep his steady hand on the helm. Even when he was home, he was preoccupied. The summer seemed a long way off. Our good times together became more and more infrequent.

Chapter 40

UP IN WASHINGTON, Payson Clemson finally chose his partner and formed the alliance that Larkin had been dreading all along. Clemson allowed himself to be purchased by Jay Gould and swung his considerable support to the implementation of laws that would advance the cause of Gould's railroad interests. Already Gould was well on his way to controlling the Denver Pacific, the Kansas Pacific, the Missouri Pacific, and the Union Pacific.

Under Clemson's governorship, new railroad companies had sprung up all over Arkansas; by the time Larkin had maneuvered Clemson to Washington, 86 separate railroads existed in the state on paper, and it had loaned these paper companies over $10,000,000. Gould had no intention of repaying this monumental sum of money. Payson Clemson had planned to allow these railroads to use their own stock as legal tender to wipe out their debt, but Larkin absolutely refused to allow this fraudulent manipulation.

In addition, Larkin announced that under no conditions whatsoever would anymore railroad bonds be issued in Arkansas. The state was too deeply indebted as it was. Payson Clemson was furious; Jay Gould was dangerous; and the result was a 30-day shooting war in Arkansas.

It began in an unlikely way. Joseph Bender — Old Brindletail — had been Larkin's opponent for the governorship nearly two years earlier. Now, Old Brindletail mostly spent his time hanging around the state house and sending extensive reports back to Payson Clemson. Suddenly, out of the clear blue sky of an April day in 1874, Joseph Bender declared himself to be the legal governor of Arkansas.

At eleven o'clock in the morning, Joseph Bender presented himself at the chamber of a loyal Clemson appointee, the judge of the county circuit court, who ruled that Bender was actually the legal governor. Within minutes, a dozen armed men appeared to escort Bender over to the state capitol. There, with muskets at the ready, they marched down the marble halls, burst through the door into the governor's office, and demanded Larkin's resignation and surrender.

Of course they got neither.

Old Brindletail Bender roared and threatened and shook his fist while his henchmen pointed guns at Larkin's heart, but Larkin refused to move. Finally, with Larkin refusing to budge and Bender's men unwilling to shoot him in cold blood, they finally dragged him out of the state house.

They threw him to the pavement, marched back onto the state house grounds, slammed and locked the iron gate, and Joseph Bender sat down at the governor's desk. In response to this signal, 300 of Bender's men marched into view and seized the state militia arsenal on the state house grounds. Nearly nine years to the day after Lee had surrendered, the shooting war for the future of Arkansas began.

With his eyes flashing and his jaw set, Larkin marched over to the Anthony House, three blocks away, established his headquarters, and proceeded to organize an attack on Bender's forces. First he wired President Grant, requesting Grant's support and the use of the arms and ammunition stored at the U.S. Arsenal. Next, he issued a proclamation stating his right to the governorship and declaring martial law. Then he asked the people of Arkansas for their support.

Grant refused to take sides. Payson Clemson had engineered the whole thing, and Grant was wary of a trap. He wired both Larkin and Bender, refusing them the use of the U.S. Arsenal.

In the meantime, Larkin armed for war. Brindletail Bender assembled his colored troops in and around the state house and dug in to withstand a siege. Larkin's supporters came in from all over the state, for he had two advantages from the start.

The first was intangible: an earned reputation as an honest man. The second was highly tangible: except for the state house and the U.S. Arsenal, Larkin controlled the city. He controlled the approaches to the city by steamboat and railroad, and he controlled the telegraph office. In response to Larkin's telegrams, men from all over the state hurried to Little Rock.

Jesse headed a company of volunteers from north-central Arkansas; from the western part of the state, Ridge led a contingent of 100 men to Larkin's defense. From eastern Arkansas, a former general of the Confederate cavalry rode up to the Anthony House and offered his services in defense of honest government. Ben Wilcox rode in at the head of a column of 100 men. In addition to the bands of grimly determined citizens who came to show their support, the prospect of conflict brought out anxious politicians, the Northern press, and two or three tootling brass bands.

From our residence on top of Petit Jean Mountain, I could do nothing except wonder and worry. The two men that I depended on most left for Little Rock as soon as they heard the news. I had assumed that Tobe would feel it his duty to stay with me regardless of circumstances, but I had misjudged him. No sooner had Cousin Ed ridden up the mountain with the news than Tobe was yelling for his horse, calling for Linney to pack his saddlebags, and preparing to join Larkin in Little Rock. Cousin Ed announced his intention of going with Tobe.

I was absolutely astonished. "Cousin Ed, do you mean to say you're going off, too? You didn't even fight in the Civil War! Why on earth do you feel called to go now?"

"The point at issue is whether or not a free people have the right to decide their own government. If a crooked man in Washington can pick out another crooked man in Arkansas, put him in the governor's chair, and use

Federal troops to keep him there, then the whole Civil War was fought in vain. I'm not doing this for Larkin. I'm answering to my own conscience." And off he went, his old felt hat set squarely on top of his old gray head.

With Larkin in Little Rock fighting the carpetbaggers and scalawags, it was up to me to get the cotton crop planted. That was a lot easier said than done. Will and Gus were nearly 11 years old and big for their age, so I put them right out in the fields chopping cotton with the darkies. I kept busy from dawn until dark, riding around the fields, checking on the plows and the mules and on the men doing the plowing, to say nothing of checking on the colored men and women and children moving up and down those long cotton rows chopping the weeds away from the bright green cotton plants. Actually, I came to enjoy it. There is something wonderful about the soft, early light of breezy spring mornings when the sun is first sending its long shadows across the land. Even in the evenings, when my body ached from long hours in the saddle, riding around those big fields and up and down that steep mountain, my sense of accomplishment far outweighed the fatigue.

For 30 days the two armies faced each other, taunting, skirmishing, and sometimes firing on each other. Up in Washington, Payson Clemson appealed to President Grant on behalf of Bender; Albert Pike organized arguments on behalf of Larkin. Finally, after the shootings and speech making and maneuvering had gone on for over a month, President Grant issued a proclamation recognizing Larkin as governor and commanded all in arms against him to return to their homes.

Larkin assembled the legislature and called for a statewide convention to focus on governmental reform. Reconstruction in Arkansas was over.

On June 4, I took the children and rode the train to Little Rock to stand pridefully by Larkin's side when he convened the new session of the legislature. Every seat in the hall was filled; the mood of the assembly was triumphant. All eyes were on Larkin. He began his address to the assembly by reading from an editorial from the *Arkansas Gazette*: "In time of public commotion and popular tumult, the rude, the ignorant, and the wicked frequently rise to power. . . . This has been the history of Arkansas since Reconstruction, and the state and the people have suffered grievously from misrule. . . . Now the people of Arkansas, for the first time in 14 years, rejoice in the full enjoyment of their civil and political rights."

He paused, faced the crowd, and continued: "Nearly 11 years ago, at Gettysburg, President Abraham Lincoln called on the people of this land to begin to heal the nation's wounds. Today I ask you to join with me in healing the wounds we have inflicted on each other and on Arkansas. I know of no better time to begin than this day."

Arkansas celebrated that day and far into the night. That evening, Larkin and I sat in state at the head table of the new legislature's celebration dinner. To Larkin's left was Mary Ann Pike; her venerable silver-haired husband was by my side. Few men could sit at a table with the massive and stately Albert Pike without having his stature diminished by comparison, but Larkin actually appeared to be enhanced by the contrast.

His prematurely silver hair emphasizing the bronzed skin and sculptured contours of his handsome face, Larkin presided over the assembly with the dignified elegance of one who was born to command. Flushed with happiness, I reflected that the hard and lonely times of work and struggle had yielded precious fruit. To my right, Albert Pike engaged my attention.

"Madam, I am sure these sentiments are not new to your ears, but I must again emphasize that your husband is a remarkable man. Not one man in a thousand would have exhibited the political adroitness to have gathered at his head table such recent adversaries as the commander of the Federal forces and the radical Republican Senator Payson Clemson. And not one man in ten thousand would have been able to convince us all that it is a most pleasurable evening marking a truly significant occasion." The shrewd eyes assessed me thoroughly. "You do the governor great credit, ma'am. Your beauty is widely acknowledged, as are your abilities."

I blushed, whether in modesty or in happiness, I do not know. The general continued. "It will be my great honor to work for further changes in our state. And to my mind, the most needful change is the replacement of our current senator, Payson Clemson, with a statesman of honesty. I have heard rumors that your husband intends returning to private life at the end of his term. May I inquire as to what your reaction would be if he were to be elected to serve as Arkansas's senator?"

I gave him an honest answer. "Sir, I have seen too little of my husband these last few years. My goal is to live with Larkin in peace and prosperity."

"Well said, ma'am. I see that your own reputation for adroitness is well earned." With a satisfied look, the general turned to his right to engage in conversation with the dignified commander of the U.S. garrison at Little Rock.

Later, as we mingled with the festive crowd in the lively ballroom, I stood with Mary Ann Pike and her husband. "A far different occasion, sir, than the one on which we first met."

The sharp eyes twinkled above the flowing white beard. "I thought on that night I had never seen a more beautiful bride, nor one more in love with her husband." He paused, then aimed his next words straight at his wife. "Except for you, Mary Ann, on the night we were wed." To my intense surprise, Mary Ann's dark eyes sparkled suddenly with the glitter of unshed tears.

"So you do still remember, Albert." Her voice was rich with remembrance, but with an effort of will and a toss of her head, she focused on the events at hand and spoke to me.

"Your reception has brought out every fashionable new gown in the state of Arkansas. Even I, as you can see, finally succumbed to these new and atrocious fashions and had my dressmaker design my new dress with a bustle." She laughed. "A fashion that flatters my figure entirely too little by exposing the lines of my large stomach entirely too much. Can you imagine, Sarah, that when Albert and I were wed, my waist measured a mere 20 inches?"

"I could span it with my two hands." General Pike, looking at his powerful hands, then at his wife's very considerable middle, shrugged aside the memory. "A skill of no great importance, as I recall."

Mary Ann pursued her own train of thought. "How can it be, Sarah, that for this festive evening, the always in-fashion Anna Strasser decided to wear a decidedly out-of-date hoop skirt?"

"It is, however, an absolutely beautiful hoop skirt." I observed. "It's got lacy ruffles and ribbons and bows and rosebuds all over it. It's so distracting and there's so much lace that it is hard to tell how much is Anna and how much is dress."

Mary Ann's wise eyes gleamed suddenly. "Could it be that the treacherous Anna has something there to conceal?"

I looked over at the Strassers, not bothering to hide my distaste. "Surely, now, we'll be seeing the last of the Strassers. Without any hope of easy pickings in Arkansas from fraudulent railroad bonds, wouldn't you think Jay Gould would transfer his attention — and the Strassers — somewhere else?"

"I expect he will." Albert Pike's tone was thoughtful. "Whether Gould's a man who seeks revenge, I do not know. But Payson Clemson does, and

I find it passing strange that Larkin was able to persuade him to be a part of this festive evening, an evening that is, in reality, a celebration of Arkansas's victory over Payson's own henchmen."

Events moved fast that summer and fall. Larkin's term was drawing to a close. I rejoiced and waited for the day when he would be home for good. It was no surprise when the Republicans again nominated him for governor and no surprise when he declined. It should have been no surprise to me, although it was, when the Democrats then held their convention and nominated Larkin for governor. Again, he declined.

But the voices of the people were still inclined in Larkin's direction. When the legislature met that fall, the first order of business was the election of a United States senator. Larkin Houston Flint was their choice. It was none other than Albert Pike himself who rode up our steep mountain road to convey the invitation to Larkin.

The general was nothing if not eloquent. "History is calling you, sir, calling you to lend your intelligence and enterprise in the building of the second century of our magnificent nation! In less than two short years, the United States of America will celebrate its first century of existence as the most noble experiment of government known to mankind! I beg you, sir, to permit Arkansas to have the honor of sending forth to Washington the most able of its native sons."

Larkin's response was measured. "Sir, please know how mindful I am of the honor being offered me. But I have longed for a life in which I once again live at home with my family and to enjoy once more the pleasures of the life I left behind." His outflung arm drew Pike's attention to our surroundings. "I do not mean to be boastful, sir, when I ask you to look around you at the finest view" — he paused, and smiled down at me — "and the finest wife in Arkansas. I am sure you can understand my reluctance to be away from both."

The general was not one to be brooked by such arguments. "I fully understand, and I completely agree. But you have an additional blessing. I am told that in your absence, your capable wife can translate your wishes with such competence as to cause your prosperity to flourish unimpeded by your absence. An advantage not enjoyed by every man in public office, I do assure you.

"Yet I would argue that there are considerations here beyond home and hearth. Whether we have in Washington an honest and enlightened government that rules in the best interests of the many rather than the enrichment of the few will depend on the caliber of men in positions of power. Ulysses S. Grant's term will soon end. Nearly a decade of graft and corruption can end with it, if the reins of government go into honest hands."

The white-maned, white-bearded head of Albert Pike assumed the aspect of Jove as he fixed his piercing gaze on Larkin. "Think of your ancestry, man! Service to your country runs deep in your blood! Over and over again, your grandfather, Sam Houston, put aside his love of hearth and home to serve his country in Washington! Will you do less?"

"What I will do I cannot say at this time, sir. What I will promise is this: Give me until the end of this week to think on the matter, and on Monday morning I will take the train to Little Rock to render my decision to you and to the legislature."

By Sunday we had talked the matter over from a dozen angles without seeing a clear answer. As a family of five — for Matt was away at his second term at the academy — we climbed into the big buggy and headed for church. I looked at Matt's empty place and missed him with the sudden overwhelming longing of a mother for her firstborn. I wondered suddenly whether I was being overly selfish in my own fierce wish to hold my husband and my children close at home within the family circle.

We made a handsome group as we walked down the aisle. I thanked God for His blessings to date and asked for His guidance for the future. Across the aisle sat Piety and Jesse Rankin, their three little boys arranged like stairsteps on the bench between them. Ahead of us I could see the substantial backs of Ben and Phoebe Wilcox, while behind us I could hear the whispers of the sisters, Vinnie and Nellie, as they made comment to each other concerning the foibles and behavior of various members of the congregation.

The morning service began in the usual fashion. There were the opening prayers and the enthusiastically sung hymns followed by the reading from the Holy Scriptures.

Our plump little butterball of a preacher announced his text with the assurance of a man who has every confidence that he speaks as the unquestioned representative of Jehovah.

"I direct your attention this morning to the 11th chapter of Proverbs: 'The integrity of the upright shall guide them: but the perverseness of transgressors shall destroy them. . . . A talebearer revealeth secrets: but he that is of a faithful spirit concealeth the matter.'"

I settled myself in for at least an hour of exhortation. Little Preacher Pierce was nothing if not long-winded.

My mind reverted to the passionate joining of our bodies that had pleasured Larkin and me so considerably during the dawning hours of this Sabbath day, and I wondered whether any of our solemn-faced neighbors had experienced a similar enjoyment. If so, they gave no sign. We sat in somber attention, anticipating the end of the sermon.

I heard with mild surprise the shrill whistle of a train as it approached the town crossing. No train was scheduled until evening, but I dismissed the noise from my mind and focused my attention on the preacher, who was steadily working himself up to a state of excitement.

I wondered for the hundredth time how such a small man could be possessed of such a large voice and such a compelling need to use it. The sermon was drawing to its close, an ending always signaled by the preacher's unvarying and thundering quotation of his favorite verse: "'Be not deceived; God is not mocked: for whatsoever a man soweth, that shall he also reap'!"

I shifted in my seat, my mind already considering various aspects of our Sunday dinner, when an alien sound brought a sharp end to the preacher's discourse.

The double doors at the back of the church were thrown open with such force as to leave them banging against the walls. Preacher Pierce, his exhoration interrupted in midsentence, regarded the new arrival in undisguised astonishment, his small mouth pursed open in amazement, his eyes as startled as those of a possum in the path of a hunter.

Down the aisle swept a tall, heavily veiled woman dressed all in black. In her arms she carried a baby, a small infant whose weak and pitiful wails were the only sounds in the sudden silence that enveloped the congregation. She approached Larkin with the swift predatory glide of one who has sighted her prey. With one quick, sure motion she dropped the crying baby into Larkin's lap. The noonday sun streaming through the church window flashed sudden fire from the large ruby ring on her long white fingers.

Her ringing tones echoed throughout our small church as she pronounced the words that were both indictment and valedictory: "That which you gave to me, I now return to you! Take this child, for you are its father!"

Her motions as smooth as those of a snake, she turned, glided back down the aisle, and disappeared out the church door. Her words hung in the air, words uttered in the unmistakeable East Side New York accent of Anna Strasser.

His face suddenly flushed with the deep red of violent anger, Larkin wrenched his eyes away from the pitiful little bundle of humanity that he now held in his arms and looked at me. I met his eyes, my own wide with the cold horror of one who has just looked into an abyss.

"Sarah, I swear to you, this baby is not mine!" His tone was anguished.

I sat in silence. Beside me, our children wondered and waited. I could feel Larky's slender body tremble. Or was the trembling mine? I did not know. What I do know is that I continued to sit in silence, my eyes dry, my head high.

Larkin stood, the baby in his arms, walked up to the front of the church, and addressed the congregation.

"As God is my witness, this is not my child! And, as God is my witness, I mean to find out what devil spawned this trick!"

He turned to Preacher Pierce, who stood standing with his prissy face now set in the stern lines of righteous judgment. Larkin held the child out to the preacher. "Here, Preacher, you take it. This baby's as much yours as mine, for I did not father this child!"

Instead, the preacher pounded his pulpit with his clenched left fist. With his right hand he pointed an accusing finger at Larkin and again thundered his favorite words: "'Be not deceived; God is not mocked: for whatsoever a man soweth, that shall he also reap'!"

Across the aisle I could see Piety's shocked and sorrowful face; all around us I could hear the stirrings and whispers of the titillated congregation. I rose from my seat, motioned for my children to follow me, and walked out the church door.

With one quick sweep of his hand, Larkin knocked the pewter plates from the offertory table and placed the baby on the table in front of the pulpit. The clang of the plates and the spatter of the scattered coins accompanied Larkin's statements to the congregation.

"If there be one among you who has it in his heart to show compassion, I ask you to look after this baby. I mean to look after my own."

His swift steps followed me to the buggy. He climbed in and took the reins, and we started off down the river road to the waiting ferry at a swift trot. As we reached the ferry, the urgent sound of a train whistle gave signal to the town of its departure.

Captain Hern was full of information. "Looks like Lewisburg Landing

got visited by its first private railroad car this morning. Pulled up, switched
its engine around, and left again in an hour's time. They say there was not
but three passengers on it. Some woman that kept her veil on the whole
time, a baby, and a little skinny darky that was brought along to look after
the baby. The conductor said the pore little brat cried the whole trip, all the
way from Little Rock." He interrupted his monologue, looked searchingly
at our silent faces, and abruptly lapsed into a silence of his own.

Not another word was spoken, not even by the children, as our buggy
began its climb to our home. When we reached Cousin Ed and Cousin
Alta's gate, Larkin stopped the buggy.

"You children get out and go over to your Cousin Alta's house and ask
her to feed you your dinner. Your mother and I need to be alone."

We rode up the mountain without another word, our fierce anger a living presence between us.

Inside the house we faced each other.

"I've said it once, but I'll say it one more time. That child is not mine.
I've never laid a hand on Anna Strasser. That pitiful whimpering brat is
somebody's bastard, I have no doubt. But it is not mine! And this is the
last time I expect to have to say so, Sarah!

"By God, when a man's own wife has her doubts about him, how in
God's green earth can a man expect others to believe him? You shamed me
today, Sarah, by letting that bitch trick you into turning against me!" His
face red, his eyes hard, his voice throbbing with a fury that his steely resolve could barely control, he stared down at me, challenging my reply.

My anger matched his own.

"How dare you talk about shame! How dare you! Even if the child is
not yours — and since you tell me it is not yours I will believe you — why
is it that every man in that congregation did not doubt that it could very
well have been yours?"

The old wounds opened up and began to throb with a pain that caused
my voice to sob. "Is it not enough that I am forced to live with a flesh-and-
blood reminder of your lust — with Ocie Casey's bastard? Must I be
forced again to look in the eyes of others and see pity? Don't you talk to
me about shame, Larkin Flint! You don't know the meaning of the word!"

"Sarah, for God's sake, that bastard is not mine! They've set a trap for
me — Clemson and Jay Gould and Strasser and others. God knows whose
child that is, or where Anna Strasser got it."

"Oh, I think it is hers. She was already showing last June, when Mary

Ann Pike remarked on the hoop skirt she wore to the ball. Who knows who got it on her — I'm sure her favors were available to many!"

He was beginning to calm down. "Then, in the name of common sense, Sarah, if you can see that it was a trick to ruin me, to cause the voters to turn against me, and to shame me out of the Senate race, then why is it that you have turned against me? Sarah, how can you look me in the eye and tell me that during this past terrible year you believe I would be fool enough — much less to have the time — to dally with the likes of Anna Strasser?"

I faced him and gritted my teeth and spoke the hard truth.

"I don't. What I believe is that lately you've been away from me far more than you've been with me. And I know your needs. I know you well enough now, Larkin Flint, to know your ways, and I know how often your body turns to mine when you are home. What I think you do on those times when the need for a woman comes on you overly strong is you go out and grab whatever whore is handy, satisfy your wants, and get on about your business!"

The quickly suppressed glint of surprise in his eyes gave terrible answer to my accusation.

We looked at each other, breathing hard, two people fighting for everything we held dear. Suddenly, the waves of nausea in my throat forced their way past my lips. The sound of my retching was no more harsh than the sounds of our words.

He waited until I was calm. When he spoke, his words came slowly. "Sarah, why God created man with needs of the flesh that cry out to be satisfied is beyond my understanding. Men differ from women. While I will admit there have been times — and they've been few — when there were temptations of the flesh of which the less said the better, none was of any importance whatsoever. Needs of the flesh that can be satisfied by any whore that comes along have nothing to do with you and me." He looked steadily at me. "You and the children are the core of my life. You know that, Sarah."

"We used to be. Power and politics have moved us to one side."

His response was swift and hard. "Don't forget, Sarah, it was you who urged me into politics in the first place. You were the one who kept telling me I owed it to the country."

"Giving service to your country and consorting with whores are two very different things! I will never believe that all men in power have such carnal knowledge of whores! Look at your own father! You know in your heart he would never consider such a thing!"

Larkin gave me a level look. "But Minerva has always been at his side. When Father was governor, he was not subjected to needless temptation."

All at once I saw my choices laid out in front of me, plain as day, but I could not bring myself to deal with them. For the first time in my life, I gave Larkin Flint a direct order.

"Pack your valise and carry that poor screaming little bastard back down to Little Rock and give it back to Anna Strasser. You're expected to meet with the legislature tomorrow, anyway. They expect to hear your decision."

We both saw clearly the trap Payson Clemson had sprung.

"You can beat him at his own game. The one thing Clemson's not expecting is to have you meet with the legislature as though nothing has happened. That's a possibility he's not counting on."

"To hell with the legislature, and to hell with Payson Clemson. Let's get this thing settled between you and me. Will you go with me, Sarah?"

I saw his drift. Likewise, I saw no need to make it easy for him.

"I'll drive you to the train. I will be seen publicly with you when it is needful. And in the here and now I mean to put a good face on this for the sake of the children. But do not think this matter to be settled. It is by no means settled. I will go through the motions of acting like your wife in public. That does not mean that our future is decided. I mean to come back home to make up my mind." I looked at him as though I was looking at a stranger. "And I would venture to suggest that you might give some thought as to how you expect to spend the rest of your life. For there is no give left in me. If I decide to remain your wife — and I may not — there will be no more whores in your life."

"Don't threaten me, Sarah." His eyes were cold as ice.

"That was not a threat."

In silence he packed his valise. In silence we climbed back in the buggy to ride back to the church. There we found Preacher Pierce, still on his knees in prayer, his loud voice importuning the Almighty in tones designed to be heard by as many as possible. The baby, now silent, remained on the table where Larkin had placed it.

I had heard enough. I picked up the soggy little bundle and handed it to Larkin without a word. Together we left the church, climbed back in the buggy, and drove to the railroad depot. God knows the thoughts that were in Larkin's mind as we sat there waiting for the train. My own mind churned with words that both pride and prudence forbade me to utter. We sat in total silence. Even the baby was quiet, whether in sleep or in sickness I could not tell. And to speak the bitter truth, I did not care. The whistle of the train came as a relief.

When he stepped down out of the buggy, Larkin turned to face me.

"Sarah, I would give everything I own if we could start over."

"I know you would." With a flick of the whip I turned the horse around and headed for home, my back straight and my head high.

Chapter 41

THE MONDAY MORNING TRAIN brought an unexpected emissary. I watched Mary Ann Pike laboriously maneuver her considerable bulk out of the rented hack that had brought her to my door. I realized anew the importance of Larkin Flint in the eyes of those who were attempting to frame Arkansas's political future. Consequently, as I walked down the steps to make her welcome, I braced myself against the persuasions that were likely to be forthcoming. But I had misjudged her motives.

Although her practiced eye appraised my surroundings in appreciation and admiration, the wife of General Albert

Pike had not undertaken her tiring journey to make small talk.

"I intend to return to Little Rock on the afternoon train, Sarah, which leaves us very little time." She waved aside my offer of dinner. "Later, perhaps. For now, I'll take a cup of tea. What needs to be said can be said better on an empty stomach. Not so much for my sake as for yours, child. Ours is a topic that needs to be discussed with clear minds."

Once seated, her regal bulk occupying most of the space on my Uncle Auguste's tapestry-covered love seat, she began her analysis.

"Sarah, you have been forced to face a hard choice, one assiduously avoided by most women, and avoided for good reason. You have been forced by painful circumstances to confront and acknowledge the possibility of your husband's infidelity. This knowledge now forces a decision that will affect your happiness — and your financial well-being — for the rest of your life."

I interrupted her in astonishment. "Mary Ann, I thought you had come here today to persuade me of the importance of Larkin's running for the Senate."

Her response was that of one wise in the ways of the world. "Sarah, Larkin would be an asset to the country, and a credit to Arkansas, but our nation will survive, with or without Larkin Flint in the Senate. No, I have come as your friend. Last night I was privy to the overly frank discussion between Larkin and Albert. I consulted neither man as to my journey here today." She paused, took a sip of tea, and proceeded. "In fact, I no longer consult anyone as to my actions. And that simple truth has a bearing on our discussion today."

I looked into her shrewd old eyes. "Mary Ann, I need all the help you can give me. I count it as an act of love that you have come here today. Please tell me what you've come to say."

"Very well. Here are your options; there are three. First, there is the option of divorce." In response to my sharp intake of breath, she held up a restraining hand. "Do not act so shocked. It is a legal and viable option, one that Larkin would fight but that you could win. You would win at great cost, both financial and emotional. Your children would suffer. Be assured they would not hold you blameless, for children infinitely prefer to have their parents preserve a facade of happiness. I understand that your inheritance formed the basis of Larkin's current wealth. Know, however, that the courts will see that wealth as belonging primarily to your husband.

Furthermore, as a divorced woman you would not be received by respectable people anywhere."

I interrupted her. "There is another option. I hold the title to my Uncle Auguste's home in Kansas City, and I have money in my own name — not a lot, but some. I could take the children and live in Kansas City among family who would receive me kindly."

Her response was matter-of-fact. "If you did so, Larkin would divorce you for desertion. Never think that any man of his iron will would so easily give up the children. Then the same penalties would apply. As a divorced woman among a family of Roman Catholics, your marital status would be a perpetual cause of embarrassment to the Chouteau family."

I argued with her. "But that's not fair! I'm not the transgressor! Why should I be the one to be penalized?"

"We are not discussing what *should* be, Sarah. This is a discussion of what would be. Do not waste my time. Believe me, divorce is an option with harsh penalties and few rewards. So I will proceed with your second option, one to which I fear you have already given much consideration. Your second option is to maintain your marriage, put as good an outward appearance on it as possible, and continue as before. You have built a magnificent establishment here on top of this mountain. It is, indeed, a small kingdom; Larkin takes well to the role of a ruler." She looked at me astutely. "And you thrive, my dear, whether or not you know it, on your role as his queen.

"As I was saying, you and the children can continue your lives here, Larkin can travel from Washington as opportunity and affection dictate such journeys, and the two of you can present the united front to which you are already accustomed."

"How can I do that knowing in my heart that he will turn to other women when he feels the need? How can I bring myself to share his bed, not knowing how many whores have already been in it? If he goes to the Senate, he'll be there months at a time. I know now that Larkin won't go that long without a woman."

Her dark eyes showed pity. "You can live that life only if you develop a hard shell, a protective armor, a shield against caring too much. But that shield has a price. Shields are built of anger and sarcasm, self-sufficiency, and loneliness. When old transgressions have not been forgiven, old wounds do not heal. Sharp anger becomes a weapon, whether for old griefs or new circumstances. The very love that still draws you together will give new flames to the embers of old angers." She thought for a while. "Were Larkin to decide to give up all political aspirations and to live here with you on top of this mountain, and were you to make that choice without forgiveness, you could not tolerate the situation.

"Jealousy is a terrible disease. It gnaws at the very vitals to breed distrust and resentment and self-pity. In the long run, Sarah, the choices we make show on our faces. Think on the faces of the women you know well. And of the men you know. Think hard, and reflect well."

I interrupted her, my voice resentful. "Why should all the penalties be mine? It was not I who sinned. Why should Larkin get off so easy? Why am I the one to suffer?"

"Be realistic, Sarah." Her tone was impatient. "I assure you that I did not make this tiring journey to redesign the world. This is a man's world. I do not plan to dwell on the obvious, except to point out that were you to have been the one to have admitted adultery, the penalties would be unbearably severe. Let us confine ourselves to the reality of the world we live in. Even Anna Strasser, decadent woman that she is, will be ostracized from the world of decent people. I have no doubt that when that private railroad car reaches New York City, Aaron Strasser will throw her back into the same gutter in which he found her! He used her to his purpose, and now her usefulness is over."

I looked at her in astonishment. "They are gone? Did she take the baby with her?"

"That train stopped briefly in Little Rock. Strasser and Clemson and their servants boarded in haste. They used the private coach of Jay Gould. I understand their destination to be New York City.

"But I have not answered your question. No, she did not take her child. The baby is dead. I have no doubt it was dead long before Larkin reached Little Rock with it. It was dead when he brought it to my door. I insisted that an immediate autopsy be performed. That baby died of malnutrition. By the doctor's best estimate, it had been deprived of its mother's milk for many days. That cold-hearted and selfish woman had simply refused to give it suck in order to dry up her own milk."

She looked at me. "A decision for which you should be profoundly grateful, Sarah." Such relief flowed through me that I trembled. "The child is buried. Let its bones lie in peace."

She proceeded. "This brings us now to your third option. You can decide to forgive. If you do decide to forgive, you must also most diligently strive to forget. You have now the choice of going forward with Larkin to build your future together. The choice must be yours."

"Ah, but the choice is Larkin's," I argued. "He must decide whether to go to the Senate or to come back home and live here with me. He is the only one who knows whether our life here will satisfy him now. After all, he's had the taste of power, and he likes the taste. He is the only one who knows what it will take to make him happy."

"Well said. Can you accept his choice if that choice leads him to the Senate? Can you not only forgive Larkin's past indiscretions, but also be willing to share him with all those people who will have a fair claim on his attentions in the future?"

I thought long and hard. "I can do so, Mary Ann, but only if I am by his side. That means that where he goes, I must go. I will not stay here to manage this big undertaking, leaving him free of any responsibilities and leaving me wondering about his faithfulness."

"Could you live in Washington without resenting the sacrifice? Are you willing to rear your children in that climate of artifice and intrigue?"

"The more important question, Mary Ann, is whether Larkin can truly be happy here on this mountain in Arkansas, now that he tasted power."

"That question is at the heart of the matter, I fear. For some men, power is an acquired taste, one readily put aside in favor of plainer, more wholesome fare. For others, like Albert Pike and Sam Houston, the lust for power runs in the blood, part and parcel of their being."

She rose. "I believe now, Sarah, I will accept your kind invitation to dinner. I am sure you have an excellent cook. Then I must go directly to catch my train."

It was when she was leaving that I finally asked the question. "Mary Ann, why is it that you decided to give me this great gift of friendship and counsel? Was it really for Larkin, or for me?"

Her eyes filled suddenly with hot tears. "I would not have you think that Albert and I have not had our times of love. I have given birth to seven children. The last two died in infancy. Of our first five — five with such promise; five with so much to offer life — only two remain. Five years ago we lost our beautiful black-haired daughter Isadore." She steadied her voice, controlled her tears, and looked at me without a trace of self-pity. "Isadore had accompanied Albert to Memphis. Albert had asked her to act as his hostess there." There was a long pause, then: "She died by her own hand. Five years ago. You remind me of Isadore. My curly-headed daughter with her honest blue eyes.

"No, Sarah, I did not undertake this journey today because of my fondness for Larkin, though I am, indeed, much taken with Larkin and count him as my friend. My reasons for coming here today may be complex, but they are grounded in love. Life is too short to make the wrong choices."

With a light kiss on my cheek, she climbed into the buggy and set her face forward.

I stood alone on my terrace and looked at my surroundings as if I were seeing them for the last time. Could I possibly bring myself to a decision that would cause me to leave this majestic mountain, this place with its whispering pines, its clear rushing streams, its fiery sunsets, its craggy bluffs, and its broad meadows? I looked down at the valley below, at the broad river rolling past the rich, flat cotton fields. I looked across, lifting up my eyes to the blue-gray ridges of the mountains that ranged on the horizon. And my heart was filled with love. Whether it was love of Larkin or love of the land or love of life, I could not determine. Nor did I waste any overmuch amount of time in the trying.

I welcomed my children home from their schooling. We ate our supper; they did their chores; I heard their lessons; we said our prayers. In short, the very routine of our ordinary activities soothed my spirits. I slept like a baby.

The next morning dawned fair. I took the crisp autumn glory to be a good omen on this day of Larkin's return. Although I had no way of knowing the decision that Larkin had reached, I had made my own, and I was content.

When I heard the whistle of the train, I walked over to the bluff to look down on the valley. In due time, the ferry began its slow crossing of the rolling river. One buggy rolled off its ramp and began its ascent up our mountain.

I stood at our door ready to greet him when he stepped out of the buggy. My silver-haired, blue-eyed husband looked at me with that dear lopsided smile that always signaled his pleasure and held out his arms. I flew into his embrace like a bird returning to its nest. Our long kiss gave testament to forgiveness of the past and promise for the future. When finally it was time for words, I asked the question that was so heavy on my mind.

"What have you decided, Larkin? Will we go to Washington, or will we stay here?"

His countenance turned somber, the face of a man who has given the matter much thought and who has come to terms with his conclusion. "Sarah, there is only one way to answer that question. I have thought on it long and hard, and the upshot of the thing is this: You must be the one to make the decision. I will not make a choice that you cannot live with. I have promised to journey back down to Little Rock tomorrow to give answer to the legislature."

He inclined his handsome head so as to look directly into my eyes and put both his hands on my shoulders to shift my body slightly against the radiant dazzle of the noonday sun.

"What is your choice, Sarah? How will we spend the rest of our days?"